Abby Maria Hemenway

Caledonia County

Abby Maria Hemenway

Caledonia County

ISBN/EAN: 9783337327552

Printed in Europe, USA, Canada, Australia, Japan

Cover: Foto ©Andreas Hilbeck / pixelio.de

More available books at **www.hansebooks.com**

Bennington and Caledonia.   **No. III.**   April, 1862.

VERMONT.

Quarterly Gazetteer

A HISTORICAL MAGAZINE,

EMBRACING A DIGEST OF THE HISTORY OF EACH TOWN,

Civil, Educational, Religious, Geological and Literary.

" She stands fair Freedom's chosen Home,
Our own beloved Green Mountain State."

" Where breathes no castled lord or cabined slave;
Where thoughts, and hands, and tongues are free.'

EDITED BY

ABBY MARIA HEMENWAY,

COMPILER OF "THE POETS AND POETRY OF VERMONT."

Terms: One Dollar per Year.   Clubs solicited.

LUDLOW, VT.:

PUBLISHED BY MISS A. M. HEMENWAY,

AND SOLD BY AGENTS THROUGHOUT THE STATE.

Press of Geo. C. Rand & Avery, Boston.

A SERIES OF TOWN HISTORIES,

GROUPED IN COUNTIES,

A Quarterly, which is a free Historical Channel for every Town.

Entered according to Act of Congress, in the year 1859, by ABBY MARIA HEMENWAY, in the Clerk's Office of the District Court of the District of Vermont.

TERMS.

**Fifty Cents a Number; $1 a year; or Fourteen Numbers for $3—Invariably in Advance.
Postage, three cents, paid at Office of Delivery.**

WANTED.—One or more Lady Assistants or Local Agents in each uncanvassed Town.

The Agents have all been instructed to solicit through or yearly subscriptions, yet to as readily take quarterly ones, with the understanding that the subscribers are to pay on delivery for each number of the work, till they may regularly discontinue the same. No subscriptions should be paid to *Travelling Agents*, unless they bear our Certificate of Agency.

CLUB TERMS.—The field is open in every Town for CLUBS, which may be sent direct to the Publisher. Terms—EVERY FOURTH NUMBER FREE; or for Four *Yearly*, or equivalent, a copy of the "Poets and Poetry of Vermont," 12mo. 400 pp.; or Six Photographs of leading Vermont Poets; or for the above list doubled, Twelve Plates, or a Plated and elegantly Gilt copy of the Poets; or for Four Yearly Subscriptions, a copy of the "Vermont School Journal,"—a work devoted to a cause that ought to bring twice the patronage it has yet received; or Dr. C. H. Cleavland's ably conducted "Medical Journal," published at Cincinnati, O.

HISTORICAL CONTENTS.

No. 3.

BENNINGTON — CONCLUDED.

Historical Contributions for Chittenden County.

Received from Henry Stevens, Esq., G. Sawyer, Esq., Rev. Mr. Flemming, Rev. Dr. Witherspoon, Rev. Joshua Young, J. N. Pomeroy, Esq., Professor N. G. Clark, James Johns, Dr. George L. Lyman, Hon. David Reed, Henry Miller, Esq., Rev. William Hough, Hector Adams, Esq., Congregational Pastor of Milton, H. Lawrence, Esq., G. H. Naramore, Esq., Hon. Rev. J. H. Woodward, and E. Rostwick's History of Hinesburg, compiled by Rev. Mr. Ferrin. Other contributions of value promised by Rev. Dr. John Hix, Rev. Dr. Foster, Rev. Mr. Converse, Professors Torrey, Benedict, and Buckham; Sketch of Hon. Hemen Allen, by Professor George Allen, of Philadelphia, Shelburne and Richmond Histories, by G. T. Sutton, A. B., and S. H. Davis, Esq., respectively.

PUBLISHER'S CARD.

THERE are no class of citizens, perhaps, as well circumstanced to render ready and efficient aid in the distribution of this work, especially to quarterly subscribers, as the postmasters of the State; and with much pleasure we embrace this occasion to return our most handsome and courteous thanks to each and all who have thus rendered most essential service: and would particularly thank, as the most obliging and *efficient*, E. S. Mason, Ludlow; C. H. Rowe, Chester; Justus Cobb, Esq., Middlebury; M. V. Baker, Weybridge; Mr. Higgins, Brandon; Mrs. Bucklin, Wallingford; Miss Newbanks, postmaster's clerk, Centre Rutland; Postmaster of Fairhaven; Postmaster's clerks, Brattleboro'; A. S. Hayward, Londonderry; Samuel Damon, Ripton; Postmaster of North Chester; N. B. Pierce, Cavendish; A. G. Hatch, Windsor; Samuel Parker, Brownsville; Postmasters of Westminster, Orwell, and Arlington. Not of the postmasters, but among our practical friends, not heretofore mentioned, men who give a hand to the circulation, we gratefully record Charles Allen, Esq., Burlington; Joshua Leland, Baltimore; Benoni Buck, Esq., Ludlow; and Mr. Weaver, merchant at Winooskie Falls. Others will be duly remembered in the patronage table continued in next number, in which we propose to give an especial "star-table" to lady live assistant and patrons—terms to admission to which will be twelve yearly subscribers, or the equivalent. The income of this publication, thus far, has been barely enough to pay its printing expenses. The editorial labor and expense bestowed upon it has never been even partially remunerated. Its completeness and forwardness will, in a great measure, depend upon the continued exertions of its practical friends. It is, therefore, most respectfully solicited of every subscriber to endeavor—and unto success—to add one or more to the present list, by calling the attention to it of each person known in their vicinity to have a taste for history or biography, a veneration for the memories and mementoes of our fathers, or that commendable town, county, or state pride that prompts individuals to lend their substantial support in the needed hour to an enterprise whose maintenance and prosperity is an honor to the present, and a legacy to future generations. Trusting the patrons and friends of this enterprise need only to be apprised of its condition to respond cordially to its wants, their immediate attention is hopefully solicited. The fourth number of the GAZETTEER will be published in April, and drawn from the press as soon as the subscriptions of its patrons cancels the printing bill. The plate of Governor Fairbanks will appear in No. 4.

VERMONT HISTORICAL MAGAZINE.

CALEDONIA COUNTY.

COUNTY CHAPTER.

BY REV. THOMAS GOODWILLIE, OF BARNET.

PREVIOUS to the American Revolution, that part of the country now known as "Vermont" was called " The New Hampshire Grants," and was claimed by New Hampshire and New York. The General Assembly of New York divided it into four counties, viz : Bennington and Charlotte on the west, and Cumberland and Gloucester on the east side of the Green Mountains.

Gloucester County was organized March 16, 1770, containing

" all that certain tract or district of land situate, lying and being to the northward of the county of Cumberland, beginning at the northwest corner of the said county of Cumberland, and thence running north as the needle points fifty miles, thence east to Connecticut River; thence along the west bank of the same river, as it runs, to the northeast corner of said county of Cumberland, on said river, and thence along the north bound of said county of Cumberland to the place of beginning." On the 24th of March, 1772, by an act " for the better ascertaining the boundaries of the counties of Cumberland and Gloucester," these limits were changed and Gloucester County was bounded " on the south by the north bounds of the County of Cumberland; on the east by the east bounds (Connecticut River) of this colony (New York); on the north by the north bounds thereof (Canada); on the west and northwest partly by a line to be drawn from the northwest corner of the said County of Cumberland on a course north, ten degrees east, until such line shall meet with and be intersected by another line proceeding on an east course from the south bank of the mouth of Otter Creek, and partly by another line to be drawn and continued from the said last-mentioned point of intersection, on a course north, fifty degrees east, until it meets with and terminates at the said north bounds of the Colony."

Newbury was fixed as the shire town of Gloucester County.

In a large map of the British province of New Hampshire (now before the writer), made by Blanchard and Langdon, and inscribed to the British " secretary of war and one of his majesty's privy council," October 21, 1761, the whole of Vermont is laid down as a part of that province. At that time none of the towns in this county were chartered, but many of the towns which were surveyed and chartered in 1762 and 1763 were laid down on this map with pen and ink.

Only three towns in this county are so laid down, Barnet, Ryegate, and Peacham ; the latter town being located west of Ryegate, which shows that Groton, which was charterted by Vermont, was surveyed long before Vermont became a State. In a large map of New York (now before the writer), constructed by order of Gen. Tryon, governor of that province, January 1, 1779, from surveys previously made, the whole of Vermont is laid down as a part of New York. On this map Cumberland County is bounded on the north by Canada and on the east by Connecticut River, separating it from New Hampshire, and on the other sides by a line beginning at the Connecticut River in Norwich, and running a little north of west to the Green Mountains, to a point probably in the town of Ripton ; thence running northerly along the mountains to a point near Onion River, probably in the town of Duxbury ; thence running northeast to Canada line, which it joins in Derby, a few miles east of Lake Memphremagog. The whole of this district is represented on this map as surveyed into townships, except some parts on the northwest.

Within the present limits of Caledonia County the towns of Barnet, Ryegate, Peacham, and Groton are laid down nearly according to the New Hampshire surveys. The most of the other parts of the county are surveyed into townships, which in number, form, and location are altogether different from the other towns now in this county.

On the Connecticut River, above Barnet, was a large township called " Dunmore," including the whole of Waterford and a considerable part of St. Johnsbury and Concord. Along the Barnet line a narrow tract of land was laid down, including parts of Waterford and St. Johnsbury, and which was inscribed "Lt. Cargills." North of Dunmore, on the Passumpsic River, was " Besborough," including the south part of Lyndon and the north part of St. Johnsbury. On the head branches of the Passumpsic was a large tract, including Burke and adjacent parts, in which was inscribed " Thomas Clark & Co." North of Peacham was "Hillsborough," embracing Danville and parts of Walden and Hardwick. These are all the towns in this county laid down on the New York map of 1779.

The New York grants were abolished when Vermont became independent, and the grantees received a portion of the $30,000 which was given to New York, 1790, to quitclaim Vermont. Thomas Clark's share was $237 05, and John Galbraith's $99 81.

In 1777, the General Convention of Vermont declared "The New Hampshire Grants" independent, and adopted a constitution for the State. In February, 1779, the legislature of Vermont, in face of the opposition of New York, divided the State into two counties, and each county into two shires, viz: Bennington on the west, and Cumberland County on the east side of the Green Mountains. Cumberland County was divided into the shires of Westminster and Newbury. In 1781, the legislature divided Cumberland into three counties, viz: Windham, Windsor, and Orange. Newbury was the shire town of the County of Orange, which embraced the northeastern part of the State to the Canada line. November 5, 1792, Caledonia County was incorporated from Orange County, including all that part of the State north of that county, and extending so far west as to include Montpelier and adjacent towns. But this county was not fully organized till November 8, 1796, when Danville was made the shire town. The whole State was divided into eleven counties in 1811, when the counties of Orleans and Essex were incorporated from Caledonia County. Four towns from this county were incorporated with Washington County in 1811, to which Woodbury was annexed in 1836 and Cabot in 1855. Caledonia County consists at the present time of sixteen towns. In 1856 the county seat was removed from Danville to St. Johnsbury, where new county buildings were erected. The court-house is a large, elegant, and commodious edifice.

The lands, therefore, in this part of the country were first of all in Gloucester County, New York; then in the shire of Newbury and County of Cumberland, Vermont; afterwards in Orange County, Vermont; and now in Caledonia County, Vermont.

The county is bounded on the north by Orleans County; on the east by Essex County; on the southeast by Connecticut River, which separates it from Grafton County, N. H.; on the south by Orange County; and on the west by Washington and Lamoille counties. It lies between N. lat. 44° 10' and N. lat. 44° 45', and immediately north of a line which if drawn east and west would divide the State into two equal parts. Its length from north to south is about forty miles, and its breadth from east to west about thirty. It contains about 700 square miles, with a population of 21,768, which gives 31 inhabitants to a square mile.

There are many flourishing villages situated in different parts of the county, containing fine churches.

It is well watered by many streams. The Connecticut River runs on the southeast side. The northern towns are watered by the head branches of the Passumpsic River, which is the largest in the county, and runs south and empties into the Connecticut River in Barnet. Wells, Stevens, and Joes rivers water it on the south, and the head branches of Onion and Lamoille rivers on the west. There are about twenty lakes and ponds in the county; the chief of which are Harvey's Lake in Barnet, Wells River and Lund's Ponds in Groton, Cole's Pond in Walden, Clark's and Centre Ponds in Newark, and Stile's Pond in Waterford. Fish of various kinds abound in most of the ponds and rivers. There are falls at different places on the Connecticut, Passumpsic, Wells, and Joes's rivers. Stevens's river, near its mouth, falls 80 feet in the distance of 20 rods. The water-power is improved by mills and factories built at the falls and other places on the streams.

The western part of the county is mountainous; but though the towns in that part are on high lands, they admit of successful cultivation. The eastern part is an excellent farming country. The intervales on the Connecticut and Passumpsic rivers are easily cultivated. From the tops of the mountains in different parts of the county extensive prospects may be obtained, and in some sites grand views of the White Hills of New Hampshire and of the Green Mountains of Vermont may be enjoyed. A mountain in Burke, whose height is 3,500 feet, is probably the highest in the county.

It is not certainly known at what time this part of the country was discovered by Europeans. It has been known to the New England settlers for more than a century. Prior to this period the Indians owned and occupied the soil, covered with the forest. The wilderness was the home and inheritance of these wild men of the woods. Here, they camped in its valleys, hunted on its mountains, and fished in its waters, over which they glided swiftly in their light canoes; and hence, they went forth to war, fighting with savage cunning and cruelty the foreigners who came over the great waters from the east, to dwell in their domains, converting the forests into fruitful fields. When it first became known to Europeans the St. Francis tribe of Indians roamed over this part of the country. They had an encampment at Newbury and cultivated "the meadows" on the Great Ox Bow. But their principal settlement was in Canada. St. Francis, a village on the south side of the River St. Lawrence, not far from the Three Rivers, was their head-quarters. The French employed them in their wars against the English colonies. With their acquaintance with the country and their deadly hatred of the English, they were formidable enemies. From none of the Indian tribes had the provinces of New Hampshire and Massachusetts suffered so much. They made their incursions along the River St.

Francis and Lake Memphremagog, and thence down the Passumpsic and Connecticut rivers. This was their highway returning from the slaughter of the English, with their scalps, prisoners, and plunder. They were much distinguished by the slaughter and destruction spread among the advanced settlements, the enormity of their cruelties and barbarities, and the number of their scalps and captives.

In the spring of 1752 a party of ten of these Indians surprised a party of four New England settlers while hunting on Baker's River in Rumney, N. H. One fled, one was killed, and the other two were taken prisoners and carried captive into Canada, to their head-quarters at St. Francis. One of these captives was John Stark, afterwards the famous General Stark, who must have been one of the first of Europeans to behold this part of the country. One of his daughters lived and died in Ryegate, and some of her descendants now reside in Ryegate and Barnet. These two men returned from their captivity in Canada in the summer of 1752, and gave an account of the country through which they had passed.

No doubt later and fuller information of this part of the country was given by Major Rogers and his rangers upon their return in 1759, by the Passumpsic River and the Coos "Meadows," from their successful expedition against the St. Francis Indians in Canada. But the sad fate of many of these brave yet unfortunate men, which took place in our county, gives a melancholy interest to the early history of this part of the county.

General Amherst being at Crown Point on Lake Champlain, carrying on the war against the French colonies in 1759, determined to make these Indians, who continued to disturb and distress the frontiers, feel the power of the English colonies. For this purpose, on September 13, 1759, the very day that the English took Quebec, he appointed Major Rogers, a brave and experienced officer from New Hampshire, who had become famous for the number, boldness, and success of his enterprises, to conduct an expedition against this barbarous tribe, carrying the horrors of war unexpectedly into their head-quarters in Canada. The night after the orders were given he set out with two hundred men in boats and proceeded down Lake Champlain. On the fourth day after they left Crown Point, while encamped on the eastern shore of the lake, a keg of gunpowder accidentally exploded, wounding a captain of the royal regiment and several men, who were sent back to Crown Point, with a party to conduct them. This reduced Rogers's force to one hundred and forty-two men, with whom he proceeded to Missisco Bay, as ordered. Here he concealed his boats among some bushes which hung over one of the streams, and left in them provisions sufficient to carry them back to Crown Point.

According to orders he left the lake and advanced into the wilderness towards St. Francis village, having left two men to watch the boats and provisions, with orders that if the enemy discovered them, they were to pursue the party with expedition and give him intelligence. The second evening after he left the bay these two men overtook the party and informed him that four hundred French and Indians had discovered the boats and sent them away with fifty men, while the rest of the party went in pursuit of the English. Rogers kept this intelligence to himself, but sent away the two rangers with a lieutenant and eight men to Crown Point, to inform Gen. Amherst of what had taken place and request him to send provisions to Coos on Connecticut River, by which route he intended to return. Rogers, in order to outmarch his enemies if they pursued him, pushed forward towards St. Francis with all possible expedition. He came in sight of the village on the 4th of October at 8 o'clock in the evening. Ordering his men to halt and refresh themselves, he dressed himself in the Indian garb and took with him two Indians, who understood the language of the St. Francis tribe, and went to reconnoitre the town. He found the Indians engaged in a grand dance, without the least apprehension of danger. He returned to his men at 2 o'clock in the morning and marched them to a distance of about five hundred yards from the town. About 4 o'clock the Indians finished their dance and retired to rest. Rogers waited till they were asleep, and at break of day he posted his men in the most favorable situation and commenced a general assault. The Indians were completely surprised and soon subdued. Some of them were killed in their houses, and of those who attempted to fly, many were shot or knocked on the head by the rangers, who were placed at the avenues. Amherst ordered Rogers and his men "to take their revenge on the Indian scoundrels" for their "barbarities and infamous cruelties," but he ordered also that "no women or children be killed or hurt, though these villains have dastardly and promiscuously murdered the women and children of all orders." But the Indian method of slaughter and destruction was adopted on this occasion; and wherever Indians were found, their men, women, and children were slain without distinction and without mercy. As the morning light increased the fierce wrath of the rangers was inflamed to the highest degree when they saw the scalps of several hundreds of their countrymen suspended on poles and waving in the air. Under this new force and irritation of their feelings and passions, they put forth their utmost exertions to avenge the blood of their friends and relations by utterly destroying the village and all they could find of its inhabitants. The village contained three hundred Indians. Two hundred were killed on the spot and twenty taken prisoners.

The town appeared to have been in a flourishing state. The houses were well furnished, and the church was handsomely adorned with plate. The whole village had been enriched by the plunder and scalps taken from the English. Two hundred guineas were found in money and a silver image weighing ten pounds, besides a large quantity of wampum and clothing, and some provisions. Collecting the provisions and such articles as they could easily transport, they set fire to the village and reduced it to ashes. At 7 o'clock in the morning the affair was finished, which broke the pride and power of the St. Francis tribe of Indians. Rogers then assembled his men and found that one was killed and six slightly wounded. Having refreshed his men for one hour, he immediately set out on his return, with the addition of five English captives he had retaken. To avoid his pursuers, he took a different route and marched up the St. Francis River, meaning to have his men collect and rendezvous at Coos on the Connecticut River. On their march they were harassed by the Indians, and the enemy several times attacked them in the rear. In these rencounters they lost seven of their men, till Rogers, favored by the dusk of the evening, formed an ambuscade upon his own track and fell upon the enemy when they least expected it; by this stroke he put an end to further pursuit and annoyance from their foes. For about ten days the detachment kept together till they had passed the eastern side of Lake Memphremagog. Their sufferings now began to be severe, not only from the excessive fatigues they had endured, but from hunger. Their provisions were expended and they were at a distance from any place of relief.

Here Rogers divided his detachment into small companies, and having ordered them all to assemble at the mouth of the upper Amonusuck River, where he expected to find food, sent them on their march. After a journey of several days he and his party reached the appointed place of meeting, having come on the Passumpsic River, which they descended.

In the mean time, by order of Gen. Amherst, Samuel Stevens and three others proceeded from Charlestown, N. H., up Connecticut River, with two canoes laden with provisions. They landed on Round Island, at the mouth of Passumpsic River, where they encamped for the night; but hearing the report of guns in the morning, and supposing Indians were in the vicinity, they were so terrified that they reloaded their provisions and hastened back to Charlestown.

Their fearful misapprehensions were soon followed by fatal consequences. Rogers and his men encamped the same night a few miles up the Passumpsic, the mouth of which river they reached about noon the next day, and discovered fire on Round Island. He made a raft and passed over to it, but to his surprise and disappointment discovered that no provisions had been left. His men were so disheartened by this discovery that a considerable number of them died before the next day.

In these dismal circumstances Rogers gave up the command and told his men to take care of themselves. Some were lost in the woods and others died of famine, but Rogers and most of his party, after almost incredible hardships, arrived at Number Four, or Charlestown, N. H.

Peter Lervey, of Haverhill, N. H., who came to Barnet to live a short time before his death, which was about the year 1817, and whom the writer has seen, was one of Rogers's party and visited the scenes of their suffering. He said that many of the rangers died on the Passumpsic River and on the meadow below on the Connecticut River. On this meadow and along the Passumpsic for two or three miles from its mouth human bones have been found at different times and places. Some of these might have been the bones of Indians who had been buried in a sitting posture, but many others were found in a horizontal position; and in one place the skeletons of two persons were discovered in the earth together. These probably were the remains of some of Rogers's men who perished in Barnet.

Lervey also said that he and some others, in order to have a better chance to find game, left the Connecticut River and went through the woods and came upon Wells River about two miles above its mouth. They killed a bear and some small game, so that none of his party perished.

The following account, taken from Major Rogers's journals, gives many interesting particulars, though it seems to differ in a few unimportant points from the histories from which the preceding account is taken:—

Maj. Rogers writes to Gen. Amherst, November 5, 1759, "It is hardly possible to describe the grief and consternation of those of us who came to Cohasse Intervales. Upon our arrival there, after so many days' tedious march, over steep, rocky mountains, or through wet, dirty swamps, with the terrible attendants of fatigue and hunger, we found that here was no relief for us, where we had encouraged ourselves that we should find it, and have our distresses alleviated. Notwithstanding the officer I dispatched to the general, discharged his trust with great expedition, and in nine days arrived at Crown Point, which was one hundred miles through the wilderness; and the general, without delay, sent Lieut. Stevens to Number Four, with orders to take provisions up the river to the place I had appointed, and there wait so long as there was any hopes of my returning: yet the officer that was sent, being an indolent fellow, tarried at the place but two days, when he returned, taking all the provisions with him, about two hours before our arrival. Finding a fresh fire burning in his camp, I fired guns to bring him back, which guns he heard, but would not return, supposing we were the enemy. Our distress on this occasion was truly inexpressible. Our spirits, greatly depressed by the hunger and fatigues we had already suffered, now almost entirely sank within us, seeing no resource left, nor

THE POETS AND POETRY OF VERMONT.

EDITED AND PUBLISHED BY

ABBY MARIA HEMENWAY.

PRINTED BY GEO. A. TUTTLE & CO., RUTLAND, VT.

"The Bargain" we copy from a beautiful volume entitled the Poets of Vermont.—*New York Independent.*

People cannot afford to read everything; hence the disposition to select works that relate to their own country, their own state, their own town, their own parish, their own family. The work before us is based on the same general principle. It was a happy thought to group together the poets of a State; and we doubt whether any State of the Union has furnished more poetry, in proportion to its population, worthy of preservation, than Vermont. —*American Baptist, New York City.*

This is an exceedingly neat edition of poems by the Green Mountain State, embracing many sweet specimens of verse, and touching upon all themes, from lively to severe.—*Gleason's Pictorial Drawing Room Companion.*

A beautifully bound volume, and contains some of the finest poetical productions of the age.—*Independence Gazette, Missouri.*

REVISED EDITION.

POETS AND POETRY OF VERMONT. Edited by ABBY MARIA HEMENWAY.

Publishers, Boston: Brown, Taggard & Chase. Brattleboro: W. Felton.

The poems embrace a great variety of topics, as well as of style and poetic merit. While they are not all brilliant, there are very few which are not good, and we question whether it would not be difficult to produce a more acceptable volume from the poetic writings of the sons and daughters of any other State, and embracing as wide a range in the selection of authors.—*Boston Journal.*

A new edition, revised and enlarged, of a book which had already been very cordially received by the press and the public. There is a great deal of excellent poetry in the five hundred and more pages; quite as much as you will find in Griswold's "Poets and Poetry of America," and kindred compilations. The book will be a popular one in Vermont, of course, and deserves to be so everywhere else.—*Boston Times.*

The volume contains a large number of poems of varied merit, as they must be, coming from many writers; and forms a collection of poetry to which any State might point with an honest pride.—*Worcester Palladium.*

Vermont has, in fact, many "poets of the people," as the volume before us abundantly demonstrates.—*Bangor Whig & Courier.*

The "Green Mountain State" need not be ashamed of her poetry, any more than of her patriotism. These poetical specimens are very creditable to their genius.—*Providence Journal.*

The degree of talent presented shows that the cold regions of the North are nurseries of poetry.—*Portsmouth Journal.*

The names of Drs. Spenser, Asa D. Smith, and Hopkins (Bishop), R. W. Griswold, George P. Marsh, and Walter Colton, are assurance enough that the land of mountain and rock has produced Arctic flowers worth transplanting. A likeness of J. G. Saxe accompanies the volume.—*Church Mirror, Portland.*

If you are a Vermonter, and want to send a handsome and appropriate present to "the old folks at home;" or if you are *not* a Vermonter, but have some particular friend who *is*, you will be tempted, we think, to buy it.—*The Lawrence American.*

The Vermont press has been as warm in encouragement as our generous neighbors; but it is not well to select out from among home-friends, where many are equally worthy.

The first edition of the Poets will be mailed, upon the reception of $1.00, to any part of the United States, or of the revised edition for $1.25.

VERMONT
QUARTERLY GAZETTEER
or
Historical Magazine.

THIS publication is to consist of a series of fourteen Quarterlies, one to be devoted to each county, commencing with Addison, and the remainder following in alphabetical order.

The whole is designed to embrace a comprehensive history of each town—civil, educational, religious, geological, and literary.

The writers in the historical department will, we think, be found to be those at once the best qualified for this work, and the most acceptable to their respective towns and the general public.

The biographical and specimen departments will be enriched by sketches of, and specimens from, such men as Ethan Allen, Thomas Chittenden, General Stark, Silas Wright, Governors Slade, Hall, Fairbanks, &c.; Senators Tichenor, Upham, Phelps, Foote, &c.; Hon. James Meacham, M. C.; Bishops Hedding, Henshaw, and Hopkins; Stephen Olin, D. D.; Amos Deane, LL.D.; Dr. Edwin James; Prof. Boardman; Carlos Wilcox; Rev. Drs. Spencer, Sheldon, Asa D. Smith, &c.; Hiram Powers, George P. Marsh, D. P. Thompson, Hon. William C. Bradley, Judge Noble, &c. &c.

We improve this occasion to give notice that each town is expected to furnish its own chapter of history and biographic sketches; each church its own records, sketches of first pastor, &c. Chapters on the geology of each county will be prepared by our best geologists.

Finally, we may be allowed to add; in order that this enterprise prove at once creditable and profitable to all concerned, we shall, of course, have to depend upon the active sympathy and hearty coöperation of every son and daughter of Vermont.

THE

ORIGIN AND SIGNIFICATION

OF

SCOTTISH SURNAMES.

BY CLIFFORD STANLEY SIMS.

The edition of this work will be limited to 150 copies; it will consist of about 100 pages in octavo, will
be printed on fine and heavy paper, with wide margins, and furnished to subscribers at $1.50 sewed and
uncut; $2 in green cloth. If any copies remain un-
sold at the time of publication they will be held at $2
in paper.
A list of Subscribers will be given.

From the Philadelphia Press.

Mr. Clifford Stanley Sims, a member of the Philadelphia bar,
has written an interesting work, entitled the Origin and Signification of Scottish Surnames, which will be speedily published by
Mr. J. Munsell, Albany—a gentleman whose name is honorably
associated with many valuable books. Only 150 copies will be
printed, to be supplied by subscription, and got up upon superior
paper, with wide margins, in Mr. Munsell's accustomed excellent
manner. The edition is very limited—we should fancy that the
St. Andrew's Society in this city alone would engross the whole of
it. We had the pleasure of perusing Mr. Sims's work in manu-
script, and cheerfully bear testimony to the research, erudition,
and full acquaintance with the subject which it exhibits. It is
entertaining as well as antiquarian, and is liberally studded with
historical and personal anecdotes.

KING PHILIP'S WAR.

It is proposed, if a sufficient Subscription can be
obtained, to publish uniformly with *Munsell's Historical Series,*

A

BRIEF HISTORY OF THE WAR

WITH THE

INDIANS IN NEW ENGLAND,

By INCREASE MATHER, together with Cotton Mather's
Account of the same War, and an *Introduction* and
Notes by SAMUEL G. DRAKE, Esq. This Work, for a
long time difficult to be obtained, is not only indispensable to all students of New England History, but
also an important adjunct to the Work on the same
Subject in the Series above alluded to, more especially
on Account of the Animadversions of Mather upon
the Statements made therein by Easton.
The Work will be printed in Old Style, in 4to form,
on fine laid Paper, containing about 300 pages, with 2
steel Portraits, at $3, in paper covers, sewed and un-
cut; or $3.50 in green cloth, top edge gilt; large paper
copies, sewed, $10. A List of Subscribers will accom-
pany the Volume, and the Edition will be limited
very nearly to the orders received before printing.
Address

J. MUNSELL, 78 State street, Albany, N. Y.

AN

HISTORICAL SKETCH

OF THE

PROVINCIAL DIALECTS OF ENGLAND.

Illustrated by numerous Examples.

By J. O. HALLIWELL.

This interesting Essay, of which only 50 copies were printed
in England for presents, will form an octavo volume of 150 pages,
printed on fine and heavy paper, in elegant style, and bound in
cloth, neatly, at $1.50; ½ turk., top edge gilt, $2. Ed. 100 copies.

VERMONT QUARTERLY GAZETTEER

OR

HISTORICAL MAGAZINE.

This publication is to consist of a series of Quarterlies, devoted to each county, commencing with Addison, and the remainder following in alphabetical order.

The whole is designed to embrace a comprehensive history of each town—civil, educational, religious, geological, literary and military.

The writers in the historical department will, we think, be found to be those at once the best qualified for this work, and the most acceptable to their respective towns and the general public.

The biographical and specimen departments will be enriched by sketches of, and specimens from, such men as Ethan Allen, Thomas Chittenden, Seth Warner, Silas Wright; Governors Robinson, Tichenor, Williams, Crafts, Slade, Hall, Mattocks, Fairbanks, Van Ness, Royce, Holbrook, &c.; Senators Upham, Phelps, Douglas, Foote, &c.; Hon. James Meacham, Hon. Rollin C. Mallory, Hon. Justin S. Morrell, M. Cs.; Bishops Hedding, Henshaw, and Hopkins; Stephen Olin, D. D.; Dr. Edwin James; Rev. Drs. Spencer, Sheldon, Asa D. Smith, Calvin Pease, &c.; Prof. J. Torrey; Hon. Amos Dean, LL. D.; Hiram Powers, George P. Marsh, Hon. William C. Bradley, Judge Noble, D. P. Thompson, Rev. S. R. Hall, Rev. P. H. White, George F. Houghton, Esq., Judge Kellogg, A. D. Hager, Esq., &c., &c.

We improve this occasion to give notice that each town is expected to furnish its own chapter of history and biographic sketches; each church its own records, sketches of first pastor, &c. Chapters on the geology of each county will be prepared by our best geologists.

Finally, we may be allowed to add, in order that this enterprise prove at once creditable and profitable to all concerned, we shall, of course, have to depend upon the active sympathy and hearty coöperation of every son and daughter of Vermont.

THE POETS AND POETRY OF VERMONT.

REVISED EDITION.

EDITED AND PUBLISHED BY

ABBY MARIA HEMENWAY, LUDLOW, VT

"The Bargain" we copy from a beautiful volume entitled the Poets of Vermont.—*New York Independent.*

People can not afford to read every thing; hence the disposition to select works that relate to their own country, their own state, their own town, their own parish, their own family. The work before us is based on the same general principle. It was a happy thought to group together the poets of a state; and we doubt whether any state of the Union has furnished more poetry, in proportion to its population, worthy of preservation, than Vermont.—*American Baptist, New York city.*

This is an exceedingly neat edition of poems by the Green Mountain State, embracing many sweet specimens of verse, and touching upon all themes, from lively to severe.—*Gleason's Pic. Draw. Room Comp.*

The volume contains a large number of poems of varied merit, as they must be, coming from many writers, and forms a collection of poetry to which any state might point with an honest pride.—*Worcester Palladium.*

The poems embrace a great variety of topics, as well as of style and poetic merit. While they are not all brilliant, there are very few which are not good, and we question whether it would not be difficult to produce a more acceptable volume from the poetic writings of the sons and daughters of any other state, and embracing as wide a range in the selection of authors. —*Boston Journal.*

A new edition, revised and enlarged, of a book which had already been very cordially received by the press and the public. There is a great deal of excellent poetry in the five hundred and more pages; quite as much as you will find in Griswold's Poets and Poetry of America, and kindred compilations. The book will be a popular one in Vermont, of course, and deserves to be so every where else.—*Boston Times.*

The Green Mountain State need not be ashamed of her poetry, any more than of her patriotism. These poetical specimens are very creditable to their genius. —*Providence Journal.*

The names of Drs. Spencer, Asa D. Smith, and Hopkins (Bishop), R. W. Griswold, George P. Marsh, and Walter Colton, are assurance enough that the land of mountain and rock has produced Arctic flowers worth transplanting. A likeness of J. G. Saxe accompanies the volume.—*Church Mirror, Portland.*

The first edition of the Poets will be mailed, upon the reception of $1, to any part of the United States; or of the revised edition, for $1.25.

any reasonable hope that we should escape a most miserable death by famine. At length I came to a resolution to push as fast as possible towards Number Four, leaving the remains of my party, now unable to march further, to get such wretched subsistence as the barren wilderness could afford, till I could get relief to them, which I engaged to do within ten days. I taught Lieut. Grant, the commander of the party, the use and method of preparing ground-nuts and lily roots, which being cleaned and boiled, will serve to preserve life. I, with Capt. Ogden and one ranger and a captive Indian boy, embarked upon a raft we had made of dry pine-trees. The current carried us down the stream in the middle of the river, where we endeavored to keep our wretched vessel by such paddles as we had made out of small trees or spires split and hewed.

"The second day we reached White River Falls, and very narrowly escaped being carried over them by the current. Our little remains of strength, however, enabled us to land and to march by them. At the bottom of these falls, while Capt. Ogden and the ranger hunted for red squirrels for a refreshment, who had likewise the good fortune to kill a partridge, I attempted the forming of a new raft for our further conveyance. Being unable to cut down trees, I burnt them down and then burnt them off at proper lengths. This was our third day's work after leaving our companions. The next day we got our materials together and completed our raft and floated with the stream again till we came to Otta Quechee Falls, which are about fifty yards in length. Here we landed, and by a withe made of hazel-bushes, Capt. Ogden held the raft till I went to the bottom, prepared to swim and board it when it came down, and, if possible, to paddle it ashore, this being the only resource for life, as we were not able to make a third raft in case we had lost this. I had the good fortune to succeed, and the next morning we embarked and floated down the stream to within a small distance of Number Four, where we found some men cutting timber, who gave us the first relief and assisted us to the fort, whence I dispatched a canoe with provisions, which reached the men at Cohasse four days after, which, agreeable to my engagement, was the tenth day after I left them. Two days after my arrival at Number Four, I went up the river myself, with other canoes loaded with provisions for the relief of others of my party that might be coming on that way, having hired some of the inhabitants to assist me in this affair. I likewise sent expresses to Pembroke and Concord upon the Merrimack River, that any who should straggle that way might be assisted, and provisions were sent up said rivers accordingly."

Having returned from his expedition up the river, Maj. Rogers waited for his men at Number Four, and having collected and refreshed a considerable part of his force, he marched to Crown Point, where he arrived December 1, 1759, and joined the army under Gen. Amherst. Upon examination he found that after leaving the smoking ruins of St. Francis he had lost three lieutenants and forty-six sergeants and privates.

This expedition, though it proved extremely dangerous and fatiguing to the men engaged in it, produced a deep impression on the enemy, carrying consternation and alarm into the heart of Canada, and convincing the Indians that the retaliation of vengeance was now come upon them.

Newbury was chartered May 8, 1763, and settled in 1764. Some of the St. Francis tribe of Indians returned to the Coos, where they lived and died, and their families became extinct. One of these was Capt. John, who had been a noted chief of the St. Francis tribe. He was in the battle of Braddock's defeat, and used to relate how he shot a British officer, after the officer had knocked him down; and how he tried to shoot young Washington, but could not succeed. He was a fierce and cruel Indian, and had repeatedly used the tomahawk and scalping-knife upon the defenceless inhabitants of Massachusetts and New Hampshire. When excited by ardent spirits, he took a fiendish satisfaction in relating his cruel and savage deeds, particularly his bloody barbarities in torturing and killing captive females, whose cries of distress he imitated, to make sport. He was, however, a firm friend of the American colonies. During the revolutionary war he received a captain's commission, raised a part of a company of Indians and marched with the New England companies against Burgoyne. One of his sons, in 1777, fought near Fort Independence, under the command of Capt. Thomas Johnston of Newbury.

Captain Joe was another of these Indians. His disposition was mild. He hated the British, and rejoiced in the success of the American colonies. Accompanied with his wife, Molly, he used to hunt in this county. His name was given to Joe's Pond, on the western border of this county, and once belonged to it; and to the stream which issues out of it and empties into Passumpsic in Barnet, where it is sometimes called Merrit's River. Her name was given to Molly's Pond in Cabot, which until lately belonged to this county.

During the revolutionary war, he with Molly visited Gen. Washington at his head-quarters on the Hudson River, and was received with marked attention. When he became old and unable to support himself, the legislature of Vermont granted him a pension of $70 annually.

The war with the French in Canada and the dread of the Indians retarded the settlements on the Connecticut River.

In 1760, no towns were chartered and no settlements made on that river north of Charlestown, N. H., 75 miles below this county. But after the courage and power of the Indians were destroyed by Rogers's daring expedition in 1759, and the termination of the war with the French colonies in Canada in 1760, the settlements on the Connecticut River rapidly increased.

In 1760, Samuel Stevens was employed by a land company to explore this part of the country, to find out the best lands for settlement. He, with a few others, began at the mouth of White River and proceeded up the Connecticut River till they came to the head branches of Onion River, which rise in the southern part of this county and not many miles from the Connecticut. Thence they went down Onion River to Lake Champlain. Then beginning at the mouth of Lamoille River, they proceeded up that stream to its head branches in the western part of this county, through which they passed to the Connecticut River.

In 1761, no less than sixty towns on the west, and eighteen on the east side of the Connecticut, were chartered. After this period Elijah King, with a party, surveyed the towns north of Wells River.

The towns first chartered in this part of the county were New Hampshire Grants. Benning Wentworth, governor of that province, chartered Ryegate, September 8, 1763 ; Barnet, September 16, 1763, and Peacham, December 31, 1763.

Barnet was the first town in the county that was settled. Its first settlers were from the New England settlements. Jacob, Elijah, and Daniel Hall and Jonathan Fowler settled in Barnet, March 4, 1770. The first house erected in the county was built by the Halls, at the foot of the falls on the north side of Stevens River in Barnet. Sarah, daughter of Elijah Hall, was the first child born in the county, and Barnet Fowler, son of Jonathan Fowler, was probably the first male born in the county. In October, 1773, there were fifteen families in town, and in 1775 it began to be rapidly settled by emigrants from Scotland, who soon composed the great majority of the inhabitants. In 1773, emigrants from Scotland began to settle in Ryegate, having purchased the south half of the town. The most of the inhabitants were Scotch, who settled in different parts of the town. The first inhabitants of the town, however, were Aaron Hosmer and his family, who had camped on the Connecticut River, two miles above Wells River. In the spring of 1775, Jonathan Elkins came to Peacham, to the lot he had pitched in 1774. Danville was chartered October 27, 1784, and a few years afterwards was rapidly settled. Dr. Arnold, of St. Johnsbury, procured the charters of that town and Lyndon, Burke, and Billymead (now Sutton), and named them for his four sons, John, Lyndon, Burke, and William. John, however, was dead. His father sainted his name and called the town named for him St. Johnsbury.*

Ryegate, Barnet, and Peacham, the towns first chartered in the county, were settled before the revolutionary war. The rest of the towns in the county were chartered by the State of Vermont between 1780 and 1790.

The first mills erected in the county were a saw-mill and gristmill built by Col. Hurd of Haverhill, N. H., in 1771, at the Falls on Stevens's River in Barnet, by a contract with Enos Stevens, one of the grantees of the town, for one hundred acres of land lying on the Connecticut River, and running back half a mile and enclosing the Falls ; Stevens, however, furnishing the mill-irons on the spot.

In 1774, a line was run from Connecticut River in Barnet through Peacham to Missique Bay on Lake Champlain, which was of great use to our scouts and to deserters from the enemy during the revolutionary war. On this line, in March, 1776, several companies belonging to Col. Bedel's regiment marched to Canada on snow-shoes.

Early in the spring of 1776, Gen. Bailey of Newbury was ordered to open a road from Newbury in Orange County, beginning at the mouth of Wells River, which empties into the Connecticut River near the southeast corner of the county, to run through the wilderness to St. Johns, for the purpose of facilitating the conveyance of troops and provisions into Canada. He had opened the road six miles above Peacham, when the news arrived that the American army had retreated from Canada, and the undertaking was abandoned. But in 1799 Gen. Hazen was ordered to Peacham with part of a regiment for the purpose, as was said, of completing the road begun by Gen. Bailey, so that an army might be sent through for the reduction of Canada. But this was probably a feint for dividing the enemy and preventing them from sending their whole force up Lake Champlain. Gen. Hazen, however, continued the road fifty miles above Peacham, through the towns of Cabot, Walden, Hardwick, Greensboro', Craftsbury, Albany, and Lowell, and it terminated at a remarkable notch in the mountain in Westfield. He erected block-houses at Peacham and other places along the road, which to this day is called the "Hazen Road," and the notch where it terminated is known as "Hazen's Notch." This road was of great advantage to the settlers after the revolutionary war.

But it appears from a letter written by Gen. Whitelaw to his father and the company in Scotland, and dated Feb. 7, 1774, that a road from Connecticut River to Lake Champlain and Canada had been designed, and the opening of it had commenced at that early period, which was probably designed to facilitate the settlement of the country. As this letter was written soon after the settlement of the county had commenced, and as it contains many interesting particulars, we quote it at length.

"RYEGATE, Feb. 7, 1774.

"We have now built a house and live very comfortably, though we are not troubled much with our neighbors, having one family about half a mile from us, another a mile and a half, and two about two miles and a half, — one above and the other below us. In the township above us (Barnet) there are about fifteen families, and in the township below (Newbury), about sixty, where they have a good Presbyterian minister, whose meeting-house is about six miles from us. There is as yet no minister above us, though there are some few settlers sixty miles beyond us, on the river (Connecticut). There are no settlers to the west of us till you come to Lake Champlain, which is upwards of sixty miles. There is a road now begun to be cut from Connecticut River to the Lake, which goes through the middle of our purchase, and is reasoned to be a considerable advantage to us, as it will be the chief post-road to Canada. We are extremely well pleased with our situation, as the ground on a second view is better than we expected, and we live in a place where we can have a pretty good price for the products of the earth. The ordinary price of provisions are as follows : Wheat, four shillings per bushel ; barley, the same ; oats, rye, and Indian corn, from one to two shillings ; pease four shillings and sixpence ; all sterling, and all the English bushel ; and the soil here produces these in perfection, besides water and muskmelons, cucumbers, potatoes, squashes, pumpkins, turnips, parsnips, carrots, onions, and all garden vegetables in the greatest plenty and perfection. They have also excellent flax, which they sell at four and a half pence sterling per pound, when swingled, which is sixpence lawful money, at Boston, in which they commonly reckon, as most of the trade here is with that part of New England. Beef sells here at one and three fourths pence per pound, pork at four and one half to sixpence, mutton from two to three pence, butter and cheese from five to six pence ; all sterling and all by the English pound. These are the real prices of provisions here, and what we ourselves pay for all these articles ; and as they have great demand for these things in the seaport towns to the eastward, the price will continue. This country seems to be extraordinarily well adapted to the raising of cattle, as it is all covered with excellent grass where it is cleared, and even in many places in the woods. As butter and cheese here sell at a good price, a good dairy here might be a very profitable business. Though this is a new country we have every necessary of life at the above prices. We have a gristmill within six miles of us, and a sawmill within two and a half. We know nothing of the hardships of settling a new place, for the first settlers in the town below, only ten years ago, had not a neighbor nearer than sixty miles, and no road but through the woods, and the nearest mill was one hundred and twenty miles down the river. The people here are hospitable, social, and decent. One thing I know, that here they are very strict in keeping the Sabbath. The winter here is far from being what I ex-

pected, for though it freezes sometimes pretty severely, yet it is not very cold. The weather is commonly clear and settled."

Barnet, Ryegate, and Peacham being New Hampshire grants, were involved in the controversy with New York, and took an active part in declaring Vermont independent, and establishing its government.

These three towns were settled but a few years before the revolutionary war commenced, no other towns in the county having been settled till some years after the independence of the United States was acknowledged by Great Britain. Though feeble frontier settlements, they contributed according to their ability to establish that independence. In 1777, when there was a general call on that part of the country for soldiers, they sent armed men to Saratoga, where they had the pleasure of witnessing the surrender of Burgoyne and his army. Afterwards they raised militia to guard the frontier, sent soldiers to the American army, and furnished provisions according to their ability.

The legislature of Vermont passed an act, Feb. 28, 1782, to raise three hundred able-bodied men for the ensuing campaign, and the men for Col. Johnston's regiment were to meet at his house in Newbury, March 1, 1782. The board of war, under this act, required two men from this county, — one from Ryegate and another from Barnet.

For the support of the troops raised by Vermont during the revolutionary war, the legislature passed an act, October 27, 1781, to levy on the polls and ratable estate of that year a provision tax of twenty ounces of wheat flour, and six ounces of rye flour, and also ten ounces of beef, and six ounces of pork without bone except backbone and ribs ; and in 1782 another act was passed to levy a provision tax on the towns, by which three towns in the county were taxed as follows, viz : —

	Flour.	Beef.	Salted Pork.	Indian Corn.	Rye.
	Pounds.	Pounds.	Pounds.	Bushels.	Bushels.
Ryegate,	1,800	600	300	54	12
Barnet,	750	250	125	24	12
Peacham	750	250	125	24	12
	3,300	1,100	550	106	36

As these towns had not fully furnished these provisions, the legislature passed an act, Feb. 22, 1783, " to remit all the arrears of taxes (except land taxes) due from Peacham, Barnet, and Ryegate, and laid on said towns before the session in October, 1782, as these towns lie so detached from the firm citizens of this State, as that they cannot be said properly to have been within the protection and to have received the benefit of the government of the State." The other towns in this county began to be settled about the time of the formation of the Constitution of the United States, in 1787 ; and their settlement rapidly increased in 1789, when the first Congress met and Gen. Washington was inaugurated President; in 1790, when the long fierce controversy with New York was amicably adjusted, and in 1791, when Vermont was admitted as one of the United States. All the towns in the county were settled before the end of the century.

The county was called "Caledonia,"—the ancient Roman name of Scotland,—out of regard for the emigrants from that country, who had purchased large tracts of land in the county, and had large and flourishing settlements in Barnet and Ryegate, and who were distinguished for their intelligence, integrity, enterprise, industry, and patriotism, as well as for their religious character. They favored the cause of American independence, and some of them served in the revolutionary army. They supported Vermont in the declaration of her independence and the formation of her constitution, in trying circumstances, which called for the highest exercise of the greatest wisdom, fortitude, and patriotism. They organized a church and settled a clergyman long before any other church was founded, or any other clergyman was installed in the county. Some of Caledonia's sons were appointed by the legislature of Vermont to high and responsible offices, which they held for many years, with credit to themselves and benefit to the State and county.

Rev. John Witherspoon, D.D., an emigrant from Scotland, owned a large tract of land in Ryegate, and his influence contributed largely to the early settlement of the county by his countrymen. He was a descendant of John Knox, the famous Scottish Reformer, by his daughter, the wife of John Welch, another reformer of Scotland. He was president of Princeton College in New Jersey, and was an able advocate of American independence. He was a member of Congress for six years, and evinced his patriotism by strenuously urging Congress to adopt the Declaration of Independence, which he himself readily signed. He was appointed by Congress on different important committees. He was a member of the committee appointed by Congress to repair to Vermont and endeavor to obtain a settlement of the matters in dispute between that State and New York, and came to Bennington, Vt., and had an interview with Gov. Chittenden immediately after his appointment. His able, humorous, witty, and sarcastic writings were greatly subservient to the cause of religion and civil liberty. That he was an eminent divine is shown by his excellent sermons, which he printed, and the admirable publications of Congress, calling on their constituents to seasons of fasting and prayer.

James, his eldest son, settled in the north part of Ryegate, where he remained nearly two years, but by his father's solicitation he joined the American army, in which he attained the rank of major. He was killed at the battle of Ger-

mantown. It is said that he was an aidecamp to Gen. Washington.

Gen. James Whitelaw, of Ryegate, was an emigrant from Scotland, being sent out as an agent to purchase a large body of land for "The Scots American Company" of Renfrewshire, composed of 140 members, most of whom were farmers, for whom he purchased, in 1773, the south half of Ryegate, from Dr. Witherspoon, at the price of "three shillings York money" per acre. He was a surveyor by profession, and was appointed by the surveyor-general of Vermont, deputy surveyor from 1778 to October, 1786. After his term he was annually elected by the legislature surveyor-general of Vermont till 1796. He surveyed a large majority of town lines in the State, and a number of towns he surveyed into lots, and drew the maps. By John Adams, President of the United States, he was appointed one of the five commissioners to execute, within the State of Vermont, an act of Congress, passed July 9, 1798, "to provide for the valuation of lands and dwelling-houses and the enumeration of slaves within the United States." In 1796, he published a large, beautiful, and correct map of Vermont, which he afterwards improved and republished.

Col. Alexander Harvey was another emigrant from Scotland, being sent as the agent of "The Farmers' Company, of Perthshire and Stirlingshire," to purchase a tract to be settled by them. In 1774, he purchased for the Company 7,000 acres in the southwest part of Barnet, the price being fourteen pence sterling (about twenty-five cents) an acre. He took an active part in the declaration of the independence of the State, and the formation of its constitution and government, having been a member of the conventions of 1777, and all the sessions of the legislature, till 1788, and also a member of the Constitutional Convention of 1791. He was appointed Associate Judge of Orange County, in 1781, which office he held till 1794. The government gave him a commission to build a fort on Onion or Lamoille River, which he declined to accept.

The emigrants from Scotland, in Barnet and Ryegate, were distinguished for religious knowledge, being well acquainted with the Holy Scriptures. They observed daily the worship of God in their families, and were careful to bring up their children "in the nurture and admonition of the Lord." They strictly sanctified the Sabbath, and loved the house of God. Feeling the want of the public ordinances of religion, they made strenuous endeavors, before and during the revolutionary war, to obtain them, and after repeated efforts they succeeded. During the revolutionary war and before and after it, several clergymen, most of whom were Presbyterians, and emigrants from Scotland came and preached in these two towns. Rev. Peter Powers, who was settled in Newbury from 1765 to 1784 was probably the first clergyman who preached in this county. Dr. Witherspoon visited Barnet and Ryegate two or three times and preached and baptized. On one of these occasions he rode the saddle on which his son sat at the battle of Germantown, and which bore the mark of the ball which killed him. The first visit was probably in 1775, and in 1782 he returned. Rev. Thomas Clark, of Salem, N. Y., preached here in 1775, and afterwards returned two or three times. Rev. Robert Annan, of Boston, Mass., preached in these parts first in 1784, then in 1785, in which year Rev. David Annan came and preached. Rev. John Houston, of Bedford, N. H., first visited these towns in the latter part of 1785, and returned in 1787, and remained a year. In 1784, the town of Barnet voted unanimously "to choose the Presbyterian form of religious worship, founded upon the word of God, as expressed in the confession of faith, catechisms, larger and shorter, with the form of Presbyterian church government agreed upon by the assembly of divines at Westminster, and practised by the church of Scotland." In 1787, the town and church of Barnet sent a joint petition to the Associate Presbyterian Synod in Scotland, for a minister, offering to pay the expense of his passage to this country. They were directed to apply to the Associate Presbytery of Pennsylvania, and informed that two clergymen had been sent out to that Presbytery, to which they made application, in consequence of which Rev. Thomas Beveridge, of Cambridge, Washington County, N. Y., came and preached in 1789, and returned in 1790. In consequence of application to that Presbytery, Rev. David Goodwillie came in the autumn of 1789, and continued his ministerial labors in Barnet and Ryegate till February, 1790, in which year a unanimous call was given to him to become their pastor, Ryegate receiving a sixth part of his pastoral labors. In this call the town of Barnet concurred. In September, 1790, Mr. Goodwillie returned and was settled as the minister of the town and pastor of the church. While yet a student in his native land, he was a friend to the American colonies struggling for their liberties. August 2, 1830, he died, honored and lamented, having labored successfully more than forty years in the county.

A Presbyterian church was organized in Peacham, by Rev. Peter Powers, January 22, 1784.

The Congregational Church in Peacham was formed April 14, 1794. Rev. Leonard Worcester was settled as the pastor of the church, Oct. 30, 1799, and continued his labors for many years. He was the second clergyman settled in the county.

At the present time there are different denominations of Christians in the county, the Congregationalists, Baptists, and Methodists being the most numerous.

Bible and missionary societies have existed in the county for many years, and many of the most honorable, useful, and influential persons have become members.

June 14, 1785, the legislature chartered the town of Wheelock, in this county, containing 23,040 acres, and granted it to the President and Trustees of Dartmouth College, and Moore's Charity School, at Hanover, N. H. The town was called Wheelock, in honor of Rev. John Wheelock, then president of the college.

The academy of Caledonia County was chartered and endowed by the legislature, and established at Peacham, Oct. 27, 1795. Alexander Harvey, James Whitelaw, Josiah L. Arnold, David Goodwillie, Daniel Cahoon, Horace Beardsly, Wm. Chamberlin, Benjamin Sias, and Jacob Davis were appointed trustees by the charter. The academy is a large, beautiful, and commodious edifice, in a fine situation, commanding a view of the White Mountains in New Hampshire, and contains a good library, and an extensive philosophical apparatus. The institution, from its organization to the present time, has been in a prosperous condition. Flourishing academies exist also in St. Johnsbury, Danville, Lyndon, and Barnet, with large and elegant edifices.

The excellent system of common schools adopted by Vermont is in successful operation in all parts of the county.

The legislature of Vermont held its session in Danville, the county seat, from Oct. 10 to Nov. 8, 1805.

The first newspaper published in the county was printed at Peacham, by Amos Farley and Samuel Goss. It was called "The Green Mountain Patriot," and commenced in Feb. 1798, and continued till March, 1807. "The North Star," published at Danville, commenced the first week in January, 1807, and still continues.

For many years the Hazen Road, according to its original design, was the highway for settlers coming into the county. At an early period a branch from that road began at Col. Harvey's residence on the North side of Harvey's Mountain, in Barnet, and ran past the north end of Harvey's Lake, and through the centre of that town to the mouth of Joes River, and was afterwards extended up the Passumpsic to St. Johnsbury. At a later date another branch from the Hazen Road was made to Danville.

The Passumpsic Turnpike Company was incorporated in 1805. The construction of the road commenced in 1807 at Joes River, and in 1808 it was made to Ryegate line, and afterwards extended to Wells River.

The Connecticut and Passumpsic rivers Railroad was constructed from White River, through Ryegate, and Barnet, to St. Johnsbury in 1850, and was extended to Barton, Vt., in 1858.

The Agricultural Society of the county has been in successful operation for many years, and its annual exhibitions show that agriculture is in a very flourishing condition. Indeed, the agricultural products of the county are greater than those of any other county in the United States, having no greater population. It is famous for cattle, sheep, horses, &c. The Scotch were early noted for making excellent butter. It is probable that no better butter is made in any other part of the world. Vast quantities are exported from the county every year, to Boston, where it always brings the highest price, and has repeatedly gained the highest premium.

For many years the nearest post-office to the county was at Newbury, Orange County, Vt. The mail was extended through Ryegate and Peacham to Danville, probably about the end of last century. In 1808, it was extended to Barnet and St. Johnsbury.

UNITED STATES AND STATE OFFICERS OF CALEDONIA COUNTY.

Hon. Wm. A. Palmer, of Danville, one of the judges of the supreme court in 1816, and senator in congress 1819-1825; was governor of Vermont, 1831-1834.

Hon. John Mattocks, of Peacham, one of the judges of the supreme court, 1833, 1834, and member of congress, 1821-1823, 1825-1827, 1841-1843; and was governor of the State in 1843.

Hon. Erastus Fairbanks, of St. Johnsbury, was governor of the State, 1852 and 1860.

Hon. William Chamberlin, of Peacham, a revolutionary soldier, who fought in the battles of Trenton, Princeton, and Bennington, and took an active part in the formation of the State government, was a member of congress, 1803-1805, 1809, 1810, and lieut.-governor of the State, 1813, 1814.

Hon. Wm. Cahoon, of Lyndon, was a member of congress, 1827-1831, and lieut.-governor of the State 1821, 1822.

Hon. Luther Jewett, of St. Johnsbury, was a member of congress, 1815-1817.

Hon. Benjamin F. Demming of Danville was member of congress, 1833-1835.

Hon. Isaac Fletcher, of Lyndon, was member of congress, 1837-1841.

Hon. Thomas Bartlett, of Lyndon, was member of congress, 1851, 1852.

Hon. Ephraim Paddock, of St. Johnsbury, was one of the judges of the supreme court, 1828-1830.

Hon. Charles Davis, of Danville, was one of the judges of the supreme court, 1846, 1847, and United States attorney for the District of Vermont, 1841-1845.

Hon. Luke P. Poland, one of the judges of the supreme court, 1848-1859, was chosen chief justice of Vermont, 1860, which office he now holds.

THE TOWNS OF CALEDONIA COUNTY, WITH THE DATE OF THE GRANTS, CHARTERS, AND SETTLEMENTS; THE NUMBER OF ACRES IN EACH; AND THEIR GRAND LIST FOR A.D. 1860.

TOWNS.	Date of Grant.	Date of Charter.	Date of Settlement.	Number of Acres.	Polls 1860.	Real Estate 1860.	Personal Property.
Barnet	Oct. 27, 1780.	Sept. 16, 1763.	Mar. 4, 1770.	26,524	728	$614,740	$107,815
Burke	Nov. 7, 1780.	Feb. 23, 1782.	1794.	23,040	610	234,650	68,550
Danville	Nov. 7, 1780.	Oct. 31, 1786.	1788 or '84.	27,511	940	668,284	124,537
Groton	Oct. 20, 1780.	Oct. 20, 1789.	1787.	28,300	334	159,633	34,954
Hardwick	Nov. 2, 1780.	Aug. 19, 1781.	Mar. 13, 1792.	23,040	620	355,818	168,453
Kirby	Nov. 6, 1780.	Oct. 27, 1790.	1788.	11,264	188	127,346	14,761
Lyndon		Nov. 20, 1780.	April,	33,040	656	461,436	10,351
Newark		Aug. 15, 1781.	1797.	23,040	252	86,646	8,400
Peacham	Oct. 27, 1786.	Dec. 31, 1763.	1775.	23,040	416	302,662	122,262
Ryegate	Nov. 7, 1780.	Sept. 8, 1763.	1773.	21,492	270	275,484	92,318
St. Johnsbury		Nov. 1, 1786.	1786.	21,167	1,538	473,057	283,166
Sheffield	Nov. 6, 1780.	Oct. 24, 1793.	1794.	23,607	390	121,466	423,225
Sutton	Nov. 7, 1780.	Feb. 26, 1782.	1790.	23,040	414	171,229	40,926
Walden		Aug. 18, 1781.	1783.	23,040	412	242,926	83,485
Waterford	June 14, 1785.	Nov. 8, 1780.	1784.	23,040	392	212,595	71,621
Wheelock		June 14, 1785.	1789.	23,040	320	340,063	16,321
					8,284	$4,786,388	$1,247,400

POPULATION OF CALEDONIA COUNTY.

TOWNS.	1791.	1800.	1810.	1820.	1830.	1840.	1850.	1860.
Bradley's Vale					21	50	107	
Barnet	477	860	1,701	1,484	1,764	2,007	2,521	2,081
Burke		98	460	841	869	760	1,109	1,158
Danville	574	1,314	2,240	2,300	2,631	2,633	2,674	2,642
Deweysburgh	48	162	200					
Goshen Gore by Wheelock			105		142	182	230	
Goshen Gore by Plainfield					44	39	20	
Groton	45	248	440	803	896	928	805	951
Hardwick	8	200	735	857	1,216	1,764	1,484	1,346
Harris's Gore								10
Kirby		20	311	312	401	620	596	478
Lyndon	59	542	1,091	1,296	1,822	1,759	1,752	1,645
Newark		8	88	154	257	791	841	741
Peacham	365	873	1,301	1,294	1,351	1,443	1,377	1,251
Ryegate	187	415	812	824	1,110	1,259	1,089	1,100
Sheffield		170	568	641	728	801	797	840
St. Johnsbury	143	615	1,334	1,404	1,592	1,887	2,758	3,472
Sutton		146	433	697	1,005	1,030	1,001	980
Walden	43	151	455	580	427	913	910	1,102
Waterford	95	505	1,289	1,347	1,758	1,848	1,412	1,172
Wheelock	32	568	954	900	834	831	630	832
	2,039	7,207	13,914	15,361	17,900	20,451	22,042	21,768

MAGNETIC VARIATION.

The magnetic variation observed by Gen. Whitelaw on the north line of Vermont, 20 miles west of the Connecticut River in 1785, was 7' and 40' west; and by Dr. Williams, at the northeast corner of the State, in 1806, it was 9° west. At the present time it is very nearly 10° west in this county.

METEOROLOGICAL TABLES for the years 1858, 1859, and 1860, deduced from the daily Meteorological Observations taken with standard instruments, at St. Johnsbury, Vt., in N. lat. 44° 25′ and W. lon. 70°, and 540 feet above tide water. These observations were kindly furnished by Franklin Fairbanks, Esq., to make these tables, which, had room in this work permitted, might have been extended, including some general observations on the clouds and winds. The thanks of the community are due to that gentleman for his diligence and care in taking these observations three times a day for years, making more than thirty daily observations to be recorded. He is one of more than five hundred regular meteorological observers in different parts of North America, taking daily observations, morning, noon, and night, for the Smithsonian Institution at Washington, to which their meteorological records are regularly returned. These observations, when properly discussed by that highly scientific institution, promise to produce, in process of time, results greatly conducive to the interests of agriculture and commerce. It is very desirable that the number of these observers were increased in all parts of the continent, and all the newspapers should publish monthly abstracts of their observations, as is done by the Caledonian, published at St. Johnsbury, and a few other papers in the country.

In the year 1859 rain fell on 95 different days.
"   "   snow "   83   "   "
"   "   total fall of snow, 104 inches.
"   "   rain and melted snow, 32.7 in.

In order to obtain information of the early history of Caledonia County, the writer has examined the public records of all the towns first settled, and made diligent search for private letters, papers, and journals; and he has succeeded beyond expectation, having had the privilege of examining very many early written and highly interesting and important documents, which belonged to Gen. Whitelaw, Col. Harvey, Rev. D. Goodwillie, Enos Stevens, Esq., and others. He is indebted to Walter Harvey, Esq., of Barnet, for the letters, papers, charts, and journal of his father, Col. Harvey; to the daughter of Gen. Whitelaw, Mrs. Abigail Henderson of Ryegate, for the general's correspondence with his father in Scotland, Dr. Witherspoon, and Rev. Thomas Clark, and other clergymen who preached in the county at an early period, and for the sketch of her father's life written by herself; and to the general's grandson, W. T. Whitelaw, Esq. of Ryegate, for the use of his grandfather's journal, papers, deeds, charts, and business correspondence, which consists of thousands of letters and several folio volumes of answers to correspondents. One of the deeds is from Dr. Witherspoon, and is beautifully written on a large sheet of parchment.

Barnet, Vt., Jan. 1, 1861.

	BAROMETER.					THERMOMETER.					Rain Gauge.	
1858.	7 A. M.	2 P. M.	9 P. M.	Highest Observation.	Lowest Observation.	7 A. M.	2 P. M.	9 P. M.	Highest Temperature.	Lowest Temperature.	Rain and melted Snow in Inches.	Snow in inches.
January ..	20.51	29.50	20.59	30.22	28.79	15	24	15	42	−8	1.41	11
February..	29.45	29.43	29.49	30.78	28.72	2	17	0	51	−19	1.34	15
March.....	29.32	29.29	29.41	29.93	28.74	13	31	18	52	−27	1.02	9
April.....	29.92	29.92	29.90	30.80	28.88	34	45	35	80	21	2.51	9
May......	29.47	29.44	29.40	30.07	28.90	45	59	45	77	35	4.15	..
June	29.42	29.42	29.42	29.68	29.20	59	70	61	90	40	4.36	..
July......	29.45	29.43	29.45	29.64	29.11	58	71	60	86	50	5.72	..
August ...	29.48	29.46	29.77	29.81	29.12	54	72	56	82	40	5.42	..
September	29.52	29.47	29.44	29.99	28.69	47	66	52	87	26	4.59	..
October...	29.51	29.52	29.54	29.99	28.86	38	51	42	70	23	5.78	1
November	29.56	29.56	29.60	29.85	29.04	20	34	28	48	−2	2.15	17
December	29.57	29.52	29.55	30.14	28.73	10	20	15	38	−25	2.10	17
	29.45	29.40	29.47	29.87	28.83	33	47	50	73	17	40.22	66
1859.												
January ..	29.55	29.53	29.55	30.05	28.90	5	22	0	38	−40	2.77	28
February..	29.45	29.43	29.44	29.78	29.00	9	26	10	40	−22	1.57	14
March.....	29.53	29.49	29.52	29.07	28.75	9	37	20	46	−10	4.01	10
April.....	29.28	29.24	29.31	30.73	29.64	31	46	36	68	22	2.42	9
May	29.50	29.42	29.55	29.84	29.17	50	67	51	87	33	1.78	..
June......	29.50	29.45	29.46	29.80	29.11	57	67	54	90	40	3.20	..
July	29.49	29.43	29.48	29.88	29.06	58	75	58	90	49	2.75	..
August ...	29.49	29.44	29.47	29.73	29.16	55	73	55	83	43	1.78	..
September	29.50	29.44	29.50	30.13	28.82	49	61	50	73	52	3.55	..
October...	29.57	29.54	29.49	30.05	29.17	26	47	38	75	18	1.50	..
November	29.26	29.32	29.51	30.00	28.74	20	40	23	53	10	3.84	18
December	29.49	29.49	29.53	30.30	28.83	2	18	10	48	−34	3.35	33
	29.40	29.42	29.45	29.90	29.05	31	48	36	68	19	32.07	104
1860.												
January ..	29.35	29.46	29.43	29.95	28.68	8	24	7	46	−32	.25	1
February..	29.50	29.41	29.46	30.03	29.65	9	31	15	53	−25	.03	10
March.....	29.32	29.31	29.38	29.77	28.80	27	38	27	65	9	1.06	7
April.....	29.49	29.35	29.41	29.58	29.70	28.61		68	77	53	.84	..
May	29.49	29.49	29.52	29.71	29.61		68		77	53	.84	..
June	29.21	29.18	29.18	29.40	28.87		71		80		1.62	..
July	29.35	29.34	29.50	29.62	29.08		75	54	90		2.75	..
August...	29.43	29.41	29.41	29.67	29.10		79		90		1.83	..
September	29.42	29.39	29.50	29.82	29.00		66		80		2.75	..
October...	29.48	29.50	29.50	29.97	28.73		62		68		4.02	3
November	29.26	29.32	29.17	29.87	28.60		34		54		.56	13
December	29.19	29.22	29.17	29.02	28.00		84		94			
	29.36	29.37	29.37	29.94	28.70		51		68		20.36	34

BARNET.

BY REV. THOMAS GOODWILLIE.

BARNET lies on the Connecticut River, at the bend where the river, coming from the northeast, turns and runs south. It is opposite Monroe (formerly Lyman), Grafton Co., N. H., in N. lat. 44° 18′ and E. lon. 4° 55′ and is 35 miles E. from Montpelier, 65 miles N. from Windsor, and 50 N. from Dartmouth College at Hanover N. H. It is bounded N. E. by Waterford and St. Johnsbury; S. E. by Connecticut River, which separates it from New Hampshire; S. by Ryegate; and N. W. by Peacham and Danville. It contains 25,524 acres, and according to the census of 1860, 2,002 inhabitants, which gives 50 persons to the square mile.

On the Connecticut and Passumpsic rivers are extensive intervales. The rest of the town is uneven and in some parts elevated. The town is well watered and the soil very productive. Harvey's lake in the southwest part of the town is nearly a mile and a half long and more than a half mile wide near the middle, and has a surface of more than three hundred acres. Ross's Pond, near the centre of the town, one third of a mile long and a quarter of a mile wide, covers about fifty acres. Moor's Pond, near the centre of the town, covers about twenty acres. All the streams of the town empty into the Connecticut. A stream from Ryegate enters Harvey's Lake at the south end, and Stevens's River issues from the north end of the lake, runs in a southeasterly direction and empties into Connecticut River about two and a half miles from the southeast corner of the town. About one hundred and fifty rods from its mouth it falls eighty feet in twenty rods, and presents a grand view when the waters are high. A stream from Peacham enters it near the lake and another considerable stream from the same town enters it about four miles from its mouth. A small stream issues out of Ross's Pond and runs through Moor's Pond and enters the Connecticut a quarter of a mile below the Passumpsic. Joes River issues from Joes Pond in Danville, and runs in a southeasterly direction through the town and enters the Passumpsic about a mile and a half from its mouth. It is the largest stream in Barnet except the Passumpsic, and is also called Merrit's River, because John Merrit owned land near its mouth.

Enerick Brook, coming from Danville, enters the Passumpsic about a mile above the mouth of Joes River.

The Passumpsic, the longest and largest river in the county, comes from St. Johnsbury through a corner of Waterford, and enters the town on the northeast part, and gradually turns and runs south and empties into the Connecticut River about two miles and a half from the northeast corner of the town. Major Rogers and his rangers came down this river from Canada in his expedition to punish the St. Francis tribe of Indians in October, 1759, and being disappointed in not receiving provisions when they came to the Connecticut River, a number of them died of starvation and fatigue, as related in the preceding history of the county.

Thompson's Gazetteer of Vermont, edition of 1824, says, "Maj. Rogers, with one hundred and fifty-six men, came to the mouth of the Passumpsic, discovered fire on the round island, made a raft and passed over to it, but, to their surprise and mortification, found no provisions had been left. The men, already reduced to a state of starvation, were so disheartened at this discovery that thirty-six of them died before the next day. An Indian was cut to pieces and divided among the survivors. David Woods, who has recently lived in this town, was one of Rogers's sergeants, and stated the above account to be correct." This account is incorrect in some important particulars. Rogers's journal and the histories of the expedition show that the soldiers and prisoners, all told, did not amount to that number, besides all the survivors were not then and there present, and that it is highly improbable that so great a number as thirty-six died in eighteen hours. Peter Lervey, one of Rogers's men, who lived in this town a short time before his death, about 1817, and who made no mention of the party eating human flesh, said that some of the men died on the Passumpsic before they came to its mouth, and others on the Connecticut River below its mouth. Human bones have been discovered in the meadows on the Passumpsic above its mouth and on the Connecticut above the Barnet depot. The story of David Woods, that "an Indian was cut to pieces and divided among the survivors" has been diligently investigated. Neither the histories of the time nor Rogers's journal mention such a circumstance, so repulsive to the refined feelings of civilized society. The story has been traced up to David Woods, who lived in an adjoining town, as the sole witness, and application has been made to living persons who knew "the man and his manner." One of these persons, who was for many years president of the Historical Society of Vermont, writes, "I have heard Woods say that he was with Rogers, and was one of his sergeants, and that they camped near the mouth of the Passumpsic, and that night snow fell several inches deep, and that a negro soldier died that night and was cut up in the morning and divided among the soldiers, and he had one hand for his share, on which, with a small trout, after being cooked, he made a very good breakfast. After breakfast, in going down the river they discovered fire on the round island opposite its mouth, and that Rogers and one man passed over to the island. Rogers became satisfied that men had been there with provisions but had left. On his return to his men a consultation was had and each soldier was told to take care of himself."

Another person writes, "Joseph Woods told me, and I think he said his father told him, that about the time the rangers expected to die of starvation, the men cast lots to see who should be killed to furnish food so that they might not all die, and that one was killed and eaten."

Another person has assured the writer that he heard David Woods say that he had "eaten a piece of an Indian."

Now all these stories can be reconciled upon the improbable supposition that Rogers's party killed one living man, a soldier; and ate three dead men, a white man, a negro, and an Indian. If Rogers and his men did these things, they had the hearts of hyenas, destitute of all good feelings and refined sentiments. Rather than attribute such horrible deeds to them, it would be far more reasonable to believe that the criminal who could boast that he "stood the pillory like a gentleman," was not a man of honor and integrity. Whatever this one witness, and perhaps some few others like him, may have done, it is safe to assert that there is no proof that Rogers and his men, as a party, killed or ate any man, white, black, or red. It is gratifying that this investigation has dispelled the cloud that has for so long time obscured, in some degree, the glory of the heroic Rogers and his brave men, who fearlessly went hundreds of miles through the woods into the enemy's country, performed exploits and endured the tortures of famine and fatigue to punish the horrid barbarities long practised by the savages of Canada, and so save the families of the frontier settlements of New England from murder, plunder, and arson.

A man by the name of Barnes lived in Barnet a short time, at an early period, who belonged to Rogers's party, and said that the silver image weighing ten pounds, which they took from the chapel in St. Francis, was hid on the way in a crevice of a rock, and covered with leaves. He said also that they took from the chapel two gold candlesticks, which they hid in the woods, under the root of a tree, near the Canada line, and that he went back after some years and searched for them, but could not find where he hid them. It is said that this part of his story was confirmed by a report in the newspaper, about 1816, that two gold candlesticks, worth $1,000, were found in the woods in Hatley, C. E., which lay in Rogers's way.

The first Geological Report of Vermont says, that beds of shell marl are found in Barnet. The second report on that subject says, "Barnet lies on the Connecticut River, in the calcareo-mica slate region. A considerable range of clay slate is found near the river. A range of granite passes through the west part of the town. The soil in the Passumpsic and Connecticut valleys is alluvial and river deposit of good quality. In the westerly part the limestone is rapidly decomposing and uniting with the drift and makes an excellent soil. The town, although considerably broken, has an excellent soil for grazing. Many valuable cattle and some horses are sent to market annually, and large quantities of excellent butter. Deposits of muck are numerous, and considerable quantities of marl are found in several places, from which a good quality of lime has been manufactured. The agricultural products of the town are abundant and of a good quality. Besides, many beef cattle and some horses and sheep are sent to market. The Scotch were early noted for making good butter." .

Almost every farmer keeps a dairy, and some of them make more than a ton of butter in a season. It brings the highest price in the market. One who has travelled extensively in Europe and America, thinks that the butter made in this part of our country is the best in the world.

For many years after the settlement of the town by the Scotch, they manufactured large quantities of oatmeal, which is a healthy and nutritive kind of food. Dr. Johnson, who had a powerful prejudice against the Scotch, defined oatmeal as the food of men in Scotland and of horses in England. Upon which a Scotch nobleman exclaimed, "Where will he find such men and such horses?" Oatmeal was highly serviceable to the first settlers, and was furnished to the surrounding towns to the Canada line and even beyond it. In one of the years of scarcity of provisions, a man from a distant town

came to Barnet, and having obtained a sufficient supply of oatmeal for his famishing family, expressed his gladness and gratitude by exclaiming, "Blessed be the Scotch, for they *invented* oatmeal!"

It was the first town settled and the second chartered in the country; Ryegate, lying on the Connecticut River, south of it, receiving its charter but eight days before. The charter is dated September 16, 1763, and was granted under the British crown by Benning Wentworth, governor of the province of New Hampshire. It is in the common form of the New Hampshire charters. It calls the town "Barnet," which it describes and bounds as follows, viz :—

"Beginning at the northwesterly corner of Ryegate, thence south sixty-eight degrees east by Ryegate to the southeasterly corner thereof, being a tree standing on the banks of the westerly side of Connecticut River, thence up said river as that tends so far as to make six miles on a straight line, thence turning off and running north twenty-eight degrees west so far that a straight line drawn from that period to the northwesterly corner of Ryegate, the bounds begun at, shall include the contents of six miles square or 23,040 acres and no more, out of which an allowance is to be made for highways and unimprovable lands by rocks, ponds, mountains, and rivers, one thousand and forty acres free, according to the plan and survey thereof made by our said governor's order and returned to the secretary's office and hereto annexed."

The plan delineated in the charter gives three sides of the town. The line on Ryegate is marked six and one fourth miles. The length of the northeast line is not given. The Connecticut River is delineated as the southeast side. A part of the Passumpsic is sketched on which the word "falls" is written, not far from its mouth. But the town is actually larger than described in the charter, which limits it to 36 square miles. As surveyed and returned to the State office of Vermont, it contains 25,524 acres, which is almost 40 square miles.

The south line along Ryegate is 6 and one half miles, being a quarter of a mile more than is mentioned in the charter. The distance from the southeast to the northeast corner, in a straight line (through New Hampshire), is more than 6 miles, the length prescribed in the charter. The northeast line, along Waterford and St. Johnsbury, is 5 miles and 52 rods, and the northwest line, along Peacham and Danville, is 10 miles and 228 rods. By the charter, the town is incorporated, and its inhabitants enfranchised; and so soon as there were fifty families settled in town it should have the privilege of holding two fairs annually, and a market opened and held one or more days each week. The first meeting for the choice of town officers was to be held on the first Tuesday of Oct., 1764, and to be notified by Simeon Stevens, who was appointed its moderator, and that the annual meeting thereafter should be always held in March. The grant of lands to the proprietors was on the following conditions, viz : that every grantee should cultivate ·five acres of land within the term of five years for every fifty acres of land owned, and to continue afterwards additional cultivation on penalty of forfeiture; that all pine trees fit for masts should be preserved for the royal navy; that before the division of the town a lot near the centre of the town should be divided into acres, one of which should belong to each grantee, and that each grantee should pay to the governor and his successor, one ear of Indian corn annually, for ten years, if demanded, and after that period one shilling, proclamation money, for every 100 acres owned, to be paid annually, forever. The town was to be divided equally into seventy-three shares. A lot of 500 acres was laid off on the Connecticut River, in the northeast corner of the town as "the governor's lot," which was to be two shares; and one share for the society propagating the gospel in foreign parts; one share for a glebe for the Church of England; one share for the first settled minister, and one share for schools, were granted forever. Sixty-seven grantees are named in the charter, which is signed by Benning Wentworth, governor and commander, and attested by T. Atkinson, Jr., Secretary. The American Revolution swept away the conditions of the charter, but the United States government confirmed all such grants.

It is not known when the town was organized, and the first meeting was held according to the charter. In Willard Stevens's collection of documents, were found some loose papers, worn and torn, containing some brief minutes of town meetings held during the revolutionary war. The following is a summary of these minutes, which are in the handwriting of Stevens Rider :

"Sept. 8, 1778. Alexander Harvey chosen Representative to the General Assembly, and entrusted with the votes (for Governor, Lieut. Governor, and Councillors) and all powers necessary, agreeable to the Constitution." Signed " Stevens Rider, T. Clerk." " Dec. 3, 1779. The town took into consideration the votes, and chose Thomas Smith constable to collect what was demanded of the town: voted Walter Brock and Peter Lang to settle the wages of the boys that were hired for this town, and they brought in that they should have eight bushels of wheat a month." " March 13, 1781. Chose Jacob Hall, moderator; Stevens Rider, town clerk; Alexander Harvey, justice of the peace for this town; Peter Lang, John Waddell, Walter Brock, select men."

Other town officers were chosen, but the mice have gnawed off a part of the paper.

" Voted that every man work six days on said road, or pay a fine of one dollar for every day he is missing without sufficient reason." " Voted, if any man let his hogs run out so as to hurt any of his neighbor's interest, the owner of the hogs should make it good to his neighbor." " May 14, 1781. Voted to raise two able-bodied men to guard the frontiers of this place and others, according to the orders Col. Johnston sent, in part of five men we had to raise according to orders that came to this town.

Voted a committee to raise one man for this town, as reasonably as they can, and the town agrees to it, by a vote of this meeting, for guarding the frontiers." "Voted Jacob Hall, James Gilchrist, and Peter Lang, a committee to write letters to Col. Beedel and Col. Johnston." " Voted Jacob Hall, captain; Daniel Hall, lieutenant."

Then follows a list of the men who have no guns, 15 in number.

" Sept. 8, 1781. Took into consideration a (despatch from) Major Childs. Voted, the major part, not to do any thing as to the last year's provisions — not to raise any at all." " Voted to raise 750 weight as to this year, to turn to the store for troops at Pencham." " Voted James Cross and Walter Brock a committee to speak to Major Childs concerning the provisions." " Voted Jacob Hall, Mr. Stuart, Mr. Gilchrist, and Peter Lang, to write a letter to Major Childs concerning getting last year's provisions. Chose two assessors; chose Mr. Harvey for a representative." "Oct. 2, 1781. Chose Walter Brock a lister, with James Cross, chosen a lister before, and likewise carried in to the listers their ratable estate."

At a meeting having no date, Alexander Harvey was chosen a representative to the General Assembly that sat at Charlestown, N.H., Oct. 11, 1781. These are certainly not the regular town records which the writer is assured Stevens Rider said, after the revolutionary war, were lost ! The State records show that town meetings were regularly held to choose Col. Harvey a delegate to the three conventions of 1777, and a representative to the legislature, from its first meeting, March 12, 1778, till the town meeting, March, 1783, which therefore was not the first town meeting at which the town was organized, as has been asserted in some histories of the town.

The regular town records begin " March 18, 1783. At a meeting of the freemen of this town, legally warned at the house of Robert Twaddell, made choice of the following gentlemen for one year : Alexander Harvey, president, and Walter Brock, clerk ; James Gilchrist, Thomas Smith, Bartholomew Somers, selectmen ; James Orr and Stevens Rider, constables ; James Cross, treasurer ; James Stuart and Peter Sylvester, listers ; John McLaren and Jacob Hall, collectors ; James Gilchrist, grand-juror ; Peter Lang, Robert Brock, tythingmen ; James Stuart, sealer of weights and measures ; Alexander Thompson, William Rider, Archibald Harvey, road surveyors ; Elijah Hall, George Garland, fence surveyors. John Shaw declined to be a selectman.

WALTER BROCK, Town Clerk."

TOWN CLERKS OF BARNET.

Walter Brock	-	-	-	1783 to 1787.
Walter Stuart	-	-	-	1787 to 1806.
David Goodwillie	-	-	1807 to 1827.
John Shaw	-	-	-	1827 to 1852.
Austin O. Hubbard	-	-	1852 to 1855.
Jonathan D. Abbott	-	-	1855 to 1859.
Thomas Goodwillie	-	-	1859 to 1861.

But though the meeting held March 18, 1783, was not the first town meeting at which the town was organized, as has been asserted, yet a list of all the freemen of the town seems to have been commenced the next year, and is recorded at the beginning of the first volume, as follows, viz : —

" Barnet, January 29, 1784. Now and formerly the persons mentioned took the freeman's oath: Peter Sylvester, Samuel Perle, James Cross, Alexander Thompson, Stevens Rider, Elijah Hall, Walter Brock, James Stuart, Samuel Stevens, John Merrit, James Orr, Daniel McFarlane, Jacob Hall, Bartholomew Somers, James Gilchrist, Alexander Harvey, William Tice, Hugh Ross, John McFarlane, Robert Twaddell, William Stevenson, John McLaren, Ezekiel Manchester, Robert Somers, John Waddell, Robert McFarlane, John Ross, Andrew Lackie, Archibald Harvey, Peter Lang, Cloud Stuart, Walter Stuart, Daniel Hall, Thomas Smith, George Garland. Jan. 29, 1784. The following gentlemen took the freeman's oath in as far as it agrees with the word of God: John Waddell, Hugh Ross, John McFarlane, John McLaren, Ezekiel Manchester, Robert Somers, Andrew Lackie, Archibald Harvey, Cloud Stuart, Walter Stuart, George Garland. Barnet, March 11, 1785. The following persons took the freeman's oath: John Robertson, Wm. Robertson, Moses Hall, Levi Hall, Robert Blair, James Buchanan, William Maxwell, Isaac Brown, Elijah Hall, Jr., Simon Perle. April 6, 1785. John Youngman, William Warden, Hugh Gammell. August 27, 1785. Joseph Bonet. Sept. 5. John McIndoe, John Hindman. 1787. John Gilkenson. May 1. John Goddard. Sept 4. 1788. Enos Stevens. March 11. John Rankins, William Gilfillan, Sen., John McNabb, James McLaren, Andrew Lang. Feb. 2, 1789. Alexander McIlroy (Roy), Samuel Huston. March 10. Thomas Hazeltine, Phineas Aimes, Phineas Thurston, Oliver Stevens, Ephraim Pierce, Moses Cross, Job Abbott, Levi Sylvester. 1790, Feb. 4. Aaron Wesson, Dr. Stevens, John Mitchell, John Stevens, Timothy Hazeltine, Cloud Somers, John Galbraith. Sept. 24. Joseph Hazeltine. Dec. 7. Thomas Gilfillan, William Innes, John Waddell, Jr., and Wm. Lang."

March 4, 1770, the first settlement in the town and county was made. The first settlers were Daniel, Jacob, and Elijah Hall, three brothers, and Jonathan Fowler. The first house in the town and county was built by the Halls at the foot of the Falls on Stevens River, and on its north side. The three brothers, and probably Jonathan Fowler, received gratuitously from the proprietors 100 acres each to encourage them to settle the town. Daniel Hall's lot was the farm where Cloud and Robert Somers first settled. Jacob Hall's lot included the meadows north of Stevens River, and Elijah Hall's lot was north of Rider's Farm. Jonathan Fowler probably settled first on the north end of the McIndoe Plain, and then in the S. W. part of the town, near Aaron and Peter Wesson's house, in the Harvey tract. Sarah, daughter of Elijah Hall, was the first child born in the town and county. She was married Dec. 27, 1787, to James McLaren, in the 17th year of her age. She was a member of the Associate Presbyterian Church of Barnet, and died at an advanced age. Barnet Fowler, son of Jonathan Fowler, was the first male child born in Barnet, and probably in the county. The Fowler family moved to Shipton, C. E. about 1810. The writer possesses documents signed by Jonathan Fowler, Sept. 3, 1791, and by Barnet Fowler, March 12, 1799.

Daniel Hall's wife was the first person who died in town after its settlement. She was buried in the graveyard at Stevens Village. She was the mother of Dr. Abiathar Wright, who was a physician in the town. Jacob Hall had but one son, Moses, to whom he sold his farm, but they afterwards moved to Shipton, C. E. Daniel Hall moved to St. Johnsbury, thence to Lyndon, and thence to Burke, where he died, having been an early settler in four towns in this county.

The town from the very first took an active part in the declaration of the independence of the State of Vermont, and the formation of its constitution and government. Alexander Harvey represented the town in the three conventions in 1777, which declared the State independent, and formed a constitution, and organized a government.

REPRESENTATIVES OF THE TOWN IN THE LEGISLATURE OF VERMONT.

Alexander Harvey -	-	1778 to 1788.
James Cross -	-	1789 to 1794.
Enos Stevens -	-	1795 to 1796.
Walter Brock -	-	1797 to 1800.
James McLaren -	-	1801 to 1803.
John Barchop -		1804.
David Goodwillie -		1805.
William Strobridge -		1806.
Enos Stevens -	-	1807.
John Duncan -	-	1808 to 1811.
Adam Duncan -	-	1812 – 1813.
Alexander Gilchrist -	-	1814 to 1816.
Henry Oakes -	-	1817 – 1818.
William Gilkerson -	-	1819 to 1823.
Walter Harvey -	-	1824 – 1825.
Henry Stevens -	-	1826 – 1827.
Hugh Somers -		1828.
Walter Harvey -		1829.
William Gilkerson -	-	1830 to 1831.
Cloud Harvey -	-	1832 to 1833.
William Shearer -		1834.
Hugh Somers -		1835.
William Shearer -		1836.
Walter Harvey -	-	1837 to 1839.
James Gilchrist -	-	1840 – 1841.
William Lackie -	-	1842 – 1843.
Walter Harvey -		1844.
Lloyd Kimball -	-	1845 – 1846.
Obed S. Hatch -	-	1847.
John Harvey -	-	1848.
Bartholomew Gilkerson -	-	1849 – 1850.
Obed S. Hatch -	-	1851.
James K. Remick -	-	1852.
Robert Harvey -	-	1853 – 1854.
(No choice) -	-	1855.

Alexander Johnston -   -   - 1856 to 1857.
Jonathan D. Abbott -   -   - 1858 to 1859.
William Warden   -   -   -   1860.

First justices of the peace appointed by the State were Walter Brock and James Gilchrist. Walter Harvey was a justice 36, Silas Harvey 33, William Shearer 29, Hugh Somers 23, and James Gilchrist, Jr. 17 years.

Enos and Willard Stevens, of Charlestown, N. H., "chief proprietors of the township of Barnet, make a contract, July 11, 1770, with Col. John Hurd of Haverhill, N. H., to build at the falls on Stevens's River in Barnet, a sawmill the ensuing fall, if convenient, otherwise by the first of July, 1771, and a gristmill within six months after that time, both to be kept in good repair during five years, the dangers of war and the enemy excepted." The saw and gristmill irons were to be furnished on the spot by E. & W. Stevens, and Col. Hurd was to have for his encouragement one hundred acres of land for a mill lot, bounded one hundred rods on Connecticut River, running back half a mile, and including the falls on Stevens's River. According to contract, the irons were furnished and Col. Hurd built the first mills in the town and county, and received for his reward a title to the mill-lot, on which he built a house and barn, and cleared twenty acres of land, and otherwise encouraged the settlement of the town. But by consent of E. and W. Stevens, Elijah Hall had previously pitched on a part of said lot when he first settled the town, March 4, 1770, and had cleared a part of it and built a house on it. For his improvements Col. Hurd gave Elijah Hall $50, and E. and W. Stevens gave him one hundred acres in a different part of the town for his quitclaim. August 14, 1774, Col. Hurd sold the land and mills to Willard Stevens.

Joseph Hutchins, of Haverhill, N. H., engaged by contract to come to Barnet and pitch a lot and begin to improve it, in the summer of 1770, but he did not receive a deed till 1780. Col. Hurd, who built the mills at the falls on Stevens's River, 1771, seems to have continued his residence in town some years.

Thomas Smith receives a deed from Enos and Willard Stevens in 1775, and Stevens Rider was in town May 5, 1776, when Willard Stevens, one of the principal proprietors of the town, writes to him "several disappointments have prevented my not being in Barnet the winter past. This spring I intended to have moved up with my family. For several reasons I cannot move up till June. I send up my brother Solomon in order to assist Thomas Smith in getting in some spring grain. I intend to be up about the middle of May." He came and settled in town, but when the revolutionary war commenced he left it, and Elijah King, who married his sister Mary, came. They resided in town till death. Archibald McLaughlin, a Scotchman,

receives a deed, 1776, for lots in the southeast corner of Harvey's tract.

According to the proprietors' records, at a meeting of the proprietors, held at Walter Brock's, in Barnet, August 23, 1785, which seems to be the first meeting held for some years, an inquiry for the charter was made, when it was found that it had been "carried out of the United States." The document before the writer is a copy of the charter, taken June 24, 1788, from the third volume of the book of charters in the State office of New Hampshire, and attested by Joseph Pearson, Secretary. The document is worn into *eight* pieces.

The records of the proprietors previous to August 23, 1785, are lost. Were these missing records "carried out of the United States" along with the charter?

According to a contract found among Enos Stevens's papers, dated April, 1770, Joseph Hutchins of Haverhill, N. H., engages to improve some part of the lands in Barnet within the term of four or six months, and to pitch and work "either one of the fifty acre lots of upland or one of the meadow lots surveyed and laid out in said township." Enos Stevens engages to deed to him "within three months three fifty acre lots of upland, and three interval lots of land as they are now surveyed and laid out in said township." No plan of this survey has been found and no reference to it is made in the record. This survey may have been entered on the plan of 1774, but that part of the chart is worn off and lost. We next read of the survey of the east part of the town.

From the existing proprietors' records, with a few accompanying papers, we learn when the town was surveyed into lots, and how they were divided to the proprietors or grantees, and the cost of procuring the charter and the surveys and division of the town. In 1773, the east part of the town was surveyed by Caleb Willard, and in 1774, the survey into large lots was completed. Among the papers of Enos Stevens was found a part of a chart of the town on a small scale. The other part, nearly one half, being worn off and lost. It is marked "a plan of Barnet, 1774," most probably in the handwriting of Solomon Stevens, surveyor. Samuel Stevens presented an account, dated Charlestown, August 18, 1785, to the proprietors at their meeting, August 23, 1785, of which we give a summary.

"July, 1762, to expense of procuring a charter, £219." This was probably dated before the charter, to include the survey of the town limits, as ordered by Gov. Wentworth, and described and delineated in the charter. Elijah King and others surveyed the charter limits of the towns immediately above Wells River in 1762 or 1763. "October, 1773, to survey of the east part of the town by Caleb Willard, £50." "June, 1774, to surveying the town into lots of one hundred acres each, £139."

These sums, together with the interest to August 13, 1785, amount to £886, for the costs of chartering and surveying the town. He charges "October; 1770, for one hundred acres given to Col. Hurd as an encouragement to build mills £50." "To mill-irons delivered there, £30." "To ten lots of land given to divers persons, as an encouragement to settle in said town, at £10 each, £100." These sums, with interest to the date of the account, amounted to £355. The sum total was £1,241. The proprietors voted to rectify and allow Samuel Stevens's account, and also voted to raise a tax of £17 on each original right, which was to be paid in silver or gold, at the rate in silver of 6s. 8d. per oz., which tax was for paying the proprietors' debts. Samuel Stevens was appointed to collect this tax, in doing which he sold at vendue in Springfield, February 27, 1786, forty-six original rights, including Benning Wentworth's two shares, to Enos Stevens. The proprietors also at their meeting, August 23, 1785, "voted to accept and establish the survey formerly made by Solomon Stevens, according to the plan by him made, and that said plan be lodged in the proprietors' clerk's office for reference. Among the proprietors' papers is a chart of the town on a scale of 60 chains to an inch, on the face of which is inscribed "A contracted copy of the plan of Barnet, taken from a plan called a true copy of the plan of the division of Barnet, accepted by the proprietors in their meeting, August, 1785, and attested by James Whitelaw, surveyor."

In the proprietors' records this plan, of which this is a contracted copy, is called "Whitelaw's plan," and agrees with the survey of the lots according to the plan of 1774, which, however, did not contain a survey of the small, irregular lots on the Connecticut River, and on the south line of the town called the "after division lots," as they were divided after the partition of the large lots to equalize the shares of the proprietors in quantity and quality.

It appears from Gen. Whitelaw's field-book that he surveyed the town lines of Barnet, in 1784, and found at the northeast corner of the town a pine-tree standing on the bank of the Connecticut River, marked "1770," which was probably done by the New York surveyors when they surveyed "Dunmore." From these facts it appears that General Whitelaw surveyed the whole town and made a complete chart of it and presented it to the proprietors at their meeting August 23, 1785, which was accepted by them, and by which the whole town was divided among them.

The writer has seen four charts of Barnet, on a scale of 30 chains to the inch, all of which were made by him. They are all soiled, worn or torn. One of these, found among the papers of Enos Stevens, attested by Gen. Whitelaw, and dated 1785, is most probably the one accepted by the proprietors, and by which the town was ultimately divided among them, which division

seems to have been nearly completed in 1785, when the proprietors' records terminate, but it would appear probable that the after division lots were not all pitched so late as 1802. The names of the proprietors are entered on all Whitelaw's maps in the lots which they pitched. Since the survey the magnetic variation of the compass needle has increased nearly two degrees westward.

Most of the town was surveyed into lots of 100 acres each. The side lines of the lots are 160 rods, and run parallel with the N. E. side of the town, which runs N. 28 deg. W., and the end lines of the lots are 100 rods, nearly ⅓ of a mile, and run parallel with the N. W. line of the town, which runs N. 48 deg. E. The lots are therefore not quite rectangular. The lots along Peacham and Danville were made to consist of 287 acres. The small and irregularly formed lots were on the Ryegate line, and along Connecticut River, at the S. E. and N. E. corners of the town.

There were 366 acres to each proprietor's right, for which he had three 100-acre lots, and such a small lot, "after division lot," as equalized the rights or shares in quantity and quality. The proprietors voted lots for public uses, according to the charter; but no part near the centre of the town was surveyed into acre-lots, that each proprietor might have one, as required by the charter. The full division of the large lots of the town to the proprietors, was finally settled and completed about 1787. The proprietors voted, Nov. 28, 1787, that "Enos Stevens, for and in consideration of his rebuilding the mills on Stevens River in Barnet, have the exclusive privilege of pitching the after division of the lands belonging to ten rights or shares." "Dec. 12, 1787, voted that lot No. 160 be for the clerk (Walter Brock), and he to pay Mr. Whitelaw, and find a book, and transfer the whole." This division of the town to the proprietors was called "the original survey" or "Grand Division of Barnet."

Nov. 6, 1774, John Clark and Alexander Harvey bought of Samuel Stevens, one of the chief owners of Barnet, 7000 acres of land in the S. W. part of the town, which was to be laid off in one body on the Peacham line, and received a bond for a deed, when the sum of £408 6s. 8d. was paid, and guaranteeing peaceable possession, in the mean time. The price per acre was 14d., or about '25. This tract occupies the S. W. part of the town, of which it is more than one fourth part, thus described: Beginning at the S. W. corner of the town, its boundary line ran along the Peacham line 5 miles to a large beach-tree marked A. H, J. W, A. T, 1776; thence, turning a right angle, it runs S. 42 deg. past the Presbyterian meeting-house, near the centre of the town, 2 miles, 188 rods, and 95 links, to a small hemlock marked A. H, I. W, 1776, on the top of the hill north of John Gilfillan's house; thence, turning a right angle, it ran S. 48 deg., W. in a direction parallel with the Peacham line, about 3 miles, 112 rods, and 32 links, to a great hemlock marked A . II, I .W, 1776; thence, turning an obtuse angle, it ran along the Ryegate town line, N. 68 deg. W. about 3 miles, to the place of beginning; the whole containing 7,000 acres, which was deeded by Willard Stevens to Alexander Harvey, March 10, 1781. Gen. Whitelaw surveyed the Harvey Tract in 1776. It is divided into 5 ranges running parallel with the Peacham line. The lots contain 50 acres each, and are rectangular, long, and narrow, and are numbered separately in each range, beginning at the Ryegate line. Their whole number is 135.

The present town clerk, by a late vote of the town, made a double index of all the land records from 1783 to the present time. The index-book is a royal folio of 500 pages, made for such a purpose. The index occupies more than 300 pages, with blank leaves under each letter for future use. It consists of a descending index, by which land titles can be traced down to the present time, and an ascending index, by which the title can be traced up to the grantees in the charter. To facilitate the process, the years in which the deeds were recorded are entered by the clerk in the double index, to make which every page of the land records, amounting to several thousand, was examined, so that, if a deed is recorded, it can be easily and quickly found, and, if it is not in the index, it is certainly known that it has not been recorded. It is believed Barnet is the first town in Vermont that has made such an index, which saves much time and trouble, and gives certain and satisfactory information in searching the records.

During the Revolutionary War, and for some years after it, the town held its meetings at John McLaren's, but more frequently at Robert Twaddell's, whose houses were near the centre of the town. June 1, 1786, the proprietors pitched lots 87, 38, and 39 for the first settled minister of the gospel, according to the charter of the town. In 1785 or 1786, 4 acres in the N. W. corner of lot 87 were cleared, each quarter of the town clearing an acre. On this a meeting house was raised. Dec. 18, 1788, the town voted to raise money by subscription towards finishing the meeting-house. "Jan. 15, 1789. Thirty-one persons declare their intention of having the meeting-house for a place of public worship." "Oct. 9. Town resolves that the house should be finished by subscription." Dec. 30, 1791. Town votes that the meeting-house was town property, and subject to town rules. Jan. 19, 1792. The town votes to constitute and appoint the meeting-house for public worship of God. Feb. 1, 1792. The lower part of the house having been finished, the pews, 28 in number, were sold at vendue, under certain regulations, for about £300, one tenth part to be paid in money,

and the rest in wheat, at 5s. per bushel. July 5, 1795. The galleries were finished, and the pews were sold, in a similar manner, for about £110, which was to be paid for the expense of finishing the house. Jan. 14, 1799. The town votes that a sum not exceeding $120 of the money due for the sale of seats be applied to purchase stoves for the house. They were not, however, procured till about 1810; still, the meeting on Sabbath was well attended in the winter, all being warmly clothed, and the women having foot-stoves, as they were called.

In 1829, the year before the demise of Rev. David Goodwillie, the first meeting-house was removed, and, on the same site, a large brick church edifice, with a steeple, was built at a cost of nearly $5,000. This edifice was accidentally burnt in February, 1849, and the congregation erected and finished the present elegant and commodious house of public worship, all ready for use, in 5 months after the former one was burnt, and the cost of erection was promptly paid.

The Revolutionary soldiers were Thomas Hazeltine, a pensioner, John Bonett, a pensioner, Daniel Hall, Caleb Stiles, John Woods, William Strobridge, a pensioner, Amasa Grout, and William Tice. The following Scotchmen also served in the Revolutionary War: Archibald Harvey, a pensioner, who was at the taking of Quebec: Thomas Clark, who emigrated to this country in 1774. He enlisted at Hanover, N. H., and served in Col. Cilley's regiment. He was in the battle of Saratoga, and was so badly wounded that he was taken to the hospital in Albany. When recovered, and on his way to rejoin the army, he was seized with fever and ague, and hired a man for $200 to take his place in the army, which sum he lost, as the Continental money was so depreciated in value. He settled in Barnet in 1792 or 1793, but, some years before his death, removed to the S. E. corner of Peacham. He was an intelligent man, and a member of the Associate Presbyterian Church of Barnet. William Johnston, a staff officer and a pensioner, was at the battles of Germantown, Monmouth, and Brandywine. He saw Gen. Putnam plunge down the frightful precipice, and escape, and witnessed Maj. Andre's execution, when, he said, the American officers wept. On one occasion, he was engaged in taking some British soldiers captive, one of whom was Alexander Emsley, who settled in Barnet, and married his widow.

Upon the first call for Revolutionary soldiers in 1777, Bartholomew Somers, John McLaren, and James Orr, all of whom settled early in town, near the centre, went to Saratoga at the time of Burgoyne's surrender. They were all members of the same church. Mr. McLaren's potatoes were not dug till the next spring, when they were found to be fresh and good, as the snow, which fell early, and was deep all winter, preserved them. Thus Providence favored the brave and patriotic.

In 1782, the State ordered a force of 300 men to be raised from all the towns in the State, except the towns on Connecticut River, above Barnet, the number to be raised according to the town lists. Jacob Hall was chosen captain of the militia of Barnet, 1779.

John Galbraith, a Scotchman, came to Barnet and bought 300 acres on the Passumpsic, at the mouth of Enerick Brook, from Enos Stevens, in 1776, intending to return to Scotland and send his sons to improve the lands, but the war prevented his return, and he built a house and lived alone. Indians often called upon him; sometimes in greater number than he thought safe; but as he was kind to them they did him no harm. Rev. Thomas Clark, of Salem, N. Y., Rev. Robert Annan, of Boston, John Galbraith, and some others, most of whom were Scotchmen, obtained a grant from New York, which lay on the Passumpsic, including Burke and parts adjacent, being about 9 miles long and 6 broad, and which they called Barnf. John Galbraith received $99 81 as his share of the $30,000 paid by this State to New York to quitclaim Vermont. He went to Canada to return to Scotland, and was seized as a spy and shipped, with Jonathan Elkins of Peacham and others, to England, where he was acquitted and set free, having got a free passage. He went home to Scotland, and, after the Revolution, his sons came and occupied his lands.

Archibald McLaughlan, another Scotchman, bought land in the southeast corner of the Harvey Tract, in 1776, from Col. Harvey. Two Scotchmen, William Stevenson and James Cross, settled in town in 1776, and took lots in Harvey's tract, on Stevens's River. They lived alone in a house for a number of years. Coming home at one time in the dusk of the evening from the mill at Newbury, with grists on their backs, when about a mile from their house, they found a bear sitting in the path. Mr. Stevenson, who was considerably ahead, while his hound engaged the bear, got an opportunity to strike it across the eyes with a cudgel of a staff that he carried, which broke its nose and stunned it in some measure; still Bruin gave fight to him and his dog; but Stevenson, watching a good opportunity, struck it across the small of the back and continued the blows till he beat the bear to death. He was a strong and courageous man, and told the writer that he did not know the nature of the beast he killed, and never thought he was in any danger till he examined the bear's great paws after death. He carried it home, while Mr. Cross, who came up during the fight and broke a fine staff over the beast, carried the two grists.

James Gilchrist, Esq., a Scotchman, about the year 1777, settled on the plain at McIndoe's Falls. At an early period he was elected to important offices in town, in which his influence was long

felt. His wife had a very vigorous mind, good judgment, and memory. She was noted for her extensive religious knowledge and piety, and was a member of the Associate Congregation of Barnet for about 40 years. She rode on horseback to Mr. Goodwillie's church, and so regular and constant was her attendance, that one day, when too feeble to attend, her horse, from long use, jumped out of the pasture one Sabbath morning, went with the neighbors to meeting, stood at the horse-block, where it used to be tied till the evening, and then went home; all this without bridle, saddle, or rider. She died in 1828, aged 95 years.

When on her deathbed she thanked her aged pastor for the precious truths of the gospel she had heard him so long preach, and kissed the young pastor's hand, saying to him, "I esteem your office higher than that of the kings of the earth." She and Mrs. Twaddel, though nearly 99 years of age, could repeat correctly the Westminster shorter catechism, besides many psalms and other parts of the Bible.

John McCulloch, a very intelligent, judicious, and religious man, and long an elder of the Associate congregation, had a son, who died lately, about 53 years of age, who had a very remarkable memory. He was well acquainted with the Bible, and could repeat more chapters after twice or thrice reading them than the teacher in the Sabbath school had time to hear. Often his memory has been tried by opening the Bible at many different parts; and reading a passage, he would promptly tell the book, the chapter, and almost always the very verse read. He was not so exact, however, as to the verse as the celebrated blind Alick of Stirling, Scotland, whom the writer has seen and tried his memory. However, his memory was most remarkable for the date of events. He could tell promptly the year, the day of the month, the day of the week, and what kind of a day it was on which the event happened. He could tell who he had heard preach, from the text, the psalm, and the tune to which the psalm was sung. The writer has tested his memory in different ways, not only by the Bible, but by records, through a course of nearly 50 years, and found it correct. February can have five Sabbaths only when it begins and ends on that day, which can occur only once in 28 years. The writer once suddenly asked when had February five Sabbaths in it? "In 1824," he promptly replied. When will it have five again was the next question, as promptly answered, "In 1852." Indeed, he was a living almanac, and so used by the family and others. His father one day was speaking of an event the date of which he did not recollect. His son was fixing the fire and not appearing to be taking notice of the conversation, when his father, according to his custom, said, "John, when was it?" He instantly replied, "Six years ago last Saturday." He was well read in commentaries on the

Bible and other religious books, and, moreover, had some talent for poetry. He composed an elegy in which he eulogized his aged minister, whose death he lamented, and also wrote a humorous and satirical song on the vices and follies of an unworthy individual. The latter, with other humorous songs, he used to sing, being very fond of music and somewhat of a proficient therein.

In 1788, the town voted to fine absentees from town meetings $1 00.

Until some years after the Revolutionary War the only way of access to the town was by the Hazen road, running through the west part of it.

At an early period a road was made, beginning at the Hazen road, on the north side of Harvey's Mountain, and proceeding by the north end of Harvey's Lake and the centre of the town, and terminated at the mouth of Joes River, and was afterwards extended up the Passumpsic River to St. Johnsbury. No road from Wells River was made up the Connecticut River till some years after the Revolutionary War.

The Passumpsic Turnpike Company was incorporated in 1805. The first mile from Joes Brook down the Passumpsic was made in 1807, and the next season it was made to Ryegate line, when the Legislature granted the privilege of taking half toll. Afterwards the road was extended to Wells River. It is said to have cost $26,000. Alterations in Barnet and Ryegate, extending in the whole to about seven miles, were subsequently made, costing more than $7,000, of which nearly $4,000 were paid by Barnet, Ryegate, and Newbury. A committee appointed by the County Court prized the turnpike at $4,000, which was paid by the towns and it became a free road.

Dr. Phineas Stevens, brother of Enos Stevens, was the first physician in town. William Shaw was the first merchant, having a store at Stevens's Falls. Thomas Dennison was probably the first lawyer who lived in town.

Mr. Wilson, a Revolutionary soldier, who had lost an arm in battle, was the first school-teacher, and taught between Stevens's and McIndoe's Falls. The log schoolhouse stood near where William Harvey now lives. William Shearer, senior, taught school at an early period near Ross's Pond. William Johnston, who served in the American army, came to town about 1790, and for a few years taught a school on the rising ground around which the public road runs, near the northwest corner of Harvey's Lake. In 1801 he moved near to the centre of the town and taught school near the Presbyterian church. He was a good teacher, and his handwriting was very plain, neat, and regular. He kept school more than 20 years in town, and many of the youth of Barnet, great and small, were taught by him. The writer possesses documents containing the signature of Jonathan Fowler, who was one of the four men who first

settled the town and county, written May 1, 1787; the signature of Barnet Fowler, his son, the first-born male in the town and county, written March 12, 1799; and a school-bill, "Jonathan Fowler to William Johnston, Dr., to one quarter's school-rate for your son Barnet, commencing November 19, 1792, $2 00."

April 1, 1788, the town is divided into four districts, according to the following description: "1st, north of Thomas Smith's Falls into Passumpsic; 2d, south of Thomas Smith's Falls to Stevens's River; 3d, south of Stevens's River to Peacham line; 4th, Great River." Now there are 18 school districts and 20 schools in town, besides a flourishing academy at McIndoe's Falls.

The spotted fever prevailed in town in 1811, and was very fatal. It returned in 1818. The typhus fever prevailed in 1815, '16, and '17, and proved fatal in many cases.

There are 4 villages, 4 post-offices, and 7 churches in town.

BARNET VILLAGE, situated at the Falls on Stevens's River, contains a large number of houses and inhabitants. Here are the Barnet post-office, an inn, a gristmill, a sawmill, two woollen factories, and two stores, the town house, and a Union church, a fine building with steeple and bell.

McINDOE'S FALLS is situated in the S. E. corner of the town, at McIndoe's Falls, on Connecticut River, so called because John McIndoe early settled and owned land at the Falls, on which are great lumber mills. The village is beautifully situated on an extensive plain, and contains a large number of houses and inhabitants. Here are the McIndoe's Falls post-office, an inn, two stores, a carriage factory, the Methodist chapel, the Congregational church, a fine building, with steeple and bell, and the McIndoe's Falls Academy, a large, elegant, and commodious edifice, finely situated.

PASSUMPSIC VILLAGE, situated at the north part of the town, on the Passumpsic River, at Kendall's Falls, at which are mills and factories. It contains the Passumpsic post-office, the Baptist chapel, two stores, an inn, and a considerable number of houses.

WEST BARNET, situated on Stevens's River, near the north end of Harvey's Lake, contains the West Barnet post-office, a neat Union church, a store, grist and sawmill.

There is a Union meeting-house in the southwestern part of the town.

POPULATION AND WEALTH OF BARNET.

The Scotchmen were generally very robust men and retained their strength to an advanced age. Many of them lived till 90 and some to 95 years of age. Robt. Twaddell's wife was nearly 99, and Claud Stuart 100 years and 4 months when they died. In February, 1774, Gen. Whitelaw writes that there were 15 families in Barnet, and in August of the same year, when Col. Harvey viewed the town to buy land for the Scotch company, he writes in his journal, August 27, that there were six or seven settlers on the river and a few in the other parts of the town.

In all Whitelaw's charts, the names of the grantees are inserted in the lots they drew, but few of the original proprietors ever settled the lands granted to them by the charter. Rev. Thomas Beveridge, who visited the town in the summer of 1789, writes that there were then 40 Scotch families in town.

In the collection of papers belonging to Rev. David Goodwillie, was found an accurately drawn map of the town, made by him about the time he came to settle, in September, 1790. In this chart all the names of the actual settlers, about 90 in number, are inserted in the lots on which they settled. From this map it appears that at that time the most of the inhabitants of the town were settled on the lots near the central parts of the town, and between these and the Peacham line, with a considerable number in the southwest part of the town. The meadow lands along the Connecticut River, from Ryegate to the Passumpsic River, were settled, and there were a few settlers between that river and Waterford. In the north and southeast parts of the town there were no inhabitants.

In 1786, the first grand list recorded gives, polls, 57, $5,816; 1790, the grand list gives, polls, 93, $13,142; 1860, the grand list gives, polls, 362, $70,213.

Population in 1791 was 477; in 1800, 860; in 1810, 1,301; in 1820, 1,488; in 1830, 1,707; in 1840, 2,030; in 1850, 2,522; in 1860, 2,002.

ENOS STEVENS, ESQ., AND FAMILY.

ENOS STEVENS, ESQ., was born October 2, 1739. There is a tradition in his father's family that the town was called Barnet from the circumstance that his great-grandfather, who emigrated to Massachusetts in 1685, came from Barnet in England, which is a market town 11 miles north-northwest from London, and is situated in a parish of the same name. "It stands on a height, and has a church, built in 1400, a grammar school founded by Queen Elizabeth in 1573, and some well-endowed almshouses. An obelisk near the town commemorates a battle fought there between the York and Lancaster armies in 1471, when the latter was totally defeated, and their leader, the great Earl of Warwick was killed. Its population in 1851 was 2,380." His uncle, SAMUEL STEVENS, was employed by a land company to explore the country, from White River to the heads of the Onion and Lamoille rivers, to find out the best lands for settlement. This he did in 1760. His father, CAPT. PHINEAS STEVENS, in 1747, with 30 men, bravely defended the fort at Charlestown, N. H., against 400 French and Indians, whose assault was carried on in different ways for three days. He repelled them without the loss of a man, while the loss

of the enemy was considerable. His father and some members of the family procured signers to the petition to Gov. Wentworth, who granted the charter of the town. They in most instances procured deeds of acquittance from the petitioners, as proprietors, giving from a few shillings to a few pounds for a share of 360 acres, so that he and his three elder brothers, SAMUEL, WILLARD, and SIMON, became chief proprietors of the town. His younger brother, SOLOMON, was a land surveyor, and surveyed Barnet in 1774.

He took the side of the British in the war of the Revolution. His father and brothers had been honored by commissions from the governors of the British provinces of New Hampshire and New York, and like many others, no doubt, he thought that the powerful crown of Great Britain would soon crush the infant American Republic. In his journal he writes : " Charlestown, N. H., May 2, 1777. Set out for New York; left my all for the sake of my king and my country." In New York, he joined a volunteer company appointed by the British Commander to guard on the coast, but it does not appear that he was ever engaged in battle. He, with six others, Sept. 30, 1782, received a commission from " his excellency, the commander-in-chief," to go to Nova Scotia "to take charge of the provisions, arms, and ammunition sent by the commander-in-chief for the use of refugees going with them, to settle in that country, and divide the same among them." He bought land and settled in Digby, Nova Scotia, where he resided till 1785. After the war of independence, he applied to the British government for indemnity for "loyalty losses, and services," but it is not probable that he was indemnified for his losses, as his lands in Barnet were not confiscated. In his journal he writes : " Feb. 25, 1785. Came to Charlestown; found all my friends well; seven years and ten months since I left this town." He came to Barnet, and was present at a meeting of the proprietors, August 23, 1785, and drew his shares in the town when the first division took place. After this, he sold his possessions in Nova Scotia, and came to Barnet to reside. He purchased the lands owned by his brothers, and obtained vendue-titles to others ; so that he owned the greater part of the town. He encouraged the early settlement of the town by giving lots to the first settlers. He engaged Col. Hurd to build grist and sawmills on the Falls, at the mouth of Stevens River, and afterwards purchased them, and they were called Stevens Mills. It is said that it was one of his brothers who built the gristmill at the outlet of Harvey's Lake, which was long owned by Robert Brock, and near which Walter Brock afterwards built a sawmill, and these were called "Brock's Mills," which were the first built in town after Stevens Mills. To Barnet Fowler, son of Jonathan Fowler, the first male child born in Barnet, he gave a lot of land in the N. E. part of the town, and the name of Barnet Fowler is written near Harvey Fowler in Whitelaw's chart of the town. Sept. 4, 1787, he was admitted to take the freeman's oath. For many years he was a magistrate, and represented the town in the Legislature in 1795, 1796, and 1807. In 1798, he was appointed by the government one of the commissioners to take the census in this part of Vermont. His brother, Willard Stevens, moved to Barnet in 1776, but soon returned to Charlestown, and, immediately after, Elijah King, who married Mary Stevens, the sister of Enos Stevens, moved to Barnet, where they lived till their death.

He was married March 4, 1791, to Sophia Grout, of Charlestown. They had 10 children, most of whom died before adult age ; only three now survive. Henry Stevens, Esq., the eldest, was born Dec. 13, 1791. He has transacted much business in town, and has been elected to different town offices, and represented Barnet in the Legislature in 1826 and 1827. For many years he has been collecting files of newspapers, pamphlets, and written documents, to illustrate the history of the Town and State, many of which he sold to the State for $4,000. He was for many years President of the HISTORICAL SOCIETY OF VERMONT. His present collection consists of 3,485 bound volumes, about 6,500 pamphlets, about 400 volumes of newspapers, and probably 20,000 letters, bearing date from 1726 to 1854. He has the old field-books of all town lines surveyed by James Whitelaw, Esq., surveyor-general, and his deputies. His son Enos graduated at Middlebury College. His son Henry, after being engaged by the government in different offices in Washington, graduated at Yale College, and went to London, and was employed in purchasing rare and valuable books for several American gentlemen, and in 1846 he was employed by the Trustees of the British Museum to make up a catalogue of American works not found in the library of that institution, and was then appointed to furnish these works, and a complete set of the public documents of each one of the United States, and a complete set of all documents published by Congress, and all such books as contain the general literature of each State.

He became, about 1848, agent for the Smithsonian Institution, and is still extensively engaged in the exchange of books between the institutions of England and America.

His son George graduated at West Point, 1843, and was appointed second lieutenant in 1844, and joined the army at Fort Joseph, commanded by Gen. Taylor, but was not long afterwards accidentally drowned.

COL. ALEXANDER HARVEY AND FAMILY.

COL. ALEXANDER HARVEY was born in May, 1747, in the parish of Gargunoch, Stirlingshire, Scotland. His credentials represent him as

"descended from creditable and honest parents ; that he had an education suitable to his station, and that he was, in his conduct and behavior, in every respect virtuous, obliging, and modest." Mr. Harvey and John Clark were the agents of a company of farmers in the shires of Perth and Stirling, appointed to search out and purchase a large tract of land in America for the company to settle. He left his father's house May 9, 1774, and they sailed for America, and landed in New York, July 22, in company with John Galbraith, Thomas Clark, and others, who came to Barnet. The agents proceeded by Albany to examine lands near Schenectady, but the quantity for sale was not sufficient. They proceeded by Ballstown, Saratoga, and Salem, to Cambridge, N. Y., but, not obtaining their object, crossed the Green Mountains, and came by Charlestown, Hanover, and Newbury, to Ryegate, one half of which Gen. Whitelaw had purchased from Dr. Witherspoon, and examined the other half of the town, as they were instructed by the directors. They then came to Barnet, where they arrived August 27, in company with Solomon Stevens, the brother of Samuel Stevens, both of whom were proprietors of the town. The next day, they went and examined 7,000 acres of land in the S. W. part of the town, attended by Mr. Stevens and a guide. In Col. Harvey's journal (now before the writer), he says " there are six or seven settlers in the township on the river, and a few in the back parts of the town." They offered Mr. Stevens one shilling sterling per acre, but he asked 18 pence, and gave them a letter to his brother in New York, "with whom they might treat at large." Returning by Albany to New York, they went by Philadelphia, and examined lands on the Susquehanna and Schuylkill rivers, and then returned to New York, where they arrived in October, 1774. They offered Samuel Stevens one shilling an acre, but he demanded 16 pence. But, Nov. 8, they " agree with Mr. Stevens to pay 14 pence sterling for each acre of 7,000 acres of land in Barnet, lying on the Peacham line, to extend 5 miles on said line, and to pay one half of the money in November, 1775, and the other to be paid them, or to bear interest for such time as it remained unpaid." His journal, under date of Nov. 23, 1784, says : "Accordingly, received a bond of Samuel Stevens of £1,600, 6s. 6d. sterling, that we were to receive a complete deed for 7,000 acres of land in Barnet, with a covenant of warrantee deed to pay and receive at Nov. 1775 ; at the same time, we granted a bond to said Mr. Stevens, of equal sum, to fulfil the promises on our part. The bond was sealed on both parts, and signed and delivered before two witnesses." Having made out an account of their proceedings to send to the company, John Clark sailed for Scotland, Dec. 11, 1774, and took the record with him.

The whole sum they agreed to pay was £408,

6s 8d., which was ultimately paid, and the receipt for payment is recorded in the town books, and Col. Harvey received deeds from Samuel, Willard, and Enos Stevens for the 7,000 acres purchased.

Having bought some tools and furniture, and hired some persons to work for the company, he, in company with Claud Stuart, Robert Brock, John Scot, John McLaren, and Robert Bentley, sailed from New York, March 23, 1775, and came by New Haven to Hartford, Ct. Having bought provisions at these places, Mr. Harvey left Mr. Stuart with Mr. Bentley to assist him in bringing the "lumber up the river in boats, and he, with the rest of the company, came a foot by Charlestown, Newbury, and Ryegate to Barnet, where they arrived March 21, 1775. His journal says they " came along Peacham line two and a half miles, struck across the breadth, came to the pond, camped all night near the pond, and cleared some part of the ground." The next day they returned to Ryegate, "the snow being too thick to work, and then to Newbury, where they bought wheat, beef, and pork, and hired a horse to carry their provisions to Barnet ; returned through Ryegate, where they tarried some days, and bought sugar and other articles, and, in company with John McLaren and Robert Brock, returned to their camp in Barnet, May 3 ; and on the 4th, built another camp ; on the 5th, viewed a proper place for improvements, and on the 6th, cut down and burnt up wood; on the 7th, Claud Stuart, John Scot, and Robert Bentley, arrived, after a long and bad passage up the Connecticut River to Newbury.

They cleared some land, sowed some grain, and planted some potatoes and beans. They prepared logs and raised a house, June 11th, with "the assistance of Mr. Whitelaw and four men from Ryegate." In July, he went to New York "to draw money to carry on the work, and to receive letters from the company," and on the way back he bought a cow of Col. Bellows. In October he sowed some wheat, and Peter Sylvester and Mr. Kimball harrowed it in with their oxen. On the 28th of October he "raised another house for two dwellers," which was completed in November, and which was inhabited by Robert McFarlane. "About the 13th of the month, snow came on so as to continue." "November 14, cut a road to Stevens Mills." During the year 1775, he received authority from the Directors of the Company in Scotland to increase his purchase of land to 12,000 acres. He purchased a number of lots in other parts of Barnet, but the Revolutionary war commencing the next year, impeded the operations of the Company, and the emigration of its members from Scotland.

The site where he first camped, and built his first house is on the farm of Jeremiah Abbott, and situated a few rods above the stone house built by William Bachop. Afterwards, he built

a house of hewn logs on the Hazen Road, in which his son Claud lived before he built a new house. In 1796, however, he sold his farm on the north side of Harvey's Mountain, and moved down the Hazen Road, and lived on the south side of the mountain, where William McPhee now lives, and where he died, Dec. 14, 1809, aged 62 years. He was a man of good abilities, widely known, and highly honored ; a member of the State Conventions of 1777, and of all the sessions of the Legislature, from the first session in 1778 till 1788, and a member of the Council of Censors, 1791. He was Associate Judge of Orleans County from 1781 to 1794, and long and early honored with office by the town of Barnet. The Legislature appointed him one of the trustees of the County Academy, and he was a president of the board of trustees till his death. The Government also appointed him to build a fort on the Onion or Lamoille River, which he declined. He and Gen. Whitelaw were attorneys appointed by Dr. Witherspoon, for the sale of lands which he owned in Ryegate, Newbury, and Walden.

He possessed a public spirit, was generous and facetious, and exerted himself for the good of the Town, County, and State, having taken an active part in declaring the State independent, and forming its constitution and government.

He was chosen colonel of the regiment formed in this part of the country.

As a proof of his "good will and favor to Mr. and Mrs. Goodwillie," he gave them a donation of some acres of land adjoining their own.

Jonathan Fowler, one of the first four men who settled in the town, named one of his sons for him, and the colonel gave him a lot of land situated in the northeast part of the town, and Harvey Fowler is entered in all Whitelaw's charts of Barnet.

On one occasion during the Revolutionary War, when soldiers were drafted in Barnet, the lot fell on George Gibson, a man of small stature, who said he would join the army, adding, " Who knows but I may be the means of establishing the independence of the United States ? " Col. Harvey observed that he never knew a means so small to produce an effect so great. A member of the Legislature, who was a great hero and patriot, boasting of his mother and six brothers, triumphantly asked the company if ever they heard of such a mother having seven such sons. Col. Harvey replied he had read of a woman who had seven just such sons, and what was very remarkable, they were all born at one birth ! " Who was she ? " asked the hero. " Mary Magdalene," replied the colonel, " who, was delivered of seven devils all at once ! "

He was married, by the Rev. Peter Powers, October 5, 1781, to Jennet Brock, a daughter of Walter Brock, Esq., of Barnet, and who was born in Scotland, October 10, 1767. They had

16 children, three of whom died when young. Eight sons and five daughters were married, most of whom lived in Barnet, of whom two sons and two daughters are now deceased. His son, Hon. Walter Harvey, was 36 years a justice of the peace, a member of the executive council in 1835, and a representative of the town in 1824, 1825, 1829, 1837, 1838, 1839, and 1844, and was associate judge of the county in 1850.

His son, Hon. Robert Harvey, was member of the State Senate in 1838 and 1839, associate judge of the county in 1848 and 1849, and member of the council of censors in 1834 and 1835, and a representative of the town in 1853 and 1854. His son, Claud Harvey, Esq., was representative of the town in 1832 and 1833. His name-son, Alexander Harvey, Esq., is married to a granddaughter of Gen. Stark, the hero of Bennington, and was high sheriff of the county in 1843. His son, Peter Harvey, Esq., was the friend and associate of Daniel Webster, and is mentioned in his life. Col. Harvey's descendants are numerous. His widow was married, by Rev. David Goodwillie, to Gen. Whitelaw, of Ryegate, August 29, 1815, and died, Dec. 28, 1854, aged 89 years.

ECCLESIASTICAL HISTORY.

It is not known at what period the Presbyterian churches of Barnet and Ryegate—chiefly composed of emigrants from Scotland—were formed, but they were organized previous to 1779, a number of years before any other church was formed in the county. Before, during, and after the Revolutionary War, several Scotch clergymen came and preached to them occasionally, and sometimes administered baptism.

The company of Perth and Stirling, whose agent was Col. Harvey, agreed to buy a large tract of land in America, in order to settle together, and have a settled minister among them, thus taking forethought for their spiritual as well as temporal interests. Harvey's tract in Barnet was purchased for them in the close of 1774, and began to be settled by them early in 1775, but the Revolutionary War checked the emigration. However, some Scotch families from Ryegate moved into town towards the close of the war, after which it was rapidly settled in different parts by emigrants from various parts of Scotland. Gen. Whitelaw, who was the agent of the Scotch Company in Ryegate, on his way thither in 1773, called on Rev. Thomas Clark, a Scotch clergyman belonging to the Associate Presbyterian Church, and settled in Salem, Washington County, N. Y., and Col. Harvey, agent of the Scotch company that settled in Barnet, on his way to town in 1774, called also upon him. To this clergyman John Gray, of Ryegate, travelled on foot 140 miles, to obtain his services. He gave them a favorable answer, April 8, 1775, and came and preached some time in Barnet and Ryegate in the latter part of the summer of that year. He revisited these towns two or three times during the Revolutionary War. Dr. Witherspoon, president of Princeton College, N. J., a signer of the Declaration of Independence, and a member of Congress, who owned lands in Ryegate, Newbury, and Walden, and whose son was settled in the north part of Ryegate, visited this part of the country three times, first, probably in 1775. In 1782, he preached in Ryegate and Barnet, and baptized Col. Harvey's oldest child. He returned in 1786, to this part of the county. Rev. Hugh White, a Scotch clergyman, preached in Ryegate at the end of 1775. Rev. Peter Powers, English Presbyterian clergyman, settled in Newbury from 1765 to 1784; preached occasionally in Ryegate, and probably in Barnet, during that period.

The proceedings of the town and church of Barnet to obtain a settled minister, are recorded at length in the town records, from which the history of the settlement of the first minister in the town and county is taken.

Jan. 29, 1784. The town "voted unanimously to choose the Presbyterian form of religious worship, founded on the word of God as expressed in the confession of faith, catechisms, longer and shorter, with the form of church government agreed upon by the Assembly of divines at Westminster, and practised by the church of Scotland." August 17, 1784. The town "voted lot No. 87, for a meeting-house and glebe; also, voted to apply to the Scotch Presbytery for a minister."

The Scotch Presbytery here mentioned was The Associate Reformed Presbytery of Londonderry, N. H., formed there Feb. 13, 1783, to which Rev. Robert Annan, of Boston, Rev. David Annan, of Peterboro', N. H., and Rev. John Huston, of Bedford, N. H., belonged. Rev. Robert Annan preached in these towns in 1784, and returned next year. Rev. David Annan preached in Barnet and Ryegate in 1785. The first leaf of the church records of Barnet is lost. The third page begins with August 27, 1786. Rev. John Huston was present with the session of Barnet, at an election of elders, August 31, 1786, when the record says "a petition was drawn up by the elders of Barnet and Ryegate, and preferred to the Associate (Reformed) Presbytery, to sit at Peterboro', Sept. 27, 1786, earnestly desiring one of their number might be sent to preach, visit, and catechise the two congregations, and ordain elders at Barnet." Accordingly the Presbytery appointed Mr. Huston for that purpose. In pursuance thereof, Mr. Huston came in October following, and visited and catechised the greater part of both congregations. He remained till May, 1787, preaching in Barnet and Ryegate, and returned November, 1788.

Previous to 1787, the emigrants from Scotland made an unsuccessful attempt to obtain Rev. Walter Galbraith, from Scotland, for their minister. In that year the town voted to apply to the year till it amount to £80 lawful, to be paid in Associate Synod, of Scotland, and sent a petition to that Synod, desiring a minister to be sent to them, and promising him a salary and the payment of expense of his passage to this country, and settlement among them. Funds were raised for that purpose. In 1787, before receiving an answer to their petition, the town voted to raise funds for the support of the gospel among them, and authorized the committee, with the elders, to employ such preachers as they could procure, agreeing with them in religious sentiments. In the beginning of 1789, information was received from Scotland that the Associate Synod in that country had sent three preachers to the Associate Presbytery of Pennsylvania, and directed them to apply to that Presbytery for a preacher to become their minister. The town having voted to make application as directed, in June, 1789, William Stevenson went to Cambridge, N. Y., and had an interview with Rev. Thomas Beveridge, a minister and member of the Presbytery of Pennsylvania, and having obtained the information desired, he wrote a letter to the Rev. David Goodwillie, a minister and member of the same Presbytery, then at New York City, informing him that "the congregation of Barnet would be exceedingly glad of a visit" from him, and referring him to certain information contained in an enclosed letter from Mr. Beveridge, who writes that the people in Barnet had made application to the Synod in Scotland, and that they had been directed to apply to the Presbytery of Pennsylvania for a hearing of Mr. Goodwillie; that there were about 40 Scotch families in Barnet, with a number in Ryegate; that some of the emigrants from Scotland in Barnet, had heard Mr. Goodwillie in their native country, and would be well pleased to have him settled in Barnet, as their minister; and that Mr. Stevenson had made application to obtain sermon for Barnet. In consequence of this information and application Mr. Beveridge came and preached in Barnet Sabbaths July 26, and August 2, and baptized several children; one of these was Walter, son of Col. Harvey. The session, in conjunction with the committee of the town, then petitioned the Associate Presbytery of Pennsylvania "for supply of sermon, and particularly a hearing of the Rev. David Goodwillie."

In consequence of this petition, Mr. Goodwillie came to Barnet in the latter part of November the same year, and remained preaching in Barnet, and occasionally in Ryegate, till the latter part of February, 1790, during which time he administered baptism, observed a public fast, Jan. 7, 1790, and occasionally preached in Ryegate.

Feb. 4, 1790. The town "voted to apply to the Presbytery of Pennsylvania for a minister, forty for and seven against it. Voted £70 a year as a salary for said minister, and to augment it £1 a year till it amount to £80 lawful, to be paid in wheat at 5s. a bushel, and stock and other produce to be conformed to the wheat. Voted to raise £60 lawful, for a settlement for said minister, £20 of which to be paid a year, and the whole to be paid in three years, to be paid in wheat, stock, and produce, the same as the yearly salary. Voted to raise £22, to be paid in wheat at 5s. a bushel to pay the present supply of sermon. Voted that the committee formerly appointed by the town to procure sermons, be requested to apply to the Presbytery of Pennsylvania for a minister.

The few who voted against this application wished to obtain a minister from the Established Church of Scotland, but did not afterwards oppose the settlement and ministrations of Mr. Goodwillie. The elders of the church and committee of town, Feb. 15, 1790, petition the Associate Presbytery of Pennsylvania "to appoint one of their number to preside in the election and call of one to be the stated minister of this town and congregation, and a supply of sermon in the mean time."

The town records, July 5, 1790, say "The committee appointed by the town, Feb. 4, last, for the purpose of applying to the reverend the Associate Presbytery of Pennsylvania, for a moderation of a call agreeable to the vote of that day, for procuring a settled minister, having petitioned said Presbytery for one of their number to moderate in the election of a minister, said Presbytery having granted the petition by appointing the Rev. Thomas Beveridge, of Cambridge, N. Y., for the purpose mentioned in the petition, and Mr. Beveridge, having agreeable to appointment, come to this town, and declared his instructions to said committee, and the public being duly notified by intimation from the pulpit, on two Sabbaths before the day appointed for the moderation, agreeable to the rule of the church in such cases, and the people being met at the meeting-house this day for the aforesaid purpose, after sermon by the reverend, the moderator, proceeded, by calling for a nomination, when the Rev. Mr. David Goodwillie being nominated by one of the elders, and upon the question being put, 'Do the people of this town make choice of the Rev. David Goodwillie for their minister?' when there appeared upwards of forty for the affirmative; and the question, 'Who are against the Rev. David Goodwillie?' being put three several times, and none appearing, the moderator was pleased to declare the Rev. David Goodwillie duly elected, and a call to the said Mr. Goodwillie to take the ministerial charge of this congregation presented and duly subscribed, in the presence of the moderator and witnesses, the tenor whereof, is as follows, viz:—

We, the subscribers, elders, trustees, and other members of the Associate Congregation of Barnet, in the State of Vermont, who have acceded to the Lord's cause as professed and maintained by the

Associate Presbytery of Pennsylvania, taking into our serious consideration the great loss we suffer through the want of a fixed gospel ministry among us, and being fully satisfied that the great Head of the Church has bestowed on you, the Reverend Mr. Goodwillie, a minister of the gospel, and member of the Associate Presbytery of Pennsylvania, those gifts and ministerial endowments which, with the exercise of them, will, through the blessing of the Holy Spirit, be profitable for our edification, — we therefore call and beseech you to take the oversight of this congregation, to labor in it and watch over it as that part of Christ's flock under your immediate charge; and we promise that, according to what is required in the Holy Scriptures, we will conscientiously endeavor to give a ready obedience to the Lord's message delivered by you, and to aid and support you in his work. And we hereby desire and entreat this Reverend Presbytery, under whose inspection we are, and to whom we present this our call, to sustain the same, and take the ordinary steps, with all due expedition, to have the said Mr. Goodwillie settled among us. In testimony whereof we have subscribed this our call at our church in Barnet, on the fifth day of July, A.D. 1790, before these witnesses, Jonathan Elkins, Jacob Guy, and Ephraim Foster, all of Peacham.

William Gilkerson, Andrew Lang, Wm. Warden, Alexander Gilchrist, James Orr, John McCallum, Ezekiel Manchester, John McIndoe, Robert McIndoe, James Gilchrist, John Waddel, Bartholomew Somers, James Ferguson, Archibald McLaughlin, John McNabb, James Warden, William Innis, Alexander Lang, John Gilkerson, David Moor, Alexander Thompson, Samuel Huston, Edward Pollard, Hugh Ross, William Maxwell, William Lang, John Gilkerson, John Ross, William Shaw, Thomas Gilfillan, John McLaren, Geo. Garland, Bartholomew Somers, William Warden, Caleb Stiles, Noah Halladay, William Gilfillan, Jr., William Hindman, John Galbraith, Cloud Somers, James McLaren, Andrew Lackie, Elijah Hall, Jr., John Robertson, John Shaw, Jr., William Gilfillan, Sen., Robert Laird, Robert Blair.

John Shaw,
Robert Twaddel, } *Elders.*
Archibald Stuart,

James Gilchrist,
John Waddel,
James Cross,
John Hindman, } *Trustees.*
William Shearer,
Wm. Stevenson,

Jonathan Elkins,
Jacob Guy, } *Witnesses.*
Ephraim Foster,

The above subscriptions, in number fifty-seven, are attested to be genuine.

THOMAS BEVERIDGE, *Minister.*

Barnet, July 5, 1790. We, the subscribers, belonging to the town of Ryegate, in the State of Vermont, though we cannot join in the call given to the Reverend Mr. David Goodwillie by the people of Barnet, not being within the bounds of that congregation, yet, as we expect some part of Mr. Goodwillie's labors will be among us, do hereby testify our concurrence with our brethren in the said call, and our readiness to join with them in endeavoring to aid and support the said Mr. Goodwillie in the Lord's work.

John Gray, William Nelson, Jr., William Craig, Andrew Brock, Alexander Miller, James Henderson, William Nelson, James McKinley, John Wallace, James Nelson, Hugh Gardner, William Craig.

Barnet, July 5, 1790. The petition of the elders and trustees belonging to the town of Barnet, humbly showeth — That whereas the congregation have given a call to Reverend Mr. Goodwillie, we entreat that the Presbytery proceed as quickly as possible to forward his settlement among us, and that, until this is done, he may be appointed to supply this place with sermon, and we hereby appoint Mr. Beveridge as our commissioner to give the Presbytery what further information may be judged necessary, and that the Lord may direct you in this and all other matters, is, and through grace shall be, the prayer of your petitioners.

James Gilchrist, John Hindman,' John Shaw, William Stevenson, James Cross, Robert Twaddel, William Shearer, John Waddel, Archibald Stuart.

New York, Oct. 21, 1790. Which day and place the Associate Presbytery of Pennsylvania met, and was constituted with prayer by Mr. Beveridge, the moderator. Present: Messrs. William Marshall, James Clarkson, John Anderson, Archibald White, ministers, and Andrew Wright from New York, and Thomas Cummings from Cambridge, ruling elders. The moderator, acting as commissioner for the congregation of Barnet, in the State of Vermont, presented a call given by that congregation to the Rev. David Goodwillie, and also gave an account of his conduct in fulfilling the appointment laid upon him at last meeting to moderate in said call. The Presbytery having been satisfied as to the minister's maintenance in that congregation, the question being put, "Approve of Mr. Beveridge's conduct or not?" it was carried unanimously, "Approve." Presbytery then proceeded to the consideration of the aforesaid call, and a member having been employed in prayer for the Lord's blessing and direction in this important matter, the question was put, "Sustain or not the call given by the congregation of Barnet to the Rev. Mr. Goodwillie?" The roll being called, it was carried unanimously, "Sustain." Wherefore the Presbytery did, and hereby do, sustain the call given to the Rev. Mr. Goodwillie by the congregation of Barnet. And in consequence of this determination, and in answer to a petition from the said congregation, presented also by the moderator, the Presbytery appoint this call to be presented to Mr. Goodwillie, and that, upon his acceptance of the same, he be admitted to that pastoral charge, according to the rules of the church, on the eighth day of February next. The Presbytery further appoint Mr. Beveridge to preside in said admission, and Mr. Anderson to preach after it.

Barnet, at the house of James Cross, Feb. 8 (1791), forenoon, which day and place the Presbytery being met, according to appointment of last meeting, and constituted with prayer by Mr. Beveridge, moderator. Present: Messrs. Goodwillie and Anderson, ministers, and James Small from Cambridge, and John Shaw from Barnet, ruling elders. The minutes of the last meeting having been read, relating to the call from the congregation of Barnet, and containing an appointment of this *interim* meeting, the call was presented to Mr. Goodwillie, and he having accepted it, an edict having been served first on the preceding Sabbath and at the opening of this meeting, the Presbytery, after waiting a considerable time, and finding no objection offered, proceeded to the admission of Mr. Goodwillie to the pastoral charge of the congregation of Barnet. Public worship being then begun in the same place, and a sermon preached by the moderator from 1 Cor. iii. 7, on these words, "God giveth the increase," the questions in the formula for ministers, excepting the seventh, were put to Mr. Goodwillie, and he was admitted, according to the usual form, as minister of the aforesaid congregation; and after a charge given by the moderator to the minister, elders, and people, the public work of the day was concluded by Mr. Anderson with a sermon from Acts xxvi. 22. "Having obtained help of God, I continue unto this day witnessing." The public assembly being dismissed, the Presbytery closed with prayer.

A true copy. Certified by

WILLIAM MARSHALL, *Moderator.*

[This account may be considered by many long, as indeed it is; but it takes up and fully explains the Scotch Presbyterian mode of setlement of pastors, etc., a part of our ecclesiastical State history, heretofore quite untouched, and which will not need be again described at length in any town.—Ed.]

After the settlement of the minister, for the period of 12 or 15 years the church of Barnet had trials arising from dissensions among a few individuals, and one or two difficult and doubtful cases of discipline, in consequence of which a few individuals left the congregation. But even during this period the church continued to flourish, the number of its members being increased more than threefold. Though the country was new and money scarce, the congregation contributed liberally every year for the payment of the incidental expenses. After this time of trial the church continued to flourish in greater peace and purity. From the foundation of this church to this time, every year, quarterly meetings of the pastor, elders, and deacons, for prayer and praise and the government of the church, have been regularly held.

Every year two public fasts were kept, one relating to the congregation, and the other to the sins and troubles of the nation and the world. Indeed, the influence of true religion has been so long and so much felt that there are probably few places in the country where the sanctuary has been more generally and punctually attended and the sacred Sabbath better observed. This church, from the beginning to this time, has contributed liberally to the funds of the Presbytery, Synod, and General Assembly, to which they are subject, for the purpose of supporting and extending the cause of Christ. Their minister's salary was augmented to £80, which was raised generally by a town tax, but sometimes by voluntary subscriptions, when almost every tax-payer in the town subscribed liberally. In 1805, the pastoral relation between the minister and town was dissolved by mutual consent. In the same year the town chose the minister to represent them in the State Legislature. In that year also the Presbyterian Society of Barnet was incorporated by the Legislature, which paid the minister's salary as long as he lived.

The members of the church of Barnet, in full communion when the sacrament of the Lord's Supper was first dispensed in Caledonia County, September 25, 1791, were 46; in '92, 68; in '96, 91; in '97, 97; in '98, 101; in 1802, 117; in '13, 140; in '23, 182: and in '30, when Mr. Goodwillie died, more than 200. During his ministry in Barnet more than 400 persons were enrolled as members, besides probably more

than 150 in Ryegate, under his pastoral care from 1790 to 1822.

Since the present pastor's ordination and settlement as his father's assistant and successor, September 27, 1826, more than 250 persons have become members of this church. In 1840, however, the congregation was divided, and Rev. James McArthur ministered to one part at Stevens's Village, one half of his time, from 1846 to '57. The whole numbers of members at present belonging to the United Presbyterian Church in Barnet is about 200, besides some who reside in adjacent towns.

Nine persons connected with the Associate Congregation of Barnet have become ministers of the gospel, viz: Rev. D. Chassell, D.D., who graduated at Dartmouth College in 1810; Rev. Peter Shaw, Rev. Robert Shaw, Rev. Thomas Goodwillie, and Rev. David Goodwillie, the sons of the pastor, who graduated in Dartmouth College in 1820; Rev. William Galbraith, a son of one of the elders, who graduated at Union College, N. Y., and settled as a minister of the Associate Church in Freeport, Pa.; Rev. Thomas Gilkerson, who graduated at Jefferson College, Pa., became a minister of the Associate Church, and settled in Conemaugh, Pa.; Rev. William C. Somers, who graduated at Union College, N. Y., and is now settled as the pastor of the United Presbyterian Congregation of Hobart, N. Y.; and Rev. Robert Samuel, who graduated at Dartmouth College in 1856.

Mr. Gilkerson's father is now one of the elders of the church in which he has held office about 50 years. He was the first person who subscribed Mr. Goodwillie's call in 1790, and has been long in office in the town, being a magistrate for many years and representing the town seven times in the Legislature of the State.

The Associate Presbyterian Congregations of Barnet and Ryegate belonged to the Associate Presbytery of Pennsylvania from the time that these congregations applied to that Presbytery for a minister till May 21, 1801, when the Associate Synod of North America was organized, when they were included in the Associate Presbytery of Cambridge, N. Y., then formed. To this Presbytery they belonged till July 10, 1840, and the Associate Presbytery of Vermont, including all the ministers and congregations in Vermont belonging to the Synod, was constituted at Barnet by Rev. Thomas Goodwillie, senior minister according to the decree of the Associate Synod. The Presbytery of Vermont has belonged, since May, 1858, to the General Assembly of the United Presbyterian Church of North America, then formed by the union of the Associate and Associate Reformed Synods.

REV. DAVID GOODWILLIE, AND FAMILY.

REV. DAVID GOODWILLIE was born in Tanshall, in the parish of Kinglassie, Fifeshire, Scotland. The mansion in which he was born stands a little south of the highway between Leslie, on the Leven River, and the church of Kinglassie, and distant from each place about half a mile. It commands an extensive prospect, Edinburgh, 15 miles to the south, being seen in a clear day. Here the good-natured Goodwillie family (as their neighbors called them) dwelt for five successive generations for more than 150 years. His great-grandfather lived in times of persecution, and encountered the opposition of the curate. His father, grandfather, and great-grandfather were "smiths" by trade. His grandfather,* David Goodwillie, was baptized October 15, 1665, and died November 7, 1745, aged 80 years. He was a member of the Established Church of Scotland and a ruling elder in the parish of Kinglassie, and was buried in its churchyard. He was married to Elizabeth Dewar, who died November 10, 1739, aged 65 years. They had four children, who survived them, — two sons, David and James, and two daughters, Christian and Elizabeth. They were possessed of considerable property in land and "movables." Their youngest son, James Goodwillie, inherited the "movables."

He was a member of the Established Church of Scotland, and a ruling elder in the Parish of Kinglassie, whose minister was Mr. Currie, who at first decidedly favored the cause of the Erskines and others who seceded from the Established Church of Scotland on account of grave errors in doctrine and practice, which the General Assembly of that church refused to condemn and correct; but who afterwards strenuously opposed by his writings the secession or Associated Church of Scotland, which cause his ruling elder espoused as the cause of God, and therefore left the Established Church and joined the Associate Church and became a member of the Associate Congregation of Abernethy, 12 miles distant from his residence. But when the Associate Congregation of Leslie was organized, he became a member and elder, and so continued till his death. He was widely known and highly esteemed as an intelligent and pious man. His letters to his children show that he exercised himself unto godliness and entertained a deep concern that the glory of God should be promoted in his own and their spiritual and eternal welfare. He was married to Mary Davidson, December 26, 1748, who was a helpmeet to him in things both temporal and spiritual. They had eight children, four sons and four daughters, three of whom died young. The parents were diligent in "bringing up their children in the nurture and admonition of the Lord," and had the satisfaction of seeing

their surviving children become members of the church, and hearing one son preach the everlasting gospel.

The father died of dropsy, which for a long time affected one of his lower limbs. One day, when rather worse than usual, he called all the family together and prayed with them, after which he told the children that he had taken solemn baptismal vows for them, which, as he had received help from God, he had endeavored to fulfil by his instructions and example, and then solemnly warned them that if they did not live a life of faith and holiness the blame would rest upon themselves. He was born in 1709, and died on the Sabbath day, January 6, 1782, aged 73 years, and was buried in the churchyard of Kinglassie. Two or three days before his death, while lying still on his bed, he broke out in a rapture, saying he was full of the joy of the Holy Spirit, and inquired when the *Sabbath* would come, expressing "a desire to depart and be with Christ." His son, having been appointed to preach at a distant place the Sabbath his father died, on the Saturday before his departure, called the family together, and having sung Psalm xxiii. and prayed, took his farewell.

——————

Extract from a letter of Rev. David Goodwillie to his brother in America, written at this time.

. . . . "Our father finished his pilgrimage on earth on the sixth of January last. He died a peaceful death at 8 o'clock on Sabbath morning, in the presence of our mother, brother, and sisters, and was buried on Tuesday, the eighth, in the family burial-place. His senses remained to the last. Great patience, Christian resignation, and other religious exercises were manifest during the whole of his last affliction, which lasted for about three weeks. Thus, my dear brother, has the Lord of life been pleased to remove from the troubles of this vain world, and, as we confidently hope, taken to the full enjoyment of himself forever, one of the best of parents, who, in a careful manner, gave us Christian instruction, and guided us by his good example. Our loss is great, but his gain by this happy change is far greater. Blessed be the God of grace and consolation, we are not left to mourn as those who have no hope. "Mark the perfect man and behold the upright, for the end of that man is peace." "Precious in the sight of the Lord is the death of his saints."

Let us then lead us to take faith's view of him who died for us, and to a firm confidence in the everlasting Father for the supply of all our wants, spiritual and temporal. Let us be concerned to be ready to enter into the joy of our Lord, for we know not how soon we may be called to go hence. Let us live by faith in "Christ who died and rose again." How full of consolation are the following subjects on which I have lately been led to meditate! Rom. viii. 18. "For I reckon that the suffer-

——————

* We are aware that this part of the sketch is not strictly *Vermont history*, yet we have such an accurate history of this old Scotch settlement, reversing the order and running from the present backward into the past, that it is much like an inclination felt when standing at the lower end of a picture gallery, to let our eye sweep up through the vista as far as our unbroken vision may extend.— Ed.

ings of this present time are not worthy to be compared with the glory which shall be revealed in us." Phil. i. 21. "For me to live is Christ, and to die is gain." 2 Tim. i. 10. "Jesus Christ hath abolished death, and brought life and immortality to light by the gospel."

Rev. David Goodwillie was the first-born of his father's family, and was baptized Dec. 31, 1749, by Rev. John Erskine, son of Rev. Ebenezer Erskine, who was the first minister of the Associate Presbyterian Congregation of Leslie, to which the family belonged.

His eldest sister, Elizabeth, was born in 1753, and married to James Blythe, an elder of the Associate Congregation of Abernethy, Sept. 1, 1775, and died in 1836.

His brother Joseph, born April 3, 1751, emigrated to America about the year 1773, and died in Barnet, Feb. 24, 1808.

His sister Christian, born July 26, 1758, was married to William Coventrie, a member of the Associate Congregation of Abernethy, where she died Feb. 14, 1806.

His brother James, born July 16, 1760, was married, had a large family, and lived to old age.

His mother died in Leslie, Scotland, June 25, 1806, at an advanced age, and was buried in the churchyard of Kinglassie. She was a Christian mother indeed, and took a deep interest in the temporal and spiritual welfare of her children. She survived her husband 24 years, and was separated, 18 years before her death, from her first-born, for whom she entertained a high esteem and strong attachment, and he proved his filial affection and regard by contributing liberally to her support as long as she lived, though his salary was not large, and his family increasing.

It is probable that Mr. Goodwillie was engaged at manual labor till about 18 years of age, when he began to study, with a view to the sacred ministry, and prosecuted his academical education at Alloa, and finished it at the University of Edinburgh. He studied theology under Professor Moncrief, at Alloa, where the Theological Seminary of the Associate Synod was established. For support when prosecuting his studies he successfully engaged in teaching, and taught at Ryelaw near Leslie, and Easter Fernie, near Capar, in Fifeshire.

After he had passed through the usual course of academical and theological studies, the Associate Synod recommended him to be taken on trial for license. His trials having proved satisfactory, he was licensed to preach the everlasting gospel by the Associate Presbytery of Kirkcaldy in the beginning of October, 1778. The next month he went to Ireland, where he remained preaching to the congregations of the Associate Church in that country for nearly a year, when he returned to Scotland. In September, 1785, he went to the north of England, where he continued more than a year, preaching in Westmoreland and Cumberland. The rest of the time till his emigration to America, he was employed in preaching in the different Presbyteries of the Associate Church in Scotland. He kept a list of all the times and places when and where he officiated, and the texts of Scripture in which he preached at these times and places, from which it appears that he was diligent in fulfilling the appointments of the Associate Synod in sending him to the different Presbyteries, and of these Presbyteries in sending him to preach to the congregations under their jurisdiction. His acquaintance and correspondence with the ministers and preachers of the Associate Synod of Scotland, were extensive.

In consequence of application for preachers, made by the Associate Presbytery of Pennsylvania to the Associate Synod in Scotland, and a petition from the church and town of Barnet, preferred to that synod, to send them a preacher, that Synod recommended him and the Rev. A. White to go to the assistance of that Presbytery. With this recommendation he complied. Taking a sorrowful farewell of his mother, sisters, brother, and many friends, both lay and clerical, he sailed from Greenock, March 15, 1788, in company with Rev. A. White, two other gentlemen, and five ladies as cabin passengers. After a passage of 51 days, he arrived at New York the fifth of May following, where he remained preaching till the last week of the month, when he went to Philadelphia, Pa., to meet with the Associate Presbytery of Pennsylvania.

He was an important and seasonable acquisition to that Presbytery, as urgent calls for preachers were numerous and increasing. That he might be qualified to exercise all the functions of a minister of the gospel in the newly organized congregations in which he should be called to labor, the Presbytery determined to ordain him at an early period, and assigned him subjects for trials for ordination. According to appointment of Presbytery, he preached in June, in Oxford and Rocky Creek, Pa., in August in Rockbridge Co., Va., and in September and October, in Mill Creek, Franklin, Rocky Creek, and other places in Pennsylvania, and attended the Presbytery of Pennsylvania, at Pequea, Oct. 1, 1788. His trials for ordination having proved satisfactory, he was ordained by the Associate Presbytery of Pennsylvania, at Philadelphia, Pa., Oct. 31, 1788, in the hall of the University of Pennsylvania. Rev. Thomas Beveridge presided, and preached from 2 Cor. iv. 1. "Therefore, seeing we have this ministry, as we have received mercy, we faint not." Immediately after which he delivered the charge to him. The sermon and charge were soon printed. Rev. John Anderson, D. D., was ordained by the Presbytery in the afternoon of the same day, Rev. William Marshall presided, and preached on the occasion. After this, Mr. Goodwillie went to New York, where he dispensed the Lord's Supper. In November he arrived in Cambridge, N. Y., where he labored during the winter, preaching occasionally in Argyle and other places in the vicinity. In April, 1789, he returned to New York and Philadelphia, where he attended a meeting of the Presbytery, and then went to Carlisle, where he labored the most of May and June, occasionally preaching in Pequea and other congregations in that part of Pennsylvania, and assisting Mr. Clarkson at his communion on the 24th of May. Returning to Philadelphia, he assisted Mr. Marshall at a dispensation of that holy ordinance, June 21st. On the next Sabbath he preached in New York, where he continued to labor till September, when he went to Cambridge, where, according to the appointment of Presbytery, he presided at the installation of Rev. Thomas Beveridge, and delivered to him the pastoral charge.

From Cambridge, probably after the meeting of the Presbytery there, Oct. 1, 1789, he returned to New York, where he attended a meeting of Presbytery, Oct. 19, with Messrs. Marshall, Beveridge, Anderson, and White. His call to Barnet, and settlement there, in 1781, we have already related in the ecclesiastical record of Barnet.

During these transactions in Barnet Mr. Goodwillie went back to New York, where he was April 10, 1790, and proceeded to Philadelphia, where he assisted Mr. Marshall at the communion, April 25. In May he probably preached in the vacant congregations west of Philadelphia, as we find he was at Marsh Creek, where he married his friend and companion, Rev. A. White to Margaret Kerr, May 27, 1790. In the first part of June he visited Alexandria and Fredericksburg, Va., and returned to Philadelphia, where he was married to Miss Beatrice Henderson, July 7, 1790. They went to New York before the end of that month, and proceeded to Barnet, where they arrived about the 12th of September, 1790. They lodged at first at John Hindman's for a few days, after which they resided, till the close of 1791, with John Ross, who lived near the south end of Ross Pond.

The charter of the town gave one share or right of land to the first settled minister of the gospel. As he was the first settled in the town and county, he obtained this right, which consisted of 340 acres of land, situated in three different parts of the town. A lot of 100 acres lay nearly a mile southeast of the centre of the town, four acres of which, on the northwest corner of the lot, were cleared when he moved into town. He gave to "the Presbyterian Society of Barnet," two acres on the northeast corner of which were the meeting-house and graveyard. 200 acres lay about a mile southeast from the centre of the town. Another lot of forty acres of inferior land lay on a hill east of the Passumpsic, above the falls near the mouth of the river. In order to obtain a better site for building, he purchased a piece of land on the north-

west line of the first-mentioned lot, on which he erected a large frame house, into which he moved, Dec. 20, 1791.

For about 12 or 16 years after he settled in Barnet, he had two difficult and doubtful cases of discipline, but his faith, patience, and perseverance finally triumphed over all discouragements. Mr. Beveridge, that "good servant of Jesus Christ," who had similar trials, writes to him at different times.

"VERY DEAR SIR: Let us not be discouraged with trials and temptations, but let us consider them as means by which the Lord fits instruments for his service. I feel in some measure the afflictions of my brethren. Let us be cheerful under them." "We must set our faces to the storm. If we faithfully serve the Lord, suffering for him, and with him, we shall reign with him. In a little while all these things which cause us grief and pain in this world shall be to us no more. I hope if we attend to our Master's service, he will not leave us without evidences, both of his fatherly care in providing for our wants, and of his gracious presence with us in his service. The more cheerful we are in his work, all things will go the better with us."

In 1804, a communication written by a clergyman of another denomination, and residing in an adjoining State, was published, in which the congregation of Barnet was said to be "a worldly sanctuary," and "no church of Christ." This occasioned a correspondence, which is still preserved, and which manifests that while Mr. Goodwillie was a man able to defend the right, he was still the Christian, full of candor, charity, and meekness. Indeed, he used arguments, drawn from reason and revelation, so powerfully, and applied the facts in the case so forcibly, that the calumniator of the congregation of Barnet was constrained to confess that "they were a body of Christians highly and generally respected."

Clergymen of another denomination, who, both in their discourses and publications, opposed the government of the United States as no ordinance of God, both from the pulpit and press, traduced Mr. Goodwillie as a traitor to the church of Scotland. But he was a firm friend of civil and religious liberty, and held fast the standards of the church of Scotland, as founded on the word of God. While he was a student in his native country, he favored the cause of the United States, then nobly struggling for their independence. Moreover, he never belonged to the Established Church of Scotland, but to the Associate Church, which, both in Scotland and America, testified against the errors of the Established Church, but held fast "the reformation principles of the Church of Scotland." Yet notwithstanding these aspersions, he continued to prosper in his ministerial labors till death dissolved the pastoral relation to his congregation, which he left in a prosperous condition; and it is remarkable that the congregations of all those clergymen who misrepresented him and his congregation, rejected them long before their death. Here it may also be proper to add that he observed through life the rule "to speak evil of no man." When he was defamed he made no defence, following a more excellent and effectual way; "when he was reviled, he reviled not again, but committed himself to Him who judgeth righteously," and obeyed the inspired injunction, "with well-doing put to silence the ignorance of foolish men."

During this long period of trial he did not labor in vain, for, as it has been before stated, the communicants numbered threefold more than at his settlement; and after this there were annual accessions till his death, when there were more than 200 living members. The whole number enrolled under his ministry in Barnet was more than 400.

When the call for him was executed in Barnet, July 5, 1790, it will be remembered that 12 members from the congregation of Ryegate attended and signed a paper of adherence to the call, expecting to receive a portion of his labors. That congregation received a sixth part of pastoral services till the autumn of 1822, when they obtained a settled minister. The records of that church were lost, but it is supposed that more than 150 members were admitted during that time, as the congregation was so strong that they gave a preacher a call in 1809, who accepted one from another congregation, and in 1814 gave another preacher a call, who had some thoughts of accepting it, but was also settled in another congregation. So that during his ministry for about 40 years in Barnet, and 32 in Ryegate, nearly 600 persons were enrolled members of these two congregations. During the whole of his ministry, even to old age, he was diligent, not only in preaching on the Sabbath, and visiting the sick, but every year paid a pastoral visit to the families of the congregations of both Barnet and Ryegate, and publicly catechised the parents and children in meetings in different parts of these two towns. The number of his baptisms of infants and adults amounts to several hundred. Once he baptized a child of the fifth generation, all living. When he was town-minister of Barnet he made a pastoral visit every year to every family in town. On one occasion a woman, the head of the household, refused to receive him as a minister. When departing, he turned round at the door of her house, and wiping his feet on the floor, said to her, "Christ commanded them whom he 'sent to preach the kingdom of God' in any house or city to 'shake off the very dust of their feet for a testimony against them who would not receive them nor hear their words,' and to depart saying, 'notwithstanding, be ye sure of this, the kingdom of God is come near to you.'" But the truth and grace of God soon prevailed, for what was said and done had such an effect that the woman soon professed her faith in Christ, and he baptized her and her children, and she continued till her death an exem-

plary member of his church. His list of marriages amounts to nearly 200. In answer to petitions sent from Canada, for preaching, the Presbytery appointed him to go on a mission to the petitioners. He left home Jan. 18, 1798, and went more than 150 miles beyond Montreal, and preached to them a few Sabbaths, and returned Feb. 24, having travelled nearly 600 miles in the winter.

During this prolonged period of trial he was called in God's gracious providence to endure two grievous losses, one of a public and the other of a domestic nature,— the death of his well-beloved brother, Mr. Beveridge, with whom he was most intimately associated in the ministry, and the death of two of his own children, which mournful events took place in his own house nearly at the same time. The sacrament of the Lord's Supper was dispensed to the congregation of Barnet the First Day, being the first Sabbath of July, 1798. Mr. Beveridge came to assist on that occasion. Coming through Ryegate he took a drink of water, which sickened him and issued in dysentery. Though much indisposed when he arrived in Barnet, he preached on Saturday before the communion. On the Sabbath his disease had increased to such a degree that he was obliged to sit while he served two tables, and after the sacred ordinance was dispensed he preached an excellent and very affecting sermon from John xvii. 11: "And now I am no more in the world, but these are in the world, and I come to thee." This was his last appearance in public; and though conflicting with a mortal malady, his talents and piety seemed to shine with uncommon lustre, while he addressed the people with all the fervor of a dying man. He was unable to attend public worship on the thanksgiving on Monday. It was not till three weeks after this that he died, and all hopes of his recovery were not lost till the evening before his death. During these three weeks he was chiefly employed in prayer and reading the Scriptures; and when unable to read he employed one of the elders who waited on him, to read such passages of the Bible as he pointed out, on which he frequently made observations as they went along. William Gilkerson, of Barnet, was sent to inform his family and congregation of his sickness, and they immediately sent James Small and Robert Oliver, two of the elders, to him.

The disease extended to Mr. Goodwillie's family, and two of his children died on Saturday, July 7th, the anniversary of their parents' marriage. The children were laid in one grave. Mr. Goodwillie himself, ere the third Sabbath of the month, was seized with the same disorder, which prevailed and proved very mortal in the town at that time. But such was Mrs. Goodwillie's exemplary prudence and tenderness, that notwithstanding Mr. Beveridge was the means of bringing the disorder into the family, of which two of her children died, she was unremitting in kindness to him; and though an affectionate mother, never shed a tear in his sight, for fear of hurting his sensibility. On the third Sabbath a number of people gathered to the house where the two distressed ministers lay. Mr. Beveridge's heart was so touched with compassion towards them, who were, at that time, like sheep without a shepherd, that he insisted on being permitted to preach to them. Notwithstanding the entreaty of his friends, who still had some hopes of his recovery, he roused himself once more and sat up in the bed, around which the people gathered, and after praise and prayer, preached a well-connected and very practical sermon from Psalm xxxi. 23, "Oh love the Lord, all ye his saints!" This discourse was delivered with great fervor of spirit, and in the application he did, in a very pathetic manner, exhort the people of Barnet to study peace among themselves, and to continue steadfast in their religious profession; warned them of the danger of apostasy, and said that if any of them should continue their contentions, which he had before endeavored to remove, he would be a witness against them in the day of judgment. He preached about an hour, and, after prayer and praise, dismissed the congregation. This exertion was far too great for his strength. In the evening he grew worse, the fever increased, and before midnight all hopes of his recovery were lost. He was fully sensible of his situation, and continued in this state till near the dawn of day, when the storm was changed into a calm. To the astonishment of his attendants, he sat up in bed and said, "I am a dying man, and dying fast; as to bodily pain, I am free of it. It is well that I am not afraid to die."

Mr. Goodwillie was then called up from his bed of sickness. When he and his family were come into the room, Mr. Beveridge said he would pray with them once more before he died; and then stretching forth his hands and speaking as fully and distinctly and with as much composure as when in perfect health, addressed the throne of grace, praying for the church of Christ in general and the Associate Church in particular; for his own congregation (in Cambridge, N. Y.); especially for the rising generation; for his brethren in the ministry, Mr. Marshall in Philadelphia and Mr. Goodwillie by name, that they might be supported under the trials they had met with in their congregations and families; and for those who had so faithfully attended him during his illness; and then, having commended his soul into the hand of God who gave it, concluded his pathetic and heart-melting prayer with these words : "The prayers of Thomas Beveridge are now ended."

After this he addressed the company around him and exhorted Mr. Goodwillie, who was a tender-hearted man and an affectionate father, not to give way to excessive grief for the loss of his children, as he would find their death among the things that were working together for good; thanked him and Mrs. Goodwillie for their kind-

ness shown to him in his illness, and desired him, when he wrote to Mr. Marshall in Philadelphia, to inform him that he had not forgotten him in his last moments. He then addressed others in the company, according to the various trials they had passed through,—in which he discovered the most perfect recollection. After which he lay down and desired two persons to sit by him, one on each side, and requested the rest of the company to withdraw. In the forenoon he lay perfectly at ease ; in the afternoon, grew worse and took little notice of any person, but called Mr. Goodwillie and asked him if he knew what time the Son of Man would come. He replied that he thought about 10 o'clock the ensuing night, or at furthest at midnight; to which Mr. Beveridge replied, "I know now," after which he lay still.

In the evening he seemed to revive, and as distinctly as from the pulpit, repeated twice that remarkable passage, "*I know that my Redeemer liveth, and that he shall stand at the latter day upon the earth; and though after my skin worms destroy this body, yet in my flesh shall I see God; whom I shall see for myself, and mine eyes shall behold, and not another; though my reins be consumed within me.*" After this he gradually sank, and about 10 o'clock expired, without a struggle, a sigh, or groan. He lies buried in the churchyard at Barnet, in Mr. Goodwillie's burial-place, where his congregation erected a monument, with an appropriate inscription, which contains the original Hebrew of the passage, "*I know that my Redeemer liveth.*"

The death of this eminent servant of Christ was deeply felt by Mr. and Mrs. Goodwillie, as he was their intimate friend, and as there were at that time so many urgent calls in the Associate Church for such sound, able, and faithful ministers. Mrs. Goodwillie, who was "a mother in Israel" indeed, expressed her pious public spirit on this mournful occasion by saying, that her loss by the death of her two children in one day was not to be compared to the loss of the church by the death of Mr. Beveridge. One of Mr. Goodwillie's elders said that he would have willingly died in Mr. Beveridge's stead had it been the will of God to spare him to preach the gospel.

Mr. Oliver, after he returned home to Cambridge, writes, after describing the saddening effect of the news of Mr. Beveridge's death on his wife and congregation, "We all join with her in our most sincere acknowledgments to you and Mrs. Goodwillie for your great care and kindness to the deceased and to us. We are anxious to hear of your recovery and Mary's, and how it fares with Mrs. Goodwillie after so much toil and trouble both in body and mind." Mr. Marshall, who was ministering to the bereaved congregation at that time, writes : "My salutations to you, who are like Joseph, separated from your ministerial brethren. Remember me in a particular manner to your dear yoke-fellow, whose praise is in this church for her many.gifts and graces."

Mr. and Mrs. Goodwillie, in 1802, were called to lament their loss by the death of Rev. William Marshall, of Philadelphia, another eminent minister of the Associate Church, and their kind and faithful friend, highly esteemed and well-beloved.

On account of the distance from his residence to the places where the Synod and Presbyteries of Pennsylvania and Cambridge met, Mr. Goodwillie was not frequently present, which was regretted by both himself and his brethren. He wished to attend to the duties of a Presbyter, and they wished to have his counsel and advice, as well as to enjoy his company, to encourage and cheer them in the duties and difficulties of the ministry. He was present at the meeting of the Associate Synod in Philadelphia, Pa., in 1803, when he was chosen moderator; in 1804, 1807, 1809, and in 1824, when he was appointed to preach the Synod sermon in the absence of the moderator.

So highly was he esteemed for his wisdom and understanding of the doctrine and order of the church of Christ that the Synod appointed him to make "a book of church government and discipline," which, after a few amendments and additions, was enacted by the Synod as "a standing rule," and which is still in force.

In his large collection of papers were found more than 1,000 letters, preserved to this time. The most of these were written by ministers of the Associate Church, both in Scotland and America, with some of whom the correspondence was maintained till death. We find letters from Rev. Adam Gibb, Rev. John Jamieson, D.D., and also from Alexander Pringle, D.D., with whom he corresponded till his death. We also find letters from Rev. William Marshall, Rev. Thomas Beveridge, Rev. John Anderson, D.D., with whom he corresponded till their death; Rev. A. White, Rev. Francis Pringle, Rev. Thomas Hamilton, Rev. John Banks, D.D., and most of the other ministers of the Associate Church in this country at an early period. From one of these clergymen he received nearly 300 letters in about 20 years. The letters of very many of his correspondents show that the writers were men of superior intelligence and piety, and many quotations might be made from them to show their high esteem of Mr. Goodwillie. They refer to his company and conversation as having been so agreeable and edifying, and thank him for his letters, as giving them so much pleasure and profit, that they desire a continuance of his correspondence and the enjoyment of his company.

Mr. Goodwillie seemed, indeed, well qualified for the station and relations in the church in which a gracious Providence had placed him. His mental endowments were suited to his circumstances, and were highly acceptable and advantageous to the people among whom he labored. From his knowledge of human nature, he accurately discerned the characters of men, and estimated and treated them according to their real worth; and was generally regarded by them to be "a very knowing man;" moreover, he was known to be amiable, peaceful, and contented; hence he was frequently consulted by all classes, and, as a blessed peacemaker, through his influence many difficulties were settled.

It was his custom on the Sabbath forenoon to expound the Scriptures. In this way he expounded all the New and most of the books of the Old Testament, — drawing inferences and observations, both doctrinal and practical, from the passages expounded. His sermons were sound and solid, well arranged, and full of the doctrines and duties of religion; and many of his people became eminent for their faith, holiness, and good works. In the pulpit he was grave and solemn, calm and deliberate in delivery, — a minister of the word who did not aspire after popular applause "with the enticing words of man's wisdom," but who, rather with great plainness of speech, preached the glorious and everlasting gospel of Christ crucified; while so deeply did his own soul experience the gracious power of the precious truths he taught that he often shed tears while delivering them to others.

His last discourse was preached in the new brick meeting-house, Sabbath, July 18, 1830, from Hebrews, respecting the sojourning of Israel in the wilderness for forty years, and the use to which the apostle applies it. "There remaineth, therefore, a rest for the people of God. Let us therefore labor to enter into that rest." The people observed, afterwards, that the discourse was remarkable, and he was himself deeply affected in delivering it, as he had been nearly 40 years settled in Barnet, and anticipated that his end was drawing near. A diary, kept by his son and assistant in the ministry, contains a particular account of his last sickness and death. On Thursday following, he seemed to be overcome by the heat of the weather, which was very oppressive, accompanied with debility and symptoms of cough and congestion of the lungs. For more than a week he was often delirious, and unable to converse much, but manifested during his sickness, by being often observed to be engaged in prayer and repeating parts of the Scriptures, that his thoughts were occupied with the things of God. After this, he grew worse, and died in the evening of the 12th day of his sickness. In the morning of that day, he became quite sensible; was aware that he had been delirious, and inquired how long it was since he was taken ill; how it came upon him; how long it was since the Lord's Supper had been dispensed, and how often he had preached since. He directed his executor to divide his library between his two sons in the ministry. After lying quiet for some time, apparently meditating, he looked up in the face of his son, to whom he had formerly observed that he would soon be left alone in his ministry, and said, in a calm but firm tone of voice, "It appears that God, in his providence, is about to put a period to my life and labors, and take me to himself. I acknowledge his goodness to me and my family and connections. Tell my absent children and relatives that I pray for every one of them, and desire that they walk in the ways of the Lord, and that they pray for each other, and especially for those who have been bereaved by death. This affliction has come on me suddenly, and has left me little time for reflection, but it is the will of the Lord, and we should submit to it with cheerful readiness. I acknowledge God's goodness to me and the church." He then exhorted his three children present "to walk by faith." Afterwards, he spoke of his being devoted to God, and acknowledged his unworthiness, but expressed his confidence in the manifold mercy of God in Christ. In the afternoon, the delirium returned, and the difficulty of breathing increased, till 6 o'clock, August 2, 1830, when he departed in peace, in the 81st year of his age, having preached the gospel nearly 52 years.

His funeral was attended by a large concourse of people, many of whom were from Ryegate and other towns around Barnet. Several clergymen belonging to adjacent towns were also present. Rev. Wm. Pringle, whose ordination and settlement in Ryegate he had lately attended, and to whom he gave the pastoral charge, read the 19th Psalm, with prayer; and he was interred beside his deceased wife and children and fellow-laborer, Mr. Beveridge. A monument was soon erected near the graves of Mr. and Mrs. Goodwillie, with appropriate inscriptions. The following Sabbath, Rev. Mr. Pringle preached to a large audience an excellent sermon, suited to the solemn occasion, from Psalm cxlii. 5. "I cried unto thee, O Lord; I said, Thou art my refuge and my portion in the land of the living." His death was considered a public loss; even his acquaintance who survive still revere and cherish his memory, which is blessed.

When he was settled in Barnet, the county was new. Except a clergyman of another denomination settled about 20 miles south of him, there was not another settled minister of any denomination within 60 miles in any other direction. This solitary state continued for 9 years.

In 1798, he procured sheet iron, and got his brother, who followed his father's occupation, and had moved his family from Nova Scotia to Barnet in 1793, in order to enjoy his ministry, to make him a stove, which for a long time was the first used in this part of the country, and considered a great curiosity and comfort. About the year 1812, he procured from the State of New York a four-wheeled vehicle, which was for some years the first carriage owned and used in Barnet.

In stature he was about 5 feet 10 inches; had a robust frame, and inclined to be corpulent in the decline of life. In his habits he was temperate and regular, and enjoyed generally good health. Thus he was enabled to endure without complaint the fatigue of travelling and the inclemency of the weather at all seasons, as well as the arduous labors of his ministry for so many years. In the last years of his life, he became deaf to a considerable degree, but his eyesight remained good, so that he could read till the last.

He brought from Scotland a good library, mostly composed of theological works, which were much damaged by the carelessness of those who transported them up the Connecticut River, permitting them to get wet. At home, he kept close to the study-room adjoining his library, continuing his labors till midnight, — a practice maintained till near his death.

In 1805, as before mentioned, his relation of pastor to the town was dissolved with mutual consent, the law of the State under which he was settled having been essentially modified. But his fellow-citizens soon gave him proofs, which continued through life, of their high esteem, as well as their confidence in his ability and integrity, in electing him to three responsible offices. In the autumn of the same year, he was chosen to represent the town in the legislature, which held its session from Oct. 5 to Nov. 8, 1805, at Danville, 7 miles from his residence. He always returned home on Saturday, and preached to his congregation on the Sabbath. In the same year, the Presbyterian Society of Barnet was incorporated, which paid his salary till his death. In 1807 he was chosen town clerk, and was annually re-elected by the town to that office till 1827, when he declined re-election.

The mail was first extended to Barnet in 1808. It was a weekly mail, and ran through the centre of the town. He was appointed the first postmaster in Barnet, and was continued in that office till 1818, when the route was changed to the Connecticut River.

His talents for business were great. He was a ready writer, and wrote a good hand, and his transactions were methodical and exact. His residence, being near the centre of the town, was convenient for the inhabitants, and the duties of these offices were light and quickly discharged, and did not interfere with his pastoral duties, which he diligently discharged with punctuality.

He labored both publicly and privately till an academy was established in the county, at Peacham, five miles from his residence, and some years before any other clergyman was settled in the county. By the charter he was appointed a trustee, which office he held till 1827, when he resigned, and the Board of Trustees passed a vote of "thanks to him for his long and faithful services." He attended all their annual meetings during this period, and was the President of the Board for many years; and annually chosen one of the examiners, and punctually attended. The pupils long remembered their examinations by the venerable minister of Barnet, who was esteemed the most learned member of the Board of Trustees. Long after his death, the 50th anniversary of the institution was celebrated, being attended by great numbers of its former pupils, from different parts of the United States and Canada. The jubilee lasted for two days. The late Chief Justice of Vermont delivered an oration, and a distinguished lawyer from Massachusetts, one of the early pupils, in his speech, eulogized Mr. Goodwillie for his talents, erudition, and piety. James Orr, a member of his congregation in Barnet, gave the County Academy $1,000 as a donation.

He was charitable, hospitable, generous; but modest and humble, and did not let his left hand know what his right hand gave to support the poor and spread the gospel. He was a life member of the Bible Society. He possessed great equanimity and fortitude,—was not uplifted by prosperity or cast down by adversity; but rather inherited and cultivated through life a peculiarly cheerful disposition, insomuch that it was remarked by the most intelligent of his people, that he appeared most cheerful in preaching when under trouble, whether of a public or domestic nature. He was esteemed a judicious man, and a faithful, affectionate friend. His brethren in the ministry sought his counsel and company, and the regret was mutual that they were settled so far apart. Rev. John Anderson, D.D., who was ordained with him in Philadelphia, and who officiated at his installation in Barnet, was a friend very highly esteemed and beloved for his superior talents, learning, and piety, with whom Mr. Goodwillie continued to correspond till the death of Mr. A., not four months before his own, which event deeply affected him as long as he lived.

Rev. Andrew Heron, D.D., who was many years clerk of the Associate Synod, writes to one of Mr. Goodwillie's sons with respect to his "venerated father's life and character." "I never heard him preach, but spent some days in his hospitable mansion, in 1814, when he was considerably advanced in life. His kindness and hospitality were unbounded. I was delighted and edified with his society and conversation. He had a rich fund of anecdotes, and a pleasing manner of telling them. I have often heard the fathers of the Associate Church, now dead, express their confidence in him and their regard for him. I have often heard my aunt, who emigrated in the same ship, tell how much she and the rest of the cabin passengers were indebted to his constant pleasantries and liveliness of manner, making the voyage to seem short and agreeable."

Besides his inexhaustible fund of good anecdotes and a good way of relating them, his sallies were ready, pertinent, forcible; and the quick wit of his replies produced sudden bursts of great laughter. When a little child, he wandered from home, and, when returning, was met by his mother searching for him. Fearing chastisement, he fell down on his knees before her, held up his hands, and said, "All obedience, mother." Such submission satisfied the mother. When a member of the Legislature of Vermont, his replies to the arguments of an opponent were so forcible and facetious, that the whole house was convulsed with laughter, at the opponent's expense, who had the magnanimity not to resent it. One Saturday evening, a young, reckless member moved "that the Legislature adjourn till to-morrow morning," which so shocked the moral sense of the house, that many members turned their eyes on the Scotch minister as a sign for him to defend the sacred Sabbath. He rose and said, "I second the motion," which greatly astonished the house; but he continued, "I second the motion, not because I approve of it, but to have the right to call for the yeas and nays, which I accordingly do, for I wish it to be known who in this house are the friends and who the foes of the Sabbath." The mover immediately withdrew the motion, knowing his name would be recorded in the journal and published in the newspapers as au enemy to the Lord's day, which would give him rather a killing notoriety. More than 40 years since, he attended commencement of Dartmouth College, after which he called on Dr. Shurtleff, one of the professors, who loved sprightly conversation as well as himself. While they were engaged in talking, Mr. A., a graduate, entered the room and took the seat of another graduate who had just gone out. Mr. Goodwillie, having been so earnestly engaged in conversation that he did not perceive the change, said, "I liked Mr. A.'s speech very well." The doctor said, "I am glad to hear it, and will introduce you to him." Turning to Mr. A., Mr. Goodwillie remarked, immediately after the introduction, "I liked your speech very well; but perhaps it was not so deep as some of the others." Thus he saved himself in some degree from the impropriety of praising a person in his presence. Dr. Shurtleff spoke highly of his public spirit and generosity. One morning at the breakfast table, with a few witty words spoken occasionally as he was eating, he kept a brother clergyman laughing so heartily that he could not get time to eat or drink, which he constantly urged him to do.

MRS. GOODWILLIE was born in Kirkcaldy, Fifeshire, Scotland, Jan. 24, 1761. David Henderson, her father, widely known for his great zeal and piety, was a member of the Associate Church. He, at first, belonged to the congregation of Ceres, 14 miles distant, but when the Associate Congregation of Kirkcaldy was organized, about 1750, he became a member and was chosen an elder, which office he held till his death, in 1775. It was his custom to rise early in the morning and engage till breakfast in reading the Scriptures, self-examination, meditation, and prayer, and continued "instant in prayer" through the day. He was a merchant, and it was his custom, when he had placed the goods on the counter, while his customers were examining what to buy, to turn his back upon them and his face to the wall, and engage in prayer.

Her mother was a daughter of William Gardner of Cupar, Fifeshire, who joined the Associate Church and became a member of the congregation of Abernethy, 14 miles distant, but after the congregation of Ceres, in the neighborhood of Cupar, was organized, became a member and continued to adorn his profession till his death in 1772, aged 90 years. He had two children, daughters, one of whom was married to John Culbert, a merchant in Cupar, who had 14 children, one of whom was Rev. John Culbert, a minister of the Associate Synod, who was in France at the time of the Revolution, lost all his property, and narrowly escaped with his life; and who was acquainted and corresponded with the eminent Rev. John Newton, of London, whose narrative he had printed in Scotland in 1783. He died in 1825.

Margaret Gardner, the youngest daughter, was married in 1744 to David Henderson. They had 7 children. The youngest was Mrs. Goodwillie, whose mother, noted for piety, died when she was but a little child, and her father when she was but 14; but his religious instructions and example had made a powerful and permanent impression, and having been afterward more thoroughly instructed in the word of God, she joined the congregation of Kirkcaldy.

She emigrated to America with Mr. Goodwillie in 1788, and resided two years with her brother, David Henderson, of Fredericksburg, Va., who came to America before the Revolutionary War, in which he suffered great losses, and enlisted in a company commanded by Capt. Washington, a brother of Gen. Washington, with whose mother he was acquainted. Mr. Henderson was a godly and generous man; for many years a member and ruling elder of the Presbyterian church of Fredericksburg, Va., and died in 1837. Among his many acts of generosity was a liberal donation, continued for many years, for the education of two of his sister's sons for the sacred ministry.

Miss Henderson was married to Mr. Goodwillie July 7, 1790, by Rev. William Marshall, in his own house in Philadelphia, Pa., and he held her in high esteem during life and made "honorable mention" of her in his life of Mr. Beveridge. To one who had always been accustomed to a city life, the change to live in a country newly settled was great; but she submitted to discomforts cheerfully, that she might be instrumental for the spiritual interests of those among whom she came to dwell. Ever very much concerned that she might be helpful to

a man of God in promoting the success of his ministry, she was indeed a great helpmeet to her husband, in things spiritual as well as temporal. So deep an interest did they naturally take in the prosperity of the church, that it was their usual practice to set apart days for fasting, humiliation, and prayer, which they observed in the family, for the peace and prosperity of the congregation, as well as the spiritual interests of the family. She had a female prayer-meeting which met in their house, and was an active member of a female society still existing in the congregation, for the purpose of contributing to Bible and missionary societies, and the support of young men studying with a view to the sacred ministry. Her friends who had the best opportunity of knowing her character and habits, represent her as conscientiously careful in discharging all personal and domestic duties, much devoted to prayer and perusal of the Word of God, and greatly enriched with religious experience. She was a faithful and affectionate Christian mother. When her husband was gone from home, she observed family worship; and so fervent were her prayers for her family and the church, that frequently the floor where she bowed down on her knees to pray was wet with her tears. And it appears that when she came to die she was well "exercised unto godliness;" yet her humility was so great that she now esteemed herself "to be nothing," and lamented that she had not lived a more useful life. But her faith in the gracious promises remained firm, and she had a desire to depart, and repeatedly prayed, "O Lord Jesus, come quickly!" When dying, her aged husband kissed her, and said, "I resign you to God from whom I received you." She died Feb. 4, 1827, aged 66 years, three years and a half before her husband. A great concourse of people followed her to the grave.

In concluding this history of Barnet, the writer would observe that he obtained materials so abundant that it would require a volume to contain a full history of the town. His chief work has been to examine, select, arrange, and condense. Besides the use of the town and church records and papers, and the extensive collections of letters, papers, journals, and charts belonging to the late Rev. David Goodwillie, he is indebted to Hon. Walter Harvey for the letters, papers, journal, and chart of his father, Col. Harvey; to Henry Stevens, Esq., for important maps and documents, and to Willard Stevens, Esq., for the papers, letters, lists, journal, and charts of his father, Enos Stevens, Esq.

Barnet, March 4, 1861.

MR. AND MRS. GOODWILLIE'S FAMILY.

BY REV. ANDREW HERON, D.D.

They had 8 children, four sons and four daughters; of whom one daughter and three sons are now living. One of the sons has been long and intimately connected with the church and town of Barnet.

MARY GOODWILLIE was born Oct. 2, 1792. She was dangerously sick when her brother and sister died, and Mr. Beveridge joined in prayer with the elders that she might be recovered. She lived to become the wife of his successor in his congregation. She was educated at the Caledonia County Academy, and married by her father Sept. 28, 1810, to Rev. Alexander Bullions, D.D., pastor of the Associate Congregation of Cambridge. Rev. P. Bullions, D. D., in the life of her eminent and excellent husband, says "she was a woman of uncommon worth and loveliness; meek, unassuming, patient under many afflictions; of sincere, unaffected piety, and beloved by all who knew her. She was the mother of 6 children, whom she endeavored to train up to fear and serve the Lord, commending them with much and fervent prayer to Him who gave them. She died in the full assurance of faith, Jan. 4, 1830." Her eldest daughter, a superior woman, was married to the Rev. Wm. Pringle, pastor of the Associate Congregation of Ryegate. Her eldest son, Rev. David G. Bullions, graduated at Union College, N. Y.; became a minister of the Associate Church, and was settled as his father's assistant and successor. The other son graduated at Union College, and became a celebrated physician, having studied his profession in Europe and America.

MILDRED GOODWILLIE, born Aug. 1, 1798, was educated in Caledonia County Academy, and married by her father, July 11, 1817, to Rev. John Donaldson, pastor of the Associate Congregation of Florida, N. Y., but afterwards settled in Scroggsfield, Ohio, where she died in 183–, greatly lamented. She deserves the good character given to Mrs. Bullions, whom she greatly resembled. She had 7 children, five of whom are living.

THOMAS GOODWILLIE, born Sept. 27, 1800, and DAVID GOODWILLIE, born Aug. 28, 1802. These two sons in 1813 went to Cambridge, N. Y., and studied under Dr. Bullions, and attended some time the Cambridge Academy, under Dr. Chassell. Returning home in the spring of 1817, they attended the Caledonia County Academy for a short time, and then entered Dartmouth College, where they graduated August, 1820. Having become members of the Associate Church a few years before, they were admitted by the Associate Presbytery of Cambridge, and commenced the study of theology in the beginning of 1821, at the Eastern Theological Seminary of the Associate Church in Philadelphia. Dr. Banks, the professor under whom they studied, was eminent for his knowledge of theology and profound acquaintance with the Greek, but especially the Hebrew language, which made him an able critic and expositor of the Holy Scriptures.

He represented them to their parents as "bearing a good character, and making excellent progress;" and the Presbytery of Cambridge, before the appointed time for the study of theology had elapsed, recommended them to the Synod to be licensed, and the Synod suspended the rule, and ordered this Presbytery to take them on trials for this end. These trials having proved satisfactory, the Associate Presbytery of Cambridge licensed them at Ryegate, Sept. 29, 1823. Their hoary-headed father was the moderator of the Presbytery at that time, and from his great knowledge and experience, with tears flowing fast, gave them suitable and sage council with respect to the duties and difficulties of the "good work" in which they were engaging. Claiming their right which was accorded to them by the Synod, they returned to the Theological Seminary, and studied another term.

Leaving Philadelphia early in the spring of 1824, in fulfilling the Synod's appointments to preach, they went to South Carolina, then into Tennessee, Kentucky, Indiana, and Ohio, and returned to Philadelphia the next spring. On their way South, their first interview with their uncle, who had so long and liberally supported them in prosecuting their studies, was very gratifying, and he was highly pleased with their company and conversation, but his greatest pleasure was to hear his nephews preach the gospel of Christ, which was dear to his own soul. Dr. Banks, the professor, writes to their "venerable father," "with much satisfaction," that his two sons were "excellent young men, who gave great attention to their studies, in which they made excellent progress;" that they preached several times in Philadelphia, and "were very acceptable to the people, among whom they left a savory remembrance of their character and abilities." The aged and venerable Dr. Anderson writes to their father, "Feb. 18, 1825: I have had much satisfaction in being visited by your two sons. They both preached to our people with much acceptance. I hope the Lord will bless them, and make them a blessing to his people." They returned home to Barnet, and assisted their father in July, 1825, in dispensing the ordinance of the Lord's Supper. So well pleased and profited were the people of their father's congregation with their ministrations that they immediately applied to the Presbytery for a moderation of a call, and on the 26th day of October, 1825, they gave Rev. Thomas Goodwillie a unanimous call to be assistant pastor and successor to his father. The aged pastor still being able to officiate, and preachers being few, and the vacant congregations many, his son continued to fulfil the appointments of Synod. Having passed satisfactory trials for ordination, he was ordained and settled as pastor of the Associate Congregation of Barnet by the Associate Presbytery of Cambridge, Sept. 27, 1826, before a large audience, many of whom came from surrounding towns. The aged father, with many tears, gave the pastoral charge to his son.

Soon after his settlement, the Legislature elected him to preach before the Governor, Council, and General Assembly, at the opening of the Legislature the next year. Accordingly, he preached at Montpelier, October 11, 1827, before the Legislature, and a vast audience of attentive listeners, and gave appropriate addresses to the Governor, Council, and General Assembly. The Legislature voted him thanks for the "eloquent and able" sermon, and requested a copy for publication, and elected him their chaplain for the session. His sermon was immediately published at the expense of the State, and gratuitously distributed to all its towns. Rev. Ashbel Green, D.D., of Philadelphia, editor of "The Christian Advocate," in noticing its publication, says:—

"It is a sensible and faithful sermon, on a text manifestly appropriate to the occasion,—Prov. xiv. 31: *'Righteousness exalteth a nation, but sin is a reproach to any people.'* We know not whether it be more creditable to the author of this discourse that he had the fidelity to deliver it, or to the Legislature of the State of Vermont that they had the good sense and piety to request its publication. We wish that such a sermon were addressed to every State Legislature, and to our congress, too, at the commencement of each of their sessions."

The sermon was afterwards reprinted. By appointment of the Presbytery to which he belonged, he went on a mission to Upper Canada in 1827. In consequence of a petition from Lower Canada, he went and preached in several towns on the St. Francis River, in 1829. While he was officiating as chaplain to the Legislature, and absent on these missions, his father officiated in the congregation in Barnet.

A few weeks after his father died, he left Barnet on account of ill-health, and for a year travelled in the Southern and Western States. In 1831 he went to the south of France, and proceeded to Sicily, and went as far as Syracuse. From thence he proceeded to Naples; visited Herculaneum and Pompeii; ascended Mt. Vesuvius, and entered the crater of this volcano; then journeyed to Rome, and saw the vast remains of antiquity, and the works of the fine arts. By Florence and Milan, he went over the Alps, by the Mt. Simplon road, to Geneva, where he saw the library of Calvin. Thence he travelled to the north of Europe; visited Scotland, and returned in 1833, with his health so far recovered as to resume his labors in the congregation of Barnet, where he has continued to labor to the present time; and his congregation has expressed their high appreciation of his character and services, and their sympathy with him in his trials, both public and domestic.

He was clerk of the Associate Synod (of the North) from 1841 to 1854, when the Synods united, except in 1852, when he was chosen moderator. After preaching at the opening of the Synod the next year, which is the duty of the moderator, the Synod, without precedent, voted him "thanks for his very excellent sermon." He was again chosen moderator of the Associate Synod in 1859. He has long been a life member of the American Bible Society.

In 1827, when his father resigned his seat in the board of trustees of the Caledonia County Academy, he was immediately chosen a trustee, to fill his place, which he still continues to occupy, and has been one of the examiners, and, most of the time, president of the board. In 1827, also, when his father declined a re-election as town clerk, he was chosen to that office, which he then declined; but, in 1859, was re-elected to the office, which was urged upon him, and he accepted, and has been since annually re-elected.

He was married, April 11, 1833, and has four children living,—three sons and a daughter,—besides a daughter who died in 1850, in the thirteenth year of her age, remarkable for her intelligence and piety. The two oldest sons have graduated at the Pennsylvania College of Dental Surgery, and settled in their profession in Philadelphia, Pa. The eldest son is one of the faculty of that college, and for some years has given great satisfaction in discharging the duties of his office, and has also become a good writer on some parts of his profession. The youngest son (who bears his father's name) is a student in Dartmouth College, preparing for the Christian ministry.

Rev. DAVID GOODWILLIE, Jr., received a call from Xenia and Sugar Creek, O.; but accepted one from the united congregations of Poland, Liberty, and Deer Creek, and was ordained and settled by the Associate Presbytery of Ohio at Deer Creek, Lawrence Co., Pa., April 26, 1826, and ever since has been a laborious minister, and his ministry has been blessed with great success. His congregations increased so much that each one desired to have a greater share of his labors, but feared the loss of the valued labors of their highly-esteemed pastor, in a division of his pastoral charge. But his labors still increased to such a degree that he was at length constrained to ask the Presbytery for a division, which was granted, and Deer Creek was disjoined in the beginning of 1833. After the union of the Associate and Associate Reformed churches, he was disjoined from Poland in April, 1859, that it might unite with another congregation in the vicinity, and he now continues his ministrations in Liberty, Trumbull Co., Pa. The number of church members enrolled under his pastoral care in Deer Creek, in 7 years, was 104; in Poland, in 33 years, 303, and in Liberty, in 35 years, extending to the present time (1861) 253, making a total of 660. For a number of years he was president of the board of trustees of Westminster College, Pa. He was married April 20, 1826. His children were three sons and three daughters, of whom two sons and two daughters survive. His firstborn, Rev. David Henderson Goodwillie, graduated at Jefferson College, Pa. ; studied theology in the seminary of the Associate Church, and was licensed to preach by the Associate Presbytery of Shenango, Sept. 2, 1853, and about the same time he was elected by the board of trustees of Westminster College, the professor of natural philosophy and chemistry, and continued to fill that office successfully, till he resigned, in December, 1854. He was ordained and settled in the Associate congregation of Stamford in Canada, four miles from Niagara Falls, Sept. 27, 1855, where he still continues.

April 11, 1861. **A. H.**

REFORMED PRESBYTERIAN CHURCH.

BY REV. JOHN BOLE, OF RYEGATE.

The Reformed Presbyterian Congregation, of Barnet, in connection with the General Synod of the Reformed Presbyterian Church in North America, was originally a branch of the Ryegate congregation of the same denomination. The congregation was organized in 1851, under the pastorate of Rev. Robert A. Hill, who demitted his charge in 1852. And in 1853, the Rev. John Bole was ordained pastor of the congregations of Ryegate and Barnet. In little more than a year after his organization, Mr. Bole demitted the charge of the Barnet congregation. Since then, this congregation has remained a vacancy under the care of the Northern Presbytery of the Reformed Presbyterian Church in connection with the General Synod. The congregation numbers about 20 members.

THE REFORMED PRESBYTERIAN CONGREGATION (OLD SCHOOL) OF BARNET.

BY. REV. JAMES BEATTIE.

This congregation was organized in 1840, the year that Rev. James Milligan was disjoined from Ryegate. It then consisted of about ten members. It was in a short time increased by the accession of members of the Ryegate congregation, who resided in that vicinity. It united with Ryegate, in 1844, in giving Rev. James M. Beattie a call, when there were 25 members, in regular standing. Mr. Beattie, who continues to be their pastor, preaches alternately to the two congregations, the two meeting-houses being five miles distant from each other. In this congregation there is a flourishing Sabbath school. The people contribute liberally to the different schemes of the church. By very liberal exertions they have recently repaired the meeting-house, which is in the southwest part of the town. Since the settlement of the present pastor there have been 48 additions. There are at present 58 communicants.

CONGREGATIONAL CHURCH.

BY REV. M. B. BRADFORD.

Nov. 21, 1816. A congregational church was organized by Rev. Samuel Goddard, then of Concord, Vt., composed of members in part of Barnet, and in part of Lyman, N. H. It was called the " Congregational Church of Barnet and Lyman." This church was small, but continued, with various degrees of prosperity, about 12 years. It appears to have been sound in the faith, and to have exerted a good influence. It was organized with 20 members, and during its continuance, received into its fellowship about 100 persons. It never had a settled pastor. Most of its members have fallen asleep. A few remain to the present time.

In October, 1829, the first Congregational Church in Barnet was formed. It consisted of three members, viz : James Gildchrist, Willard, and J. F. Skinner. After the church was organized, the Rev. A. Govan was constituted the pastor.

During the 30 years of the existence of this church, 238 members were received by letter and profession ; 111 dismissed, and 25 have died. The large number of dismissions is owing to the fact that on Sept. 10, 1858, forty-three were dismissed for the purpose of being organized into a church at Stevens Village, the first church having built a meeting-house, and established its centre at McIndoes Falls. This church has been blessed with many pastors, but only two of them have been settled. Rev. Mr. Govan continued as pastor from 1829 to September, 1832. Rev. Noah Cressey was employed a part of the time until 1835, when Rev. Joseph B. White began his labors with this church. After him, Rev. E. I. Carpenter, Rev. E. Ranney, and Rev. A. O. Hubbard were employed successively. Mr. Hubbard continued his connection with the church some six years. After him, Rev. E. H. Caswell was acting pastor about three years. In 1854, Rev. E. Cleaveland began to preach to this church, and continued two years. March 5, 1856, Rev. B. F. Ray was ordained, and dismissed Aug. 30, 1859. In December following, Rev. M. B. Bradford, the present pastor, commenced his labors.

This church is now situated near the border of the town, and is made up in part by members from Ryegate, Vt., and from Munroe and Bath, in N. H., who find it convenient to attend worship at McIndoes Falls.

BAPTIST CHURCH.

BY REV. A. H. HOUSE.

Barnet, originally settled by Scotch Presbyterians, had no other religious organization for several years. Prior to 1811, there was a small Baptist Church, called " Barnet and Ryegate Church " to which Elder Bailey — still remembered with Christian love — ministered for some time. (For twenty-four years before he became Baptist, he had been a Congregationalist; but, believing it his duty to be baptized by immersion, submitted to the rite, and united with the Baptist Church at Danville.) He was a laborious minister, and often blessed with revivals. The time of his death I do not know. Nor do I deem it a matter of importance. He lived a Christian, — best record that can be made of any man, — and died, I doubt not, in the faith. The Baptist Church in Passumpsic Village, in the north part of Barnet, was formed in 1811; but its place of worship has always been in Barnet Village, and its members have belonged to different towns, principally St. Johnsbury, Waterford, Danville, Ryegate, and Groton. At one time there was in Groton quite a branch of the Passumpsic Church, which was subsequently organized into an independent church. The records of the church at Passumpsic are in such a state I cannot state positively the number of members when organized. As near as I can ascertain, however, there were some eight or ten. The whole number received into the church was 509; baptized, 333; present number (Nov. 1, 1861), 74. This church has had ten pastors, viz: Silas Davidson, George B. Ide, D. D., now of Springfield, Mass., J. Merriam, B. Burrows, Levi Smith, John Ide, N. W. Smith, A. Boardman, and A. H. House. The average length of the pastoral relation, nearly 5 years; the first pastor 19 years and 3 months, the last pastor now in his 7th year. The church has licensed and ordained six ministers, some of whom are in heaven, and some occupying important places in the church militant. The average number of baptisms per year, during the history of the church, is six and a fraction. The church has been blessed with a number of precious revivals. In 1816, thirty-five were baptized; in 1828, forty-eight; in 1831, fifty-eight; in 1833, twenty; and in 1839, sixty-three. While some of these have turned backward, many, we trust, will be saved in the day of Christ. There were *several* years, in which every year more or less were baptized. There has been, however, no general revival since 1839. During the ministrations of the first pastor, dependence, under God, was placed on the ordinary means of grace, and God did not disappoint the expectations of his people. But since his day, more dependence has been placed on extraordinary, — *on exciting measures*, and we have been shown, what the writer has always believed, that such a course is not wise. If the Lord does not renew his work, this church, which has done so much for the truth, which has been so honorable among her sister churches, which for a long time was a model church for its discipline and benevolence, which has always been blessed with good men for its deacons, for whose welfare the Clarks, the Woods, the Parks, and the Browns have

toiled so much, will soon become extinct! Elders Davidson, Merriam, Ide, and Green have gone home. The rest of the pastors who have served this church are still in the field. I regret I am not able to give a short sketch of the life of Elder Merriam, who is remembered with so much affection by all who sat under his ministry while pastor of the church in this place. I would also speak of Elder J. Ide, did I not expect a sketch of his honorable and useful life would be furnished with the history of Coventry, where he labored many years, and where he was ordained to the work of the ministry. I will close this meagre sketch of our church — which is perhaps already too long — with a brief notice of its first pastor, Elder Silas Davidson, who was born in Pomfret, Ct., November, 1766. He came to Vermont in 1779. He united with the Baptist Church in Hartland, in 1795. In 1798, he moved to Waterford, and soon began ministerial labors there, and was instrumental in gathering a small church in that town, which, after a few years, was blended with the church at Passumpsic, with which he himself united in 1811, and was ordained its pastor, July 1, 1812, and for 19 years and 3 months after, he honorably sustained that relation; faithfully preaching Christ as the only hope of the guilty. He dwelt among *his* people, and, at his own request, was dismissed. Few men have been more useful. He was a Baptist from principle, — sound in the faith, — unswerving to the last; but a lover of all who loved the Lord Jesus. While he possessed not the advantages of an early education, his sermons were eminently acceptable to those whose minds were better cultivated, for he studied *the Book*, quoted, with great accuracy, the *Book*, and the BOOK was his guide through life. He was, moreover, a true friend of education; and all the benevolent associations of the day had his prayers and sincere co-operation. Indeed, a devout man and an excellent counsellor, few churches have been better instructed in their duty than this, of which he was so long pastor; and no man did more for the association to which he belonged, for which he was moderator six times, clerk twelve times, and preached its introductory sermon four times. Three of his sons entered the ministry, though but one lived to be ordained, and these all went before him to rest. He died in clear hope of eternal life, at his residence in Waterford, May 16, 1842, aged 76. His memory "*esto perpetua.*"

EXTRACTS FROM AN ADDRESS BEFORE THE CALEDONIA COUNTY AGRICULTURAL SOCIETY, AT THE ANNUAL FAIR HELD AT ST. JOHNSBURY PLAIN, OCT. 2, 1845.

BY HENRY STEVENS, ESQ.

By turning to the census of this State, A. D. 1790, 1800, 1810, it will be found that at each census which was taken at those periods, the people of Vermont possessed more sheep according to their population than any other State. Our household manufactures amounted to much more, according to our population, than any other State. The census shows that the inhabitants of the town of Danville manufactured 26,907 yards of linen cloth, 1,214 yards of cotton, and 16,128 yards of woollen cloth; Peacham, 13,608 yards of linen, 2,119 of cotton, and 9,824 yards of woollen cloth; St. Johnsbury, 16,505 of linen, 1,179 cotton, 9,431 woollen; Barnet, 5,535 yards linen, 319 cotton, 10,830 of woollen cloth. Caledonia County, at that period, contained 23 towns, population 18,740; number of sheep, 34,587; woollen cloth manufactured, more than 7 yards to each person. All kinds of cloth of household manufacture averaged more than 19 yards to each inhabitant. The whole quantity manufactured in this county, in 1810, was 360,516 yards. The number of females over 15 years of age was 4,485; therefore, they manufactured more than 80 yards of cloth each. There were 1,419 looms. The average quantity of cloth wove in each was more than 254 yards. The estimated value of household manufactures for each female over 15 years of age, in 1810, was more than $40.

Again, since Vermont was admitted into the Federal Union, her delegates in Congress have been the fast and firm friends in favor of encouraging industry, and promoting domestic manufactures. As a people, we have, from the time our fathers declared the New Hampshire Grants a free and independent State, 15th January, A.D. 1777, pursued this policy. It was the pursuing of this policy that enabled our fathers to meet the expenses of the Revolutionary War, to redeem the then paper issues at par, and the only State that ever did redeem their paper issues were at a discount of $40 for one. Not a single bill of purchase of woollen blankets or woollen garments, out of the State, for our brave soldiers during the Revolutionary War, has yet been discovered.

Our mothers manufactured cloth for garments, and blankets for their husbands and sons, when at home, or in the field of action. Our mothers would say to their husbands and sons, on their leaving for the army, " My dear, if anything should happen that you do not return, you will direct that my blanket be sent back."

Soon after the close of the Revolutionary War, our country was flooded with goods of the manufacture of foreign countries, which soon drained the country of most of the solid coin. Paper currency, State and government securities became nearly worthless. Tender laws and appraisement laws became the order of the day throughout the Union. The General Assembly of this State, as early as 1786, passed a law, saying that for the encouragement of domestic manufactures, the owner of sheep should be credited on his list two shillings for every pound of wool shorn, and one shilling for every yard of linen or tow cloth manufactured. This policy soon caused the balance of trade to become in favor of the State, — paper issues redeemed, private debts paid, and the State Treasurer soon reported a balance in the treasury of $14,000 in silver and gold. . . . .

We may with propriety speak of the patriotism and heroic acts of Chittenden, Allen, and Warner, and others of our citizens, in the cabinet, and in the field of action. We also must remember that at that period our mothers and sisters were cultivating the fields, harvesting the crops, and, by hand, manufacturing for their household. That spirit of enterprise and perseverance on the part of our mothers yet runs in the veins of many of those who are termed the better half. Their workmanship, exhibited to us this day, is sufficient to satisfy us that they are yet willing to contribute their proportion in rendering old Caledonia independent of our sister States, or foreign Countries. . . . .

Vermont can raise as fine wool as any section of the world. Our mountains furnish pasturage of the best kind, and roll down their thousand streams to aid us in its manufacture. Our State abounds with ores, and with forests for the miners and colliers, ample for the manufacture of iron in all its varieties, and equal to the calls of the State consumption, and ultimately, for export. Our Country and our State should follow up the mode of policy which is pursued by the greatest manufacturing interest in the world. We should sit on our wool-sacks, in order to encourage the wool-grower. We should give bounties, and grant prohibitions until the branches of our manufacturing rise to an equal level with other orders graduated to the wants they supply.

No governor of this State has at any time, in his message to the General Assembly, put forth any sentiments other than in favor of industry, economy, and the protection of the agricultural, mechanical, and manufacturing interest. You may take a candle, and search the archives of every State in this Union, and you will find no better lessons of wisdom in favor of the great and leading intererest of the State and of this Union, than are recorded in the archives of the Green Mountain State. I hope the time will come when every freeman will be furnished with the annual messages of our past governors, the answers on the part of the Assembly, and reports of committees relating to the agricultural, mechanical, manufacturing, and other leading interests of our State and Country.

Shall we who love to laud the deeds of our ancestors, and who live by the result of their toil, be content with less intelligence, or less patriotism? A STATE EXISTS IN ITS HISTORY. Take away the memory of the past, and what remains? A name, and only a name. Take away the example and the recorded wisdom of the past, and what ray of light would be left for our guidance? What could we do but grope in darkness and inexperience, and wander in the maze of perpetual childhood? If we are bound to respect the claims of posterity, we likewise owe a debt to our ancestors. . . . . .

___

BURKE.

BY A. BURINGTON, ESQ.

While adverse winds and tempests lower,
And fortune's frowns like mountains tower,
They boldly brave stern winter's power.

ONE individual alone remains of the veteran band of hardy pioneers who inhabited the town of Burke the eight years succeeding the first settlement, and this individual is a female, worn and broken by a life of toil.

Yet, with the records and papers in the archives of the town, and what still lives in story, we hope to collate and embody as many local facts and incidents as time and circumstances will permit. Burke, in the N. E. part of Caledonia County, is bounded N. by Newark and E. Haven (in Essex Co.), E. by Victory (in Essex Co.) and Kirby, S. by Lyndon, and W. by Sutton. The town originally contained a little over 6 miles square, including a gore of about 3,400 acres, lying easterly of Lyndon, and formerly called Burke Tongue. In 1807, the Legislature annexed this gore to the township of Kirby, leaving the present area of Burke about 20,320 acres, in the form of an irregular octagon, the surface somewhat uneven, rising between the rivers into high ridges, three in number, running in a northerly and southerly direction through the town, and mostly covered with a heavy growth of hard wood, among which a large proportion of sugar maple abounds. In the valleys bordering on the streams the timber is mostly evergreen, among which is some cedar and a small quantity of pine. The soil is various; the ridges or hills mostly contain a deep rich loam, and are well adapted to agricultural pursuits. In the valleys, in some localities, the soil is composed of a mixture of sand and gravel, but bordering on the streams are some meadows of a deep alluvial soil, and very fertile. Generally, the soil is well adapted to grazing, and some of the finest and best cattle and sheep found in market are raised in this town.

The Passumpsic River, a branch of Connecticut River, runs through this town, and is divided into two branches, called the East and West branches; one passing near the eastern, and the other near the western part of the town. Into these branches, which unite their waters in the town of Lyndon, flow several tributary streams, on which are many excellent water privileges adapted to the various purposes of mechanical arts.

At the eastern extremity of the township is a mountain bearing the name of Burke Mountain, lying partly in Burke and partly in Victory; the line between the towns crossing near the summit. The summit of this mountain towers nearly 3000 feet above the bed of Passumpsic River. It is mostly covered with a small growth of evergreen. Along the western base are many good farms. A small house has lately been built on the summit, for the accommodation of visitors, by Mr. Joseph S. Hall, an enterprising citizen of this place, from which a picturesque and delightful view of the surrounding country can be taken.

The original grantees of this town were a company of 65, mostly, if not all, inhabitants of the county of Litchfield, Conn., among whom were a number of females. A grant or charter was dated February 6, 1782, and signed by Thomas Chittenden, Governor, and Joseph Fay, Secretary, in behalf of the freemen of the State of Vermont, granting to said company the exclusive right to form and incorporate the same into a township, on certain specified conditions. In the year 1787, Seth Spencer and Uriah Seymour, the latter being one of the original proprietors, proceeded in the allotment of said township, and surveyed the same into shares or Rights as they were called, each share or right containing 300 acres, the town being first divided into two divisions, and a lot in each division of 160 acres was assigned to each proprietor, reserving five rights, or one lot in each division, for public uses, viz: one right for the first settled minister, one for the minister's support, one for common English schools, one for an academy in the county, and one for a seminary or college in the State of Vermont.

The first settlement of the town commenced in 1794, by Lemuel Walter, from Litchfield County, Conn. The year following, several families, mostly from Connecticut, settled. Owing to the inconveniences ever attendant upon a settlement of a new country, these worthy pioneers had to endure many hardships, sufferings, and privations. The badness of the roads, the lack of privileges of almost every description, rendered it very difficult, many times, to obtain necessary supplies for themselves and families, St. Johnsbury then being the nearest place where they could be accommodated, a distance of 16 or 17 miles. Almost the whole of the first inhabitants of the town followed the pursuit of agriculture, and for the period of five or six years little other business was done in the immediate vicinity. During many years, the inhabitants lived in cabins built of logs, and covered with bark peeled from spruce trees, and were often doomed, especially in the winter seasons, to endure cold and hunger; for, being poor, they had not the requisite means to procure comfortable clothing to screen themselves and families properly from the rigors of a northern climate. Children would frequently be seen in winter days running barefooted in the snow, and otherwise but poorly clad, sleeping on straw beds or the skins of animals, at night, in the upper loft of their bark-covered cabins, whose roofs, by the influence of the sun's rays, would but poorly shield them from the rain and snow, or the blasts of a wintry storm. Sometimes these cabins would have no chimney save a few boards fastened together in a conical form through which to convey the smoke. Sometimes they would have backs, as they were called, built against the logs at one end of their dwellings; but many were destitute of this appendage, and had nothing for a substitute but logs of wood, which when burnt away were replaced by others. Oftentimes these wooden chimneys would take fire; but, to use the common adage, "Necessity is the mother of invention." Most families had an instrument familiarly called a "*squirt-gun*," of a large size, through which a considerable quantity of water could be emitted to any part of their dwellings. This was the only *engine* made use of in those days for extinguishing fire in their dwellings, and reminds the writer of an anecdote which he heard related many years ago. At a certain time, Lemuel Walter, the first inhabitant of the town, was sitting at his table in his log cabin, with a wooden chimney, at noonday, taking his frugal meal, when a stranger on horseback rode up to his door, and with an earnest voice enquired, "Sir, do you know that your house is on fire?" Ah, said the owner, well, no matter, I will see to it as soon as I have finished my dinner. "But," said the stranger, "your house will all be in flames before that time." Be not alarmed, sir, said Walter, I am used to fire and have no fears. Thank you, sir, for your trouble. "If you are disposed to stay there and let your house burn down over your head," rejoined the stranger, "it is no business of mine," and rode off, and left the owner to take care of his own house. Whereupon, Walter deliberately took his *squirt-gun* and soon extinguished the fire.

Perhaps many circumstances and events might be here related touching the character and condition of the first settlers of the town which might serve to interest the reader; but lest the writer should extend this part of the history beyond its proper limits, it will not be prudent, perhaps, to dwell much longer on this description; yet it may not be amiss to relate some of the trials and perplexities our venerable fathers had to encounter, and the labor and toil which they experienced in subduing the forests, and braving the dangers and vicissitudes to which their condition exposed them.

Besides the labor and privations with which they then had to struggle, the country at that time was considerably infested with wolves, panthers and bears, which rendered it somewhat dangerous many times to venture a great distance from home without being properly armed and equipped to meet a deadly foe in the character of some ferocious and hungry wild beast. Still they were often under the necessity of journeying into the wilderness, and sometimes to a

considerable distance. At that time, most of the inhabitants owned but one cow, and for many years the only pasture which they had for their cattle consisted of the forest, and not unfrequently they would ramble to a considerable distance, in which case the only guide the owner had in seeking them was the sound of the bell, fastened with a leather strap to the neck of a favorite cow. I have heard of several instances in this town, in the early stages of its settlement, of inhabitants being beset by bears in their rambles in search of their cattle. Wolves, it is presumed, were not as plenty here as in many other places, still their flocks of sheep, though small, were sometimes annoyed by them. Yet wild animals, in another sense, were of benefit, especially bears, as their flesh, many times, served in part to furnish the inhabitants with meat, which from domestic animals was very scarce, and their skins were used for moccasins and various other purposes. Sometimes they were hunted in the woods, and sometimes they were caught in traps when visiting corn-fields, or by guns set in corn-fields, or by watching or lying in wait for them; various ways and means being resorted to, to entrap and destroy them. *Moose* and *deer* hunting was also resorted to, to supply the deficit of meat. The country north of this town for many miles, at that time, was an unbroken wilderness, where moose and deer were found in great numbers. It is the nature of these animals, in the winter season, to herd together in considerable numbers, especially when the snow is very deep, which circumstance greatly facilitated the means of taking them. The most hardy of the veteran settlers would resort thither on snow-shoes as soon as a sufficient depth of snow had fallen, and surprise and slay them, and after dressing them select the best part of the flesh for food, and carry it on their backs a distance of 7 or 8 miles, through the wilderness, to their homes. Not unfrequently a man would carry a burden of 100 lbs. But they soon grew wise by experience, and furnished themselves with a kind of *hand sled* made expressly for the purpose, the timber of which was made very light, and the runners, being 5 or 6 inches in width, prevented their sinking in the snow to a very great depth. On these a man would draw more than double the quantity that he could carry on his back, and the labor was not so hard. These kinds of sleds are used by many at the present time in this vicinity, and still retain the name of *moose-sleds*. For weeks, many times, they would remain in the woods, sleeping by night on hemlock boughs for beds, and in camps, as they were called, made of poles and covered with boughs, and subsisting on the flesh of wild animals, and perhaps a little bread carried from home. These camps were warmed by a fire made in front of them, one side of which was left open for that purpose. The skins of these animals, after being partially tanned by a process of their own inventing, were much used for beds, being spread upon the ground or floor of their cabins. Whole families of children would sleep upon them before the warm fire, with as much seeming composure as though they were reposing on a bed of down.

Various other means were resorted to at that time to obtain the necessary supplies for the sustenance of their families. One of these consisted in making *salts* from the ashes of wood. The new lands that were first cleared were covered with a heavy growth of hard wood, and when clearing their lands of this timber the ashes made from the wood were collected and put into leaches, generally made of hollow logs, cut from the trunks of hollow trees, and after being thoroughly leached, the lye was boiled in small kettles, generally holding no more than 12 or 14 gallons, to a consistence called *salts of lye*. These were generally transported to St. Johnsbury, and sold from $3 to $4 per 100 lbs.; the avails of which were applied in purchasing the necessary articles for family consumption. These salts, after being sold, were manufactured into pot or pearlash, and transported to Boston, or some other market. Most of the men who were not engaged in hunting found employment in this business during a large portion of the winter season. The business of making these salts was continued for several years after the town was considerably settled, when a different disposition was made in this branch of business. A man by the name of Dan. White, who emigrated from Torrinford, Litchfield Co., Ct., in or about 1800, purchased a small farm, on which he labored for several years, then purchased a few goods and opened a small store in a room in his dwelling-house, built a small potash, and exchanged his merchandise for ashes and other produce. These ashes were manufactured into potash and transported to Portland, Me., with a two-horse waggon through the Notch of the White Mountains in New Hampshire, and exchanged for such articles of merchandise as the people most needed. At that time, the road to Portland was extremely bad, especially through the Notch of the mountains, and twelve to fifteen hundred was considered to be a full load for a span of horses. In a few years, however, (the writer thinks about 1805), White sold his interest in the Potash to Chandler, Bigelow & Co., of Putney, who built a small store, and brought their merchandise from Boston, and manufactured their ashes into pearlash, and considerably enlarged the manufacturing of that article of commerce. For many succeeding years this article was manufactured on a more enlarged scale by successive merchants, and even until the timber was so much used up that it could not longer be spared for that purpose. At the present time, the business is almost wholly discontinued in this section of country.

ORGANIZATION OF BURKE.

Joseph Lord, of St. Johnsbury, a Justice of the Peace for the County of Orange, on application of a number of the inhabitants of Burke, set up a notification, warning the inhabitants of said town to meet at the dwelling-house of Lemuel Walter, in Burke, on the 5th day of December, 1796, for the purpose of organizing said town, and electing the officers thereof as required by law. At said meeting, Lemuel Walter was elected Moderator and Town Clerk unanimously; Barnabas Thurber, Godfrey Jones, and Lemuel Walter, Selectmen, and Ira Walter Constable. On the 23d day of March, following, a meeting was duly warned and holden for the election of town officers, and the transaction of other business appertaining to said town. Lemuel Walter was re-elected Town Clerk; Barnabas Thurber, David Colfix, and Godfrey Jones, Selectmen; Ira Walter, Constable; and Barnabas Thurber, Surveyor of Highways. Thenceforward, to the present time, meetings have been held annually, in the month of March, for the election of town officers, and the transaction of the business of the town. A freemen's meeting was warned and holden on the first Tuesday of September, 1801, for the purpose of giving their votes for State officers; and in December, 1802, a freemen's meeting was holden for the purpose of electing a Representative to Congress. At a freemen's meeting in Sept. 1805, Thomas Bartlett was elected the first Representative for General Assembly of Vermont, to which office he was elected the two succeeding years.

In the year 1801, the first schoolhouse was erected near the centre of the town, which answered the double purpose of a school and town house. Thomas Bartlett taught the first school in the winter of 1802. Schools were taught in this house for 8 years, and the scholars came from nearly all parts of the town, some of them a distance of 3 miles. In 1803, the town was divided into 7 school districts, but no schools were established, or schoolhouses erected in any other part of the town, till the year 1809; in that year another house was built, and schools taught therein. Other districts soon followed the example, and schools were discontinued at the old house; still it was occupied for a town house till 1825. There are now 11 school districts, all of which have schoolhouses, and schools are taught from 4 to 9 months each year. Select schools, for improvement in the higher branches of learning, are generally taught 3 months in a year in some of these districts.

Roman Fyler, an enterprising citizen of the town of Winchester, Litchfield Co., Ct., emigrated to this town in 1800, and commenced the building of a saw and grist mill on a small stream of water near the centre of the town, where the village of Burke Hollow is now located, which gave a new impetus to affairs. But the new saw-mill had but just commenced running when it took fire and was laid in ashes. This unfortunate circumstance was severely felt by the inhabitants generally, but the untiring enterprise and perseverance of the owner, in spite of many obstacles, soon found means to repair the injury. In 1802, another saw-mill was erected and put in operation, which served to supply the inhabitants with lumber for several years. After this saw-mill had been in operation several years, it was torn down, and another built in the same place by the same owner, and occupied by him until his death in 1828. A new grist-mill was also built near where the old one stood, by the same individual, in 1817, and occupied by him while he lived. In 1845, another mill was built, on a larger scale, by a company formed for that purpose, which is now in successful operation. Other mills have since been erected from time to time, and there are now 3 grist-mills, 8 saw-mills, 3 starch factories, 2 carriage shops, 2 planing machines, 1 clothing shop, and 1 carding machine, within the limits of the town; and various other machinery for artificial purposes.

The oldest person deceased in town was Reuben Lippingwell, who died about 30 years since, in the 99th year of his age. The oldest person now living is Esther Walter, the widow of Ira Walter, one of the first settlers of the town, and the first constable,— the widow being now in her 87th year. Chloe Jones, daughter of Godfrey and Sally Jones, was the first born in town; and Willard Spencer, son of Ranney and Cynthia Spencer, the first male child, who is now a prominent citizen. The first death was an infant of Godfrey and Sally Jones. The first marriage on the records of the town, John Woodruff and Esther Barbour, married Dec. 4th, 1799.

There are three small villages, known as Burke Hollow, Burke East Village, and Burke West Village. Burke Hollow is the oldest, and situated near the centre, on a stream of water called *Fyler's Mill Stream*, from the circumstance that Roman Fyler built the first mills in town on this stream, as already related. There are about 30 families, mostly mechanics and laborers. The village has increased very slowly for several years past, owing, perhaps, in a great measure, to the settlement and growth of the other two villages in different parts of the town, which possess many local and superior advantages. There is 1 meeting-house, a union house, and 1 schoolhouse, in the village; 2 stores, a grist-mill, a starch mill, a clothing machine, a carding machine, a carriage shop, a post office, 3 shoe and boot makers, a blacksmith, 2 physicians, a harness maker, and 1 lawyer. David Chadwick, Esq., is the only attorney at law who has ever had a permanent residence in the town. The village probably contains about 150 inhabitants.

(For a description of Burke East Village, see Rev. R. Godding's article.)

Burke West Village is situated near the western extremity of the town, on the west branch of Passumpsic River, at the junction where another stream of water, called Trull's Mill Stream, unites with the Passumpsic, and near the depot on the Connecticut and Passumpsic Rivers Rail Road, which passes through the western part of this town. About 28 years since, Joel Trull, Esq., of this town, purchased a water privilege, where the village is now located, and built a grist and saw mill, where a large portion of the inhabitants of the town of Sutton could be better accommodated than at any other place. The place improved but slowly for several years. In time, however, a number of dwelling-houses were built, and a store opened by Daniel Beckwith, Esq., who, with his sons, still carries on quite an extensive business in the mercantile line. In 1857, the above mentioned railroad was extended through this town, and a depot was located near the village, which soon gave a new impetus to the business transactions of this little village. Large quantities of lumber are annually brought to this place from the surrounding country, to be transported on the railroad to other markets. Present population probably about 30 families, and 150 inhabitants. Within the limits of the village, there is now but 1 store where business is done, 1 hotel, 1 schoolhouse, 1 carriage shop, 1 grist-mill, 1 saw-mill, 1 starch mill, and 2 shoe and boot manufacturers. At no distant time, this little village is destined to become the largest in town, owing to its proximity to the railroad.

Dr. Samuel Putnam was the first physician. He commenced practice here in 1804, and remained till 1808, when George W. Denison came and established himself as physician; and Putnam went to Newbury, and soon after died. He was elected town clerk in 1805, which office he held 3 years.

By the census of 1850, the number of inhabitants was 1103; and in 1860, 1138.

RELIGIOUS DEPARTMENT.

BAPTISTS.

(For a history of this denomination, see Rev. R. Godding's contribution.)

METHODISTS.

In 1804, a circuit was formed by the Methodist Conference, embracing the County of Caledonia, and in 1805, a preacher by the name of James Young appointed to this circuit, who preached in Burke occasionally, the writer thinks once in 4 weeks. In 1806, an associate preacher, by the name of Hollis Sampson, was appointed to this field; and Young and Sampson held meetings alternately at stated times. The writer thinks they continued this about 2 years, and were then transferred to another field, and other laborers appointed. In this manner, alternately changing, new preachers were successively appointed to this important charge, but no society or class formed, for the space of 10 successive years. In the year 1815, Rev. Zenas Adams was appointed to this charge, and remained 2 years, during which time he formed a class. There are no available records that describe the number, yet the writer is aware that it must have been very small. But from this time forward, the societies have been supplied with preachers, and success has, in a great measure, attended their efforts, and several successive revivals enlarged the borders of their spiritual Zion. Owing to the increase in numbers, and the extent in the field of labor, in 1824 the circuit was divided into two parts, designated as the Danville and Lyndon circuits, and a definite number of preachers were assigned to each of these respective departments. At the present time, the Sutton and Burke charge, so called, consists of 236 members, of which 124 are residents of Burke. The Methodist financial society of male members, for several years past, will probably average about 60.

UNIVERSALISTS.

During the period of 20 years and upwards, subsequent to the first settlement of Burke, there were a few among the inhabitants who were believers in the final holiness and happiness of the human race; yet no efforts were made to embody themselves into a separate denomination, hence they united with others of a different belief, — went to their meetings, and gave their influence and support as they deemed most proper. Occasionally, however, a preacher of that doctrine would visit the place and preach a short time, perhaps one or two Sabbaths; and additions were made to their numbers, and their means were increased.

On the 20th of March, 1815, a meeting was called, and a society organized, — 44 citizens of the town enrolling their names as members thereof. From that time forward, various preachers were employed, generally for a portion of the time, but no settled pastor secured for several succeeding years. In September, 1827, a church was formed, which at first consisted of only 9 members, and Rev. Daniel Wellman, a citizen of the town, was ordained as their pastor, who preached most of the time for about 5 years, and then removed to the State of Ohio, where he still lives at an advanced age. This worthy man had previously been a preacher in the Free-will Baptist denomination for several years; but after his views on religious subjects became changed, he henceforth preached the new doctrine he had embraced, ever sustaining the character of an exemplary Christian. The church and society, being thus destitute of a pastor, depended, as previously, on hiring preachers a portion of the time, for about 15 years. Under these circumstances no accessions were made, and its few members had become greatly lessened by deaths and removals.

In September, 1848, the church was again renewed, and Rev. L. H. Tabor employed for one-half of the time. Under the influence of this efficient pastor, an increased interest was soon discernible. The church consisted of about 30 members, and the society soon numbered 110. The labors of this worthy pastor were continued 6 years, when he was dismissed by his own request, to the regret of the greater portion of the people of his charge. Since that time, there has been no settled pastor over this church, but various clergymen employed for a portion of the time, and sometimes they have been destitute some length of time. Among those employed was Rev. John E. Palmer, an aged father in the ministry, who commenced his labors as a minister of the gospel in early life, and for many years was an able preacher in the Baptist denomination; but after much deliberation, his former religious views having become changed, thenceforth he became an advocate of the final holiness and consequent happiness of all our race. He is now in the winter of life, and feels sensibly the effects of age and infirmity; yet, notwithstanding, preaches occasionally to good acceptance.

Rev. Alson Scott, of Lyndon, now supplies the desk every fourth Sabbath, to good acceptance; still, the society has been on the decline since they dispensed with the labors of Rev. L. H. Tabor. The society now numbers about 80 members.

CONGREGATIONALISTS.

During several years subsequent to the first settlement of this town, there were inhabitants who cherished the fundamental doctrines of this denomination, several of whom had formerly united with Congregational churches in other places; but their numbers were so small they did not deem it expedient to organize into a separate society, but mostly gave their support to the Baptist denomination, then the only organized order in the town.

In the year 1807, 11 in number of males and females covenanted together in church fellowship, called the Congregational Church in Burke. Rev. John Fitch, pastor of the Congregational Church in Danville, officiated at the organization, and preached with them one Sabbath. Oct. 6, 1808, a meeting of the male members of this church was holden, and William Barbour chosen deacon, and Orentus Brownson, clerk. Thenceforward meetings were held at various times for the transaction of the ordinary business of the church, and to aid in the prosperity of the cause; but owing to the smallness of their number, and the want of means, the church for a long time labored under many disadvantages. Missionaries would sometimes spend a short time with them, and sometimes the little church would tax their means almost beyond their ability to procure the services of some neighboring clergyman. But they persevered in the cause they had espoused, and, notwithstanding death and removals thinned their ranks, still continued to increase gradually, though, at times, very slowly, till the year 1834, when Rev. Thomas W. Duncan was employed for a time, the writer thinks for one year. The drooping spirits of the church, and its friends, under his ministration, soon began to revive, and additions were made to their numbers. In November, 1839, he was installed pastor; but a short time after his installation requested to be dismissed, which, by vote of the church, was granted. He was succeeded by Rev. S. M. Wheelock, who continued 2 years, and was succeeded by Rev. John Clark, who remained about 10 years. For some time after Mr. Clark's dismission, they had only occasional preaching, till 1859. Since that time, Rev. Edward P. Goodwin supplied the desk — who was ordained Nov. 10th, 1859 — till Oct., 1860, when he removed to Ohio. Rev. M. Underwood now supplies this church. Present number of members about 60.

BIOGRAPHICAL SKETCHES.

BY S. N. WELCH.

CAPT. DANIEL NEWELL

Was born in Farmington, Ct., in 1755. In ——, he moved to Tinmouth in this State, where he resided until he moved to this town. While residing in Tinmouth, he was chosen captain of the artillery company there, and retained in that capacity until his removal. In 1800, he removed to this town, and settled on what is called the "West Hill."

He was, while a resident of this town, often chosen to fill town offices, such as justice of the peace, selectman, lister, etc., and he always discharged his duty with fidelity and despatch. He raised a family of 10 children, — 8 now living, — the youngest of whom is Dr. Selim Newell, of St. Johnsbury. Another (Isaac) was a Baptist preacher, for a long time settled over the Baptist Society at Danville Green, Vt., but moved West about the year 1836, where he died.

In his religious sentiments, the Captain was a Baptist, and one who exemplified his religion by dispensing with a liberal hand to the poor and needy, — consoling the afflicted, encouraging the faint-hearted, — in short, by obeying the injunction, "Do unto others as ye would that others should do unto you." Possessed of a kind heart and a large share of "sociality," he was ever a welcome guest in every circle, whether of old or young, rich or poor. Moreover, he was a very public-spirited man ; and, while unostentatious in all his acts, always one of the first to engage in any work whereby the community might be benefited, without asking or expecting re-

ward, yet having his reward in the consciousness of fulfilling the design of his creation, and in the respect, confidence and love of his fellowmen. Perhaps no man ever lived in town who was more generally respected and beloved.

Physically, he was a fine specimen of manly beauty, being above the common height, well proportioned, and very straight. His carriage was full of ease and dignity, and his countenance but the reflection of his heart. In 1824, he went to his rest.

BENJAMIN BELDEN,

Born in Farmington, Ct., in 1756; first came into this town in 1792, as an agent for distant land proprietors. He paid the town a visit every year on business for his employers, until 1805, when he became a permanent settler. He was first married about the year 1780, to Miss Rhoda Phelps, who died in 1783. In 1790, he was again married to Miss Sally Woodruff, who died in 1831. He died July 9, 1820.

ROMAN FYLER,

Born in Winstead, Ct., in 1768; married to Sally Lyman in ——. In 1799, moved with his family, consisting of his wife and four children, to Burke, and located on what is now called Burke Green, a ridge of land running N. and S. through the town, dividing it nearly in the centre. Here he built him a log house, and commenced the laborious work of a pioneer. There was at that time no grist-mill nearer than Lyndon, and he, as well as other settlers, was often under the necessity of going to Barnet to purchase grain and bringing it to Lyndon to be ground, and from thence home, his path guided by marked trees. In 1801, he built the first grist-mill in town, and subsequently added 2 grist-mills and 2 saw-mills.

In 1803, he met with a serious accident in one of his mills, having his foot and ankle severely crushed, which troubled him more or less to the close of his life. He was one of the company that, about the year 1806, built the road through the Notch of the White Mountains in N. H. He also formed one of the company that built the turnpike through the town of Barnet. He was one of the "early few" who represented the town in "olden times;" was also town clerk a number of years, besides holding many other offices of trust, always discharging his duty with fidelity and zeal. In religious sentiments he favored the Methodists, of which his wife was a member. In physical proportions he was almost gigantic. It has been asserted, moreover, that he was the strongest man ever in town. He died in the year 1828.

HON. GEO. W. DENISON, M.D.,

Born in Hartland, Oct. 16, 1779 ; about the year 1803, commenced the study of medicine with Dr. Fuller, of Cavendish ; in 1806, went into partnership with Dr. Fuller ; practised with him one year; and in 1807, moved to Burke, and purchased the farm, upon which he lived until his death.

Believing it was not good for man to be alone, in 1813 he was married, at Lyndon, to Miss Sally Jenks. From 1808 to 1813, he was town clerk; in 1822 and '23, was elected town representative, and in 1837 was chosen one of the assistant judges of the County Court, which office he held two years.

His wife died January 25, 1843. One of their sons is a practising physician in Illinois; another, a lawyer of considerable repute in Washington Territory, was formerly Judge of the County Court in Los Angelos County, Cal.; another is now in California; two remain in their native town, one upon the old homestead; another is in Canada; Charles O. (deceased) was formerly a practising physician at Lyndon; and Emeline, wife of Dr. Selim Newell, lives at St. Johnsbury.

Dr. Denison was one who was out of his element unless engaged in business. He built several mills in town, and was until his death a large land-holder, owning large tracts of wild land in several different towns. His practice as physician extended over many towns. Physically, the Doctor was a model man, 6 feet and upward, finely proportioned, with a carriage full of grace and dignity, and his countenance when at rest was but an index of his heart, reflecting all its loftier attributes, mild and gentle, yet wearing the stamp of an iron will that *must* and *would* accomplish everything it undertook. In his religious sentiments, he looked upon all mankind as brothers and sisters, travelling the same highway to one common home, — or was a Universalist. In his politics, he was a Republican. In relation to slavery, his ideas of justice were to give it no more territory, but confine it within its present bounds and let it work its own destruction. He was a capital *shot.* Nothing suited him better, even in his old age, than to take down his trusty rifle and try his skill with the young men, and if he succeeded in beating them, he would "fat an inch on the rib." He died March 4, 1847.

BY HON. THOMAS BARTLETT, OF LYNDON.

THOMAS BARTLETT,

One of the early settlers, was born in old Plymouth, Mass., May 19, 1771, and was a descendant of Sylvanus Bartlett, who emigrated from England in the year 1624. He moved to Vermont at the age of 16, and fitted for college with Judge Miles, of Fairlee. He entered Dartmouth College in the year 1794. In consequence, however, of poor health, he was obliged, after two years, to abandon his studies. While at college, he attained a high rank as a scholar, and maintained it to a respectable degree ever after. In early life he contemplated the ministry, but his state of health did not admit of his carrying out his cherished plans. He moved into Burke in 1802. Being an able writer and effective speaker,

he was often called upon to officiate at funerals, speak on the Fourth of July, etc. He was the first deacon of the Congregational church; first town clerk; first representative of the town, in 1805; planted the first apple-trees, and raised therefrom the first apples in town. Physically, he was a little above the common height, spare, and very straight, and retained his faculties in a remarkable degree to the time of his death, June 19, 1857. A man who was esteemed by all who knew him, for the excellence of his principles, can be truly written of him.

ASAHEL BURINGTON, ESQ.,

Of Burke, is one of those individuals so identified with the general history of the town, of whom a brief sketch, at the least, is requisite to complete the history thereof. A citizen of B. has furnished such sketch; but, although abounding in interest, it yet is so minute in detail, but a summary can be given.

"Asahel Burington was born in New Hartford, Ct., Feb. 17, 1791, the youngest of a family of 8 children. In 1802, the older brothers of our sketch persuaded their father to sell out his farm in Connecticut, emigrate to Vermont, and purchase lands sufficient to make farms for himself and them. The avails of the sale barely purchased 500 acres of wild land, at $2.50 per acre, and defrayed the expenses of the removal. Their cabin was thus built: spruce logs, locked together at the corners, chinked with mud, and covered with bark. Within, large logs piled against the wall-logs for a chimney, the fire being kindled in front, and loose boards floored the one room, whose area was mostly filled by three beds, curtained with blankets, and the large pine table. The one schoolhouse, near the centre of the town, was on a high ridge of land, where in winter the snow, from 3 to 4 feet deep, blowed into well-nigh impassable drifts; and even the boy of 11 could not be spared from clearing up and cultivating the farm in summer; and when at school, only reading, spelling, writing, and the first four rules of arithmetic, were indifferently taught."

Here our writer goes on to tell how young B. was destitute of all mathematical text-books, till, learning a man had moved in who had one of Pike's Arithmetics, he hastened to secure a loan thereof, and bent every energy systematically to the task, till he had mastered that tough old book. In a few years he added to this science, grammar, geography, logic, philosophy, &c. A library association had previously been formed by a number of the citizens of Burke and Billymead, (now Sutton,) which contained Rollins' Ancient History, Robinson's History of America, Josephus, one excellent novel, The Fool of Quality, &c. Embracing every opportunity rainy days, and especially evenings, mostly by the firelight, volume after volume was digested. In 1810, Martin Doyle moved in from Walpole,

N. H., bringing a respectable library for those days. Doyle and Burington were old friends. Not only were the use of Doyle's books gratuitous, but his assistance in study cheerfully given. Here Mr. B. discovered *"Ferguson's Astronomy,"* and in a year could calculate the changes of the moon and eclipses with perfect accuracy. Doyle, a self-taught scholar, imbibed his enthusiasm, and mutually assisting, these friends spent hours investigating the problems of this work. Doyle died in 1848.

From the study of this sublime science, the investigation of this "stupendous machinery," Mr. B. claims that his mind was led upward, till he, too, could exclaim,

"An undevout astronomer is mad," —

till he was irresistibly confirmed in belief of the universal mindfulness and mercy of the Creator over and toward all his creatures, particularly his offspring man.

From 1812 to '21, he was employed during the winter seasons to good acceptance in common schools, — a popular teacher, who drew many scholars from the districts around; in 1816, from thence nearly 25 years, was postmaster; and for upward of 38 years has held the office of town clerk, during which time every instrument recorded in the town, nearly or quite 5,000, has been done with his own hand. He also retains the office of town treasurer, held nearly 31 years, and justice of the peace about 24 years; in 1838 and '39, was town representative, and has from time to time held other town offices.

When not engaged in public business, his pursuit has ever been agricultural, being located on the farm on which his father settled in 1802. He is now living with his fourth wife. The Rev. L. M. Burington, mentioned by Rev. Mr. Godding in his sketch of East Burke, is his son; and H. A. Burington, in the specimen department of this chapter, a liberally educated young lady, now engaged in teaching, his daughter. And our venerable State Antiquarian Society President (H. Stevens, Esq.) may be gratified to know there is a blooming bevy of younger daughters in this family still taught to dexterously turn the somewhat antiquated spinning-wheel.

Mr. B. has from time to time written several poems, which have appeared in different journals of the day. An obituary notice to his first wife (who died of an epidemic fever in 1832) was transcribed by Rev. Hosea Ballou, 2d, into a book entitled, "Happy Deaths." In the fall of 1842, erysipelas commenced in the northern section of the State, and continued its fatal ravages for about 6 months, till a twenty-eighth part of the inhabitants of this town were its victims; a large proportion of the population clothed in mourning; a melancholy gloom visible in each countenance; and it was difficult to obtain assistance sufficient to alleviate the wants of the sick and dying. January and February, the disease was the most prevalent and fatal. The close of days this sadly eventful year he chronicled in verse, and for the fallen mourned : —

"They sank 'neath autumn's chilling blast,
And with the leaf grew pale and sere;
Their memory only with the past
Is mirrored with the dying year."

Jan. 1, 1843, which he inscribes "UNHAPPY NEW YEAR," the second Mrs. B., a lady of unusual attainments for those days, — the affectionate, the gentle, and the congenial wife, whose memory is still fragrant in the old farmhouse, — died of the fatal erysipelas. In the *"In Memoriam"* which commemorated again his dead, he thus touchingly generalizes sorrow : —

"There lives not in this world of human mould,
Not even savage Nature's rudest child,
A form so dull, affectionless, and cold,
Midst gloomy forests born, or deserts wild,
But he has sometimes felt, when doomed to part,
The last sad hopeless sorrows of the heart."

Near the close of his 69th year, he is still engaged in the active business of life. May a score of years yet crown his worthy head, who, in his waning manhood, with a pleasant pathos sings, —

FAREWELL MY YOUTH.

"Farewell my youth ! thy star was bright,
And mildly did it beam on me ;
But nevermore upon my sight
Will fall its pure, its heavenly light, —
Dear in the waste of memory.

Farewell my youth ! thy dream of love
Was like the sunset's brilliant calm,
When not a leaf the breezes move ;
But never more my soul shall prove
Its luxury and dewy balm.

Farewell my youth ! thy years are past,
Thy hopes and sunny smiles are gone, —
I knew they could not always last ;
Like roses on the torrent cast,
A moment, and their joys were flown." — ED.

WINNIE.

Down beneath the drooping willows,
By the streamlet's limpid wave,
Where the wild-birds sing above it,
Is a little, new-made grave, —
In it lieth all of Winnie
That could die,
While his soul, immortal, liveth
In the sky.

Three short summers scarce are measured
Since on earth his life begun ;
But the world was all too sinful
For our sweet and gentle one, —
All too rough for his pure spirit
Long to dwell,
And the Father called him homeward, —
"All is well."

Fare thee well, our darling Winnie,
Till we pass the river cold ;
Through the pearly gates celestial,
Through the shining streets of gold,
Thou shalt be our guardian angel,
Watching o'er,
Guiding us in paths of virtue
Evermore.

HENRIETTA ADALAIDE BURINGTON.

DIRGE.

Close gently her eyes, in their long dreamless slum-
ber,
Fold meekly the arms o'er the heart that's now
still,
Oh bear her away from that now broken number,
The place that is vacant none other may fill.

No more will her smile banish sorrow and sadness
From hearts that are swept by grief's death-flood-
ing wave,
No more will she join in the gay song of gladness, —
That voice once so sweet is now hushed for the
grave.

She's far above sorrow, nor heeds she the weeping
Of friends who on earth ever blest her with love;
Ye've paid the last tribute, she's now in the keep-
ing
Of angels, — Oh, leave her in glory above.
                                        S. N. WELCH.

EAST BURKE, &c.

BY REV. R. GODDING.

ON the eastern slope of Burke Mountain, the
Dishmill Brook rises, which takes its name from
the circumstance that in the early settlement of
the town, a man by the name of Walter built a
small shop here, where he turned wooden plates,
dishes, and bowls, of different shapes and sizes.
At the junction of this brook with the Passumpsic River, is the village of East Burke. In this
part of the town, previous to 1820, there were
but a few families. In that year the Rev. Rufus
Godding, some 10 years before he commenced
preaching, purchased the lot of land where the
village is located, and commenced clearing away
the forest to make a farm.

In 1825 he sold 10 acres, at first cost, to Joseph Wood, to encourage him to build a set of
mills and commence a village. Wood moved
into Godding's house, and commenced building
a dam across the river. Coming in one evening
from his work, he said, using his familiar by-
word, "By gracious! there are bears in the place,
and I'll have Mr. Bruin in the morning." The
next morning he and his son, with two of the
neighbors, started with dog and guns, and before
sunrise killed two bears and brought them in.
"Now," said Wood, "I will have some of the
gentleman for breakfast." He breakfasted de-
liciously, and went to his work. In that year he
completed his saw-mill, and put it in operation.
The next year he built a grist-mill.

Soon others settled in the place: Mr. C. C.
Newell, who built a blacksmith shop, and Mr. C.
Harvey, who opened a store. Wood remained a
few years, when, becoming involved in debt, he
sold his interest in the village to Willard Spencer, and removed to Victory, where, several miles
from any inhabitant, he built another saw-mill;
but his stay was short. From thence he removed
to Lyndon; then to Brighton, East Haven, and
Newark, building a saw-mill in each place, — his
last being in Newark. In his history we find one
ever ready to shake the bush, but who caught no

bird. He finally came back, and died at the
house of his daughter, in East Burke.

Spencer built a new grist-mill, dwelling-house,
shop, &c., and the village slowly increased until
A.D. 1852. In the fall of this year Spencer sold
all his property in the village to D. P. Hall.
Soon after this sale we had a heavy freshet, which
carried off the old grist-mill, bridge, dwelling-
house, shed, shop, &c., leaving the new grist-
mill tottering on its foundation, in the centre of
a deep gulf many rods in width, caused by the
flood. This took place in the night, and the
work of destruction was not so clearly seen; but
the crash of buildings, and the giving way of the
earth under the feet of those who were clearing
the house and other buildings. Some barely escaped from a watery grave, their property being
borne down the once beautiful but now dark and
terrible Passumpsic. The inhabitants on either
side, opposite their homes but a few rods, passed
the lonely night, there being no way of reach-
ing their homes without a journey of many
miles. The next morning hundreds of people
assembled to behold the devastation so suddenly
and unexpectedly made. Some remarked, East
Burke is sunk, and can never rise again.

But Mr. Hall, with an energy and enterprise
seldom equalled, repaired the dam and grist-mill,
filled in part the gulf, and built a new saw-mill,
probably the best in the county, at a cost of some
$10 or $12,000, since which time there has been
quite an increase in business and building, for a
small place. There are now 2 meeting-houses,
3 stores, 1 hotel, 2 saw-mills, 1 grist-mill, planing and clapboard machine, 2 blacksmith shops,
3 shoe shops, a post-office, starch factory, um-
brella stick factory, a repair shop, cabinet shop,
and a good schoolhouse, in which school is sustained 9 months in the year.

One incident occurred in 1846, near East Burke,
which shows that God takes care of his own
through life, and takes them home to himself as
he pleases. There was a Mr. Newell and his
wife,* some 70 years of age, poor in things of this
world, but rich in faith, and heirs of the kingdom. She was his third wife, and he was her
third husband. They lived in a small log house,
at the foot of a steep bank, in a retired place.
Being destitute of food and fuel, the neighbors
carried in a good supply of the necessaries of
life, for which they were very thankful. Mrs.
Newell, a few days after this, in conversation
with some of her neighbors, remarked that they
were poor, and that it would be difficult to support themselves, and they hardly knew what to
do. She said that her children were willing to
maintain her, but not her husband; and that his
children would support him, but were not willing
to support her, and they could not bear the
thought of being separated. She said, "We have
concluded to live together, and hope to die to-

* She was a daughter of the Rev. Peleg Hix, the
first settled minister of Burke.

gether." A short time after this conversation, there was a heavy rain during the night, which caused an avalanche or slide in the hill back of their house, which came down with such force as to carry away the roof, and fill the entire house with earth to the depth of some 5 feet. It was discovered the next morning by a man who was passing by. He informed the inhabitants of the village, many of whom immediately repaired to the place and commenced removing the earth, which in a moment of time had unroofed the house, and buried its occupants alive, while in bed, apparently asleep, as appeared when the cold, thick, heavy, earthy covering was removed from their lifeless remains. Near the bed a Bible was found lying on the stand. They had doubtless read the Word of God, and in prayer had committed to him the keeping of their souls, and fell asleep to wake no more on earth. And in this providence it seemed that their desires were granted; they were not separated in life, nor divided by death. A large congregation assembled on the day of their interment, and on many a manly face the tear stole silently down as they saw them lie side by side in death, and borne away to rest in one grave.

THE FIRST BAPTIST CHURCH

Was organized April 29, 1801, Barnabas Thurber, clerk and first deacon. Elder Peleg Hix preached in Burke several years previous to his instalment, I find by the records. In 1803, 9 were added to the church; in 1806, 27; and probably Elder Hix was installed by a council of elders, May 1, 1807. He remained pastor until April 13, 1809, when he was, at his request, dismissed from pastoral care, in full fellowship with said church. In A. D. 1810, it appears this church enjoyed a precious revival, and 30 additions, mostly by baptism. There was no other minister settled as pastor, but others were employed to preach and administer the ordinances to the church. Among the many, I name the following reverend gentlemen: Colby, Palmer, Beckwith, Ide, Davison, Fisher, Grow, Mitchel, and Doge. This church, for the want of a permanent place of worship, and the lack of means to sustain a settled minister among them, did not prosper as they otherwise might. Additions were made; but dismissions, removals, and death, reduced their numbers, and placed additional discouragements in their way.

THE GENERAL BAPTIST CHURCH

Was organized in the spring of 1830, consisting of 2 males and 4 females. Rev. Jonathan Woodman labored with them several years, and in 1831, R. Godding was licensed to preach. In 1834, Mr. Godding was called to ordination and the pastorate. From time to time additions were made and revivals enjoyed, till, in 1840, it numbered 42. At this time 8 members of the first-mentioned church united with this, and the two churches became one, and united with the Danville Baptist Association. In 1841, 25 members were added. Rev. N. Denison, who preached in several towns in this State, and Skeneateles, N. Y., with so much success, and died a few years since at Mendota, Ill., was, at his conversion, received into this church, and by it licensed to preach the gospel.

1852 and '53 were its most discouraging days, not having any place of worship but in a Union house, and their minister preaching with them but part of the time. In 1855, they decided to sell their interest in the Union house, and build a house themselves. In March, 1856, their house was finished and dedicated. It cost about $4,000, and for convenience and taste is seldom surpassed in a country village. Since that time they have had constant preaching on the Sabbath, and have been greatly prospered. Rev. Mr. Godding, who became their pastor in 1834, still sustains that relation. Within the last 4 years 75 have been received into fellowship. The aggregate number of members has been about 210. The number of members belonging to the Baptist church is about 116.

EDUCATION.

There have been a number of good scholars who have gone out from this place and became eminent teachers, who have not taken a full collegiate course, viz.: George Buckman, Rev. C. M. Cushing, and L. M. Burington. The following have graduated at college, viz.: I. D. NEWELL, an able and successful Baptist minister, who labored in this State, New York, and Illinois until his death; DANIEL LADD, now a missionary at Smyrna; B. F. DENISON, attorney at law in California; B. F. RAY, a Congregationalist clergyman in this State; and A. W. GODDING, a teacher in one of the city schools in Providence, R. I., and associate editor of the "Rhode Island Schoolmaster."

EDUCATION. — AN EXTRACT.

We once heard of an interesting little fellow, to whom was given a beautiful rose-tree. It was to be his own, to cultivate and to admire. He was delighted with his treasure, and bestowed upon it his most assiduous care. He watered it, loosened the soil about it, and watched its progress till it put forth its green foliage, and was at last covered with little rose-buds. As these were very much hidden by the thick leaves, he cut them away, and exposed them to the sun. After a few days, he saw a little opening on the side of several buds, through which he spied the colored petals. In his impatience to gather the fragrant roses, that he might carry them to his mother, he plucked away the calyx and unfolded the petals. But in the morning, he was sadly disappointed to find that his roses were all withered away. . . . . .

A profound thinker once asked, "What becomes of all the bright children?" Does not the fate of the little rose-buds furnish a practical solution? Many a parent, who would sternly chide the nurse that should attempt too soon to teach their little one to walk, do, after all, precisely the same thing in the management of their minds. The earlier years of the child are sufficiently occupied with words and things. When his mind is matured, then give him ideas, and permit him to remember, to imagine, and to reason. It is evident, that many parents and teachers, and even school supervisors, expect too much from children. It is necessary that the various faculties should be somewhat developed before mature results can be expected from their exercise. . . Besides, the minds of all children are not uniformly progressive. . . Some are more quickly matured than others. . . It is by no means a sure evidence that a pupil may not ultimately succeed, because he is backward at an early stage of his education. There is far more danger from too rapid, than from too slow progress. The anxiety of many parents to make their children proficients very often defeats itself. Thousands, who might have been able men, were spoiled in vain efforts to make them remarkable children. Shakspeare and Milton speak complainingly of their "late spring." But where are those prodigies of whom we have heard so much?

Let us then learn a lesson from the processes of nature. The leaves must shield the tender buds from the scorching rays of the sun; and the rough calyx is required to confine the petals till their color and fragrance are duly perfected. We must not expect to turn out perfect scholars to order. Indeed, it may be suspected that there is some mistake when such examples are exhibited. Let children be childlike; but when they are men, not till then, let them "put away childish things."   A. W. GODDING.

SEVEN WONDERS OF GEOLOGY.

BY MISS D. W. GODDING.

Miss G., a native of Burke, educated herself for a successful teacher without any pecuniary aid. She has taught in several places in this State, the city of Hartford, Ct., St. Louis, Mo., and is now Principal in a Ladies' Boarding School in St. Anthony, Minnesota. (1860.)

I wonder how deep,
In a fathomless sleep,
Lay the earth in her primitive state,
When Jehovah passed by,
With his fiat so high,
And each particle ran to its mate.

I wonder how low
The old primaries go,
Mysteriously building so long—
That time sped away
In long ages ere they
Could form a foundation so strong.

I wonder what power
Thus caused them to tower,

And lift their grey heads to the skies;
While the loftiest hills
Have the granite for rills,
And their tops interspersed as they rise.

I wonder how trees,
And the fish of the seas,
So ventured (the truth nature shocks)
That they should intrude,
In a manner so rude,
Even into the centre of rocks.

I wonder what time,
In old Ocean's young prime,
Little insects so busy could be,
As to form in vast piles
Those coral-reef isles,
Springing up in the midst of the sea.

I wonder, below,
What I never can know,
Of that ocean whose fiery tides lave
The crust of the earth
Since the morn of its birth,—
Lo, it rises and falls with its wave.

I wonder what hour,
By Omnipotent Power,
Creation's vast wheel shall be stayed,
And the internal fire,
Bursting forth in its ire,
Earth's funeral pile shall be made.

DANVILLE. — TO 1860.

BY M. T. C. ALEXANDER.

PART of that tract of country now known as Danville, and granted by New York, was originally called Hillsboro'* — a name at once apt, and descriptive of its most prominent natural features, being for the most part a high, elevated, and withal a notoriously hilly region, lying along the base of a still more elevated and broken range of country to the westward, known as Cow Hill, Walden Mountain, &c., and which range extends far into the northern portion of the State. The exact limits and boundaries of old Hillsboro' cannot at this time be ascertained with any degree of certainty. It was most probably given to a certain tract running north and south, and embracing all that the original State grant of 1786 covered, and also some of the western portion of St. Johnsbury. From some cause equally obscure, the old name of Hillsboro', on the issuing of the charter of 1786, or even before, was set aside, and in these latter years has, we presume, been entirely forgotten. During the early struggle of the then New Hampshire Grants for a separate state existence, the efforts of E. Allen and associates were encouraged and assisted by the French consul then at Boston, Hector St. John Crevecœur. Allen and associates, wishing to show their appreciation of these timely services, named several townships in honor of distinguished Frenchmen. Danville, in accordance with this noble intention, was named in honor of the distinguished French Admiral, D'Anville. His name is neither written on pillars of brass

* A name never put on record in the town.

or towers of stone, but fastened to the eternal hills, which are his monument.

Spring of 1783 or '84, Charles Hackett, the pioneer of this mountain region, opened a spot for his cabin just south of the house now occupied by Peter Bovee, on what is now called the "Isaac Morrill Pitch." This improvement was bought by Isaac Morrill, who subsequently settled on the farm. Mr. Hackett made a second pitch upon a spot just north of this first, now called the "Charles Sias Pitch." This improvement was bought by Capt. Charles Sias, for which he gave a cow. Mrs. Hackett was the first woman who came into this town; but, dreading the severity of the winter, remained only through the summer, and returned to Peacham.

1784, March. Capt. Charles Sias, with his family, made the first actual settlement here. His wife was the first white woman who dared to breast the long and dreary winter of this deep, unbroken wilderness. Mr. Sias drew his family and effects into town from Peacham on a hand-sled. Mr. Sias brought with him 10 children, seven sons and three daughters, as follows: Solomon, Joseph, Charles, John, James, Nathan, Samuel, Sarah, Polly, and Abigail. The snow was very deep, and the way was trackless. No mark was there to guide them, save the long line of spotted trees leading away into the dark forests. The father, with Solomon, Joseph, Charles, and John, and the three daughters, made the first company. Mr. Sias, with two men to assist, went forward on snow-shoes, and drew the sled, loaded with the girls and some goods, the boys following.

They reached their log cabin early in the afternoon, dug it out from beneath the snow, which had nearly buried it, left John and the sisters to take care of themselves through the night, — the others returned to Peacham. John was but 11 years old, and was the first male child that ever slept in Danville. The next day, came the mother with the other children, on the hand-sled. In three days more the effects were all removed, and the lone family began their hard labors upon the wilderness. They commenced by tapping the maples, which stood thick around them in the most beautiful groves, affording them sugar in abundance, and supplied, in a great degree, the lack of other food. Thus was settled the first family in this town. The father, Charles Sias, was the first captain of the first military company in town, and was one of the first members of the Calvinist Baptist Church in Danville.

In this year, Sargent Morrill commenced chopping in town.

1785. During this year, or in the spring of 1786, some 50 emigrants from New Hampshire and Massachusetts, Essex Co., had settled here as "squatters." The first settlers in Danville were Charles Sias, Sargent Morrill, Daniel Wheeler, Daniel Cross, Abraham Morrill, Jeremiah Morrill, Abner Morrill, Paul Morrill, Joseph Magoon, Timothy Batchelder, E. Howard, James Kiteridge, and Israel Brainard. In Gen. Bailey's list, of some years after, among the Proprietors' Records, the number of settlers was 54.

1786, Oct. 27. This township was granted. Oct. 31, of same year, the town was chartered to Gen. Jacob Bailey, Jesse Leavenworth, Moses Little, John McKisson, Luke Knowlton, James Whitlaw, Alexander Harvey, Ira Allen, and Thomas Chittenden. The grant covered 73 rights, of 300 acres each, which, with 17 settler's rights, and 4 public rights of same amount, gave an area of about 28,000 acres. At the approach of winter, all those that came into town during the past year or two, except Charles Sias and Daniel Cross, returned to their former homes.

1787. Those that left in the fall of 1786, returned in the spring. During the winter, 40 additional families joined the settlement, and from this time the ingress was very rapid. March 20, the town was organized, the meeting being holden at the house of Daniel Wheeler, near the centre of the town. The following is a list of the first town officers of Danville: — Sargent Morrill, Moderator; Abraham Morrill, Town Clerk; Charles Sias, Israel Brainard, Jeremiah Morrill, Selectmen; Daniel Wheeler, Constable; Zebediah Parker, Tythingman; Abner Morrill, Charles Sias, James Kiteridge, and Joseph Magoon, Surveyors of Highways; Samuel Fuller, —— Hayward, Timothy Batchelder, Fence Viewers.

The first child born in town was named Danville Howard, (sometimes in the records spelled Hayward). The date of his birth was in the summer of 1787. The conch which was blown at his birth, is still in existence somewhere in Ohio. The grant of land which the first-born was to receive, was never deeded, as the child was not long-lived, — not more than 3 years.

1788. Dec. 25, was married, by Abraham Morrill, Esq., Joseph Page to Abigail Morrill. This was the first marriage in town.

1789. Six years before this, a solitary man sat himself down among these wooded hills. Now, so rapidly has emigration been pouring in during these few years, it is estimated that there are no less than 200 families in town. The result of so rapid an increase of population, and the consequent increased drain upon the limited means of the settlers, accompanied with a severe drought, was a great scarcity of provisions. The sufferings of that time were very severe. Maple sugar formed the chief article of food. Like the manna of the ancient Hebrews, it was really a providence in the time of hunger and famine. No doubt, those stern old fathers blessed the forest trees that gave them food and life.

Large quantities of corn and other provisions were brought from Essex County, Mass., whence many of the settlers had emigrated, a distance of nearly 200 miles, and over roads barely passable.

1790. Improvements had been commenced

on nearly every lot in town. About this time, John Webber opened the first store in town, on the farm now owned by Gen. Stephen Dole, near the centre of the town, and near the site of the present Centre District schoolhouse.

1792, Oct. 29. Walden Gore, containing 2,828 acres, and situated in the western part of the town, was annexed to this township.

When Caledonia County was established from a portion of old Orange, there arose quite a strife between the towns of Peacham and Danville, as to which should be the shire town. Finally, the difficulty was adjusted by Danville's being made the shire, and Peacham's taking the grammar school. 1795.

1796, Sept. Aaron Hartshorn and Thomas Dow, for and in consideration of £30, deeded to the County a parcel of land containing 4 acres, situated in Danville Green Village, to have and to hold the same so long as the Public Buildings should remain at Danville.

1802. Soon after this township was granted, difficulties began to arise between the settlers and the several grantees, respecting the quantity of land to which they were entitled. Settlers' meetings were holden, and committees chosen; there were proprietors' meetings and conferences; but, seemingly, all to no purpose. Finally, the matter was referred to the General Assembly. Commissioners were appointed, the grounds of difference investigated, and a report made. The result of these investigations and deliberations was, that the General Assembly decided on issuing, and did accordingly issue, a new or "quieting charter" to the proprietors, November 12, 1802.

The first survey of this township was made by Eben Thompson, who came here as early as 1787, and was one of the first who settled in the north part of the town. Joshua Stevens sometime after made a re-survey, altering the former lines in certain cases, clipping certain lots, and adding to others. His survey was considered the most correct; and the lines as established by him are still adhered to in all latter transactions touching the partition of lands.

1805. The General Assembly convened here. The House met in the old Court House hall; the Council met in the hall of the hotel. The old Court House at that time stood on the west side of the Green, nearly opposite the Bank. The Jail stood on the east side of the Green, opposite the Court House.

Deweysburgh was a tract of 5,310 acres, lying between Danville and Peacham, from its shape called the Boot, and chartered to Elijah Dewey and associates, Feb. 28, 1782. It was organized as a town, and represented in the General Assembly four years.

1810, Nov. Was divided by act of the Legislature, and the southern half annexed to Peacham, and the northern half to Danville, making the area of Danville to be 33,483 acres, or over 50 square miles.

1812. During the war, a company was raised here to serve six months. This company was stationed near the line. Joseph Morrill was the captain; John A. Stanton, lieutenant; Luther Bugbee, ensign; Harvey Kelsey, Luke Swett, Plummer Sawyer, (who had already served in the war of the Revolution), Samuel Langmaid, Solomon Langmaid, John Bickford, Peter Heath, William Heath, Asa Glines, Moses Varney, Jason Wilkins, Samuel Long, James Watson, Leavitt Daniels, Stutson West, Ephraim Hartshorn, Jerry Walker, Josh Otis, Noah Willey, who was stationed at Portsmouth, N. H. At the expiration of the six months, Captain Morrill's company was discharged. He then raised a volunteer company of "years men," who served till peace was declared. Solomon Langmaid served as a dragoon at the battle of Plattsburgh. He is still living in New York, as ready to fight against tyranny as ever. Hiram Kelsey raised a company, but was not called out.

During the winter of 1812, there were two companies of Kentucky Dragoons quartered here, commanded by Captains Hall and Butler. One company was quartered on the Charles Sias Pitch, and one at the old "Mears" house, about a mile south of the Green. They came from Burlington here on account of the abundance of forage and provisions. Among them was a big, burly bully, who considered himself invincible in all rough-and-tumble fights, and was continually annoying all who came in contact with him. One day, at Cash's Tavern, in the Village, sitting before the huge fireplace, was a young man by the name of John Wilson, who had just returned from a season's work at rafting on the Canadian rivers. He was a tall, powerful man, all brawn, and sinews like whip-cord, and weighed when in "fighting trim" some 240 or '50 pounds. As Wilson was composedly sitting there, Mr. Bully took a chair, and deliberately sat down in front of him, (W.), and between him and the fire. Wilson raised his foot, and with tremendous force sent him sprawling into the fire. Bully leaped up, and made at Wilson, who met him with a blow that would have stunned an ox. Two of Bully's friends then essayed to help, but Wilson, backing into a corner, knocked them down as often as they came within reach of his arm. Wilson's sledge-hammer blows soon decided the day in his favor. "Now," says Wilson, "I have two brothers at home, and we three will be here on such a day, (naming it), when we will engage to whip the whole number of you." They came on the appointed day, but their antagonists did not see fit to appear.

1826. The Bank of Caledonia, located in this town, was chartered, with a capital of $50,000, since increased to $75,000.

1843. Erysipelas, in its most malignant form, raged here, carrying off some 30 or 40 persons, mostly young persons and women at childbirth.

During the early history of the town, it had a marked influence in the councils of the State; and for many years, even up to and during Anti-Masonic times, (from 1828 to 1835), stood among the foremost in the State for its wealth and productions, the energy and public spirit of its people. Its citizens were the recipients of the highest honors in the gift of the people. Many causes, however, both physical and moral, which we have not space to detail, have operated seriously to lessen her influence and popularity. Old Danville has settled down at length into a quiet, staid old town, shorn of her honors, and forgotten of those who once were glad of her protection.

1855. The General Assembly, setting at naught its former guarantees and obligations of 1795, and against the express wishes of a large portion of the county, removed the public buildings to St. Johnsbury.

1860. Danville generally, the northern and eastern portions especially, is not surpassed in the northern portion of the State for its depth and richness of soil, the abundance and quality of its productions. It is well watered and well timbered. There are three medicinal springs in town, strongly impregnated with sulphuretted hydrogen gas and iron. One is near North Danville Village, one about a mile east of Danville Green Village, the third is by the bank of Joe's Brook, a short distance below Greenbank's Village. The three are in a direct N. and S. line. There are five villages here. The oldest in point of time, and largest in size, is Danville Green Village, very pleasantly situated on elevated land, near the centre of the town, and in the midst of a fine farming country. It commands a surpassingly beautiful view of the far-famed White Hills and Francouia Notch, which loom up majestically against the eastern sky.

North Danville Village, five miles north of the Green, is on Sleeper's Brook, a tributary of the Passumpsic River, and is in the immediate vicinity of some of the finest land in town. Samuel Chamberlin was the first to make improvements at this point, having removed here from his former location on what is called the old Trescott Place, some a and a half miles north of the Green, in accordance with the suggestion and advice of Gen. Chamberlin, who came from Peacham on a visit. West Danville Village, Harvey's Hollow, and Greenbank's Villages, are on Joe's Brook, and have fine mill-privileges. Jesse Leavenworth, one of the original grantees of the town, settled in town very early, on or near the old Hazen Military Road, which runs through the western part of the town, and he erected the mills at West Danville Village, at the mouth of Joe's Pond. Joe's Pond covers about 1,000 acres, and was once famed in

the land for the abundance and superior quality of its trout; but now, alas! containing only the voracious pike, sucker, and other of this ilk. Some 25 or 30 years ago, some very public-spirited and benevolently-minded scamp transported a quantity of these destroyers from afar into Lyford's Pond, whose waters connect with Joe's Pond, and has been rewarded ever since with the curses of every decent man in the country.

CONGREGATIONAL CHURCH.
BY HON. A. MCMILLAN.

This church was organized Aug. 7, 1792; 20 persons then became members, some by letter, some by profession, and others belonging to different denominations. The Rev. John Fitch was then invited to take its pastoral charge, and on the 30th of Oct., 1793, was ordained and installed as their first pastor, — salary $275 per annum. His ministry extended to Oct. 1, 1816, a term of 23 years, when his pastoral relation with the church and society ceased.

Rev. Jeremiah Flint succeeded him, and was settled as their pastor July, 1817, and in March, 1818, was dismissed. Rev. Edward Hollister was settled March 26, 1823, and, on account of ill health, dismissed May 7, 1826. He was succeeded by the Rev. Elderkin J. Boardman, settled Jan. 3, 1827, and dismissed Oct. 9, 1833; 120 were added to the church during his pastorate. Rev. David A. Jones, from England, was settled March 25, 1835, and at the close of his 4th year dismissed. In the beginning of the year 1840, Rev. R. C. Hand commenced his ministry in Danville, and after about 1 year was installed as pastor. Mr. Hand was dismissed Sept. 16, 1846, after an acceptable and useful ministry of 5¾ years. Rev. David Perry was settled in Feb. 1847, and dismissed April, 1850. He was succeeded by the Rev. John Dudley, as stated supply, for the term of 6 years. The Rev. John Eastman is now acting pastor, having acceptably supplied the pulpit for the last 4 years.

While the church has had in its communion 600 members, the whole membership at present is but 140. Four meeting-houses have been built by the church and society since its organization, and their present house of worship, built in modern style, is a large, beautiful edifice, with bell, organ, and clock.

METHODIST CHURCH.
BY JUDGE HOWARD OF DANVILLE.

The first records of the Methodist Church at Danville Station show the first quarterly meeting was holden Oct. 1-2, 1803, and Elder Lewis Bates the first minister, or one of the first, as Phineas Peck appears to have been there about the same time.

Samuel Bachelder was steward in 1803, and, for anything that appears of record, the only steward at that time. Danville circuit, as early as 1806 and probably as early as 1803, embraced within its bounds the towns of Danville, Barton, Burke, Cabot, Greensboro', Hardwick, Kirby, Lyndon, Peacham, Sutton, (then called Billymead,) Walden, and Waterford. These towns were probably visited and supplied with Methodist preaching at stated periods, as the itinerants passed around the circuit.

Aaron Bickford was baptized by Elder Joseph Crawford, Sept. 30, 1803, and is probably the first person baptized on this circuit. Nathaniel Hart and John Bachelder were baptized Oct. 1, 1803, by the same elder, which were the only persons baptized on the circuit that year. In 1804, there were some 20, or more, baptized; and among the number appears the name of Solomon Sias, as receiving that ordinance July 22, and Wilbur Fisk, on the 9th day of Sept. Archelaus Sias was baptized Dec. 21, 1805, and his wife Jan. 5, 1806, both by Joseph Fairbanks, circuit preacher, and were received into the church, Jan., 1806. Solomon Sias was received into the church, and "licensed to travel and preach," in 1805, and in a very few years became quite a popular preacher, and for many years exerted a very favorable and controlling influence throughout New England. Archelaus Sias became a local elder, and spent his days in Danville, where, by his uniform, pious and consistent life, he has exerted an influence in favor of religion worthy of the man and of Methodism.

The Methodist church at Danville had no meeting-house in which to worship until the year 1822; that year they built a chapel 40 by 55 feet, on land given to the church by the Hon. B. F. Deming. It was a neat, plain house, in a pleasant location, and cost not far from $2000.

In 1825, the church built the present parsonage, with a small barn attached. A new barn has since been built, and the parsonage repaired.

In 1842–3 the chapel was moved back a few feet and raised up, and enlarged by 22 feet addition in front, with a cupola upon it, and a basement story underneath. The house is finished inside in a very neat style, all new pews, and a pulpit of a more modern height and form than the old one, all of which cost nearly, or quite, $2000.

———

[Of the Baptist church or churches in Danville, we have, as yet, received no account; but earnestly request them to send in their record for the next number.　　　　　ED.]

PHILLIPS ACADEMY.

BY HON. A. MCMILLAN.

This institution was chartered by an act of the Legislature of Vermont, Oct. 1840.

By the will of Paul D. Phillips, Esq., a citizen of the town of Danville, the sum of $2000 was bequeathed and given its inhabitants, provided they, or any part of them, should forthwith erect and finish a suitable and substantial building near the Green, to be distinguished and known as "Phillips Academy;" and also procure from the Legislature an act of incorporation.

Through the generous contributions of a few of the inhabitants of the said town, the provisions of the will were complied with, a beautiful and imposing edifice erected; and in Oct. 1841, the institution went into successful operation, under the charge of the Rev. A. Fleming. Its success up to the present day gives evidence of its usefulness.

———

TOWN STATISTICS OF 1860.

FURNISHED BY JUDGE MCMILLAN.

Population, June 1, 1860, 2547.

Productions of the year preceding June 1, 1860.

Potatoes, 58,188 bushels.
Butter, 114,980 pounds.
Maple sugar, 165,925 lbs.
Hay, 8,272 tons.

Horses, June 1, 1860,		795.
Cows,	do. do.	1,234.
Other cattle,	do.	2,290.

———

BIOGRAPHICAL.

[We here resume Mr. Alexander's MS. — ED.]

ELI BICKFORD

Was born in Durham, N. H., Sept. 29, 1754. His early life was spent on the farm with his parents; but, during his 21st year, war having broken out with England, aroused at once the spirit of independence and resistance against oppression. Being of a bold and adventurous spirit, he soon enlisted as a *private* in his country's service. Several months, however, having elapsed, and being called into no engagement with the enemy, loginging for more exciting scenes, he embarked on board a vessel privately cruising on the north-east coast. During their first engagement with an English man-of-war, he, with the rest of the crew, were taken prisoners, and for a time confined on board the " *Old Jersey.*" Soon, with others, he was sent to England, where for more than four years he was kept in close confinement. Many pleasing anecdotes are related by him, concerning this period of his life. Having found a piece of the hinge of a door, the prisoners formed a plan to escape, by digging a passage under ground sufficient to admit of their egress. One morning the keeper came into the prison and said, " Well, Bickford, I hear that you are digging out; how soon will you be ready to go?" "To-morrow night," was the reply. "Oh, that is only some of your nonsense," was the rejoinder of the keeper. To which Bickford replied, " However, this is our intention;" and when the time came the keeper found it true. After digging a passage for some distance under ground, concealing the dirt in their hammocks, made into bags for this purpose, coming under an adjoining house, they took up the brick floor, unlocked the door, and passed out. After concealing themselves for a time, hoping by some means to escape from the Island, but being unable to do so on account of the vigilant watch which was instituted, they finally made a contract with a man who should return them to the prison, and give them one half of the reward of 40 shillings sterling which was offered for their recapture. So successful was this game that it was afterward played several times, whenever their empty purses needed replenishing. At length, when peace was declared, an exchange of prisoners being made, he was set at liberty, and returned to New Hampshire, where he was soon married to Abigail Rand, of Deerfield. Owing to the depreciation in value of *Continental money* at this time, his entire property, personal and real estate, amounted to the sum of $7, one of which went to pay the parson's fee.

In 1792 and '93, many settlers emigrated to Northern Vermont; and he among the rest, with his wife and 4 children, found a home in what was then an almost unbroken wilderness. Selecting a location in the eastern part of Danville, he at once commenced the arduous work of clearing up a farm and erecting a log house. Scarcely had he commenced his labors before he was prostrated by a fever, and the strong man was laid low. Dark was the prospect which opened before him. A long, cold winter had already commenced. The settlers, it is true, were *kind*; but they, too, were poor, and so few in number that Mr. Bickford has frequently said that he has seen all the men in town *sit on one log*. Added to this, his house was not yet completed. One day, as a neighbor listened to his delirious vagaries and fearful forebodings while his reason was wandering, the man remarked that "this house must be finished." The neighbors immediately rallied, the house was completed, and Mr. B. and his family entered upon its occupancy. Often has he remarked that never was he so happy in his life as when he first took possession of his new home. With untiring energy he toiled on, until he had acquired a competency for himself and 9 children, causing his wilderness home to bud and blossom as the rose. When in after years his sons and daughters left their paternal home to go forth into the wide world, his feet still lingered around the old homestead, where were associated so many pleasant scenes of the past; and when the snows of more than 50 winters had sprinkled the brow of his youngest born, and grandchildren and great-grandchildren gathered in the old homestead, his cheerful laugh and pleasant voice was heard recounting the scenes of the long ago,—the freshness of youth that still lingered about his heart rendering him a fit companion for every age; but when a century had passed, and left him still tossed upon life's billows, thought left the busy present and wandered back to the bright scenes of the past. The old man was a child again. On the 5th of May,

1856, at the advanced age of 101 years 7 months and 6 days, he peacefully passed up to the Saviour whom he had long loved.

HON. ISRAEL PUTNAM DANA

Was born in Pomfret, Vt., April 13, 1774, and from thence came with his family to Danville in 1805. He was the fifth of a family of 12 children of John Winchester Dana, one of the first proprietors and settlers of that town, who came from Pomfret, Conn. His mother was Hannah, eldest daughter of Gen. Israel Putnam, of Revolutionary fame. She inherited and transmitted much of her father's spirit to her large family. It will illustrate the hardships which were encountered in the early settlement of Vermont, if we here put on record the narrative of an authentic tradition, that at the birth of Israel Putnam his father had to draw the midwife 6 miles over the hills and through deep snows, on a hand-sled. So exhausting was the labor, that, stopping to rest for a moment at the sugar-camp of his neighbor, Abidah Smith, he sank down insensible, and Mr. S. went on with the doctress; thus rendering an important service to his future son-in-law,—the child then born,—who twenty-four years after became the husband of *Sarah Smith*.

During his residence in Pomfret, Mr. Dana was engaged chiefly in trade. The native elements of character which marked him so decisively for a leader in whatever sphere he moved, had secured for him the rank of *Colonel* in the Vermont militia, which at that period merited and commanded respect. On his removal to Danville, he kept for 3 or 4 years the tavern on the old stand, near the present location of the Bank. He soon also resumed his mercantile pursuits, in which he continued during his active life. As a merchant he was enterprising and successful, and his store was for many years an important and well-known centre for a wide region.

He was elected high sheriff for Caledonia County, A.D. 1808, and held the office 5 years. In 1809, he took the first company of prisoners to the new state prison at Windsor, and the old-fashioned whipping-post was employed in dispensing justice to offenders no longer.

In the war of 1812, he was an earnest supporter of the national administration, and active in measures for the prosecution of the war. At one time he made two journeys to Boston and back, a distance of more than 160 miles, on horseback, in 12 days, using the same horse through the entire trip. He was much employed in raising volunteers for the service and in furnishing the commissariat for considerable numbers of the soldiers quartered from time to time in Danville. In 1814, he raised a company, and was on his way with them to Burlington as commander, when he was met at Montpelier by intelligence of the decisive battle of Plattsburg. After the war he was appointed collector, for a large district of Northern Vermont, of the direct tax levied by the United States government, to defray the expenses of the war, and in the discharge of this office found much arduous employment.

In later years, he was for a considerable period member of the Governor's Council, before that organization gave place to our present Senate, and in this position he exerted a wide and important influence on the legislation of the State. He was prominent in the formation, and for several years the *first* president of the Vermont Mutual Fire Insurance Company. The Bank of Caledonia was also largely indebted to his agency in securing its charter and organization.

Colonel Dana was a man decided in his opinions, firm in his convictions, yet always charitable to such as differed from him, and generous to an opponent. He possessed that enterprise, public spirit, courage, and discretion, which, united in any person, make their mark on a community, and exert a signal influence, especially in the development of a new settlement. It was the habit of his mind to look below the surface; to trace the underlying currents of larger, wider influences; to plant himself upon and never take his departure from sound principles. He had an eye keen to discern the right thing to be done in critical or perplexing circumstances; and, as he often said, made it a rule to act from first impressions, and that instanter. Though never inclined to protrude himself, but rather marked by a true modesty of disposition, he was, however, always ready to *act*, wherever he could do so wisely. Indolence or timidity did not tempt him to wait on the leadership of some more efficient mind. The town and the county owe much for the development of their institutions and resources to his agency and inspiration, and his name must fill a conspicuous place in any just estimate of their early history.

His mind was essentially reverent. He always held firmly, as he was early taught, the truths of the Christian religion, and he found them practically powerful and precious in his own experience. For 30 years he was an efficient and consistent member of the Congregational church in Danville, carrying his native zeal, courage, and prudence in counsel into his religious activity. His love for the cause, at home and abroad, was strong and ardent, and his house a home for ministers of the gospel and the early missionaries who labored in this part of the State. To the American Board, of which he was an early and fast friend, he contributed for the support of its foreign missionary enterprise. His eldest daughter, Frances, became the wife of Rev. Austin Hazen, whose pastoral life of more than 40 years was spent in Hartford and Berlin. Her surviving children, Allen and Sophia, became missionaries of the Board; the former in India, the latter in Persia, as the wife of Rev. David S. Stoddard.

Col. Dana died June 22, 1848, at the age of 74. The wife of his youth survived him five years.

It may be of sufficient interest to add, that the Rev. Judah Dana, of Fryeburg, Me., for some years U. S. Senator, and enjoying the confidence of Gen. Jackson, was an older brother.

HON. JOSEPH MORRILL

Was born at Brentwood, N. H., in December, 1775, and had he lived till the next December, would have been 84 years old. When about 21 years old he came to Danville, and in a year or two afterwards became a resident of our village, where he has always resided. He served in the war of 1812, was a recruiting officer, held a captain's commission, and at one time was stationed on the Canada frontier near Derby Line. At another time he recruited a company of soldiers in this town, was appointed captain, and served with them several months near Lake Champlain.

In 1822, Mr. Morrill was elected a member of the Legislature, and also, we believe, represented the town another year. In 1823 and 1824, he held the office of County Court Judge, and subsequently, for many years, held the place of County Treasurer. The best years of his life were devoted to active business pursuits. For many years previous to his death he lived in quiet retirement, in the enjoyment of his religious faith, that of the Methodist denomination, of which church he was a constant and devoted member. All men speak well of the dead. — *"North Star."*

EBENEZER EATON

Was a prominent and highly respected citizen. He was prominently known, not only in his own vicinity, but throughout the State, as the founder, and for many years the editor, of the *North Star.* He first came to Danville, with his family, in the autumn of 1806. He was then about 30 years of age. The town, prior to that period, had been established as the county seat, and the village had commenced to grow rapidly. Previous to this time, also, a newspaper had been established at Peacham, and, we believe, was still being published at the time it was determined to establish the *Star* at Danville. The paper at Peacham, however, was soon after discontinued. At a meeting of several leading citizens of Danville the name to be given the new paper was fully canvassed ; and after various names had been suggested, Mr. Aaron Porter finally proposed that *"The North Star"* be the title, which suggestion was at once unanimously adopted.

The first number of the *Star* was issued the first week in January, 1807. It was a small-sized sheet, but well filled with political and miscellaneous reading. Its politics were clearly defined, as being *Republican*, in opposition to the then styled *Federal* party. For more than 30 years, Mr. Eaton was the principal editor of the *Star ;* and during this period, his writings and the selections for his paper exerted a marked influence upon the public mind. During part of the time, the paper had a very large circulation, probably larger than any other political journal in the State. In several of the party contests of that day, it had also a wide and commanding influence. As a political writer, Mr. Eaton was frank, fearless, and honest in the expression of his opinions. In short, he was a good editor, and continued actively in that capacity until 1841, when his son, N. H. Eaton, became the principal editor and proprietor of the *Star*, which is still published by him at Danville. Up to the close of Mr. Eaton's life, however, he was associated with his son as nominal editor of the *Star*.

Personally, no man was more highly respected, yea, beloved, by all classes, than Ebenezer Eaton. Though not rich in this world's goods, yet he was rich in the honor and regard extended to him by his fellow-townsmen, and all who knew him by personal acquaintance. He was kind, social, generous, and ever compassionate to the sick and afflicted. As early as 1818, Mr. Eaton became a member of the Congregational Church; and from that time until the hour of his death, ever exemplified the character of a sincere, devoted, liberal-minded Christian. He manifested this character in all the daily walks of life; and especially during the 18 years prior to his death, when, released from the cares and perplexities of active business, his Christian light shone pre-eminent. It had a marked and salutary effect on those around him. Every one loved and honored "Father Eaton." He retained his physical and mental faculties until within about two months prior to his decease. He died, calm and happy, at his residence in Danville, January 31, 1859, at the ripe age of 82 years.

HON. WM. A. PALMER

Was born in the town of Hebron, Ct., Sept. 12, 1781. He was the son of Stephen and Susannah Palmer, who emigrated from England before the Revolution, and was the fourth son of a family of 4 sons and 4 daughters, who all came to the age of 80 years and upwards, except the subject of this notice.

At an early age during his minority, he met with a casualty in falling upon the ice with an axe, by which he lost a part of one of his hands. This occurrence seemed to be the means of determining his future course of life. By being measurably precluded from manual labor, he resolved on the study of a profession, and soon entered, with this view, the office of the late Hon. Judge Peters, of Hartford, Ct. He remained here for a time; when he resolved to seek his fortune in the new State of Vermont, about which, at that time, considerable was said as being a good place to emigrate to. Following up the Connecticut River, he finally found his way to Chelsea, Vt., where he entered the office of Daniel Buck, Esq., with whom he remained

for some time, perfecting himself more fully in the practice of his profession.

Thinking himself tolerably well qualified for the practice of law, he applied for admission to the bar of Orange County, and was admitted in due form soon after. He then very soon started on a tour of observation northward, travelling as far as Brownington, stopping a short time in the office of Wm. Baxter, Esq., who at that time and subsequently was a lawyer of considerable eminence in that place. He afterward went to Derby with a view of locating himself there, but not liking entirely his situation there, returned as far as St. Johnsbury, where he made a stand and opened an office for the practice of law. This was about the year 1805 or thereabouts.

He remained at St. Johnsbury for a term of 2 or 3 years, when he was elected to the office of Judge of Probate for Caledonia County, and removed to Danville, the then county seat. He held this office quite a number of years, and also during this time was County Clerk, — in the mean time being frequently elected to represent said town in the Legislature. He was elected Judge of the Supreme Court of Vermont in 1815 (I think). Holding this office for about 2 years, he resigned the same. In 1817, he was elected as Senator in Congress for 6 years, and also 1 year to fill a vacancy caused by the resignation of James Fisk (I think). He took his seat in Congress in December, 1818, serving in this capacity for 7 years, which terminated in 1825. For the next 2 or 3 years he held no office, except, perhaps, representing Danville 1 year in the Legislature, where he was instrumental in getting passed the charter of the Bank of Caledonia, located at Danville, — devoting himself during this time to his favorite pursuit of agriculture. In 1830, he was nominated for the office of Governor, but failed this year in the election, Hon. Samuel C. Crafts being the successful candidate. He was, however, elected Governor in 1831, holding the office 4 years, bringing it down to 1835.

This may be said to have terminated his public life, although he was chosen as delegate afterward once or twice to the Constitutional Convention of the State, — the last time in 1848. Soon after this period his health became impaired, so much so as to withdraw him from all direct or active participation in affairs of a political or public character. He continued in a state of slow decline for upwards of 10 years, only being confined for a short period before his death, which took place December 3, 1860.

Gov. Palmer was a man of strong natural abilities, possessing a decided and penetrating mind. His heart and hand were ever open to the calls of want and distress, and if he erred at all in this direction, it was in being too benevolent, loving his neighbor better than himself. He was remarkable for his intelligence, high social qualities, and unpretending simplicity of manners. In politics, he commenced as a Jeffersonian democrat, adhering through all the phases of party to the democratic side, supporting every democratic administration from Jefferson to Buchanan.

He helped make in Congress the famous Compromise line, and voted for the admission of Missouri into the Union with the constitution with which she presented herself. He always contended that his vote was cast honestly for that measure, and as he believed to be in accordance with his oath. He was, however, much censured at the time and afterwards for his vote on that occasion, but he lived long enough, however, to see that line done away by the action of the party that was mainly instrumental in its creation.

Gov. Palmer was an honest and just man in all his business transactions, a most affectionate husband and father, and in all his relations of life an estimable man. His departure was lamented by a wide circle of friends.

DR. ELDAD ALEXANDER.

At a very early period, anterior to the Revolution, three brothers, named Alexander, emigrated from Scotland to this country and settled at Northfield, Mass. One of the brothers, Thomas, was a captain in the war of Independence, on the side of the colonies. A son of one of them, named Eldad, from his father, studied medicine and resided in Hartland, Vt., and practised his profession until his death, 1829. His son Eldad, the eighth of 9 children, and the subject of the present sketch, was born May 22, 1798, in Hartland. He graduated at Yale Medical College, and yet while in his minority commenced the practice of his profession. He came to Danville in 1821, where he resided until his death, in Feb., 1859. He attained a high rank in his profession, and up to his last illness had an extensive practice. He became specially eminent as a surgeon, and probably was regarded as the most skilful in surgery of any in this whole section of country. He was much attached to his profession, making it the main business of his life; and, being a profound thinker and a great reader, added to his acquired knowledge a thorough practical experience in medical and surgical science. Personally, he was highly respected, ever maintaining the character of a good citizen, a kind neighbor, an obliging friend, and died in full hope of realizing the Christian's reward. His loss is justly regarded as a public one.

HON. BENJAMIN F. DEMING.

Digested from an obituary published at the time in the "North Star," by M. T. C. A.

Mr. Deming entered public life early. He was first chosen County Clerk for Caledonia County, in 1819. He was subsequently Judge of Probate and Councillor of the county for several years, which latter office he was peculiarly well fitted for. Several other minor offices he also held with honor to himself and the satisfaction of the public. November, 1832, as the anti-Masonic candidate, by a handsome majority, he was elected member of Congress from this, the 5th Congressional District of Vermont. He was not, however, permitted to serve his constituents but one session in the councils of the nation. Contracting, at Washington, a disease of the bowels, he started for his Northern home, in hope of benefit from the change of air and water, but only arrived at Saratoga Springs, N. Y., where he lingered a few days, and died at the Union Hall, Friday, July 11, 1834, aged 44 years. He left a wife and young family, to whom he was affectionately devoted. In whatever light we consider Judge Deming, his character will appear alike conspicuous. With more than ordinary talent, and a naturally calm and deliberative mind, quick of perception, he was well fitted for public stations and legislative assemblies. His business capacity and dealings, in which he was prompt, apt, correct, and eminently upright, have been before alluded to. As a man and citizen, he was social and winning; equanimity of temper and habits characterizing his whole general deportment. It is written of him, "He was good to the widow and the fatherless, and the poor he never sent empty away." Last, not least, he was one to whom religion was above everything else, and to whom all other things came in as of minor consequence; who was thus enabled, on his dying bed, to review his past life, and exclaim, "I have fought a good fight, I have finished my course, I have kept the faith; henceforth there is laid up for me a crown of glory."

[A notice of Hon. S. SIAS we have not yet been able to obtain. — ED.]

THE WICKET GATE.

'Mid the fast-falling shadows,
 Weary and worn and late,
A timid, doubting pilgrim,
 I reach the wicket gate.
Where crowds have stood before me,
 I stand alone to-night,
And in the deepening darkness
 Pray for one gleam of light.

From the foul sloughs and marshes,
 I've gathered many a stain;
I've heard old voices calling
 From far across the plain.
Now in my wretched weakness,
 Fearful and sad, I wait;
And every refuge fails me,
 Here at the wicket gate.

And will the portals open
 To me, who roamed so long,
Filthy and vile and burdened,
 With this great load of wrong?
Hark! a glad voice of welcome
 Bids my wild fears abate;

Look! for a band of mercy
Opens the wicket gate.

On to the palace Beautiful!
And the bright room called Peace,
Down to the silent river,
Where thou shalt find release;
Up to the radiant city,
Where shining ones await;
On, for the way of glory
Lies through the wicket gate.

JULIA A. EASTMAN.

GROTON.

BY REV. O. G. CLARK.

GROTON, situated in the south part of Caledonia County, is bounded N. by Peacham, E. by Ryegate, S. by Topsham, and W. by Goshen Gore. Its area is 38 square miles, and it contained in 1830, 836 inhabitants; in 1840, 928; in 1850, 895; and in 1860, a slight increase on the preceding decade.

Groton was chartered Oct. 20, 1789. It was settled in 1787, and consequently it is 73 years since the first settlement was made. March the 28th, 1797, it was organized by a town-meeting, held at the dwelling-house of John Darling, pursuant to a notice issued by William Chamberlin, Justice of the Peace of the town of Peacham. At this meeting were elected the following town officers, viz.:— Samuel Bacon, Moderator; Nathaniel Knight, Town Clerk; Samuel Bacon, Nathaniel Knight, and James Abbott, Selectmen; Jonathan James, Town Treasurer; Wm. Frost, Constable and Collector; Dominicus Gray, Town Grand Juror; Israel Bailey and Edmund Morse, Tithingmen; Aaron Hosmer, Jr., and Silas Lund, Highway Surveyors; Robards Darling, Surveyor of Lumber; Wm. Frost, Sealer of Weights and Measures; Jeremiah Bachelder and Samuel Darling, Hogreeves; James Hooper, Fenceviewer.

The first freemen's meeting was held Sept. 3, 1799; but the town records do not show whether there was an election or not. There is, however, a tradition that at this meeting there were two parties, viz.: the Kennebunkers, who were settlers from Sanford, Wells, and Kennebunk, Me.; and the Gaghegans, from New Hampshire, Massachusetts, and Connecticut; and that the former, being more numerous, elected Jonathan Macomber, Representative. The truth of this tradition can be ascertained only by reference to the State records.

The surface of the town is agreeably diversified by hill and valley, presenting to the eye a landscape pleasing and beautiful, rather than grand and sublime. The soil, though hard, is well adapted to grass and grain, and, when well cultivated, richly remunerates the husbandman for his labor.

Whitcher's Mountain, situated in the southeastern part, is the highest elevation of land in town, being 1,100 feet above the level of the ocean, and capable of cultivation to its summit, where there is quite a pond of water; not of sufficient dimensions and depth, to be sure, for steamboats and men-of-war, but ample enough for ducks and geese.

The soil, except in the eastern part, is hard and stony, and consequently difficult of cultivation. The rock is granite, and there is an abundance of it for all fencing purposes, and some to spare. In general, the rock of Caledonia County is primitive, and of the calcareo-mica-slate formation; but in Groton, Peacham, Danville, and the eastern part of Cabot, it is almost exclusively granite; showing that at some former period of the history of the earth, and by some powerful convulsion of her interior elements, the granite has been forced up through the primitive rock.

Wells River, which rises in Groton Pond, flows through the town from N. W. to S. E., and by its falls affords many excellent water privileges for mills and machinery, of which the inhabitants have availed themselves by erecting mills and locating machinery at various points along its banks.

In the north-western part of the town are two beautiful ponds of water, called Long Pond and Little Pond; the former 4 miles long by 1 broad, and the latter 1 mile in length by $\frac{1}{2}$ mile in width. At the foot of the latter is the "Lake House," recently erected by McLane Marshall, the present proprietor and occupant. On the latter pond, also, is a pleasure-boat 30 feet long by 10 wide, called the "Lady of the Lake," and capable of carrying 60 persons at a time. Both these ponds contain an abundance of fish, and afford the inhabitants of this and adjoining towns no little sport in catching them. They both cover an area of 2,880 acres, one being 8 times as large as the other, and are at an elevation of 1,083 feet above the level of the sea, as estimated by Zadoc Thompson.

The first settlers of the town were as follows:— Aaron Hosmer, the great-grandfather of Josiah D. Hosmer, lately deceased, is said to have been the first individual who made even a temporary residence in town. He, being a hunter, pitched his tent on the meadow now known as the Orson Ricker meadow, and from thence went north to the ponds, one of which is in Peacham, and is called Hosmer Pond. But he never made a permanent residence within the limits of the town. Edmund Morse was the first settler in the north part of the town, and James Abbott occupied the farm now known as the Jacob Abbott place, and now owned and occupied by Percival Bailey. A Mr. James settled on the next farm south of James Abbott, known afterward as the Henry Low place, and now owned by Peter Whitehill. Edmund Morse, who was the first military captain in town, and whose sword was an old rusty scythe, settled in the north part of the town, on the next farm south of Mr. James, where he continued to live till his death, which was at a good old age. Mr. Morse built the first saw and grist-mill in town, at the foot of the Little Pond. Before this, the early settlers went to Newbury to mill, some 15 miles distant, and not unfrequently carried and brought their grist on their backs. Mr. Morse's daughter, Sally, now the widow Hill, was the first female born in town.

JOHN DARLING, the father of Robert, Samuel, and Moses Darling, and great-grandfather of the present race of Darlings, was one of the first, and some say the first settler in Groton. He occupied the farm near the old burying-ground, since known as the Joseph Morrison place. He lived to a good old age, retaining his faculties to the last. At fourscore years he stood erect as a young man of twenty.

EDMUND WELCH was the first who settled on the William Frost farm, to whom he afterward sold it, and here Mr. Frost lived till his death, which was when he was about 65.

JONATHAN WELCH, brother to Edmund, first settled on the farm now owned and occupied by his son Jonathan. JOHN EMERY settled on the Timothy Morrison farm, and CHARLES EMERY, his father, on the Medad Welch farm.

The first settler in what is now called Groton Village was one DANIEL MUNROE. His house was near the present site of William F. Clark's tannery, at the east end of the village.

A. M. HENDERSON, of Ryegate, built the first saw-mill on Wells River, near the present site of Gates's carriage shop, and soon after he also built a grist-mill where the present one, now owned by A. L. Clark, stands.

JOHN HOGINS, a tailor, was also one of the first settlers in the village. His house stood where Almun L. Clark's tavern now stands.

JERRY BACHELDER first settled in the Moses Plummer neighborhood, on the farm now owned and occupied by Joseph Ricker.

JOHN HEATH first settled in West Groton, on the place now occupied by Otis Rhodes. Mr. Heath lived here quite a number of years, was a justice of the peace, and quite a prominent religious man of the Baptist order. Afterward, Mr. Heath moved to the West.

DAVID JENKINS was the first who began on the farm now owned and occupied by Charles Morrison. The next occupant of the place after Jenkins was Moses Darling, with his father, John Darling; and after them, Jonathan Darling, son of Samuel Darling, occupied it quite a number of years, until he sold it to Charles Morrison, the present owner, and moved to the "Far West," where he now lives.

The next settlers in West Groton were JONATHAN and JAMES RENFREW, of Scotch descent, one of whom made the quaint remark in reference to the soil of West Groton, viz.: "If a man should strike an axe into the ground, and it did not hit a stone, it would be sure to hit a guinea." Their farms were the two places now occupied by Nathan Darling and Moses Adams.

DAVID VANCE was also one of the first settlers of this part of the town, where he lived a good many years, and became wealthy. He was elected representative of the town a number of years, and after raising up a family of 7 sons and 4 daughters, he moved to the east part of the town, where he now lives.

EDMUND and STEPHEN WELCH, and NATHANIEL CUNNINGHAM, were the first settlers in the extreme west of the town.

BAPTIST CHURCH.

ELDER JAMES BAILEY, of Peacham, formed the first church in town, of the Calvinist Baptist order, upwards of 70 years ago. The first members were as follows:—Phebe Darling, wife of John Darling; Anna Welch, wife of Jonathan Welch; Edmund Welch and wife; Sarah, wife of Stephen Welch; Betsey Morrison, wife of Bradbury Morrison; John Emery and wife Sarah; Mary, wife of James Hooper; Edmund Morse; Josiah Paul and wife Sarah.

In 1824, Rev. OTIS ROBINSON, from the State of Maine, was installed pastor over the church, and for a number of years it continued in a flourishing condition. But at length troubles arose, Mr. Robinson became deranged and moved away, and the church received a shock from which it has not recovered to the present day. Since that time they have had no settled ministers, but have been supported from adjoining towns, till within a few years they have had no preaching at all. A few years ago their number was 35. Of late they have taken a vote not to continue their church organization any longer, but to let each member have the privilege of joining any other church he pleases. The first deacon was Wm. Hodsdon; the second, Enoch Page; the last, Hosea Welch. The first is deceased; the two last are yet living,—living, too, in the full assurance of immortality and eternal life.

FREEWILL BAPTIST CHURCH IN WEST GROTON.

BY REV. FRANCIS MORRISON, PRESENT PASTOR.

The Freewill Baptist Church in Groton was first formed in the west part of the town by Elder LATHROP, but how long ago, the records of the church do not say, but probably over 40 years since. Elder Lathrop presided over the church for a number of years with great acceptability as a preacher and a Christian, and under his labors there was a great revival of religion, by which the church was quickened, her numbers increased, and much good done. They had no meeting-house, and therefore were under the necessity of holding their meetings in private houses in the winter, and in barns in the summer. But notwithstanding the humble place of worship, the people at times came from all parts of the town to hear the word, and found it indeed a Bethel. After Elder Lathrop left the church, his place was supplied by various other ministers from other towns, but the church had no regular pastor till the year 1857, when Rev. Francis Morrison was ordained a minister over them; since which time the church, though small, has been in a prosperous condition. Their present number is 20.

M. E. CHURCH.

The records of the M. E. Church do not say who were the first Methodist preachers in town, nor how long it is since they first preached here; but the first preachers were quite successful, and soon gathered a small class, which was increased from time to time, till private dwellings and school-houses became too small for their accommodation. About the year A. D. 1837, they were enabled to build a good and commodious meeting-house, since which time, with the exception of a few years lately, they have had a preacher stationed with them all the time.

In 1838, Samuel G. Scott preacher in charge, there were on Groton circuit 107 members. During this year there was a great revival, the church was quickened, and many added to the church, some of whom continue faithful to this day.

In 1844, Benjamin Burnham preacher in charge, there were in Groton circuit 111 members.

Groton Village class contained 72 members.		
West Groton class	" 7	"
Jefferson Hill class	" 19	"
Topsham class	" 13	"
Total 111		

Since that time, by deaths, removals, and other causes, the number of members has considerably decreased, till of late, when a good work seems to be going on in the church, and some additions are being made.

HARDWICK.

BY REV. J. TORREY.

HARDWICK is the most westerly town of Caledonia County, lying 21 miles north-east of Montpelier, and 73 north of Windsor. The surface of the township is pleasantly diversified with swells and vales, but no part of it mountainous. The Lamoille River enters the town very near the north-east corner, and, after running a course of about 10 miles, affording, together with its tributaries, several excellent mill-privileges, it makes its exit a little north of the southwest corner of the town. The timber is a mixture of maple, birch, hemlock, spruce, etc. The maple-groves are remarkably fine. The rocks are granite, gray limestone, slate, and quartz, with fine specimens of rock crystals. The soil is rich and fertile — well adapted for grazing purposes. The south-eastern part of the town is on the' western declivity of the eastern range of the Green Mountains. The north-western

part has a southern inclination. Along the banks of the river, and extending for half a mile or so back from either side, are table-lands. In the southern part of the town is a mineral spring. It has been found to be efficacious in cutaneous diseases, and was formerly a place of considerable resort.

1779. Gen. Hazen came to Peacham with a part of his regiment, for the purpose, as he said, of completing the road commenced by Gen. Bailey, in 1776, that an army might be sent through for the reduction of Canada. Hazen cut, cleared, and made a passable road for 50 miles above Peacham, through the towns of Cabot, Walden, Hardwick, Greensboro', Craftsbury, Albany, and Lowell, and erected several block-houses. This road, called to this day the Hazen road, was the inlet to Hardwick in its early days, and a great benefit to the early settlers.

1780. The town of Hardwick, containing 23,040 acres, was granted Nov. 7, 1780, and chartered Aug. 19, 1781, to Danforth Keyes, and his associates.

Shortly after this, Peter Page, a native of Swansey, N. H., in the employ of Governor Robinson, one of the proprietors of the town, came to Hardwick with a man by the name of Safford. The first trees were felled by him in the commencement of a clearing near the centre of the town, on what is now the French farm. These two men brought their provisions on their backs from Cabot, 8 miles. When their first supply was exhausted, Page volunteered to go for more. On his return, — being overtaken by the rain, and thoroughly wet, — he comforted himself with the thought that when he reached the camp he should find a good fire to warm and dry himself withal; but when he drew near and saw no smoke, and nearer still and found Safford asleep, and the fire entirely out, he sat down and vented his feelings after the manner of children. There was no alternative but to go back to Cabot after fire. Page thought he could stay in Hardwick no longer, but was prevailed upon by Safford to stay until two acres or more were cleared, when both left, discouraged.

THE SETTLERS OF HARDWICK.

1792. In a certain "ciphering book," containing the names of the first settlers, Mark Norris made this record of himself: "I drove the first sleigh through the woods from Deweysburgh to Greensborough that ever was drove through by man, to my knowing, which was on the 4th of Jan. 1792. I moved into Hardwick, the first that ever moved in to settle the town, on the 13th day of March, 1792." Mr. Norris seems to have forgotten to record the important fact that he brought his wife with him. He was a mason by trade, and yet seemed to possess the faculty of turning his hand to various kinds of work; was possessed of energy, intelligence, and good judgment. He was afterwards much engaged in the public business of the town; was at different times representative, treasurer, and a preacher of the gospel.

Toward the close of March, Nathaniel Norris, a cousin of Mark, moved, with his wife, into town. He also was a mason — a good workman, but very moderate in all his movements. It is said he was never soon to run, and yet he felled his acre of trees daily for six successive days.

About the same time, March, 1792, Peter Page — the same who had a few years before left Hardwick, discouraged — took heart and returned. He built himself a rude log shanty, about three-quarters of a mile south-east of the present village of East Hardwick, and then went to bring his family. His shanty was full half a mile from the Hazen road, and the snow was deep; however, when he had moved his family and goods as near as he could by the road, he put on his snow-shoes, put his wife and three children (the youngest of whom was put in a bread-trough) on a hand-sled, drew them to their new home, and then returned for his goods. They lived a year in their rude hovel without floor or chimney, building their fire at one side, and leaving a hole in the roof for the smoke to escape. Mr. Page's wardrobe, during that winter, is said to have consisted of one pair of tow pantaloons, one tow frock, tow shirts, woollen socks, and a woollen vest. He brought all the provisions for himself and family on his back, either from Peacham, 20 miles distant, or from Cabot, 8 miles. This family afterwards suffered much from poverty. Their only cow strayed; when Mr. P. found her, ten miles from home, she had been away so long she gave no milk. The man who had kept her awhile demanded pay, and his only woollen garment, the vest, was all he could give to redeem his cow. Water gruel was substituted for milk, and was sometimes their only sustenance. The father and mother took this cheerfully themselves, but the substitution of water gruel for milk for their little babe caused them sore grief. Mr. Page was an eccentric man, and yet he was considered a Christian; loved to study his Bible, and what few religious books he had, and was a man of much meditation and prayer. He died Dec. 1852, aged 83.

John Page, the babe that rode into Hardwick in a bread-trough, afterwards removed to Westmore. He died in Montpelier in 1835, while representing his town in the Vermont Legislature.

The following year, 1793, three more families were added to the settlement — those of TIMOTHY HASTINGS and JAMES SINCLAIR, who, with an aged father, came in Feb., and that of DAVID NORRIS, a cousin of Mark Norris, in June. Old Mr. Sinclair, who emigrated from Scotland, settled in New Market, N. H., fought in the battle of

Bunker Hill, and afterwards came, with his son, to Hardwick, died shortly after his arrival. A log was dug out for his coffin, and a slab, split from another log, was nailed on or pinned on for the cover. He was buried near a spring of water not far from the Hazen road, but his remains were afterward exhumed and deposited in the Hazen Road Cemetery. Mr. Hastings soon after moved to Hyde Park.

The remaining settlers had a serious time of it. They were living at a distance of from one to three miles from each other, finding their way by means of blazed trees. Mark Norris lived near where Mr. Orrin Kellogg now lives. Nathaniel lived near where Mr. Ward Norris now lives, and David, near where Mr. J. L. Pope now lives.

In the Spring of 1793, these cousins supplied themselves with provisions sufficient, as they supposed, to last them through their Spring's work, when they were expecting to return to Peacham for a while. They had no such thing as a team or even a hoe to work with; but with their axes they hewed out wooden hoe-blades from maple chips, hardened them in the fire, and took saplings for handles. With these they hoed in, on Nathaniel's ground, two acres of wheat; but Saturday night came, when they had sowed only one acre, and they found they had only provisions enough to last them one day longer. What should they do? Neither of them were professors of religion, but they had been trained to keep the Sabbath day. However, they now held a council, concluded that it was a "work of necessity," and hoed in the second and last acre on the Sabbath. "We shall see," said Mark and David, "whether this acre will not yield as well as the other." But Nathaniel was troubled in conscience. Reaping time came; the proceeds of the two acres were stacked separately, and the time for comparing drew near. But the comparison was never made. The stack which came of the Sabbath day's work took fire from a clearing near by, and every straw and kernel was burned.

These cousins were usually in the habit of religiously observing the Sabbath day. On the first Sabbath after they came into town they held a religious meeting, and ever afterwards this practice was kept up.

1794. During this year there were added the families of Daniel Chase, Elijah True, Stephen Adams, Gideon Sabin, James Bundy, Israel Sanborne, and Elisha Sabin. Mr. Chase was a deacon in the Baptist Church. He was afterwards ordained an Elder of the Free-Will Baptist Church in 1810. He moved, in 1816, to Pennsylvania, where he continued to preach until his death. Mrs. Gideon Sabin has rendered herself illustrious by giving birth to 26 children; and surely Gideon himself deserves to be remembered if he found food, as we presume he did, for such a family, poor as he was. Mr.

Sanborne was a kind and public-spirited man, and was blessed with a family of 14 children, the third of whom, Mr. William Sanborne, now lives in Hardwick. Elisha Sabin was a hunter, led a wild life, and *allowed* his children to go *barefooted* through the winter.

1795. On the 31st of March, in this year, the town was organized. The first town-meeting was held at the house of Mark Norris. Paul Spooner was chosen the first Town Clerk, and also the first Representative.

Among the items of interest respecting these days, which we have gathered, is the fact that these men were obliged to go 40 miles to mill — Newburg being the nearest town where there was a grist-mill. We also learn of certain cases in which what was called *wild justice* was administered to offending citizens, the executive and judicial functions being combined in the person of a certain strong man with a whip.

In the fall of 1795, Elder Amos Tuttle, the first minister of the town, moved in. His son, Capt. David Tuttle, says, " There was not a cart in town; but in the following spring, two carts were constructed out of my father's wagon." He also says, " My father and I took $44 of my mother's 'savings' — money which came safely to Hardwick, sewed up in a bed — and went to Ryegate to purchase a cow; but when we got her home, she proved almost worthless. My father killed her for beef, and my mother learned to make *bean-porridge*, so we had a plenty of that instead of milk."

Between the time of Elder Tuttle's settlement as pastor of the church and town, and the year 1800, many families moved into Hardwick. Among them were several of Puritan descent, whose influence for good is, no doubt, felt to this day.

In 1796, Mr. David Philbrook and wife moved in. Mrs. Philbrook died in August, 1860, 100 years of age.

In 1797, the first public-house in town, a log building, at Hardwick Street, on the Hazen road, was opened by Col. Alpha Warner. In the same year, Capt. J. C. Bridgeman made the first settlement at South Hardwick. Also, Aug. 29th, of the same year, Mr. Samuel Stevens was the first settler at East Hardwick, thence and for some time afterwards called Stevensville, or Stevens' Mills. Mr. Stevens and his wife ate their first meal in Hardwick over a chest which contained about all their earthly possessions. He soon erected a saw-mill on the north side of the river, and in 1800 he also built a grist-mill near by.

In 1798, Thomas Fuller came to settle in Hardwick, with his wife and children. For six months he, with a family of eleven, occupied a log house, 24 feet square, with Mr. Wm. Cheever, whose family also numbered eleven. There was a stone fire-place in the centre of the house, and a hollow log for a chimney.

Samuel French moved in in 1799. His son

Daniel (now Dea. French), then aged 18 years, says, " We moved from Hardwick, Mass., to our namesake in Vermont, where we arrived the 4th of March. The last of March the snow lay 4 feet deep on a level, but the weather was mild, and we prepared for sugaring; but there came two feet more of snow, and not a tree was tapped until the 15th of April. We gathered our buckets the 15th of May. Snow-banks were visible the 9th of June. Vegetation came forward very rapidly, but not sufficiently so to save our crops. Many of them were much injured by the early frosts."

1812. Mr. and Mrs. Elisha Swett came to Hardwick; they lived together 80 years. Mr. S. died Nov. 1859, aged 96, and Mrs. S. died Feb. 1860, aged 98.

1816. About this time there were many emigrations from Hardwick to what was then called " the West;" but few went farther than the Genesee Valley. During this year, the inhabitants of Hardwick suffered much from the snow and frost. A heavy snow began to fall on the 7th of June, and continued to fall until the 9th. The sheep had just been sheared, and had to be covered again with their fleeces; but there was little or no hay for them or for the cattle, and many of them died. The forest-leaves were all killed, and the woods went in mourning through the summer. Rye sold for 3 dollars per bushel.

EDUCATION.

From an early day the people of Hardwick have manifested considerable interest in the cause of education.

1799. The town was divided into four school districts, called respectively the Hazen Road, Centre, middle, and eastern districts. The middle district was between the centre and East Hardwick, and the Eastern was on the east side of the river. The first school meeting was held in the Middle district; voted to have a two months' school, and to raise a tax on the grand list for its support. The first teacher was Anna Hill. The first part of this term she taught in a log barn, owned by Israel Sanborne; the remainder of the time in different log houses — the family occupying one room, and she the only remaining one. This was in the summer of 1800.

1800. *March.* It was voted by the town to sell the land appropriated by the proprietors of the town for the benefit of an English school. The land was sold the following year. From the fund thus raised a small dividend has been paid annually to each school district, according to the number of scholars. The whole number of scholars at that time was 85.

1801. Flavel Bailey, from Peacham, was hired to teach a six months' school in the middle district.

1802. The first school-house was built in the middle district, by Martin Fuller, for $165. This money was raised by a tax on the grand list, and was paid principally in cattle and grain.

1815. We find the town divided at this date into 9 districts, containing 339 scholars.

1821. The first select school in town was kept two terms by Miss Deborah Worcester, from Hollis, N. H., at the Centre.

1842. The first select school at East Hardwick was taught by Miss A. Stevens, a graduate of Cazenovia Seminary, N. Y.

1855. The town contains 12 school districts, and 382 scholars.

1860. By the efforts of the people of South Hardwick an Academy building, over the Town Hall, has been completed. In Nov., 1860, this Academy obtained a charter from the Vermont Legislature. Its prospects are bright. Principal, A. J. Sanborne; lady teachers, Miss L. Sinclair and Miss Bundy.

During the fall of this year measures were taken to establish the select school at East Hardwick on a permanent basis.

Of college graduates and of professional men Hardwick has raised a fair proportion.

THE VILLAGES.

There are four villages in town. The oldest, called the Street or Hazen Road, is situated on high land, near the north line of the town. The first settlement was made in 1793. This was formerly a place of considerable business, but time has wrought such changes by deaths or removals, that it has now become a *quiet* little place, with hardly a vestige of its former activity. The second village in age is East Hardwick, situated on the Lamoille River, in the eastern part of the town. The first settlement was made by Mr. Samuel Stevens, in 1797. This is at present a place of considerable business.

The third village is South Hardwick, which is also situated on the Lamoille, in the south-west part of the town. The first settler was Capt. J. C. Bridgman, in the year 1797. This is also a place of considerable business. It contains the Town Hall.

"Mackville," the fourth village in town, is situated one mile south of South Hardwick, on a branch of the Lamoille River. This small stream affords excellent water-privileges, which at present are occupied by a saw-mill, corn-mill, etc. A large building has been erected the past year, designed for a woollen factory.

The commencement of this place was about the year 1831, by the building of a saw-mill by Mr. George P. Fish. Mr. Elisha Mack built the first dwelling-house in 1834; but before he was ready to move with his family to this anticipated earthly home, death removed him to his eternal home. His eldest son, Resolved Mack, with his widowed mother, brothers and sisters, came to this new home; but eventually the family were scattered. Mr. R. Mack retained the place, and was married, in 1838, to Miss Mary Bancroft.

These families were the first settlers, and the village has been named for them.

There are now some dwelling-houses and public buildings in process of building — a Free-Will Baptist church and a large and commodious school-house.

This place has experienced a great loss in the removal by death, in February, of the present year (1861), of their first settler, Mr. Resolved Mack. He was kind and companionable in his family, a very worthy citizen, and an efficient member of the Methodist church. In the midst of *usefulness* he was called; but calmly and cheerfully met the call.

ECCLESIASTICAL.

I. BAPTIST CHURCH.

BY REV. E. EVANS.

On Nov. 18th, 1795, the members of the Danville Baptist Church who were residents of Hardwick, wishing to form themselves into a Baptist Church, for the purpose of enjoying church privileges among themselves; and having obtained permission of that church to be constituted into a church by themselves, a Baptist Church was organized on Thursday, Dec. 17, 1795. Rev. Amos Tuttle received a call to become their pastor, and was called to ordination June 16, 1796. The records of this church are lost, therefore nothing further of its history can be ascertained. Its visibility has become extinct.

Subsequent to this, there was a Baptist Church organized in Greensboro'; but as a majority of its members resided in Hardwick, it was deemed expedient to form a church in East Hardwick. In 1831, a Baptist Church was organized, consisting of 25 members. ELDER MARVIN GROW, a good man, and one whose preaching talent was very acceptable to the brethren, became their pastor. He continued his pastoral labors with them about 6 years, and becoming infirm and indisposed, requested and obtained his dismission.

He was succeeded by REV. AARON ANGIER, whose faithful and devoted labors were in a very remarkable manner owned and blessed of God. During his pastorate, A. D. 1840, a meetinghouse was built, and 92 added to the church by baptism and by letter. The church, at this time, was one of the most flourishing Baptist churches in northern Vermont, numbering 150 members. He closed his pastorate, much to the regret of the church, and went west and died.

[From Mrs. Mary Spofford, eldest daughter of Rev. Mr. Angier, we have the following additional items: "My father remained a little more than four years in Hardwick; from there he removed to Middlebury, where he remained two years, and published a paper called the *Vermont Observer.* After which he resided in Poultney a year; then in Ludlow a year, where he was associate and leading editor of a paper, named the *Genius of Liberty*—the first paper published in Ludlow; when he again removed to Cavendish, where he sojourned two years, and in the spring of 1850 went to Cato, Cayuga Co., N. Y., where he lived three years, and then accepted an agency for the Bible Union, and moved his family to Elbridge, N. Y. This, however, he retained but one year, and in 1854 became the pastor of the Baptist Church in Lamoille, Ill., where he lived but four months, when he died, the 3d of Sept., 1854, in the 48th year of his age. His family reside there still.]

REV. JONATHAN R. GREEN, an earnest and stirring preacher, who was laboring with the church in Hanover, N. H., received a call to become pastor of the Baptist Church in Hardwick. He accepted the call, and commenced his labors ; but, contrary to the expectation and wish of the church and society, he tarried with them but one year, and then returned to the people of his former charge.

ELDER NATHAN DENNISON, a zealous, enterprising, and devoted servant of his Master, next became their pastor. His unwearied efforts were blessed in the conversion of many, and the church was prospering under his administration, when some difficulty arising between two brethren, which they would not settle themselves, it was brought into the church ; and, as is too frequently the case, each had his friends, and party spirit soon became manifest. There could be no settlement of the difficulty effected ; but the state of things rather grew worse and worse. The church divided. A part went off and worshipped in the school-house, and a part worshipped in the meeting-house. This state of things continued till Rev. Mr. Jones, agent of the Convention, came into town, and induced them to come together again, and organize anew into one church.

Elder Dennison left them after a pastorate of five years, with a constitution, naturally strong and robust, broken down and enfeebled by grief.

ELDER SAMUEL SMITH, of Pen Yan, N. Y., was their next pastor ; a good man, who, though he commenced his labors under the most discouraging circumstances, yet accomplished some good. He remained three years, and returned to N. Y.

ELDER E. EVANS, of Lunenburg, then received and accepted a call to become their pastor. He commenced his labors under circumstances by no means encouraging; but the church seems to be improving; the members appear to be more united. He has been with them three, and has commenced upon his fourth year. During his stay among them, they have expended something in fixing the inside of the meeting-house ; paid $130 for an organ, and laid out about $1000 in building a parsonage, which is now occupied by their pastor.

The means of grace are well attended. The church numbers now 77.

CONGREGATIONAL CHURCH.

BY REV. C. S. SMITH.

II. The Congregational Church in Hardwick was organized July 29, 1803, at the house of Mr. Thomas Fuller. There were present, as an organizing council, Rev. Leonard Worcester, of Peacham, and Rev. John Fitch, of Danville, with their delegates. The new church consisted of 7 male members; 9 females were received to membership two days afterwards.

These first members were from New Braintree, Hardwick, and Westminster, Mass. ; from Sanbornton, Hanover, and Tamworth, N. H. ; and one from Newbury, Vt. Bro. Thomas Fuller was chosen first deacon. Rev. L. Worcester was standing moderator of the church for some years. For about three years after their organization, the church attended upon the ministrations of Elder Amos Tuttle, who in 1796 had been settled as minister of the town, and pastor of the Calv. Bapt. Church. In the year 1806, however, he was, at his own request, dismissed; and from this time until 1810, the church had no stated preaching. They met regularly for worship, however, at dwelling-houses, and received occasional ministrations of the word and of the sacraments from Mr. Worcester, of Peacham, and Mr. Hobart, of Berlin.

During the years 1809 and 1810 several missionaries visited them. Those whose names appear upon the church records, are Jonathan Hovey, Seth Payson, D. D., Solomon Morgan, —— Leland, James Parker, and J. Waters. A powerful revival followed the labors of the last two of these men. About 60 persons were added to the church during this and the following year. Some of these were men of the first ability and business talent in town.

The church now felt itself sufficiently strengthened to support a pastor, and in the fall of 1810, extended a call to Mr. Nathaniel Rawson. He accepted, and was ordained and installed pastor of the church, Feb. 13, 1811. The public services were held in a barn, on the farm then owned by Captain Hatch. During the summers of 1812 and 1813, Mr. Rawson met a company of children at his house every Friday, to hear them recite portions of Scripture. This prepared the way for the Sabbath Schools, which were established a year or two later in the several districts in town.

In 1817, Mr. R. resigned the pastorate of the church, and during the three following years the church was in a divided state.

Mr. J. N. Loomis, a graduate of Middlebury College and Andover Seminary, was ordained and installed pastor of the church, Jan. 3, 1822. The services were held in an unfinished meeting-house, just erected by Mr. Samuel French, half a mile east of the centre of the town ; but as Mr. French declined selling this house to the church, they after much perplexity in regard to a location, decided to build a house of worship upon the hill near the four corners. The meeting-house was built, but the location failed to give entire satisfaction, and the consequence was a division of the church with the advice of a mutual council.

Accordingly, a new church, called the Second Cong. Church, was organized March 2, 1825. Mr. Loomis, whose counsels were of great value to the church during the period of erecting their house of worship, and the separation that followed, continued his labors until the last of January, 1830, when, on account of the feeble state of his health, he was dismissed.

On the 25th of Sept. 1833, Rev. Robert Page, a graduate of Bowdoin College and of Andover, was installed pastor. He continued his relation until June, 1835, when he was dismissed at his own request.

In July, 1836, the church extended a call to Rev. Chester Wright. He commenced preaching to them soon after, and was installed pastor of the church June 15, 1837. He continued his labors until the beginning of the year 1840, when, his health failing, he removed to Montpelier, still retaining his pastoral relation; but he died shortly afterwards in Montpelier, — April, 1840.

Rev. Austin O. Hubbard, a graduate of Yale and Princeton, was installed July 7, 1840, and was dismissed, at his own request, May 1, 1843.

From this date until 1846, the church were without a settled pastor, when they united in giving a call to Rev. Joseph Underwood, a graduate of Bangor. He accepted, and was installed on the 18th of Dec. of the same year. During his pastorate, which continued nearly 12 years, the condition of the church and society became much improved.

In the year 1851, the old meeting-house upon the hill was torn down, and a new one erected, with great unanimity, at East Hardwick.

Several persons who had been members of the second church, when that ceased to exist, joined this. Since 1851, there has been a healthy increase of the church and congregation. The Sabbath School embraces nearly three-fourths of the entire congregation.

In Jan. 1858, Mr. Underwood, on account of the impaired state of his health, resigned his pastorate, and was dismissed, Feb. 2d.

Rev. Henry Hazen, a graduate of Dartmouth and Andover, preached one year, as stated supply, commencing Oct., 1858. In March, 1860, the church and society united in extending a call to Mr. Joseph Torrey, Jr., a graduate of Burlington College and of Andover, to become their pastor. He was ordained and installed May 30, 1860, and is the present pastor.

The whole number of members since the organization of the church is 436. Of these, about 278 have joined by profession, and 158 by letter. The present number of members is 127.

Average attendance on Sabbath about 165. Number of families represented about 70.

THE METHODIST EPISCOPAL CHURCH.
BY REV. A. C. SMITH.

Prior to the year 1803, there had been no Methodist preaching in the town of Hardwick. But during this year, the Rev. LEWIS BATES commenced his labors in this town as a Methodist preacher, and a few persons connected themselves with a society in an adjoining town, which stood connected with what was then called Danville Circuit.

In June, 1809, the Rev. NATHANIEL STEARNS formed a society in Hardwick, and was still attached to the Danville Circuit, which at this time embraced nearly all of Caledonia, Orleans, and Essex Counties. Peter Page was appointed the first class-leader, and Nathaniel Norris the first steward.

Nathaniel Norris, for several years, had been a member of, and an ordained deacon in, the Free-will Baptist Church previous to 1809, when he became one of the memorable fourteen who formed the first society. He received a license as an exhorter in the M. E. Church, bearing date July 14, 1810, and signed by David Kilburn and Benjamin R. Hoyt, who were the first circuit preachers in this town after the formation of the society.

Jan. 7, 8, 1816, the society held their first quarterly meeting in Hardwick.

For several years, the society prospered, and increased gradually until 1823, when John Ward Norris was appointed class-leader, at the age of 19, at which time the society numbered 60 members.

Several following years, the society did not increase very extensively, and they were compelled to hold their meetings in dwelling or school houses for the want of ability to build a church edifice.

In 1846, Hardwick was connected with Craftsbury, and the Rev. GEORGE PUTNAM and the Rev. O. S. MORRIS appointed circuit preachers.

At the first quarterly conference, a vote was taken to divide the labors of the circuit, by which the said Morris was to labor at Hardwick, and the said Putnam at Craftsbury.

Rev. O. S. Morris remained at Hardwick two years, during which time, through his efforts, and the concurring efforts of the society and friends, a good church edifice was erected, finished, and dedicated, at the south village, which has now become the centre of the town business by the erection of a new town hall during the last summer, and probably one of the best in the State.

The church at that time numbered 65 members. Since 1847, the desk has been supplied as follows:

1848, from the local ministry; 1849, by Rev.

A. L. Cooper; 1850, left to be supplied; 1851–2, by Rev. J. Whitney; 1853–4, by Rev. James S. Spinny; 1855–6, by Rev. L. Hill; 1857–8, by Rev. E. Pettingill; 1859–60, by Rev. A. C. Smith. The present membership, including probationers, numbers 103.

FREE-WILL BAPTIST CHURCH.
FROM A LETTER OF A. M. AMSDEN.

There are quite a number of this denomination in the south and west part of the town; those of the south belong to the Malden Church, and the west, till last June, to the Wolcott. This church is now called "Wolcott and Hardwick Church." The whole number is 26. They have had for 6 or 7 years a very flourishing Sabbath School of 35 to 48; also a good library. The pastor, ELDER CUMMINGS, died last summer. Since then they have had no pastor, but preaching three-fourths of the time by various individuals. The school-house is their place of worship.

NEW LIGHTS.
BY REV. J. TORREY.

During the year 1837, a small band of fanatics, who called themselves "New Lights," commenced a brief career in Hardwick. Their leader had been a professed Universalist, but his mind having become discomposed, and, as some thought, partially deranged, he professed to be inspired from on high, and was not long in enlisting several followers.

Great numbers were drawn together to see and hear their strange doings, and soon they began to hold their meetings in the South Meeting House. (This meeting house was built in the year 1820, by Samuel French. The motto, "*Liberty of Conscience*," inscribed on its front, expressed the design of its builder that it should be open to all, to hold such religious meetings as they pleased.) No more than 6 or 8 persons took very active parts; still, they were countenanced and encouraged by large numbers from this and neighboring towns, who preferred to spend their Sabbaths at the *Hardwick Theatre*, rather than to engage in a rational religious worship. Sabbath after Sabbath, for several months, that large house was crowded with spectators. The "drollery" of these meetings consisted of jumping, swinging the arms, rolling on the floor, frightful yelling, barking in imitation of dogs, foxes, etc. Their leader professed to have had it revealed to him that men should not shave; they accordingly suffered their beards to grow for several months, until it was revealed to another that they must all be shaved, and it was done.

It was believed that the seeds of these extravagances had been sowing for a long time in connection with the notion that the fourth commandment is not obligatory under the gospel dispensation,—that much of the religion of regular evangelical churches is composed of hypocrisy or of human tradition, and that special revelations in regard to duty, and in regard to future events, are communicated to individuals now by the inspiration of the Spirit of God.

The meetings were usually opened, after a season of sitting in silence, by the utterance of some text of scripture in a loud scream. A large portion of what was said consisted of texts of scripture. Much was also said by way of denunciation of ministers and churches, charging them with tradition, superstition, hypocrisy, etc. The irregularity and disorder of these meetings was much increased by the attempt of a young man, who thought himself called to preach, to occupy the desk on the Sabbath, in the very midst of the scenes enacted on the floor. The men with beards shouted and screamed, and the man in the pulpit exerted all the power of his lungs for hours together, to overpower the tumultuous noise below, and to gain the attention of the people.

But the career of these fanatics was short. Rev. Chester Wright, at that time pastor of the Cong. Church in Hardwick, believing that such services were calculated to bring the religion of the gospel into contempt, and to sow broadcast over this town and region the seeds of infidelity, resolved to make an effort to withstand such influence. He accordingly gave notice that on the first Sabbath in May he expected to preach with some reference to the proceedings at the South Meeting House during the past year, and invited a large audience.

Some of the most distinguished of the fanatics were present on the occasion of the delivery of these sermons, and in the midst of the forenoon services one of them interrupted the preacher by a tremendous yell, which he seemed resolved to continue. He was, however, immediately ordered into custody by a magistrate, and the services were continued and closed as usual. In these sermons, Mr. Wright aimed to show that the fundamental error of those who believed themselves, or others, to be moved by the Spirit of God, to practise the extravagances in question, was this: That the Spirit of God reveals to men truths, and inculcates duties contrary to, or above and beyond, what may be learned from the Holy Scriptures.

The influence of this strange movement was very deeply felt by the Church of Hardwick. Some of the effects were only temporary, but some were of long duration. One of the leaders hung himself not very long after the excitement ceased.

Notwithstanding the feelings of sadness and regret with which the Christian now calls to mind these scenes, he yet desires to erect a monument to their memory, that so future pilgrims may say, "It is true, *Christian* did here meet with *Apollyon*, with whom he had also a sore combat," and that they, like Christiana and her children, may see a pillar with this inscription upon it, "Let *Christian's* slips before he came hither, and the battles that he met with in this place, be a warning to those that come after."

BIOGRAPHICAL.

ELDER AMOS TUTTLE.

The following sketch will be found to contain facts of great interest, and of historical importance, presenting as they do a vivid picture of the labors, trials, and hardships of the early settlers of the town. The facts are furnished by Capt. David Tuttle of South Hardwick, the oldest son of the Elder.

Amos Tuttle was born in Southbury, Ct., Oct. 31, 1761, was married to Rachel T. Jones, June 16, 1782, lost a large property soon after his marriage through the rascality of a man in high life, and in 1788 engaged in the boot and shoe business in the town of Washington, Ct. He was at that time a noted infidel, and strong in argument; but soon, although there was no religious excitement in the neighborhood, his attention became powerfully attracted to the subject of personal religion. He began to attend worship in an adjoining town, New Preston; experienced a change of heart, and connected himself with the Baptist Church in New Preston, of which Rev. Isaac Root was the pastor. Soon after this, he prepared himself to preach the gospel, and was settled over a church in the town of Litchfield, Ct.

Rev. Mr. Root moved about this time to Danville, Vt., and was settled over the first Baptist Church in that town. Returning to Connecticut for a visit, he called upon Mr. Tuttle, and gave him such a description of the beauty and fertility of Northern Vermont, that, notwithstanding the urgent invitation of another friend calling him to Western New York, Mr. Tuttle concluded to visit Vermont the next season. Accordingly, in June, 1794, he came to Danville, and thence to Walden, Hardwick, Greensboro', and Craftsbury, became acquainted with the inhabitants, and found that a church could be organized from the four last towns, the majority of the members living in Hardwick. A church was formed. Mr. Tuttle was called to settle as minister of the town and church, and he accepted.

In the month of Oct. 1795, he started with his family from Litchfield for Hardwick. Such a journey was in those days a great undertaking. They were *fifteen days* on the way, but meeting with no more serious accident than the breaking of the wagon, they arrived at Gilman's, in Walden, during the night of the 31st of October, in the midst of a hard rain-storm. Beds were soon taken from the wagon and placed on the floor of the little bark-covered log house, and our cold, tired immigrants lay down to rest. There was not a pane of glass about the house, and so no sign of day appeared until the door was opened in the morning. Then day appeared indeed, and with it, to the great surprise of all, appeared a

white mantle of snow, covering the ground with a depth of at least 15 inches. A messenger was sent to Hardwick, requesting the friends of the family to send teams to bring them on their journey. Three sleds, with wild steers, were sent. Two of them were loaded with the goods, and the third was fitted up with boxes for seats, and with plenty of straw, to carry the sick, disheartened, and weeping mother and children. Mr. David Tuttle, who was then a boy, says, "As we reached the bottom of the awful hill by which the Hazen road descends to the Lamoille River, the sleds stopped that the bridge might be repaired. I saw my mother, brother, and little sisters all in tears, and shall never forget the expression of anguish with which my mother said, 'Dear husband, where are you taking me? I shall die, and what will become of the children?' It sobered me for the rest of that day, and brings tears to my eyes now in my old age, as I relate it."

They turned off from the Hazen road near the place where L. H. Delano, Esq., now resides, followed a narrow sled-path which wound through the woods, crossed the Tuttle brook at a place above where the road now crosses, ascended the steep bank by doubling the teams, and passed through a burnt slash to the house of Mark Morris.

The journey being thus safely over, the next care of our pioneer pastor was to find a house for his family. There was an empty log shanty to be had, but it was much out of repair. Mr. Tuttle was strong and healthy however, and, with the aid of his friends, he succeeded, by the middle of November, in making it habitable. There were, to be sure, neither windows nor cupboards nor chimney, and the hut itself was only 12 feet by 15, but he cut some holes through the logs and pasted oiled paper over them for windows, and the smoke found its own way upwards.

A successful hunt on snow-shoes on the West Hill, in which three moose were killed by his party, provided the family with meat for a time. He was so fortunate, also, as to procure a bushel of salt of a peddler by.paying five dollars in cash. The price of salt seems to have risen higher still, or else money must have become scarce, for the next year he paid six bushels of wheat for one of salt, and this in preference to paying three dollars cash.

After thus providing these "creature comforts," the next question seems to have been how to get about his parish. His gumption soon found the way. A "Tom-pung," as he called it, was hewed out and put together with wooden pins and rods, and the pieces of rope which had been used as binders on the journey he made into a kind of harness, sufficient at least to fasten the horse to the pung, and to guide him through the woods.

The town of Hardwick was organized March 31, 1795. In April, 1796, the town met and voted to unite with the Baptist Church in settling Mr. Tuttle as minister of the town. He was installed in June following. The people being poor, it was agreed that he should receive *no salary* during the first four years! By a provision of the town charter, however, he was entitled to draw three lots of land, as the first minister of the town. One of these lots he sold for a little money and a little wheat, to be paid in four annual instalments.

Soon after his installation, Mr. Tuttle went to work to clear a piece of land and build himself a log house. By the middle of November, he completed his work, and in just one year from the time the family had first huddled themselves into the little hut, they moved into the largest and best log house in town, 32 feet by 15.

The Sabbath worship was held in this house during the winter months, and in barns in different parts of the town during the summer.

But the sorest trials of this servant of God were yet to come. They were of quite a different nature from any that he had ever before experienced, nor can they be related, — for time and language would fail. Unlearned and ignorant men sowed seeds of disaffection and vanity in the church, and the little flock was divided. Only a few firm friends stayed by their pastor, and tried to comfort and strengthen him. He still continued to preach in town, and as there were Congregational church members in Hardwick, it was thought best to organize a Congregational church, and to employ Mr. Tuttle as their pastor. For three years he ministered to them, at the expiration of which time he was urged to accept a call from the Baptist Church in Fairfax, Vt. A meeting of the Congregational brethren was called, and it was concluded to consent to his departure.

During the same year, he was settled as the first minister in Fairfax, and received the portion of land granted to him ex officio. He did not retain possession of it, however, but gave it for the benefit of the town district schools. For a time, he labored here with great acceptance; but sorrow was again on his track. An Old and New School controversy arose in the church, a schism occurred, some of the most prominent men moved out of town, and Mr. Tuttle, finding that his usefulness there was at an end, requested a dismission, which was granted in 1841.

Resolving to devote himself to the work of a missionary, he visited most of the towns in Vermont, and many of the townships bordering on the line in Canada. During this time he made his home in Hardwick; but he afterwards removed again to Fairfax, where his daughters were married and settled. He remained at Fairfax until the death of his wife, when he finally returned to Hardwick to spend the remainder of his days with his son, in the very house which his own hands had built in the vigor and strength of manhood. He lived after his return to his

old home about two years, preached his last sermon at the funeral of a son of Col. Warner, soon after which he was prostrated by a painful disease, and died a lingering but peaceful death, February, 1833, aged 72 years. His body was buried in the Hazen Road Cemetery, where he had attended the first burial ever made there. On that occasion he had remarked to those present, that, in all probability, his own body would moulder to dust in that ground. A short time before his death his two sons were expecting to carry his remains to Fairfax and deposit them near those of his wife; but their father said that although this seemed pleasing to him at first view, yet the travelling was so bad and the distance so great, that it was his preference to be buried at the Hazen Road Cemetery. And so his prophecy came true.

ELNATHAN STRONG.

Dea. Elnathan Strong was born in Chatham, Ct., March 25, 1787. He was the son of Rev. Cyprian Strong, who was for many years a minister of the gospel in Chatham. He left home when quite young, and lived with a relative in Windsor, Vt. He afterwards removed to Danville, where he abode until the year 1808, when he removed to Hardwick. About two years after coming to this town, he united himself with the Congregational Church. He was married to Jane Chamberlain, Oct. 17, 1820. Was chosen deacon of the church in the year 1826, which office he continued to hold until his death, which occurred June 19, 1843.

In a discourse preached on the occasion of his death, the Rev. O. A. Hubbard says: "I should shrink from anything like mere *eulogium* in regard to *any* individual, and certainly in regard to one, a leading trait of whose character was *modesty*, and of whom it is well known that he rather *shunned* observation than *sought* it. Deacon Strong possessed a native discrimination of mind, and an accuracy of judgment, that fall to the lot of exceedingly few. Scarcely ever have I seen the individual that would investigate a complex subject with greater readiness, or pronounce, in regard to it, a more correct decision; for while he was quick of apprehension, he was careful and deliberate in arriving at his conclusions. Although in early life his opportunities for education had been quite limited, yet he was, at least, in the *practical* sense of that word, a close and accurate scholar."

Deacon Strong was especially distinguished in regard to the extent and accuracy of his knowledge of the Bible. He also possessed a peculiar power of illustrating scripture truth, which fitted him to fill with great acceptance the place of a teacher in the Sabbath School, and made his presence always welcome in the conference meeting.

He was a man of marked *integrity* and *uprightness*. His prevailing tone of Christian character was that of a meek, spiritual, and consistent disciple; never giving utterance to common-place or cant expressions in regard to feeling, exercises, etc.; but exhibiting a heart softened, humbled, and elevated by the Divine grace, directed to the extension of the church and the salvation of the world,—one of those men whose religion seems to consist in *being* and *doing*, and that *heartily* and liberally. His home was always open to the servants of God, and they loved to linger there. Favored by Providence with large means, he exemplified much of the principle, " It is more blessed to give than to receive." His memory will long be cherished by all who knew him, and especially by the members of the church, of which he was the *father*, the *counsellor*, and the *almoner*.

ADDITIONAL BIOGRAPHY.

BY MISS STEVENS,

ISRAEL SANBORN

And wife emigrated from Lee, N. H., to Hardwick, in 1794. They were a valuable addition to the new settlement. He was first town treasurer, which office, with others, he held many years. A benevolent regard for others was a characteristic of Mr. and Mrs. Sanborn. Their log barn was often occupied as a school-room, and their house for a church and town hall; and at one time, when the people had been exposed to the small pox, was thrown open for a pest house. Families in need of a temporary home till they could build, were kindly received here. They were both church-members. As an illustration of the Christian character of Mr. S., we may be allowed to offer the following anecdote. There existed a little difference between him and a neighbor in regard to a road. The neighbor called to see about it. Mr. S. was at the barn. Going out to the barn, he did not see him, but heard the voice of prayer. Mr. S. was imploring a blessing upon each neighbor by name. The *one present* was not omitted. Never afterward did the latter doubt the honesty of his neighbor S. In a word, his was in every way a noble nature. But, " Our fathers, where are they ? "

DEA. THOMAS FULLER

Was a native of Cape Cod, and early left an orphan. At the age of 16 he went to Hardwick, Mass., where some years after he married Lydia, daughter of Colonel Page, and in 1798 removed to Hardwick, Vt. He was of Puritan descent, and strictly carried out their principles in the training of his family, and matters pertaining to the church and society generally.

His public spirit and capability to serve the town gave him frequent offices and the confidence of the people. He aided in the organization of the first Congregational Church, and was elected its first deacon, which office he held till his death, in 1823.

SAMUEL STEVENS,

Son of Capt. Simeon Stevens, an officer in the army of the Revolution, was a native of Newbury. Early bereft of father and mother, the promise to the orphan was verified to him ; for in the midst of corrupt examples, compelled to hear profanity, exposed to all the allurements of vice, he yet never defiled his lips with an oath, or followed the multitude to do evil. He was apprenticed to a man who required various kinds of service, and who, contrary to agreement, gave him few opportunities for mental improvement, a deprivation he deeply lamented during his life. In his minority he gave proof of his native strength of mind, enterprise, and rare business talents for which he was afterwards distinguished.

In 1798, he came to Hardwick, and, with a small patrimony left him by his father, together with his own gains, he purchased a wild lot, erected a log house, and, the same year, was married to Miss Puah Mellen, of Holliston, Mass. They were the first settlers of the flourishing village East Hardwick, formerly called Stevens's Village. He built the first mills in town, a saw-mill in 1798, and a grist-mill in 1800, and prosecuted various branches of business ; was remarkable for his promptness in making contracts, for the energy with which he carried forward whatever he undertook, and his strict integrity in all his dealings. For 21 years he was town treasurer ; was one of the first in the temperance reform, practising abstinence from all intoxicating drinks, and requiring the same of all in his employ. He gave land on which to build a store on condition that it should be a temperance one. The carrying out of these temperance principles exerted a moral influence that is still felt in the village. " Mr. and Mrs. S. manifested a deep interest, also, in the cause of education. They were, moreover, noted for hospitality. Ministers, friends generally, and the travellers, as well, seeking entertainment, always found a welcome. Both members of the Congregational Church, they manifested their piety by their willingness to support the gospel, and by their regard for the requirements of God. They lived happy and died happy, and their memory is blessed.

SIMEON H. STEVENS,

" Third son of the foregoing, was a young man of much promise ; a graduate (   ) at the University of Vermont ; conducted for a season the Craftsbury Seminary ; and commenced the study of theology in the Bangor (M. E.) Theological Seminary. In consequence, however, of failing health, he was obliged to abandon all anticipations in reference to the ministry. He, nevertheless, was married about this time to Miss M A. Young, daughter of Hon. Augustus Young, and settled upon a farm in his native town. But with returning health, desiring a wider field in which to labor for the good of his fellow-men, he removed to Johnson, and became Principal of the Lamoille Co. Grammar School. A year had not elapsed, when he was suddenly removed by death. His remains were interred in Hardwick. It was remarked upon the occasion of his funeral that the large audience were all mourners."

LEVI GOODRICH

Settled from Massachusetts in 1798. A worthy and efficient man in the town and the church.

SAMUEL FRENCH,

Born in Hoosich, Mass., came to Hardwick, Vt., about 1800. He married Tabitha Dow, a sister of the far-famed Lorenzo Dow, a woman of talent, and agreeable and lady-like. "He was considered a man of talent, especially in public speaking." He was one of Nature's noblest sons, but was peculiar in his religious feelings; yet it was true of him that he entertained no sectarian views. Sectional variances delayed the building of a church for worship, and he was led to feel a special order from heaven to build a house for the Lord. This he did almost wholly unaided in 1820, which was the first church-building in town to be occupied by all denominations. He never would sell or deed it to any sect; the Congregational Church made repeated efforts to purchase it. Although it is conceded that his motive to furnish the town with a church was good, yet the result was, contrary to his expectations, deleterious to the town. The inscription, "Liberty of Conscience," gave all a right of occupancy; but finally it was used in a way foreign to the worship of God, and the intent of the builder. He was repeatedly urged to serve the town in a public capacity; though a philanthropic man, he always despised office. On once being asked to run as a candidate for representative, he declared "he would not go if elected." He was very kind in his family, a good neighbor and citizen. He died in 1848, aged 69 years.

DR. AMASA MORSE

Was the first physician in Hardwick. He came into town with his family in 1800, and continued in practice until his death. "He was a very kind and feeling man, and a good family physician." He died in 1820, aged 46 years. His wife survived him nearly 40 years — an active woman, who energetically met the wants of a large family. She was a very shrewd but useful woman in community, and a professing Christian. She died in 1859, in the 82d year of her age.

CAPT. JOHN C. BRIDGEMAN,

From Coventry, Conn., to Hardwick, the first settler in the south part of the town, served the town in different ways. Was a very kind man to his friends, and in his family.

FRANCIS WHIPPLE

And wife came into Hardwick with their son, Joel Whipple, and family, in 1804, from New Braintree. He was a very jovial man, much given to anecdote, but firm in principle, and a very industrious, economical, and useful citizen. In his last sickness his prayer was especially for the welfare of the church. He died in 1823, aged 81. His wife, Mrs. Whipple, was a woman of superior mind, and a mother in Israel, beloved by all, young and old. She possessed a great fund of cheerfulness, and was often very shrewd. A fanatical minister once called, and said, "You sometimes entertain ministers." "Yes, if they have a recommendation." "And what would you say at one from heaven?"—"Go straight back, 'tis a poor country here for such a man!" When a widow, an aged man asked her to become his wife. In answer, "Why, Mr. B., we are nothing but old children. You have one foot in the grave, the other will be there soon. You had better go home, read your Bible, and prepare to die, than to be here on such an errand!" She was very industrious; some of her last work was spinning linen for a web. She warped it, forgot to tie the leases, and, as she took it from the bars, a gust of wind blew the whole into an irrecoverable snarl. "And is this the great Babylon I have built? a just rebuke to my pride and vanity!" She was a friend to the sick and needy, and such was her great disinterestedness and every-day piety, she was a fit counsellor for all. The last years of her life she made her friends a yearly visit. She always chose to walk. People, sick or well, ever gave her a cheerful welcome. "Grandma is coming," has been echoed from many a child's glad heart. The words of wisdom and instruction which were dropped from her lips are as golden treasures in the memory of those who knew her. The last visit she made was in December. She walked half a mile to see a sick man. The effort was too much, and proved the occasion of her death. Her last audible prayer was, "Clothe me in the righteousness of Christ, and may I, in the morning of the resurrection, rise in the image of my Saviour!" She died Dec. 1833, aged 89.

DEA. JOEL WHIPPLE

Inherited the ready wit of his mother, and the firmness of his father. Was very active in town business, and in promoting schools. He was elected deacon of the Congregational Church in 1821, which office he held till his death, in 1827. During this time, the church was subjected to severe trials, and a division, caused by the locating a house of worship.

He gave liberally, and was firm and persevering in his efforts to accomplish the work of building a house for the Lord. The brethren were nerved on to action by his cheerful, hopeful spirit; the pastor encouraged; religion honored by his love to God, to the church, and his fellow-man, and in the promotion of peace and harmony, for which he was especially distinguished.

MRS. MARTHA WHIPPLE,

His wife, was a woman of great refinement, meek, and Christ-like. She, and also her husband, joined in singing praises to God in his house till their death. The tones of her voice were sweet and melodious. She died in 1836, aged 54 years.

FRANCIS P. WHIPPLE,

Their oldest son, a graduate of Middlebury College, and principal of an academy in Granville, N. Y., died in 1830, aged 25. He was intending to enter the ministry.

HORATIO NELSON,

Their third son, two years in Amherst College, was taken sick, and obliged to leave. Having partially recovered, he engaged in teaching in Medway, Mass. He taught but a short time, however, before he went to his uncle Levi Whipple's, in Putman, Ohio, where he died of consumption in 1835, aged 26 years.

He, too, had decided to be a minister. He was a very devoted, useful Christian; unassuming, pleasing in his ways, and had the love and esteem of all who knew him.

CHARLES WHIPPLE,

The youngest son and brother, commenced a preparatory course of study, with the ministry in view, but relinquished his cherished wishes to live with and care for his widowed mother; but the angel of death claimed yet another. He died in 1832, aged 21.

REV. J. B. HARDWICK NORRIS,

Son of Deacon Nathaniel Norris, the second man who came, with his family, to settle in Hardwick, was the first child born in town (1792), and named HARDWICK in honor thereof. In early life he became a preacher and member of the Vermont Methodist Conference; and, notwithstanding the accumulating care of a large family, was an itinerant for many years — for more than forty a faithful minister of the gospel. January, 1861, he left the vineyard of toil for the banqueting house above.

COL. ALPHA WARNER.

BY A. J. HYDE, M. D.

COLONEL WARNER was born in Hardwick, Mass., Dec. 1770, and removed to Hardwick, Vt., 1796, following the old military road to Canada, opened through the wilderness by Col. Hazen. Soon after he came here, he was married to Miss Lydia Cobb, of Hardwick, Mass.

As the old sign shows, bearing the date of 1797, he, this year, opened a house of entertainment on the Hazen Road, and presided in the capacity of host for nearly 60 years. This house was one of the most noted in Vermont, and many

a traveller would ride a little later or go a little further to get to "Warner's." In 1816, he had the misfortune to lose, by death, the companion of his early years. In 1818, he was married again to Mrs. Anna Burton, whose death preceded his but a short time. He went West in 1853, and died Jan. 1854, at Chillicothe, Ohio, in the 84th year of his age.

Col. Warner was one of the principal men by whose influence the name of the town was called after "Old Hardwick, Mass." He was one of the early representatives of the town in the State Legislature. A member of the church, he continued in his Christian profession up to his death. He was a very public-spirited man, always favored improvements, especially of roads.

He was considered a man of good judgment upon matters of every-day life. This father of the town had the gratification to witness repeated rewards of his usefulness and public generosity, the waving grains take the place of the wilderness, the town teem with life and activity, the thoroughfares busy with the hurried traveller, and society flourish under the nurture of truth and virtue.

[We are also indebted to Dr. Hyde for helping gather and copy other historical material, both in and near this section. — ED.]

EXTRACT OF A LETTER.

FROM MISS STEVENS.

Mr. David Tuttle, son of Rev. Amos Tuttle, the first minister of Hardwick, who has lived in town longer than any other person now living, says we are mistaken in one item of history — that is, of the first burial of an adult in town. In the history, we have written of a Mr. Sinclair, an aged man, that he died in 1796, and was buried in a log dug out, etc. Mr. Tuttle says he was 13 years old; remembers well of his death, funeral, and burial. His father attended or heard the exercises. He says his coffin was made of pine boards, and painted black. Still Mr. Sinclair, a great-grandchild of the one in question, claims *that he was* interred in a log, as described. He says, his mother was at the funeral, etc. In Greensboro', two miles away, there was a good saw-mill; with means at hand, we can hardly suppose so rude a coffin would have been preferred.

Mr. Tuttle says, before the town was settled but after the clearing made by Messrs. Safford and Page, a Mr. Safford, the one who worked with Mr. Page, or a man by the same name, was moving with his family through Hardwick to Cambridge. They encamped for the night in the hut built by Peter Page. He was taken with bilious colic, and died; and Mr. Tuttle says, Mr. Safford's son told him that they were obliged to dig out a bass log to bury him in. He was interred near the stopping-place. This, perhaps, gave rise to the story of Mr. Sinclair's being buried in such a coffin.

THOUGHTS OF THE PRESENT, AND REMINISCENCES OF THE PAST.

I am an old man, seventy-eight to-day. I am the only person living in this town that was living in it at the time it was organized. I have seen its growth for the last sixty-six years; have shared in its trials, prosperity, and honors, and have now retired from business with little capital, except a middling clear conscience, excellent health for one of my age, many friends, and not an enemy that I know. If I have any, we never meet; so I am pleasantly situated at the present, and visit my friends often, in which I take great satisfaction.

I meet citizens of this town, with their splendid equipage, on a good smooth road, where I, sixty odd years ago, found my way through then a dense forest, by blazed trees. Not long since, I was on an eminence where, in by-gone days, I followed my sable line. Then I could see but a few rods into the great woods; now, from that stand-point, I can see many splendid farms and residences, and even look in upon adjoining towns. I stood for a time enjoying the beautiful prospect, contrasting it with the past, when thoughts crossed my mind of the great West; and I said, What is this, compared with that I have seen there? *Here*, it has taken over half a century to bring about this change. *There*, I have seen on the shores of the great lakes, and on the banks of the Father of Waters, villages grow up in a few months larger than this town owns at the present. But soon my thoughts were again on the landscape before me, and I said, mentally, though this has been a slow work compared with some of young America for a few years past, yet it has been *sure*. The splendid farms and residences that I see here, the occupants own, and have money to let; whereas those I have seen grow up so rapidly at the West, some capitalist living East holds a mortgage for much more than they can be sold for in these hard times. Although I admire those Western States, — believing they are destined to be the heart of the greatest republic on earth, — I am compelled to say, Vermont is a good little State to live in, after all that is done and said. The Vermonters have ever done their own work and thinking, and will continue to for a long time to come, I am confident.

Ladies and gentlemen, citizens of the town of Hardwick, Caledonia County, and State of Vermont, I wish you all the prosperity and happiness that belongs to a correct and virtuous community.   DAVID TUTTLE.

South Hardwick, Feb. 20, 1861.

[We thank most cordially this Hardwick father for his contribution. How many other towns will send, for our Literary Department, a tribute from their *oldest man* living? When old men talk, we love to listen. — ED.]

I AM PASSING THROUGH THE VALLEY.

Miss Jane Ann Porter, born in East Hardwick, in 1832, died December, 1855. The following lines were written three weeks before her death: —

I am passing through the valley
    Called by mortals dark and drear;
Where the dread death-angel reigneth,
    Striking stoutest hearts with fear.

Round me rolls the rapid river,
    And the breaking waves dash high;
But they shall not overwhelm me,
    For my Saviour still is nigh.

One strong arm around me circles,
    While the other points above —
And he whispers to my spirit
    Words of holy peace and love.

Ah! this valley, dark and lonely,
    Is not dark and lone to me;
For the Star of Bethlehem gleaming
    Through the rippled clouds I see.

Brighter yet it grows, and brighter,
    Till the shadows disappear;
And the shore of life eternal
    Rises to my vision clear.

Forms of loveliness excelling
    All I've ever seen before,
Wait to welcome me to glory,
    When my pilgrimage is o'er.

THE LIFE OF A MISSIONARY.

BY MRS. E. S. INGALLS.

Many long years since, I can just perceive in the distance a ruddy youth of beautiful countenance, full of animation, of kindly disposition, dearly beloved by all his friends, full of zeal for the extension of the Redeemer's kingdom, ready to triumph over filial, fraternal, and social affections, to go far hence among the aborigines of the Western wilds.

Distances were not then shortened to the extent that they now are. It was a long, long way over hill and dale, terminating at last in literally a howling wilderness, with no other road than an Indian trail, where the wolves played well their part.

This young missionary was among the pioneers to the Cherokee nation, therefore subjected to all the privations incident to a first expedition. He at once fixed his habitation among red man's wigwams, where the forest was not only to be felled, but the wild man tamed. At the very commencement he reared the standard of Immanuel, and to the nations around told the story of Jesus. Faster than his means would allow, he would have collected the youth and children into schools.

That knowledge might be diffused the whole length and breadth of the nation, he often itinerated. More than once on the excursions was he compelled to subsist on the productions of nature, without any material modification of art to render his dish palatable. In a letter to his friends he remarked, "I often make my breakfast of a water-melon, and my dinner and supper on cucumbers and green corn.

"All day have I rode in the rain, swam deep creeks, and at night laid down in my drenched clothes on the ground, and slept quietly, uninjured by exposure. So you see I have great reason to praise God for a good constitution."

In process of time other missionaries were sent to the Cherokee nation, among whom some whole families, that the nations might have a sample of good order and industry to awake their dormant energies. From one of these families this missionary selected a companion. This was the first Christian marriage celebrated in the Cherokee nation, therefore publicly solemnized in the presence of many natives, who soon learned the propriety of the institution.

A single instance out of thousands will show that they were mutual sharers of trials of no ordinary kind. Once when they were journeying on horseback from one station to another, the distance of 50 miles or more, the sable curtains of night encircled them while they were still in the midst of a dense forest, the rain descending in torrents. There was no alternative but to remain through the night. The first effort to obtain fire, doubtless by friction, forced the whole apparatus from his grasp, while the darkness rendered the search for it wholly unavailing. A shelter composed of their saddles and a few barks was all a tender female and helpless infant had to shield them a whole night from the pelting storm. The little one, notwithstanding all the defence its mother could afford, was so completely drenched as to wear marks of its 'green cap until its hair was of sufficient length to be cropped from its head.

While on a visit to his friends in Hardwick, relating some of the various scenes through which he had passed, his friends inquired "Why he did not mention in his public addresses some of the many trials he had to encounter on missionary ground?" "I should blush to hold up to public gaze my trials, while the goodness and mercy of my Heavenly Father have followed me all my days," he replied. Very true, indeed; praise might well dwell upon his tongue.

He did not spend his strength for naught. In the course of a few years, the entire aspect of the nation was changed. "Instead of comfortless wigwams," he wrote, "I now find good framed or brick houses; instead of sleeping on the ground, I now repose on feather beds; instead of partaking my scanty meal with my fingers, I now find good, wholesome food placed on a neatly-furnished table; and, what is far better, instead of the heathen, the blind worshippers of the 'Great Spirit,' I now find a well-organized community, the meek and humble followers of Christ Jesus, — not that it is true of the whole nation, but a good proportion."

Here I would gladly leave the Cherokee nation, and the devoted missionary, quietly and faithfully pursuing his labors of love; but the white man coveted the highly productive land of the Indians, who, after long and grievous abuses, were removed from their cherished homes, to the uncultivated regions of the "far West," where thousands, victims to the change, found an early grave.

The missionary, after laboring more than 20 years with the Indians, was employed by the Home Missionary Society to labor in Illinois. But he has gone to his reward. He died 1841, while attending the Presbytery at Alton, Ill.

His name was Rev. Wm. Chamberlain, a native of Bradford, Vt. He passed several years in Hardwick, where he was converted, and sent forth to the missionary work.

While visiting his friends in Vermont in 1835, an uncle inquired if he had made any provision for his future support? "Certainly." "Where?" "In Heaven," was the emphatic reply. "I commit all to the care of my Heavenly Father." Subsequent events proved his faith genuine, and the gracious promises immutable. On his return, provision was made for the education of two of his daughters. Mr. Fanshaw, of N. Y., well known as the printer and agent of the American Tract Society, educated one; a lady in Brooklyn, another. When the faithful missionary was called suddenly away, aid was immediately proffered. Rev. S. Worcester, of Salem, Mass., whose father was the first Secretary of the Board of Foreign Missions, and died at Brainard, Cherokee Nation, at the house of Mr. C., who closed his eyes, and committed dust to dust, claimed the privilege of educating one; all the others were kindly educated by benevolent individuals.

KIRBY.

BY CHARLES H. GRAVES.

A township lying in the easterly part of Caledonia County, and very well adapted to agricultural pursuits — the soil being generally free from stone, and consisting of a rich gravelly loam; is well adapted to the raising of all kinds of grain and grass, and in most parts to the growing of Indian corn successfully. Fruit, also, grows well here; there are some fine specimens in town. The winter of 1858 was, however, rather unfavorable for the apple; the old growth already shows signs of decay. With the exception of a range of mountains in the easterly part, the town is susceptible of cultivation; and even those mountain-lots, after being cleared of their heavy growth of timber, produce the best of pasturage. Indeed, there is very little waste land in town. The low lands, that in the early settlement were considered too wet and swampy for cultivation, are now the most productive and valuable. The township is well watered with springs and brooks that rise among the hills, and wind their way through the valleys to the Passumpsic and Moose Rivers, the latter of which passes through a corner of the town. Along its borders are a few excellent farms, but no sites for mills. Near the centre of the town there is quite a mountain-ridge which somewhat divides the business of the town. Here is also a small pond, from which issues Pond Brook, on which are erected 2 saw-mills and 1 starch factory, which do good business; there are also 2 other saw-mills in town in successful operation a part of the year. In the easterly part of the township is an excellent quarry of granite, known as the "Evans quarry," which, for beauty and feasibility, excels anything of the kind yet found in this section, and will, doubtless, at some future day, be extensively used for building purposes. The town did not settle very rapidly, and has never numbered much more than 500 inhabitants. There was nothing unusual or remarkable in the events connected with the early settlement. In common with the early settlers of the rest of this region, the first inhabitants of Kirby suffered much inconvenience and many hardships — living as they did in a wilderness country, far from any market or source of supplies, and destitute in almost every instance of a team.

The exact date of the first permanent settlement made here is not known. Theophilus Grant and Phineas Page removed thither about 1799, locating near the town line adjacent to St. Johnsbury. In 1800, Jonathan Leach came into the north part of the town, then called Burke Tongue, and cut his first tree. He was soon joined by Josiah Joslin, Jude White, Jonathan Lewis, Ebenezer Damon, Asahel Burt, Antipas Harrington, and others, mostly from Massachusetts and New Hampshire. Jonathan Leach and wife are still living upon the same farm upon which he first settled, and are the only survivors of the first company of settlers. They still enjoy comfortable health, and their mental faculties are as yet very little impaired. The age of Mr. Leach is 85; of Mrs. Leach, 88 or 89. He was a native of Bridgewater, Mass. He made his first "pitch" in the town of Burke — purchasing a lot of land near the centre of that town. While absent, however, engaged in removing his family from Massachusetts to their new home, the proprietors obtained a new draught of the town, bringing his number some five miles to the southward of the spot where he had commenced clearing, in an unbroken wilderness. Procuring, on his return, the assistance of a neighbor as a guide, started out in quest of his number, which, after some difficulty, he succeeded in finding. In this new location he commenced his labors, in the month of April, 1800. He erected at once a log house, though, as the reader may readily imagine, "under difficulties," innasmuch as he was destitute both of shingles and boards, not to mention numerous other articles usually deemed indispensable in order to con-

venient and successful house-building. Into this rude structure, and while his gable-ends were still open, he removed his family, consisting of a wife and two small children. Addressing himself now to clearing away the forest about him, and preparing the soil for cultivation, he succeeded the first year in raising a sufficient amount of grain to meet the wants of his family. By another year, without the aid of a team, he had subdued enough of the forest to gather in 150 bushels of wheat. By the third year, he had put up a framed barn — the building in which he thinks was taught the first school and held the first religious meeting in town (A. D. 1804). That barn is still standing, and is in a good condition. The first saw-mill in town, moreover, was built by Mr. Jonathan Leach.

The town charter was granted Oct. 20, 1786, and chartered Oct. 27, 1790, to Roswell Hopkins, by the name of Hopkinsville, containing 11,284 acres. Subsequently, 2527 acres were added from the town of Burke, known as Burke Tongue, and the name of the township altered, by an act of Legislature, in 1808, to Kirby. The town was organized on the 8th of August, 1807, and on the 29th of the same month, the first town-meeting was called to elect town officers. Selah Howe was chosen Moderator, Jonathan Lewis, Town Clerk, which office he held 17 years. Benjamin Estabrooks, Joel Whipple, Arunah Burt, first Selectmen; Philomen Brown, first Constable; Josiah Joslin, first Town Representative.

Dr. Abner Mills removed into town about 1810, practising medicine in this and adjoining towns; but did not remain long, with the exception of the year 1813, when the prevailing epidemic proved very mortal here, there being 21 deaths in town, and mostly of adults. The people have ever enjoyed a very good degree of health. The oldest person deceased in town appears, from the record, to have been Zebulon Burroughs, aged 84. The first birth (June 2d, 1801) was that of Lavina Harrington. The first marriage celebrated was that of Nathaniel Reed and Sukey Sweat, Feb. 8, 1804. The first death was that of Henry White, Sept. 3, 1803. There are now seven organized school districts in town.

In 1812, there was a Congregational Church organized, consisting of 11 members. Timothy Locke was chosen first deacon, which office he held until his death in 1850. This church has never had a pastor ordained over it; but has been improved a part of the time by itinerant ministers from abroad. In 1824, Rev. Luther Wood united with this church, and continued to preach a portion of the time, until, on account of the infirmities of age, he was no longer able to perform pastoral duties. In 1828, the church erected a comfortable house of worship, in which they continued to meet until about 1840, at which time the church numbered 45 members. About the same year a new church was formed at East St. Johnsbury. In order to enjoy better privileges and accommodations than what they had hitherto been able to, a portion of the Kirby Church asked and obtained dismission from the latter with a view to uniting with the former. This exodus from the old church left it in such a feeble condition that it was no longer able to sustain stated preaching. In consequence, most of the members have taken letters to churches in adjoining towns.

There was a Methodist Society established here as early as 1804, the class being formed under the supervision of the Rev. Mr. Peck, of the Lyndon charge. They were for a long time supplied with preaching from adjoining towns. At present, however, this society is in a flourishing condition, about 25 having been added the past year. They now number about 75 members, and enjoy stated preaching, — Rev. Mr. Bullard, pastor.

REV. LUTHER WOOD.

Father Wood, as he was more familiarly called, was born in Lebanon, N. H. In 1800 he removed to St. Johnsbury, Vt. He obtained a license to preach about 1804. I think he was never ordained over any church. His early history was marked with affliction, privations, and losses, — having been burnt out once or twice, and thrown upon the charities of the world with a large family of small children to sustain. His motto, however, was ever onward and upward.

At an early day he purchased a farm, and removed his family to this town. About 1824, he, with his wife and some of his children, united with the Congregational Church here, which at that time was very feeble, and the timely aid which this connection afforded was joyfully received by its members. He continued to preach to them at intervals until he was called to his reward. Although he never possessed so much pulpit eloquence as many, yet his sermons were deep and impressive, and full of gospel truth. They were more deeply impressed on the mind by the fact that they came from a warm and feeling heart, without any affectation of over-heated imagination. He lived to the advanced age of 79, and retained his mental faculties almost to the end of life. Of him it was emphatically true, he was a faithful servant of his Master. In his death the church and community sustain no ordinary loss. In his will he bequeathed $1800 to carry forward missionary enterprise.

HON. ALBERT WESLEY BURROUGHS.

Judge Burroughs, son of Seth and Olive Burroughs, was born April 18, 1815. Although he never enjoyed the advantages of what is termed a classic education, being by nature a scholar, he early manifested an ardent love for books; and being possessed of a discriminating mind and a disposition to improve, was, while quite young, initiated into the business interests of

the town. Not only was he disposed to succeed, but was eager to excel in all his pursuits. At the age of 19, he was appointed county surveyor, and after that did most of the surveying in this vicinity. He entered the militia company, and was in due time placed at the head of the same. In 1843, he was elected Representative to the General Assembly; in 1850 and '51 elected one of the Assistant Judges of the County Court for this county; and, although he was a practical farmer and never entered the school of law, yet his knowledge of the science was quite extensive, and his practice considerable. His opinions, indeed, were often sought, and his decisions considered very reliable, scarcely less so than the majority of the bar. His death occurred on the 3d day of September, 1858.

LYNDON.

BY HON. GEO. C. CAHOON.

LYNDON is a six miles square township, situated a little north of the centre of Caledonia County, in the valley of the Passumpsic, the natural northern terminus of the beautiful valley of the Connecticut. It is bounded S. by St. Johnsbury, cornering on the S. W. by Danville, W. by Wheelock, N. by Sutton and Burke, and E. by Burke and Kirby, and lies in latitude 44 deg. 32 min. N., and in long. 4 deg. 54 min. E. Its surface is uneven, interspersed with hills and valleys, carved out by the many tributaries of the Passumpsic, flowing from other towns, and uniting in this, and forming one beautiful river. Its waters are uncommonly cold and pure. These rivulets divide the town into a fair proportion of meadow and upland. The soil is a rich loam, easy of cultivation, and very productive. There is scarcely any barren or waste land in the town, and the highest hills are arable to their summits, and are usually as fertile and productive as the low lands, and will yield abundant harvests of any crop the farmer may choose to cultivate; and they also afford excellent grazing for neat cattle, sheep, and horses. The intervales, which are overflowed by the spring and fall freshets, and sometimes — unluckily for the growing crops in the summer — are sufficiently enriched by the alluvial deposit thus given them, as not to require the manure-dressings which uplands need to restore the exhaustions of frequent harvests. In addition to these benefits, the beauty of the scenery is greatly enhanced by the variety of hill and dale produced by these various streamlets. Several sites of excellent water-power for mills and machinery are located in the town. The most noted of these are the "Great Falls" and the "Little Falls," both being on the main branch of Passumpsic River, and the Great Falls on the entire river as it leaves town; the head of the Falls, over which the railroad passes, being some 60 rods north of the south line of the town, and having a descent, in about 30 rods, of 65 feet. The Little Falls are one mile above, having a descent from the bed of the river of about 20 feet.

Both sites of Falls having rock beds, and rockbound shores, afford good facilities for the erection of factories, mills, and machinery of any kind — the river being of sufficient breadth, depth, and capacity for all needed practical purposes. The Great Falls have a capacity of operating an almost unlimited amount of machinery.

The Connecticut and Passumpsic Rivers Railroad, which runs through the town north and south near its centre, passes near both these Falls, and affords ready transportation for the manufactured or raw material.

The town was located in the summer of 1780, by Hon. Jonathan Arnold, Daniel Cahoon, and Daniel Owen, of Providence, R. I, an Exploring Committee of an association of about fifty of the most enterprising citizens of that city and its vicinity, to select ungranted territory for a township in which to settle a colony in the new State of Vermont — then famed for its beauty and fertility — and to procure its charter. Barnet, Peacham, and Ryegate were the only towns then chartered in the present limits of Caledonia County. The approach of the committee to the ungranted territory was by way of the Connecticut River Valley; and, as a natural continuation of the same valley, they followed up the Passumpsic River to its Great and Little Falls, and its extensive meadows on the main river, and its many tributaries; and made such further reconnoissances as they deemed necessary, to be sure that they were right. They then, from the summit of the high conical hill south-east of the "Corner Village," with the eye fixed the outlines now forming the boundaries of the town of Lyndon, as best comporting with the interests of their mission; and all will agree that it was a very judicious selection. Before its chartergrant, the territory thus selected was called Bestbury. The author of the name is unknown, but it is indicative of the same sentiment in the sojourners in the wilderness, which has been entertained by its settlers — that it is the better land for an earthly habitation. It appears to have been the hunting and fishing-ground of the native American; and many arrow-points of flint, and other implements — made and used by Indians — of stone, were found by the early settlers about the Falls, in the river, and on the late Gen. Cahoon's farm, indicating that those pleasant fields, which have been the chosen grounds for military parades and mock-fights, in modern times, were also the battle-grounds of the aborigines at an earlier period.

The St. Francis Indians were the last known to occupy this part of Vermont, and scarcely a year passes without some of the descendants of that tribe come out of Canada in families, and select some favorite grove to encamp in, to make and peddle baskets and nick-nacks peculiar to their race; and they make themselves quite at home, and if reminded by the owner of the premises that they are too free-and-easy with the lands and property of others, they adroitly set up prior right by priority of possession, saying, "Indians were here before white men." With such squatter sovereigns to contend with, a few presents to the matrons of the tribe, with an intimation that you wish them to leave, is the most effective way for their removal.

The town was granted by the General Assembly of Vermont, Nov. 2, 1780, to Jonathan Arnold and his associates — in all 53, inclusive of the Governors of Vermont and Rhode Island, and the Rev. James Manning, D.D., of Providence, and the others, mostly his parishioners, uniting the interests of church and state in favor of the adventurers. The name Lyndon was given it in honor of the oldest son of the first grantee, Doct. Arnold, whose name was Josias Lyndon. Historically it was chartered Nov. 20, 1780; but that recorded in the Town Clerk's office bears date June 27, 1781, after its survey, and confers on the township the usual privileges and immunities of corporate towns, dividing the proprietary shares into seventieth parts, and reserving six for public uses, viz. College, County Grammar Schools, Town Schools, minister's settlement, minister's support, and mill-right, and 9 1-7 acres of each share for roads; a whole right containing 329 1-7 acres. Also, reserving that each share have a settlement, with a house 18 feet square on it, in four years, or so soon after the war as safety will allow. Josias Lyndon Arnold was a native of Providence, liberally educated, and professionally a lawyer, and also a poet. He settled at St. Johnsbury at an early day, but it is said that his social and educational tastes did not perfectly harmonize with backwoods life. He was probably the first lawyer settled within the present limits of the county. He died in 1792, and left a widow and daughter. The widow afterwards married the Hon. Charles Marsh, of Woodstock, and was mother of the Hon. George P. Marsh, the present American Minister to Sardinia. The Hon. Jonathan Arnold, first grantee of the town, having afterwards obtained the charters of Billymead and St. Johnsbury, and settled in the last town, died therein in 1793.

The natural productions of grain are wheat, rye, oats, barley, corn, potatoes, and the usual culinary vegetables of the State; these are grown for home consumption, and some for market. More oats are raised than all other grains, as they furnish good forage both by the grain and the straw, and they find a more ready market, and are a very sure crop. Wheat used to be grown in great abundance, and formed quite an article of traffic, and the soil is well adapted to its culture at the present time; but the weevil has been its great enemy, and the cause of the failure of the crop for years; but many farms have recently successfully tried the crop again, and others will do well to follow the example. Potatoes have given good profits for their cultivation for several years, and particularly since the construction of the railroad through the town for exportation, and were before that much grown for starch, as at a previous period for the making of whiskey. Rye and barley were formerly grown here for malt and distillation; but the worm of the still has long since ceased to devour either the potatoes, the rye or the barley, and they are all much more used for the feeding of cattle than formerly.

The growing of grain is not always so ready paying as the raising of neat-cattle, sheep, and horses. In all these, Lyndon holds a prominent position. The Shearman, the Root, and the Demiss Morgans, have enjoyed a world-wide reputation. About a year since, a purchaser from the State of Georgia came here to buy a colt at a price of one thousand dollars. For symmetry of form, and for beauty of action, and for speed, they are unrivalled. Vermont horses rank high, and Lyndon horses rank with the highest. And so as to neat-cattle and sheep. Lyndon furnishes her full share of good oxen and good cows, and stock of every description, and a fair proportion of the Vermont butter found in market comes from this quarter; and many beef cattle, sheep, lambs, and calves, are marketed from this same region. Another rich product of the town is maple sugar, relieving the North from subserviency to the South for the sweets of life.

The native forest-trees are white pine, spruce, hemlock, fir, and cedar, of evergreens, and of annual foliage the sugar-maple is predominant; beech, birch, bass-wood, butternut, elm, ash, and tamarack, interspersed with a variety of trees of smaller growth, both ornamental and useful, as the cherry, the moosemissa, the raspberry, and blackberry — the two latter, with the delicious strawberry of the hay-field, yielding rich nutritive fruit, contributing much to good living.

The grant of the township being to citizens of Rhode Island, so most of its early settlers came from that State and its vicinity, Seekonk and Rehoboth, Mass. Others came from the interior of Massachusetts, and the valley of the Connecticut River in Massachusetts, Vermont, and New Hampshire; and some from the interior of New Hampshire, — Sandwich, and its neighborhood.

The first settlement was commenced by Daniel Cahoon, Jr., a native of Providence, R. I., then coming from Winchester, N. H. He, with a few chosen men, commenced a clearing on Right No. 3, allotted to his father, as original proprietor, in April, 1788. The first season was devoted to clearing land and building the log house, and growing scanty supplies of provisions; he having the honor of falling the first tree for the settlement. As the woods were full of game, and the river of trout, they fared more

sumptuously than such adventurers would now. His first experience in housekeeping was in a camp of boughs; and then in one covered with bark peeled from the trees in large sheets, and afterwards in the log house, covered with the same material, keeping bachelor's hall. After his beginning, others followed in his wake, and shortly many a new opening was made in the forest, and many a smoke, rolling upward, indicated that human habitations were there in progress of construction. Jonathan Davis, Jonas Sprague, Nathan Hines, and Daniel Hall, were of the number. They did not attempt a winter's residence, but retired to their friends for more comfortable quarters; and, after rest and social enjoyment, and obtaining supplies of necessaries, the former adventurers returned the next spring, 1789, invigorated and with new zeal in their enterprises, — and one at least with a new stimulant to action, — and that was Davis, with his wife, the first female settler of the town, they making it their home in Mr. Cahoon's new log house. This year, most of the beginners of the previous year, with several others, moved their families into town; and this year and the next were so well prospered and increased, that in 1791, so many had commenced settlements in different parts of the town, that it became desirable to have it organized for the making and repairing roads and bridges, and the better managing the prudential affairs of the community; and with the patriotic purpose of duly honoring the 4th of July, they fixed on that day for its organization; Abraham Morrill, Esq., of Wheelock, warning the meeting, and presiding until it was effected by the choice of Elder Philemon Hines, Moderator. Daniel Cahoon, Jr., was elected Town Clerk; James Spooner, Daniel Reniff, and Daniel Cahoon, Jr., Selectmen and Listers; Nehemiah Tucker, Treasurer, and Nathan Hines, Constable and Collector. There were, at the time of taking the census this year, 59 inhabitants.

It was "Voted to have the Selectmen divide the town into six highway districts, to convene the inhabitants in working on the highways near home," and surveyors were chosen; then voted to adjourn the meeting to August 1st.

At the adjourned meeting, as expressed by the record, "Thinking it necessary, and highly conducive to the settlement of the town, that measures be taken to open new roads, and erect bridges for the convenience of the inhabitants of this and other towns, where the roads are almost impassable," and declaring the inability of the inhabitants of the town to do it — Voted that the Town Clerk make and forward a petition to the next General Assembly, for a tax of two pence on each acre of land in town for the purpose. And voted to purchase the Statute Laws and suitable record books for the town, and raised money by subscription, on the credit of the town, to pay for said books.

VERMONT

Quarterly Gazetteer

A HISTORICAL MAGAZINE,

EMBRACING A DIGEST OF THE HISTORY OF EACH TOWN,

Civil, Educational, Religious, Geological and Literary.

' She stands, fair Freedom's chosen Home,
Our own beloved Green Mountain State."

" Where breathes no castled lord or cabined slave;
Where thoughts, and hands, and tongues are free."

EDITED BY

ABBY MARIA HEMENWAY,

COMPILER OF "THE POETS AND POETRY OF VERMONT."

Terms: One Dollar per Year.   Clubs solicited.

LUDLOW, VT.:
PUBLISHED BY MISS A. M. HEMENWAY,
AND SOLD BY AGENTS THROUGHOUT THE STATE,
ALBANY, N.Y.: J. MUNSELL.

A SERIES OF TOWN HISTORIES,

GROUPED IN COUNTIES.

A FREE HISTORICAL CHANNEL FOR EVERY TOWN.

Entered according to Act of Congress, in the year 1859, by ABBY MARIA HEMENWAY, in the Clerk's Office of the District Court of the District of Vermont.

TERMS:

Fifty Cents a Number; $1 a year; or Fourteen Numbers for $3—Invariably in Advance.

Postage, three cents, paid at Office of Delivery.

WANTED.—One or more Lady Assistants or Local Agents in each uncanvassed Town.

The Agents have all been instructed to solicit through or yearly subscriptions, yet to as readily take quarterly ones, with the understanding that the subscribers are to pay on delivery for each number of the work, till they may regularly discontinue the same. No subscriptions should be paid to *Traveling Agents*, unless they bear our Certificate of Agency.

CLUB TERMS.—The field is open in every Town for CLUBS, which may be sent direct to the Publisher. Terms—EVERY FOURTH NUMBER FREE; or for Four *Yearly*, or equivalent, a copy of the Poets and Poetry of Vermont, 12mo. 400 pp.; or Six Photographs of leading Vermont Poets; or for the above list doubled, Twelve Plates, or a Plated and elegantly Gilt copy of the Poets; or for Four Yearly Subscriptions, a copy of the Vermont School Journal—a work devoted to a cause that ought to bring twice the patronage it has yet received; or Dr. C. H. Cleavland's ably conducted Medical Journal, published at Cincinnati, O.

HISTORICAL CONTENTS.

HISTORICAL CONTRIBUTIONS

FOR ESSEX COUNTY.—Bloomfield, by Hon. A. Burbank; Brighton, by N. P. Bowman, Esq.; Brunswick, by Mrs. Margaret G. Marshall; Canaan, by Geo. W. Hartshorne, Esq.; Concord, by J. E. Woodbury; Granby, by Loomis Wells; Guildhall, by Milton Cutler; Lemington, by Arthur T. Holbrook; Lunenburgh, by Hon. Jonah Brooks; Maidstone, by Hon. Charles Rich; County Chapter of Natural History, by H. A. Cutting. East Haven, Granby, and Victory, to be supplied.

FOR FRANKLIN COUNTY.—Introductory, or County Chapter, by George F. Houghton, Esq.; Bakersfield, by Rev. Caleb W. Piper; Berkshire, by Hon. Stephen Royce; Enosburgh, by Hon. Alvin H. Baker; Fairfax, by Pres. Upham and John Ufford; Fairfield, by Col. Samuel Perley; Fletcher, by Benj. A. King-ley, Esq.; Franklin, by Edwin R. Towle, Esq.; Georgia, by Rev. Alvah Sabin; Highgate, by Amos Skeels, Esq.; Montgomery, by Nelson W. Clapp, Esq.; Richford, by Rev. B. J. Livingston; Sheldon, by Hon. Alfred Keith and Hon. D. D. Weed; St. Albans, by Rev. J. E. Rankin; Swanton, by Rev. John B. Perry; Geology of the County, by Rev. John B. Perry.

No. V, CHITTENDEN COUNTY (now in press), will be embellished with portrait of Gov. Van Ness. The succeeding Nos. of the *Gazetteer* may now be expected to go to press quarterly, and to be drawn as fast as the subscriptions of its patrons cancel its printing bills.

LYNDON.

BY HON GEORGE C. CAHOON.

[Concluded.]

At town meeting, March 12, 1792, Elder Philemon Hines was chosen moderator; Daniel Cahoon, town clerk; Daniel Cahoon, Philemon Hines and James Spooner, selectmen and listers; Nathan Hines, constable; and Nehemiah Tucker, treasurer. "Voted, that the selectmen be paid four shillings per day for services actually performed for the town."

"Voted, that a tax of six pounds be assessed for exigence expenses of the town. At freemen's meeting, 1792, Daniel Cahoon, Jr., was elected the first representative of the town.

Prior to 1792 all taxes and assessments for highways and other purposes were by common consent and voluntary subscription, and enforced by self-will and patriotic purpose. The first grand list was made this year, composed of 30 persons, and the total of each item and the amount of the whole was as follows: polls 28; 26 acres of land, 22 oxen, 22 cows, 6 3 years old cattle, 7 2 years old cattle, 2 yearlings and 11 horses—amount £359, equal to $1,196.66. Of those who composed that list, William Fisher, the last survivor, died in town, June 30, 1861, aged 96 years 3 months. The family name of only six of the number remains in town; Cahoon; Easterbrook (there were in the list two of this name—Benjamin and Caleb), three Fishers, Jeremiah, William and James; and two McGaffeys, John and Andrew; Jonas Sprague, and Zebina Wilder.

1793, at March meeting, Daniel Cahoon was re-elected town clerk, and Daniel Cahoon, Daniel Reniff and Nehemiah Tucker were elected selectmen and listers; and Andrew McGaffey, constable. In the early period of the settlement milling and marketing had to be done at Barnet, over 20 miles, and at Newbury, about 35 miles distant, on

44

almost impassible roads, as best they could; Col. Wallace of Newbury, was the wholesale commissariat of Northern Vermont; at a later period they obtained ample supplies at Barnet, and still later at St. Johnsbury. Their luxuries, though few, were with a keen relish enjoyed with each other. In a brief period the patron of the enterprise, Daniel Cahoon, Jr., nurtured under milder skies and kindlier influences, not having a constitution of sufficient power and vigor to keep up with his mental and bodily exertions, became prostrate with that insidious and flattering but fatal disease, the consumption, long ere the meridian of life; but to the last he sought the faithful performance of all trusts, and the best good of the infant plantation. He had rendered himself useful to other settlements, as St. Johnsbury, Billymead, now Sutton, and Barton, presiding at Barton at its organization. To the great sorrow of his friends and neighbors, it remained for him to fill up with his death the notable coincidences of his relationship to the history of Lyndon, that he was its first settler, first town clerk of the first board of selectmen and listers, the first justice of the peace, the first representative, and holding all these offices at the time of his death, finally to be the first person who died in town, which occurred June 11th, 1793, aged 26 years 4 months. His son, Benjamin P. Cahoon, then nearly 2 years of age, was the second male child born in town, Lyndon Hines being the first, and Lydia Wilder being the first female born in town. B. P. Cahoon removed from Lyndon in 1817, and in the year 1861, died at Kenosha, Wisconsin, a noted gardener. It remained for a younger brother, William Cahoon, then 19 years of age, who had come to the rescue, to take the helm of affairs and go ahead, which he did, from that time forth, successfully to the close of his life, May 30th, 1833. During that period he had the pleasure of seeing the town become thickly populated, and supplied with all needful advantages for home comfort and for common school and academic education and religious worship, with a competency of property, himself having sustained meekly all the offices of honor, profit and trust in town, county, and state, which he could desire, and the last four years of his life represented the state in the congress of the United States.

In May, 1793, Daniel Cahoon, Sen., one of the locating committee and a charter grantee of the township, moved his family into town, occupying a portion of the log house erected by his son in 1788, which had been essentially enlarged and otherwise improved for comfort. He was the only one of the original proprietors who settled in town. His transition from the wharves and storehouses of the importing merchant, and the councils of the city, and the counting room of the forge and furnace, in which he had spent the vigor of his manhood, to this backwoods settlement, was very great; but such as the devastations of the war of the Revolution occasioned to him as to many others. He did not possess physical strength sufficient to endure the rugged labor of the farmer, but he had the mental ability and ready tact to render himself very useful in the management of the financial and prudential affairs of the community, and on the death of his son Daniel, he was immediately chosen to fill the town offices thus made vacant, and performing their duties acceptably, he was re-elected thereto many years; having been town representative 8 years, selectman 11, and town clerk 15 in succession, to which offices his son William succeeded on his retirement, and held the latter office 21 years in succession, resigning it in 1829, on being elected to congress. In 1808, when Daniel Cahoon retired from the office, he received high commendation from a special committee appointed to report in the premises, and a vote of thanks from the town for the faithful and satisfactory manner in which he had performed the duties of the various town offices which he had held, and particularly of town clerk, which is of record. He died September 13th, 1811, aged 74 years, being gored by a bull not known to be vicious, when passing through a barnyard, and not on his guard. The concourse at his funeral was much the largest that had then ever assembled in the town on such an occasion, numbering eight or nine hundred, and many from other towns.

In 1793, 43 were listed, one deceased being omitted, showing an increase during the year of 14, some of whom were young men arriving at manhood, others were from immigration; in which latter class we find Daniel Cahoon, Sen., Widow Cynthia Jenks, and her two sons, Nehemiah and Brown Jenks, Calvin and Jesse Doolittle, John and Roswell Johnson, Joel Fletcher, Ephraim Hubbard, Job Olney, Samuel Winslow, and others, active, useful citizens. The amount of the list was £479 personal property, 34 oxen, 35 cows, cattle 2 years old 6, cattle of 1 year 10, and 8 horses, showing an increase of 32 neat cattle. John Johnson was the first merchant in town. In 1794, 50 were listed. Its amount was £583, the increase in neat cattle was 8, of horses 6. Joel Ross, Simeon Smith, Peter Tibbets, Benjamin Bucklin, Jonathan Parks, Jonathan Robinson and others, moved into town. Mr. Robinson at an early day moved into Barton. During the current year from June, '93 to June, '94, the settlers though well prospered in their agricultural pursuits were sorely afflicted by the sickness and sudden death of several of their members; first, of Daniel Cahoon, Jr., as already noticed, in June '93, and, in the same month, of a son aged 12 years of Samuel Winslow, by a falling tree: in May '94, of a daughter of Daniel Hall of canker-rash, aged 12 years; on the 4th June, '94, of Philemon Hines, a Baptist elder of estimable character, by suicide — verdict of jury of inquest, cause insanity — and 12th August, of Widow Cynthia Jenks, of lockjaw. Mrs. Jenks commenced the first settlement of the Corner village, occupying the grounds where the Fletcher buildings stand, now owned by E. A. Cahoon. After her death her log house became noted as the temporary residence of many a new settler entering town, and as the first school-house, being first occupied as such by Abel Carpenter, Esq., and afterwards by Dr. Abner Jones, who then was or subsequently became a Baptist preacher. This year was also notable for the one in which they began to marry in the settlement, and the first transpiring was that of Jeremiah Washburn and Hannah Orcutt, June 16th. Mr. Washburn previously living in Lyndon, and the ceremony having been performed by Daniel Cahoon, Esq., it has been reputed to have been the first that occurred in town, but the bride's father resided in Billymead (now Sutton) and the wedding was at her home, and the first marriage in Lyndon was of Roswell Johnson and Naomi Bartlett by the same magistrate, Oct. 5, 1794.

1795, at a freemen's meeting in February,

to elect member to congress, Wm. Cahoon and three others were admitted freemen, Daniel Buck had 14 votes, and Nathaniel Niles 4. At March meeting, Daniel Cahoon, Jesse Doolittle and Nehemiah Tucker were elected selectmen and listers. The number of lists were 65, and the amount of the list £732, or $2440, an increase of nearly $500, arising from immigration, internal improvements, and increase of cattle and horses, of the former 36 and the latter 10. Joel and Wait Bemiss, John and Josiah Brown, Caleb Parker, Wm. Ruggles and Ziba Tute, all good citizens, moved into town this year, and others also. Some of the notable occurrences of the year, were the building of the first framed house by Nathaniel Jenks, Esq., a scientific and practical surveyor who about this time moved into town, and a Mr. Arnold put up some imperfect mills on the site now occupied by Mr. Kimball's planing mill, on the branch near the Corner, with a view to acquire the mill right, but the town not accepting them, voted said mill right to William Cahoon, if he would build thereon suitable mills, which he did to acceptance. Mr. Ziba Tute, who some years after removed to Windsor, was a man stout and athletic, and of noble daring, as is shown by an occurrence at the burning of the Tontine building at Windsor. The building had many occupants, merchants and others; when the fire was raging and no hopes of saving the building, it was told that in one of the rooms, in an upper story there was a quantity of powder stored, which if not removed would soon explode and imperil the lives of many, and spread the fire. The avenues to the powder were all closed except by a long ladder — Mr. Tute had no personal interest in the matter, but seeing others unwilling to run the risk, dashed forward and promptly ascended the ladder, opened the window and entered the almost suffocating room, seized the powder cask with its hoops on fire, clutched it under his arm, and descended the ladder with it but little singed, extinguished its burning hoops, and put it in a safe depository, much to his own comfort, and the great joy of all others.

In 1796 Wm. W. McGaffey was elected selectman and lister in lieu of Mr. Doolittle. The lists were 73, neat cattle, 209, an increase of 74; amount of list, £1054.15 or $3515.83; and Abel Carpenter, Esq., Capt. Elias Bemiss, S. Smith Matthewson, Gains Peck, Ely Dickerman, Joseph Harris, Peleg Hix and others came to reside in town. Esquire Carpenter, as he was familiarly called, or

captain in reference to his military proclivities, was a lieutenant and commissary in the Rhode Island line in the army of the Revolution, carrying in his person, as an evidence of his valor, one of the enemy's bullets received in battle, for which he received immediately an invalid pension of small amount, and afterwards a more munificent pension under the general pension laws, commensurate with his official position in the army; which were in this case meritoriously bestowed, as he was a brave man and good officer. He used facetiously to call his invalid pension his short staff and his Revolutionary pension his long staff, saying that Uncle Sam made better provision for him when old than when he was young; he was thankful for what he could get. It so occurred that he did not, when living, receive the pension that he should as commissary. By a new construction of the law his children obtained it after his decease. At the time he moved into Lyndon he possessed a good practical business education, acquired in part by his official services in the army, and having an aptitude to turn the same to account, and also to impart it to others, he soon became the first school master in town, and a principal officer to manage the town affairs for some 20 years, in various capacities. Capt. Bemiss was also a prominent man, as also his sons, two of whom, Elias and Welcome, were state senators. A military company was organized this year of about 50 persons, and soon increased to 76.

In 1797, Daniel Cahoon, Nathaniel Jenks and Abel Carpenter were elected selectmen and listers. They were also the principal trial justices for several years; and integrity of purpose seems to have characterized the courts of that day, for an early lawyer is reported to have said of the first, that if he had a bad cause, he would be the last man in the world he would have try it, but if he had a good one, the very first. The same might have been said of the others. Mr. Cahoon was the favorite justice in the court of matrimony, usually receiving his fees, if paid at all, in the currency of the times— "change of works" with the swain in his peculiar vocation or calling, the contrast sometimes rendering it amusing. There were 75 lists, amounting to $4374.50, exceeding the list of last year $858.67. Neat cattle, 229, and 31 horses. Timothy Ide, two families of Houghtons, two of Evans and two of Norris, Caleb Parker and three or four other families moved into town. In 1798, the same were elected selectmen and listers. There were 85 lists, 264 neat cattle and 43 horses—increase of neat cattle, 35; of horses, 12. Total lists, S5126; increase of the year, $751.50. The town this year had quite an ingress of valuable citizens, of whom were Leonard and Henry Watson, Eben Peck 1st, Levi Lockling, Jacob Houghton, Elijah Ross, Zerah Evans, Jude Kimball, John Woodman, Nathan Parker, Benjamin Walker, and Nathan Hubbard. Mr. Woodman was father of the Rev. Jonathan Woodman, a popular Freewill Baptist preacher.

In 1799, selectmen and listers same as the three years preceding. The lists were 100; neat cattle, 336, and horses, 63—increase of neat cattle, 72; of horses, 32. Total list, $6669.25; increase, $1543.25. A number of good citizens moved into town this year, of whom were Isaiah Fisk, the father of the Rev. Dr. Wilbur Fisk, late president of the Wesleyan University at Middletown, Conn., who, at that time being six or seven years old, came with the family, and remained here until he commenced his academic education, some ten or more years afterwards; also the Hoffmans, the Sheldons, the Winsors, Bacons; Dr. Abner Jones, who was also a preacher; Eleazer Peck and Josiah Gates, whose daughters, Elizabeth, Lucy and Sally, became the good wives of Elijah Ross, Eliphas Graves and David McGaffey; Mrs. Lucy Graves marrying Capt. Elias Bemiss for her second husband and his second wife. Mr. Job Sheldon, though he resided in town but a short time, left behind him the lasting remembrance of the generosity of the sailor, by his donation to the town of ten acres of valuable land, near its centre, for a public cemetery and common.

In 1800, Daniel Cahoon, William Winsor and Isaiah Fisk were elected selectmen and listers. There were 110 lists, 347 neat cattle, and 77 horses—increase, 11 cattle and 14 horses. Amount of list, $7186.50—increase, $517.25. The town received a good recruit of new settlers this year, of whom were the Blys, Browns, Wilmarths, Alphs, Fletcher, Field; John Gates the miller; Haskell the clothier, the Scotts, Ripley, and others. There is incorporated into the town records of this year the formation of a religious society for the purpose of settling a minister, and a vote of the town of 100 acres of the minister's settlement right to any acceptable preacher who would settle in town, and of said society's tendering such settlement to Elder Stephen Place, understood to have been a Baptist, who did not accept the offer.

In 1801, Daniel Cahoon, Nathaniel Jenks and Isaiah Fisk were selectmen and listers. The number of lists were 133; there being 439 neat cattle, and 103 horses and colts—whole amount, $8608. Of those who moved into town this year, were James Ayer, Joel Bemiss, Abel Brown, Oliver Chaffee, Ira Evans, Wm. Houghton the tanner, Samuel Park, Job Randall, Abraham Smith, James Shearman and Aaron Walker. Mr. Randall and Mr. Smith have both represented the town and held various offices. Mr. Randall still lives, in a vigorous old age, much respected, and is probably now the oldest person living in town. Mr. Shearman obtained a celebrity for good horses.

In 1802, ten years from taking the first grand list, Daniel Cahoon, Wm. Winsor and Isaiah Fisk were the selectmen, and William Cahoon, Abraham Smith and Nehemiah Jenks, listers. The lists were 147; neat cattle, 450; horses, 75; and sheep, 420; amounting, inclusive of the valuation of improved real estate—as is to be considered in all the lists—to $9118.75; thus giving the progress of events in town for the first decenary after its organization, its gradual increase and means, and the basis of its taxation. At this period, the settlement had got under good headway, and, owing to the uniform goodness of the soil, and the charter provision that settlements should be made on each right, to prevent forfeiture, "as soon as safety would allow after the war," 50 acres being accorded by common consent to such settler; and being thus obtained scot free, the settlements became very general and nearly simultaneous on each right; roads were opened to every section of the town, encouraging others to follow, which they did rapidly; so that soon the town became populous. Like gregarious animals, the early settlers were a little clannish—grouping together in clusters coming from the same locality, state, or territory, so far as circumstances would allow, which phase is not entirely obliterated; but many of the old landmarks are removed by time, and a denser population succeeding, with the amalgamation of the second and third generations by marriage, it is less noticeable.

It may well be believed that the old folks were a merry set of jokers by the nick-names they gave the different localities in town in its early settlement, as Pudding Hill, Squabble Hollow, Mount Hunger, Hard Scrabble, Hog Street, Shanticut, Musquito District, the Whale's Back, Owlsboro', Egypt, and Pleasant Street, from being the residence of some fair ladies; and most of these names are yet familiarly known, but not confessed to be truthfully descriptive of the present condition of those localities. A good degree of shrewdness characterized the inhabitants, and being frugal and industrious, they made themselves comfortable with what they had and could acquire, and happy in the anticipation of possessing a competency for ordinary gratification, and obtaining an additional store for the evening of life, and if they have not succeeded to their utmost wishes, it should not be attributed to want of calculation and forethought, so much as to unforeseen events.

About this time the town canvassed the matter of putting up a building to answer the double purpose of a town hall and meeting house, and fixed its location at the Centre, but deferred the enterprise. It was finally erected in 1809, but the expense exceeding the estimate after an expenditure by the town in its corporate character of over $1000, it was left unfinished, and occupied with temporary seats and desks for several years, being finally completed by the sale of pews, to be occupied by the different denominations in proportion to ownership, reserving to the town its use for town meetings. But other appropriate churches, needful for worship having been built, the old house by common consent, was yielded up to the town, and the same has recently been remodeled and renovated exclusively for a town hall.

In 1812, by the concurrent votes of the town, and a religious society associated for the purpose, Elder Phinehas Peck, a Methodist minister who had preached in town some years before, was permanently settled as the first minister of the town, and in consideration thereof the selectmen, by vote of the town, conveyed to him a lot of land, being a third of the right reserved for minister's settlement. Mr. Peck continued to officiate as such until about 1819, acceptably and with good success; when his health failing, he ceased from his labors here, and his charge in 1820 was supplied, in the person of the Rev. Daniel Fillmore, a very talented man and able preacher of the Methodist itinerant ministry, and has ever since been cared for in the same manner, the last 2 years by the Rev. Lewis Hill, and the present by the Rev. P. M. Granger. The Methodists built a new chapel in the Corner village in 1840, with a small basement vestry, and in 1855 or 6, the house was renovated, the vestry enlarged to the size of the house, with an ante-room and stair-way from the basement,

and the whole new painted and papered. Since that period the Congregational Meeting House, which was built in 1826-7, at the Corner, has been new modeled and thoroughly fitted up inside and out. In 1848 the Freewill Baptists, built a neat church at the Centre. The Universalists built another of the same dimensions soon after. The last is noticeable for its singular vane—an angel in the act of blowing his trumpet. The academy was built in 1831, and was incorporated that year by the name of "Caledonia County Grammar School at Lyndon," and subsequently endowed by an act of the General Assembly of the state with a portion of the Grammar School lands lying in the county of Caledonia reserved by the charters of the towns for the use of county grammar schools within, and throughout the state, and to be under the control of said General Assembly for ever, "subject to the opinion of the Supreme Court as to the validity of said act against an act establishing a County Grammar School at Peacham," which decision was that said lands were irrevocably granted to the Peacham corporation, and that the corporation of the Lyndon School could take nothing by their grant, which decision, in view of the charter reservations, and the evident intent of the legislature making those reservations, and the spirit of the government itself to confer equal privileges on all, was never relished as good law by the Lyndonenses, compelling them individually to raise funds which they believed should emanate from another source. Henry Chase, Esq., a graduate of Yale College, and his sister, Miss Ada Chase, a lady highly educated, and a graduate of Mount Holyoke Seminary, are present principals and worthy of good patronage. The churches and academy have each a cupola, and all have good bells, excepting the Universalist. The religious community who keep up public worship are divided into four congregations, two at the Corner, the Methodist and Congregationalists, and two at the Centre, the Freewill Baptists and the Universalists. Each is well attended. The Methodists when they held their meetings for worship at the Centre were much the most numerous, and are probably so now, but many of their members were discommoded by the erection of the new chapel at the Corner, one and a half miles further from them, and have since attended other meetings at the Centre, generally the Freewill Baptist, whereby their numbers were considerably increased, the congregation formerly worshiping at the north part of the town gathered by Elder Quimby having also united with it. Its desk has been supplied by very worthy preachers, Elders Quimby, Moulton, Woodman, Jackson, Smith, and the present incumbent, the Rev. M. C. Henderson. The Congregationalists have usually been supplied by able preachers, the Revs. Messrs. Tenny, Scales, Thayer, Greenleaf and Hale, are of the number. And the Universalists by their best, the Rev. Messrs. Tabor, Scott and others. There are some Calvinistic Baptists in town, and others who would prefer the Episcopal church service, but neither sufficiently numerous to maintain the public worship of the order. The writer does not possess the present statistical numbers of any of the denominations, having expected that they would be furnished from another source.

In 1802, '03, '04, '05, the Graves, Mathewsons, Roots and Williams, and other farmers; and the brothers Nathaniel and Samuel B. Goodhue, lawyers; and Doctors Hubbard Field and Olney Fuller; and the Cushings, house joiners, cabinet and chair makers, settled in the town; and from that period to 1810, Charles F. H. Goodhue, Bela Shaw, Jr., Asa S. and Alanson and George B. Shaw, brothers; and Benjamin F. and Reuben H. Deming, his brother; at a later period all the last engaged in merchandise in stores of Chandler, Bigelow & Co. at Lyndon and elsewhere, and of Daniel Chamberlin & Co. and Chamberlin & Deming. Alpheus Houghton and his brother Elijah, farmers, with their families, and the Emerys and Bundys, also farmers; Major Elias Clark, Jr., saddler; Samuel Hoyt, 1st, farmer, soon after his brother Dr. Moses Hoyt; Dr. Meigs, John M. Foster, attorney; Ephraim Chamberlin, Esq., innkeeper, and afterwards mill owner; James Knapp, mill wright; Josiah Rawson, and afterwards his brother Dr. Simeon Rawson. In 1811, Isaac Fletcher, an educated man and well read lawyer, came in town, and soon after William and Joseph and their father Ichabod Ide; Daniel Bowker, cabinet maker, now the oldest resident at the Corner; Warren Parker, clothier; Jonathan and Nehemiah Weeks, tanners and shoemakers; Richard and Nathan Stone, saddlers; Abel Edgell, Bela Shaw, Senr., and Charles Stone, farmers; Richard and Charles Stone, brothers, were both afterwards deacons; and not far from the same time, Josiah C. and Samuel A. Willard, brothers, who came into the country at an early day with their mother and grandfather, Daniel Cahoon, Sen., but resided part of the time in Sutton and Burke and elsewhere, became permanently settled in Lyndon. Mr. B. F. Deming went to Danville to fill official positions of which we shall speak elsewhere. Mr. R. H. Deming after quitting trade became a Methodist preacher, and removed to Wisconsin, and has officiated as county and city clerk at Kenosha; Mr. Bela Shaw, Jr., removed west, and at Rockford, Illinois, held the office of judge of probate several years. About the year 1816, '17, quite a colony of good citizens came to Lyndon as settlers, from Sandwich, N. H., and its vicinity, headed by three brothers, Major Anron and Elders Joseph and Daniel Quimby, with their large families. They were of the Freewill Baptist denomination of Christians, the major devoting himself to farming, and the elders dividing their time between secular and ecclesiastic pursuits, as they appeared to have a call in either vocation; never being idle, but always actively and usefully employed. They drew in their train the Gilmans, Prescotts, Rices and Randalls, and others, with their families. Elder Joseph left the town after a few years, yet it can hardly be believed to return to Sandwich for agricultural purposes, for the comparison between Lyndon and Sandwich, both for ease of culture and the amount of product, must have been greatly in favor of Lyndon. After his departure, Elder Daniel doubled his diligence, and mostly at his own expense built a meeting house near the centre of that settlement, and not far from his own house in the north part of the town, and succeeded in collecting a large church, which continuing to worship there until 1840, when the Methodists having vacated the meeting house at Lyndon Centre, and some of the Freewill denomination residing in that vicinity, it was deemed good church tactics to remove their place of worship to the Centre, which was done, consolidating the different memberships in one communion at that place; by so doing, they had the accession of the Methodists in that locality disaffected by the building of their new chapel at the Corner. Their congregation being very much enlarged, the effect was to raise the standard of their meetings by calling into their pulpit their best preachers before named, and occasioned the demand for a better house of worship, which was built in 1848. There was no better man than Elder Quimby, but his severe secular labors would not allow him as a preacher to equal his worthy brothers in the ministry, who devoted themselves exclusively to the gospel.

The descendants of the early settlers arriving at maturity, nurtured in the school of industry and economy, became important members of the community. Since that period others have come from abroad, who, from their business capabilities or professional skill, have filled large spaces in public estimation, of whom are Gen. E. B. Chase and Halsey Riley, merchants at an early period. Philip Goss, Esq., and Doctors Phineas Spalding, Freedom Dinsmore, and Abel Underwood, Nicholas Baylies, Thomas Bartlett, Jr., Moses Chase, Henry S. Bartlett, and Samuel B. Mattocks, lawyers by profession, but not all in practice; and subsequently Doctors Hoyt, Carpenter, Sanborn, Darling, Mattocks, Newell, Denison, Blanchard, Scott and Stevens; Doctors Cahoon and Houghton of the town helping to fill the ranks — as a class distinguished for high professional attainments — and more recently Jonathan W. Colby and Wm. H. McGaffey, merchants; L. R. Brown, goldsmith; J. N. Bartlett, silver plater; G. T. Spencer, marble engraver; Hill, Howe, Baker, Welton & Currier, harness makers and carriage trimmers; E. Underwood, merchant tailor; and the Millers, carriage makers; there are two establishments, one, Miller & Trull, very extensive; the other, C. C. Miller & Co. — both do excellent work, in good times employing about 30 men. The Weeks, Quimbys, and W. H. McGaffey, merchants, and the Cahoons, lawyers and physicians, were descendants of the early settlers; and in all parts of the town there are those equally meritorious in their places, as Messrs. Bigelow, Baker, Pearl, Folsom, Thompson, Ingalls, Cunningham, Chaffee, Knapp, Fletcher, Sanborn, Spalding and Wakefield, but where all are equal it is impossible to discriminate, and we have no space to enroll all. The mass of the population are thrifty, well-to-do farmers, with a proper sprinkling of mechanics and professional men to inculcate good principles, keep good order and assuage and alleviate pain and sickness.

Of the selectmen, listers and other town officers, since the time specifically given, our limits will not allow the detail; all were competent to perform those duties, but the experienced could do so with greater ease, hence the old gentlemen, Daniel Cahoon, William Winsor and Abraham Smith were held in the service a few years longer; and then Judge Fisk, Gen. William Cahoon and Abel Carpenter, Esq., succeeded them in those offices very many years, some of them till 1827. Alpheus Houghton, Job Randall, Elias Be-

miss, Samuel A. Willard, Samuel W. Winsor, William Way, Benjamin F. Deming, Josiah C. Willard, Bela Shaw, Jr., Halsey Riley and Jerry Dickerman participating as selectmen, or listers, and the last five principally in the latter office, for a period of some 20 years. Since then there has been more change, either on the principle of rotation in office, or taking turns in doing the drudgery of it. New comers and younger men, as the Bemisses, Bigelow, Baker, Chase, Chamberlain, Cunningham, Chaffees, Evanses, Fletchers, Folsom, Goss, Graves, the Houghtons, Hoyts, Ingalls, Ide, McKoy, McGaffeys, Parks, Pearl, Pierce, Pike, Prescott, Powers, C. Randall, Ray, Sanborns, Spauldings, Thompsons and Weeks, with some others, alternately being the ins and the outs of said offices most of the time since — all, from first to last, tinctured with the infallibility of town rights and town prerogatives as against an individual. And the longer retained in office, the more tenacious, apparently on the principle of regal government that "the king can do no wrong," the officer acting in the representative character, embodying himself in the corporation, arrogates for it all he could desire it to have. We suspect that these sentiments are not confined to town corporations, but pervade much larger communities, though justice requires the admission that this arises, probably, from an over anxiety to faithfully perform their official duties, making individual rights subservient to the public good. We are apt to flatter ourselves that we possess greater merits and virtue than our neighbors, and may consider ourselves exemplary and praiseworthy in many particulars, for good qualities and good acts incident to all, yet in two things, if the Lyndonenses do not excel, they at least are commendable for their well doing, the one is for their care for the poor, the other their liberal expenditures, both publicly and individually, for the support of education, fostering public and private schools. For many years furnishing a throng of students to academies abroad, they have since, by private munificence, erected an academy at home, supplied it with a good apparatus, and then without funds, sustained it. Before this several had fitted for and completed their college course. Several have since fitted here and elsewhere, and received degrees at college, at a much less expense in preparing than formerly, and it is a noticeable fact that many more young men in this town than in any other town in the county or this section of the state, with perhaps the exception of Peacham, have obtained liberal educations, and many others, not graduates, with finished academic and professional educations, have gone forth to do honor to themselves and their country in their appropriate spheres. The late

REV. WILBUR FISK, D D.,

the eloquent divine, and learned president of Wesleyan University at Middletown, Conn., a model of Christian excellence and purity, stands at the head of the list of Lyndon graduates in 1815 of Brown University. He was son of the Hon. Isaiah Fisk of this town, was born August 31, 1792, at Brattleboro, fitted for college at Peacham, and first entered college at Burlington; but that institution being suspended by the war, he transferred his relationship to that at Providence, R. I., where he graduated with distinguished honor. He entered the law office of the late Hon. Isaac Fletcher, and grasped the elementary principles with avidity, but the practice did not harmonize with his views of Christian duty and inclination, and after a year or two, a portion of which was spent in Maryland as tutor in a gentleman's family, he yielded to his sense of duty and became an itinerant Methodist minister in 1818. This as some would think it, was not placing his light under a bushel, but where his talents like a luminous body became resplendent and shone all around. As is usual in the conference, as the representative body of the denomination is called, he was stationed here and there, where his experience and talents would seem to indicate, and to some places where his innate modesty and infirm health would make him, in anticipation, quail, but where the reality fully justified the appointment; he never failed to be most acceptably received wherever he went, and there were probably but few, if any, his superiors in his order. He was soon appointed principal of the institution at Wilbraham, at which place he labored hard and successfully, and was appointed a bishop, which he declined, and afterwards first president of the Wesleyan University which he accepted, having presided over the institution at Wilbraham 5 years, being elected to the last office in 1830, 15 years and 4 months after graduating; over this new institution, in its commencement laboring under many difficulties, and the greatest the want of funds, he presided with distinguished ability the remainder of his life, about 9 years, dying the 22d of February, 1839. During the term of his presidency, for the double purpose of solicit-

ing aid for the university, and promoting his health and also enriching his mind, he visited Europe, or to use the phrase of his biographer, Prof. Holdich, "at the meeting of the joint board of the Wesleyan University it was resolved to give the president a commission to Europe for the two-fold purpose of benefiting his health and advancing the interests of the institution, particularly having in view, for the university, additions to its philosophical apparatus and library. On the 4th September, 1835, Rev. Dr. Wayland, president of Brown's University, officially communicated to the Rev. Mr. Fisk that the board of fellows of Brown's University had conferred on him unanimously the degree of doctor of divinity. This was very acceptable from his *alma mater* on the eve of his departure for the tour of the east, which occurred on the 8th day of September, 1835. His wife and a Mr. Lane, afterwards professor in the university, accompanied him; they were absent over a year, making an interesting and profitable tour to the most important cities and places of Europe, including England, France, Italy, Ireland and Scotland, and returning in November, 1836, invigorated with health and well laden with very valuable donations as desired for the university. All were well satisfied with the result of his mission. During his absence, the maxim, Out of sight, out of mind, was not true in regard to him, for the general conference elected him to the office of a bishop, his former election to that office being in 1829, by the Canada conference. He declined this also, considering his duties to the university paramount, preferring duty to honor, and also disregarding great offers of wealth if he would accept that office, and continued to do his whole duty to the university as long as health would admit, and it continued to increase in popularity and numbers under his administration. His incidents of travel in Europe, published by request, is an interesting work; he published other works of interest, some were election sermons, and upon other occasions, and some dissertations on matters of ecclesiastical polity, all well worthy of perusal. In placing the name of Fisk at the head of the list of Lyndon graduates, I have made a biographical digression unintended in this place, yet perhaps more appropriate with his friends than if placed elsewhere alone as intended in some niche of our sketch, as we should deem it imperfect without him; for we think or speak of him but to admire and venerate. His last sickness was of pulmonary complaints, which troubled him through life, and it is said were in the last stages extremely painful, yet borne with great fortitude and meekness. He died as the good man dieth, aged 47½ years nearly.

GEORGE B. SHAW, ESQ.,

Was the next on the list graduated at the University of Vermont in 1819, aged about 19 years, and was immediately appointed tutor in the university. He subsequently studied law in the offices of Messrs. Griswold and Follett of Burlington, and of Hon. I. Fletcher of Lyndon; was admitted to the bar in 1822, opened an office at Danville, and received a generous patronage of the business done there, which was not great, acquitting himself handsomely in its performance. By the influence of his father-in-law, Hon. Wm. A. Griswold, who formerly resided in Danville, he was induced to move to Burlington in 1823, where he remained some two years, and then returned to Danville; afterwards, when Lowell, Mass., broke like a meteor on the horizon, he removed there, and, after remaining a year or two, removed to Ottawa, Canada, and remained several years, and then returned to Burlington, which he made his permanent residence for life. When young, Mr. Shaw was remarkably precocious, possessing maturity far beyond his years; and in early manhood was characterized by the same trait, coming forward as the learned scholar and accomplished gentleman much earlier than his youthful associates. He was an elegant penman, a good accountant and a ready debater; of uncommon suavity of manners, he could render himself, with ease, the centre of any social circle in which he mingled. The young and the old alike regarded him as a shining ornament of society. After his return to Burlington he became absorbed in other matters than his professional pursuits, in part relative to the estate of Mr. Bigelow, father of his second wife (the first having died young, when at Danville). And at this time, while residing at Burlington, he was elected by the general assembly, several years in succession, reporter of the decisions of the Supreme Court; and afterwards his partner, William Weston, Esq., received the same appointment several years. Previously to this, during the administration of Governor Crafts, Mr. Shaw held the office of secretary to the governor and council, combining the present offices of secretary of the senate and secretary of civil and military affairs; both offices of secretary and reporter were very efficiently and acceptably filled by him. His son, Wm. G. Shaw, Esq., has since, under Gov. Fletcher,

held the office of secretary of civil and military affairs, and has for a number of years been supreme court reporter, and now holds the office. The father died in 1853, of epilepsy.

GEORGE C. CAHOON

Graduated at the University of Vermont in 1820, and his name is under the head of the practicing lawyers in town.

REV. JOHN Q. A. EDGELL

Graduated at the same institution, and was settled in Massachusetts as a Congregational clergyman, possessing good talents and a genial disposition, and presumed to be an ornament of his profession, and is supposed to be still living.

REV. JAMES L. KIMBALL,

Of the same order, graduated at Dartmouth College about the year 1823 or '24, and having studied divinity, was ordained, and enjoyed bright prospects of eminence and future usefulness, when the destroying angel entered the abode of his father, Jude Kimball, Esq., with the flattering but insidious disease of consumption, and first took a beautiful and accomplished sister, Mary, in 1826, and in quick succession, an elder brother, Benjamin, and himself. And the flowers of youth were faded, and the early hopes of parents and friends blighted.

EDWARD A. CAHOON

Also graduated at the University of Vermont in 1838, and is in the list of Lyndon lawyers.

FREDERICK H. STONE

Graduated at Hanover, and is settled in Iowa.

WILLIAM W. CAHOON

Graduated at Dartmouth in 1845, and at the Medical College at Woodstock in 1848, and subsequently at a medical college in New York, where he was afterwards connected with the institution, under Doctor Mott, as assistant physician, where he made good progress in science and made himself useful about a year, when he contracted a pestilential disease and died. None had better abilities and higher aspirations for excellence and professional usefulness than he had. Having studied with able and skillful physicians and surgeons, attended the best lectures in the state, and received his diploma, in pursuit of still higher attainments, he sought the fountain heads of the profession in New York, resolved to never unskillfully tamper with human life in the practice of his profession, if adequate knowledge could be attained, and in his laudable endeavors to make himself more useful by garnering from the purlieus of the hospital, he became a martyr to the cause of humanity. The following tribute erected in New York city to him and thirteen others, speaks for itself:

Hæc mea ornamenta sunt (These are my jewels). "Gorham Beals, William W. Cahoon" and 12 others, strangers here, "students of the College of Physicians and Surgeons, died of pestilential disease while serving in the Public Hospitals of New York. *This Tablet* is erected by the Faculty that the memory of these *Martyrs of Humanity* may not die, and that taught by their example, the graduates of the College may never hesitate to hazard life in the *performance of professional duty.*"

The editor of the newspaper from which the above is taken, adds: "Many of our readers will remember one whose name is given above — W. W. Cahoon of Lyndon — a young man of much promise, whose sun went out ere it had reached the meridian." He was the son of the late Hon. William Cahoon, and died August 31st, 1848, aged 23 years and 6 months. He was a favorite of the family, and wherever known was appreciated.

CHARLES B. FLETCHER

Was a graduate at the Catholic College, Montreal, C. E., of him we have spoken elsewhere, he makes the fifth of the honored dead of the Lyndon graduates.

HON. CHARLES W. WILLARD,

A lawyer and editor at Montpelier, is a graduate at Dartmouth, belonging to Lyndon.

HENRY CHASE, by profession a lawyer in Illinois, at present principal of the Academy at Lyndon, is a graduate of Yale College; GEO. W. CAHOON, attorney at Lyndon, and CHARLES M. CHASE, attorney and editor in Illinois, were classmates, graduating at Dartmouth; HENRY S. BARTLETT, now a lawyer of R. I., was a graduate of the same institution; Messrs. GEORGE E. CHAMBERLIN and HENRY NEWELL, should rightfully be classed as Lyndon students, who have recently graduated at Dartmouth (but it would be characteristic of St. Johnsbury to claim them); Mr. GEORGE W. QUIMBY of Lyndon, is also another recent graduate at Dartmouth, and two others hold a student's relation to the same, WM. HENRY PECK and DENNIS DUHIGG. The other gradu-

ates living in town, are MOSES CHASE, Esq., the Rev. WILLIAM SCALES, Hon. SAMUEL B. MATTOCKS, the last two of Middlebury; Dr. ENOCH BLANCHARD, Messrs. CHASE and BLANCHARD of Dartmouth; Messrs. ISAAC FLETCHER and NICHOLAS BAYLIES, deceased, also being graduates — and much is due to Mr. Fletcher for his influence in behalf of a liberal education. Others of the class are probably inadvertently overlooked.

Under the head of education we may appropriately include professional teaching, in law, medicine and divinity, for Lyndon at different periods, and almost constantly, has possessed among her citizens able tutors in all these sciences; and it is within the recollection of the writer that nearly an hundred young men belonging to the town, or coming from abroad for the purpose, have received their professional education here, and more' particularly in the professions of law and medicine; many have in this and in neighboring states, become ornaments in their professions and valued members of society. Their numbers being proportioned about 20 theologians to 30 medical and 50 law students.

Of residents in town, of gentlemen in these professions, there have been nearly 50 clergymen settled acording to their order: 30 Methodists, one settled by the town and preaching 8 or 10 years, the others stationed annually by Conference, and most of them continued 2 years each, of whom are dead, Messrs. P. Peck, Fillmore, Fisk, Cahoon, Dow, Perkins and Mann; 8 or 10 Freewill Baptists, one, elder Quimby,* and nearly the same number of Congregationalists, though not more than 6 technically settled permanently; some others preaching for a limited time on probation or otherwise, one, Mr. Kimball, dead,* particularly spoken of elsewhere, and some 4 or 5 Universalists. We have elsewhere alluded to the merits of this worthy class of our citizens.

There have resided in town over 20 different physicians, most of whom we have named; some were eminently skilled and all of good repute for science as well as morals. Some of the most scientific and skilled still live, of whom it is not my purpose to make remarks in any department other than general, yet it may not be deemed invidious to name as such, Drs. Spaulding and Newell, who are neither now residents here, and Dr. Fuller, deceased, one of the earliest, was a very learned and skillful man, having visited

* Only two died in this town.

France to perfect his education ; Dr. Field, also deceased. was noted for his prudent care and good nursing. Since its settlement about 25 practising lawyers and some 4 or 5 out of practice, have lived in town, "the keepers and doers of the law." All have had a share of patronage. It is lucky that they were not all here together, for it would have been dry pickings, and some might 'have obtained a bad name ; but spreading them over a space of nearly 60 years, they all have had opportunities to make themselves useful. Some look upon the lawyer as a sort of harbinger of evil, but this is illiberal, his duty is to suppress evil ; and if governed by principle, he will endeavor to do it. The virtuous should not complain of him ; but the rogue when caught undoubtedly would, for

"No rogue e'er felt the halter drawn,
With good opinion of the law."

As a class, the lawyers of Lyndon have compared favorably with those elsewhere, and their general deportment has been courteous, manly and honorable ; but we do not intend to speak of the merits of the living, but to the dead would give a passing tribute.

NATHANIEL GOODHUE,

The first of whom we have knowledge, coming here in 1804 or '05, was a courtly gentleman, and as a town lawyer, very acceptable and efficient. As he left no record of his legal learning, we can not speak of it with certainty, not then being a correct judge of such matters ; but coming from Windham county, the old school for good lawyers, we infer that it was respectable. He returned there after a few years, and his brother,

SAMUEL B. GOODHUE,

Took his place, but was very unlike him in appearance, and eccentric and erratic in his movements, a crusty old bachelor, who was reported to have been soured and shattered by an unfortunate amour in his youth. Like other eccentric bodies, he had his bright scintillations, but not very enduring. He appeared to be a harmless, upright and conscientious man, remaining here till 1811 ; when last heard from he was in a lunatic asylum.

JOHN M. FOSTER

Came next. He had been in practice elsewhere, and being naturally bright and kinky, he was a troublesome opponent for our bachelor friend, and particularly so, when he was a little warmed up by the *spirit* of the bar. Mr. Foster joined the army in 1812, and left town, probably in turn having been a little worried by the next coming lawyer. We have said that "in 1811

ISAAC FLETCHER,

An educated man and a well read lawyer came to town ;" he was a native of Massachusetts, and a graduate of Dartmouth College. After receiving his diploma, he taught in the Academy at Chesterfield, N. H., and there formed an acquaintance with Miss Abigail Stone, his future wife, and read law with Mr. Vose of New Hampshire, and Judge White of Putney, Vt. He possessed an ardent temperament, with an ambition to equal, if not excell his competitors; prompt, energetic and unremitting in his efforts for his clients, he soon attained a good reputation and an extensive and lucrative practice, competing successfully with the most noted of the bar in the state, giants of their time. In doing this, he overwrought both his bodily and mental powers, participating in the trial of almost every cause in the supreme and county courts in Caledonia, Orleans and Essex counties, and being 8 years in succession state's attorney of Caledonia county, from early morn to a late evening hour, while attending court, being thronged with clients, or pressed with business ; and when it was the period of repose for others, it came his time for genial social intercourse, which he greatly relished, endowed with kindly feelings, and greatly needing relaxation from his severe labors. In addition to his ordinary labors was the care at different periods of some 30 students, some of these however lightening his burdens by assistance in writing and ordinary office business. He also entered the political arena, first in the house of representatives of the general assembly of the state, to which he was elected four times, and at the last session he was chosen speaker of that body. He was twice elected member of congress, but his health failing him from over exertion and mental and bodily prostration, he could not distinguish himself as he did in his profession, nor as his native talents and learning would entitle himself and friends to anticipate ; yet when others would have been negligent, he was constant and faithful in his duty to the end of his term. His motto seemed to be, to do with all his might whatever he had to do. He acquired his military title by being appointed adjutant general in the staff of Governor Van Ness. He died in October, 1842, the year after the close of his congressional term, literally worn out, aged 58. Less ambition and less labor would probably have saved him many years to his family, his friends, and the world. His only son

CHARLES B. FLETCHER,

A young man of brilliant intellect, who was necessarily with his father most of his congressional course, and became well posted in matters of state, succeeded to his father's business in the office with Mr. Bartlett, his late partner, and remained at Lyndon a year or two, afterwards removed to Nashua, N. H., and then to Boston, Mass., to practice law with his father-in-law, Mr. Farley, a distinguished lawyer there; but he returned to Lyndon in 1852, with consumption, and died soon after, aged 34.

HON. NICHOLAS BAYLIES

Came to Lyndon to reside in 1835. He was a graduate of Dartmouth College, and afterwards a student and partner of the Hon. Charles Marsh of Woodstock, and afterwards of Senator Upham of Montpelier. He was a native of Massachusetts. While residing at Woodstock, he married Mary, daughter of Professor Ripley of Hanover, and sister of Gen. Eleazer W. and James W. Ripley, of the army of 1812, and since of congress. He moved to Montpelier in 1810, and had Judge Prentiss and other able men to compete with; yet, by industry, besides laboriously attending to his office and large court business, he composed several volumes of Indexes of Common and American Law, arranged under appropriate heads, affording ready references for practical use, and very valuable to the profession, three good sized volumes of which were published, entitled Baylies' Digested Index. Other volumes, written afterwards as an addenda, have not been published. He also published a treatise on the powers of the mind, considered valuable. He was an able practitioner of his profession till 1833, when he was elected judge of the Supreme Court, and reëlected in 1834, discharging the duties of the office with distinguished ability. His wife having deceased, on retiring from the bench he ever after made it his home with his only daughter, Mary R., Mrs. George C. Cahoon; and, although advanced in life, yet, possessing good health and a vigorous constitution, he entered into the practice of law again with the ardor of youth, especially of chancery, in which he delighted, and at his death, in 1847, aged 79 years, was esteemed one of the most learned lawyers of the state. His mind was not so much characterized for brilliancy as for patient and indomitable perseverance in investigation and in arriving at correct conclusions. His family consisted of three children, the oldest a son, Horatio N., who was a merchant, and died in Louisiana in 185-; and his youngest a son, Nicholas, Jr., a lawyer, who resides in Des Moines, Iowa. The daughter, Mary Ripley, Mrs. George C. Cahoon, died at Lyndon, July 18, 1858.

There are two considerable villages in the town, LYNDON CORNER and LYNDON CENTRE, and some other places which aspire to the name, not very numerously settled, as the Red Village and East Lyndon.

Lyndon Corner is a centre for several other towns to do much of their mercantile and mechanical business, and is noted for being a brisk business place. The villagers having in their number those who professionally deal in almost all the necessaries and comforts of life, they transact business of nearly every kind found in the country, and there are enough of each trade and profession, so that a person can have a fair opportunity to select with whom to deal, and the subject matter to deal about. It contains 2 church edifices, an academy, and 2 school-houses; a public house, livery stable, and two buildings with large halls for public occasions; 2 retail stores, in one of which Lyndon post office is kept; 1 merchant tailor's clothing store, 1 other tailor's shop, 1 extensive tin and sheet-iron factory and stove and variety store; 1 flour and grocery store, 1 medical store, 4 shoe stores and shops, 2 harness shops and 2 carriage trimmers, 2 jewellers, 1 daguerrean gallery, 1 silver plater; 2 extensive carriage factories, one operated by steam, the other by water, both making excellent carriages; marble works, cabinet makers, house-joiners; 4 blacksmith shops, 2 planing-mills, sawmills, grain mill, oil mill, plough shop, blind-maker, sash and door makers, coopers, painters, mason, butcher, cattle dealers; also 2 clergymen, 4 physicians and 4 lawyers. The private dwelling-houses are about 120, with 150 families and from 700 to 1000 inhabitants. This village lies in the southerly part of the town, and derives its name from the junction and course of the roads.

Lyndon Centre, deriving its name from its locality, is about two miles north from the Corner, situate in which are 2 church edifices, the town hall and school-house, and a public house. It has 2 clergymen, 1 physician, 2 merchants, 2 shoe shops, 2 blacksmiths, several house-joiners, 1 rail road contractor, 1 starch factory, 1 sawmill, 1 tannery, 1 harness shop, and about one-third of the number of houses at the Corner, and families and people in proportion; also a post office. The cemetery is also in this village, and, although it may not possess great interest to strangers, yet their own is a very interesting feature to the people of every town and locality. It is situated in rear of the town hall, as now called, being for many years the only meeting-house in town, and the ground in the cemetery first used for burial, is part of that donated to the town by Mr. Job Sheldon. It was first used in 1803, by the burial of Lucy, daughter of Capt. Joel Fletcher, and none other in town has been used since, unless a few in the Elder Quimby neighborhood, long ago. It contains a large congregation of our loved and honored dead. The old part was indiscriminately used without reference to order, but on adding the new part at the west, it was allotted out as well as it could be, and laid out in good taste. Another addition, on the whole length of the north side, was made a year or two ago. Since this purchase, the whole grounds have been encircled with a nice new painted fence, and ornamented by terraces and flower beds; costly family monuments and a very large number of beautiful head-stones are erected to our friends, and high above them all, on elevated ground at the west end of the centre avenue, stands a tall Italian obelisk upon marble pedestals and granite base of appropriate dimensions, inscribed to the memory of about twenty Revolutionary officers and soldiers who have died in town. This was erected under the superintendence of a town committee, with funds raised by private and voluntary donation; an appropriate tribute from the right source—a spontaneous outpouring of the treasures of the heart to the champions of freedom. There is an expensive tomb near the centre of the ground, with hewn granite front and iron doors, erected by Elder Daniel Quimby for private family use, which has occasionally been used as a receiving tomb. The family monument of Abel Carpenter, Esq., one of the Revolutionary officers, whose name is familiar, was the first erected here. Its base was granite, and its column white Vermont marble, good for its time, but less than those of recent structure. The next erected, was to the family of Jude Kimball, Esq. This, for the purposes intended and the number of its inscriptions, is probably better proportioned and more symmetrical than any other in the cemetery.

It is placed in the centre of the group of graves of father, mother, her mother, two sons, two daughters, and two grandsons. A beautiful bed is made over the graves, and the shaft of the monument rests on appropriate bases of marble and granite. The surviving son who caused its erection, Lucius Kimball, Esq., of Brooklyn, N. Y., must have cultivated his taste in Greenwood Cemetery. The monument of Dr. Charles B. Darling, of rich Italian marble, octagonal, fluted and otherwise ornamented, and of elegant proportions, is the most beautiful in the cemetery. Its truthful tribute is "He was a good man." A few weeks since his beautiful wife was laid by his side, to claim another tablet to departed worth. The family monuments of Hon. Isaac Fletcher, Capt. Joel Fletcher and Josiah C. Willard, Esq., are as large and expensive, and some of them more so, than Mr. Kimball's, and of similar materials, but vary in form and finish, to suit the taste of the purchaser. The Trull, Bemiss, Curtis and Bowker, are also good ones, but not so large nor of the same order. In proportion to the whole, the monuments are but few, but there are an unusual number of beautiful head stones, and many of them of the richest Italian marble of good size and proportions, very thick and highly polished on all sides, and set in appropriate granite bases.

In other parts of the town there are some 8 blacksmith shops, also other mechanics, such as are needful and will make themselves useful in every community, such as house joiners, chair makers, sash and blind makers, mill wright, 7 or 8 saw mills, carding machine, starch factories, &c., &c., and at the rail road station a large wholesale store, besides the capacious depot and storage store. More with propriety might be said of the convenience and benefit of the rail road to the town. Freight for the Lyndon stations is usually deposited in the depot, but might be taken off at the Folsom crossing, three miles north, where there is a side track convenient to East Burke, where many cars are loaded from the north part of the town and Burke, and from Wheelock and Sheffield; but all those towns usually take their freight to and from the depot, situated about ¾ of a mile southeast from the Corner. Large numbers of cattle, sheep and horses are sent from here, also large quantities of butter, potatoes and starch, and of whatever is marketable; and a great number of carriages and harnesses made in town for the sunny south and California, in better days, to order.

There is not great ornamental beauty in the location or structure of the buildings of the main village, the site being uneven and lacking compass and space for building and pleasure grounds; but it is adapted to its use of being a busy central business place not only of the town, but of a large surrounding country. Its surroundings are high, but verdant hills of pasture ground and cultivated fields, and if the mind is weary of confinement in the seeming fastnesses, the body has but to climb to the summit, and there will be ample space in which to breathe free and easier, and for thought to soar.

The census shows the population to have been in 1791, 59; in 1800, 542; in 1810, 1092; in 1820, 1296; in 1830, 1750; in 1840, 1753; in 1850, 1754; and 1860, number not known by the writer, but understood to have diminished a trifle. For several years the town has not increased much in population, and probably for the last decenary not quite held its own.* This arises from a variety of causes, one of which is that the inhabitants are mostly engaged in agriculture, and that there is but little unsettled land in the home market, and that held at so high a price as to be eclipsed by the large amount of lands at the west at government prices. Another is the golden bait for the greedy at California, Pike's Peak and Australia, both these causes have greatly tended to deplete this and other towns in the vicinity of their richest treasures, their enterprising young men and women, to people the wilderness or delve in the mines. And many young men and women have gone abroad to find broader fields in which to disseminate learning, mete out justice, administer the potent pill, or declare peace on earth and good will to man. It is no wonder then, that our numbers should decrease under such a process: yet we have a healthful and intelligent population left, with as fair prospects of prosperity and happiness as usually falls to the lot of man.

STATE, COUNTY AND TOWN OFFICERS,
RESIDENTS OF LYNDON.

Town Clerks.

1791, '2, '3, Daniel Cahoon, Jr.†
1793–1808, Daniel Cahoon, Sr.†
1808–1829, William Cahoon.†
1829–1843, Elias Bemiss, Jr.†
1843–1845, Andrew J. Willard.
1845–1855, John M. Hoyt.
1855, John McGaffey.

*See Chapter County Census Table, page 270.

1856, Edward A. Cahoon.
1857, William H. McGaffey.
1858–1861, Isaac W. Sanborn, incumbent.

State Councillors.

1814, Nicholas Baylies† (then of Montpelier).
1815–'20, William Cahoon.†
1820–22, Wm. Cahoon,† Lieut. Gov. and ex-officio Councillor.
1826–32, Benj. F. Deming.†
1833–34, George C. Cahoon.
Office abolished in 1836, and Senate created.

State Senators.

1836, Joseph H. Ingalls.†
1840, Elias Bemiss, Jr.†
1841, '2, Thomas Bartlett, Jr.
1843, '4, George C. Cahoon.
1845, '6, Welcome Bemiss.
1847, '8, Sam'l B. Mattock, now of L.
1849, '51, Eph. Chamberlin.
1856, '7, Edward A. Cahoon.

Council of Censors.

1806, Isaiah Fisk.†
1813, Nicholas Baylies.†

Representatives.   Years.

1792, Dan. Cahoon,† . . . 1
1793, Josiah Arnold, ... 1
1794–1802, inclusive, Daniel Cahoon, Sr.,† 8
1802, '5, '8, '9, '10, '11, '12, '25, '26, William Cahoon,† 9
1803, '4, '13, '14, '15, '16, '17, '18, '21, '23, Isaiah Fisk,† 10
1806, '7, Abraham Smith,† . . 2
1819, '20, '22, '24, Isaac Fletcher,† 4
1827–33, Job Randall, ... 7
1834, '52, '53, E. B. Chase, . . 3
1835, George C. Cahoon, . . . 1
1836, '7, Elias Bemiss, Jr.,† '. 2
1838, '9, Benjamin Walker,† . . 2
1840, '41, '48, '49, Stephen McGaffey, . 4
1842, '3, Benaiah Sanborn, . . . 2
1844, '5, Asaph Willmarth,† . . 2
1846, '7, Lucius Kimball, · . . 2
1850, '54, '55, Thomas Bartlett, Jr., . 3
1851, John D. Miller, ... 1
1856, Daniel L. Ray, ... 1
1857, '8, William H. McGaffey, . 2
1859, '60, Sumner S. Thompson, 2
1861, George Ide, incumbent.

Delegates to Constitutional Convention.

1793, Josiah Arnold.†
1814, '28, William Cahoon.†
1822, Isaac Fletcher.†
1836, '43, George C. Cahoon.
1850, '57, Thomas Bartlett, Jr.

† Deceased.

JUDGE OF SUPREME COURT.

1833, '4, Nicholas Baylies.* Judge Baylies formerly resided at Montpelier but in Lyndon the last 12 years of his life.

JUDGES OF THE COUNTY COURT.

1807 (1st), Isaiah Fisk.* Years,
1822 (last), in all 14 years, being chief
  justice, ... 8
1811–19, William Cahoon,* . 8
1824, '5, Samuel A Willard, . . 2
1839, '42 '3, Ephs. B. Chase, . . 3

STATE ATTORNEYS.

1820–29, Isaac Fletcher,* . . . 8
1835, '6, '7, '47, George C. Cahoon, . 4
1839, '41, '2, Thomas Bartlett, Jr., . . 3
1851, '2, 3, Henry S. Bartlett, . 3
1854, '5, Edward A. Cahoon, . . . 2
1860, '1, George W. Cahoon, incumbent, 2

SHERIFFS.

1815, '16, Jude Kimball,* . . . 2
1828, '9, '30, '31, Silas Houghton,* . 4
1832, '3, '4, '5, Charles Roberts, . . 4
1851, '2 '3, George Ide, ... 3
1854, '5, Horace Evans at St. Johnsbury, 2
1856, '7, Orenso P. Wakefield, . . . 2

Mr. Evans's family were early settlers of Lyndon, where he lived many years and officiated as deputy there a long period, previously to his election as sheriff.

JUDGES OF PROBATE.

1821–32, Benjamin F. Deming,* . . 12
1836 (1st), '47 (last), Samuel B. Mattocks, ... 9

REGISTERS.

1821, '2, George B. Shaw,* . . 2
1823, '3, '5, George C. Cahoon, . . 3
1826 (1st), '38 (last), Samuel B. Mattocks, 8

COUNTY CLERKS.

1817–32, Benj. F. Deming, . . . 16

Mr. D. was a merchant at Lyndon, and relinquished it to very faithfully perform his official oppointments.

1837 (1st), '48 (last), Samuel B. Mattocks, 12

Mr. Mattocks formerly resided at Danville, and represented that town 3 years, and was cashier of the Bank of Caledonia 8, and has been cashier of the Bank of Lyndon 5 years, and now holds it.

MEMBERS OF CONGRESS.

1829–33, William Cahoon,* . . . 4
1833, '4, Benjamin F. Deming,* . 2
1837–41, Isaac Fletcher,* . . 4
1851–53, Thomas Bartlett, Jr., . 2

* Deceased.

PRESIDENTIAL ELECTORS.

Of President Madison, William Cahoon;* of President Lincoln, Edward A. Cahoon. Both were messengers to Washington.

PRACTICING ATTORNEYS.

Thomas Bartlett.
Edward A. Cahoon.
George C. Cahoon,
George W. Cahoon, partners.

PHYSICIANS.

Charles S. Cahoon.
Horace Stevens.
Daniel Trull.
Edward Mattocks, Allopathy.
Chester W. Scott, Homœopathy.
  Lyndon Centre.
Enoch Blanchard, Allopathy.

POST MASTERS.

Lyndon.
John M. Weeks,
1861, Aug., Wm. H. McGaffey.
  Lyndon Centre.
Elisha Sanborn.

In the 71 freemen's meetings, holden since the organization of the town, it is a remarkable fact that there has always been an election of a representative, and never but one failure of his attending the legislature, and that of General Cahoon in 1810 by reason of sickness. Farmers have represented 48 years, lawyers 9, merchants 9, physician 2, carriage-maker 1, and rail road contractor, 2; the representatives of 40 years are known to be dead, the others except one, are known to be living.

CALEDONIA COUNTY FARMERS' CLUB.

BY THE SECRETARY.

A convention was called at the Town Hall in Lyndon, the 5th day of September, 1860, to organize an agricultural society to accommodate more particularly the citizens of Northern Caledonia. A large number were in attendance, the convention enthusiastic and harmonious. After a temporary organization by choosing Hon. E. A. Cahoon, president, and I. W. Sanborn, secretary, and spirited remarks from gentlemen of the several towns represented, a county farmers' club was permanently organized, with the following officers: Elisha Sanborn, president; Sullivan Ranney, vice president; I. W. Sanborn, secretary; Charles Folsom, treasurer.

The first exhibition was held at Lyndon

Centre on Thursday, the 20th of the same month, with very satisfactory results. Nearly a thousand head of cattle were exhibited, including 792 oxen! The other departments were well represented, especially the ladies, or Floral Hall.

At the second annual meeting, held Jan. 30, 1861, the same officers were reëlected with an additional vice-president and secretary.

The second exhibition was held on the same ground, Oct. 2, 1861. The fair was very successful.

The society is founded upon a basis in many respects dissimilar to any other in the state. Diplomas are awarded instead of cash premiums, thus rendering the expenses of the society comparatively small, the necessary funds being raised by membership subscriptions. The results thus far have proved very satisfactory.

THE FARMER'S GIRL.
A GREEN MOUNTAIN SONG.
BY ISAAC W. SANBORN.

For the farmer's girl, hurrah, hurrah!
  Hurrah for the farmer's girl!
Light is her step o'er the grassy lawn,
As that of the playful, agile fawn,—
  Hurrah for the farmer's girl!

For the farmer's girl, hurrah, hurrah!
  Hurrah for the farmer's girl!
Her cheeks are tinged with a roselike hue,
Her lips are red and her eyes are blue,—
  For the farmer's girl, hurrah!

For the farmer's girl, hurrah, hurrah!
  Hurrah for the farmer's girl!
She's hale and hearty, noble and true,
Ever ready for the work she has to do,—
  Hurrah for the farmer's girl!

For the farmer's girl, hurrah, hurrah!
  Hurrah for the farmer's girl!
She's truthful, trusting, generous, kind,
Happy and gleeful—just to your mind,—
  For the farmer's girl, hurrah!

Extracts from "Lelia Lyndon" (Miss Susannah S. Burt).
SOMETHING NEW.
In reply to an article in The Aurora of Nov. 24, 1860.

We have found the priceless dower,
  We've obtained the fitting gem,
And it sparkles bright this hour,
  In our nation's diadem

Would you know the thing selected,
  As the "something new" we scan?
'Tis that "Honest Abe" 's elected
  Champion in the truth's bright van,

'Tis that error now shall crumble
  'Neath the power of justice's might,
Truth shall cruel tyrants humble,
  Bringing "hidden things" to light.

Now the fettering curse of thralldom
  Shall *extend not* with its sin,
Since our Ruler we've installed him,
  Lincoln's rails will fence it in!

WEARY NOT.

Weary not tho' each endeavor
  Brings not now success to thee,
Work in faith — remember never
  Acts of goodness lost will be.

Sit not down with heart despairing,
  Weary not within the strife,
There's a goal that's worth the sharing,
  Brighter than this tear-dimmed life.

NEWARK.
BY J. P. SMITH.

The history of this town contains little to interest that class of readers whose homes are among the thriving towns and villages of our state, surrounded by wealth and luxury, and who have little or no sympathy for the rough backwoodsman and hardy pioneer. Those, however, who cherish the memory of our forefathers, and sympathize with those who encountered so many difficulties and hardships in subduing the dense forests, and preparing a home for themselves and their descendants, will love to read their humble story, and draw the parallel between their *own* comfortable times, and those of their ancestors. This town is situated in the north or northeast part of the county, and was laid out in the form of a square, containing 36 square miles. It was formerly a part of Essex county. It was chartered August 15, 1781, to William Wall and others.

The first land that was cleared in its limits was near the boundary of Burke, in the year 1795. In September, 1797, James Ball came with his family, and settled upon the farm now occupied by his son, Mr. Perley Ball. In 1801, Eleazer Packer came and settled some two miles deeper still in the forest. Charles Palmer came in 1804. These were the first settlers. Others came in soon after, and the town was organized in 1809. These families suffered many privations. The nearest grist mill was at Lyndon, 12 miles away, and the cold summer of 1816 destroyed nearly all their crops. In the course of a few years, however, large tracts of forest land were cleared of their timber, and bountiful harvests repaid the settler for his labors and placed his family in comfortable circumstances. The soil of this town is naturally fertile and well adapted to the growth of wheat. 40 bushels to the acre have been raised on the farm now owned by D. D. Hall, and from 30 to 40 bushels on fields of from 40 to 75 acres on the farm of Alpheus Stoddard. But the ravages of the weevil (or midge, as it is now called), has led to the cultivation of other crops to the almost total neglect of wheat. The present year (1860), however, the weevil has not made its appearance, and strong hopes are entertained by our farmers that wheat will yet be raised abundantly as in "days of old." The failure of the wheat crop turned the attention of our farmers especially to the raising of potatoes and herds grass seed.

The last named gentleman above who settled here in 1820, has cleared 600 acres of timbered land for this purpose. He has reaped some years 100 acres of grass for seed. The labor of clearing a heavy growth of timber from the soil, is immense; to engage in it extensively and successfully, requires men of muscle and strong constitutions. Among the enterprising farmers of this town who have added much to its wealth in this way, are Henry Dolloff, Eleazer Davis, Marshall Stoddard and Samuel Gray. In 1852, M. Stoddard raised 8,600 bushels of potatoes, all upon newly cleared land; he has also reaped 100 acres of grass seed in a single year.

The township is well watered. Here the Passumpsic river takes its rise. The settlement has extended gradually. It is a post town, and has four school districts.

This town is also celebrated for its large productions of maple sugar. The original growth of timber upon two-thirds of its area, consisted of maple, beech and birch, maple being in the excess; many beautiful groves of this useful tree have been cut down, but many yet remain. The eastern slope of a mountain which extends from East Haven to the centre of the town (a distance of three miles), is covered for two miles or more with a continuous forest of sugar-maple. Many tons of sugar are made here annually. Another remarkable feature of the town, is the great number of perennial springs. There is scarcely a farm that does not contain one, and some six or seven. On the farm of Mr. A. P. Taft is a beautiful spring of clear water, which sends off from its fountain-head a stream sufficient to turn

a saw mill. On the road from Newark to Island Pond is a mineral spring, the waters of which are supposed to run through a stratum of coal, as it is strongly impregnated with carbonic acid. There are three large ponds of water in the town, one of which is situated exactly in its centre, and is called Centre Pond. The manufacture of lumber is carried on to a considerable extent; there are 7 saw mills, 1 grist mill and 2 starch factories. The number of school districts is 9, and the population is 567.

One serious drawback to the interests of this town, has been its geographical position, though we trust the time will come when it will cease to be felt. It is divided by ranges of hills in such a manner that it is difficult to establish a central locality where the citizens may meet to transact their business. One palpable effect of this is, that the merchant in the adjoining towns receive the benefit of our trade. Another is, that though there are 3 religious societies in town, there is no meeting house. Several attempts have been made to erect one, but have failed by reason of disputes as to the location. A proposition is now before the town to build a town hall in connection with a church, which will probably succeed.

[The meeting house has been erected and dedicated the past season—*Ed.*]

OBED JOHNSON

Moved into Newark from —— in 1812, and began clearing his land. He was a man of uncommon energy and industry; an excellent and skillful farmer. As a citizen, he was obliging and trustworthy; as a christian, he was of exemplary piety, and an invaluable member of the church. Practically benevolent, it was his custom when a subscription was in circulation in behalf of any religious enterprise to give a sum double that of any other contributor. He acted as class leader in the Methodist church for 40 years. He died in 1858, aged 72.

ADDITIONAL FACTS.
BY L. M. SLEEPER.

List of first town officers, 1809 — Eleazer Packer, James Ball, John Sleeper, selectmen; David Pike, treasurer; Miles Coe, constable.

First justice — Eleazer Packer, 1808, 20 years; others, Lauren M. Sleeper, 19; Amos Parker, 15; Philemon Hartwell, 13; and Miles Coe, 12.

First representative — Eleazer Packer, 1811 (1858).

45

First merchant — James Morse, 1832.

First teacher of common school — Ursula Newell, 1810.

First birth — Arnold, son of James Ball.

First death — Eleazer Jr., son of Eleazer Packer, April 3, 1806.

First marriage — Philemon Hartwell and Sally Hartwell, by Eleazer Packer, June 28, 1812.

The oldest person among the early settlers who has deceased, was Mr. Billings.

The oldest now living, is the same Eleazer Packer, who was at the head of the second family that moved into town. From the organization of the town till age demanded his retirement from public services, he was among the first and foremost in all business transactions; he held many of the most important town offices year after year, and many times represented this town in the general assembly of the state; was justice of the peace until he refused longer to serve, and is a member of the Methodist church.

[About 21 years since, in the northeast corner of Newark, lived Calvin Hudson, first settler on the east road from Burke line to Brighton, which was then only brushed out. Here he and his brother, Kitridge Hudson, had bought a right of land, and Calvin had built a log house, and moved his family, a wife and 7 children, in the fall before. In the winter he made shingles. One morning his family being in want of "necessaries," he took his knapsack and started for Burke. Not being very well, he declined waiting for breakfast, and started before the family had risen. At Burke he made his purchases, and started for home. A storm came on, and the snow fell fast; at Seymour Walton's, last house in East Haven, still 5 miles distant, he stopped to warm, and again, not to be detained, pushed on homeward. Two days afterward (I had the narrative from the lips of his brother, and give it from memory), within 40 rods of home, he was found frozen by the wayside. Coiled up at his feet (the snow melted beneath the devoted animal), lay his own faithful little dog. And after the funeral several days — the family having been removed — some one visiting the deserted house, found this same affectionate creature had stayed behind and crawled beneath the blanket that wrapped the body of his dead master before the burial, and had been left upon the shelf in the entryway; and with difficulty was he coaxed from the sacred relic and solitary house. — Ed.]

PEACHAM.

BY REV. A. BOUTELLE.

Peacham received a corporate existence by charter from Benning Wentworth, governor of New Hampshire, Dec. 31, 1763. This charter made over to seventy grantees, "inhabitants of N. Hampshire and of our other governments, and to their heirs and assigns forever," a tract of land — 23,040 acres — "six miles square and no more."

A tract of land lying between Danville and Peacham, which afterward received a township charter under the name of Deweysburg, was by act of the legislature divided in 1810, a part added to Danville and a part to Peacham, which gave it a territory of 25,695 acres.

Peacham is in the second range of townships westerly from Connecticut River, and its principal village is 7 miles northwesterly from its rail road station at Barnet. A high ridge of land passes through the westerly part of the town, running northeast and southwest, which divides the waters of the town running into Lake Champlain, from those passing into Connecticut River. The territory of the town lies chiefly on the eastern slopes of this dividing ridge, and though a varied surface, has many excellent farms, well adapted for all kinds of grain, grass and pasturage. We can say in truth, both valleys and hills possess a remarkable fertility, some of our best farms being on high swells of land.

From the summits of some of our high hills beautiful prospects are obtained. On one of these, called by way of legendary distinction, Devil Hill, looking west and north, the eye gazes upon an almost unbroken wilderness, extending from the base of the hill directly beneath your feet for several miles, while by just turning around, without other change of position, the cultivated farms of Peacham and Barnet, lie spread out to the beholder's view. From Cow Hill, a still higher eminence, the vision is bounded north and west by the Green Mountain range and to the east by the Franconia and White mountains in New Hampshire. Looking west, or looking east, the whole intervening country lies spread out in all its untold variety of hills, valleys, forests, ponds, farms and villages.

Within the limits of the town are several ponds, or small lakes, some of which, environed with forests, and fed by mountain springs, are remarkably clear and much visited by those fond of piscatorial diversions. Onion River Pond—so called as the source of one of the principal branches of Onion, or Winooski River—is in the westerly part of the town, covering an area of about 300 acres. Little Osmore Pond, one mile west of Onion—a long sheet of water wholly surrounded by forests—has on its bed a deposit of *infusorial marl*, much admired by geologists for its fineness and freedom from foreign ingredients. Shell marl of coarser quality is found in other places in town, from which lime, in considerable quantities has been manufactured.

There are several streams of water running easterly, affording numerous mill privileges, upon which are 4 sawmills, 2 gristmills, a starch factory, a carding machine, a tannery, a blind and sash factory and 2 wagon shops.

According to charter prescription, the first town meeting of the proprietors of Peacham was held in Hadley, Mass., Jan. 18, 1764. Hadley is distant from Peacham 164 miles. It is an honored town, and Peacham need never be ashamed of the place of its birth. There the machinery of the town was put into working order, but the power to work the machinery was in the city of London, while the chief overseer had his dwelling in Portsmouth, N. H. Affairs slumbered, and for nearly 20 years the town remained in almost unbroken silence.

After long intervals the proprietors held an occasional meeting, and made some progress in surveying lots and running lines around the town. Their first meeting held in Peacham, bears date August 20, 1783, 6 months previous to the first regular town meeting of which there is any record. The disturbed condition of the country, arising from the contested claims of New Hampshire and New York, and the American Revolution retarded the growth of the town. A very few inhabitants tried to carve out homes for themselves and families as early as 1775, but lived in constant peril by day and night. Early in the spring of that year, Dea. Jonathan Elkins* came with a few others, and began cutting down the forest; but from fear of the enemy, soon after returned to Newbury. In 1776 the solitude was broken by the marching of several companies of soldiers along a line made by blazed trees from Newbury to Champlain. It was in early spring, and they marched on snow shoes. But upon hearing of an invasion from Canada, they soon marched back again. The few people who were here, fled with them. Dea. Elkins, however, with John Skeele and Archey McLaughlin, returned in the fall and

spent the winter together in Peacham. These were the first white men who wintered here, and may be called the fathers of the town. But the few increased a little from year to year till the close of the war.

In October, 1777, was born Harvey Elkins, the first white male child born in Peacham; and next year, Ruth Skeele, the first female child born in Peacham, and who died Sept. 25, 1860, aged 82 years.

In 1779, Gen. Hazen, stationed at Newbury, had orders to clear a road from that place to Champlain, and thus gave name to the so-called Hazen Road, which for a long time thereafter was a great convenience to the inhabitants. As usual in those early days, that road did not avoid the high hills. In 1780 a Capt. Aldrich built a picket around James Bailey's house for security from the enemy, and this was probably the only block house in the limits of P. Generally the people had to take care of themselves as best they could, and seasons of alarm were not unfrequent; though it is not known that any one was killed in the limits of the town by Briton, Tory or Indian. A few were taken prisoners, among whom were Cols. Elkins of Peacham, and Johnson from Newbury in 1781, and two by the name of Bailey, in 1782. Col. Elkins was carried to Quebec, thence to England, and was there exchanged for one of equal rank. Col. Johnson returned on *parole.*

After the war closed, population rapidly increased. It was a point of considerable commercial importance in Indian trade, and as the Hazen Road became famous as a medium of transit across the country, the land rapidly came under cultivation. People began to forget past trials in the prospects opening before them, and population became respectable in numbers, intelligence and character. By December, 1784, there were 24 freemen in the town, and a population of some 200. The census of 1791 shows a population of 365. In 1800, there were 873—only 374 less than at this present year (1860). Thus in 1784 the town was fully organized, and on that same year, it was voted to raise $60 for preaching, to be paid in wheat at 6s. per bushel, and the selectmen were the committee to hire ministers and appoint places for preaching.

In 1791, was agitated the question of erecting a meeting-house. The vote stood *contents* 33, *non-contents* 28. But the people could not agree on the place of building, for even when they agreed to abide the decision of men appointed from out of town, who should "stick the stake," they were very reluctant to stick to their vote. Happily in 1795, their thoughts were turned to the question of erecting an academy, and of using the same building, both for a school and a sanctuary, and the question prevailed, and Caledonia County Grammar School, located in Peacham, received its charter, bearing date Oct. 27, 1795. It seems the question was agitated whether the County School should be here or the Court House and Jail, and the people wisely decided to have the School, and posterity thanks them for the wisdom of the choice. For Peacham, it was a happy day when she said, Danville may have the Court House, we will have the School; and Danville was satisfied, rejoiced and was glad. The academy located here, drew to it the eyes and the hearts of the people. The meeting house wrangle was hushed. The men called from New Hampshire, to "stick the stake," were not needed. The people this time stuck their own stake, and on the brow of the noble eminence called afterward Academy Hill, the stake was stuck and all the people said amen. The town agreed to support the principal three years, and in addition, erect a commodius building. On the 1st of December, 1797, it was opened for the reception of pupils, and Ezra Carter, Esq., was the first principal. From that time to this, it has gone its way prospering, with an annual average aggregate of 200 pupils. It has had 35 different preceptors, of whom 24 were graduates of Dartmouth, 3 of Yale, 2 of U. V. M., 4 of Middlebury and 1 of Harvard. Among these are the honored names of Ezra Carter and Jeremiah Evarts, Esqrs., David Chassell, D. D., David Merrill, Prof. Bartlett, Evarts and Noah Worcester, Daniel Christie, John Lord, Mellen Chamberlin and C. C. Chase. Hon. Thaddeus Stevens, Hon. Samuel Merrill, Chief Justice Redfield, Rev. Wilbur Fiske, D. D., were among its pupils. Its present principals are Lyman S. Watts, A. B., and Miss Jane E. Chamberlin.

RELIGIOUS INTERESTS.

The people of the town have ever taken a warm interest in its moral and religious welfare. In 1784, when it does not appear there were more than 6 freemen in town, it was voted to raise $60 for preaching, and in that same year a church was organized by Rev. Mr. Powers of Newbury, consisting of 18 members of the Presbyterian order. That church did not prosper, and at length disbanded. On the 14th of April, 1794, the present Congregational Church was organized with 12 members. The last survivor of this number was Mary Bailey, 2d, who died in Glover in 1844, aged 92 years. In the same year 23 others united with the church, three of whom lived till after the present pastor was settled over the church. Jonathan Elkins and Reuben Miner were its first deacons. In 1800 there were 41 members, of whom Rev. Leonard Worcester was the 40th, who was ordained pastor of the church, Oct. 30, 1799.

Thus we come down to 1800. Within less than 30 years the wilderness had been invaded, and before the sturdy blows of the woodchopper the forest had rapidly disappeared, and these now beautiful and fertile slopes of land laid open to the light of the sun, and bountiful harvests crowned the labors of the husbandman. Substantial dwellings took the place of log cabins, roads were opened and graded, an academy built and set agoing under auspicious influences, a printing press established from whence for several years a weekly newspaper was issued, a church organized and a pastor settled. The people worked — earned their bread by the sweat of the brow. The idle and shiftless were not wanted, and were summarily reminded they might return whence they came. The Elkinses were brave men, the six gigantic Blanchards were not behind, while William Chamberlain run lines both for land and conduct. Others too, as the McLaughlins, Skeele, the Baileys, Minors, Merrills, Martins, made their mark, and posterity honor their memory. Among its freemen at that time were William Chamberlain, afterward member of congress and lieutenant-govenor of the state, John Mattocks, for 6 years member of congress, governor of the state and a judge in the supreme court, Leonard Worcester, for 40 years a wise, devoted and successful minister of the gospel; not to mention the boys and girls, who in after years grew up sturdy yeomanry, bowing not, nor doing reverence to king, pope or bishop, abhorring slavery, and titled aristocracies of all grades.

From 1800 its prosperity has been steadily onward to this day, comparing favorably with any other town in a rural region for health, wealth, enterprise, thrift, intelligence and positive religious influences.

The Academy has had a very happy influence on the resident population as upon other hundreds who have gone from us. In 1840 Mr. Worcester stated in a published sermon; "No less than 26 young men from among the inhabitants of this town have obtained a college education, having been fitted for college in this institution." It is believed this was the first academy building erected in the state of Vermont.

THE CONGREGATIONAL CHURCH AND SOCIETY.

As before remarked, the church was organized in 1794. Rev. Leonard Worcester was ordained as pastor Oct. 30, 1799, and till 1840 labored faithfully in the work of the ministry. He appears to have been the right man in the right place, and in the memories of a grateful people his words and deeds are still garnered up. It was a ministry of great prosperity, and generally during the period of his labors the church occupied a very commanding position among those of the denomination in the state. In the 18th year of his ministry there began a revival of religion which continued for two years, when 225 were received to its membership on profession of faith. Again in 1831, in a time of great darkness and no little alienation among brethren, the Spirit was wonderfully poured out from on high, and in the course of 14 months 154 were added; when the total of its membership arose to 370, and except Middlebury, it was the largest church in the state. During Mr. Worcester's ministry 571 were added. His formal connection as pastor was not dissolved till his death, which occurred May 28, 1846. He was succeeded by Rev. David Merrill—a native of Peacham, and a member of the church,—who was installed September 9, 1841. Mr. Merrill was pastor nearly 9 years, dying suddenly, July 22, 1850. During his ministry 99 were added to the membership. The present pastor, Rev. A. Boutelle, was installed February 13, 1851. Since his ministry commenced, 132 have been added, leaving a present membership of about 260. Since its organization in 1794, there have been added 877.

This church and society have always taken a warm interest in the cause of humanity, temperance and missions. Forty years ago there were some 30 distilleries in operation here, but for more than 25 years they have ceased to be, and the places they occupied will be known as such no more forever. So far as votes are tests of temperance, this town has sometimes been called the "banner town" in Vermont, and the same may probably be said of the attendance upon public worship on the sabbath day. The statistics of contributions for benevolent purposes in the Congregational Church and Society can

be given only for 10 years—from 1851 to '61. These amount to about $5,844; beside some $22,000 in legacies by Dr. Josiah Shedd.

The first meeting-house of the Congregational Society was built in 1806 on Academy Hill, and for the times was a large and beautiful building, and what was better still, usually filled with hearers from sabbath to sabbath. Its cost was more than $5,000. The present pastor of the church is the third from its beginning.

[Not long since while on a visit at the Peacham parsonage, the present lady there (Mrs. B.) remarked unto us, "This church can claim what probably not another church of its age can in the state. It has had but three pastors—two are in the grave yard over there, the other in the parsonage here."—*Ed.*]

METHODIST EPISCOPAL CHURCH.
BY REV. D. PACKER.

The M. E. Church in Peacham was organized by Rev. D. Field in 1831. There had been occasional preaching in the east part of the town, some three years previous, by the Rev. Mr. Fairbank, stationed preacher at Danville, and Rev. A. Sias.

The following ministers have been regularly appointed at Peacham:

D. Field, .	1831,	1 year
John Currier, . .	1832,	2 do
O. Curtiss, . .	1834,	1 do
J. A. Sweetland, .	1835,	1 do
C. Lyscomb, .	1836,	1 do
Roswell Putnam, .	1837,	1 do
J. H. Patterson, .	1838,	1 do
J. N. Hume, . .	1839,	1 do
W. Evans, . .	1840,	1 do
John Clark, . .	1841,	1 do
J. D. Rust, . .	1842,	2 do
R. Bedford, . .	1844,	2 do
F. T. Albee, . .	1846,	1 do
H. P. Cushing, .	1847,	2 do
A. G. Button, .	1849,	2 do
H. Hitchcock, . .	1851,	2 do
D. S. Dexter, .	1853,	1 do
E. D. Hopkins, .	1854,	2 do
N. W. Aspinwall, .	1856,	2 do
George F. Wells, .	1858,	1 do
D. Packer, . .	1859,	1 do

The Society built a chapel in 1832, which was dedicated January 1, 1833. During the first decade to 1840 the Society numbered 111, including probationers. In 1850 it numbered in full membership and probationers 123. In 1860 we reported in full and probationers 141. In 1859 the number was 74 only; but the Lord of the vineyard blessed us with a glorious revival during our first year, nearly 100 professed faith in Christ. We have expended during our two years, in repairs in the chapel, and parsonage $725. Well may we say, "What hath God wrought," to Him be the praise.

[We here resume Mr. Boutelle's MS.—Ed.]

Peacham had in 1791 the largest population of any town in the county, and in 1800 the largest except Danville. In 1840 it had 1443; in 1850, 1377; in 1860, 1257.

INCIDENTS.

Aloof from scenes of war, in which the towns bordering on Lake Champlain so much participated, we have scarce anything to speak of as unusual or marvelous.

The first millstones for a gristmill in Peacham were drawn from Newbury on an ox sled, by Col. Johnson, of N. He tarried over night with Dea. Elkins. Somehow, the Tories found out he was there. They had a special dislike to Col. Johnson, Gen. Bailey, and Rev. Peter Powers. They hated Bailey for his influence over the Indians; they hated Johnson for his bravery at the taking of Ticonderoga; and Powers, for he now and then preached on *freedom* and *human rights*, and that was preaching *politics*. Knowing Johnson was staying with a defenceless farmer, about midnight they surrounded the house, and entering, took prisoners whom they would, at the point of the bayonet. Resistance was useless, and Johnson, with Jacob Page, Col. J. Elkins and a younger brother, were marched off before daylight, prisoners of war. Johnson told the Tories the younger Elkins would not live to get through the woods, as he was feeble, "having been drowned when a little boy," and they let the boy return, to his great joy and that of his parents. Col. J. found many old acquaintances among the Tories, now bitter enemies. There were eleven of them under the command of a Capt. Prichard. This affair happened March 6, 1781.

At another time during the war, several men were clearing land not far from Cow Hill. One morning, as they went for lunch in their camp, leaving axes behind, an Indian stole down from the hill—where also were two Tories and other Indians—and counted and examined the axes, and fled back. The Tories insisted on going down to scalp and massacre. "No," said the Indian, "we no meet men who use such *big axes.* We want three Indians to fight one big white man. We no go." The Tories yielded, and they went away.

At another clearing, at P. Blanchard's place, about dark, one thought he saw an Indian. The dog soon began to bark and snarl. The cabin fire was put out, the dog seized, his jaws held together to keep him still, and the family fled into a slashing of timber, where they spent the night in darkness, taking turns in confining the dog's mouth till light, when they fled to the garrison.

One day, at the farm of Mr. Aaron Bailey, the hog made an outcry. Upon looking, it was found a large bear had laid hold of the porker, resolved on a good meal. Mrs. B. seized a cudgel, and in the true grit of those early days, dealt out upon him blow after blow, till Bruin gave up and fled, and so she delivered the hog out of the paw of the bear.

In the cold summer of 1816, snow began to fall on the 9th of June and continued next day till it was several inches deep. Mr. Joseph Walker, aged 82 years, went to a distant pasture to drive in some lately sheared sheep, became bewildered in the snow-storm, lost his way, laid out in the woods two nights, and when found on the third day was near perishing. His feet were badly frozen, rendering amputation of some of the toes necessary. He was found on Sunday, and so general was the rally to search for him, that it is said only two men were present at church that day.

In 1811, a malignant fever swept over the town—called the *spotted fever*—particularly fatal to children. There were 59 deaths that year, out of a population of 1300, of whom 34 were under ten years of age. Almost every house was a house of mourning. From 1800 to 1838, the average mortality was 16¾ per year. From Jan., 1851, to Jan., 1861, the number of deaths has been 192, an average of 19¼ per year, the largest annual mortality being in 1852, when the deaths were 33. The erysipelas and scarlet fever were very prevalent that year.

Mrs. Ruth Watts was instantly killed by lightning July 13, 1813.

FIRST THINGS.

It is believed the first trees felled by white men for clearing, were on the Dea. Elkins farm, and the first log cabin was on that farm.

The first religious meeting was at the house of Mr. Moody Morse, where Thomas Morse now lives, and at or near the same place was assembled the first common school.

James Bailey was the first town clerk, the first town treasurer, and the first representative to the state legislature. The first selectmen were James Bailey and Simeon Walker. The first justices were Wm. Chamberlain and James Bailey.

The first *recorded* death of an adult was that of Gen. John Chandler of Newtown, Conn., father of Hon. John W. Chandler, March 15, 1796.

The first salary pledged by the town to the principal of the academy, for the ensuing three years, beginning with 1796, was $333.33. Tuition free to the youth of the county, and *twenty-five cents* a quarter for pupils residing out of the county.

The first call to a minister to settle in the town in the work of the ministry, was as follows: "At a town meeting held in Mr. Reuben Miner's Barn, July, 1791, Voted to offer Rev. Israel Chapin one half of the minister's lot and a salary of fifty pounds annually, which sum be paid in wheat at five shillings a bushel, or neat cattle, rating six-feet oxen at twelve pounds per yoke."

The following are the names of the 12 persons, members of the Congregational Church at its organization, April 12, 1794:

James Bailey,	died 1808,	aged 86.
Dea. Jonathan Elkins,	do 1808,	do 74.
James Bailey, Jr.,	do 1828,	do 77.
Ephraim Foster,	do 1803,	do 72.
Dea. Reuben Miner,	do 1829,	do 93.
William Varnum,	do 1814,	do 68.
James Abbott,	do 1815,	do —.
Mary Bailey,	do 1818,	do 84.
Mary Bailey, 2d,	do 1844,	do 92.
Mary Walker,	do 1834,	do 74.
Phebe Skeele,	do 1836,	do 80.
Anna Bailey,	do ——,	do —.

BIOGRAPHICAL.

DEA. JONATHAN ELKINS,

Born at Hampton, N. H., 1734; married Elizabeth —— of Chester, N. H., 1756, and in 1760 removed to Haverhill, N. H., being among the first settlers of that town, and coming there in very troublous times. From thence in 1776 he removed with his family to Peacham. His was the first family to settle in town, and his house the first public house kept in P. He was also the first deacon of the Presbyterian Church in P., and when that ceased to be, filled the same office in the Congregational Church. More than any other man, he may be called the father of the town. As a pioneer, he was patient, peaceful, persevering; as a citizen, trusty, worthy and honest; as a Christian, exemplary, kind, quiet, submissive.

He loved peace, and to maintain it, would make almost any sacrifice. When the Tories took possession of his dwelling, he yielded rather than defend it, as being in his circumstances the wisest course, and they left his house standing, and him with his family in it, excepting his two sons, and one of those returned the day after, and the other in the space of two years. His idea was, conquer by mildness, more than by fighting; to persuade rather than drive, and beseech rather than fret and threaten; and by his gentle, yielding temperament, may have averted trouble and calamity from the infant settlement. He died Dec. 4, 1808, aged 74 years. His wife died in Peacham, March 7, 1809, aged 71 years.

COL. JONATHAN ELKINS,

Son of Dea. E., born in Haverhill, N. H., Oct. 23, 1761, came with the family to Peacham, and was taken captive by Tories in his father's house, March 6, 1781. He was marched away on foot, in deep snow, direct to Canada, first to Quebec, then carried to Ireland, then to England, from whence by exchange of prisoners, he returned to his friends the following year. He removed from P. about 1836, to Albion, N. Y., where he died. He possessed a soldierly element, was fearless, hardy, able to endure, met perils and dangers with firmness, and could mingle in stirring events with self-possession and confidence. His memory is held in high esteem by those who knew him, as a citizen of Peacham in the stirring times of its early history.

HON. WILLIAM CHAMBERLAIN,

Born at Hopkinton, Mass., April 27, 1753; removed with his father to Loudon, N. H., 1778; enlisted a volunteer in the army 1775, where he held the office of orderly sergeant; went with the army at the invasion of Canada; suffered all sorts of privations while so doing, especially in the retreat, and was one out of the nine officers and privates who remained of a company of 70 to take part in the battle of Trenton, N. J., that same year. At the expiration of his enlistment he returned to New Hampshire, but went forth again at the invasion of Burgoyne, as a volunteer, was in the battle of Bennington, from whence he is said to have brought away some trophies of personal contest with his Hessian enemies. About 1780 he removed to Peacham, being then clerk of the proprietors of the town. He was town clerk 12 years, justice of the peace 24 years, was a member of the convention for framing a state constitution, town representative 11 years, member of congress from 1803 to 1805, and from 1809 to 1811, and lieutenant governor in 1814, the last of his public and civil offices. He died Sept. 27, 1828.

In private life Gen. C. was upright, a friend of order, learning and religion. For 15 years he was president of the board of trustees of Peacham Academy and held the same office for some years in the County Bible Society. He lived to see the wilderness become a cultivated and populous region, and as a matter of far higher moment to himself, closed a long, useful and eventful life on earth in humble trust of a better life in heaven.

THE BLANCHARDS.

Abiel, Peter, Joel, Abel, Reuben and Simon, six brothers born in Hollis, N. H., came to Peacham about 1780. Strong, stalwart, fearless men, well fitted for the privations and hazards of pioneer life, they have left a numerous posterity; and while many are dispersed abroad, very many still bear the name around the old homestead. The children of these six brothers, as shown by the town records, amount to 44.

EZRA CARTER, ESQ.,

Born at Concord, N. H., Feb. 15, 1773; graduated at Dartmouth College, 1797; was the same year appointed first principal of the academy in Peacham, which office he held 10 years, and died Oct. 10, 1811, aged 38 years.

Though a lawyer by profession, he devoted himself principally to teaching. In that vocation he was strict almost to sternness, and in discipline resorted pretty freely to *arguments* that were more *telling* and *impressive* than words. He had to cope with the rudeness and independence of a forming period in society, and determined to make heaven's first law the motto of his doings. In the early history of the town he filled an important and useful sphere of action, because he had so much to do with its moral and mental culture, to give shape and tone to methods of study, application and industry. Many of his surviving pupils, now aged men and women, though not forgetting the discipline, bear testimony to his fidelity as a teacher, and his worth as a man.

HON. JOHN WINTHROP CHANDLER,

Born in 1767, the son of Gen. John Chandler of Newtown, Ct., who died at Peacham, March 15, 1796. He was one of the early settlers of the town, was successful in his business transactions, amassed a large property, and after filling many offices of trust and honor, died July 15, 1855, aged 88 years. He was assistant judge 6 years, treasurer of the Grammar School, and of the town of Peacham 34 years, when both these offices were transferred to his son, Samuel A. Chandler, Esq., who held them till his death, Feb. 11, 1855.

REV. LEONARD WORCESTER,

Born in Hollis, N. H., Jan. 1, 1767; he was the third son of Noah Worcester, and of the 6th generation from Rev. William Worcester, who came from England and was settled pastor of the first church gathered in Salisbury, Mass., about 1640. The descendants of William may be reckoned by hundreds, if not thousands, widely scattered over the Union. Noah (the father of Leonard) was the father of 16 children, and before he died, August, 1817, having nearly completed his 82d year, had noted the natal day of 77 grandchildren. In a record in his family bible, Sept., 1798, he says: "I had eighteen children of my own and by marriage at my table to-day." In all he had 95 grandchildren, and of these 94 were born to 6 sons and 2 daughters. Of his descendants, 17 have regularly graduated at college, nearly half of whom entered the ministry. Six others have been in the sacred office.

The brothers of Leonard who entered the ministry were Noah W., D. D., settled in Thornton, N. H., Thomas W. settled in Salisbury, N. H., and Samuel W., D. D., settled in Fitchburg, then in Salem, Mass.

Of the sons of Noah, two, Samuel and Thomas, entered the ministry.

Of the sons of Jesse, Henry Aikin W. entered the ministry, while his 2d son, Joseph Emerson W., LL. D., devoted himself to literary pursuits, noted as the author of gazetteers, geographies and dictionaries.

Of the sons of Samuel, Samuel M., D. D., was successor of his father 25 years in the ministry at Salem.

Leonard of Peacham, was the father of 14 children, of whom Samuel Austin, Evarts, Isaac Redington and John Hopkins entered the ministry. Four of his sons regularly graduated at college, from which it will be seen he well sustained the ancient character of his ancestors. He served an apprenticeship, beginning in his 18th year, in the printing office of Isaiah Thomas, Esq., in Worcester, Mass., after which he was for several years editor, printer and publisher of the Massachusetts Spy. This occupation gave him great facilities for reading, and presented a stimulus for correct composing, and he diligently improved his opportunity. He learned grammar, not from grammar books, but from a careful reading of standard authors, and there he learned the power of the English language and how to use it. In 1795 he was chosen deacon of the first church in Worcester, of which Samuel Austin, D. D., was pastor, and turning his attention to the study of theology, was licensed to preach the gospel March 12, 1799, at the house of Dr. Emmons, Franklin, Mass. He came to Peacham in June the same year, preached a few sabbaths, and being unanimously invited to settle in the ministry, was installed Oct. 30, 1799. It was a prosperous ministry of 40 years; during that time 571 were added to the church. He succeeded admirably in uniting the people in himself, and for more than 31 years of his pastorate, his was the only organized church and society in Peacham, and when he closed his ministry, it was in point of numbers among the foremost in the state. At that time one-fourth of the population of the town were professing Christians.

The writer of these lines never heard or saw Mr. W.; but he sees among the people the presence of an influence, which he trusts will not soon pass away. Few ministers leave behind them a more healthy and abiding impression. His habits of punctuality, exactness in the common dealings of life, his conscientious regard for right and wrong in all public and private transactions, his indignant rebukes when judgment was perverted by men in power, his kind and gentle treatment of the serious and thoughtful, both young and old, his style of preaching, so free from effort at effect and sensation, so straightforward, so simple, yet solemn and earnest, grave, methodical, evangelical, these gave him power, and his memory is blessed. Such a ministry of 40 years could hardly fail to do a great and good work for the people. The town, indeed, owes much to him for the orderly, moral, religious elements yet existing in the habit of attending public worship, punctuality therein, and a prevalent bias of feeling toward evangelical religion. The house in which he so long lived still stands, and his grave is among us. A massive granite monument marks the spot — fitting memorial of such a man. In a sermon preached on the occasion of his death by Rev. D. Merrill who knew him well, he thus speaks:

"His personal appearance was tall, commanding, and of full proportions in middle life, erect to the last, strong, compact, and capable of much endurance, a fit habitation for such a mind. He never appeared in the pulpit without full written preparation, and what he had written, he had written. His voice was strong, clear, and sweet, and his manner ardent and energetic. Yet with all his resolution and force of mind, he was naturally bashful, and easily put to the blush. His defects were such as belong to his peculiar cast of mind — an independent spirit could scarcely brook control or desert a position once taken — a sanguine temperament that could hardly conceive itself wrong. There was the *honest*, the *just*, and the *pure*; but too slight an admixture of the *lovely* and the *amiable*. But these defects disappeared in great measure as he advanced in life. May 28, 1846, he finished his course and retired to rest, but his works live after him, not only in this, the principal scene of his labors, but wherever the young people of Peacham are scattered. They will feel when they learn of his death, that a great man has fallen."

Mr. Worcester was town clerk of Peacham 34 years, a trustee in the Grammar School 27 years, and president of the board 10 years. Several sermons of his preached on special occasions, were published.

He married for his first wife, Elizabeth, daughter of Rev. Samuel Hopkins, D. D., of Hadley, Mass., Nov. 1, 1793; for his second wife, Eunice Woodbury of Salem, Mass., Jan. 25, 1820, who survived him only about 3 months.

REV. DAVID MERRILL,

The successor of Mr. Worcester, and son of Jesse and Priscilla Merrill, was born at Peacham, Sept. 8, 1798. He was of the 7th generation from Nathaniel Merrill, who settled in Ipswich, Mass., in 1638. His parents came to Peacham in March, 1789. Their children, all born in Peacham, were 10 sons and 3 daughters. Three of their sons have been members of Dartmouth College; James, the oldest, graduated in 1812; David in 1821.

He made a profession of religion in 1817, along with 69 others, who united with the church the same day. Turning his attention to the work of the ministry he graduated at Andover, in 1825; was licensed to preach the gospel the same year, and the year after emigrated to the west. After preaching in various places in Indiana and Illinois, he came in 1827 to Urbana, O., was installed over the Presbyterian Church in that town, and there remained 14 years. Unanimously invited to succeed Mr. W. at Peacham, the invitation was accepted, and he was installed Sept. 9, 1841.

Mr. Merrill was the author of the popular temperance tract — *Ox Sermon.* It was written and published in a village newspaper in Urbana, in 1832. The Temperance Society next published it in an extra newspaper form, issuing more than 2,000,000 copies. Next it was adopted as a permanent tract by the American Tract Society, who printed more than 200,000 copies. In this way it has had an immense circulation, and no doubt done great good. That sermon reveals the cast of his mind, as original, shrewd, logical, sagacious. One who knew what he was going to say, and having said, knew when to stop. Having taken his position, he was not easily driven therefrom. He respected human authorities, but his convictions were superior to authorities, the Bible being his great guide in policy and theology. As a preacher, earnest, sincere, awakening, he made a most faithful application of truth to the hearts and consciences of his hearers. Dying in "manhood's middle day," he still lives, and will long live in the hearts of many, both east and west. He died of erysipelas, after a short and distressing sickness of four days, July 22, 1850, aged 51 years.

A volume of his sermons, compiled by Thomas Scott Pearson, was published in 1855, to which is prefixed a short biographical memoir. It is a fact of interest that the last sermon in the volume, from the text "What I do thou knowest not now, but thou shalt know hereafter," was never preached. He left a widow and 10 children, of whom all but one are living at this writing.

REV. ORA PEARSON,

Born in Chittenden, Oct. 6, 1797, graduated at Middlebury College in 1820, and at Andover Theological Seminary in 1824. In 1826 was settled as pastor at Kingston, New Hampshire, where he remained seven years, after which he labored 3½ years as a missionary in Canada East, and next settled over the churches of Glover and Barton, where he remained 6 years. The last 6 years of his life was spent in Peacham, where he died July 5, 1858, aged 60 years. Bereft of his eyesight, at about 50 years of age he ceased to act as pastor, though continuing to preach as opportunity presented till his

last sickness. He was a good man, of unfeigned humility of spirit, Christlike, tender, peaceable, conscientious, earnest in his work and in his convictions, a man of prayer, of faith and love, dying in calm and joyful hope of entering the saints' everlasting rest.

REV. SAMUEL AUSTIN WORCESTER,

Born in Worcester, Mass., Jan. 19, 1798; the 3d son of Leonard W., graduated at the University of Vermont, 1819, and at Andover, 1823; went as a missionary to the Cherokee Indians in 1825; was stationed at Brainard, East Tennessee, till 1827, then removed to Georgia. In Sept., 1831, was imprisoned in the Georgia Penitentiary for refusing to comply with unjust state requirements, bearing on the Indians within its borders, where he continued till Jan. 14, 1833 — 16 months, when he was released and returned to his former place of labor. After various removals, he finally went with the tribe to the Indian Territory, and died at Park Hill, April 20, 1858. He was a man of great wisdom, firmness, courage, consistency and devotedness, eminently fitted for the post he held among the Indians in the turbulent scenes through which he passed, occasioned by the forcible removal of the Indians from the state of Georgia.

REV. EVARTS WORCESTER,

Fourth son of Leonard, was born at Peacham March 24, 1807; graduated at Dartmouth, in 1830, was principal of Peacham Academy, one year, a tutor in Dartmouth College one year, and resided in Hanover, pursuing theological studies till 1836, when he was ordained pastor of the Congregational Church in Littleton, N. H., where he died the same year, Oct. 21. He was a distinguished scholar, and had he lived would unquestionably have attained a high rank in his profession.

REV. ISAAC R. WORCESTER,

Fifth son of Leonard, was born at Peacham, Oct. 30, 1808, received a medical degree at Dartmouth in 1831; ordained pastor of the Congregational Church in Littleton, N. H., 1837; dismissed 1842; now an assistant secretary of the American Board, and resides at Auburndale, Mass.

REV. JOHN H. WORCESTER,

Sixth son of Leonard, born at Peacham, May 28, 1812; graduated at Dartmouth, 1833; tutor at Dartmouth one year, ordained over Congregational Church at St. Johnsbury, 1839; dismissed in 1846; installed at Burlington, 1847; dismissed Oct. 11, 1854; now resides at Burlington.

JOSIAH SHEDD, M. D.,

Born at Rindge, N. H., 1781. He received a medical diploma at Dartmouth College. Spent nearly all his professional life in this town; was regarded as a skillful practitiouer, a successful financier, a man of integrity, energy and firmness of character. He died suddenly of apoplexy, Sept. 4, 1851, aged 70 years.

HON. THADDEUS STEVENS.

He. fitted for college in our Grammar School, and graduated at Dartmouth College, A. D. 1815; for a time pursued the study of law in the office of John Mattocks, Esq., of this town; and this town, more than any other place, was his early home. Here lived the family, and the graves of his parents are among us. From Peacham he went to Gettysburg, Pa., thence to Lancaster, Pa. He is at this time a member of congress (1861), and for several preceding sessions has served his country in that position. He has just been reëlected by a large majority to the next congress.

HON. JOHN C. BLANCHARD,

Was born in Peacham, 1787, and graduated at Dartmouth in 1812. After graduating he taught in York, Pa., two years, reading law at the same time. He then went into practice at Bellefont, Pa. Was elected to congress in 1844, and took his seat in 1845. He died in 1849 at Lancaster, Pa., while on his way home from Washington.

MELLEN and WILLIAM CHAMBERLAIN,

Sons of Hon. William Chamberlain. MELLEN, born June 17, 1795, graduated at Dartmouth in 1816; was in the practice of law some years in the state of Maine, and while making the tour of Europe, drowned in the river Danube, May 14, 1840. His grave is on the banks of the Danube, province of Servia, empire of Austria.

WILLIAM, born May 24, 1797; graduated at Dartmouth in 1818; in 1820 was elected professor of languages in his *alma mater*, and so continued till his death, July 11, 1830.

The following inhabitants of Peacham are graduates of college:

Clergymen.—Samuel A. Worcester, Evarts Worcester, John H. Worcester, David Merrill, Horace Herrick, Ephraim W. Clark, John Mattocks, William Walker, Elnathan Strong.

Lawyers.—Thaddeus Stevens, John C. Blanchard, Nathaniel Blanchard, William C. Carter, George B. Chandler, S. A. Chandler, O. P. Chandler, William Mattocks, James Merrill, David Gould, A. A. Rix, James Stuart, John A. Gilfillan.

In other callings.—Leonard Worcester, Enoch Blanchard 1st, Enoch Blanchard 2d, Mellen Chamberlain, William Chamberlain, George Mattocks, Moses Hall, William Varnum, Willard Thayer, William Bradlee, William W. Moore, Ephraim Elkins, Lyman S Watts. Total, 35.

PUBLIC LIFE AND CHARACTER OF GOVERNOR MATTOCKS.

BY REV. T. GOODWILLIE OF BARNET.

Editor of the Vermont Hist. Magazine:
You write to obtain information of the public life and character of Gov. Mattocks, from one who was acquainted with him. It is true I was long acquainted with him, but not intimately, till the last years of his life. I send you the following sketch drawn from personal knowledge and other sources:

Hon. John Mattocks was born at Hartford, Conn., March 4, 1777. His father, who was treasurer of the state of Vermont from 1786 to 1801, came with his family about the year 1778 or 1779, and settled in Tinmouth, Rutland county, Vt. His youngest son became the fourteenth governor of Vermont. Having been admitted to practice law before he was 21 years of age, he opened an office in Danville, Caledonia county, and commenced the practice of his profession in 1797, but the next year removed to Peacham in the same county, where he resided till his death. In a few years he became a celebrated lawyer, and ultimately a very popular man, being elected to every office for which he was a candidate. He was one of the great men of Caledonia county, indeed he was one of the eminent men of the state of Vermont. He practised law about 50 years, the most of the time in the courts of four counties. He has often been engaged in every jury trial at a whole session at the county court, and won every case. He represented Peacham in the legislature of Vermont in 1807, and again in 1815 and 1816, and also in 1823 and 1824; and was a member of the constitutional convention of 1835, when the measure for a state senate was adopted, and which he advocated. During the last war with Great Britain he was brigadier-general of militia in this part of the state. He was judge of the supreme court of the state in 1833 and 1834, but declined a reëlection on

368 VERMONT HISTORICAL MAGAZINE.

account of domestic afflictions. He was a representative in congress from Vermont in 1821–1823, 1825–1827, and 1841–1843, and was governor of Vermont in 1843–4. It is the opinion of good judges that in many respects he resembled the celebrated lawyer, Jeremiah Mason of New Hampshire.

He did not receive a liberal education, but was a self-educated man. " My brother," said he, "rode through college to the law, but I came up afoot." He possessed in an uncommon degree "the sanguine temperament," as physiologists call it, being distinctly characterized by vigor, vivacity and activity of mind, a ready and retentive memory, lively feelings and a humorous disposition. Indeed so strong and active were his mind and memory, that a book which a good lawyer would take a number of days to master thoroughly for practical purposes, he could devour and digest in a day, storing its contents away in his capacious memory ready for future use. His wonderful talent of appropriating the contents of books enabled him, though altogether a practical man, to obtain a tolerable knowledge of standard English, and the current literature of the day, as well as a considerable acquaintance with history. His style, as may be seen in his reported judicial opinions, was direct and forcible, using few words to convey his thoughts. His concentration of mind and power of analysis and illustration were so great that he had an admirable faculty of presenting facts and points in a clear and convincing manner, and his address had a peculiar aptitude to the case under consideration.

In stature he was about 5 feet 10 inches high, with a large robust frame inclined to corpulency, but with a very healthy appearance. Active, energetic, industrious and prompt, he did much work, which was well done and done in due season. He had a superior way of examining witnesses, but his great and universally acknowledged power as a lawyer was advocacy before a jury. Here he stood unrivaled among great lawyers. His success was almost certain, especially when he had the closing argument. His power as an advocate was not owing to his eloquence as an orator. It did not consist in long and loud speaking. He had not a copious flow of fine words "like flaxseed running out of a bag" to use one of his own comparisons with respect to flowery pleading and preaching. He employed no rhetorical flourishes or fanciful sketches to fascinate the jury. But in a familiar and colloquial

manner he talked the whole matter over with them and he talked his side of the case into them. In a manner really ingenious and artful, but apparently frank, fair, and artless, he convinced them that his client was in the right, and ought to gain the case. He seized upon the strong points of his case with consummate skill and ability and urged his natural and simple logic with such power and perspicuity, that any man of common sense could easily comprehend the case. He excelled also in making the most out of a series of circumstances, not always harmonious, and was long celebrated for his skill and tact in managing criminal cases. His knowledge of human nature, which was deep and extensive, he successfully employed in his profession. As a book lawyer he was not so remarkable, for although he had such an acquaintance with the books as readily to find what he wanted, yet his mind was too active and impulsive to plod patiently among authorities. So acute and rapid were his mental operations that he grasped a knotty point instantly, as if by intuition, and solved the legal problem in some quick mysterious manner quite incomprehensible to ordinary minds. As a judge he was cautious and upright, desiring to do justice to all. His reported dissenting opinion given in the Supreme Court with respect to the Christian sabbath agrees with the word of God and the laws of the state. His views on this important subject were sound and Christian. He had warm sympathies for his fellow-men, and could not have been an oppressor, a persecutor, or an inquisitor, had he lived in the dark ages when oppression and superstition prevailed. Ever ready to relieve the poor, his charities were like numerous rivulets which water a wide space. When a member of congress and governor of the state he took an early and decided stand against human bondage. In a speech he made in congress when he presented a petition for the abolition of slavery in the District of Columbia, he said, "I present this petition because I believe in my soul, that the prayer thereof ought to be granted, so as to free this land of liberty from the national and damning sin of slavery in this our own bailiwick, the District of Columbia."

As he was intelligent and social, his conversation was interesting and instructive. He was universally acknowledged to be a keen and ready wit. The lightning-like operations of his mind and his prompt memory, always gave him ready command of all his resources, which were numerous and diversified. His wit consisted in combinations of these materials adapted to the subject and occasion. His witty sayings were sometimes very pungent, but in general they were harmless pleasantries. His fund of anecdotes was inexhaustible, and both in public and private, he illustrated the subject with pertinent anecdotes well told in few words. His conversation was sprightly, and he enjoyed a hearty laugh. He was fond of joking, even with strangers. One evening at the place of his residence, he heard an agent of the Colonization Society represent its claims in a manner so forcible that he thought him a *good beggar* in a good cause. The next morning the agent called upon the governor and in a general conversation, asked him "what is the chief business in this place at present?" "*Begging,*" quickly replied the governor, "is *now* the chief business," at the same time slily slipping some gold into the agent's hand, for which he thanked him. "Not at all," said the governor, "*I thank you,* sir." "Why thank me?" asked the agent. "Because," answered the governor, "*you let me off so easy.*" In a tight pinch he was very adroit in devising ingenious and prompt expedients for effectual deliverance from difficulty. He wrote such a hasty and imperfect hand, that sometimes he could not read it himself, but which, his brother, a lawyer in the country, could decipher. Going to trial before the County Court on one occasion he had such difficulty to read the writ, though written with his own hand, that the judge questioned the correctness of his reading, when he instantly gave it to his brother, saying, "You are college learned, read that writ." At one time when returning from the court at Guildhall, he lodged on Saturday night in the town of W., then a new settlement, where they had no public worship. The next day he went home through Barnet, intending to worship with the Presbyterians in that town (whose religious principles and practices he esteemed so highly as to refer to them with approbation in a reported opinion he gave from the bench of the Supreme Court), and to hear their venerable minister, Rev. David Goodwillie, whom he held in high estimation, preach. The next morning the sheriff from Barnet arrested him at his residence in Peacham and took him to Barnet, to be tried upon a charge of violating the law of the state by traveling on the sabbath in prosecution of his secular affairs. Arraigned before a sage Scotch Presbyterian justice, he called for a jury, and by exercising his right of challenge, he got a number of Presbyterians on the jury, knowing they were strict observers of the

sanctity of the sabbath. Having produced his testimony, he freely admitted that he went home from court on the sabbath, but in his defence he said, "The court at Guildhall sat so late on Saturday I had not time to go home that evening. The next morning I found that there was no public worship in the town of W., where I lodged on Saturday night. It being my custom to attend church on sabbath, I came to Barnet to worship with the Presbyterians whom I know to be sound in the faith and right in practice, and to hear their intelligent and pious pastor preach. But I was disappointed, for when I came to their church door I found that their worthy minister was officiating out of town that day. I was then half way home, and instead of returning to the place whence I came that morning, I went home, knowing my residence was in a *better place* than the *wicked* town of W. where there is no church, no clergyman, no public worship, *no sabbath and no religion.*" The court having heard his witnesses and *defence,* immediately withdrew the action and discharged him from arrest. He then generously entertained the court and company at his own expense.

About the time he became governor of the state, I was sent to him by the board of trustees of Caledonia County Academy to procure from him a piece of his land to complete the site for the new academy. When shown what was wanted, he instantly gave it as a donation to the academy, although the land was a part of his mansion garden. After returning to his house, we engaged for some time in relating anecdotes, respecting the folly and wickedness of dueling, as a member of congress had been lately murdered in a duel. About to depart I related an anecdote, which convulsed the governor with laughter. I bid him farewell and left him still laughing heartily, but the next time I saw him, which was not long afterwards, oh how sadly changed! The shocking death of his youngest son, a college graduate, then at home, produced lamentable effects upon his mind and body, which lasted as long as he lived, although he recovered from them in a good degree. But there is reason to believe that a gracious Providence overruled this heart-rending event for his spiritual interest and eternal welfare. At the grave of the deceased, he said to the multitude that attended the funeral, "With the mangled body of my son, I bury my ambition and love of the world, and God grant that they may never revive." Regretting the errors and delinquencies of his past life, he settled his worldly affairs, made his last will and testament, declined a re-election to the office of governor of the state, and joined the Congregational Church of Peacham, of which he continued a member till death. His creed was Calvinistic, embracing the great doctrines of the gospel. He always preferred such sermons as were deeply doctrinal and practical. Through life he refrained from secular affairs on the sabbath, and it was his constant practice to attend church on that holy day. He was never rude nor insolent, but courteous to all. He was particularly spoken of, and is gratefully remembered by many, for the assistance and encouragement he almost uniformly gave to young men, and markedly so to those of his own profession. He always acted in an honorable manner towards his fellow lawyers and judges, and his clients were his firm friends. His great success as a lawyer, though his charges not were exorbitant, laid the foundation of an ample fortune. Besides the donations bestowed on his children after he gave them a liberal education, his property at death was valued at $80,000. He died August 14, 1847, aged 70 years. His funeral was attended by a great concourse of people from different and distant parts. Three sons survived him—one of whom became a clergyman, another a physician, and a third a lawyer.

THOMAS SCOTT PEARSON,

BY MRS. L. H. KENDALL.

Son of Rev. Ora and M. K. Pearson, was born at Kingston, N. H., Sept. 14, 1828. His religious birth dates about the age of seventeen. He entered Middlebury College in 1847, and was graduated in 1851; for the year subsequent was principal of Addison County Grammar School, at Middlebury, and librarian of the College.

In 1852, he became principal of Caledonia County Grammar School, Peacham, which position he filled with great acceptance until compelled by ill health to resign in the spring of 1855. The summer of 1855 was passed under medical care, and in traveling for his health; the autumn and winter of the same year, in part, in completing a catalogue of the library of Middlebury College. In the spring of 1856, he became connected, as teacher, with Kimball Union Academy, at Meriden, N. H.; a post, however, he was soon obliged, in consequence of increasing feebleness, to relinquish. In August, he left his home in Peacham to try the effect of the western climate upon his still failing health;

but death had placed his seal upon him. He died at Indianapolis, Ind., Nov. 10, 1856. To a stranger, this is but a short and common-place story; to those who knew Mr. Pearson, a brief outline of an earnest, well-spent life.

As "the boy is father of the man," so there early appeared in the subject of this sketch those traits of character which enabled maturer years. Orderly, conscientious, truthful, *eminently* persevering, obtaining a ready mastery of the rudiments of knowledge, and exhibiting withal a marked predilection for the gathering up and classification of facts, he became early distinguished as a reliable, intelligent boy, and in later years as the devoted son and brother, the faithful friend, the trusted pupil, the indefatigable teacher, the upright citizen, and the consistent Christian. As a Christian, he was always in his place. His seat in the prayer-meeting was seldom vacant, nor his voice silent there; as a sabbath school teacher and superintendent, it is believed he accomplished much good.

Although gifted with unusual conversational powers, having rare fluency of utterance, an inexhaustible fund of anecdote, and a keen perception of the ludicrous, he rarely, if ever, indulged in unseemly mirth, or uttered a word inconsistent with his profession as a Christian. In religion, as in every thing else, he was in earnest, doing with his might whatsoever his hand found to do. His early fondness for collecting facts, alluded to, strengthened with his years. He was always on the alert for items of value, for all which he had a place and a use. While maintaining a high rank as a scholar, and defraying most of his college expenses by teaching, he made this remarkable talent effective in the preparation of several important works, viz., the triennial catalogues of Middlebury College, which he greatly improved; an elaborate catalogue of the college library; the biographical catalogue of the graduates of Middlebury College, believed to be the most thorough and complete work of the kind ever published in this country; obituary notices of deceased members of the alumni; the literary remains and memoir of Rev. David Merrill. And in addition to these, a large amount of unpublished material, which, had he lived, might have been wrought into works of value. The remarkable manner in which all this was accomplished, clearly indicated the work for which he was peculiarly adapted. His talent was becoming widely known and appreciated. He was elected resident member of the N. E. Historic-Genealogical Society, and his death was noticed by this and several other societies.

But there was another, a moral trait, as beautiful as rare, deserving of especial mention; it was filial piety. Loss of eyesight and impaired health had rendered his father unable to labor for the support of the family as in former years, and so this noble son assumed and fully met the heavy responsibility.

Reluctant to lose even a day, he had resumed his duties as teacher, after an attack of illness, before health had become fully established. Reduced as he was previously by unremitting toil, it was too much for him; and his system gave way and consumption began its insidious work. While it was evident he was gradually loosening his hold on earthly things, still there was so much work to be done, he would make one effort more for health and life. Counseled by physicians, he decided to try the west. He arranges his study,* sacred to him by many hallowed associations, gives a parting glance at his varied treasures gathered there. One more prayer and he turns the key upon the place dearest to him on earth. With a full heart but chastened spirit, and a calm, manly bearing, he gives to each member of the household a tender, affectionate farewell and goes forth from his home forever. A few weeks of weary, fruitless wandering among strangers, were terminated by distressing sickness and death. It was a mysterious providence that led him from home only to suffer and to die, away from the affectionate ministrations of his kindred. This it was, doubtless, that in his delirium caused him to utter in vain the bitter cry, "My mother! take me to my mother!" It was, perhaps, the last needful refining process with which God often visits his children, just before he takes them to himself.

Neighbors and friends in Peacham, to whom he had become greatly endeared, rested not until his remains were brought from their grave in the distant prairie to rest on the sunny slope of one of their own green hills. The marble that marks the spot bears the fitting sentence, "Not slothful in business; fervent in spirit; serving the Lord."

* This room is kept as he left it—large accumulations of newspaper files, books, manuscripts, as his own hands arranged. In collating Addison county for the *Gazetteer*, his biographical catalogue of the college had been a favorite text book. We stood as in our dead master's room—a large, well-filled, antiquarian treasure-room—during a day spent with this interesting family, in the summer of 1860.—*Ed.*

EXTRACTS FROM A LETTER OF REV. MR. WORCESTER,

Requesting Mr. Merrill to prepare a Sermon to be Preached on the occasion of his Death.

St. Johnsbury, Jan. 3, 1844.

It has long seemed to me that, in obituary notices of Christians and Christian ministers, in funeral sermons and in Christian biographies, there is, much too commonly, something like high wrought panegyric—something which approaches very near, and sometimes quite reaches to gross adulation—to me, things of this nature are always unpleasant—I had almost said disgusting. In relation to myself, I am sure any thing of this sort would be utterly out of place; and it is my earnest desire that, by every one who may have occasion to say anything concerning me, after my decease, it may be most carefully avoided. Living and dying, my prayer must be, "God be merciful to me a sinner." And though I would not dictate as to the text for a sermon at my funeral, I do not think of one better adapted to the occasion than this prayer of the publican, or the declaration of Paul to Timothy, which has been a favorite text in my preaching, "It is a faithful saying and worthy of all acceptation that Jesus Christ came into the world to save sinners." I think that neither of these texts could legitimately suggest any inflated eulogy in speaking of a poor unworthy sinner.

A word or two now in relation to my desire that my remains may be laid in the grave in Peacham. When I was sick at Littleton, a respected and beloved brother of our church made me a visit; and having understood that I had expressed such a desire, in allusion to it, remarked that *he* had felt that it would be of no consequence where *he* should be buried; intending I suppose to intimate that he thought my desire to be, to say the least, a childish one. His remark however, produced no change in *my* feelings. And when I find in my Bible, that good old Jacob exacted an oath of his son Joseph, that he would bury him in the cave of Machpelah with his venerable grandparents and parents, and one of his deceased wives, which was done at no little expense; and that Joseph himself also exacted an oath of the children of Israel, that they should take his bones with them when they should return to Canaan, that they might be buried in the land of promise, I can not but hope it need not be thought either unreasonable, or very strange, under all the circumstances of the case, that I should desire that my poor remains may be interred in Peacham, in preference to any other place. There for almost forty years of my life I found a pleasant home, and in my poor way performed the duties of the ministry, endeavoring "to testify the gospel of the grace of God." There, too, I was made the humble instrument of gathering a goodly number into the visible fold of the Good Shepherd, no small proportion of whom, I humbly trust, will be found among those on his right hand, in the day of his appearing. There is the grave of the beloved wife of my youth, the mother of my numerous family of children, and the graves of more than half these dear children themselves. Yes, and there too no small number of the members of that beloved church and society, to whom I ministered the gospel of the Son of God so long, have been gathered into the congregation of the dead; and there, no doubt, many more of them, and you my dear brother, it may be, among them, will yet be gathered together into that same congregation. There too, I freely own, if the Lord will, I *would* that my poor remains may rest with them until "the voice of the Archangel, and the trump of God" shall call us all from thence. And O, that we may all, together

"Then burst the chains in sweet surprise,
And in our Saviour's image rise,"

and go away to be forever with the Lord.

I add one item more. It seems to me a somewhat remarkable fact that, although thirty ministers have been ordained or installed pastors of churches in Caledonia county, only seven of whom, including myself, now retain that relation, and four of whom certainly, and others not improbably, have deceased, yet no one of them has ever died, or found his grave among the people of his charge here. One only (Brother Wright) has deceased, sustaining his pastoral relation; and he died and was buried, not among the people of his charge, in Hardwick, but among his former charge in Montpelier village—my son Evarts is the only minister of our order who has yet found his grave in this county.

Your very affectionate brother
In the bonds of the gospel,
LEONARD WORCESTER.

Rev. David Merrill.

EXTRACTS FROM THE OX SERMON.
BY REV. DAVID MERRILL.

Among the laws given by the Divine Lawgiver through Moses to the Jews, was the following: "If an ox gore a man or a woman that they die, then the ox shall be stoned — but the owner shall be quit. But if the ox *were wont to push* with his horn in time past, and it hath been testified to his owner, and he hath not kept him in, but he hath killed a man or a woman, the ox shall be stoned, and his owner also shall be put to death."—*Exodus*, XXI, 28, 29.

The principle of this law is a very plain one — and a very broad one — here applied in a specific case, but extending to ten thousand others. It is this. Every man is responsible to God for the evils which result from his selfishness, or his indifference to the welfare of others. ＊ ＊ ＊ ＊
The principle of this law is a principle of common sense. ＊ ＊ ＊ Every man is responsible for evils which result from his own selfishness or indifference to the lives of men. In other words, to make a man responsible for results, it is not necessary to prove that he has malice, or that he intended the results. The highwayman had no malice against him he robs and murders, nor does he desire his death, but his money, and if he can get the money he does not care. And he robs and murders because he loves himself and does not care for others; acting in a different way, but on the same selfish principle with the owner of the ox, and on the very same principle is he held responsible.

In the trial of the owner of the ox, the only questions to be asked were these two: Was the ox *wont to push* with his horn in time past? Did the owner *know* it when he let him loose? If both these questions were answered in the affirmative, the owner was responsible for all the consequences. This is a rule which God himself has established.

I. Is *Intoxicating Liquor* wont to produce misery, and wretchedness, and death? Has this been testified to those who make and deal in it as a beverage? If these two things can be established, the inference is inevitable—they are responsible on a principle perfectly intelligible, a principle recognised and proclaimed, and acted upon by God himself.

Turn then your attention to these two facts:

1. Intoxicating liquor is wont to produce misery.

2. Those who make or traffic in it know this. * * * * * * *

The greatest wretchedness which human nature in the world is called to endure, is connected with the use of inebriating drink. There is nothing else that degrades and debases man like it — nothing so mean that a drunkard will not stoop to it — nothing too base for him to do to obtain his favorite drink. Nothing else so sinks the whole man — so completely destroys, not only all moral principle, but all self-respect, all regard to character, all shame, all human feeling. The drunkard can break out from every kind of endearing connection and break over every kind of restraint; so completely extinct is human feeling, that he can be drunk at the funeral of his dearest relative, and call for drink in the last accents of expiring nature.

Now look at a human being, whom God has made for noble purposes and endowed with noble faculties, degraded, disgraced, polluted, unfit for heaven, and a nuisance on earth. He is the centre of a circle — count up his influence in his family and his neighborhood — the wretchedness he endures, and the wretchedness he causes — count up the tears of a wretched wife who curses the day of her espousals, and of wretched children who curse the day of their birth. To all this positive evil which intoxicating liquor has caused, add the happiness which but for it this family might have enjoyed and communicated. Go through a neighborhood or a town in this way, count up all the misery which follows in the train of intoxicating liquor, and you will be ready to ask, can the regions of eternal death send forth any thing more deadly? Wherever he goes the same cry may be heard — lamentation, and mourning, and wo; and whatever things are pure, or lovely, or venerable, or of good report, fall before it. These are its effects. Can any man deny that "the ox is wont to push with his horn?"

II. *Has this been testified to the owner?* or are the makers and venders aware of its effects? The effects are manifest, and they have eyes, ears, and understandings as well as others. * * * * * *

Look at the neighborhood of a distillery — an influence goes forth from that spot which reaches miles around — a kind of constraining influence that brings in the poor, and wretched, and thirsty, and vicious. Those who have money bring it — those who have none bring corn — those who have neither

bring household furniture — those who have nothing bring themselves and pay in labor. Now the maker knows all these men, and knows their temperament, and probably knows their families. He can calculate effects, and he sends them off, one to die by the way, another to abuse his family, and another just ready for any deed of wickedness. Will he say that he is not responsible, and like Cain ask, "Am I my brother's keeper?" The ox was wont to push with his horn, and he knew it; and for a little paltry gain he let him loose, and God will support his law by holding him responsible for the consequences.

But a common excuse is, that "very little of our manufacture is used in the neighborhood: we send it off." And are its effects any less deadly? In this way you avoid *seeing* the effects, and poison strangers instead of neighbors. What would you say to a man who traded in clothes infected with the small-pox or cholera, and who would say by way of apology, that he sent them off, he did not sell any in the neighborhood? Good man! he is willing to send disease and death all abroad! but he is too kind hearted to expose his neighbors. Would you not say to him, you may send them off, but you can not send off the responsibility? The eye of God goes with them, and all the misery which they cause will be charged to you. So we say to the man who sends off his intoxicating liquor.

"But if I do not make it and traffic in it, somebody else will." What sin or crime can not be excused in this way? I know of a plot to rob my neighbor; if I do not plunder him somebody else will. Is it a privilege to bear the responsibility of sending abroad pestilence and misery and death? "Our cause is going down," said Judas, "and a price is set upon the head of our Master, and if I do not betray him somebody else will. And why may not I as well pocket the money as another?" * * * *

Says another, "I wish it were banished from the earth. But then what can I do?" What can you do? You can keep one man clear; you can wash your hands of this wretched business. And if you are not willing to do that, very little reliance can be placed on your good wishes. The days of ignorance on this subject have passed by; every man acts with his eyes open.

Look at the shop and company of the retailer. There he stands in the midst of dissipation, surrounded by the most degraded and filthy of human beings, in the last

40

stages of earthly wretchedness. His business is to kindle strife, to encourage profanity, to excite every evil passion, to destroy all salutary fears, to remove every restraint, and to produce a recklessness that regards neither God nor man. And how often in the providence of God is he given over to drink his own poison, and to become the most wretched of this wretched company. Who can behold an instance of this kind without feeling that God is just. "He sunk down into the pit which he made, in the net which he hid is his own foot taken." Another will say, "I neither make nor traffic in it." But you drink it occasionally. As far as your influence supports it and gives it currency, so far are you a partaker of its evil deeds. If you lend your influence to make the path of ruin respectable, or will not help to affix disgrace to that path, God will not hold you guiltless. You can not innocently stand aside and do nothing. A deadly poison is circulating over the land. Its victims are of every class; and however wide the difference in fortune, education, intellect, it brings them to the same dead level. An effort has been made to stay the plague, and a success surpassing all expectation has crowned the effort. Still the plague rages to an immense extent. What will every good citizen do? Will he not clear his house, his shop, his premises of it? Will he not take every precaution to defend himself against it, and use his influence and his exertions to diminish its circulation and thus diminish human misery? If he fears God or regards man, can he stop short at this? "I speak as unto wise men: judge ye what I say."

ANNIVERSARY ODE,

Sung at the Semi-Centennial Celebration of the Incorporation of the Caledonia County Grammar School, at Peacham, July 1, 1846.

BY OLIVER JOHNSON,

Who was born in Peacham in 1809, and served an apprenticeship in the office of the *Montpelier Watchman.* He was one of the twelve who formed Jan. 1, 1832, the present Massachusetts Anti-Slavery Society, and from that day has been prominently indentified with the anti-slavery cause; aiding it as lecturer, and editing several of its leading papers in the country. He was associated with Garrison in the *Liberator,* three years; an associate editor of the *New York Tribune,* four years, 1853 (1858); has edited the *Anti-Slavery Standard,* New York.

When forests crowned these verdant hills,
  Full fifty years ago,
And ringing through these fertile vales
  Was heard the axman's blow;
When Peace and Thrift came hand in hand
  These woodland wilds among,
Above the settler's humble cot
  A modest Temple sprung.

In Faith our fathers reared the shrine
  To Truth and Knowledge given,
And lifted high a beacon-light
  To guide the soul to Heaven!
That light, though kindled long ago,
  Is burning brightly still;
Its rays are now in beauty shed
  O'er valley, plain, and hill.

The Fount of Knowledge opened here,
  From purest source supplied,
Hath sent afar its healing streams,
  And showered its blessings wide;
The dusky Indian of the West
  Hath felt his soul reclaimed,
And e'en to heathen isles its sons
  The Gospel have proclaimed.

In honored places of the land
  Its sons have served their age,
And won for it a noble name
  On History's glowing page;
In Pulpit, Court, and Council Hall,
  Their words of Truth are heard,
And through the Press their clarion voice
  The Nation's heart hath stirred.

On this dear spot, in youth's fair morn,
  While yet our hopes were bright,
Wise Teachers sought to guide our feet
  In paths of love and light;
And now we come in manhood's hour
  To pour our grateful song,
And offer up our fervent prayer
  Where holiest memories throng.

The Father, leaning on his staff,
  This day renews his joy,
And in the mother's listening ear
  Talks proudly of her boy;
The Widow's broken heart revives
  To see her son return,
And Friendship's fires, once more renewed,
  With holy fervor burn.

O Father! in this joyful hour
  Our thanks to Thee we bring,
And with united heart and voice
  Thy glorious praises sing;
Thy love is boundless as the sea —
  Thy mercy ever sure —
O may the shrine our Fathers reared
  To latest time endure!

May Education's holy light
Extend on every hand,
Till War's foul blot, and Slavery's curse
Be banished from the land ! '
And O may Freedom's sacred fires
On every altar flame,
And Temperance, Righteousness and Peace
Exalt our Nation's fame!

RYEGATE.

BY REV. JAMES M. BEATTIE.

The town of Ryegate was chartered by New Hampshire, to Rev. John Witherspoon, D. D., Sept. 8, 1763. In the winter of 1773, a company was formed by a number of farmers, in the vicinity of Glasgow, Scotland, for the purpose of purchasing a tract of land for settlement in North America. This company was called the Scotch-American Company of Farmers. In March of the same year, David Allen and James Whitelaw, were commissioned by the company to carry out their purpose. Accordingly, on the 25th of March, they sailed from Greenock, and reached Philadelphia, May 24. On their arrival, they providentially met with Dr. Witherspoon, who was then president of New Jersey College, Princeton. He informed them that he had a township of land called Ryegate, in the province of New York on the Connecticut river, containing about 23,000 acres, which,. if they could not suit themselves elsewhere, he would be glad to sell to them, professing at the same time, to take a deep interest in the success of their enterprise. After spending five months in exploring the country, north and south, they returned to Dr. Witherspoon, then in Princeton, N. J., and bargained with him for one half of the town of Ryegate. On coming to New York, they met with James Henderson, a carpenter, and one of their shipmates, who had been sent to assist them in their undertaking. Leaving Mr. Henderson to come in a sloop by way of Hartford, with their chests, tools, and other necessary articles, they left New York, on the 19th of October, and arrived in Newbury, Vt., November 1, where they were hospitably entertained by Jacob Dailey, Esq., to whom they had a letter of introduction from John Church, Esq., who was connected with Dr. Witherspoon in the proprietorship of Ryegate. One week after their arrival, James Henderson appeared in a canoe freighted with the chests and tools aforesaid. On the 10th of November, Mr. Church came to Newbury. The town of Ryegate was then divided. The south half fell to the Scotch American Company. This was considered preferable to the north half for reasons given by Gen. Whitelaw.

"The south," he says in his journal, "has the advantage of the north in many respects.

"1. It is the best land in general.

"2. It is nearest to provisions which we have in plenty within three or four miles, and likewise within six miles of a grist mill, and two miles of a saw mill, all which are great advantages to a new settlement.

"3. We have several brooks with good seats for mills, and likewise Wells river runs through part of our purchase, and has water enough for a grist mill at the driest season of the year, of which the north part is almost entirely destitute.

"We are within six miles of a good *Presbyterian Meeting*; and there is no other minister about that place."

The last reason is particularly worthy of notice. These sons of Scotia in seeking out a home for themselves and others in the new world, were influenced in their choice not merely by the fertility of the soil, and other natural advantages; but by considerations of a religious character. Noble example! Worthy the imitation of all immigrants from the old world.

When they came to Ryegate, they found John Hyndman, one of their own countrymen, who had with his family moved into town a few months before. He was engaged in building a house. "So," says the journal, "we helped him up with it both for the conveniences of lodging with him till we built one of our own, and also that he might assist us in building ours."

These houses, built of logs and covered with bark, were finished about the 1st of January, 1774. John Hyndman's house stood a little northeast of the present house of · John Bigelow. James Whitelaw's was situated near where William T. Whitelaw's house now stands.

Aaron Hosmer and family were the only persons, and the shanty in which they lived about one mile north of Samuel More's, was the only house in town previous to this time.

The remainder of the winter was spent in making an opening in the wilderness; the whole of the town being covered with trees of various kinds, among which were beech, maple, hemlock, spruce, birch and pines. James Henderson was employed part of the time in manufacturing wooden bowls, dishes, and other articles for domestic use. James

Whitelaw went to Portsmouth and Newbury-port for a sleigh load of such necessaries as they needed. In the month of April they made 60 pounds of maple sugar — a business that has been followed up in the town ever since, large quantities being manufactured annually, both for domestic and foreign use. In May, James Whitelaw commenced the survey of the company's half of the town.

On the 23d of May, David Ferry, Alexander Lynn and family, Andrew and Robert Brock, John and Robert Orr, John Willson, John Gray, John Shaw, and Hugh Semple, came over from Scotland; and in July when the survey was completed, drew their lots, and commenced a permanent settlement. These were among the first settlers. They were men of sterling worth. And some of their descendants are among the most respectable at the present time.

In the survey of the southern portion of Ryegate, a lot extending from the parsonage to the foot of the hill below John O. Page's, was laid out for a town. This was divided into small lots. Each purchaser of a lot in any other part of the township received a town lot. It was the expectation that a large town or city would, in the course of time, grow up in that place. But time has rolled on, and the city is still unbuilt. Like many cities in the West, it is but a city of faith. Whenever the early settlers had occasion to refer to that part of the township, they called it the town, although the only building upon it was a small log house. The hill at John O. Page's is still called the town hill.

The company's half of the town having been surveyed and allotted, David Allen, James Whitelaw's associate, left for Scotland. It was an affecting occasion. All the inhabitants accompanied him to Col. Bailey's in Newbury, where they took farewell of him. James Henderson was unwilling to part from him even then, but journeyed with him all the way to Newburyport, before he took his leave. These early settlers, far from their native land, and exposed to danger, both from the Indians and wild beasts, were bound together by strong ties. It is no wonder therefore, that they were so loth to part with one of their number, and especially as that one had been a leader among them. Soon after the survey of the south half, the north half was surveyed and allotted.

In 1774, the settlement realized another accession from Scotland, John Waddle, James Neilson, Thomas McKeach, Patrick Lang and family, William Neilson and family, and David Reed and family, Robert Gemmil and son, Robert Tweedale and family, and Andrew and James Smith.

About this time, it was found necessary to erect a house to accommodate the immigrants on their arrival, until they could build houses of their own.

On the 22d of October, Andrew Smith departed this life. This was the first death that occurred. About a mile south from the Corner, a lot was selected for a burying ground, and here he was interred. The remains of a number of others of the early settlers lie in the same place.

And is it not highly discreditable to the town that that sacred spot — sacred by containing all that is mortal of men, whose memory, on account of their toils and perils in exploring and subduing our forests, ought to be dear to us all—should be unmarked by any monument. As the trees and bushes have been recently cleared off, why not proceed a step further, in honoring the memory of our worthy ancestors, by erecting upon the place of their interment, a monument with an appropriate inscription?

In January, 1775, Gen. Whitelaw purchased a lot of land of Newbury, on the north side of that part of Wells river which contains the great falls, with the privilege of one half the river, for the purpose of erecting mills thereon. Accordingly, James Henderson commenced to prepare materials, and in October of the same year, a grist mill was finished, and put in operation. In this same month, the frame of a saw mill was erected, but not completed until July, 1776. These mills although in Newbury, were only two and a half miles from the centre of Ryegate. They stood where Bolton's Mills now stand.

In April, 1775, the settlement was enlarged by the arrival of Archibald Taylor and family in February, and John Scot in April. About this time the war of the Revolution commenced, and, in consequence, few additions were made to the settlement for a number of years. After peace was concluded, the spirit of emigration revived, and the town received many valuable accessions from Scotland. As a general rule, the Scotch, especially those of the Presbyterian faith, with their habits of industry and economy, their knowledge of the scriptures, their regard for the sabbath, and the institutions of religion, are a blessing to any community where their lots may be cast.

The town was organized on the third Tuesday of May, 1776. James Whitelaw, first town clerk; assessors, John Gray and James

Whitelaw; treasurer, Andrew Brock; overseers of highways, Robert Tweedale and John Orr; overseers of the poor, Patrick Lang and John Shaw; collector, John Scot; constables, Archibald Taylor, James Smith, William Neilson and David Reid.

The high estimation in which these persons were held, is evinced by the fact that at the expiration of the year for which they were chosen, they were by a vote of the town, continued in office for another year. In this year James Taylor was born, the first male child born in town. He died at the age of 64 years.

In common with the other early settlements, the people of Ryegate were subjected to great hardships and privations, a minute account of which would fill volumes. Take the following as a specimen :

In the summer of 1776, a year so memorable in the history of the United States, a message was received that St. Johns was retaken by the British, and that the Indians, who were a terror to all the early settlers, would be sent to lay waste the country. They were greatly alarmed, and at their wits' end to know what to do. After some consultation, they concluded the only course was to remove to some place of greater safety. Accordingly with what of their effects, they could carry in their flight, they left for Newbury, where a fort had been erected, and soldiers stationed, both to protect the settlers from the Indians and Tories in the surrounding country, and to check the incursions of the Indians and British from Canada. Before leaving, William Neilson filled a large Scotch chest with sundry articles, and buried it, and then to prevent the suspicions of the sons of the wilderness, burnt a pile of brush upon its *grave*. They soon found, however, that if they remained long at Newbury, a greater calamity, if possible, than war, would befall them. They had commenced to clear and cultivate the land; their crops were in the ground, and they must secure them, or die of starvation. These brave men again held a council and all agreed that there was no alternative but to return at the risk of their lives. Tradition reports that William Neilson preceded the rest. He bravely said, "It is better to die by the sword than famine;" and tearing himself away from his weeping wife and children, went boldly back, trusting in Jehovah's arm for safety. During the day he worked hard, and slept at night with his door barricaded, and his gun at his pillow. The expected invasion, however, did not occur, and

consequently all in a few days returned to their own habitations.

Beasts of prey proved a greater annoyance than the Indians. The latter, by kind and hospitable treatment became the friends of the settlers, but the wolves and bears which were very numerous, were not so easy to subdue. For some time, John Henderson was the only person that owned a cow. One evening the cow not returning home as usual, Mrs. Henderson, her husband being absent, went in search of the cow. Soon after Mr. Henderson came in, and missing his wife, asked the children where their mother was? They replied, "Mother has gone for the cow." It then being dark, it at once occurred to him that she was lost. With a pine torch in one hand, and a gun in the other, he sallied forth to find her. He fired off his gun, but no reply being given, he proceeded further into the woods, and discharged his gun the second time. She answered. Following the direction of her voice, he found her lodged in a tree, where she had taken refuge from wild beasts. At another time, George Reynolds, on his way to pay a visit to one of his neighbors, encountered, as he supposed, a very fierce dog. After a sharp contest with the animal, he succeeded in putting it to flight; left however, in anything but a good humor, on arriving at his neighbor's, he gave the good woman of the house, a severe reprimand for keeping such a cross dog, and on examination it was found to be a wolf.

One day in the summer of 1778, Mrs. John Gray saw a bear carrying off a sheep. With a courage with which probably few ladies in this age are endowed, she followed the bear by his trail, till she suddenly came up within a few feet of him. Greatly terrified, she screamed outright, whereupon Bruin not accustomed to such noises, dropped his prey and betook himself to flight; and Mrs. Gray putting the sheep on her shoulder, returned home in triumph.

There was a long time before the bears were completely destroyed, particularly in the northeastern part of the town. In 1804, four bears that had been making havoc among the sheep, were killed on Robert Dickson's farm.

Bear's meat was much used by the early settlers. The lean part of the bear being like beef, and the fat like pork, it was a good substitute for both. When salted a little it was called corned beef.

Besides the perils from the Indians and wild beasts, there were other difficulties that the early settlers had to surmount to put their descendants into the possession of their present inheritance. There were no bridges and no roads, but spotted trees. When they went to mill which was in Newbury, 10 miles distant from the central part of the town, they carried their grists on their backs. This was also the mode of conveyance, in carrying articles to and from the store, which was also located in Newbury. There, too, was their place of worship. Not only men, but women also, traveled all that distance on foot, that they might have an opportunity of worshiping the God of their fathers in the public congregation. "When the ladies," says Mr. Powers, "came to Wells river (there being no canoe), they would bare their feet, and trip it along as nimbly as a deer, the men generally went barefooted, the ladies certainly, wore shoes."

Money was a scarce article, as is shown by the following incident: Gen. Whitelaw purchased a corn-broom, the first that was used in the settlement. His daughter being very much pleased with it, remarked that she would never again be at the trouble to make a broom of hemlock brush, when one so much superior could be bought for twenty-five cents. "Marion," said her father, "I have seen the time when there was not twenty-five cents in Ryegate." (For the incidents that we have just related, and for many other facts in these sketches, we are indebted to Mrs. Abigail Henderson, daughter of Gen. Whitelaw, in her 78th year. She is a pious lady, and endowed with a remarkable memory).

January 9, 1777, James Henderson was married to Agnes Lynn, and on the 17th of the same month, Robert Brock to Elizabeth Stewart. These were the first marriages in Ryegate. Mr. Brock moved into Barnet, and settled. Mr. Henderson took up his residence in Ryegate. He was the first carpenter in town. Besides being very useful as a mechanic during the infancy of the settlement, he afterwards served the town as representative, and in various town offices to which he was elected. He was a consistent member of the Associate Church. He died at the age of 85 years. His farm is owned and occupied by his son, William Henderson, in his 80th year (1861).

While exploring and subduing the forests, the early settlers did not neglect the intellectual and religious culture of their children. In the year 1787, the first regular school was established in James Whitelaw's house. The first teacher was Jonathan Powers. The school continued to be kept in private

houses until 1792, when the first school house was erected. This was built of logs, and stood on the town lot, southeast of John O. Page's.

Previous to this time, James Whitelaw had been appointed surveyor general of the state of Vermont; and, in consequence was under the necessity of resigning his office as agent of the Scotch-American company.

Accordingly, he intimated to the company in Scotland, that they must appoint some other person to be their land agent in this country. In accordance with his request, they authorized the members of the company, residing in the town of Ryegate, to call a meeting for that purpose. This meeting was held in March, 1793, at which William Neilson, James Henderson and Hugh Gardner were appointed managers, and it was "voted that James Whitelaw, who now holds the deeds of the company's land shall to him deed it to the managers and their successors in office."

Up to this date, Gen. Whitelaw held all the deeds of all the land that had been sold in the south half of Ryegate. He then delivered them all up with the disposal of all the lands belonging to the Scotch-American company not taken up, to the said managers. This was Gen. Whitelaw's last act as agent for that company, which he had served so long and so faithfully; and yet all his valuable services received but very small compensation.

In 1795, the town was divided into two school districts. These were afterwards subdivided to meet the wants of the people. There are now in the town 9 school districts. The school-houses with one or two exceptions, are neat and commodious. A growing interest is also taken in the schools; and it is the determination in most of the districts, that none but competent teachers shall be employed. The number of scholars between the ages of 4 and 18, are 342.

The attention of our forefathers was turned to the education of the heart and conscience, as well as the head. At one time they were under the impression that they would enjoy the ministrations of Dr. Witherspoon, the Rev. proprietor. But disappointed in that, those of them that did not find it convenient to attend church at Newbury, held meetings for prayer and Christian conference, read good books, and attended particularly to the religious education of the children. In March, 1797, they "voted to raise forty bushels of wheat by a tax, to support the gospel in the town for the ensuing year." They then engaged a part of the services of Rev. David Goodwillie of the Associate Church, who had been settled in Barnet over a colony also from Scotland. And it may be remarked in passing, that it was from the first settlers of these two towns, Ryegate and Barnet, that the county received the name of Caledonia.

Another event of some importance that occurred in 1797, was the erection of the frame of a meeting house on the hill west of the Corner. It was soon enclosed and meetings held in it. But it was not finished until in the year 1800. This was the first meeting house in town. Previous to this time, civil and religious meetings were held in private houses. For sixteen years after the erection of the meeting house, the people worshipped in it without any stove. It was used as a house of worship till 1850, when it was abandoned for a new and tasteful meeting house, built at the Corner south of the brick house, by the Reformed Presbyterian (old school) and Associate congregations of Ryegate. Town meetings, however, continued to be held in it till 1855, when it was pulled down, and a town house erected in the same place.

In the same year that the meeting house was finished, Rev. William Gibson of the Reformed Presbyterian Church, was settled. And being the first settled minister, he drew one right of land, which is now owned and occupied by James Beattie, Esq.

For some time after, Mr. Gibson's settlement, there were no carriages in the town. The only modes of locomotion were on foot and on horseback. It was not an uncommon thing on a sabbath morning, to see the worshipers, some on foot and some on horseback, flocking to the house of God. A man and his wife, each holding a child, frequently rode one horse. And notwithstanding these difficulties, many that lived from 4 to 6 miles distant from the place of worship, were seldom absent on the sabbath.

From the time that Mr. Gibson became pastor in Ryegate, the town has been well supplied with gospel ordinances.

The professors of religion in Ryegate are, with a few exceptions, Presbyterians; and are divided into three denominations—the Reformed Presbyterian (old school), Reformed Presbyterian (new school), and the United Presbyterian.

About the time of Mr. Gibson's installment, a lot of land consisting of two acres, south of the meeting house, was purchased of Andrew Brock, for a burying ground. Being ledgy, and therefore not well adapted for a

place of interment, another lot south of it has recently been purchased, by a company formed for that purpose. Some improvements have been made on it. When ornamented with walks and trees, it will be a neat yard. It is called the Blue Mountain Cemetery. Besides those mentioned, there are two other burying grounds in the town, one in the western part, and one near South Ryegate.

The surface of this town is generally uneven. The northern and eastern portions are hilly and broken. The only mountain, called Blue Mountain, is situated in the northwest part. This, though a bleak, barren mountain, is valuable for its quarries of granite, from which monuments, mill stones, &c., are manufactured. Its summit affords a commanding view of the surrounding country. Indeed Ryegate abounds in picturesque scenery. Limestone is found in different parts of the town.

Connecticut river bounds it on the east, and Wells river runs through the southwest part of the town, affording ample water power. Ticklenaked pond, in the southern part, discharges its waters into Wells river, and North pond in the northern part, empties itself into Connecticut river. The whole town is well watered by springs and small streams.

The soil is mostly of clay and loam. The interval land on the Connecticut and Wells river, is level, and the soil of an excellent quality, producing abundantly all kinds of garden vegetables and grain. The other portions, though hilly, are also well adapted to the production of grain, and yield luxuriant crops of grass. The attention of the farmers is chiefly occupied with cattle raising and the dairy. This town has long been celebrated for its excellent butter.

There are two small villages in town, Ryegate Corner and South Ryegate, with a post office at each. Besides the meeting house already mentioned, there is another place of worship at Ryegate Corner, which belongs to the United Presbyterians. There is also a Union Church at South Ryegate where the Ref. Presbyterians (new school) worship.

There is no high school in town. But this is not felt to be a want, as in each of the adjoining towns of Peacham, Barnet and Newbury, there is an excellent academy. Hence the youth are well instructed, and care is taken to have the school attainments sanctified by lessons of Christianity. The inhabitants of Ryegate, are a plain, unassuming, honest, industrious and peaceable people. The Puritan and Presbyterian principles are finely blended in their manners and character.

The professional men that claim Ryegate as their birth place, are Rev. Robert Gibson, for many years pastor of the 2d Reformed Presbyterian Church, New York city, now deceased; Rev. John Gibson, and Rev. William Gibson, ministers in connection with the Presbyterian church in the south; Rev. A. M. Milligan settled in New Alexandria, Pa.; Rev. S. T. Milligan in Michigan; Rev. J. K. Milligan, pastor of the 1st Reformed Presbyterian Church, New York; Rev. James M. Dickson, pastor of the Church of the Covenanters, Brooklyn, Long Island; Rev. John Lynn, pastor of a Presbyterian church in Maryland; Dr. William Neilson, a distinguished physician and surgeon in Cambridge, N. Y., deceased.

Dr. Eli Perry came to Ryegate in 1814. He was the first physician in town, and is still with us, aged 70 years.

George Cowles is at present town clerk; and so completely does he enjoy the confidence of all parties that he has held that office for 18 years.

For the last half century the town has advanced rapidly, and we stand to-day amid fields of waving grain, and under trees bending with luscious fruit; we look at the beautiful green meadows, and neatly painted farm houses, the well cultivated gardens and tasteful yards, the white school-houses, warm and comfortable; we see from a distance the church spire; all this to-day we see, where 86 years ago was a wild and unbroken forest. Thanks to the strong arms and brave hearts of our forefathers! Thanks to the Great Protector, who amid all their toils and perils, blessed them with health and strength, to accomplish the great work which they had undertaken.

BIOGRAPHICAL SKETCHES.

JAMES WHITELAW,

Who may be called the father of Ryegate, was born at New Mills, parish of Oldmonkland, Scotland, February 11, 1748. He came here in 1773. The circumstances connected with his arrival and settlement, have been already stated.

He certainly was the chief agent in the settlement of the town, and for about 40 years his influence was felt in almost every movement. He built the first framed house in the town, which stood where the late Wm. Whitelaw's house now stands.

He was surveyor-general of the state of Vermont, and not only surveyed this town, but many of the town lines in the northern part of the state were run by him, and some of the towns allotted. This was done when there were no roads but dotted trees, and but few houses, and these many miles distant from each other. Hence his way, in many places through which he traveled, was obstructed by logs, rocks, mountains, and other obstacles. He was always attended, at such times, by three or four men, whose business it was to carry the chain, mark the trees, and render him such assistance as was needed. They carried their provisions on their backs, in knapsacks; slept at night in the woods, on beds of hemlock boughs; and often when they awoke in the morning, found themselves covered with a soft, white blanket, more than a foot thick, it having snowed during the night.

Surveying was his employment for 12 or 14 years, yet during all this time there is no record of his ever having been molested by any savage, beast, or venomous reptile. He always enjoyed good health and spirits, and submitted to the trials and hardships of his occupation with patience, and even cheerfulness.

In the year 1796 he completed a very correct map of the state of Vermont. He afterwards established himself in a land office, in which situation he continued the residue of his life.

He was three times married. In 1778 he was married to Abigail Johnstone of Newbury, by whom he had two sons and two daughters. The sons, who were useful citizens, are dead. The daughters are still living. His first wife died July 13, 1790. His second wife, Susanna Rogers, died in 1815. He married for his third wife, Jannet Harvey, a widow, who died in 1854, aged 88. She came from Scotland before the Revolutionary War, and lived to see the wilderness blossom.

We will bring this sketch to a close, by quoting from the communication of a person who had excellent opportunities of becoming acquainted with Gen. Whitelaw. Says Mrs. A. Henderson: "As husband, father, brother, or friend, he was not surpassed by any in his day. His townspeople had the utmost confidence in him. He was their town clerk for upwards of 40 years; and town treasurer and postmaster, from the time of their establishment in the town, to the day of his death. He had always great care and government of his own words and actions. There was no pride or passion in his intercourse with mankind, but a wonderful serenity of mind and evenness of temper were visible in his very countenance. His benevolence and philanthropy were always equal, if not beyond his means. He was ready on all occasions to administer to the necessities of every one he saw in need. Few men have been more beloved in life, or more lamented in death." He died April 20, 1820, aged 81 years.

JOHN GRAY

Was born in Ederslie, near Paisley, Renfrewshire, Scotland, in 1749. At the age of 28 he joined the Scotch-American Company of Farmers. As already mentioned, he came with others to Ryegate, in May, 1774. On his arrival he had but one shilling in his pocket. He selected a lot about half a mile north of the Corner, on which he erected a log-cabin, and commenced to clear the land, but spent the subsequent winter in Newbury, in laboring for the necessaries of life.

In 1777 he was married to Jean McFarland, by whom he had 7 children, 5 of whom died in 1796 and '97, leaving the eldest daughter and one next the youngest, a son. During the war he was occasionally molested by the Tories and Indians passing through this part of the country.

He was, from the commencement of its settlement, devoted to the interests of the town. Being a man of energy and decision of character, and withal generous and public spirited, he gained the confidence and esteem of all, and occupied a prominent position in the community. Several times he represented the town, was first captain of the militia, and held various town offices.

He was an efficient elder in the Associate Church, and a zealous advocate for the divine right of the Presbyterian form of church government. He was a peace-maker. "He was," said one that knew him well, "the noblest work of God—an honest man."

He died in Nov., 1816, leaving a widow, a daughter and son—the daughter since deceased. The son, William Gray, Esq., occupies the homestead, is the father of 11, and grandfather of 40 children, all alive.

HUGH LAUGHLIN

Was a native of Ireland, who emigrated to the United States and settled in Ryegate, Aug. 2, 1799. Possessed of considerable attainments, and a benevolent heart, he soon rose in the estimation of the people. Thrice he represented the town, was many years a justice of the peace, for a long time an active member of the bible society, and a deacon in the Congregational Church. He died June 30, 1826, in the 65th year of his age. He had 3 children.

ARCHIBALD PARK,

Born in Scotland in 1780, came to Ryegate when he was 14 years of age. In 1806 he married Margaret Renfrew. They had 12 children, 6 of whom, with their families, reside in town, within a few miles of each other.

Mr. Park took an active part in all the public movements of the town, was several years selectman, many years justice of the peace, and at different times overseer of the poor. He departed this life Dec. 12, 1847, in his 68th year.

WILLIAM GIBSON,

Born in Renfrewshire, Scotland; came to Ryegate with a family of 9 children (7 sons and 2 daughters), in June, 1801. He was a quiet, peaceable, and useful member of society, held various offices in the town, and was also an exemplary member and zealous office bearer in the Associate Church. Very generous and public spirited, he contributed liberally towards the support of the gospel.

All his children, except one son and a daughter, settled in Ryegate, and with one exception, have large families. His sons and grandsons are for the most part thrifty farmers, and honest, upright men.

Mr. Gibson died Jan. 2, 1844, in his 90th year. At the time of his death he had between 50 and 60 great-grandchildren.

JAMES NEILSON,

Son of William Neilson, was born in June, 1779. He possessed, in a high degree, the confidence of his townsmen. He represented the town 5 successive years, was justice of the peace many years, and held other offices.

In 1808 he was married to Agnes Gibson. They had 11 children. His son, Dr. William Neilson, now deceased, was an eminent physician. In early life he became a member of the Associate Church. As a professor he was exemplary. He died in June, 1840, in his 61st year.

JOHN CAMERON,

A native of Scotland, came to America and settled in Ryegate in 1790. He purchased 1000 acres of land in the western part of the town, and afterwards at the Corner, 1½ acres of John Orr, on which he built the first store in town. The land is now owned by his son, John Cameron, whose dwelling house occupies the place of the store. He represented the town more than 12 years, was several years member of the council, a judge in 1814, and although a Democrat, he was retained in office under the Federalists.

Judge Cameron was a man of large mental endowments, whose influence was not only felt in the community where he resided, but throughout the state. He died in 1837, aged 76 years. His first wife was a daughter of Gen. Stark.

JONATHAN COBURN,

Was a native of New Hampshire, but spent the most of his life in Ryegate, his father having removed to Vermont in 1789, when he was but 7 years of age. At the age of 24, after a careful examination of the principles of the Ref. Presbyterian church, becoming satisfied of their agreeableness to the Scriptures, he embraced them by public profession in the congregation of Ryegate, and continued an upright and exemplary member till his death, January 8, 1860. He was a consistent covenanter, who had no sympathy with defection. By his death the church sustained a great loss, where as an elder he was an active, zealous, and faithful office bearer for 40 years, exemplary in all his attendance upon the ordinances.

He was moreover a peacemaker, often instrumental in removing offences and healing divisions. A man of comprehensive benevolence, his heart was full of love to all, and his hand ready to perform kindness to any of whom he knew as in need. He also took a deep and lively interest in the cause of missions, sabbath schools, temperance, and the oppressed Africans in our land. He died as he lived. "Let me die the death of the righteous, and let my last end be like his." Mr. Coburn left a widow and several children.

JOHN NEILSON, ESQ.

BY REV. JAMES M'ARTHUR.

In Ryegate, Sept. 6 (1853?), died John Neilson, Esq., in the 79th year of his age. Mr. Neilson was born in the memorable year of the Declaration of American Independence. He was the second male child born in the town of Ryegate, and therefore intimately acquainted with its early history. He was born of religious parents, brought up in the fear of the Lord, and educated in

the principles of the Associate Presbyterian church. These principles he espoused some 40 years since, in connection with the Associate congregation of Ryegate, and maintained them with an unwavering faith unto the last. He was an active member of the congregation in the weakness of its early history, and in its struggles of a later day stood firm in its cause; was liberal in his support of the gospel, and not only *sound* but *strong* in the faith.

He was ever modest and humble, but under afflictive providences, and in times of danger, when others were alarmed and disturbed, calm and peaceful he would say, "we are in the hands of a good providence," and therefore neither unduly feared nor murmured. He further manifested his faith by a truly Christian deportment in all his relations of life. As a husband, ever tender and affectionate; as a parent, maintaining that kindness and intimacy that ever endears; as a friend and neighbor, peaceable and obliging; possessing in an unusual degree that Christian courtesy and politeness proceding from a kind and generous heart.

Though his long life was one of almost uninterrupted good health, yet he had acquired in a high degree the patience of the saints, which is usually through much tribulation. This he ever indicated as occasion offered, but especially in sickness, a severe attack of which brought him near to the gates of death about four years since, and which seemed to have been specially designed to discipline his mind and heart preparatory to his last illness, which in a few weeks reduced the strong man to the extremity of death.

A few days before his death he remarked that he thought he could say with another, that he would place all his good deeds in one scale, and his evil in another, and flee from both to the merits of his Saviour. Let us then "Mark the perfect man, and behold the upright? for the end of that man is peace."

JAMES WHITEHILL.

BY REV. JAMES MILLIGAN.

The subject of this memoir was born in Renfrewshire, Scotland, emigrated to America about the year 1798, and was for many years a ruling elder in the Reformed Presbyterian congregation of Ryegate; was charitable to the poor, and liberal in support of the gospel; but in imparting his benefactions, seemed from principle to shun ostentation.

His habits were those of industry, serenity, and piety. Even in advanced life, he was "diligent in business," and "fervent in spirit." His modesty and diffidence even to a fault, was probably one reason why he did not pursue his education farther, and fill a place in one of the learned professions, for he had made in his youth considerable progress in the Latin language, besides having acquired a very ample English education. He was well supplied with religious books, which he read with great care and spiritual discernment; but the Bible was his chief delight, especially towards the close of his life. On his death-bed he remarked to the writer of this, that in secret prayer, morning and evening, he had great comfort, and also endured terrible conflicts with the adversary. "Many a time," said he, "the adversary tried to drive me from that post, but by the grace of God did not prevail." As a ruler in Israel, he was eminently useful, having an extensive knowledge of church history and government, as well as of didactic and practical theology. His attachment to truth and ecclesiastical order, united to his love of peace, made his services invaluable. During his last illness his ejaculations were frequent and transporting. His conversation became more and visibly in heaven. Reserve was laid aside, but humility continued, adding weight to his piety. His path was remarkably that of the just, which "shineth more unto the perfect day." A short time before his death he sent for his pastor, and requested him to take the following statement from his lips:

"I was baptized in the established church of Scotland, and before I was 20 years of age, renewed the baptismal bans avouching God to be my own God in Christ. Long I felt the obligation to commemorate Christ's dying love, but was afraid, until I had more evidence that I had passed from death to life. I was from early life persuaded that the Revolution was not so pure as the Reformation Church, but delayed joining the latter until I was 30 years of age. * * * "I have found great advantage and comfort in consecrating and keeping my birthday as a day of fasting, prayer, and self-dedication. I had frequently attended to this occasionally, but never statedly, until about 14 years ago. It affords an opportunity of ascertaining and comparing our spiritual progress from year to year.

"I approve of the American Revolution. The Colonies had a right to be free from Great Britain. But oh! they have declared their independence of God, as if they needed

not His wisdom to direct, nor His power to protect them. The nations need to be taught their dependence upon the Lord, and allegiance to the Prince of the Kings of the Earth. I have endeavored, though in great meekness, to promote the interests of the Covenanted Church in this place. * * * * I should like to see all my children take an active and growing interest in the Reformation cause, and hope they will; but in the meantime, I desire to say with David — 'though my house be not so with God, yet hath He made with me an everlasting covenant, ordered in all things and sure.' * * I have no desire to live any longer, though I do not despise my life. I think it lawful to pray for an easy passage through the valley of the shadow of death, but leave it altogether with my God, who has been with me in all the *six* troubles of life, and who will not forsake me in the *seventh*. * * * * Oh! that He would hasten the consummation of His work, sanctify and deliver me from this body of sin and death, and take me to Himself, all through Jesus Christ my Lord."

CHURCH HISTORY.

THE ASSOCIATE CONGREGATION, NOW THE UNITED PRESBY. CHURCH OF RYEGATE.

BY REV. THOMAS GOODWILLIE OF BARNET.

It is not known at what period the Presbyterian churches of Barnet and Ryegate were formed, but they were organized previous to 1779. Before, during and after the Revolutionary war, several Scotch clergymen came and preached to them occasionally, and sometimes administered baptism. Gen. Whitelaw who was the agent of that company, on his way to Ryegate in 1773, called on Rev. Thomas Clark, a Scotch clergyman belonging to the Associate Presby. Church, settled in Salem, N. Y., and Col. Harvey, agent of the Scotch company that settled in Barnet, on his way to town in 1774, called also upon him, and to this clergyman John Gray of Ryegate traveled on foot 140 miles to obtain his services. He gave them a favorable answer April 8, 1775, and came and preached some time in Barnet and Ryegate, in the latter part of the summer of that year. He revisited these towns two or three times afterwards, during the Revolutionary war.

Dr. Witherspoon, president of Princeton College, N. J., a signer of the Declaration of Independence, and a member of congress, who owned lands in Ryegate, Newbury and Walden, and whose son was settled in the north part of Ryegate, visited this part of the country three times, first probably in 1775. In 1782 he preached in Ryegate and Barnet, and baptized some children. He returned in 1786 to this part of the country.

Rev. Hugh White, a Scotch clergyman, preached in Ryegate at the end of 1775.

Rev. Peter Powers, English Presbyterian clergyman, settled in Newbury from 1765 to 1784, preached occasionally in Ryegate, and probably in Barnet during that period.

Previous to 1779, the congregations of Barnet and Ryegate were associated in joint endeavors to obtain preachers. In that year a petition was sent from Ryegate to the church in Newbury, to obtain a share of the ministerial labors of Rev. Peter Powers. Rev. Robert Annan preached in these towns in 1784, and returned next year. Rev. David Annan preached in Barnet and Ryegate, in 1785. Rev. John Huston was present with the session of Barnet, August 31, 1786, when, the record says, "a petition was drawn up by the elders of Barnet and Ryegate, and preferred to the Associate (Ref.) Presbytery, to sit at Petersboro', Sept. 27, 1786, earnestly desiring one of their number might be sent to preach, visit, and catechize the two congregations, and ordain elders at Barnet." Accordingly the Presbytery appointed Mr. Huston for that purpose. In pursuance thereof, Mr. Huston came in October following, and visited and catechized the greater portion of the congregations. He remained till May, 1787, preaching in Barnet and Ryegate, and returned in November, 1788.

In 1789 and 1790, Rev. Mr. Goodwillie of Barnet, preached occasionally at Ryegate. And this church, from his settlement in 1790 (see *Barnet Ecclesiastical History*, pp. 205 and 206), received one-sixth of his labors till 1822.

For 32 years Mr. Goodwillie was diligent in preaching, pastoral visitation of families, and public catechisings, and never failed to fulfill his appointments except twice, when prevented by sickness. During this time, however, they occasionally had preachers sent to them by the Presbytery. In 1809, they gave Mr. Musbat, and in 1813, Mr. Francis Pringle, Jr., calls, but they settled in other congregations. In 1822, Rev. Thos. Ferrier was ordained, and settled as their pastor. He resigned in 1825. In 1827, Rev. Thomas Beveridge was called to the pastorate of the Associate congregation of Ryegate, but did not accept the call.

After being a considerable time supplied by Rev. William Pringle, he was ordained and settled as their pastor, June 29, 1830, by the Associate Presbytery of Cambridge, Mr. Goodwillie, their former pastor, giving him the pastoral charge. He was the son of the eminent Rev. Alexander Pringle, who was for more than 60 years pastor of the Associate Congregation of Perth, Scotland, and married to the daughter of Rev. Alexander Bullions, D. D., being the granddaughter of Mr. Goodwillie. The greatest number of members at one time was 140. Mr. Pringle ministered till 1852. The congregation, however, divided in 1840. Rev. James McArthur ministered in Ryegate one-half of the time, from 1846 till 1857, when he resigned. The congregation, after serious difficulties, is now happily united. The town hall and meeting house, finished in 1800, was the only church edifice in Ryegate till 1825, when the Associate congregation built a good church on a fine site at Ryegate Corner.

May 21, 1801, Barnet and Ryegate congregations were included in the Associate Presbytery of Cambridge, N. Y., to which they belonged till July 10, 1840, when they were included in the Associate Presbytery of Vermont. (See *Barnet*, p. 287.)

THE REFORMED PRESBYTERIAN CONGREGATION (OLD SCHOOL) OF RYEGATE.

BY REV. JAMES M. BEATTIE.

This congregation was organized in 1798 or 1799. About the time that Rev. Wm. Gibson, who was driven from Ireland, because of his republican firmness, and participation with the United Men, emigrated to this country, and preached in Ryegate. In 1800, the Covenanters, then few and feeble, not numbering more than 8 in full communion, gave Mr. Gibson a call, which he accepted. He labored among them with some success until 1805, when his connection with them was dissolved.

While vacant, Rev. Jas. Milligan preached for them by Presbyterial appointment, and in 1817, became their pastor. The number of members at this time was 80. Mr. Milligan's labors were very abundant. He not only cultivated his own field, but for many years he visited and preached to the congregations in Topsham and Craftsbury. He continued to labor among the people in Ryegate till 1840, when he received and accepted a call from New Alexandria, Pa. The congregation again became vacant, and remained destitute of a pastor for 4 years. It was, however, for part of that time supplied with preaching, by Presbytery. In the winter of 1843 and '44, James M. Beattie, a licentiate, preached to them, and in the spring received a unanimous call, which was by him accepted. In June, Mr. Beattie was ordained and installed in the pastoral charge of the united congregations of Ryegate and Barnet, the Barnet congregation having united with Ryegate in the call.

At the time of Mr. Beattie's settlement, these congregations were in a somewhat broken and scattered condition. Owing to the troubles that arose towards the close of Mr. Milligan's pastorate here, they had decreased in numbers. In Ryegate there were only 82 communicants, when Mr. Beattie took the spiritual charge.

By the blessing of God, the people soon became more united, and a new impulse was given to the cause.

Some very valuable members have been called to the congregation of the upper sanctuary, but others have arisen whom we trust will fill their places. The sabbath school, in connection with Ryegate congregation, promises to do much good.

Besides supporting their pastor, the people contribute yearly to aid the funds of the foreign and domestic missions, and of the Theological Seminary. Since the settlement of the present minister 89 have been added to the congregation; and notwithstanding the losses that have been sustained in removals and deaths, there are at present 129 members.

THE REFORMED PRESBYTERIAN CONGREGA-
TION OF RYEGATE, IN CONNECTION WITH THE
GENERAL SYNOD OF THE REFORMED PRES-
BYTERIAN CHURCH IN NORTH AMERICA.

BY REV. JOHN BOLE, PASTOR.

The origin of the Reformed Presbyterian Church in Ryegate, is nearly coeval with the first settlement of the town itself. The first pastor, the Rev. James Gibson, was settled in the year 1798. Mr. Gibson labored faithfully and successfully in building up a Reformed Presbyterian congregation amongst the early settlers in Ryegate. He was succeeded by Rev. James Milligan, who was translated from Coldingham to Ryegate in the year 1817. Mr. Milligan spent a long and useful pastorate amongst the green hills of Vermont, and the seed which he sowed here amid much toil and trouble is still bringing forth fruit to the Master's praise. Mr. Milligan removed from Ryegate, leaving the congregation vacant, in 1839. In the meantime a division had taken place in the Reformed Presbyterian church in America,

respecting the use of the elective franchise. One party maintaining that those who exercised the elective franchise under the constitution of the United States, ought to be subjected to the discipline of the church, the other maintaining that this should be made a matter of forbearance. This resulted in the formation of two separate synods, each claiming to be the Synod of the Reformed Presbyterian Church. This unhappy division occurred in the year 1833. Its influence was soon felt in the congregation in Ryegate; and ultimately in the year 1843, the congregation were divided in respect to this question of using the elective franchise. Those in the congregation who believed that the exercise of this political privilege, ought not of itself, to be regarded as a sufficient ground for church censure, gave in their adherence to the General Synod of the Reformed Presbyterian Church, and were by that body recognised as the Reformed Presbyterian congregation of Ryegate, in connection with the General Synod of the Reformed Presbyterian Church in North America. We have thus stated (as we believe impartially), the ground of the division which took place in the congregation, respecting the elective franchise; we have also defined, as distinctly as we could, the position occupied by the congregation with which we stand connected. It would evidently be out of place in a work like the present, to enter into any particular defence of the ground which we occupy as a congregation. However willing we might be to do this in other circumstances, yet in the present connection, as a matter of taste and courtesy, we confine ourselves to a simple statement of the facts in the case.

In the year 1848, the Rev. Robert A. Hill, was ordained pastor over the congregation. Mr. Hill continued to labor in Ryegate with much zeal and acceptance for upwards of three years, when he was removed to another field of labor. The present pastor was ordained over the congregation, in the year 1853. He has had much comfort in his pastoral connection with his people. There are now 135 members on the roll. Preaching is sustained all the time at South Ryegate, a sabbath school is in successful operation, and a large and valuable library is established in connection with the congregation. In reviewing our history there as a congregation, from the beginning down to the present time, surely we have abundant reason to erect our "Ebenezer," and inscribe upon it, "Hitherto hath the Lord helped us."

ELEGIAC EXTRACT.

On Rev. David Goodwillie, who died Aug. 2, 1830.

BY MARY JANE LAUGHLIN.

"I have waited for thy salvation, O Lord."—*Gen.* XLIX, 18.

And long thou waitedst, venerable man,
While more than eighty circling periods ran,
Full fifty years through many a dreary scene,
Proclaimed a Saviour's grace with modest mien,
While Time, his desolating havoc spread,
. . . . . .
Stood at thy work and choose still to remain,
. . . . . .
Pleased with God's service to thy latest year.
. . . . . .
Not long ago, did I behold thee stand,
With consecrated symbols in thy hand,
With hoary head, with aspect kind and meek,
The tears fast flowing down thy aged cheek,
Discoursing of thy Saviour's dying love,
And pointing to the boundless bliss above,
Like pilgrim past the dangers of the way,
Almost at home, thy looks appeared to say,
"My friends no more will I partake with you,
Till we in heaven our intercourse renew"
. . . . .

WHERE?

BY CARRIE S. GIBSON.

Where can I look for peace, to heal
My weary soul; and sorrow steal
From out my mind, and heaven reveal?
In the Bible?

What Book, unto our hearts doth bring
Good cheer; and never leaves a sting;
And give us hope, God's praise to sing?
The Bible.

SONG OF THE INVALID.

BY CARRIE S. GIBSON.

An invalid, we have been told, for many years; yet the first one to send the *Quarterly* a club from Caledonia county. Unable to go out into the neighborhood around, she laid the enterprize before her visitors. We appreciatingly commemorate this fair example of practical sympathy, and cheerfully find a modest niche in the department of her birthtown for this dear girl:

I'd love to climb the mountains high,
To wander thro' the valleys green,
To look athwart the azure sky,
And o'er the lakelet's silver sheen.

I'd love to wander with some friend,
Some dear, congenial, tender soul;
And view the blessings God doth send,
And watch the bright waves gleam and roll.

But ah! it may not — can not be,
And I must try to bow in love;
To leave my lot, O God, to thee,
And hope for happiness above.

MEMORIES.

BY MRS. M. S. BEATTIE.

Like gleams of the far-off heavenly —
One by one in vision bright,
How the by-gone memories come,
To brighten the spirit's night.

I am kissing now a dimpled cheek,
I am smoothing golden hair,
I am thinking now, with a mother's pride,
My babe is wond'rous fair.

Two little snow-white arms of love,
Hold me in a soft embrace,
Two tender eyes of the sweetest blue
Look up to my happy face.
. . . .

But the twilight deepens to night,
And I hear the wind's low moan;
And it whispers sad as it passes by,
"Alone, young mother, alone!"

O! it is true that the sunshine fled,
That lighted our home so bright;
O! it is true that the music died,
When those lips grew still and white.

ST. JOHNSBURY.

Lat. 44° 27'. Long. 72° 1' W.

BY EDWARD T. FAIRBANKS.

Prior to the independence of New Hampshire Grants, and 16 years before the settlement of St. Johnsbury, a tract of land on Passumpsic river was granted by King George III, to certain of his "loving subjects of the Province of New York." This tract contained 39,000 acres—including the whole or nearly the whole of St. Johnsbury, together with a portion of Concord and Waterford—was granted to 39 petitioners under leadership of John Woods and Wm. Swan, and formally chartered by Cadwallader Colden, who in 1770 was governor general of New York. The charter was issued at New York city on the 8th August, 1770; and in honor of the Earl of Dunmore, who on the 19th October following was appointed under his majesty, governor of the province, the new township received the name of Dunmore. From this document, which is still preserved in the State Hall at Albany, the following sections are transcribed:

"George the Third, by the Grace of God—of Great Britain, France and Ireland, King, Defender of the Faith and so forth—To all to whom these Presents shall come, Greeting: "Whereas our loving subjects John Woods and William Swan in behalf of themselves and their Associates, by their humble petition presented unto our trusty and well-beloved Cadwallader Colden Esquire, our Lieut. Governor, and Commander in Chief of our Province of New York and the territories depending thereon in America—and read in our Council for our said Province on the 31st day of Jan. now last past—did set forth among other things—That the Petitioners had discovered a certain Tract of vacant Land situate on the West Branch of Connecticutt River in the County of Gloucester, within our said Province, containing about 39,000 acres, and that the said Lands are not included in any grant heretofore made by the Gov. of New Hampshire and are still lying vacant and vested in us.

"Know ye, That of our especial Grace, and certain Knowledge, and meer Motion, we have given, granted, ratified and confirmed, and do by these Presents, for us our Heirs and Successors, give, grant, ratify and confirm to them, the aforesaid John Woods, William Swan and Associates their heirs and assigns forever — All that Tract of Land aforesaid set out, abutted, bounded and described in the Manner and Form as aforesaid, together with all and singular the Tenements, Hereditaments, Emoluments and Appurtenances thereunto belonging or appertaining, and also our Estate, Right, Title, Interest, Possession, Claim and Demand whatever of, in, and to the same lands and Premises, and every Part and Parcle thereof. And the Reversion and Reversions, Remainder and Remainders, Rents, Issues and Profits thereof, and of every Part and 'Parcle thereof—Except, and always reserved out of this our present Grant unto us, our heirs and Successors forever, All Mines of Gold and Silver and also all White or other Sorts of Pine Trees fit for Masts, of the growth of 24 inches diameter and upward at 12 inches from the Earth, for Masts for the Royal Navy of us, our heirs and Successors—To their only proper and separate Use and Behoof respectively forever as Tenants in common and not as joint Tenants. Yielding, rendering, and

paying therefor yearly and every year forever unto us our heirs and Successors, at our Custom House in our City of New York, unto us, our or their Collector or Receiver General there for the time being, on the Feast of Annunciation of the Blessed Virgin Mary, commonly called Lady Day—the yearly Rent of two shillings and Six pence Sterling, for each and every 100 acres of the above granted lands, and so in proportion for every lesser Quantity thereof. And we do by our especial Grace, and certain Knowledge and meer Motion, erect, create, and constitute the Tract or Parcle of Land herein granted and every Part and Parcle thereof, a Township, forever hereafter to be and continue, and remain—and by the Name of DUNMORE forever hereafter to be called and known. And for the better and more easily carrying on and managing the public Affairs, and Business of the said Township, our Royal Will and Pleasure is, that there shall be forever in the said Township, 2 Assessors, 1 Treasurer, 2 Overseers of Highways, 2 Overseers of Poor, 1 Collector and 4 Constables, Elected and chosen out of the Inhabitants of the said Township, yearly and every year on the first Tuesday in May at the most publick place in said Township, by the majority of the Freeholders thereof, then and there met and Assembled for that purpose. In testimony whereof. We have caused these our Letters to be made Patent and the Great Seal of our Province to be hereunto affixed. Witness our said trusty and well-beloved Cadwallader Colden Esquire, our said Lieut. Gov. and Commander in Chief of our said Province of New York, and the Territories depending thereon in America. At our Fort in our City of New York, the Eighth day of Aug. in the Year of our Lord one thousand seven hundred and seventy, and of Our Reign the Tenth.
Signed, &c.

The conditions of the above grant were as follows: "That some or one of the grantees should within three years next after date, settle on the tract granted, so many families as should amount to one family for every 1000 acres of land—or plant or effectually cultivate at the end of three years, at least three acres for every 50 acres of land granted capable of cultivation." That no one should "by their Privity, consent or Procurement, fell, cut down, or destroy any of the Pine Trees suitable for the Royal Navy. Otherwise the Grant should be void, and the land should revert to, and be vested in the Grantors."

Whether any of the grantees undertook the fulfillment of these conditions, we are not informed, but it is highly probable that the difficulties which shortly after arose in adjusting the claims of landed proprietors in New Hampshire grants, prevented the actual settlement and tillage of the Dunmore lands.

Seven years after the grant of Dunmore, the state of Vermont threw off her shackles, and declared herself an independent sovereignty. In the conflict which thence arose respecting the right of lands granted under the seal of neighboring states, a board of commissioners was appointed to adjust the claims of the New York grantees. These latter had the choice of paying ten cents per acre on their lands, and retaining them, or giving up their title thereto and removing to new grants in western New York. Probably most of the grantees of Dunmore sold or relinquished their claims in Vermont, and settled in other quarters. From records preserved at Albany, we learn that the township lines had been surveyed previous to the issuing of the charter, and that two warrants of surveys had been filed on the first of January, 1770, but the field books of the surveyor general from this quarter are not found. We learn further, from a petition presented to the general assembly of this state in 1787, by one Moses Little, that the proprietors of Dunmore had completed the lotting out of the township, and that this had been done at great expense. The same petition proceedeth to show "that the Petitioner, not in the least doubting that the said Grant had been legally made by the said Governor of New York, had purchased at a very high Price, Ten Thousand Acres of Land in the said Dunmore, situate about 20 miles north of Newbury in the Co. of Orange. That since the State of Vermont had Exercised Jurisdiction, the whole of said Tract of Land had been granted by the said St. of Vt. to the Proprietors of St. Johnsborough and other towns, whereby the Petitioner hath suffered greatly by the loss of his property, and hath no redress besides applying to the Hon. Assembly of the State." This comprises all that can be found relative to the township of Dunmore. On a map of "His Majesties' Province of New York," published in London about 1779, may be seen this township, located according to the boundaries designated in the grant, on either side of the Passumpsic (west branch of Connecticut), and extending on the east nearly to the boundary line of New

Hampshire. It is not known that any permanent settlements were made within its limits, until the year immediately preceding Gov. Chittenden's charter of St. Johnsbury. It is certain however, that the valley of the Passumpsic was often traversed by surveyors, hunters and trappers, and had probably been spied out and examined by the future proprietors of St. Johnsbury, sometime before its forests had been opened by the squatter's axe.

On the 27th October, 1786, Thos. Chittenden, then in the 10th year of his service as governor of Vermont, made an official grant to Dr. Jonathan Arnold and associates, of a tract of land in old Orange county, to be known as the "Township of St. Johnsbury." The shorter and more euphonious name which Cadwallader Colden had bestowed on this tract in 1770, and by which he thought to immortalize the memory of the British earl, was now repudiated by the less loyal mountaineers, who had already assumed the control of the state. Among the French people they had found a man, whose love of liberty, and disinterested friendship for the Green Mountain State, challenged their respect, and won their gratitude, and as a most appropriate testimony of their regard for his character and services, the new township was named the borough or town of St. John de Crevecœur, the French consul at New York. This was done at the suggestion of Gen. Ethan Allen, who was a warm personal friend of St. John, and who successfully advocated the claims of the latter before the governor and council. The following letter, addressed by St. John to Gen. Allen, evinces in a striking manner the characteristics of the man, besides containing an allusion to the name in question:

New York, 31st May, A. D. 1785.

"Gen. Allen: In consequence of the leave you have given me, with pleasure I will communicate to you the following thoughts, earnestly desiring you'd be persuaded that they have not been dictated by any vanity or foolish presumption, but by a sincere and honest desire of being somewhat useful to a state for the industry and energy of which I have a great respect. I am an *American* by a law of this state passed in the year 1763. I have lived and dwelled in it ever since. I married in 1770. I have three children. I have drained 3000 acres of Bog Meadow, built a house, cleared many acres of land, planted a great orchard. I have had the pleasure of publishing in Europe a work which has been well received by the public;

wherein many interesting facts are recorded of the bravery, patience and suffering of the Americans in the prosecution of their last war. Such, dear sir, are the titles whereon I presume to found and establish the liberty I am now taking. First, I offer to have the seal of your state elegantly engraven on silver by the king's best engraver, and to change somewhat the devices thereof. I offer with pleasure to get another engraved for the college which the state of Vermont intends erecting, and I will take upon myself the imagining of the device thereof. I will do my best endeavors to procure from the king some marks of his bounty and some useful presents for the above college. If the general approves what I told him formerly concerning national gratitude and the simple though efficacious way of showing it to such French characters as have amply deserved it, no opportunity can be so favorable as the present, since new counties and districts will soon be laid out. If the general dont think it too presumptuous, in order to answer what he so kindly said respecting names, I would observe that the name of *St. John* being already given to many places in this country, it might be contrived by the appellation of *St. Johnsbury.* But the most flattering honor that the citizens of Vermont could confer on me would be, to be naturalized as a citizen of that state, along with my 3 children — America Francis St. John, William Alexander St. John, Philip Lewis St. John. As soon as any resolution will be taken towards giving to the new townships and districts, some of the new names, I earnestly beg the general would write the account of it, which I should beg of him to send me by 2 or 3 different ways, so that I should not fail to have that part of it translated and put into the French newspapers with the name of the general. Wishing your state every prosperity, your good governor and council and yourself, my dear sir, I take my sincere leave of you, and beg you will look on me as a true friend and your very humble servant, St. John."

From Allen's reply to the above we extract the following:

"Sir, in behalf of the people of Vermont I return you thanks for the honor you have done me and them in your correspondence and assure you that we esteem it a great honor to be noticed by the *French nation,* the *guarantees of American independence,* more especially as we are not as yet confederated with the United States, and we flatter ourselves that a mutual interchange of friend-

ship and good offices amounts nearly to an alliance. We have not as yet made an accurate plan or map of the state, but are now doing it, which, when done, we will send to France, to be completed by the king's engraver with the seal of the state, as you propose. With regard to the other matters, the people of Vermont confide in Mr. St. John, and are his humble servants. I should have written you much earlier could I have obtained an opportunity of laying the subject of your letter before the governor and council of the state, which I have since done. They readily conceived your good intentions, and nothing will be wanting on their part to promote your laudable requests in every particular.

"I have the honor to be, sir, with every sentiment of respect and esteem,

"Your friend and very humble servant,

"Ethan Allen."

Besides St. Johnsbury, the names of Danville and Vergennes were adopted at the request of Mr. St. John.

The township of St. Johnsbury, which was granted to the petitioners "for the due encouragement of their laudable designs, and for other valuable considerations thereunto moving," comprised 71 equally divided rights, each right including 310 acres, 1 rood, 22 poles, the whole being estimated at 21,167 acres. Besides the rights appropriated to the several grantees, we find one 71st part reserved for the use of a seminary or college, and the same for the use of county grammar schools in the state. Also "lands to the amount of one 71st part for the purpose of settlement of a minister or ministers of the Gospel in the said township, and the same amount for the support of an English school or schools in the said township." The two first mentioned reservations were to be under the control and disposal of the state assembly, the latter to be located "justly and equitably or quantity for quality" in such parts of the township as would least incommode the settlement thereof. At the first proprietors' meeting it was determined that the college and grammar school reservations should include two full rights in the extreme north-eastern corner of the town — the others were variously located, in no case comprising more than one-third of the same right. Provision was also made in the charter for the erection of the first grist and saw mills out of the proceeds of the public lands and 9 acres in each 71st part, and the same proportion for each lesser part were so reserved by the charter, that the profits arising there-

47

from should be applied to the construction of public roads and highways. The conditions and other reservations of this charter were "that each proprietor of the township should plant and cultivate 5 acres of land, and build a house at least 18 feet square on the floor, or have one family settled on each respective right in said township within the time limited by law of the state. Also, that all pine timber suitable for a navy be reserved for the use and benefit of the freemen of the state." The penalty of non-fulfillment was forfeiture of each non-improved right of land, the same to revert to the freemen of the state, and by their representatives be regranted to such persons as should after appear to settle and cultivate them.

Thus was granted the town of St. Johnsbury. The quaint memorials of olden days, will hardly be sought in the annals of a town, whose birth dates so late in New England history. A hundred and sixty-six years had already passed since the Mayflower first dropped her anchors in Plymouth Bay. Nine years since the squatter sovereigns of New Hampshire Grants, had declared their green hills an independent territory. Full twice nine since the boys of the Green Mountains had first raised the arm of resistance against the tyranny of the Granite and Empire states. The straight forward policy and decision of the incipient commonwealth had been felt to the east of the Connecticut, and west of the Lake, and the time had come when "tall grenadiers of the King's army, stood and trembled in the day of her fierce anger." But not as yet had this little state been accepted by Congress, as one of the confederated union. Her repeated applications had been treated with an evasive policy which at the time was regarded as alike unfortunate for the state, and discreditable to Congress. Nevertheless, her very disappointment resulted eventually in good to the state, since it served to develop a greater self-reliance and energy on the part of the citizens, and furthermore released them from the heavy governmental taxation, necessitated by the expenses of the Revolution, just concluded. This consideration, together with the strength and efficiency of the state government, and the cheapness of lands, induced a large immigration of young and enterprising men, who came up to clear her forests and settle within her borders. Such were the men whose axes first rang in the wood lands of St. Johnsbury. Earnest, hardy, and vigorous, they sought not the refinements of

society so much as a lordly independence around their log cabin firesides.

The names of the grantees were as follows: Jonathan Arnold, Esq., Samuel Stevens, Esq., John James Clark and Joseph Nightingale, Joseph Lord, Ebenezer Scott, Jr., David Howell, Thomas Chittenden, Esq., John Bridgeman, John C. Arnold, Joseph Fay, Esq., Ira Allen, Esq., Simeon Cole, Benjamin Doolittle, Josiah Nichols, James Adams, Jona. Adams, J. Callender Adams, Thomas Todd, William Trescott and Jona. Trescott. Thomas Chittenden, the governor, in accordance with the usage of the day received one 71st part as remuneration for his services in drawing up the charter. His right was located on the east bank of Passumpsic river, north of the Center village, Ira Allen of Irasburgh, and Joseph Fay of Bennington, men of influence and position in the state were also non-resident proprietors to the amount of four 71st parts. The principal proprietor was Samuel Stevens, Esq., who held 18 rights or about 5400 acres. Being a non-resident, however, he subsequently transferred most of his lands to Dr. Arnold and others who were ready to settle. Arnold at the date of the charter held 3900 acres, 13 rights, or a tenth in amount of the old township of Dunmore. Of the other grantees, the last eight in the list, obtained the rights of proprietorship, by virtue of settlement previous to the chartering of the town, and held respectively one 210th part, or about 100 acres.

In the latter part of 1786, before the boundaries of the township had been fixed, or its charter issued, James Adams, Martin Adams, James Callender Adams, and Jonathan Adams, came up the valley of the Passumpsic, to the meadow south of Railroad street, and there began the first clearing in the town. About the same time Simeon Cole, whose old pasture gate subsequently swung on the edge of Cole Gate Hill, established himself on the meadows south of Center village. Before the close of this year Benj. Doolittle, Josiah Nichol-- Thomas Todd, Jonathan and William Trescott had all obtained the right of proprietorship. It is difficult to trace the history of these early pioneers, inasmuch as most of them removed to other settlements, and of those who remained no very reliable record can be found. The two Trescotts lived and died in this vicinity. Jonathan, on a certain occasion, sent out the following *"Friendly Salutation:"*

"Know all men by these lines, that th

undersigner is expecting to leave this country, and wishes all his friends, or foes if any, to call on him by the 20th May instant, and he will endeavor to make them satisfaction. Sheriffs, Constables and Lawyers are desired to make their demands or otherwise hold their peace. Adieu! Wishing all, God's blessing here on earth, and eternal life hereafter, when I hope to meet you all again. JONATHAN TRESCOTT."

He died at the age of 88, and from the rough hewn stone which marks his resting ing place in the cemetery, we learn that "He was one of the first settlers in town, being the seventh inhabitant." His brother William died in a kind of subterranean habitation near Joe's pond in Danville. He was something of a hero in his day as we shall find in a subsequent part of this narrative.

A winter of primitive simplicity was that of 1786–7 in St. Johnsbury. A great settlement had not as yet sprung up on the ruins of Dunmore. To the few and scattered families who braved out the first winter in this wilderness, the distant stores and grist mills of Barnet, furnished rum, sugar and flour. No bridge had been erected, no roads established, and the lines of travel were as yet but rough cut sled paths through the "forest primeval."

Early in the spring of 1787, came Jonathan Arnold, Joseph Lord, and Barnabas Barker, with 14 others. Dr. Arnold, the principal proprietor of the three towns Lyndon, Billymead and St. Johnsbury, was much the most efficient and enterprising man among the settlers of this vicinity. He was now in his 46th year, and had already seen much of public life both in state and national assemblies. For several years he was a member of congress from Rhode Island, and while serving in this capacity, he was suspected by many of being over friendly to the interests of Vermont, and in particular, of communicating to men in this state certain doings of the continental congress while in secret session. The following extracts from a letter addressed to Hon. Daniel Cahoon of New Hampshire (afterwards a resident of Lyndon), indicate the position of Dr. Arnold, respecting the affairs of Vermont; but whether he advocates the independence of the state solely as a safety measure for New Hampshire, may be doubted. He says, writing from Philadelphia:

"Congress has been on the affair of Vermont for several days, and upon the whole, s appears that the present members will do nothing to its advantage. I have it from the friends of New York, that a new state will probably be formed on Connecticut River, having for its western line the Green mountains, and its eastern they care not where. I think it would not be amiss to suggest to the friends of New Hampshire, that New York policy will probably set such a project on foot (if Vermont is not supported in her present claims), in order to secure the land west of the mountains and on the lake to themselves at Hampshire's expense—and that as the only sure means of preventing such an event, it is the policy of the latter to concede in the clearest and most decided manner to Vermont's independence. Propositions, I doubt not, have passed between some individuals of your state and New York to divide Vermont between them by the height of land, but from what I can discover, it will be dangerous for New Hampshire to depend on such a division; and if New York agrees to it, I think it must be with a view to effect a future division of your state. I am the more confirmed in this opinion from sentiments discoverable in the persons lately banished from Vermont, viz: Phelps and his companion, who are now in this city, and who are daily and nightly propagating every false and scandalous rumor that malice can invent to injure the people of that country, who have no agent or other person to contradict them. I must therefore again repeat, that New Hampshire can only be safe in holding jurisdiction to the river—by leaving Vermont to its present limits, *Independent*."

If Dr. Arnold anticipated at this time a future settlement in Vermont, he was well aware that his own interest would be furthered by the independence of the state, without regard to the policy of New Hampshire; but it is more probable that as a true patriot and a disinterested observer of the struggles which he here witnessed for freedom, he threw his influence and sympathies in favor of the oppressed. It was shortly after the close of his term in congress that Dr. Arnold immigrated to St. Johnsbury. He had served as a sergeant and surgeon in the Revolutionary war, and received his compensation in continental money, which he desired to invest in landed property. We learn however, that a few years after his removal here, the state effected a trade with Arnold, according to which he was to supply the medical chest of the state which was kept at Bennington, and receive in compensation his charter fees. The value of these charter fees may be determined from a resolution passed in council at Rutland, Oct. 27, 1786, in which it is declared that the "grant of land made to Jonathan Arnold and associates, be under the following terms, viz: That each proprietor agreeable to the grant, pay for each right in said grant, nine pounds hard money, on or before the first day of June next, in order to be appropriated to the exigencies of the state." Subsequently, the sum of £537 13s. 7d. was discounted on the charter fees of St. Johnsbury and Danville, being due bills given by Surveyor General Whitelaw for services rendered in the town surveys. The survey of the lot lines and the division of the township into rights, was not completed until the summer of 1787, as we learn from a call for proprietors' meeting, published in the *Bennington Gazette*, and also from a letter addressed by Dr. Arnold to Esquire Whitelaw, the surveyor. This letter which was dated at Bennington March 8th, 1787, runs as follows:

James Whitelaw, Esq.:

Sir—The surveyor general has appointed me to look out, cut and make a road from the west line of St. Johnsbury, beginning where Capt. Leavenworth ends the road he is to make through Danville, and thence crossing the Passumpsic river at (or as near as the land will suit), the best falls in the said river, which I suppose is between Cole's and Adams [now Paddock's village], thence on a course which will bring it through some part of the gore east of Lyndon, to the west line of Lunenburg—which road will not only be necessary for facilitating the transport of provisions for the surveyors and their parties, but will serve valuable purposes for general roads in that part of the state. The surveyor general having also consented that you should complete the outlines of St. Johnsbury, and lay the same into lots of 300 acres each before you enter upon the general survey, I am to desire you to get Josiah Nichols and Martin Adams to assist you to make the same, which I would *wish to be done plain and distinct;* and if Mr. Adams or Nichols can not attend to that service, the old gentleman, or Mr. Simeon Cole may be applied to, although I hope and expect that Mr. Cole will be otherwise engaged for me at that time. You will please call on Mr. E. R. Chamberlin for pork and flour for this service, and get some rum from Col. Thos. Johnston. I hope to be with you early in May, and fix the magazine for

your supplies for surveying that quarter. I enclose a sketch of the manner which I think will lay the lots to best advantage in St. Johnsbury—if you can better it, you will. I am the less anxious about matters there, from having the fullest confidence in your ability, will and friendship. Desiring you to make my compliments agreeable to all friends in that quarter, I am sir, with esteem, your assured friend and humble servant,

JONA. ARNOLD.

Squire Whitelaw was subsequently appointed surveyor general, and from his *Field Book of Surveys of Town Lines in St. Johnsbury* we extract the following as a specimen of the manner in which he filled some forty or fifty pages of the journal while surveying in this quarter:

"Began the W line of St. J. at NW being Birch tree marked Lyndon SW corner Nov. 16, 1786, and ran S 6°, 20′ E. At 18 Ch. brook 10 links wide runs SW. At 63 Ch. little brook runs W. 1 *Mile*, on W. branch of brook 10 links wide running S. Easterly by an Alder marked M. 1, 1787, and an alder meadow (m) 2 *Miles*, a stake 12 links S. 40° W. fr. a fir tree on land descending east (g) the wood elm, fir, beech, ash and maple, excellent land for grass. At 8 Ch. a stream 3 rods wide runs NE. * * * 7 *Miles*, a stake 8 links westerly fr. a little birch on the south side of a hill (g)—this mile chiefly uneven—the wood beech and maple, good for grain and pasture; at 51 Ch. Barnet Corner at a hemlock tree marked Barnet Cor. March 23, 1784, standing on flat land on the edge of brook running SE. wood chiefly hemlock (g) A lot in St. J. 310 A. 1 R. 22 P."

Under a later date, and after the surveys of town and lot lines had been completed, we find the account of James Whitelaw against the state as presented to the treasurer for settlement; from a portion of this account we quote as follows:

	£	s	d
To Provisions and assistance furnished by Dr. Jona. Arnold, .	52	4	5½
To 1 Quart of Rum, . .	0	1	0
To 7 Males' Victuals at 10d, .	0	5	10
To 10 Days surveying. . .	5	0	0
To 2 Days settling acc'ts with Jona. Arnold, Esq., . .	1	4	0
To a man and horse 1 Day, .	0	6	0
To 2 Camp Kettles, . .	0	8	0
To 1 Quart West India Rum, .	0	2	0
To 3 males' victuals at 10d, .	0	2	6
To Entertainment (?) for Hands,	0·10	0	
To 2 Bags worn out in the Surveys, ...	0	12	0

To Dr. Arnold's Account, . £118 5 0½
To 7 lbs. Salt Pork of Capt. Colt
and 2 Galls. Rum, .   .   . 0 17 0
To 35 Days Surveying, .   . 21 0 0
To 4 Days making Plan to lay
before Commissioners ap-
pointed to locate the Flying
Grants, ... 2 8 0

A single tradition in connection with the surveys of this town, although it occurred at a later date, is perhaps worthy of mention. Dr. Arnold was in town at the time, and in company with Squire Whitelaw and others, was laying out certain lines in the vicinity of Sleeper's River, then known as West Branch. The provisions and equipments of the party were left in charge of Thomas Todd, who was instructed to keep a careful watch over the same, while the others penetrated into the forest to finish their surveys. Meantime Todd removed his effects from the bushes to the river bank, and on the return of the party was found rolled up against a log and fast asleep. "Henceforward," said Dr. Arnold, "let the West Branch be known as *Sleeper's River*," and to this day its waters flow along the sandy bed whose name recalls this legend of our "Sleepy Hollow."

After the settlement and before the organization of the town in 1790, all matters of township business were transacted in proprietor's meetings held at some one of the houses in the town. In the *Bennington Gazette*, vol. 4, No. 182, we find an advertisement signed by Isaac Tichenor, afterwards governor of the state, in which the "Proprietors of St. Johnsbury are warned and notified to meet on the eighth Feb., 1787, for the purpose of choosing committees to complete the division of lands then undivided in the township — to hear report of committee appointed to settle with new residents in township — to make provision for erecting mills in the course of the ensuing summer — to take measures for the furtherance of the settlement, and transact other business deemed necessary." It is doubtful whether this meeting was ever called to order, and if it was, probably no business of importance was transacted, as no record of proceedings can be found. Another meeting was called in the June following, and in the meantime Dr. Arnold had removed to the township and erected a house, as we infer from the following minutes, taken from the first page of the town records:

"At a meeting of the Proprietors of the Township of St. Johnsbury held at the House of Jonathan Arnold, Esq., in the said Township, in the Co. of Orange, on the 18th Day of June, A. D. 1787, Alex. Harvey, Esq., was chosen Moderator, Dr. Joseph Lord, Proprietors' Clerk. Voted, that the several rights in said Township (exclusive of two Lots of One-Third Right each to the 10 persons who had entered the town in 1786 and who were admitted as Proprietors by reason of actual settlement — also one Full right for building mills in said Township and Five public Rights, all which said Rights are located and designated on the said Plan) be now drafted for."

Thereupon Alex. Harvey, Jos. Lord and Enos Stevens, were authorized to prepare lots with numbers affixed, the same to be shuffled and drawn against each proprietor's name. Dan'l Cahoon, Jr., and William Trescott "in presence of and under superintendance of the Assembly, made draft of the lots, and in the said draft the lots came out to each proprietor's name" in the order recorded in the proprietors' record book.

The "one full right" which was reserved according to charter for building mills, was located on the Passumpsic at the most available place for water-power, just above the mouth of Moose River. This property including about three hundred acres was assigned to Dr. Arnold, and during the spring of '87 he put up a saw mill. The following year a grist mill was erected, and the business importance of the settlement largely increased. These were days when our modern Paddock village was known as "Arnold's Mills," and before the "big moose" which was afterwards victimized on the bank of East Branch, had left to that dashing stream a more historic name. The house of Dr. Arnold was located in the wood lands at the northern extremity of the plain, just above the park which still bears the family name. The erection of this house began the settlement of the plain, and within its walls, during succeeding generations, no less than seven several families found a home, and last of all the owl and the bat. We could wish that the "boys" who in 184- brought down its old timbers with fire, to the ground, had reserved their torches until some artist could have sketched the "rough exterior" of the *first frame house* erected in St. Johnsbury.

To this house it was that Dr. Arnold carried home his third wife, Cynthia Hastings. Now the way in which Cynthia came to be the wife of the doctor was as follows: On a certain occasion the latter was journeying down the river, and quartered for the night with one Enos Stevens of Barnet. In the course of the evening it was determined with great unanimity of feeling that their condition bore a forlorn resemblance to that of the old Romans before the visit of the Sabines — pioneers in a new settlement and hopelessly destitute of wives. Nothing could be done to remedy the matter in this northern wilderness; accordingly an expedition to Charleston "No. 4" (N. H.) was immediately planned, to take effect on the morrow, the object being to spy out the available daughters of the land. Arrived in Charleston they called on Samuel Stevens, Esq., and made known their wishes. After some consultation invitations were issued to Cynthia Hastings and Sophy Grout requesting their company at tea, it being understood by the contrivers of this plot, that the two strangers from Vermont should accompany them back to their homes. In anticipation of a possible emergency it was judged advisable that Mrs. Squire West should also be in attendance to play the part of umpire in case both gentlemen should claim the same lady. Tea time arrived, and so did the unsuspecting maidens. The evening passed, but when the hour of departure came, Cynthia Hastings seemed to be in double demand. The ladies still remained in blissful ignorance of the conspiracy. Mrs. Squire West was called for, and constituted referee. She very sagely argued that Sophy Grout was admirably adapted to be the companion of a *farmer* (Mr. Stevens was a tiller of the soil), but as for Cynthia it was much more suitable that she should be attended by a professional man. This wise decision of Mrs. Squire West (especially grateful to Dr. Arnold), prevailed, and before separating that night each of the gentlemen from the north made known to parties most concerned the special object of their visit to Charleston. Sophy Grout suffered somewhat from paternal interference, grounded on the fact that Stevens was a tory, but she was finally told that if she *would* marry an old tory she *might*, only she should carry nothing from the ancestral domain but *herself* and a *cow*. A few days later the afflicted Grout family witnessed the departure of Sophy and the old cow with a tory. The doctor experiencing less difficulty in preliminary arrangements, went forward to Rhode Island where he remained a few days, and on his return was accompanied to St. Johnsbury by the aforesaid Cynthia of Charleston. She became the mother of Lemuel Hastings Arnold, who was born at St. Johnsbury, educated at Providence, governor of Rhode Is-

land in 1841-42, member of governor's council during the Dorr rebellion, member of congress in 1845-47, and died at Kingston June 27th, 1852. We learn from the political journals of the day that Mr. Arnold met with some opposition while a candidate for the office of governor. "During the canvass and in the heart of the electioneering campaign conducted upon the high pressure principle, a zealous Jackson man lustily accused Mr. Arnold of the enormous crime of having been *born in Vermont!*" Thereupon a question arose, as to whether a man could be held accountable for being born in any particular age or country. This kind of accountability was hardly recognized in the political creed of the Green Mountain boys, and does not appear to have been sanctioned by the sons of Rhode Island, for Mr. Arnold, notwithstanding he was born "way up in Vermont," was elected by a decided majority, and did honor both to the state of his birth and the state of his adoption.

After the mills were established, the rights assigned, and the settlement of the town fairly under way, the population increased rapidly by immigration from the south. Most of the new comers were citizens of New Hampshire, Massachusetts or Rhode Island. No regular record of marriages, births and deaths was kept, until after the organization of the town, in 1790. The marriage service was commonly performed by Dr. Arnold, the first on record being that of Eneas Harvey and Rhoda Hamlet, who "were married 17th Jan'y., 1793, by Jonathan Arnold, Esquire, in presence of several witnesses." The earliest recorded births are those of Polly, daughter of David Doolittle, Dec. 14, 1789; and Polly, daughter of John McGaffey, Aug. 28, 1788. About this time a tax was imposed on the township to raise funds for the purpose of procuring a record book, wherein such interesting events might subsequently be preserved. Something of the condition of the town in the third year of its existence, may be gathered from the following petition presented to the general assembly by Dr. Arnold; the original of which is in the state department at Montpelier:

"To the Hon. Gen. Assembly of the State of Vt., convened Oct. 1789. The subscriber humbly showeth—That he hath with great difficulty and expense begun a settlement in the northern part of this state. That he hath since the 25th April, 1787, introduced more than Fifty Industrious men as settlers (which number would have been much greater, but for the scarcity of Provisions in that Country), and some of whom have families now there. That a principal difficulty we have had to encounter, hath originated from the want of passable roads to the Townships by which we are planted, and which we have had no means of procuring to be made. And this difficulty is still likely to continue, unless by the interposition of your Honors we are relieved."

The location of the contemplated roads is then described, the principal one being through Barnet, corner of Waterford, St. Johnsbury, Lyndon, &c., which is now the regular river road.

Doubtless the scarcity of provisions alluded to in the above petition, resulted chiefly from the want of roads and suitable conveyances; and this indeed might have been expected in days when men carried the necessaries of life on their backs for miles through the forest.

It is said that the old pioneer, who was afterwards elected first representative to the state assembly, used to make periodic journeys on foot to Barnet, and return with a two bushel bag of grain on his back, and a galllon of rum in his hand. Of course the measurement of the latter was taken at Barnet. Another illustrative tale is told of a certain eccentric individual, who bought a bag of potatoes "down below," and having with the assistance of two or three able bodied men, secured the same upon his back, set out for St. Johnsbury. Unfortunately and greatly to his dismay, a small rent in the corner of the bag, became so enlarged in the course of the homeward trip, as to permit the escape of one of the esculents, and how to recover this was a problem which gave ample scope to his available eccentricity. Fearing to stoop, lest the weight of the bag should prevent his subsequent perpendicularity, and unwilling to lose so dainty a morsel, he proceeded to inflict upon the said potato sundry well-directed kicks, which in due time propelled it with variable velocities to the floor of his kitchen, whence it met its appropriate fate. For the authenticity of the above we are incompetent to vouch, but we accept it as a practical treatise on the times. Probably very few of the early settlers were burdened with a surplus of hard money. Wild meat, grain and furs were the legal tender. A letter has been found, written by one Merritt, who lived in the south part of the town a year or two after the settlement was begun. It seems that he had been dunned

by Capt. Lovell for a debt. His reply states "that he had just *hoed in* three acres of wheat, a few potatoes and some barley, which was all the property he had in the world, save flint, powder and gun. He proposes to set out on a hunt the following day, and if Providence is pleased to give him usual success, he pledges within a limited time to redeem his credit with furs."

For many years moose were abundant, and contributed much toward supplying the wants of the settlers. How Daniel Hall, in 1793, gat for himself the necessaries of life, and the name of a mighty hunter, may be gathered from the following notes, inserted as they were taken from the narrator:

"Hall had grant of land from Dr. Arnold—hundred acres—in St. Johnsbury—west of Passumpsic—above Plain—by mistake, deed not given—next year Doctor dies—alarming apprehensions—Hall applies to Josias Lyndon—son of Doctor—J. L. gives him hundred acres—up in Lyndon—Hall satisfied—next morning up early—packs wife and goods on hand sled—travels to Lyndon—on crust—unpacks wife and goods—builds fire—sets up wigwam—moves in wife and goods—all settled—sundown— Next morning, nothing to eat—takes gun— sallies into forest—tracks a moose—big one—shoots moose—skins thigh—cuts out steak—carries home—wife delighted—heard gun go off—thought breakfast coming— roasts meat on forked stick—eats—no butter, pepper, salt—after breakfast calls up all neighbors—they skin moose—each takes a piece—Hall gets out hand sled—loads on moose meat and pelt—goes to St. Johnsbury—trades—gets three pecks potatoes, half bushel meal, peck salt—carries home to wife—wife delighted—sundown."

In the year 1790, the first town meeting was held at Dr. Arnold's house, and the organization of the town effected. The record of this meeting stands as follows:

"At a meeting of the Inhabitants of the Township of St. Johnsbury, legally warned and holden at the Dwelling house of Jonathan Arnold Esquire, in the said township, on Monday the 21st day of June, Anno Dom. 1790, being the first town meeting ever held in the said Town.

Jonathan Arnold, Esq., was chosen Moderator; Jonathan Arnold, Town Clerk; Jonathan Adams, Town Treasurer; Asa Daggett, Constable; Asa Daggett, Collector of Taxes; Jonathan Arnold, Sealer of Weights and Measures; Joel Roberts, Joseph Lord, Martin Adams, Selectmen; The Selectmen, Listers and Assessors; Barnabas Barker and Four others, Surveyors of Highways and Fence Viewers. Meeting Dissolved.

JONA. ARNOLD, Town Clerk.

The selectmen immediately proceeded with the duties of their office, and sent up to the assembly an urgent petition for roads, in which it is

"Humbly shown—that they suffer under great inconvenience from the want of Roads and Bridges in the Township of St. Johnsbury, and although the Inhabitants have exerted themselves equal at least to those of any new Settlement, and have also had the Assistance of a small Proprietor's tax; the whole is utterly inadequate to what is absolutely necessary for their convenience, the advantage of Land Owners, and the Interest of the State. For the circumstances of the Town is such as requires much more to be expended for such purposes than falls to the Lot of such Townships in General, it being so Situate as to be the Key to a very fertile Country northward, and the only practicable and nearest communication between the towns on and about the Onion River, to those on the Connecticut at the Upper Coös; which render necessary an extent of about 35 miles of Roads for general purposes, besides many others for more private and particular uses therein. And the said Township having nearly through its center from North to South the Passumpsick, a River about 12 rods wide, and on the East part the Moose River about 6 rods wide, and runs therein an extent of about 5 miles, and on the West part the Sleepers River about 4 rods wide, and runs therein an extent of about 7 miles—requires a large number of Bridges, two at least on the Passumpsick, one near the Mills, and the other near the North line of the said Township; two on Moose River, and three at least on Sleepers River. Wherefore your Petitioners humbly pray Your Honors for leave to bring in a Tax of 4 pence per acre on the lands in St. J. for the purpose aforesaid. And as in duty bound will ever respectfully pray."

Signed, &c., by Selectmen.

To this petition were also affixed the signatures of Jonathan Arnold, Joseph Fay, Enos Stevens and Thomas Chittenden, as proprietors, to the amount of 32 rights, joining in the prayer of the petition; and upon the 30th June following, we find that the committee appointed by legislature for laying out and making these roads in St. Johnsbury, "allowed £30 for Bridge over the Pass. River at the Mills—£20 for ditto

across the East Branch or Moose River near its mouth, and six pence per rod for completing a road (1 rod wide) from one bridge to the other." Jonathan Arnold undertook the job, and in building the first bridge, "tradition says that his inflexible will compelled the workmen to commence the planking at the opposite end from which the plank were, so that they were compelled to convey all the plank across the river as best they might, instead of laying them down in advance of their own steps." During this year, 1790, the plain was mostly cleared of its forests, and contained three habitations; Dr. Arnold's at the northern extremity, Joseph Lord's log hut at the southern, and a rude cabin on the site now occupied by the St. Johnsbury House. A road was cut across the plain, corresponding to Main street as it, now lies—charred stumps on either side and dense woods beyond. A ravine about 20 feet deep ran across the street near the corner of Church street, which was afterwards spanned by a dry bridge. By especial vote, and at expense of the township, a guide-post had been erected. The population of the town was 143; grand list, $590; first freeman's meeting was held Sept. 26th, 1791, and Joel Roberts was elected representative of the town in state assembly. His certificate, which is preserved in the secretary of state's office, runs as follows:

"This certifies that at the Freeman's Meeting in St. Johnsbury on the day assigned by law, Mr. Joel Roberts was Chosen to Represent in the General Assembly of the State of Vt. for the year thence ensuing, the Town of St. Johnsbury aforesaid.

"Attest,   ASA DAGGETT, Constable.

"St. J., Sept. 26, 1791."

The first freemen's oaths taken in St. Johnsbury were administered on the 2d Sept. 1794. Only one of the eleven young men who on that day first exercised their elective franchise, is still living, and he, through the infirmities of three score and thirty years, but faintly recalls the scene. On the same hills where, in 1791, he began his clearings, Mr. Goss, our oldest citizen, is still residing, and the beautiful valley which his axe first opened along the upper waters of Sleeper's River, preserves the memory of his labors in the name of "Goss Hollow." The freemen's oaths alluded to were taken by John Barker, Jeriah Hawkins, P. Gardner, Moses Melvin, David Goss, Wm. Hawkins, B. Bradley, Steph. Houghton, Nath. Daggett, Danl. Smith and Nath. H. Bishop. On the same day, was held the first recorded election for governor, with the following result:

For Governor.—Nathaniel Niles had 16 votes, Thomas Chittendon 8 votes, Isaac Tichenor 6 votes.

For Lieut. Governor.—Jona. Hunt, had 30 votes, Nath. Niles 1 vote.

For Treasurer.—Saml. Mattocks, had 23 votes.

In the state election for this year, Thomas Chittendon was for the 17th time elected Governor, Jonathan Hunt Lieut. Governor, and Samuel Mattocks Treasurer.

The first hog constables in the town were James Thurber, James Wheaton, Martin Wheeler, Eneas Harvey and Alpheus Houghton, elected on the first Monday of March, 1793, and as record declares "all married within the year last past." The first merchant in St. Johnsbury was a Mr. Sumner, who, about 1794 or '5 opened a store in the house of Jonathan Trescott, which stood on the road to Passumpsic, just below the county fair grounds. Afterwards Stephen Hawkins and Reuben Alexander came from Winchester, and commenced trade about 1798. Hawkins married a daughter of Capt. Arnold the *miller*. This Arnold was an old sea captain, a brother of Dr. Jonathan, and was the first person employed to tend the gristmill. His successor was Daniel Bowen, who lived in a rude hut by the corner of the bridge at the rail road crossing, which was the first house built in that village. The first store kept on the Plain was opened by Fred. Phelps as early as the year 1800, at the north end of the street. He carried on a potash factory near the mills, which was afterwards converted into a distillery of whiskey. Amaziah D. Barber kept a store somewhat later near the head of Maple street, which was subsequently occupied by Chamberlin & Paddock, afterwards fitted up as a house of worship for the Second Congregational Church, then in its infancy, and finally moved to its present location nearly opposite the post office, where it is still occupied as a dwelling house. The first public house or tavern was opened by Dr. Lord soon after the settlement of the town, at the southern extremity of the Plain. In 1799, the building now occupied as a bakery was built and opened as a tavern by Maj. Thomas Peck. It is said that Dr. Lord, after he had erected his great two story red house, distinguished himself and astonished his neighbors by importing from Montreal an enormous metallic structure, known as the first cooking stove brought into town. It is

reported to have been cast in Scotland. The first clock in St. Johnsbury was purchased before 1800, by Nath. Edson in Danville, for $75, and is still to be seen in running order at the house of Mrs. J. Clark on the Plain. It is one of those lofty relics of antiquity which used to stand guard in the corners of old kitchens, surmounted with brazen balls, and the moon's disc. It was on the lawn fronting Edson's house (now Mr. Butler's), that the first public muster and training was held. A few years after when Edson was preparing to remove to the west, he experienced some difficulty in making his exit from the town. His wagon was packed up with moveable property, ready for an early start on a certain morning, but during the night some mischievous person purloined one of the wagon wheels, rendering it impossible to proceed. The vexation of the Edson family was great, for it was not until two or three days had passed that the wheel was found, buried in a thistle bed half a mile from the house; and this vexation was greatly increased when it was discovered that a vast multitude of spectators had assembled on the Plain to witness the progress of a wagon that had gained so much notoriety. This same man subscribed in company with one of his neighbors for Spooner's *Vermont Journal*, which was the first paper that circulated in this part of the state. As one of them lived away from the main road, it was proposed that all the papers be left at Edson's house until the *end of the year*, and then equally divided between the two. Among the earliest lawyers in St. Johnsbury were Lyndon Arnold, Goodhue, Bissel, Dorr, and Gov. William A. Palmer. The row of maple trees front of the court house and along the east side of the street were set out by Gov. Palmer, who brought them all out of the woods on his back as early as 1805. He died in Danville, December, 1860. Hon. Ephraim Paddock is the first lawyer that can be said to have had a permanent residence in St. Johnsbury. Very soon after the settlement of the town, Joel Roberts, Gardiner Wheeler, Ariel Aldrich and Martin Wheeler, each purchased a 100-acre lot about two miles north west of the Plain. They commenced clearing at the same point which was the common corner of the four lots, and in process of time the title "Four Corners," which was at first applied to this clearing simply, came to embrace the whole region now known by that name, and where the descendants of the original proprietors are still residing.

About three years after its organization, the town was deprived of its most efficient leader in the death of Dr. Jonathan Arnold. He had risen rapidly in public estimation, and was regarded by all as one of the most able men in this section of the state. The following notice of Dr. Arnold's death is quoted from a series of letters published in London, about 1797. "The first principal inhabitant and proprietor of St. Johnsbury, Vt., was the truly patriotic and learned Dr. Jonathan Arnold, who is now no more. The Doctor emigrated from Providence in the state of Rhode Island. How sincerely his death is lamented, those only who had the happiness of knowing him can tell. His son (Josias Lyndon) was bred to the law, to which profession he does honor. His attainments are great. With the Greek and Roman authors he is familiar, and however strange it may appear, perhaps Mr. Arnold is the only person in Vermont, who is perfect master of the French language, and who speaks it in its utmost purity. Saint Johnsbury lies on the Passumpsic river, and to this town is attached some of the best land in the whole state." From one who was for more than half a century an active citizen of the town, we learn that the Doctor was a strong minded independent man. Yet accessible and companionable, but in St. Johnsbury always maintaining a complete ascendancy over all about him. He was a member of the governor's council at the time of his death. On a marble slab in the cemetery overlooking the valley of the Passumpsic and the beautiful village he founded, we read the simple inscription: "Hon. Jonathan Arnold, died Feb. 1st, 1793, Aged 52."

After the death of the Doctor, his eldest son Josias Lyndon, referred to in the above quotation, removed from Rhode Island and settled in St. Johnsbury. His career was short, although uncommonly brilliant in prospect. He was graduated at Dartmouth College with high honors in the class of 1788, admitted to the bar of Rhode Island—elected a tutor in Brown University—received in '91 the degree of A. M., from Brown, and was admitted *ad eundem* at Dartmouth and Yale. He removed to Vermont in 1793, married Miss Susan Perkins of Plainfield, Ct., and died June 7, 1796, aged 28. The year following Arnold's death a small volume was published in Providence, entitled, *Poems by the late Josias Lyndon Arnold, Esq., of St. Johnsbury, Vermont.* From the preface to this volume we make the following extract: "Mr. Arnold, before leaving college,

had given splendid proofs of his practical talents, and acquired the reputation of uncommon attainments in all the ornamental and useful branches of literature. His acquaintance with the Greek and Latin classics and the best English writers in history and belles-letters was intimate; with the vernacular and learned languages he was familiar and critical. With an imagination bold and fruitful, he possessed an understanding cool and discriminating; and while indulging the fanciful flights of the muse, he was equal to the calm discussions of reason. No man was better calculated to command the voice of popular applause. No one of his age received more flattering proofs of public approbation. He was an early candidate for fame. His political prospects were bright and promising, and few had stronger reasons for attachment to life; but alas! the strength of his constitution was unequal to the vigor of his mind." As representative of Mr. Arnold's versification, we quote the following

Lines on a Young Lady embarking for a Sea Voyage.

Ye winds be hushed — forbear to roar
  Ye waves, nor proudly lash the shore;
Be hush'd, ye storms, in silence sleep,
  Nor rage destructive o'er the deep.
Aspasia sails — and at her side,
The *Beauties* on the ocean ride.

Rise, Neptune, from thy coral bed,
  And lift on high thy peaceful head;
Calm with thy rod the raging main,
  Or bid the billows rage in vain.
Aspasia sails — and at her side
The *Graces* on the ocean ride.

Attendants of the watery god,
  Ye Tritons, leave your green abode;
Ye Nereids, with your flowing hair,
  Arise, and make the nymph your care.
Aspasia sails — and at her side
The *Muses* on the ocean ride.

Thou sea-born Venus, from thine isle,
  Propitious on this voyage smile;
Already anxious for the fair,
  Thy winged son prefers his prayer.
Aspasia sails — and at her side
The *Loves* upon the ocean ride.

Let ALL attend — and bid the breeze
  Blow softly — bid the swelling seas
Swell gently — for such worth before,
  The ocean's bosom never bore.
Aspasia sails — and at her side
The *Virtues* on the ocean ride.

July 22, 1791.

The following lines have perhaps more local interest than intrinsic merit, being a brief extract from

An Ode Written on the Banks of Passumpsic River, in September 1790.

PASSUMPSICK, hail! who glid'st along
Unknown to melody and song,
.   .   .   .
Reflecting in thy watery glass
Wide spreading elms,   ·   ·   ·
And pines that kiss the ambient sky.
Thy stream which runs like Fancy's child,
Irregular and sweetly wild,
Oft on its margin has beheld,
The Sachem and his tawny train,
Roll the red eye in vengeful ire,
And lead the captive to the fire.
Now, fairer scenes thy banks adorn;
Yellow wheat and waving corn
Bend in gratitude profound,
As yielding homage to the ground.
PASSUMPSICK, hail! who glid'st along,
The theme of many a future song.
Had'st thou a wish, that wish would be
Still on thy banks such scenes to see.
Where innocence and peace are found,
While vice and tumult fill the earth
around.

Mr. Arnold at the date of his death held the offices of town clerk and town representative. His widow, Mrs. Susan P. Arnold, afterwards re-married, and was the mother of the Hon. Geo. P. Marsh of this state.

An old chronicler, who half a century ago was recording passing events, makes the following allusion to the death of the Arnolds:

"The father had chosen for his family seat, a plain near the south part of the town. The son occupied the same. They looked to that spot as the seat of the future village. Every thing was favorable. The leading roads almost unavoidably centered there. The situation was favorable for building. On its border were excellent seats for mills, and all kinds of machinery requiring the aid of water. The short life of the father, and still shorter of the son blasted all these prospects, and destroyed the design of the Doctor, which was to build up a city around him."

It is further stated that Dr. Arnold intended to have parceled out the Plain lands into "small lots, sufficiently large for garden and necessary buildings," allowing no one more than one or two lots, and thus to have controlled and superintended the building up of the village.

In turning over the early records of our town clerks, we find the business transactions of town and freemen's meetings to have partaken largely of the miscellaneous. These meetings were commonly held at the dwelling house of Dr. Arnold until his death, after which they were "held around." Sometimes they convened at Nathaniel Edson's barn, and sometimes in the new dwelling house of the said Edson. In 1798, it was unanimously "voted, that the town will agree to hold their meetings at Asquire Edson's house in future." Apprehending certain contingencies however, it was judged advisable to appoint a committee "to enquire of the said Edson for liberty of the use of his house." This committee after a conference with said Edson, reported "that the said Nath. Edson gives his consent that the town shall hold a meeting at his House on March next and not thereafter." The house in question is the same now occupied by Mr. Beaumon Butler south of Center village.

In 1792 it was "Voted, that a Bounty of $10, be paid to any Inhabitant of this Township who shall take track of a Wolf in town and kill the same in any part of the state."

In 1795 "Voted, that a committee be appointed to procure powder and lead if necessary.

Voted, that the town be *districted* for schools, and that the Selectmen be committee for the said purpose."

1796, "Voted, that Surveyors of Highways shall see that Canada thistles are cut in the season directed or complain.

"Voted, that the Selectmen shall take invoice of ye rateable properties by going to their several dwellings."

1797, "Voted, that Henry Hoffman have the Improvement of the Burial Yard in the South Parish in St. Johnsbury (Plain), provided he clear the same, and does not interfere with the use heretofore made thereof, until such time as the said town shall put the said land to some other use."

1798, "Voted, to dispose with such part of the fine imposed on John K—t for theft, as belongs to the town of St. Johnsbury."

1799, "Voted, that Nath. Edson receive from the town $70 in grain, *for the use and trouble of his house.*"

1800, "Voted, that Hogs shall not run at large during the ensuing year."

Sheep, cattle and swine had for the most

part, been suffered to ramble at large. So long as this was the case, it became necessary for each animal to submit to the process of *marking*, which operation generally involved the mutilation of one or both ears. We find the following "cattle marks" recorded in 1795: "The mark of Josias L. Arnold, Esq., is a swallow's tail in the end of the right ear, and a crop off the left ear, being formerly the mark of Jonathan Arnold his father. The mark of Barnabas Barker is a hole through the left ear (simplex munditiis). The mark of Nathaniel Edson is a hole through the right ear and a slit in the same. The mark of Joseph Lord is a cut of half an inch on the top of the right ear and about the middle thereof, and a half penny on the upper side of the left ear near the head. Recorded March 2, 1795, J. L. Arnold, T. Clerk."

Before the XVIIIth century closed St. Johnsbury had grown to be a thriving town, and was fast increasing in population and wealth. In 1800 the town numbered 663 inhabitants, and the grand list was figured at $8628. The table from which this list was made out is here inserted; probably the ten houses mentioned did not include the log cabins in which most of the settlers were quartered:

Town of St. Johnsbury, County of Orange.
Grand List, A. D. 1800.

No. of Polls, . 124;	Assessment,	$2480.00
No. a. imp. land, 1059;	"	1853.25
No. of Houses, 10;	"	61.00
Other property to value of, . . .		5754.00

$10,148.25

Deduct 76 Militia Polls, assessed at 1,520.00
do   Horses of Cavalry, none.

Bal., or true list for State Taxes, $8628.25

To show the comparative increase of property in the town, a table of grand lists is here quoted from the date of organization down to the year 1800:

1790, . . $408.10	1796, . . $1415.10
1791, . . 590.00	1797, . . 6295.25
1792, . . 863.15	1798, . . 7286.50
1793, . . 1033.15	1799, . . 7261.75
1794, . . 1200.00	1800, . . 8628.25
1795, . . 1500.00	

In the year 1797, St. Johnsbury was set off from Orange county, and with eighteen others united to form the new county of Caledonia. This year we notice an increase in the grand list over preceding years of nearly $5000. The increase of population by births

and immigration for the first five years after settlement of the town was not far from 50 a year or 250 in all. The exact number is not known.

As yet no established post roads had been constructed, and the arrangements for carrying mails were every way inadequate to the wants of the settlers. All the southern mails were conveyed from Barnet to St. Johnsbury, over the bill road through Peacham and Danville. The post riders made their periodic circuits on horseback, fully equipped with saddle bags and tin horns. Prominent among these public functionaries, and well known for his daring, was the man William Trescott. He had been endowed by nature with a versatile genius. His attainments in astronomy and capacity for ardent spirits were alike immense, and his genius was especially exercised in the construction of almanacs and the destruction of bears. He it was, who encountered and vanquished Bruin on the edge of the gravel bank south of the Plain. It happened on this wise: Trescott had been employed in clearing and burning over the tract of hill land to the south of Dr. Lord's house. The fires which required "tucking up" in the evening, had excited the curiosity of a certain bear, who after dark, prowled out of the woods to investigate proceedings. In the course of their wanderings over the hill-side Trescott and Bruin most unadvisedly met, each being astonished at seeing in the darkness an undefined phenomenon standing on two feet. No very considerable space of time elapsed before an acquaintance was effected, and warmly embracing each other, the two rolled in alternate victory and defeat down the hill-side, until cradled in the hollow of an uprooted stump. Trescott was now underneath, uninjured and unterrified. His right hand was free, with which he straightway produced a knife from his pocket, and after opening the blade of the same with his teeth, applied it with fatal effect to the jugular vein of the quadruped. Thus ended the tragedy; but the bear meantime had suffered untold agonies from the incessant worrying and yelping of Trescott's dog, and it is said that the personal comfort of both combatants had been seriously endangered by the showers of fire brands that came blazing down the hill-side at the instigation of a certain terrified youth above. Now in giving the minor particulars of this transaction, authorities somewhat differ, but as to the *essential facts*, that Bill Trescott met, hugged and rolled down hill with a *bear*, and thereupon instituted a course of proceedings highly disgusting to the latter, all agree.

Several years after the above adventure, and indeed within the recollection of many eye witnesses still living, a movement was made which evinced a unanimous determination on the part of the citizens, to wage a war of extermination against the bears. The fact that the latter had greatly multiplied in the land, and had long waxed corpulent over the plundered cornfields of the settlers, was regarded as ample provocation for this belligerent movement. In due time Dr. Calvin Jewett as commander-in-chief, mustered all the effective forces of St. Johnsbury, who took up their fowling-pieces and followed him into the haunts of the taciturn offenders. An ample range of forests was enclosed by the encompassing hosts, and the point of convergence determined upon, was the steep bluff on the east bank of the Passumpsic, opposite the bend in the river road, midway between Center village and the Plain. Hither in course of time, were gathered nine distracted bears. Furthermore it is a very suggestive fact, that shortly after the advent of these bears over the hill-top, nine black pelts might have been seen, spread out on the grass plat front of Edson's tavern. Equally suggestive is the fact that these nine pelts were "all sold of for the necessaries of life — rum, bread and butter."

Previous to the year 1800, vigorous and repeated efforts had been made by various citizens of the town to establish a place of public worship, or some building to answer the two fold purpose of a church and town house. It was not however until the year 1802, that the town voted an appropriation for this purpose. On the 2nd September of this year, a meeting was called "by request of 18 substantial freeholders," to consider the question of building a town house.

"Met at the house of Lieut. Pierce, and made Choise of Alexander Gilchrist Moderator. On motion, voted to raise $850, Payable in good wheat at the market Prise, for the purpose of building a house for holding town meetings — one half to be paid in the Town treasury by the first of January next, viz: $425 at each payment. On motion, voted to erect said house on a certain Peace of Land given by Lieut. Thomas Pierce for Publick use near his house in said Town. On motion, voted to choose a committee of three to superintend building said House, and that Joel Roberts, Asquire Aldrich, and Thomas Pierce, Esq., be the Committee, who eccepted the appointment. On motion, voted

that said Committee have Liberty to Dispose of the floors of the house to individuals, in such a manner as they in their wisdom shall Judge best, the avails of which to be appropriated in order to finish said house Sutible and Convenent to attend Publict Worship in, and for a Town House. On motion, voted that the said Committee prosead as soon as may be, in the line of their appointment. On motion, voted to dissolve said meeting. Attest, NATH. EDSON, T. Clerk."

During the following year $80 more were appropriated to the same object, and in the autumn of 1804, the building was raised. At this raising all the able bodied men and boys in town were assembled. After the frame had been erected, a gymnastic entertainment was executed by Zibe Tute, who about the going down of the sun, ascended one of the rafters, stood on his head at the end of the ridge pole, and thence, after emptying the contents of his flask, descended with head downwards to the ground. The temperance reform had not yet begun. Tradition tells us that all the shingles used on this building were taken from a single tree. The floor of the house was divided up into the square pews which were characteristic of olden days, 51 being placed on the lower floor and 25 in the galleries. This building, which stood for more than 20 years the only meeting house in town, was built on the high hill west of Center Village, in the central right of the township, which had been originally alloted to Ebenezer Scott, and by him deeded to Lieut. Pierce, with a special reservation of 2 acres for the use of the town. From its high and bleak location, it overlooked the valley of the Passumpsic, from Lyndon Falls, past the mouth of Moose river and Arnold's Mills to the meadows at the mouth of the Sleeper. Within its spacious walls it received on town days the representatives of every family, and on the sabbath the worshipers of every denomination. For 41 years its brown old timbers stood on the hill top, until in 1825 it was removed to its present location in the Center village, and as late as 1855 the lower floor was used for the accommodation of town meetings. The former site is now a green sward, with no relic of former years, save the projecting end of ledge which was known as "Whig Rock" in the days when it was used as a rostrum for political haranguers. The first town meeting held in this house was on September 1, 1804. Respecting this building the following action was subsequently taken by the town :

"Voted, that Capt. John Barney be employed to keep the Meeting House clean, and that he sweep it at least twice during the year.

"Voted, that no person or persons be alowed to enter the Pulpit on town meeting Days, unles speshely Directed by the town.

"Voted, that Five persons be appointed to Expel dogs from the Meeting House on Sundays, and that they be authorized to take such measures as they think proper, and that the town will indemnify them for so doing."

Gen. Joel Roberts, Capt. John Barney, Gen. R. W. Fenton, Simeon Cobb and Abel Shorey, were appointed dog committee, and accepted the responsibilities of the office. One of the ways in which expenses of public worship were met may be gathered from the following note, in which the subscriber promises to pay "three midling likely ewe sheep as to age, size and quality, on demand, and to keep the said three sheep five years, free from expence to the said Society, and to pay the Wooll to the committee in June, and the lambs on or Before the first day of November yearly. All the Wooll and all the lambs and all the proffits arising from the said Sheep, to be laid out yearly for Congregational Preaching."

The first district school house built by the town has led a more restless career than its predecessor the meeting house. No less than six distinct localities on Main street have sustained this classic edifice. Originally it stood on Main street, corner of Winter; thence it was moved southward to a place opposite the Bank;' thence northward to the foot of Mt. Pleasant; thence southward to the corner of Church street; thence northward over against Arnold park; thence southward a short distance to its present location, a few hundred yards north of its original site. The first school in this building which is now attached to a dwelling house, was kept by Miss Rhoda Smith. Rev. Dr. Goodell of Constantinople was also at one time a teacher on the Plain. A few years later a small building was erected on the south side of Moose river, and was known as the Branch Bridge school house. In this house a party of soldiers returning from the war of 1812, were quartered for a night, making use of the hemlock fire wood for pillows, and the handkerchief of the mistress for bandages. No record of dates is found to indicate the time when the different school houses in town were erected. The present number of school districts is 17, the number of schools

23, and the amount expended for their support per annum, about $3000.

It must have been after the erection of the meeting house and the establishment of the first school on the Plain, that a petition was sent in to the legislature by the land owners and settlers in the west part of Littleton (now Waterford), praying to be set off from that town and united to St. Johnsbury. For in this petition "it is humbly shewn that the Inhabitants of St. Johnsbury being Organized, and amongst whom Law is known, and Order is duly observed, and having begun to provide for the introduction of regular Schools, and the Preaching of the Gospel; for these reasons in an especial manner, as well as others, we are desirous to be united with them that we and our Children may as Citizens and Christians enjoy those valuable advantages as early as may be, and which without such Union we cannot expect to do, if ever, for many years." It would seem that the Governor was not opposed to such a change, for he states in a foot note to the petition that "in case the foregoing facts are truly stated, he has no objection to the prayer of the petitioners being granted."

St. Johnsbury at this time was rapidly improving. The publication of its weekly paper, the increase in the number of its churches, and the subsequent establishment of the Academies, tended much to elevate the character and influence of the place.

On the 3d of July, 1828, was issued at St. Johnsbury Plain, the first number of The Farmer's Herald, a weekly Whig journal, edited by Dr. Luther Jewett. This publication was continued about four years, when the failing health of the editor caused its temporary abandonment. In July of 1832, however, it was revived by Samuel Eaton, Jr., under the name of The Weekly Messenger, or Connecticut and Passumpsic Valley Advertiser. In the course of the following year, the establishment passed into the hands of A. G. Chadwick, Esq., who commenced in August, 1837, and for 18 years continued the publication of The Caledonian. Since 1855, this paper has been under the management of Rand & Stone and Stone & Co., has nearly reached its XXVth volume, and attained a circulation of about 1900 copies.

Dr. Luther Jewett,

Whose enterprise established and whose literary talent ably sustained the first paper in St. Johnsbury, was for many years an active and honored citizen of this town. He was born in Canterbury, Ct., 1772 — graduated at Dartmouth College, class of 1792 — removed to St. Johnsbury in 1800, and immediately commenced the practice of medicine. In 1817 he represented the north-east district of Vermont in Congress, and took his seat by the side of Daniel Webster, then in his second term. He was licensed to preach the year following by the Coos Association, and supplied the pulpits of Newbury and other towns in this vicinity for a period of ten years. His varied acquirements, and experience in public life especially fitted him for the post of a journalist, and in the editorial management of the *Herald*, he displayed much practical tact and ability. He was honest and straightforward in every expression of opinion, and no less firm in his support of justice and right, than unsparing in his rebuke of existing evils. Slavery, intemperance and anti-masonry, he denounced in the most fearless manner, and to combat the ultraism of the latter, he issued during the year 1827, a weekly sheet entitled *The Friend*, whose columns were entirely devoted to the discussion of this and kindred subjects. A late member of Congress from Massachusetts, and intimate friend of the Doctor, writes as follows : " To us, the name of Luther Jewett will always recall some of the most pleasant memories of life. He was eminently good, and scrupulously just in all his ways. In a delightful village, unsurpassed for its picturesque beauty by any in New England, his bright example has contributed largely for half a century in the development of its character for enterprise, as well as for moral and intellectual elevation. On revisiting the town a few years since, we sought out the venerable old man at his retired house, and found him so feeble that he scarcely ventured from his door. His snowy locks and patriarchal mein lent impressiveness to his words as he conversed of current events with the zest of one who was never content to be a mere spectator of the world's progress. It was our last meeting. We left him

'—— in a green old age,
And looking like the oak, worn, but still steady
Amidst the elements, while younger trees
Full fast around him.'"

He died in 1860, aged 87.

ST. JOHNSBURY FEMALE SEMINARY.

On the 27th November, 1824, was incorporated the St. Johnsbury Female Seminary. This institution owed its existence to the efforts of Judge Paddock and Deacon Luther Clark, by whom the charter was obtained, and a small school opened the year follow-

ing in the hall of the brick house built by Capt. Martin, the ruins of which are still standing near the Union school house. Owing to the want of sufficient funds, no organization under the charter was effected, but for several years the seminary was sustained with much success, until after the grant of St. Johnsbury Academy 18 years later, when it was given up and merged into the latter institution. The persons employed as teachers in this seminary were 8 in number, extending their instructions over a period of nearly seventeen years, viz: Miss Trowbridge of Worcester, Miss Giles of Walpole, Miss Newcomb of Keene, Miss Almira Taylor of Derry, Misses Susan and Catharine Clark of St. Johnsbury, Miss Bradley of Peacham, and Miss Hobart of Berlin.

HON. EPHRAIM PADDOCK,

One of the originators and warmest supporters of this Seminary, was a strong-minded, self-educated man, and well-known for many years as one of the ablest lawyers in this part of the state. His early education was that of the common school only, but in this he made such proficiency that on removing to this state from Massachusetts, he was for two or three years employed as an instructor in Peacham Academy, then the only institution of the kind in the county. His opportunities for professional studies were very limited, and the standard of legal acquirements at the time was by no means a high one ; yet after he had commenced practice in St. Johnsbury, he applied himself with such diligence to judicial investigation, that he was quickly enabled " to take rank with the most learned lawyers of the state." He always maintained a high position as a lawyer, and did much to elevate the standard of the legal profession in this vicinity. We find the following record of his public services : " He was representative of St. Johnsbury in the state legislature from 1821 to '26, inclusive — a member of the constitutional convention in 1828 — one of the council of censors in 1841 — judge of the supreme court from 1828 to '31. In 1847 he retired from professional duties, having well earned a quiet old age by a long life of activity and usefulness." He died July 27, 1859, aged 79.

ST. JOHNSBURY ACADEMY.

Early in the year 1842 a movement was made by several persons who were warmly interested in the cause of education, to establish on a permanent and liberal basis a high school or academy on the Plain. This movement resulted in the establishment of the St. Johnsbury Academy, an institution, which from a small and unpretentious beginning has grown to become one of the most flourishing of its kind in this part of the state. A constant and efficient religious influence, systematic thoroughness in everything undertaken, and cultivation of the mental faculties rather than mere accumulation of knowledge, were the objects specially aimed at in the establishment of this institution, and by which it was thought that a foundation might be laid for a consistent, sound, and useful character. The first session of this academy was opened on a small scale in the fall of 1842, and during the following year a building of ample accommodations was erected at the south end of the Plain. The subsequent growth of the town and increasing demands of the school, have required a more appropriate and commodious building. From the commencement, with exception of a short interval, the school has been under charge of the same principal, who is still at its head. There have been connected with the instructing department of the institution, 21 male and 17 female teachers assistant, and nearly 1800 different names are recorded on the 18 catalogues which have already been issued. The rate of increase for the first five years may be seen from the following enumeration : Number of scholars during first year, 101 ; second year, 164 ; third, 196 ; fourth, 206 ; fifth, 257. Greatest number in any one year subsequent to 1847, 223 ; James K. Colby, principal ; J. C. Cutler, principal in 1856–7. The springing up of other similar institutions in this vicinity, has withdrawn somewhat from the patronage which it formerly received, but it is believed that the high standard, and well earned reputation of St. Johnsbury Academy, will still give it that favor and influence in the community to which its antecedents so justly entitle it.

We'would not in this connection, omit the name of one, who but a few years since, was actively identified with the interests of religion, education, and social progress in this community, and whose memory is yet warmly cherished in the hearts of those who knew him. In early manhood and the full tide of usefulness, he passed from earth, but not until by an earnest, benevolent and guarded Christian character, he had faithfully accomplished "life's great end." Another's pen, if any, should eulogize, but ours is the privilege to make grateful mention of an honored parent, a liberal and worthy man — JOSEPH P. FAIRBANKS.

CHURCHES.

Nearly 8 years were numbered after the settlement of the town, before any active movement was made to establish public divine worship. Not a large proportion of the first settlers were religious men, and after the rough labors of the week were closed, the sabbath seems to have been regarded rather as a day of physical relaxation than religious observances. We are told that in those days they were wont to spend the sabbath in rambling the fields, visiting each other's homes, and planning those labors which called for the public arm, and aimed at the public good. The first town meeting was held in 1790, but not till 1794 was the question put, "Will the town raise money by tax to pay for preaching of the gospel?" It was determined in the negative, and during the following year, J. L. Arnold, Joseph Lord, Stephen Dexter, John Ladd and Jona. Adams, were chosen committee to draw up a subscription paper with the same object in view. No record of their labors is found, and in September, 1797, it was voted that a minister be hired at the expense of the town. Before the close of the meeting however, this vote was recalled, and a committee of three appointed to find how much money could be raised for this purpose by voluntary contributions. What success attended their labors we are not informed, but at the next March meeting in 1798, we find that the town voted to raise $80, payable in grain within the year for the support of preaching. It was also voted "that the town build a house for public use or a town house, to be framed, enclosed with rough boards, and shingled by Nov. 1st, 1799; to be 56 by 46 feet square on the ground, and to be located wherever a committee appointed for the purpose should designate." On the 18th day of June following, a meeting was called, in which the last mentioned vote respecting the town house was revoked, and it was then and there determined that the town should not build a meeting house. The month following a meeting was called to consider the question of hiring a minister. Committee of seven was appointed to consider the subject, and report within one hour. According to the records, they reported it as their opinion "that the town ought to hire a minister, and therefore to raise $230, payable in wheat, rye, corn, pork and beef, for his yearly salary. Also that said minister preach one half the time on the Plain, and the other half at the most convenient place toward the north end of the town. On motion, voted to hire a minister. A minister was accordingly engaged, who probably remained a few weeks only, for in September of the same year "it was put to vote to see if the town would raise money to pay for further preaching and determined in the negative. But, voted to raise $15 to pay expense of preaching already incurred." One year later, September, 1799, a motion to hire a minister by the town was again negatived. On the 25th of May, 1801, it was "voted, to raise $100, payable in grain by the 1st of Feb. next, to pay for preaching." The first of February came—the grain and the minister came not.

On the 2d September, 1802, one more, and finally successful effort was made by the town to erect a church edifice, and establish at last a place for the observance of sabbath worship. Record of this meeting, which is one of interest [and somewhat anomalous, as the town subsequently seemed to abide by its action], has been transcribed, and inserted in a previous section, page 401. A large and commodious building was erected in the fall of 1804, and so finished off as to answer the purpose of town and meeting house, although it was some years before the formation of any church body.

THE FIRST CONGREGATIONAL CHURCH,

Was organized Nov. 21st, 1809, fifteen years after the settlement of the town, and five after the raising of the meeting house. Rev. Leonard Worcester of Peacham, Rev. John Fitch of Danville, and Rev. Asa Carpenter of Waterford, constituted the ecclesiastical council. The little band of nineteen whose names constitute the first church roll of the town, formed the nucleus of four large Congregational churches which now stand in its place. Six were males, and thirteen females. Hubbard Lawrence was chosen moderator and David Stowell clerk, both of whom were subsequently appointed deacons, and both of whom were recorded as "good men and true.":

Six years passed away before the church obtained a pastor, but public worship is said to have been uniformly maintained, sometimes with, and often without preaching. The sisters of the church frequently walked from three to six miles in mid-winter to attend worship, and sat in a cold room through the service. The following list embraces all who have been settled over the church:

Pastors.	Installed.	Dismissed.
Pearson Thurston,	Oct. 25, 1815,	Oct. 17, '17.
Josiah Morse, M.D.,	Feb. 21; 1833,	May 3, '43.
James P. Stone,	Sep. 29, 1846,	Sep. 23, '50.
H. Wellington,	Jan. 4, 1855,	Oct. 25, '60.
George H. Clarke,	Jan. 15, 1862.	

During the 2 years' ministry of the first pastor, 52 members were added to the church, and during the 7 years of the third, 66. This church still worships in the old meeting house, which was moved from the hill into Center village, in 1845, and located east of the burial ground. About 15 years after the organization of the First Church, in consequence of the scattering of the families and the increase of population in town,

THE SECOND CONGREGATIONAL CHURCH

Was set off as a colony from the first, and organized on the 7th April, 1825. It is a noticeable coincidence that this church also was established with 19 members, of whom six were males and thirteen females. They were set off by their own request, and with full consent of the church then existing, and adopted the same Confession of Faith and Covenant. This church worshiped on the Plain, and over it we find the following list of pastors, settled and dismissed:

Pastors.	Installed.	Dismissed.
James Johnson,	Feb. 28, 1827,	May 3, '38.
John H. Worcester,	Sep. 5, 1839,	Nov. 6, '46.
William B. Bond,	Oct. 14, 1847,	June 29, '58.
Ephraim C. Cummings,	May 10, 1860.	

The church was very much enlarged during the ministrations of its two first pastors, and especially during the revivals of 1827, 1831 and 1832. The additions embraced a large number who resided in and near the East village of St. Johnsbury, and in accordance with their wish, to be set off in a separate body,

THE THIRD CONGREGATIONAL CHURCH

Was organized, Nov. 25th, 1840. A meeting house was erected for their accommodation in the East village, and the church at the date of its organization, consisted of 26 individuals from neighboring churches, to wit, two from the First and eleven from the Second in St. Johnsbury; five from the church in Kirby; and two from the church in Lyndon. This church subsequently received large additions under the ministrations of its successive pastors, as follows:

48

Pastors.	Installed.	Dismissed.
Rufus Case,	May 4, 1842,	Feb. 26, '50.
J. H. Gurney,	Feb. 27, 1850,	'55.
John Bowers,	Feb. 4, 1858.	

The Second Church, located on the Plain, by reason of the increase of its congregation, found it necessary to erect a new house of larger dimensions, which was completed in 1847, standing on the corner of Church and Main streets. But the population of the parish still continued to increase. The new house was found insufficient to accommodate all who wished to attend public worship; and in the spring of 1851, it was determined, after mature deliberation, that the interests of religion rendered expedient the formation of a new church, and the erection of a new house of worship on the Plain. Accordingly a

FOURTH CONGREGATIONAL CHURCH

Was organized Oct. 28, 1851, consisting of 65 members—it having been previously voted that 'not less than one-quarter, nor more than one-third of the members of the Second or North Church should be designated to the new organization. The church edifice, located near the academy at the south end of the Plain, was built at the expense of the whole society, and became the property of the new church, its rents being appropriated to the support of their own pastor, and other expenses of public worship. After the establishment of this colony, the two churches on the Plain, Second and Fourth became known as the North and South Congregational churches of St. Johnsbury. Pastors of the South Church have been as follows:

Pastors.	Installed.	Dismissed.
S. G. Clapp,	Jan. 13, 1852,	Jan. 18, '55.
Geo. N. Webber,	Dec. 4, 1855,	Sep. 13, '59.
Lewis O. Brastow,	Jan. 10, 1860.	

Respecting churches of other denominations, our records are incomplete. The Universalist Church at Center village, was built about the year 1830; the Methodist in the same village, a few years later. Of the other two Methodist churches in St. Johnsbury, one is located at the East village, the other on Central street, at the Plain, which latter was completed in 1858, and is at present supplied by Rev. H. W. Worthen. Early in 1859, an association was organized for the purpose of sustaining Episcopal worship, but as yet no church has been built, or permanent preacher obtained. The corner stone of a Catholic church was laid in the summer of 1860, and when completed,

there will be numbered in St. Johnsbury 9 church edifices—two at the East, and three at Center village, and four on the Plain. Yet, less than 40 years ago, not a church spire was to be seen in either of the villages.

The influence of the strong religious element, which after the formation of the first church, began to prevail over the immoralities of former years, has been great. It is said that few towns have at different periods of their history, developed such marked changes of character as this. Originally the standard of morality was low; in a few years, with the influx of a mixed population, it became still lower; but by degrees the influence of good men, and the increasing facilities for religious and intellectual cultivation, imparted a more salutary tone to society, and elevated the social condition of the place to such a degree, that it soon acquired, and has for many years retained, a high character for morality, industry and intelligence. And it is a fact worthy of mention, that at the present time (1861), the heads of both the executive and judiciary of this state, are residents of St. Johnsbury — Gov. E. Fairbanks, and Chief Justice L. P. Poland.

The relative increase of population in the town since 1800, may be seen by comparing the following tables quoted from the census reports: 1800, 663; 1810, 1334; 1820, 1404; 1830, 1592; 1840, 1887; 1850, 2758; 1860, 3470. In 1857, the first registration report was made, recording for that year 114 births, 59 deaths, 10 marriages. The increase in post office business has been great. Thirty years ago there was but one office, the compensation of the post master being about $50. Now, of the three independent offices located at the Plain, East and Center villages, a single one receives twenty times the compensation which was paid in 1830. Within the last decade, the town has made its most rapid growth and internal development. The opening of the rail road — chartering of the bank — removal of county buildings, and the extensive manufacturing and rail road interests here established, have all tended to increase the importance of the place as a business center. Passumpsic Bank was incorporated in 1849 — capital, $100,000. Mt. Pleasant Cemetery was laid out and dedicated in the summer of 1852, and is probably unsurpassed in natural beauty and location by any other in the state. Caledonia County Court House was built in 1855, at an expense of $15,000. Of this amount, $3,000 was raised by the town for furnishing a hall, $1,770 paid as share of county tax, and $1,000 by voluntary subscription in the village, making a total of $5,770, or about two-fifths the whole expense. The ground occupied by the Court House, was originally granted to the town by Jonathan Arnold for a burial yard, and was used for this purpose until the new cemetery was opened in 1852. The Union School House on Summer street, was built in 1854, providing for the primary, intermediate and high school departments in the same building. Caledonia County Fair Grounds were first opened south of the Plain in the autumn of 1858.

The manufacturing interests of St. Johnsbury are varied and extensive, embracing almost every variety of wooden and metalic wares, machinery, agricultural and household implements. The business villages which have sprung up on the banks of each of the rivers, witness to the natural endowments of the town, and these all with a single exception are of modern date. In 1821, before Center village had ceased to be known as Sanger's Mills, not a single dwelling house had been erected on the marshes which then covered that region. As late as 1848, the only building on the flat now intersected by rail way tracks, was the little farm house which still stands at the southern extremity of Rail road village. Arnold's Mills, built in 1787, give to Paddock village the right of priority in settlement, but before Huxum Paddock had built his foundries and revived the importance of the village which has since then borne his name, grist and saw mills had been put up on the banks of Sleeper's river, by a man from Brimfield, whose descendants have originated and developed on the same water privilege the manufacture of "weights and balances." By request of the publishers, more particular details of this manufacture are here inserted.

THE FAIRBANKS SCALES.

About the year 1830, a business company was established at St. Johnsbury, for the purpose of cleaning hemp, and preparing the fibre for market. The location of this business was in Mooso river valley, on the site of the large red mill, which was burned in the summer of 1860. After commencing operations, it was found that a machine or scale was very much needed to facilitate the operation of weighing the hemp. This necessity led to an investigation of the principle of levers as combined in a weighing machine, and resulted ultimately in the invention and development of the platform scale, by Mr. Thaddeus Fairbanks. The invention of this machine—the first grand idea which has resulted in profit not only to the manufacturers, but to almost every branch of human industry — was by no means an accident; and yet, hardly less mental ingenuity was required to originate the idea, than in after years to perfect the manufacture, a work to which the skillful mechanical genius of the inventor has been constantly and most successfully directed. Labor-saving machinery, and all the appliances which years of study can develop, are employed to facilitate the work; and the delicate accuracy, strength and unchanging quality of the scales are due in a great measure to the minor improvements successively introduced. The success of the establishment has been a natural sequence of skill in construction, care in management, and increasing demand for the article manufactured. The limited resources of Sleeper's river, have proved utterly insufficient to supply the power required for driving the thousand machinery wheels of the factory. And even since the employment of steam, one engine after another has been removed to make room for others of higher power. The works at present employ an average of 300 men, on wages of about $130,000 annually— consume 2500 tons pig iron, 200 tons bar iron, 38 tons steel, 26 tons copper, 300 tons anthracite coal, 100,000 bushels charcoal and 1,000,000 feet of lumber. The annual product of scales amounts to $500,000. Up to January 1st, 1861, there had been made 96,658 portable scales; 8,872 hay and track scales, and 94,712 counter and even-balances; making an aggregate of more than 190,000 in all, including a hundred different modifications, and a range of capacity from half an ounce of the even-balance to five hundred tons of the canal scale.

A correspondent of the New York press, after visiting this manufactory, remarks: "There is no business worthy of New England, but will afford employment for all the skill and care which can be commanded, but the scale manufacture seems in an especial degree to require experienced and intellectual labor. The three hundred workmen employed in the scale works at St. Johnsbury are unequaled by any like number of operatives collected together in the world.

"This is due partly to the nature of their employment, their isolated situation, the influence of employers, but more than all, no doubt to the traits of character inherent in the people of this section. The village is purely New England—the proverbial air of freshness, neatness and industry, being no where more strongly marked than in this locality."

Well does the author of the above allude to the prosperity and thrift of the employees in this manufactory, and justly may our community congratulate itself on the general intelligence, public spirit and energy which characterize this class of its citizens. From their daily workshops, where indeed "thought is embodied in iron and brass," the delicate emblems of Astrea have gone out to every quarter of the globe, and in distant resting places their quick responses have silently witnessed to the industry and skill of this Green Mountain town.

THE ABORIGINES.

In closing this imperfect record of historical sketches, it is fit that a passing mention be made of our lost Aborigines, and of the traces which they have left to us of a sovereignty here, anterior to the date of even most of the traditional history.

The records of early adventurers, and the comparative scarcity of Indian relics, induces the belief, that in this immediate vicinity the numbers of the warlike red men were few. Not, indeed, because nature here refused them ample means of subsistence, for within the memory of men now living, game was abundant — numberless trout leaped in our brooks, and rotund bears rioted through the forest. But this was contested land. The powerful and dreaded tribes of the Iroquois on Lake Champlain, and the Abenâquis or Coossucks, who ranged the Connecticut valley and the forests of Canada, each laid claim to the fair hunting grounds of Northern Vermont, and this being border land between them, never became permanently settled or abundantly stocked with their rough-hewn relics. Yet now and then, even at the present time, there is found some rudely fashioned implement of savage days. Arrow points are turned up from time to time in the furrows of the plow. And within the year last past, a more formidable object—a veritable stone battle axe was discovered on the pasture ground south of the plain. This Indian axe head is verily an object of interest, a grim old reminder of those taciturn tribes, who stalked of yore along our thoroughfares. It bears a rough and venerable look, as characteristic of those days " when the

rank thistle nodded in the wind, and the wild fox dug his hole unscared "—when the hand of some patient squaw chipped it into fashion, and the stout arm of an Algonquin brave sent it crashing on its fatal errand. Its granite edge seems to tell of tracts away to the east of Connecticut river, and how of old the fierce Coossucks

"Armed themselves with all their war gear,
Sang their war-song wild and woful."

and journeyed hitherward on their way toward the hunting grounds of the mighty Iroquois.

But a few years have passed since our Aborigines took up their farewell marches. When Lord Cornwallis surrendered his sword, not a white habitation had been seen within the boundary lines of St. Johnsbury. Scarce fifty years have gone since old Joe, the "last of the Coossucks" passed away to the "kingdom of Ponemah," and only a hundred since Major Rogers sacked the Indian villages of St. Francis, and saw his brave rangers on their return starving on the islands at the mouth of Passumpsic river. Strange and sad, that in these regions, over which contesting tribes of Indians roamed and hunted and fought, the traces of their existence should have been so quickly and thoroughly obliterated. We might almost think to find their lodge poles undecayed, and shelving rocks still blackened with the smoke of their camp fires.

Note.—For facts and valuable assistance in compiling the above sketches, especial acknowledgments are due to Henry Stevens, antiquarian, whose abundant resources were readily tendered to the writer. The preparation of the narrative has involved many difficulties, in combining at the same time the requisites of a readable article for the *Quarterly*, and a faithful record of the town history; and if inaccuracies have crept into the text, or too much incoherence characterises the whole, it must be remembered that the limited space and the nature of the case, forbid a thorough and systematic treatment of the almost endless variety of subjects introduced.

Saint Johnsbury, Dec. 31st, 1860.

EDITORIAL GLEANINGS.

The Catholic Church.

Until the erection of Burlington into an Episcopal see, in 1853, St. Johnsbury had received occasional visits from missionary priests of Canada, and Rev. H. Drolet, who was then stationed at Montpelier.

Soon after the arrival of the oblate fathers at Burlington, they were appointed to attend St. Johnsbury, and one of them, Rev. R. Maloney, visited there once every month on Sunday, until the fall of 1856. The lot on which stands the present church was brought at his suggestion.

Rev R. Maloney officiated for the congregation in 'a public hall, hired for that purpose, and service continued to be held there until lately, when the church was far enough completed to allow it to be used for worship.

Rev. Charles O'Reilley of Bellows Falls, attended the congregation after Rev. R. Maloney, until July, 1858, when Rev. Stanislaus Danielou was appointed resident pastor of the place. To his exertions is due the erection of the handsome church of St. Johnsbury, named Our Lady of Victories, after a celebrated church in Paris, situated on the Place des Petits Peres.

Rev. Stanislaus Danielou purchased also a lot for a cemetery, which he laid out with great taste.

The Catholics of St. Johnsbury and vicinity number about eighty families."

CAPTAIN JOHN BARNEY,

Said *The Caledonian*, in an obituary notice, "was one of our oldest citizens; had been a resident of this town 50 years or upwards, was widely known and much respected." Mrs. Curtis, his daughter, who resides at St. Johnsbury, thus writes:

"Your kind offer to insert something in the St. Johnsbury chapter, if I would furnish it, of my father, stirs me up to attempt. I shall fail to write an article that will read well — would that I could borrow some able pen to write a history of that lovely man — but I will endeavor to give you a few facts. From the large family Bible (bequeathed to me), I find in the record, 'John Barney, born in New Haven, Conn., Jan. 4th, 1775; married in St. Johnsbury, Vt., July 17, 1802, to Betsy Carlton.' He resided in his native place till about 21 years of age. After his settlement in St. Johnsbury he became the captain of a military company, which office he acceptably filled several years. He built the second public house of entertainment on the Plain. A part of the building now remains, connected with the St. Johnsbury House. This house he kept for many years, and as was customary in those days, it had its *bar*, but when the temperance cause awoke in Vermont, and came up like a bannered host from the wilderness, he was one of the first to enlist in this great moral reform, and

stand ever afterward by its sacred standard. He held several town offices in his day; was deputy sheriff from 1809 a number of years; also justice of the peace several years; and was known as a townsman always one of the first in all patriotic, enterprising and benevolent movements. I have often heard my parents narrate various incidents connected with their habits of living, social, moral and physical. True, I find as I dwell upon them none of the superfluities and elegancies of life that constitute the luxuries of the present, but I find instead, a homely but hearty sufficiency, with frugality and cleanliness withal, and a home ever made desirable and appreciated. A characteristic picture of their sociality was the winter evening visit: Some long and pleasant December or January evening, the noble yoke of oxen were 'whoa'd' and 'gee'd' to the kitchen door, hitched to the sled, and the first family started; calling for the next family and the next, on the way, till the last family on the road joined the party. Arrived at their destination — as our old fashioned surprise party came steadily up to the log mansion, and shaking off their 'buffalo of hay,' the sleds were unloaded upon the great stone door step — the welcomings and greetings were sometimes as hearty as to be almost deafening. The well fatted turkey must be prepared for the spit, and pies and puddings well flavored, placed for baking; meanwhile a mug of hot flip came not amiss after their cold ride of eight or ten miles. A good supper, joviality and sincere good will crowned the hour. I could dwell at much length on many adventures of these early settlers, deer huntings, &c., but others will recount for you similar narrations. And of my father's Christian character I would speak more fully. In or about 1827, he made a profession of the Christian religion—a public profession, and erected a family altar, where from thenceforth prayer went up daily from a heart overflowing. Even now I seem to hear the kindness that lingered in his voice as he reproved our childish follies, or see the patient, beaming smile, as he encouraged our feeble efforts to do the right. Thus a sainted father's heavenly influences still shines out sweetly and clear upon the path of his child, guiding on like a beacon star to right purposes — activity, patience here, and the hope of the beyond. It is an inestimable blessing to have such a father. And to lose him ——. But I write of the dead, and would 'not wrong the messenger that gathered back the breath,

'For his touch was like the angel's,
Who comes at close of day,
To lull the willing flowers asleep,
Until the morning ray.'

"He died Oct. 12, 1860, suddenly, of heart disease, at the house of his daughter in Lancaster, N. H., aged 76. At his funeral, one of the deacons of the church arose after the sermon, and amid the tearful congregation, spoke at some length of the power of holy example. 'I know,' said he, 'it is not according to our custom to thus speak in the funerals of our dead, but a good man has departed, and I cannot refrain from this just tribute.' [This deacon was Gov. Fairbanks.] Our aged mother, who has already seen 81 summers, resides in her old home with her son George. Her children are all living, four in number."

A niece of the departed, from Connecticut, present upon the funeral occasion, published at the time, a poem, in *The Caledonian*, from which we extract:

A Good Man has Departed.

'Twas a solemn gathering. A day
Long to be treasured in the kindliest hearts
That worshiped in that temple. An aged man,
A man whom all had known for many years,
A friend, a Christian, honest and sincere,
Had by that shaft, which nothing can resist,
Been called to part with earth and earthly scenes.
"A good man had departed" — full of years
'Tis true, and ready for his sudden change;
But happy in his love of brotherhood,
His old familiar friends, his kindred ties,
And ripening for his immortality.
An aged man, of whiten'd locks, he stood
Whene'er the sabbath came, in his own pew,
To show his reverence for the sacred word,
And love for holy things. I see him now
With form erect, and noble brow, as o'er
The sacred hymns he pondered oft. . .
Within this temple now — silent unseen,
His spirit hovers o'er that chosen pew,
And bids them look above, with faith's clear eye,
Above the cares of earth — these sordid scenes,
To purer joys. . . . .
                              SARAH ELIZABETH.

ELEAZER SANGER,

Born in Keene, N. H., married Sabrina Whitney of Winchester, Mass., and settled in St. Johnsbury at the Four Corners, about 1790. Mrs. Roxana Sears, a daughter of Mr. Sanger, from whom we have the account,

says her parents came immediately after their marriage to St. Johnsbury, moving in on an ox sled, and she thinks her father was, after Mr. Cole, one of the first five settlers in town. Here his 12 children were born and he lived, till his death about 17 years since, and died aged nearly 70, being insane some 18 years before his death. Dr. Arnold, Gen. Roberts, Martin and Gardiner Wheeler, and Mr. Sanger, all settled at the Four Corners. Three of the families, the Roberts and Wheelers, have always lived there. Mr. Sanger soon removed to the Centre, where he was the first settler, and owned the land upon which the Centre village now stands — some 200 acres. Here he built a large "hopper-roofed" house for his family, and though he never opened a public house, yet, as he was himself a teamster, the teamsters and so many others put up with him, that he kept about as many travelers as the tavern. After his death, the ample old house was rented at one time to some five families; it may still be seen standing near the Methodist chapel. He also built several other houses to rent, and the first saw and grist-mill at the Centre. After many years these mill privileges were sold to Reuben Spaulding from Cavendish, who built new mills on the old sites. Ezra, Mr. Sanger's son, kept the first store at the Centre. Mr. Sanger never coveted any part or lot in town offices, but appears to have been a prominent business man, helping well toward first building up the Centre Village. He was, moreover, one of the first free masons of St. Johnsbury — to whose lodge also belonged General Roberts, Gardiner Wheeler, Capt. Barney and Gen. Fenton, who moved in somewhat later, and carried on the manufacture of earthen ware, which business his son Leander, has since followed. In those pleasant olden days, town meeting was a great day; the farmers for miles around were accustomed to bring their wives into the village for a visit. For years at St. Johnsbury Centre, Mr. Sanger's was a general rendezvous where the men left their wives to visit while they went to the meeting, and then came back to supper. Speaking of suppers — we are told Mrs. Sanger kept the first anniversary of her birthday in St. Johnsbury with a supper, to which Dr. Arnold, Gen. Roberts, the Wheelers, and the wives of all were invited, and came — and "all went merry as a marriage bell." The pine table was loaded, and the jovial guests around — when suddenly the floor, unsupported by crossbeams or props (they lived in the little log hut at the Corners then,) began to slide and cave and tunnel cellarward — down went the table, pewter, turkey, gravy, Doctor, General, host, ladies, floor and all. Great was the smash, the scare and the laugh, after the party had all crept safe from the hole — for cellars were but holes in those primitive huts, and men and women both could laugh heartily over little mishaps — the pewter plates were not broken, the floor could be relaid.

Mrs. Sanger died about 3 years after her husband, while on a visit to a daughter in the west. None of the family reside now in St. Johnsbury. But three of the children survive, a son and a daughter in Ohio, and Mrs. Sears, now a resident of Ludlow, before alluded to. "At St. Johnsbury Plain," says Mrs. S., "43 years ago, old Dr. Lord lived in a large two story house at the lower end of street; Dr. Calvin Jewett about the middle of the Plain; his brother, Dr. Luther Jewett, who was the oldest, lived just opposite, and old Mr. West, a 'dreadful good' old man, lived next door to Dr. Luther, and John Clark kept store with his brother at the north end of the village."

St. Johnsbury Plain.
August, 1860.

The railway hugging close the river-land as we come up the Passumpsic valley, gives no hint of the handsome village we are approaching till we are there, landed at the convenient and respectable depôt under the hill — nor indeed, then and there, the village proper is on the plain over above. Only a few sightly residences like light-houses at sea, hang off the hill. Winding up the ascent to the village — rather steep for an invalid or the aged — though pleasantly assuring the hearty they are getting up in the world — arrived at the street of the Plain which runs north and south, if you turn to the right and go up, you pass presently offices, shops, stores, &c., while a conspicuous block over the left labeled in gilt, the "St. Johnsbury House" (the stand where old Captain Barney used to keep tavern), looks over to you, and you to that. Anon you come to dwellings — pleasant residences with pleasant yards, till you have passed up — I can not measure distance safely by memory two years back — it is 1862 now — but till you have gone a long way up the street — till the last house is left — and the village passed in this direction.

A little further on, through an entrance way, about which there is nothing remarkable, a new road leads by a gradual curve downward, and around the hillside, away at once from all sight and sound of the other. You stand in the beautiful cemetery of St. Johnsbury, a broken landscape, more hillside than dell; in sacred seclusiveness, so holily shut away from the world, you feel you would love to be buried here. Each picturesque site has its headstone and grave, and a good carriage way winds through the handsome grounds. Here you stand by the monument of Joseph P. Fairbanks, whom you will remember as the benefactor of Middlebury College,* the liberal patron of education and works of worthy promise. Let his memory be blessed: and let especially the history of the just and liberal man be written. And here is the monument and grave of Judge Paddock. But turn with me and search now for the grave of Josiah L. Arnold, the poet of St. Johnsbury. The St. Johnsbury cemetery is indeed the most beautiful yard of burial we have found in the state.

Returning to the head of Eastern avenue, if you take the left hand and go down the main street southward, you directly pass the handsome court house and county buildings, churches, academy, &c., and soon arrive at the terminus of the village; and at the natural head of this street, fronting the street, commanding an extensive view down through the street, stands the residence of the same late Joseph P. Fairbanks, by whose tomb we stood in the cemetery. The beautiful, under the hand of elegant culture, begins to develop more markedly here in the parterre of shrubs and flowers fronting the pleasant porches. Crossing the street to the right-ward, on the road leading toward Danville, the house and flower grounds upon the right, of Horace Fairbanks, may not be passed without receiving a full tithe of admiration. You recognize the place at once, having been told he has this summer the most beautiful garden in St. Johnsbury. It can not be other than this. The beds in their arrangement are markedly unique — the flowers in their glory of bloom. As you go down yet farther into Fairbanksville, the road winding through a natural glen or narrow defile in the hills, one house in particular, upon the hillside leftward, from its several terraces of earth, verdant and velvety smooth, looms up like the olden towers on a rock, looking down upon you as you pass. But where all

*See page 55, No. 1.

is beautiful, who may with just delicacy designate? We will individualize but one other. At the foot of the village on your right — up and away from the street beneath where you only catch a partial view of a pillared porch — you ascend a marble flight, where upon the topmost stair, from within a natural recess in the hills, the mansion, with its quietly perceptive swell of graded ground between, serenely develops. The hills hang over and above and half around. At the westward or right wing of the building, knots of flowers spread away, and over beyond the flower plat, lies a miniature lake beneath. This is the home and family seat of Governor Fairbanks.

St. Johnsbury has grown very much, we are told, within a few years. It is now, indeed, one of the handsomest villages of the state. Nature made it beautiful at first, and architecture and horticulture have lavished upon it since. Several fine views of the place, and especially of Fairbanksville, by B. F. Gage, the artist of St. Johnsbury, decorate the picture saloons of some of the first artists in New York.

THE DOOMED WILLOW.

The sun had set,
And night's black shadows hung once more,
O'er Saint Helena's distant shore;
The god of storms o'er land and tide,
Had flung the banner of his pride,
And mustered all his legions there,
To battle in the midnight air,
Or revel in their reckless mirth,
And scatter ruin o'er the earth.

The storm grew wild —
The guarded Exile heard the sound,
That shook the midnight air around,
Anon he saw the lightning's flash,
And started at the thunder's crash,
As if he deemed he heard once more
The music of the battle's roar;
Yet as the tempest raved and moaned,
Low on his couch he raved and groaned
In mortal pain.

Gasping, he spake
In accents low—" Ye know the tree
That waves beside the distant sea,
Where I have loved to sit all day,
And watch the billows in their play.
There ye shall lay me down to rest,
And heap the turf above my breast,
And long its drooping bough shall wave,
Above my low and lonely grave,
Wild birds their mournful lays shall weave,
And nature o'er my ashes grieve,

And all earth's nations yet shall weep,
Where the great hero lies asleep,
And curse the foul deceit and hate,
That gave him to the arms of Fate,
That crushed his heart and closed the strife,
E're waned the glorious noon of life."

Night rolled away,
The sun returned with quiet smile,
To Saint Helena's lonely isle,
But that sweet smile came not to him,
The mighty chief whose eye was dim,
Whose iron frame and royal brow,
In death were cold and pallid now.
Sweet sounds the murm'ring breezes bore,
And balmy scents were in the air;
The glad waves rippled on the shore,
And wild birds carol'd gaily there; •
Yet the proud chieftain's favorite tree,
Waved not besides the solemn sea,
Torn by the fury of the blast,
And on the shore in fragments cast,
The tree lay dead!
.   B. F. GAGE.

SHEFFIELD.

BY ALFRED S. LAMB.

Several years elapsed after the settlement of the southern portions of the county before settlers were willing to locate within the wilds of the more northern towns. Hence so late as 1793, the dense forests of this town were still standing wholly unharmed by the woodman's axe.

In this year, October 25, the town was chartered by the legislature of Vermont to Stephen Kingsbury and associates, with five rights for public purposes.

In the latter part of the following winter several families from New Hampshire came on and commenced a settlement in the southern part. The town was organized the 25th of March, 1796. Moses Foss, moderator; Archelaus Miles, Jr., first town clerk, an office which he held 12 years in succession; Stephen Drown, Archelaus Miles, Jr., and Isaac Kenaston, selectmen; Jonathan Gray, constable. The first representative, was Stephen Drown in 1806; first physician, —— Mitchell; and first merchant, John Green; no lawyer ever yet resided in town. The first settlement was made in the spring of 1794, by John and Richard Jenness, and James and Jonathan Gray with their families.

It is impossible at this day to form a just conception of the hardships encountered by early settlers, leaving the comforts and conveniences of an older country, moving to a distant wilderness into dwellings insufficient to protect them from the wintry blast, and with but scanty fare; yet with unremiting toil they sought to clear them up a home. The first year proved favorable for the growth of grain, and as early as the 28th of July, they had wheat harvested and at the mill. At no time since, has wheat been harvested in town so early.

And yet with all their industry and frugality, for the first few years they were unable to raise sufficient provisions to subsist upon. Their corn had to be brought from the river towns upon horses, a great part of the distance through the forest, guided by marked trees. At one time being out of provisions Jonathan Gray and a neighbor started for the Connecticut valley in quest of corn. Not being able to find any upon this side of the river they resolved to cross to the New Hampshire side. No boat was near and although late in the evening they mounted their horses and attempted to swim them to the other shore, but the darkness was so great that they reached the shore at a considerable distance below the landing place, where a steep bank covered with a heavy growth of bushes prevented their horses from obtaining a footing. A few lusty halloes, however, brought a sturdy farmer to the bank who exclaimed with a strong Scotch accent: "Hoot, mon, what do ye here?" A few words sufficed to explain to him their situation and with the assistance of himself and sons they were soon upon *terra firma* once more, where wet and benumbed with cold they gladly availed themselves of the invitation extended to them by the hospitable Scotchman to spend the night at his house. The following morning having procured their corn, they crossed the river by means of a boat and proceeded homeward.

The first buildings erected by the settlers were rudely constructed log cabins, with a bark roof and stone chimney outside the house. The floors were of short, thick plank split from the bass, sometimes from other trees, and confined with wooden pins in place of nails. The doors were formed in the same rude manner, and all combined to give the cabins a unique and shaggy appearance. If they could secure a few panes of glass and a pound or two of nails, they considered themselves provided with a very convenient and tasty dwelling.   •

While the men were laboring in the field, their wives with commendable zeal were striving, what time they could well spare from other duties, to improve the condition of their cabins. The wife of Richard Jenness, unwilling longer to perform her cooking upon the hearthstone, with her own hands constructed an oven of stone, daubing it well with mud in lieu of mortar, and in this for several years she performed the baking for her family.

Although good crops of grain were raised the first year, yet they found it hard to procure sufficient fodder to winter their stock. At that time there was no English grass nearer than North Danville, but they fortunately discovered a beaver meadow in the western part of the town covered with a heavy growth of wild grass, which they cut and stacked, drawing it the following winter upon handsleds, four miles, through a dense forest, and thus were enabled to supply their cows with food through the rigors of a Vermont winter.

John Jenness worked at his trade as a tanner for several years, in the early settlement of the town, using for a vat a large trough dug from a tree with his axe, and pounding his bark for tanning purposes by hand. He built the first framed house in town.

The following year Deacon Stephen Drown and wife moved in. Mrs. Drown is still living, at the advanced age of 85 years. Her mental faculties are yet good, and she recollects incidents which occurred in the early settlement of the town distinctly. She says that when she first came into town the only covering to their cabin consisted of strips of bark confined to the roof by means of large timbers placed at right angles. A few plank were split out, upon which was placed their bed; while two more pinned together served them for a door; and in such a dwelling, surrounded by wild beasts, and exposed to the vicissitudes of a New England climate, they lived and labored. No hardship so great, no labor so severe, no undertaking so hazardous, as to daunt their spirits or cause them to waver from their firm determination to build them up a home; but true to their purpose they struggled on against difficulties, still laboring for that "better time" which they could then but faintly discern in the distance, yet afterwards so happily realized.

The first male child born in town, was William Gray, July 28, 1794. He still resides in town. The first female, Hannah Jenness, born Oct. 15, of the same year— her death occurred April 4, 1860. The first marriage in town was that of Capt. Samuel

Twombly, to Miss Elizabeth Gray. Oldest person deceased in town, Samuel Drown, aged 96 years. Oldest person now living in town, Ward Bradley, Esq., aged 88. The first death in town, was that of a child of Richard Jenness, caused by eating pieces of isinglass. First school-house built in 1805, on land now owned by Sylvester Hall— Stephen Drown was the first teacher; present number of districts, nine. Three convenient school-houses have been erected quite recently. The remainder are wholly unfit for the purposes for which they were intended.

Heretofore there has been too little interest manifested in educational matters; but for the few past years the prospect has looked more cheering; public feeling has been roused somewhat to the importance of the subject, and it is sincerely to be hoped that this feeling will continue to be strengthened, until a subject of such vital importance shall receive that attention which it demands from every enlightened community.

The town was first surveyed by Jesse Gilbert, a man well fitted to perform the arduous duties of a surveyor. A beautiful tract of land situated in this town, consisting of about 1000 acres, was named in honor of this surveyor, Gilbert Square, an appellation which it still retains.

The soil of this town is mostly of a loamy nature; some portions are quite stony, while others are entirely free from stone.

The town is well adapted to the raising of stock, and our farmers are beginning to see the importance of an improved system of farming.

This town remained as it was originally chartered until Nov. 23, 1858, when a corner consisting of 3000 acres was annexed to the town of Barton. A mountain range passes through the northern and western portions of the town, which separates the waters of the Passumpsic and Barton rivers. Notwithstanding this elevation is a continuance of the "water shed" between the valleys of the Connecticut and St. Lawrence, the altitude is not sufficient to produce sterility of soil or failure of crops. Upon the very summit the soil is fertile, producing well all kinds of grain usually raised in this section, excepting corn.

This elevation of land, unlike most mountain ranges, does not seem to penetrate the distant sky, nor is it characterized by craggy cliffs, abrupt precipices, or sharply pointed peaks, but rather by gently sloping sides, and rounded summits heavily wooded to the very top.

The town is watered by several brooks, which rising upon the mountains, unite a short distance north of the village and form a considerable stream, which flowing onward empties into the Passumpsic at Lyndon.

That portion of the town upon the other slope of the mountain is watered by streams that flow into the Barton river. But a small portion of the town lies upon the western side, and consequently no good mill privileges are found; but in the southern and central portions, water power is abundant.

In this town are several ponds romantically situated among our green-clad hills. At the outlet of one of these, years ago, when the country in that vicinity was all a wilderness, a man by the name of Bruce attempted to build a saw-mill, but after erecting the frame and getting his mill in running order, he suddenly abandoned his project, removed the machinery, and left the country. The ruins of the mill are still to be seen, a part of the timbers still standing. From this circumstance the body of water received the name of Bruce pond. Another pond, called "Duck pond," from its having been a favorite resort for wild ducks, has the appearance of once having covered a much greater surface than now, the position of the land and growth of timber denoting the place it once occupied. It appears gradually to be growing less; what occasions this diminution of its waters is a mystery.

One feature of the town is the abundance of excellent springs which every where abound. Upon nearly every hill side, gushes forth the pure, limpid stream. The climate is healthful, although our winters are more rigorous than in towns situated upon large streams. There is one limestone ledge in the extreme western portion of the town, which has been worked but little.

Bears were numerous in the early settlement of the town, and often disturbed the settlers by their nocturnal visits. At one time, Hiram Jenness, then a lad of 12 years, was sent by his father to a bear trap which he had placed in the forest adjacent to his clearing. Not finding the trap sprung, the lad sauntered leisurely along through the forest, musket in hand, in search of game. Wandering on among the thickly wooded hills, he at last found himself several miles from home, and nearly to the summit of the mountain range which runs through the western portion of the town. Halting to view the scenery around, he espied a large bear lying beside a log quietly gnawing a bone. As he stepped forward to reconnoiter, the bear, evidently considering this as an intrusion upon his rights, rose upon his hind legs and growled defiance at the invader. The boy, nothing daunted, cooly leveled his musket and laid the beast dead at his feet. The bear weighed upwards of 400 pounds.

In conversing a few days since with Mr. Haines, an aged man, who resides a short distance from the writer, he related the following circumstance, which so strikingly exhibits the dangers to which early settlers were subjected that we are inclined to give it place in our columns, nearly verbatim, as related to us at the time.

He was then a young man just commencing in life. His family consisted of a wife and one child. They lived at the time in a rude log house, the door of which was without suitable fastenings. One night, weary with the labors of the day, they had retired to rest: when about midnight they were awakened by something traveling upon the outside of the bed.

They at first supposed it to be a dog, but upon looking up, they at once discovered that their visitant was in fact a full grown bear. They were terribly frightened, but Mr. Haines quickly springing upon his feet caught him by the hind leg, and endeavored to pull him from the bed, but Bruin, it seems, was as much frightened as the rest, for quickly extricating his foot from the grasp, he sprang from the bed, leaned for the door, and put for the forest with all speed. Our mountain streams were formerly a favorite resort for the beaver tribe, There are several meadows in town which were formed by these industrious little creatures, all of which produce a luxuriant growth of grass, and which from the earliest settlement of the town, until these lots were taken up and settled, was yearly cut, stacked and drawn to the barns upon sleds the ensuing winter.

Some of their dams still remain almost entire, but the greater part of them have been leveled by the plough of the farmer.

Previous to the extension of the Passumpsic rail road from St. Johnsbury to Barton, stages ran regularly through the town, giving us a daily communication with other parts of the country; but since the building of the rail road we are obliged to content ourselves with a semi-weekly mail. In 1850, an accident of a serious nature occurred upon this line of staging, by which a Dr. Flanders of N. H. was instantly killed, and

several other passengers were more or less injured. The accident was occasioned by the upsetting of a coach within the limits of this town. Blame was attached to the town at the time for not keeping a suitable railing beside the road at this place, and also to the driver for not exercising suitable caution; the night in question being extremely dark and foggy. Probably both parties were somewhat to blame, and a compromise should have been effected, and a settlement made with the friends of the deceased; but bitter feeling was engendered, and an expensive litigation entered into, which for intensity of feeling manifested has rarely been excelled in our courts.

Dense forests yet cover a considerable portion of the mountain range which passes through the town; and encircled by these timbered hills, lie several beautiful sheets of water. Tiny ponds half a mile in length, and perhaps half that distance in width, with their clear, sparkling waters now glistening in the sunbeams, then flowing in graceful ripples along the wooded shore. Nothing can be more pleasing to the student of nature, than to roam through these grand old woods and behold the diversity of scenery so wild and picturesque everywhere unfolded to view. It was a lovely morning in autumn, accompanied by a friend, we started upon such excursion. Not a cloud obscured the clear, blue sky, as the bright beams of the sun began to tinge every hill-top with a golden light, richly in contrast with the deep gloom of the vales below.

Moving leisurely along, we at last reached the confines of the most remote clearing, and climbing the brush fence which ran along its border, at once entered the forest wilds. Not a sound disturbed the surrounding stillness, save the joyous carol of some warbler as perched upon a slender twig, he poured forth his song of praise, or the merry chitter of the bright-eyed squirrel as he nimbly sprang from tree to tree, or peered forth from his sly retreat far up among the branches. All was lovely, and everything seemed fresh with the impress of Divinity.

Beauty, utility, and perfection, exist in nature's laboratory. She brings forth nothing but what is perfect. Now pausing to enjoy the romantic wildness of the scene, then pursuing a tortuous course through some winding vale, covered with its tangled growth of alders, and anon climbing some thickly wooded hill side, we, at last, reached one of those mimic lakes which lie embosomed among these green hills.

At its eastern extremity lies a tract of several acres, destitute of timber, covered with a rank growth of brakes and wild grass For a considerable distance around extends one unbroken wilderness. Standing upon a slight eminence near the center of this little clearing, we have a fine view of the surrounding scenery. Below lies the miniature pond with its pebbly shores and gleaming waters, while around far as vision sweeps, extend the huge forest trees that raise their heads reverently toward Heaven, and wave in silent praise, their bright foliage in the gentle breeze. We stood upon that gentle eminence, we looked down upon those limpid waters and beheld the dancing ripples as they broke upon the solitary shore. A thousand new beauties everywhere spread around us, we almost imagined ourselves in the primitive Eden, and could but wonder if any could be found so insensible to the influences of these exhibitions of beauty and grandeur as not to be led from this contemplation of nature to look away to nature's God.

This little tract of land was cleared by nature, in 1806, by a tornado passing through this section of country. Prior to this time, a road had been cut through the wilderness, now known as the Duck Pond road, to accommodate travelers passing between the northern and southern portion of the state. It was barely passable for wagons and a journey from the settlements of this town to Barton was considered quite tedious. At the time of which we are speaking, a gentleman and his wife were passing through the forest in the vicinity of Duck Pond; they heard the roar of the rushing blast, and its nearing approach, but escape was impossible. The tornado burst upon them in all its fury. The huge forest trees came crashing around in confused and tangled heaps, here piled and crossed in multitudinous confusion, there broken and crushed in one shattered mass; yet strange to narrate, our travelers, although so completely hemmed in by fallen timbers that it required considerable time, with all the assistance which could be procured to extricate their team from the tangled mass, were wholly unharmed. But we have wandered with our story. Let us return to the little eminence where we stood. We soon left this position and followed down the western shore of the pond, across a tract of land, dry, free from stone and apparently well calculated to reward the labors of the husbandman; and we venture to predict that at no very distant day we shall find in this section, a district of well

cultivated farms. Following the little stream which forms an outlet to the pond which we had left behind, we soon reached another sheet of water somewhat smaller and occupying a much lower position, yet surrounded by the same wild beauty which characterized the former. This pond is situated less than a mile from the main road, and is not far distant from the dividing line between this town and Glover. But all days have their end, and we reached home as the gray shadows of twilight were fast deepening into night, feeling ourselves amply repaid for the toils and fatigues of the day.

All the wild land in this town is now taken up, yet there are several lots that have not yet been settled.

Perhaps it would be well to state before closing this cursory sketch, that General Hull once owned a large portion of the town, but previous to his disgraceful conduct in the war of 1812, he exchanged with Isaac McLellan, Esq., for lands in Newburyport, Mass. Lumber has for several years formed quite an article of export, and six saw-mills in different parts of the town, find abundant occupation during the sawing season.

Our little village is situated about one mile from the southern boundary of the town, in a pleasant and fertile valley through which flows a small creek designated as Millers run, which furnishes to the people all necessary water power, and adds much to the appearance of the place. The first trees were felled in this place by Jonathan Gray and Samuel Daniels, in 1794, near where the school-house now stands, on land then owned by Deacon Wm. Hawkins. The first house was built by Deacon Hawkins in 1794. In 1797 he also built a saw and grist-mill, upon the above mentioned stream, near where the mills now stand. The clothing mill was built by James Townsend, in 1822; the first hotel in the village, by Sewall Bradley, in 1832; though there were taverns kept in town as early as 1800; the first church in town was erected by the Freewill Baptist society, A. D. 1829; one store, one church, a school-house and several dwelling houses have been added quite recently. Old antiquated buildings have been repaired, or have given place to more elegant structures, and a spirit of improvement which is really commendable, seems at present to be manifested among our citizens. The village has 2 churches, 2 stores, 1 grocery, 1 saw-mill, 1 shoe shop, 1 starch factory, 1 carding mill,

1 hotel, 2 blacksmith shops, 1 school house, 1 town hall, and 21 dwelling houses.

ECCLESIASTICAL.

The early settlers of this town were mostly of the Freewill Baptist persuasion, and they early began to hold religious meetings upon the sabbath. In 1800, six years after the town was first settled, the Baptists of this town and Wheelock united, and the first church was organized. The first monthly meeting was held October 6 of that year. The church at that time, counting the members from both towns, consisted of 77 members. Although destitute of a pastor, and with no suitable place to meet for public worship, yet they continued their meetings, preserved their discipline, and enjoyed frequent religious revivals, as the fruit of their labors, until 1829, when a church was built at the village, where they afterwards met for worship. They had occasional preaching, but no steady pastor until March 9, 1836, when they organized anew—the members of the different towns having become sufficiently numerous to render a separate organization expedient. The Rev. Zebina Young was this year installed pastor, being the first settled minister in town. To him consequently fell the right of land granted by the state at the time of the original charter. Since his removal, the church has enjoyed the labors of several different clergymen.

In 1850, Rev. Jonathan Woodman, the present pastor, was installed. He has the pastoral care of two churches, preaching alternately at this place and Wheelock. The society originally built their house without a steeple; but during the past season, they have caused some repairs to be made. The long wished for belfry has been added, and an excellent bell procured and placed therein. The society now consists of 51 members.

SECOND BAPTIST CHURCH.

We have not been able to procure the statistical facts in connection with this church, but will here insert what information we have been able to ascertain. The church was organized soon after the great revival of 1839, and made up mostly of people residing in the eastern part of the town. The Rev. Mr. Bugby was their first pastor. For several years they held religious meetings at a school house in that part of the town, but about 1850, erected a convenient house for public worship, and are now in a prosper-

ous condition. The Rev. Mr. Hill is their present pastor. Number of members about 25.

WESLEYAN METHODISM IN SHEFFIELD.

BY REV. JOHN DOLPH.

In the fall of 1854, the Rev. Mr. Hall, a Wesleyan Methodist minister, who was then stationed on Albany and Glover circuit, came into this town and commenced laboring among the people in the vicinity of Gilbert Square. There were soon such an interest manifested, and such an attachment to the principles of Wesleyan Methodism displayed, that Mr. Hall deemed it best to organize a small class as a branch of the Glover church. This may be considered as the commencement of Wesleyan Methodism here, although there had been previous to this time, a few lectures by Wesleyan ministers, who preceded Mr. Hall on the charge above mentioned. In the spring of 1856, the Rev. Dyer Willis succeeded Mr. Hall, and during his stay of two years he held a few evening meetings. Mr. Willis was succeeded in the spring of 1858 by the Rev. John Croker.

During Mr. Croker's stay of one year, he held a few meetings in this town. In the latter part of the year he preached a few times in the school-house on what is called Glover road, four miles from Sheffield village. Some interest was manifested by the inhabitants, and they expressed a desire to have regular preaching among them; accordingly, a regular appointment for preaching every fourth Sabbath was established. In May, 1859, Mr. Croker was succeeded by Rev. John Dolph, the present pastor, who took up his residence in Sheffield. Soon after Mr. Dolph commenced his labors, it became apparent that a church organization in this town would be beneficial to the cause of religion; accordingly on the 25th of July, 1849, the friends of the cause met and organized a church of about 40 members. From that time to the present, although they have met with strong opposition, which grew out of prejudice, the Wesleyans have gradually increased in numbers and influence. Prejudice is, however, dying away, opposition has partially ceased, and they are now in a prosperous condition, and number, at present, about 60 members. During the past summer (1860), they have erected a convenient and tasty chapel for religious worship, at Sheffield village, which was dedicated on the 20th of Oct., 1860. Rev. P. A. Field of Shelburn officiating.

We would here return our thanks to individuals who have furnished us with items of facts pertaining to the early history of the town, and especially are our thanks due to the Hon. John P. Ingalls and Dr. A. M. Ward, by whose efforts much of the material for this sketch has been collected.

BIOGRAPHICAL SKETCHES.

This town has never been prolific in what the world denominates great men, yet many are deserving of an honorable mention.

JAMES GRAY,

One of the first settlers of the town, was born in Barrington, N. H. He married Hannah Burrill of the same place, and moved to this town with his family in the spring of 1794. There being no bridge across the river at Wheelock at the time, they crossed upon the dam, and passed on to their claim which was upon lot 36, now owned by Mr. Holmes. Mrs. Gray was the first white woman that ever came into this town. The following year Mr. Gray moved, and commenced anew upon the lot where Isaac Pearl now resides. Here he lived until a year before his death, when feeble in health, and bowed down with hard labor and the infirmities of age, he left to spend the remainder of his life with his son George, upon the place now owned by his grandson, L. M. M. Gray, Esq., and here he continued to reside until his death. His son Jonathan also came the same year with his father. To him belongs the honor of having felled the first tree in town.

The hardships incident to early settlers bore heavily upon Mr. Gray. At this time there was no gristmill near, and he was obliged to take his grain sometimes even to Newbury to be ground, and often for the want of a horse, he carried it upon his own back. Yet with all his labor and hardships he was healthy and vigorous, and lived to the good old age of 85 years.

SAMUEL DROWN,

Was born at Rochester, N. H. He came into this town in 1795. He was an old revolutionary soldier, having been attached during some part of the war to an artillery corps. His grandchildren have often heard him relate incidents of different battles in which he had been engaged, and of the difficulties they sometimes encountered in drawing their pieces into battery in places inaccessible for horses. He was first engaged in the battle of Bunker Hill, and served his country faithfully for several years afterwards. He died at the advanced age of 96 years, being the oldest person deceased in town.

DEACON STEPHEN DROWN,

Son of Samuel Drown above mentioned, was born in Rochester, N. H., September 17th, 1770, was married at the age of 21, to Sarah Gray, daughter of James Gray, a brief sketch of whom we have before given. They moved to this town in 1795, four years after their marriage, and settled upon the farm now owned by Elisha Davis, Esq., where they continued to reside until his death, which occurred April 6, 1841. His wife survived him, and is now living with her son Horace, and is the oldest female now residing in town, and but so short a distance is she now removed from the scenes of her earlier years, that she can sit at her window and look upon the farm where she and her husband first commenced their labors, and for nearly 50 years lived and toiled together. They commenced in town poor, and often suffered for the necessaries of life. For some time during the first year, they subsisted entirely upon the milk of one cow. In the spring they had been unable to obtain potatoes for seed, but had planted a few parings given them for the purpose, which had sprouted and grown and were now in full blossom. To this field the wife turned her footsteps, when she could no longer behold her husband exhausted with the labors of the day, and no suitable food to prepare for the evening repast. Having dug a half-pint of potatoes of diminutive size and killed a small chicken, she prepared a meal which may well be called the first product of the farm.

But they did not long remain in such circumstances. Industry and economy worked wonders in their case, and they were soon surrounded with plenty. Mr. Drown represented the town for several years in the legislature of the state, was 22 years town clerk, and taught the first school in town. He experienced religion in 1800, was the first convert, and ever after one of the main pillars of the church. To him the people were indebted as to a pastor for visiting the sick, attending funerals, holding meetings, baptizing converts, and performing all other pastoral duties which devolved upon him. He lived an exemplary life, sustaining his Christian profession unblemished until death closed his labors.

CAPT. STAPLES,

Served in the war of 1812. It is said that in one engagement he. slew with his own hand three British soldiers that had attacked him, and afterwards joined his company in safety. He continued in service until the close of the war, when he moved into this town and labored for several years at his trade, being the first blacksmith in town.

HON. JOSEPH H. INGALLS,

Father of the Hon. John P. Ingalls of this town, was born in Madbury, Mass., A.·D. 1774. Came into Wheelock about the year 1797, where he married Comfort Weeks, daughter of Capt. Joshua Weeks of that town, and continued to live in Wheelock until 1806, when he moved with his family to Sheffield, where he resided until his death. He came into Wheelock with little or no property, but by industry and strict attention to business became a wealthy man.

At one time he owned nearly all the land where our village is now situated. He was one of the most influential citizens in the place, and for a long series of years held responsible offices in town.

He was a member of the Vermont Legislature 13 years, and of the senate one year. As a man of sound judgment and thorough business habits, he probably never had a superior in town. His decease occurred June 14, 1850, aged 76 years.

ELDER MOSES CHENEY.

BY S. P. CHENEY.

Moses Cheney was born in Haverhill, Mass., December 15, 1776, in an old "garrison house" still standing.

Mrs. Hannah Dustin, famous in our history for having killed the ten Indians that captured and carried her from Haverhill up the Merrimac river to where Concord, N. H., now is, was his great grandmother.

When he was 5 years old, the family moved to Sanbornton, N. H., where his father purchased 60 acres of wild land, and with much hard labor reared a family of 9 children.

Moses was the second child, a weakly boy; kept in doors pretty much in childhood. He sat on the split basswood floor by the side of his mother, and learned to read of her while she spun linen. Their library consisted of the English Primer, Watts' Psalms and Hymns, and the Bible. The first he committed to memory and much of the New Testament, which he retained through life.

The family was *emphatically poor*. Moses never had clothes proper to wear from home till after he was thirteen. That spring, in imitation of his father and brother who were making sugar, he split troughs and dug them out, tapped several trees, obtained sap, and after the others were done boiling and retired to rest, and he could have the kettles, in the dead hours of the night, boiled his sap alone. He made wooden "clappers" for shoes, drove nails through the bottoms to keep them from slipping on the crust, and with some rags wound about his feet for stockings and the clappers on, he was able to brush about and do his work. With his sugar he bought 8 yards of tow cloth, which was colored black with white maple bark, all but enough for a shirt, which was bleached as white as snow, and made up by his mother, who also made his whole suit; and when it was completed he put it on, and went into the field to show his father and Daniel. When his father saw him coming he exclaimed, " There comes our clergyman ; see there, Daniel, I guess our Moses will make a minister." It is to be borne in mind that only clergymen wore *black* in those days.

Now, then, he would go to church, and for the first time. He had even then, as ever after, a great taste for sabbath day meetings. He went to school a few days at different times, but it all amounted to pretty nearly nothing.

At the age of 17, when he had grown tall and had better health, his father gave him his time, and he went out to work on a farm. At 20, he went to learn the joiner's trade; and the next year, attended school during the winter, kept by Elder John Drew, as also to singing school, by Mr. William Fenney of Goffstown, N. H. At the close of these two schools, his teachers give him the credit of having done *very well;* and the latter, as was his custom, to his best scholar, at the close of a winter's school, "gave Moses Cheney his pitch-pipe and singing book."

He was now a healthy and powerful man, stood 6 feet and an inch in his boots, broad-shouldered, with long and strong arms. He was a great chopper, and at one time, felled two acres of trees of heavy growth in two days, finishing the second day when the sun was two hours high. Moreover, he was not only strong, but remarkably *quick*, and could leap a line that he could walk erectly under with his hat on.

At the age of 24 he married Abigail Leavitt, eldest daughter of Moses Leavitt of

Sanbornton, N. H., and pursued his trade with much ambition. But at the close of about three years of excessive labor, his health was gone, and in addition to this, within six months, they lost their two little children. In his own words, "he was at that time brought to a childless state — a healthless state — a comfortless state — a hopeless state — a sinful state — and a state of condemnation." He also adds, "When the breath left the body of our little boy, I lifted my right hand and said, I have now done with the happiness of this world, unless I find it in God."

He suffered much for about four weeks, when he was urged to go into social company; and he was inclined so to do; but a voice said to him, "What did you promise? It will be four weeks to-morrow, at 9 o'clock, since you made that promise—wait!" And he did. The morning came, and as the hour drew near he was impressed to go to a certain wood; he went and there sat as he felt directed, and took from his pocket a leaf of of the Bible, which he had secretly put there, and read: "This shall be written for the generation to come, and they shall praise the Lord." In an instant his sorrows were all gone, and he was leaping and praising God. He hastened home and told his wife of his happiness. Ran to neighbor Copp, who was mowing close by, and told him. He dropped his scythe and met him, and both rejoiced with great joy.

"After the turn about in my mind," he writes, "I applied myself to the Bible, being unable to do any work. The word of God became my meat and drink; I really thought I loved God's law. I thought I loved to pray. I thought I loved to praise. I thought I loved to speak, and I thought I loved to hear. I thought I loved to mourn and to rejoice—in a word, that I loved all that God loved, and hated all He hated. I attended all the meetings that I could, and I think I always had something given me to say."

The loss of his health brought him to think of the study of medicine, and the next spring he commenced it with Dr. Daniel Jacobs of Gilmanton Corners. At the same time he entered the academy for one term, and it was said he went ahead in both. He also taught a singing school in the academy. After that he taught town schools, and pursued the medical study for a while; but at length gave that up and taught summer and winter for four years.

But all this time he had "impressions" that he must preach, and one passage of Scrip-

ture followed him day and night for one year till he "did preach" from it, and then it was gone; but another took its place, and so on. He thought he could not preach, and after trying a few times, declared he would not. Then came terrible trials and temptations, all the while growing worse and worse, till a certain time, concerning which, let him speak for himself:

"It came to pass one day, as I was on the way to school, crossing a pasture, in a deep hollow, out of sight of all flesh, I came to a sudden stop, and stood still. I could not so much as turn to the right or to the left, nor could I go forward a single step, till the great question was decided about preaching. I stood, I know not how long; at length I began to repeat the following words: 'Lord, open doors and provide places for me to preach in—open ears to hear me, and give me food and raiment convenient for myself and family, and I am thy servant forever.' Never was there an agreement more thoroughly ratified. I believe the Holy Spirit was the editor on my tongue to print a word at a time until the whole was finished."

The next sabbath he preached, and from that time forward he continued to preach until his death. The first few years of his ministry he was with the Freewill Baptists; but a most singular vision caused him to leave them, and join the Calvinistic Baptists, to the principal doctrines of which sect he adhered through life.

We can not follow him through his long ministry; but it must be said that probably no man ever preached, prayed and sung more for 30 years than "Old Elder Cheney." He was a great Bible student, prepared his sermons well, but never wrote them. He was a natural, spirited, and gifted orator. always so plainly setting forth his ideas, that all who heard *understood* and were pleased. His large, white head, and proportionately large Roman nose, gave him a most dignified look. His voice was a pure tenor, and whether you heard him sing or preach, you could but feel that he possessed great vitality, and capability of most protracted vocal effort.

He was a man capable of the most deeply solemn feelings and looks; but he enjoyed a little fun at proper times, as well as any other man, and was capable of using sharp words, and was sometimes sarcastic, but never bitter. He used to say he was "sorry to have people laugh under his preaching, but they *would* sometimes." Yet tears were as common as smiles. A stranger to him once told it about right, when she said, "Father Cheney, I heard you preach once, and I never laughed and cried so much in one sermon."

He was a most intense lover of music, and his musical talents were of great service to him. He imparted them to his children, all of whom could sing before they could remember. The family consisted of five sons and four daughters; four of the sons and one of the daughters were teachers of music, and at one time were known as the Cheney Family. The whole nine are still living.

In the early years of his ministry, he was accustomed a good deal of the time to go here and there, in a sort of missionary style, as he was invited, and so was from home a great deal. It was a singular fact, that if there was any trouble or sickness *at home*, he was informed of it, and that too, without any visible messengers; and many times he went home, when he had arranged far differently, because he "was impressed" to go; and sometimes he knew the precise nature of the cause that called him home. There is scarcely a town in all New Hampshire in which he has not preached, and ever after he was 40 years old he was familiarly known all abroad as "Old Father Cheney," or "Old Elder Cheney"—not because he was decrepid, for he had very little of that up to the last year of his life, but his *hair* was abundant and white at 40, having been *red* originally.

In the summer of 1823, he moved to the town of Derby, Vt., where he was the pastor of a church for several years. During his residence there, he occasionally accepted a call for a few weeks or months from towns in other parts of the state, and even in New Hampshire and Massachusetts, and spent one entire summer in the town of Littleton, Mass. He loved "the sea-board." He also preached in Beverly, and 30 years ago, he was well known in the towns and cities of Exeter, Portsmouth, Salem, Chelmsford, Lowell and Groton.

At length he sold out at Derby, and went back and lived and preached two or three years in Sunbornton, N. H., and towns around. In 1843, he finally moved to Sheffield, Vt., where he lived till his death, Aug. 9, 1856. During these last 13 years he had the charge of no church, but continued to preach till his last sickness. He was always, but particularly in his old age, much called upon to preach funeral sermons, and to officiate at weddings.

49

For 20 or more of the last years of his life, he was free from all sectarianism; and ceased to be interested in the new movements of the Baptists, or to attend their associations. While he was living in Sanbornton, the Meridith Association to which he had belonged, held a meeting at New Hampton, which was close by him. The association appointed a committee "to go and visit Father Cheney, and ascertain where he was." They called on him and made their business known. He told them, very pleasantly, that they "might return to the association, and tell them that Old Father Cheney was away back behind, *right in the middle of the road, with the good, old Bible under his arm*"—and that was all they could get from him.

He believed, and made known his belief, that the Baptists had ceased to be the spiritual people they were when he joined them, and were "too much conformed to this world." He believed that a man, to be a true and genuine preacher of the Gospel, must verily "be called of the Spirit to preach," and when he was so called, "must go to *preaching*, and not to a theological seminary to *learn* to preach. He must preach and study, and study and preach, *and God would take care of him.*" He claimed that the Scriptures sustained him in this belief; and could we, in this brief sketch, lay before the reader the thrilling accounts he has left on record of the numerous revivals of religion that followed his preaching, and the numerous churches that were built up from them, he might see *other* reasons why *he* should believe as he did.

In politics he was a thorough-going old fashioned Jeffersonian Democrat from first to last.

He abhorred dishonesty in any man, and hated above all things to be cheated; we give an anecdote to illustrate this: The Baptist Society in Derby, on a certain time thought they ought to do more than they were doing for the Elder, so they appointed a committee to purchase a cow and present her to him. They did so, and he was very grateful. But upon trial, the milk of the cow was found to be *skimmed* milk, and that continually. She was faithfully tried for one week; during which time the Elder ascertained that the committee had bought her of a man who had once made him 'pay for a pair of blinders twice,' and that, together with the fact that there was "*no cream* on the joke," determined the Elder to return the cow. So one morning he called one of his boys to him, and said: "Here P., take this whip, and drive that cow back to where she came from, and tell Deacon Carpenter that your father says he will stand a law suit before he will take the gift of her." It was done as he commanded, as the writer of this personally knows, and that was the last of "the present" on both sides.

He was a high-tempered man, but usually kept that temper under his control, or as he used to say, he "kept down the Dustin blood." He was not in the habit of doing things hastily; but when it was necessary for any work of severity to be done, he was not the man to flinch.

Among other peculiar things in his history we may mention his numerous escapes with his life, when there seemed but a step between him and death. He was once drowned till he "lay still." Once barely escaped from freezing, having fallen into the water on a very cold day, and having miles to go before he could reach a house. At two different times it was thought he must die with fever. His life was despaired of when he had the measles; and he was once thrown from a carriage and his neck nearly broken.

At about the age of 18 years he had an encounter with a cross bull, which so well sets forth his physical powers, and so well proves that the Dustin blood was "strong blood" even to the fourth generation, we are tempted to a description of it in his own words:

"I was requested by my employer to go to a certain pasture and drive said animal to the bars. I had heard, by the by, that he was cross, and drove his owner out of his barn yard only a few days before. I did not wish to discover cowardice; so not a word was to be said, but out into the large pasture I went in pursuit of the chap. But by the way, it looked proper enough to furnish myself with a tough beech sprout about six feet long. I thought it best to go at him as one having authority. At first he seemed to consider me so, and started off very peaceably; but suddenly, as we were rising a steep bank, he whirled and came at me with great fury. I voided out of his way, and flew to a large clump of bass bushes that surrounded a great stump. Round the bushes I went, and he after me, on the clean jump. I soon overtook him, and put on the cudgel the whole length of his back. Then he whirled again after me, and I after him, and as often as I overtook him he took six feet of beech. In this way we played circus till my antagonist gave a frightful roar, and

took off for the bars. I was still at his heels laying on the beech, till I saw the battle was won. That was a terrible fight! It was both furious and long. I was very warm and *rather short* for breath; and as for curl-head, if he did not puff and blow and sweat, no matter!"

Last to be mentioned, but the first narrow escape he had, was in this wise: When a little boy, he went to carry his father his dinner, where he was felling trees. He had arranged a "drove" of trees, so that by starting one, they would all go down. He did not see his boy approaching, until the trees had started. In an instant he cried out, "Run, Moses!" but Moses had no time to run. He was close to a large hemlock, when he saw his danger, and dropped between two large roots that had grown in such a way as to leave a cavity just large enough to receive him. The thick limbs fell all round about and over him. His father shrieked "I have killed my boy," but Moses was not hurt. His father cut away the limbs and took him out, and was so much affected, "he went home, related the story to the family and went to bed." The stump of that tree lasted many years, and Moses went often to visit it, while the family lived there, and he says: "After my father moved away, I was often back to visit the old hemlock stump. At length I sought in vain for any remains of it. *I have not been there since.*" Then he wrote the following:

Farewell to the Old Hemlock Tree.

Old Hemlock, you're gone—ah how lonely I
    feel!
When I knew where you stood—then I knew
    where to kneel;
'Twas thither I flew, when no other could
    save;
And the tall evergreen saved the boy from
    the grave.

My God! didst Thou plant that strong-root-
    ed tree
On the side of this hill, just to save one like
    me?
Yes, answers my Lord, when 'twas small as
    a hair,
I bid it stand there and watch and take care.

My Lord and my King! your command was
    obeyed,
When the fast falling trees threatened death
    o'er my head.
And the lad was secure by Eternal decree
Through the watch and the care of the Old
    Hemlock Tree.

Old Hemlock, you're gone, yet I see where
you stood
And pointed your green, spriggy hands up
to God,
Ne'er shall I forget, with my heart full of joy,
How thou kept the command and protected
the boy.

Old Hemlock, you're gone—'tis a warning to
all,
That just as thou didst, so must we all fall;
Farewell, then, old friend, but this pledge
take from me,
I'll be kind unto others, as thou wast to me.

Thus we have briefly considered a few of
the leading incidents in the life of this singular, but natural and noble-hearted man.
At no period of his life was he more interesting as a man and a Christian, than during
his last illness. Through all that long and
terrible ordeal of more than three months'
suffering, he was never known to be impa-
tient for a moment, nor breathe a word of
regret. At one time, he said to his daughter
who was almost constantly with him, "if
you see any symptoms of impatience about
me at any time, *tell me;* and may God forbid
that one who has tried to preach his word
for half a century, should murmur at his
will at last."

His disease was dropsy of the chest; but
all its pains could not exclude him from moments of most ecstatic joy, and even at times
he would wish he could be out of doors, that
he might have *more room* to praise in. A
brother minister asked him if he was happy? He replied, "Yes, but not all of the
time; sometimes there is a cloud in the
way; *but I know who is behind the cloud.*"
A few hours before he expired (his speech
having been many days gone), his son Moses
sung a portion of the "Dying Christian,"
commencing with, "The world recedes and
disappears." Instantly his dying father
seemed to be inspired; he had known the
music and words long before the son was
born, and when he came to the line, "Lend,
lend your wings, I mount, I fly," he raised
both hands, neither of which he had been
able to move for more than a week, and beat
the time throughout to the end; and when
the last words "Oh death where is thy
sting" were sung—shouted a loud and ex-
ulting "Amen!"
That was his last loud word; he expired
without a struggle, and, as we trust, is now
reaping the rewards of a long, thoughtful,
and active Christian life.

SUTTON.

BY JOHN BECKWITH, ESQ.

Sutton is a town on the north side of Caledonia county, on a latitude of about 44° 30′
north. It is bounded south by Lyndon, east
by Burke, north by Westmore and Newark,
west by Sheffield. It lies about 40 miles N.
E. of Montpelier and 18 northwesterly from
St. Johnsbury.

Sutton was chartered by the name of
Billymead, Feb. 26, A. D. 1782, to Jonathan
Arnold and his associates, by his excellency
Thomas Chittenden, then governor of the
state of Vermont, and contains 23,140 acres.
In 1812, the name was changed to Sutton.
The settlement of the town was commenced
in the year A. D. 1790, by Mr. Hacket, who
was soon after joined by several other families from Sandwich and Moultonboro in the
county of Stafford, N. H., together with a
few families from Lyndon and the adjoining
towns. The town was organized July 4th,
A. D. 1794. Samuel Orcutt was chosen moderator; James Cahoon, town clerk; John
Anthony, Samuel Cahoon and Samuel Orcutt, selectmen; and Jeremiah Washburn,
constable. The surface of the town is generally level, laying in four swells or ridges,
which are called the south, middle, north
and east ridges. These divisions are made
by three branches of the Passumpsic river,
which have their sources in the north and
west part of said town, and running south-
eastwardly unite in Lyndon. These streams
afford plenty of water power.

There are in the N. W. part of the town
several ponds, which are well supplied with
fish, and are situated on an elevation where
the waters divide, a part running southerly
to the Connecticut river, a part north to the
St. Francis river. In some places a few
hours' labor would cause rills or brooks to
flow to the St. Lawrence river or Long Island
sound. There are several bogs of marl of
which lime is made; also, several sulphur
springs, some iron ore and a quarry of
slate.

The natural timber was principally syca-
more or sugar maple, with some beech, birch
and ash; but along the streams are large
quantities of spruce and white cedar. The
soil is generally free from stone, and is well
adapted to the raising of oats and grass.
The inhabitants are chiefly engaged in agriculture. There is a small village near the
centre of the town, consisting of about 30
dwelling houses and about 200 inhabitants.

The Passumpsic rail road passes through the centre of the town from Burke to Barton. There is but one mountain worthy of notice which is in the northwest part of the town near Lake Willoughby, and is called Mount Pisgah or Millstone Mountain; it is about 4000 feet above tide water and 200 above the waters of the lake. The inhabitants of the town have ever been celebrated for the manufacture of maple sugar; according to the census of the state they have always made a larger quantity than any other town in the state of equal population.

HISTORICAL SKETCH OF THE FREE-WILL BAPTIST CHURCH.

BY REV. L. T. HARRIS.

In the early settlement of the town, a few families from Sandwich, N. H., located here, who were either Freewill Baptists or favorable to their doctrines and usages. They soon established social meetings, which were held in private houses and school houses; but were seldom favored with preaching until December, 1799, when Rev. Joseph Quimby from N. H. visited them, and found an interesting revival of religion in progress. There being no organized church in town it was thought proper to organize a Freewill Baptist church, which was effected in December, 1799, consisting of 8 or 9 members; Bradbury M. Richardson was chosen deacon. The church was organized in the house of a Mr. Cahoon, where a serious, yet fortunate accident occurred. Being assembled in a room directly over the cellar, the sleepers gave way and the congregation were precipitated into the cellar. But as the falling floor assumed a tunnel shape, they all rolled or tumbled into a confused pile in the centre; and fortunately no one was injured. Rev. Mr. Quimby remained with them some time and the revival increased in interest, and for several years scarcely a month passed without some additions to the church, which in October, 1810, numbered 117. The first meeting house was built in 1812, by Rev. John Colby, under peculiar circumstances. The fact that they were destitute of a suitable place of worship impressed his mind very deeply with the importance of proceeding to build. He accordingly drew a plan for a convenient house, and laid the subject before the people of the town and tried to encourage them to build. A few were zealous for the enterprise. Some were too poor, others had their land to pay for. They were

expecting a war with Great Britain, and the people of the town gave him little encouragement.

Elder Colby, however, was so strongly impressed that the Lord would clear the way before him and assist him, that he resolved to build at his own expense. His engagements were such that he had only about one week to stay in town. During this time he selected a spot near the centre of the town, adjoining a grave yard, purchased the land, contracted for the lumber, nails, glass, &c., and also with a workman to complete the outside of the house by the 20th of June following. He then gave out an appointment to preach in the new house on the last Sabbath in the same June; while the timber was yet growing in the forest. At the day appointed he preached in the new house agreeable to his notice. This house has long since gone to decay, and in the year 1832 another neat and commodious house was erected by the society, which is still occupied. About the year 1838 or 1834, while the church was under the pastoral care of Rev. Jonathan Woodman, its name and policy were changed to correspond with the general Baptists in England, but did not meet with the favor of many members of the old church, and in October, 1837, it was again organized into a Freewill Baptist church, by a council consisting of Revs. D. Quimby, J. Quimby and David Swett. The church was now composed of 20 members, but soon large additions were made. Rev. J. Woodman, now of Wheelock, filled the pastorate of this church with marked ability and success for nearly 30 years. Rev. R. D. Richardson preached here some 10 or 12 years, and succeeded well as a preacher and pastor. The labors of several other ministers have been enjoyed by this church whose names are not here given. Rev. L. T. Harris is the present pastor. The church now numbers about 100.

We have a neat and pleasant parsonage in the village, a congregation of about 200, a prosperous sabbath school with about 600 volumes in its library. In the fall of 1859, the people were called out to pursue a bear which had been seen in the town. After a chase of two or three hours by about 40 men and boys, the bear was shot; after which the company were called together to determine in what way to dispose of the avails of the hunt. It was agreed, without a dissenting voice, to appropriate the money ($11) to purchase books for the Sunday school library.

GIANT BOY OF SUTTON.

Frank Rice, son of John M. Rice, was born April 12, 1854. When 5 years of age he weighed 105 pounds. In the fall after he was 3 years old a basket containing one bushel of potatoes was placed before him, which he readily raised from the ground by the ears of the basket. He is now 8 years old, and weighs about 130 pounds, not having grown as fast for two or three years past as formerly. His form is good, being in about the usual proportions. He is also much in advance of his years in intelligence and judgment. A few years since a caravan was exhibiting at the village, which drew out the usual crowd of people attendant upon the traveling menagerie and circus in the country town. Our little hero came down to the show—and the people from abroad, we are told by an eye witness, gathered around him with as much curiosity as they evinced for the wonders of the menagerie. Indeed, our reliable narrator rather carried the idea that the "big boy" eclipsed the caravan.—*Ed.*

THE HARRIS TWINS.

John Wesley and Charles Wesley Harris, sons of Rev. L. T. Harris, born Sept. 11, 1851, in Brookfield this state, are noted for a similarity unusual even for twins in their looks, size and general appearance. At their birth there was a difference of but one ounce in their weight, one weighing 6 lbs. 10 oz., and the other 6 lbs. 11 oz., and there has never been known since, at any one time, a greater difference than one pound, and usually the difference has not exceeded the original ounce. While infants their mother distinguished them by strings of different colored beads, till when from eight to ten months old, first one and then the other broke the beads from their necks, whereupon a string of red yarn was tied around the ancle and worn for a long time as a distinguishing mark. When they were about one year old, one of them being unwell, the mother after getting them to sleep, prepared some medicine to give the sick child when it should awake. At length the child as she supposed, aroused, and the medicine was administered, but shortly after, by consulting the red string on the ancle, it was found the well child had taken the medicine. Their present weight is 91½ pounds. They still retain the same similarity in their looks, and those best acquainted with them can not distinguish the one from the other. Charles, however, is able to get his lessons in school

more readily than John, and on one occasion, when they were called to recite, John failing to have his lesson committed was sent back to study it over. Upon which the boys quietly changed seats, and when John was called out to recite again, Charles came promptly and recited the lesson, and the teacher was satisfied. "The resemblance is still so perfect," their father writes, "I do not often attempt to distinguish them, and can not do so without the closest inspection."—*Ed.*

WALDEN.

BY HON. JAMES D. BELL.

Walden is 6 miles square, situated in the western part of Caledonia county, having Cabot on the S. W., Danville on the S. E., Goshen Gore on the N. E., and Hardwick on the N. W. It lies 25 miles N. E. from Montpelier, and 12 W. from St. Johnsbury.

Walden belonged to Orange county until the organization of Caledonia county in 1796; was granted Nov. 6, 1780; chartered August 18, 1781, by the legislature of Vermont, to Moses Robinson and 64 others, on condition that each grantee put under cultivation 5 acres and build a house 18 feet square or more within 3 years after the close of the war, the state ever reserving all pine timber suitable for naval purposes. The town was surveyed in 1786.

The surface is broken, laying upon the high lands that divide waters flowing from a marsh near the center of the town east into the Connecticut river, and west into the St. Lawrence by way of the river Lamoille and lake Champlain. The soil is good, producing grass and the English grains in abundance. The highest point of land is under cultivation, and is probably the most elevated, improved land in the state. The snows fall very deep, covering the earth nearly one-half the year. One of the early residents described the town as being a first rate place for sleigh rides, for the reason that we have nine months winter and the other three months were very late in the fall. There has been but little emigration west from Walden, the farms of the first settlers are generally occupied by their sons. There are now probably in town 25 voters by the name of Perkins who have descended from two persons of that name among the early settlers, thus showing the peculiar attachments that surround mountain homes.

Joe's brook, which has its origin in Cole's pond in the north part of the town, runs southerly into Joe's pond in Cabot, thence into the Passumpsic, is the largest stream. Cole's pond was discovered by a hunter by the name of Cole from St. Johnsbury, thus deriving its name. Lyfford's pond in the south part of Walden was also discovered by one of Gen. Hazen's men of that name. A small portion of Joe's pond is situated in town.

Joe's brook and pond derived their names from a friendly Indian of the St. Francis tribe who first discovered them, and used to fish and hunt in and around them. He had a cabin in town for himself and his squaw Molly, for some years after its settlement. He rendered valuable service to the early settlers by warning them of danger from his red brethren, and in assisting them to explore the wilderness around. He died at an advanced age in Newbury in 1819. His memory was ever kindly cherished by those whom he had befriended. Capt. Joe, as he was familiarly called, in his old age received a pension of $70 per year granted by the legislature of Vermont.

In 1779, Gen. Hazen built a military road from Peacham through Cabot, Walden, Hardwick, and north to Hazen's notch in Westfield. Hazen's road, as it is still called, passes through the S. W. part of Walden, and was of essential service to those who early came into town. Gen. H. built a block house on the land now occupied by Cyrus Smith, and left a small garrison to man it until the next year. The name of the officer left in command was Walden, who requested that the town should receive his name when chartered, which was accordingly done.

The block house remained for some years and was temporarily occupied by many of the first settlers, having the honor of having the first school, the first sermon and the first birth in town, and at one time a family by the name of Sabin, consisting of father, mother and 26 children within its walls.

Walden was mainly settled by emigrants from New Hampshire. Nathaniel Perkins moved his family into town in 1789, being the only family for the three succeeding years. Nathan Barker was the next. Mr. B. was soon followed by Joseph Burley, Samuel and Ezekiel Gilman, Elisha and Benjamin Cate, Samuel Huckins, Robert Carr, Major Roberson and many others, who mainly settled on or near the Hazen road; and so rapidly was the settlement increased, that in 1800 the inhabitants numbered 153; at which time numerous families arrived, among whom were Timothy Haynes, Stephen Currier and

John Stevens, who were the first settlers on or near the county road—a road running nearly centrally through the town east and west, which was laid out by a special act of the Vermont legislature, probably in 1801. The land upon which they originally settled is still occupied by their sons, and it may not be amiss to say in this connection, that they were men possessed of sterling qualities, and met the exigencies incident to the hardships of life in a new settlement with patience, courage and hope largely developed; lived to a good old age, and departed leaving the impress of their exertions on the religious, educational and other institutions of the town.

Walden was organized March 24, 1794,—Nathaniel Perkins, town clerk, Nathan Barker, Nathaniel Perkins and Joseph Burley, selectmen, Samuel Gilman, treasurer, Elisha Cate, constable. In March, 1795, Samuel Huckins was first grand juror, and in the same year Nathaniel Perkins was elected first representative.

March, 1796, the town voted to raise 30 bushels of wheat to pay for preaching, 30 do. to pay for schooling, $10 worth to defray town expenses; and appointed a committee of three to hire preaching. Thus early evincing their interest in the cause of religion and education.

In March, 1797, voted to raise $5 for town expenses for the current year, being the first money raised by the town for any purpose, and $25 for schools likewise, and selected the first petit jurors.

First sermon in town by Elder Chapman, at the house of Nathaniel Perkins, in 1794. Dr. George C. Wheeler came into town in 1828; remained about one year; was the first physician. James Bell, the first lawyer, being the only professional man that ever permanently resided in town.

Nathaniel Farrington, Jr., was first merchant. Jesse Perkins, son of Nathaniel Perkins, first child born in town, is still a resident. No settled minister has ever had a residence in Walden.

The first death in town was that of Samuel Gilman, caused by the burning off and falling of a stub of a tree where he was clearing on the farm now occupied by Otis Freeman. He left his house in the evening to roll together the brands of the piles that were burning; not returning, his wife went in search and found his lifeless body crushed to the earth, and was obliged to obtain assistance of a neighbor before it could be extricated. The second death was that of Mrs.

Melcher, who was buried with her infant a few days old. The third, Ezekiel Gilman, killed by the rolling of a log upon him while engaged in rearing a log cabin. First marriage, Mr. Melcher. First school taught by Nathaniel Perkins. The oldest person deceased in town was Mrs. George aged 102. Her son Moses is now 90 years of age. Edward Smith is the oldest now living, aged 91 years.

There have been five college graduates from this town, viz: Rev. Samuel H. Shepley, now a teacher in Pennsylvania; Mark Durant, now a teacher in Kentucky; James S. Durant, now a physician in Danville; Daniel W. Stevens, teaching in Ohio; and Giles F. Montgomery, now a theological student in Ohio.

Present number of school districts, 13. The first church built was a Union house in South Walden, in 1826; the second, a Congregational house, in 1844, in the north part of Walden; the third and last, a Union house, in 1856, in the southerly part of the town.

Walden has suffered for the want of a common center. There is no village in town, and no mills that do business to much amount, excepting saw mills. Population in 1860, 1102, showing an increase during the last decade of about 200.

CHURCHES.

The first church organization was Congregational, organized in 1805. Its deacon, Theophilus Rundlet, was a man of fervent piety, and conducted public worship on the sabbath, with the help of occasional preaching, for many years. He left town, and was gathered to his grave like a shock of corn fully ripe, at an advanced age, a few years since. This church has lost its organization, and none of its records are to be found. In 1828 a new Congregational church was formed, and by the aid of the Vermont D. M. society and other sources, it was supplied with the services of a clergyman for some years, but is now essentially disbanded. Its two first deacons, Merrill Foster and Gilman Dow, being dead, and others of its members, united with the Congregational church in Hardwick.

In 1810 a Methodist E. church was formed by Elders Kilbourn and Hoyt. Nathaniel Gould and wife, Timothy Haynes and wife, and Nathaniel Perkins and wife, were among its original members. It is the leading denomination in town; has had constant preaching for a long series of years. Its present membership is 107.

A Universalist society was formed in 1829, and a Freewill Baptist in 1837. The two last have only occasional preaching.

BIOGRAPHICAL SKETCHES.

Capt. Enoch Foster,*

Was born at Bow, N. H., in the year 1770. At the age of 13 he removed to Peacham, Vt., with his parents, where he lived until the year 1800, when he removed to Walden. Much of his early manhood was spent in the woods. He was often employed as a guide by the early settlers, to conduct them to different parts of the country. Indian Joe was his constant companion in the woods for a number of years. Capt. Foster was a man of stern integrity and possessed great energy, which together, made him a friend of all.

Many are the strangers that remember his generous hospitality. He lived to follow four of his six children to the grave, and died at the age of 84 years. He was a member of the Congregationalist church for 40 years, and died as he had lived, a zealous Christian.

Nathaniel Farrington,

Came into Walden from New Hampshire in 1799, and settled on the farm now occupied by Jacob Dutton. He was possessed of property to some extent—a man of energy, so much so that in 1802, he raised 1300 bushels of English grains, accumulated property rapidly, kept the only hotel in town, for a number of years, and in various ways exerted a controlling influence over his townsmen. He represented Walden in the state legislature in 1801-2-3-8-9 and 1811. He lived to old age, and left a large property to his children.

Nathaniel Farrington, Jr.

Came into town when a lad with his father. He early developed business tact, was the first merchant in town, and engaged to the time of his death, in 1854, in farming, merchandizing, building mills, &c., ever doing a large miscellaneous business, thereby adding largely to his own estate, and to the material wealth of the town. He was possessed of a cool, sound judgment, and exercised an influence rarely attained, over his fellow townsmen for a long series of years. He was town representative in the years 1828-29-30-31-36 and 37. Simple

* This article furnished by a friend.

and unostentatious in his own habits, he disbursed of his means with great liberality for the maintenance and education of his large family, and ever exercised a kind, considerate care over the interests of those whom he had assisted by pecuniary aid, to better their fortune, and his memory is cherished gratefully by the poor and needy.

NATHANIEL PERKINS

Moved his family into town in 1789, being the only family there for the three succeeding years.

He was possessed of uncommon energy, which enabled him to overcome the difficulties and hardships incident to living thus separated from the neighborhood of men. On one occasion he went to Newbury, a distance of 30 miles, on foot, and procured a bushel of Indian corn meal and returned with it on his shoulders.

His house was the home of all the first settlers for the time being, and no weary traveler was denied its shelter, or a share in its sometimes extremely scanty stores. He represented his town in the state legislature in 1795, being its first representative, also in '96–99–1800–1804–5 and 6.

Mr. Perkins was one of the original members of the Methodist church, and ever one of its pillars. He lived to see great changes in the town of his early adoption, and died at the age of 90 years, leaving numerous descendants.

A friend has kindly furnished the following:

JAMES BELL.

John Austin of pure Norman extraction, a native of Glasgow, Scotland, invented the tulip-shaped bell—for which he was knighted by Queen Elizabeth, and took the name of Bell. He was a staunch Presbyterian, and during the religious controversy was obliged to flee, and went to the north of Ireland. From thence a large family of brothers emigrated to the United States, and settled in various parts of the Union. James, the second son, settled in New Hampshire, from whom the subject of the following sketch descended.

James Bell was born in Lyme, N. H., in December, 1776. His father, James Bell, was accidentally killed by falling on the point of a scythe which he was carrying on his shoulder. His son was then but two years old. Mr. Bell's mother was a woman of strong sense and Christian character, for whom he ever cherished the strongest affection and respect. She married for her second husband, Col.

Robert Johnston of Newbury, Vt., in which town Mr. Bell was brought up to manhood. Not far from 1800, he went to reside in Hardwick, Vt., and was married to Lucy Dean of Hardwick, Mass., in 1801. Soon after this, he became entangled with a lawyer for whom he had done business as deputy sheriff. A legal quarrel arose which lasted for years; litigation stripped him of his property, and threatened to ruin him. The struggles of that season of his life required more courage than to fight with physical giants. The inevitable privations of the early settler, the scarcity of provisions, when the clearings were small, and shaded by the thick forests which encircled them, so that the grain which had struggled through the summer was likely to be nipped by untimely frosts; the fearful drain upon pecuniary means, and the excitement attendant upon litigation; the wants of a young family of children, whom he tenderly loved; the pain to think that he had made the sharer of his trials a woman who had seen better days,—a woman of the strictest principles, ambitious—and who must have been more than human to be always patient under the allotments of fortune;—was enough to tempt a less buoyant spirit to do as another individual was advised to when sorely tried. Still, he never yielded, but rather pressed onward. The "divinity that shapes our ends," used this roughhewing as a means of showing to himself and others the talents that were in him. He became too poor to employ counsel, and was obliged to defend himself and plead his own causes; and soon displayed wit and a native eloquence, which, in those primitive times were more than a match for his mere legal antagonist. He eventually drove him from the field, and was ever after engaged in legal business, though not admitted to the bar for a number of years after.

He settled in Walden in 1804 or 5; in 1810 he commenced the farm where he ever after lived, and where his son, Hon. James D. Bell now resides. The place was entirely wild, and the first tree fallen was the foundation log on which his cabin was erected. In 1815 he was elected to the state legislature, after having had conferred on him the office of justice of the peace, captain of militia, &c., which honors in those days were not without their significance. He was again elected to the legislature in 1818, and was a member of that body for 10 years in succession. He was an eloquent debater, and few men had more influence in the house. Few were there whose political sway was felt more throughout the state than Mr. Bell.

At the time that Mr. B. was admitted to the bar of Caledonia county, it was composed of a constellation of many of the first order of talents, among whom he was received as a peer, and in mother wit surpassed perhaps any one of them. Intellectual sport he enjoyed from the foundations of his being, and his irrepressible 'laughter was genial and sparkling, as the bursting forth of sunshine. He moreover had an immense persuasive influence with a jury; his sympathies being strong, he intuitively hit upon those points which would sway them in the direction he wished.

The *man* was the *man* in his esteem, whatever the texture of his coat might be; his client's wrongs were his own wrongs, and he defended him with a zeal and enthusiasm that never flagged till his point was gained. He was a hard man to face, for perhaps when his legal antagonist had finished a labored plea, and thought his mountain stood strong, a few playful sallies from Bell, or a stroke or two of the scalpel of satire directed to the weak points of his argument, and he would find the whole fabric tumbling about his ears. A case of this kind occurred once, when he was attending court in a neighboring state, where he was a stranger. The counsel on the other side was a man of pretension, wealthy, influential, and much of an egotist. He made a great effort for his client, represented the wrongs he had suffered as without a parallel, labored to excite the sympathy by the presentation of arguments drawn from no very apparent facts, and worked himself up to a very high point of commisseration for his much abused client, and sat down. Mr. Bell arose with a very solemn face, but a queer twinkle of the eye, and said he thought they would all feel it a privilege to join in singing, "Hark, from the tombs a doleful sound,"—he struck the old minor tune in which the words were then sung, and sung the verse through. The speech of his opponent, in the minds of those present, was upon the poise between the pathetic and ridiculous—the ridicule flashed upon them, and the house was in a roar. When the merriment subsided he went on with his plea. The advocate who preceded him had indulged in invidious remarks, not only in reference to Mr. Bell, but to the Vermont bar generally, and Mr. B. mentioned that he had been both surprised and pained at the ungentlemanly and narrow allusions which had been made by one who had the honor of belonging to one of the most liberal professions in the world; and the man afterwards ingenuously said, that he was never so used up.

In 1832, Mr. B. made a public profession, and joined the Congregational church in Hardwick; and was ever after a conscientious and constant attendant at the sanctuary, when his health permitted. He was a lover of freedom, and a hater of oppression. Well, do we remember his relating the following anecdote. He was standing in front of the Capitol at Washington, when a gang of slaves, manacled together, and driven by their keeper, passed by. When they came opposite the Capitol, they struck up, "Hail! Columbia!" and the refrain was kept up until their voices were lost in the distance. He said: " What a satire upon our brags of freedom was that music from those unconscious wretches! Oh, how I longed to stand upon the floor of that house and say what I wanted to say." He was an earnest temperance advocate. During the political and other conflicts of his manhood, he was a firm, warm friend, and a most whole-souled despiser of those he disliked; but, as age advanced, and the tumults of life receded, the affections became predominant, and embraced all. His sportiveness almost went with him to the grave. After he was so infirm that his step was almost as uncertain as an infant's, he said to some one, alluding to his infirmities, that there was one thing he could do as quick as ever. "And what is that?" said the person addressed. " I can fall down as·quick as ever I could !" was the answer. He was chosen a member of the council of censors, in 1848, which was the last public service in which he engaged.

There is but one sketch of any of his public efforts remaining. That was reported by S. B. Colby, Esq. of Montpelier, and which we take the liberty to insert in this article.

Orleans County, January Term, }
                A. D. 1847. }

Brother Bell has made one of his great speeches to-day in defence of Mrs. Hannah Parker, on trial for the murder of her own child. I have never heard or felt a deeper pathos than the tones of his voice bore to the heart, as he stood up in the dignity of old age, his tall, majestic form over-leaning all the modern members of the bar (as if he had come from some superior physical generation of men), tremulous, slightly, with emotions that seemed thronging up from the long past, as the old advocate yielded for a moment to the effect of early associations, and introduced himself and his fallen brethren whom his eye missed from their wonted seats, as it glanced along the vacant places inside the bar. He said:

May it please your honor,
      and gentlemen of the jury:

I stood among giants, though not of them: my comrades at the bar have fallen. Fletcher! the untiring and laborious counselor, the persuasive advocate, the unyielding combatant, is where? Eternity echoes, here!

Cushman, the courtly and eloquent lawyer, the kind and feeling man, the polished and social companion and friend, where now is he? The world unseen alone can say.

Mattocks lives, thank God; but is withdrawn from professional toil, from the clash of mind on mind, the combat of intellect and wit, the flashing humor and grave debates of the court room, to the graceful retreat of domestic life.

I am alone, an old tree, stripped of its foliage and tottering beneath the rude storms of seventy winters: but lately prostrate at the verge of the grave, I thought my race was run; never again did I expect to be heard in defence of the unfortunate accused. But Heaven has spared me, another monument of His mercy, and I rejoice in the opportunity of uttering, perhaps my last public breath in defence of the poor, weak, imbecile prisoner at the bar.

Gentlemen, she is a mother. She is charged with the murder of her own child! She is arraigned here a friendless stranger. She is without means to reward counsel; and has not the intelligence, as I have the sorry occasion to know, to dictate to her counsel a single fact relating to her case. I have come to her defence without hope of reward; for she has nothing to give but thick, dark poverty, and of that, too, I have had more than enough.

But it gives me pleasure to say that the stringent hardship of her case has won her friends among strangers, and the warm sympathies which have been extended to my client, and the ready and useful aid I have received during this protracted trial, from various members of the bar, strongly indicate the great hearts and good minds of my departed brothers, have left their influence upon these, their successors.

Soon after Mr Bell's return from court he received the following from Mattocks:

"Peacham, 16th January, 1847.

Brother Bell: In the *Watchman* I have just seen a specimen of your speech in the murder case. It is worthy of being inserted in the next edition of '*Elegant Extracts in Prose*.'' Sir, you are the last of the Mohicans and the greatest, and when you die (which I fear will be soon, for from the account I hear of your effort in the cause of humanity, it was all but a superhuman brightening before death), the tribe will be extinct. You have justly called our two lamented friends giants, and with the discrimination of a reviewer, have'given to each the distinguishing traits of excellence; and although your introducing me with them was gratuitous, it was kind, and the traits you have given me I owe to your generosity.

You say 'I was not of them;' this was a fiction, used in an unlawyerlike manner to prevent self-commendation, unless, indeed, you meant as Paul might have said, that *he* was not of the prophets, because he was a head and shoulders above them. I am proud that you have sustained and surpassed the old school of lawyers. Sir, you are the Nestor of the bar, and may be truly called the 'Old man eloquent.'

I am, sir, with the greatest respect,
      your friend and humble serv't,
            JOHN MATTOCKS.

N. B. I reserve the all important part of this letter to stand by itself. Let us hold fast to our hope in Christ. We near the brink."

Bell survived his friend a few years, encompassed with infirmity, and died of paralysis, 17th April, 1852.

WATERFORD.

BY T. A. CUTLER.

This town is pleasantly situated on the Connecticut river, lying along the 15 miles fall S. S. E. of St. Johnsbury, and 45 miles E. from Montpelier. The surface is generally broken, presenting that diversified scenery of mountain and valley so common to Vermont. The soil is fertile and well adapted to agriculture, especially to grazing, which has ever been the favorite pursuit of the inhabitants, and in which they have gained an honorable reputation. The valleys produce bountifully the usual varieties of grains and grasses, while the hills, arable to their tops and thickly dotted with maple groves, abound in rich pastures. The rocks are primitive and belong to the calcareo-mica slate formation, and there is a range of clay slate running north through the town from which superior specimens of slate for roofing have been quarried by Messrs. Hale & Bracket. There are also many specimens of a peculiar formation of granite, sometimes called nodular granite. "It contains balls, usually a little flattened, scattered in it like plums in a pudding. These balls are usually about an inch in diameter, and are composed essentially of black mica, having the plates arranged in concentric layers with a very thin deposit of quartz between the layers."

Except the Passumpsic, which flows through the west corner of the town, Waterford has no rivers, though it is well watered by numerous brooks and springs. Styles' pond, covering an area of about 100 acres, lies in the north part of the township.

Of the early settlement of Waterford, though probably attended with the trials and hardships incident to all early settlements, nothing has been handed down worthy of record. The town, by name of Littleton, was chartered Nov. 8, 1780, to Benjamin Whipple and his associates. The name was changed to Waterford in 1797. Tradition says that James Adams was the first settler. The exact time of his coming is not now known. Thompson dates the first settlement at 1787, but we find by the proprietors' records that a proprietors' meeting, held at Barnet in the fall of 1783, was adjourned to the house of James Adams in "said Littleton," which shows that Mr. Adams was here as early, at least, as 1783. The next settlers were Joseph and John Woods, who came as early as 1784 or '85, and settled on the Passumpsic river. Very soon after came the Pikes, who were the first settlers in the east part of the town. The first person born in town was Polly Woods, daughter of Joseph Woods. The first male born in Waterford was William Morgan.

The town was organized in 1793. The first town officers were: Selah Howe, clerk; Peter Sylvester, Daniel Pike and Nehemiah Hadley, selectmen; Levi Aldrich, Luther Pike and Levi Goss, listers; Samuel Fletcher, constable; Abel Goss, town treasurer. Population in 1791, 63; in 1800, 565; in 1810, 1289; in 1820, 1247; in 1830, 1358; in 1840, 1388; in 1850, 1412; in 1860 (see census table in county chapter, No. 3).

There being no valuable water power manufacturing establishments or central place of business, the occupation of the people has been confined exclusively to agriculture, and much of the business of the town goes to the adjoining towns of Barnet, St. Johnsbury and Concord; consequently the population has for many years remained nearly stationary, and the two little villages present to-day nearly the same appearance as in early days, when a rhyming son of Vulcan sang of his beloved village as

——"A very fine place,
Adorned with majesty and grace;
Situated under Rabbit Hill,
With a tavern, store and a clover mill."

With this change, however, a beautiful church now stands in each village, and the clover mill has been changed to a starch mill, which suits the wants of the people quite as well, though it might *grate* a little in the poet's measure. In 1798, a

CONGREGATIONAL CHURCH.

Was organized, consisting of 8 members—4 males and 4 females. The Rev. Asa Carpenter, the first minister, was born Oct. 4, 1770, in Ashford, Conn. He graduated at Dartmouth college when about 25 years of age; studied theology with Rev. Mr. Burton of Thetford, Vt.; preached a short time in several towns in the state as a missionary of the Connecticut Home Missionary Society; moved to Waterford in the fall of '97, and was ordained pastor of the Congregational church at its organization. He labored in Waterford until June, 1816, when he removed to Pennfield, N. Y., where he died in 1827 or '28. In 1818 the first Congregational Meeting House was built, and in October of the following year, Rev. Reuben Mason was settled as pastor, and sustained this relation 5 years. Soon after the first, another meeting house was built at West Waterford, and meetings were held at the two houses until a church was erected in Lower Waterford in 1837. In Sept., 1825, Rev. Thomas Hall was installed; dismissed in 1830; reinstalled in 1834, and sustained his pastoral relation until January, 1844. During the interval of Mr. Hall's labors from 1830 to 1834, the pulpit was supplied by Rev. Messrs. White, Bradford and others. Mr. Hall was succeeded by Rev. Eben Smith, whose pastorate continued until Jan., 1848. Immediately after, Rev. Francis Warriner commenced his labors with the church; was installed in 1854, and sustained the pastoral relation till Oct., 1860, when he was dismissed on account of ill health, and Rev. Geo. J. Bard, the present pastor was ordained. In 1818, a meeting house was erected in the N. W. part of the town and occupied by the

FREEWILL BAPTIST SOCIETY,

Over which the Rev. Rufus Cheney was installed. How long he preached, or how long the society remained in existence the writer is not informed, nor are the records of the church to be obtained. A religious society called

THE FIRST UNIVERSALIST SOCIETY

In Waterford, was formed on the 17th of May, 1824, consisting of over 100 members. The society has never had a settled minister, but has been supplied a portion of the time by different preachers. At the present time, and for a year past the society have occupied the Union meeting house in the upper village and have had preaching regularly on the sabbath by Rev. Carlos Mantin. Connected with the society is a sabbath school, furnished with a good library. The society is not as large, owing to death and removals, now as it has been, but at the present is prospering.

PROFESSIONAL MEN

Born and educated in Waterford:

Clergymen.—Wm. H. Hadley,* Alfred Stevens,* Samuel A. Benton,* James H. Benton, E. I. Carpenter,* Prosper Davidson, Thomas Kidder, Eben. Cutler,* Zenas Goss,* Samuel Hurlbert, Silas Gaskill, Philander Carpenter.

Lawyers.—J. D. Stoddard, R. C. Benton, R. C. Benton, Jr.,* Jacob Benton, A. H. Hadley, O. T. Brown, A. J. Hale, Jona. Ross,* E. Cutler, Jr.,* A. P. Carpenter,* Luther Kidder.

Physicians.—A. Kinne,* A. Farr, C. Farr, R. Bugbee, Jr., A. G. Bugbee, Frank Bugbee, N. S. Goss, Wm. Benton.

Representatives.—1795, Jona. Grow; 1796-98, John Grow; 1799-1801, Asa Grow; 1802-5, Jos. Armington; 1806, Silas Davidson; 1807, Jos. Armington; 1808-16, S. Hemingway; 1817, Jos. Armington; 1818-19, Nathan Pike; 1820-21, Jacob Benton; 1822, S. Hemingway; 1823, Jonah Carpenter; 1824, S. Hemingway; 1825-26, Silas Davidson; 1827-29, S. Hemingway; 1830-32, Robert Taggard; 1833-34, J. D. Stoddard; 1835, S. Hemingway; 1836-37, Lyman Buck; 1838-39, James Works; 1840-41, R. F. Rowell; 1842-44, Royal Ross; 1845-46 Dennis May; 1847-48, Joseph Ide; 1849-50, Barron Moulton; 1851-52, A. P. Bonney; 1853-54, Wm. Adams; 1855, Dennis May; 1856-57, J. D. Stoddard.

Town Clerks.—1793-95, Selah Howe; 1796-1801, John Grow; 1802-5, S. Hemingway; 1806, Samuel Gaskill; 1807-16, S. Hemingway; 1817-23, J. Carpenter; 1824-41, S. Hemingway; 1842-57, L. S. Freeman.

* Graduates.

WHEELOCK.

BY HON. T. C. CREE.

This town embraces a territory of about six miles square. It lies about six miles from the line of the Passumpsic Rail Road. In 1785, the legislature of this state gave by charter, this town to Dartmouth College and Moors Indian Charity School, institutions situate at Hanover, N. H., one moiety to the college and the other moiety to the school. In the same instrument the town was incorporated, and named after President Wheelock, the first officer of the aforesaid institutions. In the charter it is provided that so long and while the said college and school actually apply the rents and profits of this land to the purposes of the college and school, the land and tenements in town shall be exempt from public taxes; so that the town have never been called upon to pay state taxes. This, in the mind of the writer, was a great oversight in the legislature, and it is doubtful whether such wholesale exemption from the public burthens is constitutional. The town enjoys all the rights and privileges of other towns, and yet pays but little of the expense of maintaining the state government. There being no list of the real estate returned to the legislature accounts for the smallness of the grand list reported.

The town was organized March 29, 1792. Abraham Morrill, first clerk; Dudley Swasey, Abraham Morrill, Joseph Venen, first selectmen; Gideon Leavett, first constable.

The settlements commenced about 1780. I am unable to ascertain the names of the first settlers; they were a hardy race of men and women, and were compelled to bear burthens and hardships that would now be insupportable to some of the "young America" of the town. For several years after the first settlement there were no roads to the older and adjacent towns, so that their grain for grinding had to be transported to Danville, a distance of 12 miles, upon their shoulders or upon handsleds, the route being indicated only by spotted trees.

The general surface of the town is rather uneven. One range of the Green mountains runs through the west part of the town, but is no where very steep or stony. Roads cross the summit in several places. The land upon the mountain is well timbered, and susceptible of cultivation to the summit; and what has been cleared affords some of the best grazing land in the state. The eastern part is more level, and all good land for farming purposes. Large quantities of hay, oats and lumber are carried from this town to Lyndon and St. Johnsbury, and large quantities of maple sugar are also annually manufactured here.

Miller's river runs through the north part of the town and empties into the Passumpsic at Lyndon. This river affords some excellent mill sites, and along its banks is some of the most fertile land in the country.

In November, 1796, the town voted to build a meeting-house — the first one in town. It was built the following year, was a large, two-story edifice, and, like others of its kind, was never finished. Enough was done, however, so that meetings could be held in it. It was never lathed and plastered overhead; a hail storm broke some of the windows in the upper story, which invited the swallow and wren to make it their abode. The writer occasionally attended meeting there in 1829-30; the monotonous tone of the preacher, the cheerful twitter of the swallow and the crying of the *babies*, that used then to be carried to meeting, formed rather a medley of sounds.

One curious vote was taken by the town in relation to this house, that I must not omit. It appears by the record that they had a town meeting for the purpose of selling the pews, and the first vote passed was as follows: "Voted that the town be at the expence of *rum* for the vendueing off the meeting-house pews;" and from the subsequent bids it would appear that some of the pews were very valuable; however, I suppose it was then customary to have rum at all vendues to stimulate people to bid for that they did not want, and was thought to be well enough even in selling church property. It would hardly do now, in these temperance times, for even a town to furnish or give away rum to sell anything, particularly pews in a meeting-house.

MINERAL SPRINGS.

There are 2 in town; one in the village and one about 50 rods north. The waters have never been analyzed, but it is said by those who profess to know, that they are the strongest impregnated in the state. Their properties are the same as those at Alburgh and Newbury in this state. There is no doubt they possess medicinal qualities. The water of the one in the village is used for common drinking purposes by the whole village in the warm part of the year, and more or less at other times; and to this fact

is attributed the unusual healthiness of the inhabitants. These springs are not affected by great rains or drouth, but the water flows at all times alike. Persons subject to headache, humors, and the like, have found relief and cure by drinking and bathing in the water.

THE VILLAGE

is situate near the northeast corner of the town, on the bank of Miller's river, and contains about 30 dwelling houses, 1 meeting house, 1 tavern, 1 grist mill, 2 saw mills, 1 machine shop, 1 tannery, 1 planing mill, 1 store and post office, 1 law office, 2 blacksmith shops, 2 shoe shops, and 1 starch factory. The population in 1860, was 858. The town has been the home of a large number of soldiers of the Revolution and the War of 1812; the last of the former has now gone to his rest.

ECCLESIASTICAL.

The prevailing denomination of Christians is the Free-will Baptists. There are 2 societies in town, one South, the other North; both have meeting houses. The South Church was organized about 1800, by Elder Joseph Boody of Stratford, N. H. Among the names of ministers who have had charge of this church may be mentioned Elders Benjamin Page, Robinson, Mainard, Gillman and Allen. The society do not support preaching all the time. The North Church was organized Feb. 11, 1831, Elder Jonathan Woodman. They organized with 6 members; have 30 members; their house of worship is at the village. Elder J. Woodman is their present pastor.

There are quite a number of Congregationalists and Methodists in town, but no organized church or society of those denominations.

The town is divided into 10 school districts. All except one have summer and winter schools. Most of the districts have 3 months each term. Most of the school houses are poor; but a better feeling is manifest in relation to them, and it is evident, from some late demonstrations that better times are coming for the youth, as to good, commodious school houses — as one has been built at the village, worthy of the name.

[The reader will observe that no biographic sketches appear in connection with the history of Waterford or of this town. The historian whose well written sketch appears above, writes us, in extenuation of his seeming neglect, in connection with the matter, that they have up there "neither presidents nor fools to write about." We have not received the "extenuation" of Waterford yet.—*Ed.*]

GOSHEN GORE.

BY JOSEPH CLARK.

There are two Gores in Caledonia county by this name. The largest contains 7339 acres; lies in the northwest part of the county, is bounded north by Wheelock, east by Danville, south by Walden, and west by Greensboro'. The smaller Gore contains 2828 acres, and lies in the southwest corner of the county.* These Gores derive their name from the town to which they formerly belonged. By a singular act of the legislature, these two Gores in Caledonia county, and one still larger in Addison county, 70 miles distant, containing 13,000 acres, were incorporated into a town, by the name of Goshen; chartered Feb. 1, 1792, to John Rowell, Wm. Douglass, and 65 others, and re-chartered to the same, Nov. 1, 1798. The inhabitants of the part of the town in Addison county, organized March 29, 1814. The Gores in Caledonia county were severed from the town of Goshen by the legislature in 1854. There have been frequent petitions by the inhabitants of the larger Gore in this county to become organized into a town, the first being presented to the legislature in 1835; but an organization has never been granted.† The larger Gore in this county, being most accessible to East Hardwick, as a place of business and post office address, is distinguished from the other, by "Goshen Gore, near Hardwick." This tract of land lies sloping from the valley of Lamoile river, rising to form one limb to the fork of the Y.

The first settlements were made by Elihu Sabin and Warren Smith in 1802. Smith did not settle permanently. Sabin built a frame house which he occupied until his decease, some 41 years. Other settlements were made soon after that of Sabin, by Reuben Smith, Elisha Shepard, Reuben Crosby, Thomas Ransom, Azariah Boody, Ephraim Perrin and Andrew Blair. Improvements were made about the same time by several other transient residents. Although the settlement of the place was at comparatively a late date, the hardships incident to new settlements had to be encountered. Supplies of grain and necessaries had to be procured in a measure from adjoining towns; the method of transportation frequently upon their backs, and the method of payment,

† The people, for the most part, are not dissatisfied with their present situation, being exempt from the demands of the tax-gatherer, and the expenses incident to a town organization.

generally, by day's work. The frosty season of 1816, and others which occurred previously, was severely felt. Mary Sabin was the first child born. Freeman Smith was the first male child, and Edmund Barker and Betsy Sabin, the first couple married.

The western portion of the Gore, towards Lamoile river, comprising about two-thirds of the territory, is improved by resident occupants. The number of families is over 40. The soil is a mold, in some parts black, in others reddish; but little clay or loam. It is strong and well adapted to grass and English grain; the timber chiefly maple, birch, spruce and fir. Two or three farms on the eastern extremity, adjoining Danville, have been under improvement since 1805. James Clark and Thomas Young made the first improvement there.

The eastern portion is chiefly unimproved and mountainous, but well timbered. In the northern part, there is a pond covering about 80 acres, the outlet of which finds its way to the Connecticut river. A steam saw mill was erected by this pond in 1856, by T. G. Bronson. Bronson died in 1857, and the mill passed into the hands of others—Hawkins & Ross, present proprietors. Nearly 1,000,000 feet of lumber is manufactured at this mill annually, which is principally drawn to St. Johnsbury, and used in the manufactory of E. & T. Fairbanks. About a mile west of this pond is a "beaver meadow, also called "Blueberry Meadow," where vestiges of the labors and dwellings of this sagacious animal are yet to be seen. A stream arises from this meadow, called Gore Brook, which empties into Lamoile river.

The first saw mill was built by G. W. Cook, on a stream which is the outlet of a pond in Wheelock. This mill was burnt, and another built by William Shurburn on the same spot. The second was burned, and the third was built by Enoch Foster in 1833, which is still in operation. There was also another built in 1840, by Levi Utley, on the Gore brook, leading from Beaver meadow.

The first meeting house, first public house, first grist mill, first physician, and first lawyer, are among the things that never were. The first school was kept by Barilla Morse, in Reuben Crosby's barn, in 1812. Judith Chase, Betsy Sabin and Lucretia Washburn were the next succeeding teachers. Mrs. Andrew Blair sent her girl to the first school, and paid the tuition with a pink silk handkerchief. "Schoolmarm know'd I had it, and she wanted it to make her a bonnet." (Good old Mrs. Ann Blair's testimony.) The first frame school house was built in 1823. In 1834 a second school district was formed.

A Freewill Baptist Church was organized here in August, 1841, and Elder John Garfield ordained pastor. It consisted orignally of 12 members; upwards of 50 have since belonged to it. Two of their quarterly meetings were held here. In 1855, H. W. Harris became their minister, who was succeeded by Elder Geo. King, ordained pastor of the church in 1857. Elder King has left the place, and the church is now supplied only by itinerant ministers. In 1850, this church "Resolved themselves into a society for the purpose of aiding superannuated ministers and poor widows and orphans, and to do all they could for their aid and support."

ELIHU SABIN

Born in Dudley, Mass., in 1772, died in "Goshen Gore, near Hardwick," July 9, 1843, aged 71. He was one of the 26 children of Mr. and Mrs. Gideon Sabin, commemorated in the Hardwick History (No. 3, p. 324).

As has been before mentioned, he was the first permanent settler of this Gore. A generous-hearted, worthy man, talented for his day and opportunities, energetic and persevering, he had the respect of all the settlers of the neighboring towns, and was, for about 20 years, a justice of the peace. He was, moreover, distinguished for uncommon muscular strength, in so much that the history of the Gore is not without an example of the courage and prowess requisite for a hand-to-hand mortal combat.

Once on a time, well verified it is said, Sabin did face the foe in a single-handed struggle for life. It appears that he had caught a cub, whose cries brought forward the bear robbed of her young, whom Elihu unflinchingly smote with the breech of his gun; the bear was dispatched, and so was the breech of Elihu's gun. Lest, however, it may be said, in cavil, that sudden desperation which has been known to give supernatural strength, nerved our hero's arm, we have a more deliberate feat with which to crown our point—the prodigious strength of Elihu Sabin—a feat of no thrilling moment, a plain, practical test, however, evincing not less arm-strength in the man. A living witness testifies that he has seen Mr. Sabin knock down with one blow of his fist, a two year old bullock, striking him between the fore shoulders, and breaking a rib. Can the state show a stronger man?

EPHRAIM PERRIN

From Connecticut, came into the Gore in 1807, and lived entirely alone 8 years in a log hut, which he constructed by the side of a large rock, which served the purpose of fire-place, and one end of his apartment. It is said all the bedding which this man had, "was a rag coverlet and a second-hand great coat which Mrs. Sabin let him have." Finally, his affairs prospered, and one of his neighbors, a good old lady, told him he must get married, and "picked a wife out" for him, Miss Polly Cheever, whom he married, and then built a frame house. This wife died in a few years, and he married the second time to Maria Cutler, and reared a numerous family. He justly merited the reputation he obtained, of being a remarkably honest, hard working man; was rather tenacious in his opinions and prejudices, but not forward to assert them. He died in 1859.

REUBEN CROSBY

One of the first settlers, accumulated a handsome property, but becoming partially insane, meditated self destruction. For this purpose he made his escape from his house, and seated himself upon a large rock, where he remained till his limbs were frozen. But by a change in the weather the process of thawing, much more painful than freezing, commenced. This led him to creep to the house, but he lived only a few days. He died in 1830.

REUBEN SMITH

From Warren, N. H., was another of the early proprietors. He died Jan. 30, 1860.

ISAAC STEVENS

Came into the place about 1820. An excellent variety of potato, extensively known as the Stevens potato, was propagated by him from the balls. He died in 1859.

ANDREW BLAIR.

Had the Olympic races come down to our times, Mr. Blair, according to report, might have become a successful competitor for a crown. It is current that he once ran down and captured a fox, and was overheard holding a parley with the captive, whether the thing was done fair. But, unlike the Olympic races, not having an impartial judge to decide the points, the fox seemed to dissent from his victor's boast of fair play. "Now," says Mr. Blair, "if you think the thing was not done fair, we'll let try it again." Whereupon the fox was let go, and was allowed to have a few rods the start, when Blair took the track. Away went the fox—away went Blair; one for life, the other for victory, over hill, over fence, over brush, till Blair caught the breathless trophy, a second time, in triumph.

Mr. Blair was one of the pioneer settlers. Andrew M. Blair, Esq., son of Andrew Blair, was late a member of the Wisconsin state senate.

MILITARY CHAPTER.

THE ADMINISTRATION OF GOVERNOR FAIRBANKS IN RELATION TO THE REBELLION OF 1861.

[Desirous of obtaining from the most authentic source, a full and correct account of the organizing, officering, equipping, subsisting and sending into the field the first six Vermont regiments raised during the late administration, we made application to Gov. Fairbanks for such historic paper, who complied with the request and forwarded the following account. With his characteristic modesty, he gives his account as in the third person, and has evidently avoided speaking of the labors to which he was necessarily subjected during the last six months of his official year. It was necessary, under the law, that he should give his personal attention to the details in the formation of each regiment, and every bill and voucher in an expenditure of more than half a million, was audited by him, assisted only by his valuable secretary, Col. Merrill. (See reports of the legislative committee. In other states, such duties are divided among other boards of officers.) There was also the signing of 500,000 of state bonds, and drawing his warrants on the state treasury for accounts and bills allowed. In brief, an amount of business which could hardly have been accomplished, had he not been accustomed to active business habits; all which, however, and much more, he passes over, submitting the following valuable record, which we give verbatim.—Ed.]

Governor Fairbanks accepted the nomination for the executive office in 1860, with the distinct understanding that it should be but for a single term only. The country was at peace, and all the interests of the state were prosperous. The annual October session of the legislature was marked by no unusual features.

The governor, in his address, recommended a few important measures for the consideration of the two houses, and closed by congratulating the members upon the general prosperity of the state and country.

The result of the presidential election in November, was the signal for the development of dark schemes for the overthrow of the government and the dismemberment of the Union.

Immediately after the assembling of the 36th congress, the insolent bearing of southern senators and members—the development of treason in the cabinet—the threatening tone of the southern press, and the disloyal resolves of southern legislatures and conventions, indicated but too clearly the probable necessity of effective military preparations to protect the country and the United States government from the deep and fast maturing plans of traitors.

Vermont had no effective military organization. Her uniformed militia consisted of a few unfilled companies, in some of the principal villages, while the enrolled militia was a myth. The duty devolved upon the town listers to make returns of citizens liable to be called to do military service, but that duty had been extensively neglected, and, at best, the provision of the statute was practically inefficient. In view of the possibility, not to say probability, that a requisition for troops would be made upon Vermont by the general government, Gov. Fairbanks issued an order, dated the 25th of January, 1861, requiring the officers charged with the duty, to make returns of the enrolled militia forthwith; and at the same time a general order, Nov. 10, was issued, requiring the commanding officers of the uniformed militia companies to adopt measures for filling all vacancies, and to have their men properly drilled and uniformed. A few of the companies responded to this order, but very little was accomplished until after the requisition of the secretary of war.

On the 15th of April, a requisition was received by telegraph from the secretary of war, upon the governor of Vermont, for one regiment of infantry, being the quota for Vermont of the 75,000 troops called for by the president's proclamation of the same date.

Governor Fairbanks immediately issued his proclamation for a special session of the legislature, and gave the necessary orders for detailing ten companies from the uniformed militia, and for furnishing the regiment with its outfit. The legislature assembled at the capital April 23d, when Gov. Fairbanks delivered the following address before the joint assembly:

Gentlemen of the Senate and House of Representatives:

We are convened to day in view of events of an extraordinary and very alarming character. The element of disunion which, in a portion of the United States, for many years, vented itself in threats and menaces, has culminated in open rebellion; and an unnatural and causeless civil war has been precipitated against the general government.

Unprincipled and ambitious men have organized a despotism and an armed force, for the purpose of overthrowing that government which the American people have formed for themselves, and of destroying that constitutional frame-work, under which we have enjoyed peace and prosperity, and from a small and feeble people, grown and expanded to a rank among the first nations of the earth.

The enormity of this rebellion is heightened by the consideration that no valid cause exists for it. The history of the civilized world does not furnish an instance where a revolution was attempted for such slight causes. No act of oppression, no attempted or threatened invasion of the rights of the revolting states, has existed, either on the part of the general government, or of the loyal states; but the principle has been recognized and observed, that the right of each and every state to regulate its domestic institutions, should remain inviolate.

The inception and progress of this rebellion have been remarkable; and characterized, at every stage, by a total absence of any high honorable principle or motive in its leaders. Its master spirits are composed, essentially, of men who have been in high official position in the general government; and it has transpired that members of the late cabinet at Washington, while in the exercise of their official functions, were engaged in treasonable plots for seizing the public property and subverting the United States government. Conventions of delegates in the revolting states, chosen, in some instances, by a minority of the legal voters in those states, have, with indecent haste, adopted ordinances of secession, which ordinances have in no instance been submitted to the people for their ratification.

These proceedings have been followed by a convention of delegates from the several revolting states, which convention has organized a confederate government, adopted a constitution, elected its executive officers and subordinate functionaries, constituted itself into a legislative body, and enacted a code of laws — all which proceedings have been independent of any action of the people of those states.

The authorities of the revolting states, and subsequently that of their confederacy, have proceeded to acts of robbery and theft upon the property of the United States, within their limits. Forts, arsenals, arms, military stores, and other public property, have been seized and appropriated for use against the power of the general government; and custom houses and mints in southern cities, with large amounts of treasure, have been feloniously robbed.

These acts have been followed by military demonstrations and strategetical operations against the United States forts at Pensacola and Charleston, the latter of which, under its gallant commander, Maj. Anderson, after a bombardment of thirty-four hours, from beleaguering batteries of the insurgents, was evacuated on the 13th instant, and the flag of the Union withdrawn. But the crowning

act of perfidy, on the part of the conspirators, is the proclamation of Jefferson Davis, styling himself the president of the southern confederacy, "inviting all those who may desire, by service in private armed vessels on the high seas, to aid his government, to make application for commissions, or letters of marque or reprisal:" thus instituting a grand scheme of piracy on the high seas, against the lives and private property of peaceful citizens.

These acts of outrage and daring rebellion have been equalled only by the forbearance of the general government. Unwilling to precipitate a conflict which must involve the country in all the calamities of civil war, the present government of the United States has exhausted every effort for peace, and every measure for bringing back to their allegiance these disaffected and misguided states.

The duty of protecting the forts and government property, not possessed by the insurgents, was imperative upon the administration; but further than this, no measures for coercing the revolting states into obedience to the constitution and the laws were adopted; and in the matter of the beleaguered forts, the government acted only on the defensive, until the conflict was commenced by the insurgents.

Such forbearance on the part of the government, while it has served to place the conspirators in a moral wrong, is no longer justifiable; and the country hails, with entire unanimity and with ardent enthusiasm, the decision of the president to call into requisition the whole power of the nation for suppressing the rebellion and repelling threatened aggressions.

From every part of the country, in all the loyal states, there is one united voice for sustaining the Union, the constitution, and the integrity of the United States government. All partizan differences are ignored and lost in the higher principle of patriotism. In this patriotic enthusiasm, Vermont eminently participates. Her citizens, always loyal to the Union, will, in this hour of peril, nobly rally for the protection of the government and the constitution.

On the fifteenth instant, the president of the United States issued his proclamation, "calling forth the militia of the several states of the Union, to the aggregate number of seventy-five thousand, in order to suppress treasonable combinations, and cause the laws to be duly executed."

The quota required of Vermont, for immediate service, is one regiment of seven hundred and eighty officers and privates.

On receiving the requisition from the secretary of war, for this regiment, I ordered the adjutant and inspector general to adopt the proper measures for calling into service such of the volunteer companies as are necessary to make up the complement; and the quartermaster general was directed to procure, with the least possible delay, the requisite outfit of knapsacks, overcoats, blankets,

50

and other equipments; which duty he has performed.

Having adopted the foregoing preliminary measures, for responding to the call of the president, I availed myself of the constitutional provision for convening the general assembly in an extra session; not doubting that you, gentlemen, representing the universally expressed patriotism of the citizens of this state, will make all necessary appropriations and provisions for defraying the expenses already incurred and carrying into execution further measures for placing our military quota at the service of the general government.

Conceiving it imminently probable that, at an early day, further calls will be made upon this state for troops, I respectfully call your attention to the importance of adopting immediate measures for a more efficient organization of the military-arm of the state.

During the long interval of peace which we have enjoyed, while our citizens have been uninterrupted in their lawful industrial pursuits, the importance of a military organization and discipline has been lost sight of. Our laws in relation to the militia have been subjected, during nearly a quarter of a century, to numerous isolated amendments and alterations, until as a code, they are disjointed, complicated, and altogether too cumbrous for the basis of a regular and effective organization. I therefore recommend that the legislature should promptly remedy these defects, and adopt such enactments as shall provide, effectively, for organizing, arming, and equipping the militia of the state, and for reasonably compensating the officers and privates, when required to meet for exercise and drill.

I desire, also, to urge upon you the duty of making contingent appropriations of money, to be expended under the direction of the executive, for the outfit of any additional military forces which may be called for by the general government.

The occasion is an extraordinary one. Intelligence reaches us, that the Virginia convention of delegates, elected under the express provision that any ordinance adopted by them, should be submitted to the people for their approval or rejection, has, in secret session, passed an ordinance of secession, and that the governor of the state has assumed to order the seizure of the United States forts, arsenal and vessels within the limits of that state.

The Federal capitol is menaced by an imposing and well armed military force, and the government itself, and the national archives, are in imminent peril.

Such is the emergency, in view of which I invoke your immediate action. The legislatures of other states have made liberal appropriations and extensive military arrangements for aiding the government, and their citizens are hastening to the rescue of our country's flag. We shall discredit our past history should we, in this crisis, suffer Vermont to be behind her sister states, in her patriotic sacrifices for the preservation of the Union and the constitution.

I feel assured, gentlemen, that you will best reflect the sentiments and wishes of your constituents, by emulating in your legislative action, the patriotism and liberality of the noble states which have already responded to the call of the government.

It is devoutly to be hoped that the mad ambition of the secession leaders may be restrained, and the impending sanguinary conflict averted. But a hesitating, half-way policy on the part of the administration of the loyal states, will not avail to produce such a result.

The United States government must be sustained and the rebellion suppressed, at whatever cost of men and treasure; and it remains to be seen whether the vigorous preparations that are being made and the immense military force called into service by the president, are not the most probable and certain measures for a speedy and successful solution of the question.

May that Divine Being, who rules among the nations, and directs the affairs of men, interpose by His merciful Providence, and restore to us again the blessing of peace, under the ægis of our national constitution.

ERASTUS FAIRBANKS.

On the 25th, the legislature passed an act appropriating $1,000,000 for arming, &c., the militia of Vermont; and, on the 26th, certain acts were passed for organizing and paying the aforesaid regiment of the uniformed militia.

The legislature also passed "an act to provide for raising six special regiments for immediate service for defending and protecting the constitution and Union."

This last mentioned act was independent of any previous militia law; and, without naming any other officer, placed the responsibility of raising, organizing, uniforming, arming, equipping and subsisting the regiments solely in the hands of the Governor, with authority to draw his warrants on the state treasurer for all expenditures.

The legislature adjourned on the 27th, and on the same day a general order was issued by the commander-in-chief, designating the companies detailed for the first regiment, and requiring them to hold themselves in readiness to march to the place of rendezvous, to be thereafter designated, on twenty-four hours' notice.

On the 2d day of May the regiment was mustered at Rutland, under the command of Col. J. W. Phelps and Lt. Col. P. T. Washburn; and on the 9th it left its encampment, fully armed, uniformed and equipped, *en route* for Old Point Comfort — being only 24 days after the requisition by telegraph from the secretary of war,

This regiment did important service at Newport News, and was honorably discharged at Brattleboro after the expiration of its term of three months.

On the 7th of May, commissions were issued for recruiting the 2d and 3d regiments of volunteers, for three years' service, or during the war. The impression was common in the state, that these regiments could only be filled by drafting; but the result showed that the sons of Vermont needed no compulsory process to rally them for the defense of their country's flag. The regiments were filled with great despatch, and were mustered at Burlington and St. Johnsbury early in June.

The 2d regiment, under the command of Col. Henry Whiting and Lieut. Col. G. F. Stannard, left their encampment for Washington city, June 24th, and soon afterwards participated in the battle of Bull Run, in the brigade under the command of Col. (now Brig. Gen.) C. C. Howard. They were in the hottest of the fight, and suffered the loss of 66 men in killed, wounded and prisoners. (See Stannard's report.)

In response, afterwards, to an address from the non-commissioned officers of the regiment, Gen. Howard remarked: "I remember you on the march before the 21st of July, at Sangster's, at Centreville, and on the memorable day at Bull Run. I often speak of your behavior on that occasion; cool and steady as regular troops, you stood on the brow of *that* hill and fired your 36 rounds, and retired only at the command of your colonel."

This regiment was afterwards ordered to Fort Griffin, and forms a part of the Vermont brigade.

The 3d regiment remained in camp at St. Johnsbury until the 24th of July. During the time they were thus encamped, there were between two and three hundred cases of measles, and some fifty men were unfit for service when the troops were ordered forward. The regiment, under the command of Col. Wm. F. Smith and Lieut. Col. B. N. Hyde, arrived in Washington city, July 27th, and was immediately ordered forward to Chain Bridge. Here the men performed important work in throwing up intrenchments and making rifle pits, on the Maryland side of the Potomac, and were afterwards sent across the river into Virginia, without tents, being in near proximity to the enemy, and for ten consecutive days and nights *bivouacked*, while constructing the *abattis* and earth works at Fort Marcy. They were afterwards exposed to severe service, as skirmishers and pickets, and are now with the Vermont brigade at Camp Griffin.

At the time of the passage of the act to raise six special regiments, it was not expected that more than two regiments would be called for. The act "authorized and *required* the governor to raise *two* regiments without delay, and, at such time as in his discretion it may be necessary, four other regiments." On the 30th of July, the governor issued the following proclamation:

STATE OF VERMONT, }
Executive Department, }
St. Johnsbury, July 30, 1861. }

By an act of the legislature, passed April 26th, 1861, the governor was "authorized and required to raise, organize and muster into service of the state, without delay, two regiments of soldiers; and at such time as in his discretion it may appear necessary, four other regiments," &c. Under this provision, two regiments — being the 2d and 3d Vermont volunteers — have been raised, uniformed, armed, equipped, and mustered into the service of the United States for the term of three years, or during the war.

The 1st Vermont regiment, having been detailed from the companies composing the uniformed militia of the state, were mustered into the service of the United States, for three months' service, on the 2d day of May last. This regiment, under the command of Col. J. W. Phelps, rendered important service at Newport News, Va., and during their term of enlistment have nobly sustained the honor of the state and the country. Their term of service will expire early in August.

The 2d regiment having been ordered to Washington, participated in the disastrous battle of the 21st. The 3d regiment has been ordered to Washington, where it still remains.

The events of the 21st instant, and the retreat of the United States army from the field near Manassas Junction, demonstrate the necessity of a greatly increased national force; and, although no formal requisition has been made upon me by the secretary of war, nor any apportionment of troops as the quota for this state communicated, yet the events referred to, indicate clearly the necessity of exercising the discretionary power conferred on me by the aforesaid act, for raising and organizing additional regiments. Orders will therefore be issued immediately, to the adjutant and inspector generals, for enlisting the 4th and 5th regiments of volunteers for three years, or during the war, to be tendered to the general government, so soon as it may be practicable to arm, equip and discipline the troops for service.

ERASTUS FAIRBANKS.

By his excellency the governor,
GEO. A. MERRILL, Private Sec'y.

Commissions were issued August 6th, for enlisting the 4th and 5th regiments, and a call having meantime been made by the secretary of war, the governor, on the 20th, issued the following proclamation:

EXECUTIVE DEPARTMENT, }
St. Johnsbury, Aug. 20, 1861. }

To the citizens of Vermont:

An emergency has arisen which demands the active and prompt coöperation of every lover of his country, in efforts to raise and organize troops for the aid and protection of the general government.

In view of imminent danger, an earnest call has been made upon the executive, by direction of the president of the United States, for the two regiments which, under my general order of the 5th inst., are being enlisted—requesting that the troops may be forwarded to Washington with the utmost despatch.

Deeply impressed with the importance of the crisis, I earnestly call upon the citizens, and especially upon the young men of the state, to enroll their names at the several recruiting stations, for the service of their country. Vermont has never been delinquent when called to defend the honor of the national flag, and at this critical juncture, when our invaluable institutions, our dearest privileges, and our national existence even, are imperiled, let it not be said that the Green Mountain state was among the last to fly to the rescue.

ERASTUS FAIRBANKS, Governor
and Commander-in-Chief.

This call was nobly responded to, so that before the middle of September, two full regiments of volunteers were enlisted and mustered—the 4th at Brattleboro, under Col. E. H. Stoughton and Lt. Col. H. N. Worthen, and the 5th at St. Albans, under Col. H. A. Smalley and Lt. Col. S. A. Grant. These regiments arrived at Washington, Sept. 24th-26th, and were assigned to the army of the Potomac, in the Vermont brigade.

A requisition having been made by the secretary of war for the 6th Vermont regiment, commissions were issued on the 17th of September for recruiting; and, in the remarkably short space of thirty days, a full regiment was raised, uniformed, armed, and equipped, under the sole direction of the governor.

This 6th regiment, under the command of Col. N. Lord, Jr., and Lt. Col. A. P. Blount, left their encampment at Montpelier, October 19th, and form a part of the Vermont brigade in the army of the Potomac.

All these regiments were armed with rifle muskets of uniform calibre—the 6th with the Springfield rifles, and the 2d, 3d, 4th, and 5th, with the Enfield rifle muskets.

Two companies of sharp shooters for Berdan's regiment were enlisted in August and September, and left their place of rendezvous at West Randolph for Washington city — the first under Capt. E. Weston, Jr., and the second under Capt. H. R. Stoughton.

Valedictory Address of Erastus Fairbanks, Governor of the State of Vermont, to the General Assembly, at their Annual Session, October, 1861.

The Honorable, the General Assembly of the State of Vermont:

The extraordinary events of the present year—the critical condition of the country, and the very responsible and difficult duties assigned to the executive, under the provisions of the acts of the late extra session of the legislature, furnish a sufficient reason why I should depart from the usual custom in retiring from the executive office, and communicate briefly, in an address to the general assembly, the transactions of the past few months, and especially those pertaining to the organization and equipment of troops for the service of the United States.

Immediately after the passage of the act of April 26th, providing for "the appointment of regimental and field officers," the 1st regiment was detailed from the uniformed militia for three months' service, under the requisition of the president of the United States, and on the 2d day of May, mustered at Rutland.

This regiment, under its accomplished commander, Col. Phelps, did important service at Newport News, and was honorably mustered out of the service of the United States, at Brattleboro', on the 13th of August.

On the 7th of May, orders were issued for recruiting the 2d and 3d regiments of volunteers, under the provisions of the act of the 26th of April, entitled "an act to provide for raising 6 special regiments." These were filled with great dispatch, and mustered at Burlington and St. Johnsbury, early in June.

The 2d regiment, under Col. Whiting, left Burlington for Washington city, June 24th.

The 3d regiment was ordered forward by the secretary of war, July 18th, and left St. Johnsbury, under the command of Col. (now Brig. Gen.) Smith, July 24th.

On the 6th of August, commissions were issued for raising the 4th and 5th regiments of volunteers, which were filled nearly or quite to the maximum number of 1046 men each, and mustered at Brattleboro' and St. Albans, September 12th-14th.

The 4th, under Col. Stoughton, left Brattleboro' for Washington city, September 21st, and the 5th, under Col. Smalley, left St. Albans, September 23d.

These several regiments have been uniformed, equipped, furnished with army wagons and horses, and armed with rifled muskets, at the expense of the state.

On the 17th of September, recruiting officers were appointed for raising the 6th regiment of volunteers, which was filled with great promptitude, and mustered at Montpelier, the first week in October, under the command of Col. Lord—being fully equipped and uniformed, ready to be ordered forward to the seat of war.

These five regiments are composed, principally, of the mechanics and yeomanry of the state, and under their educated and experienced commanders, will, it is believed, form a Vermont brigade.

On the 7th of August, I issued a commission to Capt. E. Weston, Jr., to raise a company of practical sharp shooters, to be organized upon the plan of Col. H. Berdan, as approved and authorized by the president and secretary of war. This company was recruited to the maximum number, and left West Randolph for Col. Berdan's regiment in the army of the Potomac, on the 4th of September.

On the 25th of September, I issued a commission to Capt. H. R. Stoughton, to raise a second company of sharp shooters.

These companies have been or are to be armed, uniformed and equipped by the general government.

A regiment of cavalry has been raised by voluntary enlistment, under a commission of the secretary of war to Col. L. B. Platt.

I have authorized Capt. L. R. Sayles of Leicester, to raise a squadron of cavalry, to form a part of a regiment apportioned to the several New England states, to be organized, uniformed, and equipped, by Gov. Sprague of Rhode Island, and denominated the New England regiment of cavalry. This order is subject to the direction of the legislature.

These several corps are composed of intelligent, independent citizens — volunteers — enlisted for three years, or during the war; and the alacrity with which they have volunteered and entered into the service of the country, is a remarkable and gratifying expression of the devoted patriotism of our citizens, and an unmistakable pledge of the loyalty of Vermont to the government of the United States and the cause of the Union.

I should do injustice to my own feelings, as well as to the officers and men in service, should I fail to mention the uniform testimony which has been communicated to me, of the excellent conduct of our troops. Those of them who have been in active service, have been under excellent discipline, and have, when in posts of danger and fatigue, displayed a coolness, courage and endurance, not excelled by soldiers in the regular army; while their moral bearing and exemplary deportment has won for them the confidence and approbation of their superior officers.

I doubt not that the regiments which have recently joined them, as well as the one soon to follow, will do themselves equal credit, and prove an honor to the state and the country.

It will be recollected that the acts of the extra session, authorizing the raising of these special regiments, is independent of any previous military organization or statute. The responsibility of raising, organizing, uniforming, arming and equipping them, is made the sole duty of the governor. In the absence of any existing military organization or authorized code, this duty has been embarrassing and laborious; and not unfrequently responsibilities were assumed for which no specific authority existed. But in all cases, care has been taken to conform to the obvious intent and meaning of the act aforesaid.

By the provisions of this act, the term of service is limited to two years; and each non-commissioned officer, musician and private, is entitled to receive from the state of Vermont, $7 per month, in addition to the compensation paid by the United States.

The requisition of the president of the United States for troops for three years, or during the war, made it expedient and necessary to adopt a form of contract in accordance thereto, while at the same time it was made to conform to the provisions of the act aforesaid, as follows: "We enlist and agree

51

to serve for the first two years under and by virtue of the provisions of the act of the legislature of this state, entitled an act to provide for raising six special regiments, for immediate service, for protecting and defending the constitution and the Union, approved April 26, 1861, and are to receive the compensation therein provided, and for the third year, under the laws, rules and regulations relating to the army of the United States, and such further compensation, if any, as the legislature of the state of Vermont may hereafter provide." It will be seen, therefore, that should the term of service be extended to the third year, the soldiers thus serving will not be entitled to the $7 per month extra pay, without further legislative provisions.

Every consideration of equity and justice demands that provisions should be made for placing the several corps of citizen soldiers upon the same footing in this regard.

Owing to circumstances beyond my control, it has, until the present time, been impossible to obtain all the vouchers necessary for preparing properly the abstracts to be presented to the treasury department, for the reimbursement of expenses incurred by the state.

An estimate, certified by me to be within the amount actually expended for the first, second and third regiments, was forwarded to Washington by J. W. Stewart, Esq., inspector of finance, early in September, upon which estimate 40 per cent, or $123,000 has been refunded and placed in the state treasury.

The amount of warrants drawn by me upon the Treasurer, up to and including the 4th of October, is $512,362.59; which amount has been disbursed upon proper vouchers for the six regiments aforesaid, under appropriate heads, to be submitted hereafter. Of this amount, $123,000 has been reimbursed by the secretary of the treasury, as above stated.

A few bills for expenses of the 4th and 5th regiments are yet unsettled, as also the recruiting service, transportation, subsistence and incidental expenses of the 7th. There is also a class of claims, which I have not felt authorized to allow, which will probably be presented.

By the act of congress of July 27th, it is provided as follows: "That the secretary of the treasury be, and he is hereby directed, out of any money in the treasury, not otherwise appropriated, to pay to the governor of any state, or his duly authorized agents, the costs, charges, and expenses properly incurred by such state, for enrolling, subsisting, clothing, supplying, arming, equipping, paying and transporting its troops employed in aiding to suppress the present insurrection against the United States, to be settled upon proper vouchers, to be filed and passed upon by the proper accounting officers of the treasury."

I respectfully request the appointment by the legislature, of a commission to examine the accounts for disbursements already made by me for the above purposes, to adjust and settle all outstanding bills, to arrange the vouchers and prepare the necessary abstracts of expenses, to be presented to the secretary of the treasury for allowance under the act aforesaid.

Early in June, I received a letter from T. W. Park, Esq., of San Francisco, Cal., covering a check for $1000, as a patriotic contribution to his native state, "towards defraying the expense of fitting out her sons for the service of the country," which amount I placed in the hands of the state treasurer.

Under the provisions of the act of November 27th, 1860, entitled "an act for the better protection of the treasury," I appointed John W. Stewart, Esq., of Middlebury, inspector of finance, which office he has accepted.

In common with the executives of the other loyal states, whose legislatures were not then in session, I appointed commissioners to the peace convention, so called, which assembled in Washington in February last. The question of providing for reimbursing the expense of this commission is respectfully submitted for the consideration of the legislature.

In accordance with general order No. 25, of the war department, I appointed a board of medical examiners, for the examination of candidates for the office of surgeons of regiments, consisting of Samuel W. Thayer, Jr., M. D., Burlington, Edward E. Phelps, M. D., Windsor, Selim Newell, M. D., St. Johnsbury, who have attended to the duties of their appointment, and the expenses of the board are included in those of the volunteer militia.

I have appointed the Hon. Joseph Poland of Montpelier, a special financial agent to visit and remain with the Vermont regiments at the seat of war, for the purpose of being a medium of communication between the soldiers and their friends and consignees at home, giving information to the men, and receiving and transmitting such portion of their pay as they may desire to send home for investment and safe keeping, or for the use of their families or friends.

Mr. Poland has been constituted by me a trustee of the soldiers aforesaid, for the above service, and has executed a bond, with ample sureties, for the faithful execution of the trust.

The importance of this appointment, both to the officers and men of the regiments and to the state, can hardly be over-estimated; but, as it is not provided for by law, I commend it to the favorable consideration of the legislature.

The multiform and onerous duties relating to the raising, organizing and furnishing the several regiments, the auditing of bills and accounts, the disbursement of funds, &c., imposed upon the executive by the acts of the extra session, rendered it impossible that I should attend to the appointment and correspondence of town agents for the support of families of citizen soldiers; and at my request, the lieutenant governor kindly consented to take charge of that department of the public service.

By his report, which is herewith submitted, it will be seen that the amount drawn from the treasury prior to October 1st, is $1,778.22.

I submit herewith a copy of instructions, prepared by me for the observance of the several town agents, but the experience of the lieutenant governor has shown the importance of a more perfect system, and I respectfully commend the suggestions contained in his report to the consideration of the general assembly.

Under my directions, the quartermaster general has sold a quantity of Windsor rifles belonging to the state, at $13.50 each. These rifles are a good arm, but being without bayonets, and not adapted to the use of our soldiers, they have long remained practically useless to the state.

It has been my purpose to confine this communication to the history of the past, earnestly hoping that the governor elect, who is detained by illness, will, at an early day, be able to lay before you the appropriate business for the session. I therefore omit to call your attention to measures which, under other circumstances, I might deem important.

Gentlemen of the Senate and House of Representatives:

In retiring from the arduous duties of the political year now closing, I desire to express, through you, to the citizens of Vermont, my high appreciation of their confidence and patrotic coöperation in carrying into execution the important measures required by the acts of the special session, and to assure you that I shall carry with me into private life a sacred devotion to the interests of the state and to the cause of our common country.

You, gentlemen, are called to deliberate upon measures more important and vital to the interests of the state and the country, than any which have ever before occupied the attention of the general assembly; requiring your patient, careful and dispassionate deliberation. May an all-wise Providence guide you; and may our Heavenly Father interpose to deliver our beloved country from its present calamity and from the perils which threaten it, and restore to it again the blessings of peace, union and prosperity.

[Careful historians will be engaged to furnish historical papers for this department, which will continue to give an accurate summary of our legislative acts pertaining to the war, and also an account of the part taken by the Vermont soldiers in every engagement in which they have or may be called to participate, so soon as the facts can be gleaned and established for a reliable history — lists of the killed or wounded will also be given by counties, or companies, and anecdotes of the soldiers.—Ed.]

OFFICERS OF REGIMENTS OF VERMONT VOLUNTEERS AS ORGANIZED—(*First 8 Regiments*).

BRIG. GEN. P. T. WASHBURN.

First Regiment.

Colonel, J. Wolcott Phelps.
Lieutenant Colonel, Peter T. Washburn.
Major, Harry N. Worthen.
Chaplain, Rev. Levi H. Stone.

Co. A.—Captain, Lawrence D. Clark; 1st Lieut., Albert B. Jewett; 2d Lieut., John D. Sheridan.

Co. B.—Captain, William W. Pelton; 1st Lieut., Andrew J. Dike; 2d Lieut., Solomon E. Woodward.

Co. C.—Captain, Charles G. Chandler; 1st Lieut., Hiram E. Perkins; 2d Lieut., Freeborn E. Bell.

Co. D.—Dudley K. Andros; 1st Lieut., John B. Pickett, Jr.; 2d Lieut., Roswell Farnham.

Co. E.—Captain, Oscar S. Tuttle; 1st Lieut., Asaph Clark; 2d Lieut., Salmon Dutton.

Co. F.—Captain, William H. Boynton; 1st Lieut., Charles C. Webb; 2d Lieut., Francis B. Gove.

Co. G.—Captain, Joseph Bush; 1st Lieut., William Cronan; 2d Lieut., Ebenezer J. Ormsbee.

Co. H.—Captain, David B. Peck; 1st Lieut., Oscar G. Mower; 2d Lieut., George J. Hager.

Co. I.—Captain, Eben S. Hayward; 1st Lieut., Charles W. Rose; 2d Lieut., Orville W. Heath.

Co. K.—Captain, William Y. W. Ripley; 1st Lieut., George T. Roberts; 2d Lieut., Levi G. Kingsley.

Second Regiment.

Colonel, Henry Whiting.
Lieutenant Colonel, George J. Stannard.
Major, Charles H. Joyce.
Chaplain, Rev. C. B. Smith of Brandon.

Co. A.—Captain, James H. Walbridge; 1st Lieut., Newton Stone; 2d Lieut., William H. Cady.

Co. B.—Captain, Samuel Hope; 1st Lieut., John Howe; 2d Lieut., Enoch Johnson.

Co. C.—Captain, Edward A. Todd; 1st Lieut., John S. Tyler; 2d Lieut., Henry C. Campbell.

Co. D.—Captain, Charles Dillingham; 1st Lieut., William W. Henry; 2d Lieut., Charles C. Gregg.

Co. E.—Captain, Richard Smith; 1st Lieut. Lucius C. Whitney; 2d Lieut., Orville Bixby.

Co. F.—Captain, Francis V. Randall; 1st Lieut., Walter A. Phillips; 2d Lieut., Horace F. Crossman.

Co. G.—Captain, John T. Drew; 1st Lieut., David L. Sharpley; 2d Lieut., Anson H. Weed.

Co. H.—Captain, William T. Burnham; 1st Lieut., Jerome B. Case; 2d Lieut. Chester K. Leach.

Co. I.—Captain, Volney S. Fullam; 1st Lieut., Sherman W. Parkhurst; 2d Lieut., Isaac N. Wadleigh.

Co. K.—Captain, Solon Eaton; 1st Lieut., Amasa S Tracy; 2d Lieut., Jonathan M. Hoyt.

Third Regiment.

Colonel, William F. Smith.
Lieutenant Colonel, Breed N. Hyde.
Major, Walter W. Cochran.
Chaplain, Rev. M. K. Parmalee of Underhill (resigned). Rev. Mr. Mack succeeded.

Co. A.—Captain, Wheelock G. Veazey; 1st Lieut., Frederick Crain; 2d Lieut., Horace W. Floyd.

Co. B.—Captain, Augustine C. West; 1st Lieut., Enoch H. Bartlett; 2d Lieut., John H. Coburn.

Co. C.—Captain, David T. Corbin; 1st Lieut., Danford C. Haviland; 2d Lieut., Edwin M. Noyes.

Co. D.—Captain, Fernando C. Harrington; 1st Lieut., Daniel J. Kenneson; 2d Lieut., Charles Bishop.

Co. E.—Captain, Andrew J. Blanchard; 1st Lieut., Robert D. Whittemore; 2d Lieut., Burr J. Austin.

Co. F.—Captain, Thomas O. Seaver; 1st Lieut., Samuel E. Pingree; 2d Lieut., Edward A. Chandler.

Co. G.—Captain, Lorenzo D. Allen; 1st Lieut., John H. Hutchinson; 2d Lieut., Moses F. Brown.

Co. H.—Captain, Thomas F. House; 1st Lieut. Waterman F. Corey; 2d Lieut., Romeo H. Start.

Co. I.—Captain, Thomas Nelson; 1st Lieut., James Powers; 2d Lieut., Alexander W. Beattie.

Co. K.—Capt. Elon O. Hammond; 1st Lieut., Amasa T. Smith; 2d Lieut., Alonzo E. Pierce.

Fourth Regiment.

Colonel, Edwin H. Stoughton.
Lieutenant Colonel, Harry N. Worthen.
Major, John C. Tyler.
Chaplain, Rev. S. M. Plymton.

Co. A.—John E. Pratt; 1st Lieut., Albert K. Parsons; 2d Lieut., Gideon H. Benton.

Co. B.—Captain, James H. Platt Jr.; 1st Lieut., Alfred K. Nichols; 2d Lieut., Samuel H. Chamberlin.

Co. C.—Captain, Henry B. Atherton; 1st Lieut., George B. French; 2d Lieut., Daniel D. Wheeler.

Co. D.—Captain, George Tucker; 1st Lieut., George W. Quimby; 2d Lieut., John H. Bishop.

Co. E.—Captain, Henry L. Terry; 1st Lieut., Stephen M. Pingree; 2d Lieut., Daniel Lillie.

Co. F.—Captain, Addison Brown, Jr.; 1st Lieut., William C. Holbrook; 2d Lieut., Dennie W. Farr.

Co. G.—Captain, George P. Foster; 1st Lieut., Henry H. Hill; 2d Lieut., Joseph W. D. Carpenter.

Co. H.—Captain, Robert W. Laird; 1st Lieut., Abial W. Fisher; 2d Lieut., J. Byron Brooks.

Co. I.—Captain, Leonard A. Stearns; 1st Lieut., Levi M. Tucker; 2d Lieut., Albert A. Allard.

Co. K.—Captain, Frank B. Gove; 1st Lieut., Charles W. Bontin; 2d Lieut., Wm. C. Tracy.

Fifth Regiment.

Colonel, Henry A. Smalley.
Lieutenant Colonel, Nathan Lord, Jr.
Major, Lewis A. Grant.
Chaplain, Rev. V. M. Simons.

Co. A.—Captain, Charles G. Chandler; 1st Lieut., Alonzo R. Hurlburt; 2d Lieut., Louis M. D. Smith.

Co. B.—Captain, Charles W. Rose; 1st Lieut., Wilson D. Wright; 2d Lieut., Olney A. Comstock.

Co. C.—Captain, John D. Sheridan; 1st Lieut., Friend H. Barney; 2d Lieut., Jesse A. Jewett.

Co. D.—Captain, Reuben C. Benton; 1st Lieut., James W. Stiles; 2d Lieut., Samuel Sumner, Jr.

Co. E.—Captain, Charles P. Dudley; 1st Lieut., William H. H. Peck; 2d Lieut., Samuel E. Burnham.

Co. F.—Captain, Edwin S. Stowell; 1st Lieut., Cyrus R. Crane; 2d Lieut., Eugene A. Hamilton.

Co. G.—Captain, Benjamin R. Jenne; 1st Lieut., Charles T. Allchine; 2d Lieut., Martin J. McManus.

Co. H.—Captain, Charles W. Seagar; 1st Lieut., Cornelius H. Forbes; 2d Lieut., Charles J. Ormsbee.

Co. I.—Captain, John R. Lewis; 1st Lieut., William P. Spalding; 2d Lieut., Henry Ballard.

Co. K.—Captain, Frederick F. Gleason; 1st Lieut., William Symons; 2d Lieut., George J. Hatch.

Sixth Regiment.

Colonel, Nathan Lord, Jr.
Lieutenant Colonel, Asa P. Blunt.
Major, Oscar S. Tuttle.
Chaplain, Rev. S. H. Stone.

Co. A.—Captain, George Parker, Jr.; 1st Lieut., Riley O. Bird; 2d Lieut., Frank G. Butterfield.

Co. B.—Captain, Alonzo B. Hutchinson; 1st Lieut., La Marquis Tubbs; 2d Lieut., Barnard D. Fabyan.

Co. C.—Captain, Jesse C. Spaulding; 1st Lieut., George C. Randall; 2d Lieut., Hiram A. Kimball.

Co. D.—Captain, Oscar A. Hale; 1st Lieut., George H. Phelps; 2d Lieut., Carlos W. Dwinnell.

Co. E.—Captain, Edward W. Barker; 1st Lieut., Thomas R. Clark; 2d Lieut., Frank B. Bradbury.

Co. F.—Captain, Edwin F. Reynolds; 1st Lieut., Elijah Whitney; 2d Lieut., Dennison A. Raxford.

Co. G.—Captain, William H. H. Hall; 1st Lieut., Alfred M. Nevins; 2d Lieut., Edwin C. Lewis.

Co. H.—Captain, David B. Davenport; 1st Lieut., Robinson Templeton; 2d Lieut., Luther Ainsworth.

Co. I.—Captain, Wesley Harelton; 1st Lieut., William B. Reynolds; 2d Lieut., Edwin R. Kinney.

Co. K.—Captain, Elisha L. Barney; 1st Lieut., Lucius Green; 2d Lieut., Alfred H. Keith.

Seventh Regiment.

Colonel, George T. Roberts.
Lieutenant Colonel, Volney S. Fullam.
Major, William C. Holbrook.

Co. A.—Captain, David B. Peck; 1st Lieut., Heman Austin; 2d Lieut., Hiram B. Fish.

Co. B.—Captain, William Cronan; 1st Lieut., Darwin A. Smalley; 2d Lieut., Jackson V. Parker.

Co. C.—Captain, Henry M. Porter; 1st Lieut., Erwin V. N. Hitchcock; 2d Lieut., John G. Dickinson.

Co. D.—Captain, John B. Kilburn; 1st Lieut., William B. Thrall; 2d Lieut., George E. Cross.

Co. E.—Captain, Daniel Landon; 1st Lieut., George W. Sheldon; 2d Lieut., Richard T. Cull.

Co. F.—Captain, Lorenzo D. Brooks; 1st Lieut., Edgar N. Ballard; 2d Lieut., Rodney C. Gates.

Co. G.—Captain, Salmon Dutton; 1st Lieut., George M. R. Howard; 2d Lieut., Leonard P. Bingham.

Co. H.—Captain, Mahlou M. Young; 1st Lieut., Henry H. French; 2d Lieut., George H. Kelley.

Co. I.—Captain, Charles C. Ruggles; 1st Lieut., Charles Clark; 2d Lieut., Austin E. Woodman.

Co. K.—Captain, David P. Barber; 1st Lieut., John L. Moseley; 2d Lieut., Allen Spalding.

Eighth Regiment.

Colonel, Stephen Thomas.
Lieutenant Colonel, Edward M. Brown.
Major, Charles Dillingham.

Co. A.—Captain, Luman M. Grant; 1st Lieut., Moses McFarland; 2d Lieut., Gilman S. Rand.

Co. B.—Captain, Charles B. Child; 1st Lieut., Stephen T. Spalding; 2d Lieut., Frederick D. Butterfield.

Co. C.—Captain, Henry E. Foster; 1st Lieut., Edward B. Weight; 2d Lieut., Frederick J. Fuller.

Co. D.—Captain, Cyrus B. Leach; 1st Lieut., Alfred E. Getchell; 2d Lieut., Darius G. Child.

Co. E.—Captain, Edward Hall; 1st Lieut.

Kilburn Day; 2d Lieut., Truman Kellogg.

Co. F.—Captain, Hiram E. Perkins; 1st Lieut., Daniel S. Foster; 2d Lieut., Carter H. Nason.

Co. G.—Captain, Samuel G. P. Craig; 1st Lieut., Job W. Green; 2d Lieut., John B. Mead.

Co. H.—Captain, Henry F. Dutton; 1st Lieut., Alvin B. Franklin; 2d Lieut., William H. H. Holton.

Co. I.—Captain, William W. Lynde; 1st Lieut., George N. Holland; 2d Lieut., Joshua C. Morse.

Co. K.—Captain, John S. Clark; 1st Lieut., Adonirum J. Howard; 2d Lieut., George F. French.

First Cavalry Regiment.

Colonel, Lemuel B. Platt.
Lieutenant Colonel, Geo. B. Kellogg.
Major, William B. Collins.
Major, John D. Bartlett.

Co. A.—Captain, Frank A. Platt; 1st Lieut., Joel B. Erhardt; 2d Lieut., Ellis B. Edwards.

Co. B.—Captain, George B. Conger; 1st Lieut., William M. Beaman; 2d Lieut., Jed. P. Clark.

Co. C.—Captain, William Wells; 1st Lieut., Henry M. Paige; 2d Lieut., Eli Holden.

Co. D.—Captain, Addison W. Preston; 1st Lieut., John W. Bennett; 2d Lieut., William G. Cummings.

Co. E.—Captain, Samuel P. Rundlett; 1st Lieut., Andrew J. Grover; 2d Lieut., John C. Holmes.

Co. F.—Captain, Josiah Hall; 1st Lieut., Robert Schofield, Jr.; 2d Lieut., Nathaniel E. Hayward.

Co. G.—Captain, James A. Sheldon; 1st Lieut., George H. Bean; 2d Lieut., Dennis M. Blackwer.

Co. H.—Captain, Selah G. Perkins; 1st Lieut., Franklin T. Huntoon; 2d Lieut., Charles A. Adams.

Co. I.—Captain, Edward B. Sawyer; 1st Lieut., Henry C. Flint; 2d Lieut., Josiah Grout, Jr.

Co. K.—Captain, Franklin Moore; 1st Lieut., John S. Ward; 2d Lieut., John Williamson.

Sharp Shooters.

1st Co.—Captain, Edmund Weston, Jr.; 1st Lieut., Charles W. Seaton; 2d Lieut., Martin V. Bronson.

2d Co.—Captain, Homer R. Stoughton; 1st Lieut., Frederick Spalding; 2d Lieut., Henry M. Hall.

3d Co.—Captain, Gilbert Hart; 1st Lieut., Henry Herbert; 2d Lieut., Albert Baxton.

Light Artillery.

1st Battery.—Captain, George W. Duncan; Lieutenants—1st, George T. Hebard,

Edward Rice, Jr.; 2d, Henry N. Colburn, Saimon B. Hebard.

2d Battery.—Captain, Lensie R. Sayles; Lieutenants—1st, Benjamin N. Dyer, Coridon D. Smith; 2d, John A. Quilty, John W. Chase.

NAMES OF VOLUNTEERS,

With their residence, to what regiment and company attached, and their respective ages.

BARNET.

Third Regiment.

Co. C.—Wm. H. Ash; Henry Brock, 30; Jacob C. Goodale, 25; David Somers, 28.

Co. G.—Henry Farewell, 45; Benj. Farewell; Henry C. Thompson, 20; Charles E. Peabody.

Co. I.—Nelson Blodget, 23; John Sulivan, 23; John A. Sutherland, 24; Reynolds A. Kenady.

Fourth Regiment.

George N. Harvey (com. sergt.); Francis Page, 17; Horace Page, 23; Wm. Page, 21; Henry Gilchrist, 20; John Welch.

Sixth Regiment.

Co. B.—Archibald Hariman, 34.

Co. E.—James Gray, 45; Nelson T. Scott; John McGill, 40.

Eighth Regiment.

Co. C.—A. P. Hawley; Geo. Goodale, 23; Eben Goodale; Charles Newman, 20; Robert Morse, 19; Geo. H. Hazeltine, 19; Nathaniel Annis.

First Cavalry Regiment.

Co. D.—Josiah H. Moor; Henry A. Moor; Elijah Page; Byron Morrill; Horace Ide, 22; Loren Brigham, 21; Jas. Davies, 21; James Asden, 19; Wm. Cummings; Bartlett Beard, 50; Charles Beard; Oscar Beard, 20; Henry H. Beard, 24; John Beard; Guy E. Clement.

Berdan's Sharp Shooters.

Augustus Page.

New Hampshire Regiments.

Henry H. Dewey, 22; Wm. Morgan; Geo. Morgan; James Morgan; Azro Morgan.

Massachusetts Regiments.

Albert Hardy; 15th, Benj. P. House.

Miscellaneous.

Robert Cowen, 22; John Farewell, 19; Geo. Ryan, 21; Loren Winslow, 23; Henry Matthews, 22; Edwin Peabody, 20; Joseph Clark; G. C. Clement (corp. cav.); Thomas Guthrie, 20; James Ramsey; Carlos F. McNab, 19.

[From Peter Lindsay, 1st Selectman.]

BURKE.

First Regiment.

Co. D.—Russel B. Page, 48 (cavalry).

Third Regiment.

Co. E.—Charles W. Wells, 16; Charles

Eggleston, 20; Myron Eggleston, 23; Joseph Eggleston, 24; Franklin J. Thomas, 16.

Co. G.—Albert H. Jenkins, 24; Porter Morse, 30; Henry Bruce, 32.

Fourth Regiment.

Co. B.—R. G. Hayward (corp.).
Co. D.—Henry C. Carleton, 22.
Co. G.—James R. Page, 19; Albert Carpenter, 18; Charles C. Clogston, 16.

Seventh Regiment.

Co. H.—Ephraim Orcutt, 18.

Eighth Regiment.

Co. K.—Oramel Parker, 23; Perry Porter, 20; Kingsley Stoddard, 20; Henry Woodruff, 19; Franklin Cheney, 18; Alanson White, 26; Charles C. Burt, 26; Joseph Crotean, 21; Willis Jenkins, 34; Harrison Hunter, 24; Azro H. Henison, 17; Warren S. Norris, 19.

[From A. Burington.]

DANVILLE.

Third Regiment.

Co. G.—Franklin L. Badger, 30; John Gorman, 34; Harvey D. Judkins, 20; Alvin B. Danforth, 25; Charles Danforth, 19; Charles Northrop, 18; Franklin B. Caswell, 19; John Doney, 40; Edward Dana, 21; Nathan Davenport, 35; John Cook, 30.

Wells River Co.—1st Lieut., Danforth C. Haviland.

Fourth Regiment.

Co. H.—Capt., Robert W. Laird, 35; 1st Lieut., Abial W. Fisher, 28; 2d Lieut., Franklin Bradbury, 24; 1st Sergt., Lewis W. Fisher, 24; 2d Sergt., E. H. Stewart, 26; 1st Corp., Silas H. Stone, 25; 5th Corp., Charles P. Hatch, 28. Privates—Wm. S. Allen, 19; Charles Cook, 18; William Ellis, 34; Jacob Forrest, 30; John B. Harris, 19; Hiram Hawkins, 24; Geo. A. Hawkins, 22; Payson S. Hawkins, 23; J. Lundry, 30; John Mc Millan, 22; A. S. McDonald, 26; H. B. Morse, 22; George Parker, 32; Wm. Picket, 34; Horace E. Rowe, 26; Edward Taylor, 36; J. F. Vincent, 18; Ezra B. Weeks, 40; W. Armstrong, 19; Amos C. Barber, 26; Franklin Harris, 25; Calvin J. B. Harris, 25; B. F. Faylor, 34; Morris Aaron, 22; Charles Adams, 24; Wm. J. Sly, 19; Abram Sulham, 30; Edw'd Sulham, 28; Simon Russell, 23; Charles Cowdery, 35.

Allen Guards.—Oliver M. Badger, 18; Charles M. Badger, 22; H. D. Morrill, 18; Daniel Adams, 20; Ward Rollins, 20; John Rollins;* James Morrill, 24.†

First Cavalry Regiment.

Capt., Addison W. Preston, 30; 4th Sergt., Martin V. B. Sargent, 28; 2d Corp., John B. Chace, 33. Privates—Benjamin F. Clefford, 28; Harvey J. Bickford, 26; Charles Bickford, 22; Kyron Morrill, 20; Austin A.

* Of Danville, is serving in an Illinois regiment in Missouri.
† Served in the 5th Massachusetts regiment, and was in the battle of Bull Run.

Bailey, 28; Benjamin F. Carr, 26 (deceased); Amos B. Chace, 35; Edwin Hall, 32.

Butler's Regiment.

Eleazer Morrill, 40; Trefrew Paquien, 22; William W. Bacon, 36 (artillery); Henry A. Crane, 20.

[From M. T. Alexander and Wm. B. Palmer.]

GROTON.

Third Regiment.

Co. C.—Geo. Stebbins, 24; Leveret Page, 24;† Morris Vance,† 23; Charles Burnham, 20;† Charles Burbank, 17;† Charles Jones, 26;† Gardner Orr, 21.†

Co. H.—Moses Page, Jr., 20;† Charles Emery, 23.†

Co. K.—William Scott, 22.†

Fourth Regiment.

Co. B.—George Philbrick, 35.*

Sixth Regiment.

Co. B.—Charles Brock, 20.†
Co. E.—Everett Ricker, 25;† Robt. Taisey, 25.†
Co. K.—George Scott, 2d, 20.†

Eighth Regiment.

Asa Emery, 21;† Charles Emery, 2d, 19.†

Sixth Massachusetts Regiment.

Co. E.—Frederic Glover, 25.*

Seventeenth New York Regiment.

Benjamin Emery, 25.

Forty-Fifth Illinois Regiment.

John Brown, 20.†

[From Rev. O. G. Clark.]

HARDWICK.

Second Regiment.

George T. Brown, 17;† Wyman C. Allen, 21;† Benjamin F. Stuart;† Abial Foy, 21;‡ Isaac Bowen, 28;‡ George Bridgman, 21;† Wm. F. Norris, 20;† Daniel George, 22;† Charles E. Remick, 20;† Charles Canmy.†

Third Regiment.

Orson Marsh, 30;† Albert J. Hoyt, 20;† Andrew J. Dutton, 33;‡ Marshall T. Hatch, 22.†

Fourth Regiment.

Co. D.—Lyman Kibbee, 21;† Charles W. Cade, 24;† Thomas W. Griffin, 28;‡ Wm. Cunningham, 23;† John Bedel, 24;‡ Oscar E. Johnson, 21;† Joseph Houston, 20;† Isaac W. Clifford, 30;‡ Wm. G. Scribner.

Sixth Regiment.

Charles Paine, 21;† Joseph Wakefield, 22;† Chester Smith, 21;† Giles Smith, 21.†

Seventh Regiment.

Co. C.—William H. Ward, 22;† Chas. W. Ward, 19.†

Eighth Regiment.

Oscar E. Rice, 35;‡ Leonard O. Sanborn,

* Married.   † Single.   ‡ Family.

20;† Charles W. Ransom, 20;† Charles F. Goodwin, 24;† Samuel Davison, 18;† Willis Lowell, 19;† Joel T. Houston, 28;‡ Geo. Root, 19;† Philip Root, 17;† Augustus Remick, 17;† George Barrett, 82;† Levi W. Barrett, 28;† Charles Barrett, 24;† Pardon Allen, 18.†
[From Miss A. Stevens.]

Ninth Regiment.

Chas. Warren,† John Gray,† Frank Page.†

First Cavalry Regiment.

Bernard E. Walker, 80.‡

KIRBY.

Second Regiment.

Co. G.—Ephraim Harrington, 28.†

Third Regiment.

Co. I.—Julius Duplissa;* George W. Newhall, 25.†

LYNDON.

Third Regiment.

Co. G.—Charles W. Allen, 20;† John Aldrich, 19;† William Aldrich, 17;† Warren Bradley, 24;† George F. Brown, 23;† Beniah S. Carpenter, 20;† Haynes Carpenter, 23;† Jacob Chapman, Jr., 20;† Orrin Farnsworth, 30;† Russell U. Farnsworth, 22;† George N. Harriman, 20;† William H. Hubbard, 28†; (1st sergt.); Albert H. Jenkins, 21;† Edward Mattocks, M. D., 45 (sergt. maj.);* Edward N. Mattocks, 19;† Felix A. Merchant, 25;† Abel B. Quimby, 19;† George J. Quimby, 24 (corp.);† Romanzo V. Quimby,† 21; Aaron W. Quimby, 56;* Francis B. Root, 82;† Albert F. Scruton, 23;† John W. Whipple, 20;† Chas. W. Hill, 19;† William H. Hunter, 22.† Co. D.—Edson I. Harriman, 18.†

Fourth Regiment.

Geo. Henry Fisher,† 18; Chas. Burt,† 22.

Seventh Regiment.

Dr. Enoch Blanchard, 83 (asst. surgeon);* Leonard Balch, 40;* Charles Balch, 18;† Robert McVicar, 42;* Charles A. Ward, 20.†

Additional Volunteers.

Albert Baker, Austin Miles, Charles Butterfield, Alex. McVicar, Henry Pierce, Henry Deos.

Navy.

Wm. A. Baker, 34;* Abram Hicks,27.*
[From I. W. Sanburn.]

NEWARK.

Third Regiment.

Co. G.—Levi West (died in hospital); Lawrence Ryan (discharged).
Co. K.—Wesley P. Carroll.

Fourth Regiment.

John Ryan.

Sixth Regiment.

Co. E.—B. T. French, Asa B. French, Henry F. Sheldon.

Eighth Regiment.

Co. K.—James W. Smith, Rufus D. Smith, Demming D. Fairbanks, John G. Gordon, Charles R. Carroll, William Bunker, Daniel Cole, Wm. A. Hart, Wm. C. Hudson.

First Vermont Cavalry.

Co. D.—Joseph W. Gordon.
[From H. Bugbee, P. M.]

PEACHAM.

Third Regiment.

Alvin Jones;* Francis E. Sargeant;† Joseph N. Sargeant;† Charles Inman;† Charles Dubois;† Nathaniel Heath;† Lucius O. Morse;† John Glass;† Carlos Parker.†

Fourth Regiment.

E. D. Palmer;* Charles Gilbert;* Francis Field;† William Armstrong;† Nelson West;* Isaac Mann;† David Mann;† Horace E. Rowe.†

Sixth Regiment.

Willard T. Brown;* John Somers;* Wm. F. Jones;* Archibald Gillis;* David Merrill.†

Cavalry Regiment.

Jacob Trussell;† Harvey A. Marckres;† Geo. P. Blair;* Lorrin Chase;* John Gracy, Jr.;† John F. Morse;* Mark Wheeler;* Dennis White.†
[From Miss M. L. K. Pearson.]

RYEGATE.

W. J. Henderson (Capt.);* Thomas Nelson (Capt.), 48;* Alex. Beattie (1st Lieut.), 32;† Henry C. Miller (corporal), 22.† Privates—Charles Lamb, 18;† Samuel Scott, 21;† David Scott, 20;† Henry Gibson, 22;† David Wright, 49;† James Wright, 19;† Henry C. Wright, 17;† Archibald McCall, 21;† Henry McColl, 19;† Henry Neilson, 17;† James A. Chamberlin, 19;† Henry M. Currier, 20;† Albert Langmail, 22;† Horace Page, 22;† Francis Page, 18;† H. W. Gardner, 28;* Thomas Guthrie, 18;† Archibald Guthrie, 17;† James Guthrie, 28;† John R. Holmes, 21;† George W. Hayward,* John Whitcher,* J. T. H. McLure, 27;*—— Wheeler,† John S. Cameron, 21;† Elmore Vance.†
[From Rev. James M. Beattie.]

ST. JOHNSBURY.

Third Regiment.

Co. C.—C. R. Kellum, David E. Harriman, Geo. W. Bonnett, Thomas Howard, William Norris, Alonzo H. Nute, Daniel S. Lee, John W. Ramsey (2d Lieut.), Thomas Bishop, Johb S. Kilby, Hiram Hanscorn, William L. Jackson (hospital steward), John A. Paddock, Ephraim P. Howard, Henry N. Crossman (principal musician), A. O. Kidder, Curtis R. Crossman (clerk to brigade surgeon), Amos H. Robinson, William H. Hawes, Wm. Tuohy, Chas. Hodgdon, D. C. Haviland (1st Lieut., dis.), Franklin Belknapp.

* Married.   † Single.   ‡ Family.

Co. D.—Hugh Montague, James Doyle, Thomas Whalan, Joseph Gartland.

Co. G.—John H. Hutchinson (1st Lieut.), James Dickerman, Moses F. Brown (2d Lieut.), Michael Foly, John McDonnall.

Co. H.—Edward Bailey, Cha.s McCarthy.

Co. I.—Justus Duplesee.

Co. K.—Charles Kennedy.

Band.—Arthur E. Worthen, Oliver W. Hoyer, W. H. Herrick, Charles L. Paddock, Fred. E. Carpenter, Leonard Miles.

Teamster.—W. H. Stevens.

Fourth Regiment.

William Howard.

Co. A.—Oscar F. Guy.

Co. B.—John C. Shay.

Co. G.—J. W. D. Carpenter (2d Lieut.), Stephen H. Brockway.

Co. K.—Charles N. Blake.

Fifth Regiment.

Band.—Edward P. Carpenter (dis.).

Sixth Regiment.

Lieutenant Colonel, Asa P. Blunt.

Co. C.—John F. Murdock, Walter E. Murdock, Dennis Townsend, Daniel W. Cutler.

Co. E.—Elmore W. Pierce, Rensselaer Bickford, George W. Bickford, A. F. Carpenter, Edwin W. Barker.

Seventh Regiment.

Co. C.—Dwight Knapp.

Eighth Regiment.

Co. C.—John Gilman, Orange F. Lyme, Charles E. Dunton, O. F. Haywood, Geo. Hannet, Geo. Howard, John A. Ripley.

Co. C.—Henry V. Severance, Lewis Clark, W. I. Heyer (dis.), George Knapp, Turrill E. Harriman, Nathan F. Jay, Harvey G. Perigo, Michael Carr, Asahel M. F. Dean, Amos Belknapp, Martin H. Wilcox, Francis Cushman, —— Annis.

Co. K.—Edgar Blake.

Cavalry Regiment.

Co. C.—Martin G. Davis.

Co. D.—Darwin J. Wright, John W. Woodbury, Charles Knapp, Joseph Hutchinson (prisoner).

Co. I.—John P. Eddy.

Thirteenth Massachusetts Regiment.

Co. B.—F. O. Baker, John B. Curtis.

Miscellaneous.

Alexander Livingston, Charles West, Orville Hutchinson, R. C. Vaughn, George Mc Curdy, Lewis Merchant, Enos Webber, Lyndon Arnold, William Hannet (died in service), William Pierce, —— Leavit, Orville W. Hutchinson, Hiram Gorham, Benjamin F. Cummings, George G. McCurdy, Charles H. West, Alexander Livingston, Calvin J. Humphrey, Roswell C. Vaughan, Benj. D. West.

[From Dr. I. D. Kilbourne.]

SHEFFIELD.

Warren Bradley, Asa C. Brown, Joseph Barber, Elmere Berry, Edwin Berry, Stephen Berry, Stephen E. Drown, John Elllins, Leon Gorman, Silas E. Gray, William Gray, Sanford Gray, Azro Gray, Jerry Gray, Hiram Gray, William Green, Cyrus Root, James Sympson (deceased), Jacob Miles, Alanson Switzer, Albert Serriton, Aaron Sympson, Charles Sandborn, Alonzo Taytroe, George Walcott.

[From Dr. A. M. Ward.]

SUTTON.

Perry C. Dean, 24;† Hugh Crow, 25;† A. R. Stone, 28;† Charles Hodgdon, 23;† S. W. Cobleigh, 21;† Silas Cobleigh, 23;† Luther B. Harris, 16;† A. P. Blake, 17;† L. P. Clark, 21;† Amos Ham, 26;† Loren Ayers, 26;† David Ratery, 28;† Lawrence Ryan, 22;† Perry Porter, 21;† B. L. Caswell, 20;† L. W. Young, 58.*

[From Rev. L. T. Harris.]

WALDEN.

Marshal Montgomery, Austin Bailey, Amos Cushion, E. D. Dutton,* C. O. Gibson,* Geo. Lowell,* David W. Stevens, Wm. H. Hunt, Alonzo Woodard, Dudley Bixby, Jas. Bailey, Nathan Chamberlin, Geo. P. Foster (Capt.), John Hibbard,* James J. Snow,* Moses S. Clefford, Louis B. Paquet, Levi B. Richardson, John N. Smith, Alanson C. Kitteredge,* Thomas Ferrin,* Freeman Capron,* H. W. Capron, Wm. Smith.

[From Hon. James D. Bell.]

WATERFORD.

Third Regiment.

Co. I.—Samuel C. Chaplin, Samuel S. Stoddard, Jacob Goodell, Ebenezer Goodell, Nelson Blodgett, Joseph S. Bean, Carleton Felch, Alfred Prouty, jr.

[From L. S. Freeman.]

Samuel Fletcher, 27;† Jerome Fletcher, 25;† Dan Rowell, 22;† Ronold Kennedy, 27;† John McDonald, 25;† Geo. Hoag, 20;† John Lee, 26;* Geo. Bonett, 23.†

[From T. A. Cutler.]

WHEELOCK.

[Ages between 21 and 30 years; all single men.]

Third Regiment.

Co. G.—Bial Jones, Henry Folsom.

Fourth Regiment.

Co. G.—Amos Cushion.

Co. H.—Augustus Londry.

Sixth Regiment.

Co. E.—Patrick King, Charles Hill, Austin Copsan,‡ Wm. Judd, Joseph Barber, George Wolcott, Frederick Whitney, Harrison S. Way, Osias D. Matthewson, Daniel S. Jones, Stephen M. Jones, Isaiah Piper, Sanford Gray, David Allard, Roswell L. Copsan, Jas. Riglesby, Frederick Shouty.

[From Hon. T. J. Cree.]

* Married.   † Single.   ‡ Family.

‡ Died at Camp Griffin, Nov. 29, 1861.

CALEDONIA COUNTY VOLUNTEERS —
CONTINUED.

BARNET.

THREE YEARS' MEN.

Tenth Regiment.

Recruits.—Lemuel Shaw, B. H. Fuller, Walter Harvey, Jr., Peter M. Abbott, Hiram B. Somer, Thos. J. Miller, Warren W. Somer. *Co. A.*—H. H. Dewey, Calvin Dewey, M. F. Gerald, William Cady, Atkins Moore, Wm. Wallace, Lyman Bemis.

Eleventh Regiment.

Recruits.—Oliver H. Woods, Austin Goodell, Arthur Wright, William Brierly, Samuel C. Stevens, John A. Collins, Nath, Batchelder, Chester Orr, Waller D. Brock, Peter M. Wilson. *Co. A.*—John C. Stevens, Wm. A. Aiken, Henry Lackie, Samuel Brock, Thomas Gilkerson, Stephen P. Carter, Norman D. Goss.

NINE MONTHS' MEN.

Fifteenth Regiment.

Co. F.—J. C. C. Stevens (Capt.); Moses Lyman, Jr. (2d Lieut.); A. Scott Laughlin, Henry A. Gilfillan, John Sullivan, Magnus D. Brock, Olin H. Harvey, Henry Smilie, William H. Johnston, William S. Brock, Jr., Leonard W. Brock, Peter M. Buchanan, John Conway, Thomas W. Gibson, Alexander P. Gilchrist, James Gilchrist, 2d, Charles Johnson, Joseph Lester, Samuel McLeram, Wm. J. McMullan, Joseph A. Mercer, Arch. J. Miller, Bart. G. Somers, Lewis M. Gibson, George B. Somers, Robert Stevenson, James B. Stuart, Virgil Townshend, David Vance, John S. T. Wallace, Peter Chompeow, George L. Williams, Robert M. Brock, Frank Bedell, Thomas Gilfillan, Robert S. Kelly, Wm. Somers, Henry M. Townshend, Oscar F. Rankin, Daniel W. Phelps, Henry O. Peck, William S. Gilchrist, Thomas Gilkerson, 2d. *Recruits for Company.*—George Galbraith, Stillman Nutting, Benjamin Gadley.

[From Peter Lindsay, first selectman.]

BURKE.

THREE YEARS' MEN.

Third Regiment.

Co. C.—John Carrington. *Recruits for Company.*—James F. Gray, George W. Gates, Halsey H. Packer. *Co. G.*—Aaron Q. Ladd, Porter Morse, Virgil Ladd, George Decamp (recruit). *Co. H.*—Alva P. Bell. *Co. I.*—Harlow W. Jones.

Fourth Regiment.

Co. G.—Alonzo H. Bell.*

Eighth Regiment.

Co. C.—James McHubbard, Phelix Merchant. *Co. H.*—George Gates (substitute); Daniel Cole.

* Dead.

Tenth Regiment.

Co. A.—John Bertheaume, Samuel Merriam, Charles Woodruff, Edward Duval, James Shields, Frank W. Hudson, George Walter.

First Cavalry Regiment.

Co. D.—Warren S. Norris, Azro H. Kenison.

NINE MONTHS' MEN.

Twelfth Regiment.

Co. H.—Sylvester Hall, Elbridge Hall.

Fifteenth Regiment.

Co. E.—Joseph S. Hall, John Andrews, Albert Hendrick, Elbridge C. Freeto, Henry Dudley, True B. Walter, Emery C. Buell, Joseph W. Martin, George W. Humphrey, Willard S. Smith, Sumner Page, Obadiah Moultrix, Jonathan S. Lougee, David W. King, Felix Purhey, Charles Philips, Solomon Petrie, Abram P. Brown.

Miscellaneous.

Horace B. Houston, Marcelles Colby, Geo. Latham, Benj. F. Jenkins, Hiram Farmer.

[From D. W. Cushing, selectman.]

DANVILLE.

Third Regiment.

Co. C.—Edward J. Deane, W. Armstrong. *Co. H.*—William H. H. Stevens. *Co. I.*—John F. Cook (corp.); Alvin B. Danforth.

Fourth Regiment.

Co. G.—Chas. F. Badger (corp.); Samuel D. Rollins. *Co. H.*—Lewis S. Fisher (1st sergt.); Silas H. Stone (sergt.); Nathan B. Stone (corp.); Solon M. Haddock, John F. Colby,

Sixth Regiment.

Co. E.—Brigham D. Ames.

Eighth Regiment.

Co. C.—Silas Houghton, Erza Bedard, John Adams, Josiah Brown. *Co. I.*—Eleazer D. Morrill.

Ninth Regiment.

Co. E.—John Bolton.

Tenth Regiment.

Co. A.—Trefly Payuin, Allen J. Morrill.

Eleventh Regiment.

Co. A.—Francis S. Chase, James Ranson, Orwell R. Kelsey, George N. Frost, Peter M. Wilson, Oliver M. Morse, Martin S. Sanbourn, Charles H. Sanbourn, H. D. Bolton, John W. Hooker, L. J. Weeks, Orra S. Chase, Samuel H. Scales, Andrew Bryan, Morris F. Hunt, Calvin E. Bruce, William H. Nunn, William D. West, James Stuart, Clarke W. Powers, William Salter, Albert C. Scales, Noah Lane, Albert Sulham.

First Vermont Cavalry.

Co. D.—William Cummings (2d Lieut.); Hiram Danforth, Michell Brown, Thomas Murray, J. Page, Frank H. Caswell.

NINE MONTHS' MEN.

Fifteenth Regiment.

Co. B.—Capt., James M. Ayre ; 1st Sergt., Charles D. Brainard ; George E. Sias ; 2d Corp., Joel C. Goodwin ; 5th Corp., W. H. H. Wilbey ; 8th Corp., N. H. Page ; Drummer, Walter Sulham. Privates—Elicom C. Bascom, Charles Burdick, Noah Burdick, Albert Carr, Alonzo Carr, Ethan Carr, Jas. W. Carr, Cyrus B. Clark, Samuel E. Davis, John Dana, Wm. P. French, George H. Galbraith, Rodolphus Goodale, John L. Goodall, Oliver M. Green, Wm. H. H. Haviland, Gardner L. Heath, George W. Howe, Edmund C. Little, Joseph Martin, Samuel P. Martin, Robert Meader, Abner W. Miner, Augustus Morrill, Alden W. Morse, Oliver L. Morse, Henry C. Nute, Stillman N. Nutting, Nathan P. Parker, Edwin L. Reed, Henry M. Roberts, Wm. H. H. Rollins, Lyman Russell, Wm. W. Sias, Fred. G. Stanton, John P. Tilton, Wm. Wallace, Isaac P. Woodward, Putnam D. McMillan, Quartermaster ; George Varney, Wagoner.

[From Miss A. F. Preston, copied from the records of the town, Nov. 23, 1862.]

GROTON.

THREE YEARS' MEN.

Third Regiment.

Co. F.—Charles Dow, Aaron Darling, Wm. Hays, Morris Page, Alva Page, Horace Wood, William Annis.

Co. H.—Jerrie Emery, Reuben Goodwin, Timothy Emery, Isaiah Frost, Rufus Lund.

Sixth Regiment.

Co. B.—John Scott.

First Cavalry Regiment.

Marshall Darling, John Whitehill, Sylvanus Lund.

NINE MONTHS' MEN.

Twelfth Regiment.

Co. B.— Scott Darling, Isaac Ricker, Charles Lamphire, Isaiah D. Ricker, David Miller, Silas B. Morrison, Lafayette Carpenter, Andrew Jackson Carpenter, Augustus M. Heath, Thaddeus Millville, Isaac Goodwin, Willis Vance, Nathan Usher, Daniel Wormwood.

[From Rev. O. G. Clark.]

HARDWICK.

THREE YEARS' MEN.

Milo Scribner, Albert J. Burnham, John C. (illegible), Wm. H Allen, C. O. Gibson, Wesley Alexander, Joseph H. Lane, Prentiss Scribner, D. G. Whitcher, J. G. Parker, M. D. Chandler, Levi Henis, Charles B. Sewall, Jr., Philip Cameron, Harry P. Philbrook, Oliver W. Cross, John Cass, Geo. W. Stevens, Orra C. Cole, Wm. J. Utley, George R. Beach, Pardon W. Allen, Joseph A. Houston, Charles A. Ward, Brainard E. Walker, Saml. B. Davison, Joel G. Houston, Oscar F. Rice,

Orison Marsh, Benj. F. Page, Wm. C. Norris.

[These last ten names are probably the same corrected as on pp. 445-46.—Ed.]

NINE MONTHS' MEN.

Fifteenth Regiment.

William A. Morse, Dean J. Woodbury, Sylvanus Crandall, G. H. Walton, Joseph S. Walton, Corrie W. Sanborn, Josiah Chum, Nathan Field, Wm. W. Gifford, Wm. Kenaston, Wm. H. Stuart, E. T. Howard, Zenas A. Badger, Lucius S. Gissey, Archibald D. Nelson, Charles S. Wakefield, Geo. H. Drew, E. M. Woodbury, B. F. Smith, Joseph H. Magoon, Orrin B. Hall, John Cunningham, Charles E. Cheever, Geo. M. Stevens, Geo. P. Sanborn, Norman J. Kingsbury, Asael Hall, V. M. Currin, Pyam Hovey, John M. Giffin, E. T. Howard.

[From S. R. Goodrich, L. W. Delano, J. W. Blanchard, selectmen of Hardwick.]

KIRBY.

Third Regiment.

Recruits.—Reuben Pease, Jr., Loran Page, Chas. A. Hoadley, Homer S. Young, Wm. Merchant, Bazalael Archer, Benj. C. Wood.

Fourth Regiment.

Co. C.—John S. Russell.

Co. G.—Orvil D. Cobleigh.

Eighth Regiment.

Co C.—Oscar Haywood.

Co. K.—Willard Wood.

Tenth Regiment.

Co. A.—Henry Brown, Merritt Parker, Henry Bailey, George Bailey.

First Cavalry Regiment.

Recruit.—Franklin G. B. Ennet.

Co. I.—Josiah Grout.

NINE MONTHS' MEN.

Fifteenth Regiment.

Co. G.—Sewell H. Bonett, Ransom Smerage, Edson H. Ranney.

Co. K.—Ira Quimby, Franklin E. Cobleigh, Henry A. Joslin, Robert Gunston, Ezra Copp, Jr., Joseph Chasteney, John A. Moore.

[From Charles H. Graves, Esq.]

LYNDON.

THREE YEARS' MEN.

George C. Latham, 25 ; Orville J. Magoon, 21 ; James Courrell, 18 ; Silas Farnsworth, 2d, 21 ; Samuel B. Hadgdon, 19 ; Hobart S. Homer, 29 ; James A. Perry, 18 ; Hiram Taylor, 45 ; David Connell, 20 ; James S. Simpson, 19 ; John Harrigan, 30 ; Samuel Winchester, 32 ; Daniel J. Weed, 45 ; Jonas G. McLoud, 48 ; George L. Sawtell, 18 ; Hubbard O. Stockwell, 25 ; Willard P. Chaffee, 22.

NINE MONTHS' MEN.

Stephen R. McGaffe (Capt.); Henry E. Graves (1st sergt.) ; Charles E. Hammond (3d sergt.); Francis A. Fletcher (4th sergt.); Curtis G. Mooney, Austin M. Bean, Nicholas Ryan, Samuel G. McGaffee, Edwin C. Russell, Porter Williams, Frank Valcoure, Chas. Sidney, John Williams, Jr., Harvey J. Flanders, Arthur McLaughlin, Charles H. Fisher, Mark P. Goodell, Hugh O'Donnell, Moses Miles, Dennis Dubigy, James N. Capron, Joseph Lefo, Sewell H. Bonett, Silas E. Dunton, Hubbard Gaskell, Leon Valle, Frank Hill, Don C. Ayer, Raben W. Ayer, Joseph C. Stevens; Zeno Willey (Corp.) Joseph Aldrich, Edwin Dickerman, and two foreigners, names unknown.

[From Wm. Harvey.]

NEWARK.

Sixth Regiment.

Co. E.—Joseph French, David H. Hudson.

Tenth Regiment.

Co. A.—Thomas J. Drew, James Gordon, Ira B. Cole.

Eleventh Regiment.

Co. A.—Augustus B, Fullerton.

Fifteenth Regiment.

Co. E.—Geo L. Hudson, Russell T. Sleeper, Rufus G. Allard, James B. Ball, Denison F. Corliss, Desany Gould, John P. Smith.

[From D. F. Johnson, John A. Smith, M. W. Stoddard, Selectmen.]

PEACHAM.

Second Regiment

Recruits.—Hazen Hooker, Benjamin H. Merrill.

Eighth Regiment.

Recruit.—Oscar Daniels.

Tenth Regiment.

Co. A.—Arthur McLaughlin, Jr., Robert Haskell, Jerry Fields, Martin Hardy, Wm. Wallace, Charles Lyford, Samuel Mann, Geo. M. D. Dowse.

Eleventh Regiment.

Co. A.—Newell Blanchard, Newcomb Martin, Austin Wheeler, William Mattocks.*
Co. I.—Tisdale Eddy.

Fifteenth Regiment.

John C. Blanchard (1st Lieut.); Leigh R. Pearson (1st sergt.); Harvey Hand, B. John Hand, James Cassady, Wm. Cassady, Chas. P. Varnum, Jonas G. Varnum, Alvin Harriman, Henry N. Clarke, Albert Gould, Stephen Heath, Elijah W, Sargent, Ira H. Waldo, Chas. B. Bickford, Edw. C. Palmer, John Ray, John S. Hight, Enoch G. Barker, George F. Nute, Nelson Bailey, John C. Hendry, Asa Sargent, 2d, Hiram C. Varnum, Samuel M. Farrow.

First Battery.

Recruit.—Alexander Ferguson

ST. JOHNSBURY.

NINE MONTHS' MEN.

John Allen, Henry M. Ayer, Roseme E. Bacon, Milo A. Barbour, Silas M. Beede,

James R. Beede, Horace E. Brockway, Oscar C. Bickford, Oliver A. Brown, Gates B. Bullard, William A. Chapman, Daniel P. Celley, Albert M. Cook, Nelson Cary, Charles C. Chapman, Charles E. Davis, Nathaniel P. Dean, Jr., Henry G. Ely, Albert F. Felch, Ezra B. Gates, George E. Goodall, Nathan P. Harrington, Samuel W. Hall, Albert Harris, Ira A. Harvey, Alfred Howard, Hoyt Dunbar, George H. Ide, Edward M. Ide, James B. Jones, William Lamb, Charles Little, Josiah McGaffy, Elbert W. Miles, Joseph Mudgett, Wm. D. C. Nichols, Hiram T. Page, Edward Potter, Horatio N. Roberts, Chas. H. Ramsey, Edward D. Redington, Franklin Roberts, Solan S. Roberts. Benjamin Rogers, Henry P. Sawyer, Charles F. Spalding, Cyrus Sargent, Theron W. Sernton, George Shorey, Henry Shorey, William H. Sherman, James T. Steele, George A. Stickney, John R. Thompson, Harrison W. Varney, George B. Woodward, Edward P. Warner, Albert F. Wheeler, James D. White, Charles H. Walter, Chauncey L. Welch, Oscar L. Whitelaw, Chas. W. Witcomb, Leslie G. Williamson, Edgar W. Young, Henry S. Young, Carleton P. Frost.

[From Dr. I. D. Kilborne].

SUTTON.

Third Regiment.

Co. G.—Henry Bruce, Mark W. Gray

Fourth Regiment.

Co. D.—William H. Goodwin, Martin H. Bartlett, Marcellus L. Colby, George H. Ball, William F. Stoddard, Charles H. Ball, John Blake, Joel Ball, N. R. Moulton.

Seventh Regiment.

Co. H.—Alvah Elmer.

Ninth Regiment.

Co. H.—Freeman Haswell, Ambrose Allard, Chauncey Allard.

Eleventh Regiment.

Co. D.—Nathan Smith.
Co. H.—Ambrose Allard.
Co. K.—Reuben C. Moulton.

Fifteenth Regiment.

Co. G.—George H. Blake, William C. Gliddon, Lewis W. Gordon, Lucius J. Campbell, Otis Ham, Alvin Jewell, Charles Bundy, Daniel R. Densmore, Sargent J. Whipple, George Bundy, Thomas C. Green, Calvin R. Stone, John B. Webster, Freeman Hyde.
Co. I.—Charles Flint, Aaron Willey.

First Cavalry Regiment.

Co. D.—William Daniels, John N. Frost, Alonzo Wilson, William R. Roundy, Ira S. Bryant.

WATERFORD.

Third Regiment.

Recruit.—Austin H. Hall.
Co. C.—Alonzo C. Armington, Moses A. Parker, Charles Prouty, Lorenzo Hutton.
Co. G.—Charles W. Hall, John McDonald
Co. H.—Gordon Smith.

Co. I.—Valentine N. Blodgett, Wm. Crawford, Frank Hadley, Oliver Sanborn, George Green, Baxsted Bowman, Hiram Davis, Edward C. Morrell.

Fourth Regiment.

Co. G.—Joseph Moreau.

Eighth Regiment.

Co. C.—Eben C. Goodell, Lorin P.Winslow, Harvey Perigo, James K. Bonett, Hiram L. Whipple, Nathan P. Jay.

Tenth Regiment.

Co. A.—Isaac L. Powers, Geo. H. Conley, Charles A. Conley, Charles R. Hoagg, John A. P. Gammel, Jefferson Packard

Eleventh Regiment.

Co. A.—John C. Burnham, Dennis S. Hurd, Charles Ross, A. Harlan, P. Ross, Edward P. Lee, Ellery H. Carter, Warren Phillips, Jas. N. Joslin, Luther C. Bonett, Joseph W. Hutchinson, Marshal J. Packard.

Miscellaneous.

Dorrick Bodett, Ira B. Bennett (U. S.A.); Alanson Priest (N. H. regt).

Cavalry Regiment.

Recruits.—Charles A. Cory, Loren Packard, Thomas Brigham, Chas. W. Brigham.

Co. D.—Elisha C. Page, Geo. B. Davison, Loren Richardson.

NINE MONTHS' MEN.

John Bowman, S. F. Aldrich, E. R. Clark, Emery L. Hovey, Edwin E. Hovey, Samuel Fletcher, Charles J. Stoddard, Jas. C. Lewis, F. J. Dalton, Edgar O. Matthews, J. W. Curtis, Charles W. Davis, Asa L. Hurlburt, Daniel P. Rowell, George B. Rowell, Calvin Green, Lander C. Ormsby, Allen Carpenter, Joseph Valley.

[From Lorenzo Green, Jonathan Farr, Dennis May, selectmen].

WHEELOCK.

Asa Allard, Clark Willey, Oscar Bogue, William H. Jones, John F. Kelly, William J. Ranney, John Wines, Asa Miles, Robert Alston, Artimas C. Whitney, James Highly, Edwin C. Clement, Chester A. ——, Stephen O. Elkins, Levi A. Smith, Stephen S. Cree, Walter W. Chase, Isaac K. Gray, Spencer Drake, Jr., S. R. Willey, Hiram M. Thomas, William L. Ayer, John Sheldon, Norman W. Caswell, John Gadley, Milo Blodgett, Reuben Kelley.

[From Hon. T. Cree.]

Catalogue of a Valuable and Extensive Collection

OF

BOOKS RELATING TO AMERICA,

COMPRISING

Local and State Histories, Revolutionary War, Antiquities, Voyages and Travels, Works on the Indians and the War of 1812–15, American and Foreign Biography, Genealogies, Chronology, &c., &c.,

FOR SALE AT THE PRICES AFFIXED,

BY J. MUNSELL, 78 STATE STREET, ALBANY, N. Y.

Postage on books sent by mail, is one cent an ounce.

ADAIR. *History of the American Indians,* particularly those Nations adjoining to the Mississippi, East and West Florida, Georgia, South and North Carolina, and Virginia; containing an account of their origin, language, manners, religious and civil customs, laws, form of government, punishments, conduct in war, and domestic life, their habits, diet, agriculture, manufactures, diseases, and methods of cure, and other particulars sufficient to render it a complete Indian system, with observations on former historians, &c., and a map of the country. London, 1775, 4o, bds. scarce. $12.

Natural History of the State of New York. 21 vols. cloth, and Map on roller, good copy. $100.

FORCE's *American Archives,* Fifth Series. 3 vols. thick folio, ½ russia. $25.

—— do. vol. 6, Fourth Series. $8.

BURGOYNE. *State of the Expedition from Canada,* as laid before the house of commons, by Lieut. Gen. Burgoyne, and verified by evidence; with a collection of authentic documents, and an addition of many circumstances which were prevented from appearing before the house, by the prorogation of parliament; written and collected by himself, and dedicated to the officers of the army he commanded. London, 1780, 4o, Map of the expedition and 5 plans of battle fields, bds. $10.

—— Another copy, 8vo, bds., $5.

REES. *Cyclopædia,* or Universal Dictionary of Arts, Sciences and Literature. Lond. 1819, 45 vols., 4o, 6 vols. plates, ½ cloth. $40.

HUMPHREYS. *The Illuminated Books of the Middle Ages;* an account of the development and progress of the art of illumination, as a distinct branch of pictorial ornamentation, from the 4th to the 17th centuries; illustrated by a series of examples of the size of the originals, selected from the most beautiful MSS. of the various periods, executed on stone and printed in colors. London, 1849, royal folio, full bound in tur. mor., gilt edges (magnificent work), $50.

WESTWOOD. *Pæolographia Sacra Pictoria :* being a series of Illustrations of the Ancient Versions of the Bible, copied from Illuminated Manuscripts executed between the Fourth and Sixteenth Centuries. Large 4o, 50 splendid plates, ½ turk, top edge gilt. $20.

The *Game of the Chesse* by Wm. Caxton, reproduced in facsimile from a copy in the British Museum, with Remarks on Caxton's Typographical Productions. London, 1860, 4o, $10.

BERJEAU. *Speculum Humanae Salvationis :* le plus ancien Monument de la Xylographie et de la Typographie réunis. Reproduit en facsimile avec Introduction Historique. London, 1861, folio, cloth, $20.

WATT. *Bibliotheca Britannica;* or a General Index to British and Foreign Literature. Edinburgh, 1824, 4 vols., 4o, half tur. mor., neat. $45.

OETTINGER. *Bibliographie Bibliographique*, ou Dictionnaire d
anciens que modernes, relatifs à l'histoire de la vie
hommes célèbres de tous les temps et de toutes les n
dispensable supplement à la Biographie Universelle d
dictionnaires historiques. Leipsic, 1850, 4º, cloth. $

NAUMANN. *Serapeum : Zeitschrift für Bibliothekwissen E
ältere Literatur. Leipsic, 1840-59, 20 vols., 8vo, i
plates, &c., ½ calf, neat. $65.

HONE. *Every Day Book and Table Book*, or everlasting cal
ments, sports, pastimes, ceremonies, manners, custom
each of the 365 days, in past and present times, forn
of the year, months and seasons, and a perpetual ke
don, 1831, 4 vols., 8º, 436 engravings, half sheep. $

AMERICA.

1 BOND, Minnesota and its Resources, 12°, cloth, plates, $1.
2 BRADFORD, Notes on the North West, or Val. of the Up. Mississippi, 12°, p. 302, sewed, 50c.
3 BROWN, History of Illinois, 8°, map, cloth, $2.
4 BROMWELL, History of Immigration to the United States, 8°, cloth, $1.
5 BUCCANEERS of America, Hist. of, 8°, cloth, $1.
6 CALIFORNIA Sketches, with Recollections of the Gold Mines (Kip), 12°, pp. 57, stitched, 15c.
7 CLAVIGERO, History of Mexico, 2 vols. 4°, map and plates, bds., $7.50.
8 COGGESHALL, Hist. American Privateers and Letters of Marque, 1812-14, 8°, plates of naval engagements, cloth, $2.
9 COOPER, History North America, 12°, lacks last leaf, sheep, 38 cents.
10 CURTISS, Western Portraiture and Emigrant's Guide, description of Wisconsin, Illinois, Iowa, Minnesota, &c., 12°, cloth, 50 cents.
11 DANA, Great West, complete Guide to Emigrants, 12°, 1861, cloth, new, $1.
12 DONIPHAN'S Campaign in New Mexico, 12°, map, sewed, 25 cents.
13 DUANE, Visit to Colombia, 1822, 8°, ¼ mor. neat, $1.50.
14 DUNN, Oregon Territory and British North American Fur Trade, 18°, cloth, 50 cents.
15 EMORY, Notes of a Military Reconnoissance in New Mexico and Cal., 1846, 8°, clo., plates, $1.
16 EMORY, Military Reconnoissance from Fort Leavenworth to San Diego in California, including part of the Arkansas, Del Norte, and Gila Rivers, maps and plates, 8°, sheep, $1.25.
17 FREMONT, Geographical Memoir upon Upper California, and map of Oregon and California, 8°, pamphlet, 50 cents.
19 FRENCH, Historical Collections of Louisiana, vol. 1, 8°, $1.75.
— do. vol. 5, port. Bienville, 8°, clo., $1.50.
20 FROST, Pictorial Hist. California, 12°, clo., $1.
21 GAYARRE, History of Louisiana under the French and Spanish, 3 vols. 8°, cloth, $5.
22 GIHON, Kansas; complete History of the Territory to 1857, 12°, pp. 348, stitched, 25 cents.
23 HALL, Sketches of Life and Manners in the West, 2 vols. 12°, cloth, scarce, $1.50.
24 —, Western Land Owner's Manual, 12°, cloth, $1.50.
25 HAMILTON, Hist. National Flag of the United States, 8°, colored plates, cloth, $1.
26 HEAP, Central Route to the Pacific from Mississippi to California, 1853, 8°, plates, cl., 75c.
27 HERNDON and Gibbon, Exploration of the Valley of the Amazon, 4 vols. including maps, 8°, numerous plates, $4.
28 HILDRETH, Pioneer History of the Ohio Valley, &c., 8°, maps and plates, sheep, $2.

29 HINES, Oregon, Prospects, &c.,
30 HISTORICAL Ma concerning the graphy of Amer
31 — vols 1 and 2
33 JANSEN, Strang the genius, m people, and fact &c., 9°, plates, t
35 LONGCHAMP, I lution du Parag torial du Do.te gilt, neat, $1.50.
36 McCLUNG, Ske and Settlement sheep, 75c.
37 MEXICAN War, vols., 8°, numer
38 MIRANDA'S Exp America, 1806,
39 MORMONS. Gui Lake Valley, 12
40 — Book of N
41 SMITH, Nuts fo (Cadwallader p &c.), 8°, cloth,
44 STEAM Boat Dia 12°, engravings,
45 ST. DOMINGO,
46 THORBURN, Fi New York, 18°,
47 TOWNSEND, N the Rocky Mou Sandwich Islan
48 WHITE, Histor thick 8°, map, p
49 — Statistics description by cloth, $2.
50 NEILL'S History est Explorations cloth, $2.
51 PARKER, Iowa cloth, 62 cents.
52 PAYNE, Geral M in a Brazilian bds., 25 cents.
53 PIDGEON, Trad tiquarian Resea $1.50.
54 ROBINSON, Me 2 vols., 8°, port calf, $2.50.
55 — do. Am
56 SABINE, Addre Death of Gen. W
57 SAN FRANCISC portraits and pl

58 SCHOOLCRAFT, Discovery of the Sources of the Mississippi, 1820 to 1832, 8°, maps and plates, cloth, $2.

59 SHELDON, History of Michigan from first settlement to 1815, portraits, 8°, cloth, $1.50.

60 SITGREAVES, Expedition to the Zuni and Colorado Rivers, 8°, plates, sewed, $2.50.

61 WILKIE, Davenport Past and Present, its Early History and Personal Reminiscences, 8°, numerous fine port. and plates, cloth, $1.50.

62 YOAKUM, History of Texas, from 1685 to 1846, 2 vols., 8°, cloth, $5.

Carolinas.

64 CARROLL, Hist. Collections of S. Carolina, embracing rare and valuable pamphlets, &c., 2 vols. 8°, map, cloth, $4.50.

65 FOOTE'S Sketches N. Carolina, 8° cloth, $2.

66 WHEELER, Hist. Sketches North Carolina, 2 vols. in 1, 8°, cloth, plates, $1.50.

Kentucky.

67 ARTHUR & Carpenter, History of Kentucky, 16°, cloth, 50 cents.

68 COLLINS, Hist. Sketches Kentucky, 8°, sheep, map and plates, $2.25.

Connecticut.

69 BARBER, Historical Collections of every town in Conn., 8°, 200 engravings, cloth, $2.50.

70 COTHREN, Hist. of Ancient Woodbury, thick 8° (350 pp. genealogy), portraits, cloth, $2.50.

71 COLLECTIONS Conn. Historical Society, 8°, cloth, $2.25.

72 DE FOREST, Hist. of the Indians of Conn., royal 12°, map, port. and plates, $2.

73 DOD, East Haven, 12°, portraits (Dod Family Record, pp. 24, bound up with it), $1.

74 DWIGHT, Hist. of Hartford Convention, 8°, cloth, $1.50.

75 EVEREST, Poets and Poetry of Connecticut, 8°, cloth, $1.50.

76 HOLLISTER, History of Connecticut, 2 vols. 8°, portraits, cloth, $5.

76*MEAD, Hist. Greenwich, 12°, cloth, $1.25.

77 PHELPS (R. H.), Hist. of Newgate, its insurrections and massacres, and the working of its mines, small 4°, cloth, 1.25.

78 PHELPS (N. A.), Hist. Simsbury, Granby and Canton, 8°, stitched, 75 cents.

79 —— History Copper Mines and Newgate Prison, and Captivity of Daniel Hayes, 8°, pamphlet, 37 cents.

80 STEDMAN, 200th Anniversary of Norwich, 8°, map and colored plates, sewed, $1.50.

Florida.

81 FAIRBANKS, Hist. and Antiquities of St. Augustine, 8°, port., map and plates, cloth, $1.50.

82 LATOUR'S Florida, 8°, ½ sheep (lacks title), $1.

83 SEWALL, Sketches of St. Augustine, 12°, cloth, 50 cents.

84 VIGNOLES, The Floridas, 8°, bds., $1.

Maine.

85 ALLEN, Hist. Norridgewock, 12°, plates, 75c.

86 COLLECTIONS, Historical Society, 6 vols. 8°, cloth, $15.

87 FOLSOM, Saco and Biddeford, 12°, bds., $2

88 LOCK, Hist. Camden, 12°, cloth, $1.50.

89 PIERCE, Hist. Gorham, 8°, cloth, $2.

89*THURSTON, Hist. Winthrop, 12°, cloth, $1.25

90 WILLIAMSON, Hist. Maine, 2 v. 8°, sheep, $5.

Maryland.

91 FISHER, Gaz. Maryland &c., roy. 8°, map, cl. $1.

91*RIDGELY, Annals of Annapolis, 12°, plate, cloth, $1.50.

Massachusetts.

92 ABBOT'S Hist. Andover, 12°, cloth, 75 cents.

93 BARRY, History of Framingham, 8° (200 pp. genealogies), cloth, $2.

94 —— History of Hanover, with family genealogies, 8°, plates, cloth, $2.50.

95 BERKSHIRE Jubilee, 1844, 8°, pl., sewed, 75c.

96 BOSTON, Drake's Hist. of, thick 8°, portraits and plates, cloth, $5.
do.   do. ½ turk., $6.

97 —— List of the Inhabitants of, 1822, place of residence, the valuation of their real and personal property, and amount of taxes assessed upon them, 8°, pp. 200, stitched, $1.

98 —— Massacre, 8°, map and plates, cloth, $1.

99 —— By Laws and Orders of the Town of, 1818, 12°, autograph Wm. Bainbridge, ½ sheep, 62c.

100 BROOKS, Edward, Reply to John A. Lowell respecting Boott estate, thick 8°, privately printed, cloth, $2.

101 CHASE, History Haverhill, thick 8°, portraits and plates, cloth, $2.50.

102 CLARK, Centennial Anniversary at Athol, 8°, pamphlet, $1.

103 ESSEX Institute, Proceedings of the, 2 vols. 8°, vol. 1 in cloth, 2 in paper, $4.

104 —— Hist. Collections of the, 3 vols. small 4°, in Nos., $6.

105 HUTCHINSON'S Massachusetts Bay, 3d vol., wanting to many sets, 8°, paper, $1.

106 LAWS of the Commonwealth, 1780 to 1816, 4 vols. 8°, sheep, $5.

107 MASS. School Returns, 1845–6, 8°, ½ cloth 50c.

108 MINOT, Hist. Mass. Bay, 2 v. in 1, 8°, cl., $2.

109 MITCHELL, Hist. Bridgewater 8° (300 pages genealogies), ½ cloth, $2.

110 NATURAL Hist. of Massachusetts, 5 vols. 8°, plates, various bindings, $20.

111 NORTH American Review, 16 vols., from 13 to 28 inclusive, 8°, ½ sheep, $8.

112 PIERCE, Hist. Harvard University, 8°, ½ calf, plates, stained, 75 cents.
—— do. 8°, cloth, $1.

113 QUINCY'S Municipal History Boston, cloth, plates, $1.25.

114 RAIL Road Jubilee, 1851, 8°, cloth, map, 75c.

115 SIBLEY, History Union, thick 12°, cloth, portraits, $1.25.

116 WARD, History Shrewsbury, 8°, portraits, ½ sheep, $2.

117 WASHBURN, History Leicester, 8°, map, portraits and plates, cloth, $3.

118 YOUNG'S Chronicles of First Planters, 8°, port., cloth, $2.50.

New England.

119 DRAKE, Researches among the British Archives for information relative to the Founders of New England, made in 1858–60, 4°, maps and portrait of Drake, cloth, $3.

120 ELLIOTT, History New England, 2 vols. 8°, portraits, cloth, $4.

121 HAYWARD, New England Gazetteer, 12°, map, sheep, $1.

122 MATHER'S Providences of New England, London, 1856, 12°, port., cloth, $1.25.

123 NEW England Society in New York city, Hilliard's Address and Proceedings at Dinner, 1852, 8°, pamphlet, 25 cents.

124 NEWS from New England, being a True and Last Account of the present bloody wars, 1676, small 4°, reprint, cloth, 50 cents.

125 VOYAGES and Commercial Enterprises of the Sons of New England, 12°, cloth, $1.

126 WINTHROP'S History New England, 2 vols. 8°, port., cloth, $4.50.

126*REVIEW of Savage's Winthrop, 8°, portraits, cloth, 50 cents.

New Hampshire.

127 BARSTOW, History of New Hampshire, 1614 to 1819, 8°, cloth, $2.

128 CHARLTON, New Hampshire as it is, 8°, cloth, portraits and plates, $1.50.

129 COLLECTIONS N. H. Historical Society, 6 vols., 8°, bds., $12.

130 FARMER & Moore's Collections, 8°, 3 vols., bds., $7.50.

131 STONE, Festival of Sons of New Hampshire, 1849, 1853, 2 vols., 8°, cloth, portraits, $2.

New Jersey. .

132 BARBER & Howe, History and Antiquities of New Jersey, thick 8°, new ed., numerous plates, cloth, $3.

133 MULFORD, Civil and Political History of New Jersey, 8°, cloth, $2.

134 PRINCETON Semi-Centennial Jubilee, 1862, 8°, pp. 72, stitched, 38 cents.

135 THOMAS, Pensilvania and West New Jersey in America, 12°, fac simile of edition of 1698, map, cloth, privately printed, $1.25.

136 WHITEHEAD, History of Perth Amboy and Sketches of Men and Events in New Jersey during the Provincial Era, 8°, portraits, cloth, $1.50.

137 CARPENTER & Arthur, History of New Jersey, 12°, cloth, 31 cents.

Pennsylvania.

138 BELISLE, History of Independence Hall, and sketches of the sacred relics preserved there, and Biographies of the Signers, thick 12°, plate, $1.

139 CRAIG, History Pittsburgh, 12°, maps, cloth, $1.25.

New York.

140 ADJUTANT General's Report, New York, 1862, 8°, stitched, 50 cents.

141 BARBER, New York Historical Collections, thick 8°, numerous plates, cloth, $2.50.

142 ———, Pictorial History New York, 8°, map and plates, sheep, $2.50.

143 BELDEN, New York, Past, Present and Future, 12°, cloth, 50 cents.

143*WEEK in Wall Street, 1841, 12°, ½ cloth, 62c.

144 BENTON'S History Herkimer County and Upper Mohawk Valley, 8°, maps and plates, cloth, $2.50.

145 BLAKE'S History Putnam Co., 12°, cloth, $1.50.

146 BOLTON, History Church in Westchester County, thick 8°, portraits, &c., cloth, $3.

147 BRICE, Account of Captivity of Capt. Deitz and John and Robert Brice, and Horrible Massacre of the Deitz Family, &c., 8°, pamphlet, 50 cents.

148 CAMPBELL, Border Warfare of New York during the Revolution, or the Annals of Tryon County, thick 12°, cloth, $1.50.

149 CLEVELAND, Greenwood illustrated, 12°, cloth, loose, 62 cents.

150 COLDEN'S Vindication of the Steam Boat Right, Duer's Letter, and Sullivan's Letter, 3 vols., 8°, ½ calf, neat, $2.50.

151 CONSIDERATIONS in favor of a great state road from Lake Erie to the Hudson River, 8°, pamphlet, 25 cents.

152 COOPER, Battle of Lake Erie, 12°, stitched, 50 cents.

153 DAVIS, Discovery of America by the Northmen, 8°, pamphlet, 25 cents.

154 ———, Shekomeko, or the Moravians in Dutchess County, 8°, pamphlet, 37 cents.

155 DENTON'S New York, 1670, Notes by Furman, 8°, cloth, $1.

156 DE PEYSTER, The Dutch at the North Pole and the Dutch in Maine, 8°, pp. 80, stitch, 25 cents.

157 DE VOE, Market Book, Historical Account of the Public Market in the cities of New York, Philadelphia and Brooklyn, with a brief introduction of every thing sold therein, the introduction of cattle in America, and notices of many remarkable specimens, 8°, cloth, $2.50.

158 DOCUMENTS relative to the Colonial History of the State of New York, procured in Holland, England and France, 11 vols., 4°, cloth (1 vol. index), $36.

159 DOCUMENTARY History of the State of N York, 4 vols., 4°, mor., maps and plates, $

160 ——— 4 vols., 8°, cloth, $8.

161 DUER, New York as it was during the l Century, 8°, pamphlet, 25 cents.

162 DUNLAP'S Hist. of New York, 2 vols, 8°, po and plates, cloth, $3.50.

163 ——— do. for Schools, 2 vols., 12°, cloth, !

164 EMMONS, American Geology, 8°, plates, pa 1, 2 and 5 (all that is published) sheets, $4.

165 GORDON'S Gazetteer of New York, 1836, sheep, map, diagrams of cities and counti $2.50.

166 HAMMOND, Political History of New York notes by Gen. Root, 3 v., 8°, plates, sheep, $

167 HEADLEY, J. T., Report on Criminal Statistics of the State of New York, 1857, 8°, cloth 50 cents.

168 HOUGH'S New York Civil List, 12°, last e mor., $1.

——— do 1858, 12°, mor., 75 cents.

169 ——— St. Lawrence and Franklin Countie thick 8°, maps, portraits and plates, cloth, $

170 ——— Jefferson County, maps, portraits a plates, $3.

171 ——— Lewis County, do, ½ sheep, $2.

172 JOGUES, Captivity among the Mohawks, & by J. G. Shea, 8°, pp. 69, stitched, 75 cents.

173 JONES, Annals of Oneida County, thick t sheep, $3.

174 JOURNAL of the Legislative Council of th Colony of New York, 1691 to 1775, full inde by Dr. O'Callaghan, 2 v., folio, ½ sheep, $

175 JOURNAL of the Votes and Proceedings the General Assembly of the Colony of Ne York, 1743 to 1765, by Hugh Gaine, 2 vol folio, sheep, $10.

176 LEAKE'S Life and Times of Lamb (Revoli tionary History), 8°, maps and port., cloth, $

177 LIVERMORE, Cooperstown and Cooper, 12 cloth, just published, $1.25.

178 LIVINGSTON, Law Register, 8°, port. Ec monds, cloth, 50 cents.

179 LOWVILLE. Academy Semi-Centennial, 8 pp. 133, plates, 50 cents.

180 MARRIAGE Licenses issued by the Secretar of the Province of New York, previous to 178 8°, cloth, $1.50.

181 MEMORIAL of St. Lawrence, Franklin an Clinton Counties in 1825, for a canal survey t the St. Lawrence river, 8°, pamphlet, 25 cents

182 MULTER, Farmer's Law Book and Town Offi cer's Guide, 12°, sheep, $1.

183 OBSERVATIONS on Penitentiary Discipline 8°, pamphlet, 25 cents.

184 O'CALLAGHAN, History of New Netherland or New York under the Dutch, 2 vols., 8° maps and plates, $4.

185 PARKS' Troy Conference Miscellany and Hist Sketch of Methodism, thick 12°, cloth, $1.50

186 PICTURE of New York in 1848, 18°, map and plates, ½ calf, neat, $1.

187 POLITICAL Code of the State of New York 8°, 1860, pp. 607, cloth, new, $1.

188 PRELIMINARY Report of Census 1855, 8°, pamphlet, 25 cents.
189 PRIEST, American Antiquities and Discoveries in the West, 8°, sheep, $2.
190 RANDEL on Erie Canal, 1822, 8°, ½ mor., $1.
191 REPORT on the Condition of the N. Y. State Cabinet of Natural History, and the Historical and Antiquarian Collection, revised edition, 8°, cloth, numerous colored plates, $2.
192 Another copy, a little soiled, 75 cents.
193 REPORTS Regents University, 8°, stitched, odd vols.
194 REPORT of the Debates and Proceedings of the Convention for the Revision of the Constitution of N. Y., 1846, 8°, ½ turk. neat, $3.
195 RUTTENBER, History of the Town of Newburgh, sup. royal 8°, in numbers, maps and plates, $2.50.
196 SIMMS, History of Schoharie County, 8°, plates, sheep, scarce, $5.
197 SIMMS, Trappers of New York (account of celebrated hunters and Sir Wm. Johnson), 12°, cloth, plates, $1.
198 SMITH, History of New York, Albany, 1814, 8°, hds., soiled, $1.
199 SQUIER, Antiquities of New York and the West, 8°, cloth, plates, $1.25.
200 STATE Engineer's Report, 1861, valuable rail road map, cloth, $1.
201 THOMPSON'S Long Island, 2 vols. 8°, portrait and plates, cloth, $5.
202 TOMPKINS' Letter to McIntyre, 1819, 8°, pamphlet, 62 pp., 25 cents.
203 TOWER, Appeal in favor of Chenango Canal, 1830, with statistics, 8°, pamphlet, 25 cents.
204 TRANSACTIONS State Agricultural Society, 8°, cloth, 1849–61, odd vols., each $1.
205 VALENTINE, History of the City of New York, 8°, cloth, maps and plates, $2.
206 WATSON, Annals New York in the Olden Time, 8°, plates, cloth, $2.
207 WOODWORTH'S Reminiscences of Troy, 8°, pamphlet, 25 cents.

Ohio.

208 CIST, Sketches and Statistics of Cincinnati, 12°, portraits and views, cloth, $1.
209 CUMINGS, Western Pilot, charts of Ohio and Mississippi Rivers and Gazetteer of Towns, 8°, plates, ½ sheep, 75 cents.
210 OHIO, Historical Sketch of State Library, 8°, cloth, 50 cents.
211 REPORTS of Commissioner of Statistics, 1857-8-9-60, 4 vols., thin 8°, cloth, $2.

Delaware.

212 FERRIS, original Settlement on the Delaware, and History of Wilmington, 8°, maps and plates, cloth, $1.50.

Pennsylvania.

213 BOWEN, Pictorial Sketch Book of Pennsylvania, 1852, 8°, cloth, $1.
213*Another copy, 1853, with map, $2.
214 BUCK, History of Montgomery Co., within the Schuylkill Valley, royal 8°, cloth, $1.25.
215 BURROWES, State Book of Pennsylvania, maps of counties, 12°, cloth, 50 cents.
216 COLONIAL Records and Archives of Pennsylvania, 28 vols. 8°, ½ sheep, $20.
217 GARRARD, Chambersburg in the Colony and the Revolution, 8°, cloth, 75 cents.
218 HARRIS, Pittsburgh and Western Pennsylvania Directory, 1837, 12°, cloth, 50 cents.
219 MINER, History of Wyoming, 8°, 2 maps, cloth, $1.50.
222 PEARCE, Annals of Luzerne county from the first settlement at Wyoming to 1860, 8°, map and plates, cloth, $2.50.

221 RECORD of Upland County, Pa., and Military Journal kept by Maj. E. Denny, 1781-95, 8°, portraits, map and plates, cloth, $2.50.
222 SANFORD, History of Erie county, Pa., 12°, map and portraits, cloth, 1.50.
223 SIMPSON, Lives of Eminent Philadelphians, thick 4° (large paper copy), 44 steel portraits, cloth, $10.
224 ——   do.   8°, cloth, $5
224 SMITH, Philadelphia as it is in 1852, 12°, map and plates, cloth, 75 cents.
225 THURSTON, Pittsburgh as it is, 12°, map, stitched, 50 cents.
226 WATSON, Annals of Philadelphia and Pennsylvania in the Olden Time, 2 vols. 8°, portraits and plates, cloth, $5.50.
227 WILSON, Picture of Philadelphia for 1824, 12°, plates, sheep, cracked, $1.

Rhode Island.

228 BARTLETT, Rhode Island Colonial Records, 1636 to 1740, 6 vols. 8°, clo. (1st v. sheep), $12.
229 COWELL, Spirit of '76, in Rhode Island (revolutionary history, army lists, &c.), 8°, last ed., cloth, $2.25.
230 KEACH, Burrillville as it was and as it is, 12°, cloth, 50 cents.
231 NEWPORT Illustrated, 12°, engrav., cl., 50c.
232 PETERSON, Hist. Rhode Island, 8°, cl., $1.50.
233 WHITE, Memoir of Slater and History of the Rise and Progress of Cotton Manufacture, 8°, portraits and plates, cloth, scarce, $2.

United States.

234 GRAHAM, Colonial History of United States, 2 vols. port., cloth, $3.50.
—— do. 2d vol. cloth, 50 cents.
235 HAMILTON, History Republic U. S., 4 vols. 8°, port. and plates, cloth (pub. at $10), $6.
236 POUSSIN, The United States, its Power and Progress, 8°, cloth, $1.50.
237 WARDEN, Statistical, Political and Historical Account of the U. S., 3 vols. 8°, maps, bds. (pub. at $10), $4.
238 WILLSON, American History, 8°, maps and plates, cloth, $1.
239 WINTERBOTHAM, View of the U. S., 4 vols. 8°, portraits and maps, $4.

Vermont.

240 EASTMAN, Hist. Vermont, 18°, ½ sheep, 37c.
241 HALL'S History Eastern Vermont, thick 8°, cloth, $3.
242 HEMENWAY, Vermont Gazetteer, 8°, ports., 4 Nos. (as far as printed), issued quarterly, $1.
243 THOMPSON, History Montpelier, 8°, portrait, cloth, $1.25.

Virginia.

244 BIRKBECK, Notes on a Journey from Virginia to Illinois, 8°, ½ calf, map, $1.50.
245 —— another, ½ cloth, 62 cents.
246 BEVERLY, History Virginia, 8°, numerous plates, cloth, $2.
247 CAMPBELL, History of the Colony and Ancient Dominion of Virginia, thick 8°, clo., $3.
248 FOOTE'S Sketches of Virginia, 2d series, 8°, portrait, cloth, $1.50.
249 FORREST, Sketches of Norfolk and Vicinity, including Portsmouth and the adjacent counties, and principal objects of interest in Eastern Virginia, 8°, cloth, $2.
250 HAAS'S History of Western Virginia, $2.
251 HISTORICAL Collections of Virginia, 8°, map and plates, sheep, $3.
252 HISTORY of the Early Settlement and Indian Wars of Western Virginia, 8°, plates, cloth, $2.50.

253 MARTIN & Brockbrough's Comprehensive Description of Virginia and the District of Columbia, 8°, sheep, $2.

254 RICHMOND in By-gone Days, 12°, clo., 75c.

254*SMITH'S History of Virginia, 1819, 2 vols. 8°, plates, sheep, $5.

255 TAYLOR, Lives of Virginia Baptist Ministers, 12°, sheep, $1.

256 VIRGINIA Springs and Natural Curiosities, 12°, cloth, maps and plates, 50 cents.

257 VISIT to Red Sulphur Spring, 8°, paper, 25c.

Wisconsin.

258 CITY of Watertown, map, 12°, pamphlet, 12c.

259 DRAPER, Report on the Common Schools and Educational Interests, 8°, port., cloth, $1.

260 HAINES, Laws for Organization and Government of Towns, 8°, stitched, 25 cents.

261 LAPHAM, Wisconsin, 2d ed., 12°, map, cloth, $1.

262 MADISON City Charter, 8°, pamphlet, 25c.

263 PRAIRIE du Chien, 8°, pamphlet, 12 cents.

264 REVISED Statutes and Laws of, 1859, '60, '61, 4 vols., 8°, ½ sheep, $4.

265 SMITH, History Wisconsin, 2 vols., 8°, cloth, $1.75.

266 WHEELER, Chronicles of Milwaukee, 8°, cloth, $1.25.

267 WISCONSIN Historical Collections, 4 vols., 8°, 2 stitched, and 2 in cloth, $6.

Canada, &c.

268 ANSPACH, History Newfoundland, Fisheries and Trade, 8°, maps, ½ sheep, $1.50.

269 BONNYCASTLE, Canada and the Canadians, 2 vols., 12°, cloth, $1.50.

270 BOSWORTH, Hochelaga Depicta, early history and present state of Montreal, 12°, plates, $1.

271 HALIBURTON, Historical and Statistical Account of Nova Scotia, 2 vols., 8°, map and plates, bds., $3.

272 HERIOT, Travels through the Canadas, 12°, bds., 75 cents.

273 MURRAY, Historical Account of British America, 3 vols., 12°, map and cuts, cloth, $2.50.

274 PERLEY, Handbook for Emigrants to New Brunswick, 12°, map, pamphlet, 25 cents.

275 SERVENTES de Dieu en Canada, 8°, pp. 158, stitched, $1.

276 THELLER, Canada in 1837-8, causes of the late Revolution and its failure, personal adventures of author, &c., 2 vols., 12°, cloth, $1.50.

American Revolution.

277 BOTTA, History of the War of Independence, 2 vols., 8°, sheep, $5.

278 LOSSING'S Pictorial Field Book of the Revolution, 2 vols., 8°, cloth, $8.

279 MOORE, Diary of the American Revolution, 2 vols., 8°, port ., cloth, $5.

280 MORSE, Annals American Revolution, &c., 8°, plates, sheep, $1.75.

281 NEW York City during the American Revolution; a collection of original papers in the Mercantile Library, 4°, map, privately printed on tinted paper, cloth, $5.

282 RAMSEY, History American Revolution, 2 vols., 8°, sheep, $1.50.

283 SPARKS, Correspondence of the Revolution, 4 vols., 8°, cloth, $5.

284 SIMCOE, Military Journal; operations of the Queen's Rangers, 8°, sheep, plates, $5.

285 THORNTON, Pulpit of the American Revolution (political sermons of the period), with introduction and notes, 12°, plates, cloth, $1.50.

286 BURGOYNE, State of the Expedition from Canada, with a collection of authentic documents, &c., 4°, bds., 6 folding maps of battle fields, &c., $8.

287 —— 8° edition, maps, ½ calf, $4.50.

288 WALSH, Appeal, an historical outline of the merits and wrongs of the United States as colonies, and strictures upon the calumnies of the British writers, 8°, bds., $1.25.

289 WATSON, Men and Times of the Revolution, 8°, cloth, $1.50.

290 LEAKE'S Life and Times Gen. John Lamb, 8°, sheep, $2.

American Church.

291 AMERICAN Congregational Year Book, 1858, 8°, stitched, 50 cents.

292 BERRIAN, History Trinity Church, New York, 8°, plates, cloth, $2.

293 BROWN, Old School Presbyterians Vindicated, 8°, cloth, 50 cents.

294 CAMBRIDGE Platform, 1648, 12°, cloth, 30c.

295 CLARK, History St. John's Church, Elizabethtown, N. J., 12°, cloth, $1.

296 CONVERSATIONS with a Churchman, 12°, stitched, 25 cents.

297 CUSHMAN, History Bowdoin Square Church, Boston, 18°, cloth, 25 cents.

298 ECCLESIASTICAL History Connecticut, 8°, cloth, $3.

299 HAWES, Tribute to the Memory of the Pilgrims, and Vindication of the Congregational Churches of New England, 12°, bds., 75 cents.

300 HUMPHREY, Historical Society for the Propagation of the Gospel in Foreign Parts, 8°, cloth, 50 cents.

301 JOBSON, American Methodism, 12°, plates, cloth.

302 KEYSER, Religion of the Northmen, 12°, cloth, $1.

303 MATHER'S Magnalia, 2 vols., 8°, portrait, sheep, neat, $3.50.

—— cloth, new (pub. at $5), $3.

304 MORAVIANS in New York and Connecticut, 8°, plates, cloth, $1.25.

305 REED and Matheson, Visit to Am. Churches by, deputation from the Cong. Union of England and Wales, 2 vols., 12°, cloth, $1.50.

306 RITTER, History Moravian Church in Philadelphia, 8°, portraits, cloth, $1.

307 ROBBINS, Second or Old North Church, Boston, 8°, portraits, cloth, $1.

308 SCHAF, What is Church Hist. ? 12°, cl., 38c.

309 SMITH, Old Redstone, History Western Presbyterianism, early ministers and perilous times, 8°, portraits, &c., cloth, $2.

310 SPRAGUE, Annals of the American Pulpit, 7 vols., 8°, ½ calf, new, $21.

West Indies.

311 COLERIDGE, Six Months in the West Indies, 1825, 16°, map, cloth, 50 cents.

312 EDWARDS, Bryan, History British Colonies in the West Indies, 4th ed., 3 vols., 8°, port., plates and maps, bds., $4.50.

313 RAYNAL, History of the Indies, 5 vols., 8°, port. and maps, calf, $5.

American Indians.

315 ADAIR, History of the American Indians, &c., 4°, map, bds., scarce, $12.

316 ADVENTURES of Hunters and Travelers and Narratives of Border Warfare, 12°, pl., cl., 50c.

317 BRADFORD, Am. Antiquities and Origin and History of the Red Race, 8°, cloth, $1.25.

318 BUCHANAN, History, Manners and Customs of North Am. Indians, 8°, map, ½ cloth, $1.

319 CHATEAUBRIAND, Atala, with Notes, 18°, ½ sheep, 50 cents.

320 DE FOREST'S History of the Indians of Connecticut, 12°, cloth, map, portrait and plates, $2.

321 DRAKE'S Indians of North America, 8°, portraits and plates, cloth, $2.50.

322 EVENTS in Indian History, 8°, numerous folding plates, sheep, $1.50.

324 FROST, Hist. Sketches of the Indians, 12°, numerous wood cuts, cloth, 75 cents.

325 —— The Indian on the Battle Field and in the Wigwam, 12°, wood cuts, cloth, $1.

326 INDIAN Treaties of New York, 1783-92, 4°, maps, ½ turk., $10.

327 JOHNSON'S Narrative of his Captivity and Sketches of Indian Character and Manners, 1890, 12°, ½ cloth, $1.25.

328 McCOY, History of Baptist Indian Missions, &c., 8°, cloth, $1.50.

329 MORGAN'S League of the Iroquois, 8°, map and plates, cloth, $2.

330 PARKMAN, Conspiracy of Pontiac, 2 vols. 12°, cloth, $2.

331 PENHALLOW'S Indian Wars, 4°, cloth, $2.

332 SIMMS, Trappers of New York, 12°, plates, cloth, $1.

333 SCHOOLCRAFT'S Notes on the Iroquois, 8°, portrait and plates, ½ sheep, $1.50.

334 THATCHER'S Indian Biography, &c., 2 vols. 8°, cloth, $1.

335 WHITE, Indian Battles, &c., 12°, cloth, $1.

Government Expeditions, &c.

336 BARTLETT, Explorations in New Mexico, Texas, California, Sonora, and Chihuahua, 2 vols. in 1, 8°, maps and plates, cloth, $4.

337 BLODGETT, Climatology of the United States, and full comparison with Climatology of same latitudes of Europe and Asia, with isothermal and rain charts, sup. royal 8°, sewed, $1.50.

338 CONGRESSIONAL Globe, 1855-57, 6 vols. 4°, ½ russia, $6.

339 EXPLORATIONS and Surveys for a Rail Road Route from the Mississippi River to the Pacific, 12 vols. 4°, cloth (8 vols. ½ russia), numerous plates and maps, $35.

340 —— vols. 1, 2, 3, 4, ½ calf, $6.

341 EMORY, Report on the United States and Mexican Boundary Survey, 2 thick vols. 4°, numerous colored plates, cloth, $10.

342 GILLIAM, Travels in Mexico, 1843-4, and description of California, 12°, cloth, $1.50.

343 LANMAN, Tour to the River Saguenay, and Doniphan's Campaign in Mexico, bound together, 12°, ½ mor., $1.25.

343*PERRY'S United States Japan Expedition, 3 vols. 4°, numerous plates, cloth, $12.

344 REPORT of the Commercial Relations of the United States with all Foreign Nations, 5 vols. 4°, cloth, $5.

345 —— vols. 1, 3, 4, cloth, $3.

346 UNITED States Naval, Astronomical Expedition to the Southern Hemisphere, 4 vols. 4°, ½ calf, numerous plates, $10.

347 UNITED States Coast Survey, 1853-60, 8 vols. 4°, cloth, $10.

Directories and Registers.

348 ALBANY Directory, 44 vols. 12°, bound in 28 half sheep, and 6 vols. 8°, half cloth, complete set, $50.

349 DISTURNELL'S New York State Register for 1858, 12°, cloth, 50 cents.

350 GREAT Metropolis, 1846, 18°, cloth, 20 cents.

351 HANDBOOK for the Stranger in Philadelphia, illustrated, map, stitched, 25 cents.

352 MAINE Register and Business Directory for 1856, 8°, cloth, $1.

353 MAP of Albany, colored, 25 cents.

354 MASSACHUSETTS State Record and Year Book for 1847, 12°, cloth, 50 cents.

355 MASSACHUSETTS Register, 1852, 57, 58, 59, 4 vols. 8°, cloth, $2.

do and Military Record, 1862, 8°, cloth, $2.

356 MILLER'S New York as it is, Stranger's Guide Book, 18°, map and plates, cloth, 25 cents.

357 NEW ENGLAND Business Directory, 1856, thick 8°, half cloth, $1.

358 NEW YORK State Register, 1845, thick 8°, half sheep, 50 cents.

359 RHODE ISLAND Register, 1853, 1856, 2 vols. 12°, cloth, $1.

360 WALTON, Vermont Register, 1853, 18°, stitched, 25 cents.

361 WILLIAMS, New York Annual Register, 4 vols. 12°, 1830, 31, 33, 34, half mor., $1.

362 WILLIAMS' Traveler's Guide United States and Canada, 18°, cloth, 50 cents.

363 DIRECTORIES of Albany, Boston, Cincinnati, Buffalo, Chicago, Pittsburg, New York, Baltimore, Philadelphia, Detroit, New Albany, Indianapolis, Milwaukee, Poughkeepsie, Hudson, Utica (1817), Rome, Schenectady, Syracuse, Troy, Toronto, Newburgh, Jersey City, Hartford, Brooklyn, Fall River, Charlestown, Lynn, Salem, Taunton, Roxbury, Newburyport, Manchester, Kingston, Rondout, Newport and Hoboken, various sizes and prices.

Genealogy.

364 ABBOT Family, 8°, cloth, $1.

365 ADAM Family, 8°, pamphlet, 25 cents.

366 ADAMS Family of Kingston, Mass., 8°, cl., $1.

367 BOND, Genealogies and History Watertown, Mass., 2 vols. in one, thick 8°, portraits and plates, cloth, $4.

368 DUDLEY Family, 8°, cloth, $1.50.

do   do   paper, stained, 75 cents.

369 DURRIE, Steele Family, sup. royal 8°, plates, new ed., cloth, $2.50.

370 HOLGATE, Amer. Genealogy, 4°, sewed, $10.

371 HOYT, Hoyt Family, 8°, portraits, &c., cl., $1.

372 NEW ENGLAND Historical and Genealogical Register, 16 vols. 8°, numerous portraits and plates, half mor., $40.

373 REDFIELD Family, 8°, portraits, cloth, $2.50.

374 SILL Family, 12°, cloth, $1.

375 STETSON Family, 8°, stitched, 63 cents.

376 PREBLE, Genealogical Sketch of the Preble Families, resident in Portland, Me., 1850, 50 copies privately printed, pamphlet, $1.

377 WETMORE Genealogy of America, and its Collateral Branches, with genealogical, biographical and historical notices, 8°, ½ turkey, top edge gilt, $5.

378 WHITMORE'S Handbook American Genealogy, a catalogue of family histories and publications, containing genealogical information, chronologically arranged, 4°, cloth, top edge gilt, $3.

379 WILLIS, McKinstry Family, 8°, paper, 50c.

American Wars.

380 ATHERTON, Suffering and Defeat of the North Western Army under Gen. Winchester, 1812, 18°, half morocco, 75 cents.

381 BATTLES, Sieges and Sea Fights, 18°, sheep, 50 cents.

382 BREWERTON, Wars of the Western Border, 12°, cloth, $1.

383 BURGESS, Battle of Lake Erie, with Notices of Com. Elliot's conduct in that engagement, 12°, plates, cloth, 75 cents.

384 COOPER'S Battle of Lake Erie, 12°, stitched, 38 cents.

385 DAVIS, History Late War, 12°, half morocco, loose, 75 cents.
386 ENTICK, History War in Europe, Asia, Africa, and America, 1748-63, 5 vols., 8°, calf, $5.
387 GILLELAND, History Late War with Great Britain, 12°, sheep, 50 cents.
388 INGERSOLL, History Second War with Great Britain, 8°, sewed, 50 cents.
389 MEXICAN War and its Heroes, with biography of its officers, and account of the conquest of California and New Mexico, 12°, cloth, numerous portraits on wood, $1.
390 NAVAL Battles of U. S., 20 cuts, 12°, cl., $1.
391 STEDMAN, History of the American War, 2 vols., 4°, maps, half calf, $12.

Travels.

392 AMERICANS as they are, tour through Mississippi Valley, 12°, bds., 62 cents.
393 ANBUREY'S Travels through the Interior Parts of America (accompanied Burgoyne's army), 2 vols., 8°, plates, calf, lacks map, $6.
394 Another, half calf, $6
395 BELTRAM'S Pilgrimage in Europe and America, 2 vols., 8°, maps and plates, bds., $2.50.
396 BRADBURY'S Travels in the Interior of America, 1809-11, 8°, bds., $1.25.
397 BRISSOT de Warville's New Travels in U. S., 1788, 8°, sheep, $1.50.
398 COLTON, Three Years in California, 12°, lacks ports., cloth, 50 cents.
399 CATLIN, Notes of Eight Years Travels in Europe, with his North American Collection, 2 vols., 8°, plates, cloth, $2.
400 COCHRAN, Trav¹ls in Colombia, 2 vols., 8°, map and plates, ¹·lf calf, $2.50.
401 COLLECTION of Travels : Sansom in Lower Canada, 1817 ; Mollien in Africa, 1818 ; Maximillian in Brazil, 1815 ; Graham in Portugal and Spain, 1812 ; Bowring in Spain, 1819 ; Brackenridge in Buenos Ayres, 1817, thick 8°, numerous plates, half morocco, $1.50.
402 DWIGHT, Travels in New England and New York, 8°, 4 vols. bds., uncut, $5.
403 ———, Travels in North Germany, 1825, 8°, stitched, $1.
404 EXCURSION through the United States and Canada, 1822-3, 8°, map and plates, $1.50.
405 FAUX'S Tour in U. S., 1818, 8°, bds., $1.50.
405* FIDLER, United States and Canada, 1832, 12°, half cloth, $1.
406 HALL, Francis, Travels in Canada and United States, 1816-17, 8°, half sheep, $1.50.
407 HALL, Capt. Basil, Travels in North America, 1827-8, 2 vols. 8°, bds., $1.
408 HARRIS, Collection Voyages and Travels, 2 vols. thick folio, maps and numerous plates, half calf, uncut, $8.
409 HERIOT, Travels through Canada, and description of picturesque scenery of rivers and lakes, 4°, map and numerous folding plates in colors, calf, neat, $5.
410 HODGSON'S Letters from U. S. and Canada, 1819, 2 vols. 8°, half cloth, $2.
411 HOWITT, Tour in 1819, Indians' descent from lost Ten Tribes, 12°, bds., 75 cents.
412 JOHNSTON, Notes on North America, agricultural, economical and social, 2 vols. 12°, map, cloth, $2.
413 LONG, Voyages and Travels of an Indian Interp reter and Trader, manners and customs of Indians, Posts on the St. Lawrence and Lake Ontario, and Vocabulary, 4°, map, calf, $5.
414 ——— Voyages chez differentes nations sauvages de l'Amerique septentrionale, 12°, sewed, 75 cents.
415 MARCY'S Explorations of the Red River, 8°, with vol. of maps, cloth, $2.

416 MACKENZIE, Voyages from Montreal to the Frozen and Pacific Oceans, 1789-83, maps and port., 4°, calf, $5.
417 MARRYAT, Diary in America, 12°, cloth, 75c.
418 MONTGOMERY, Journey to Guatemala in 1838, 8°, cloth, 50 cents.
419 NOAH, Travels, 8°, sheep, scarce, $2.
420 PIKE, Expedition to the Sources of the Mississippi, through Louisiana and New Spain, 1805-7, 8°, sheep, $1.50.
421 ———, Exploratory Travels through the Western Territories of North America, &c., 4°, map, bds., $5.
422 ROCHEFOUCAULT Liancourt's Travels thro' U. S. and Canada, 1795-7, 2d ed. (3 vols. in 2), 8°, half sheep, $3.
423 STUART, Three Years in North America, 2 vols. 8°, bds., $2.
424 SMITH, Early Indiana Trials and Sketches, thick 8°, portrait, cloth, $2.
425 STANSBURY, Expedition to the Valley of the Great Salt Lake of Utah, and authentic account of the Mormon Settlement, 8°, numerous plates, cloth, $3.

BIBLIOGRAPHY.

426 ANTONIO, Bibliotheca Hispana, 2 vols. folio, calf, $8.
427 ASTLE, Origin and Progress of Writing, as well hieroglyphic as elementary, illustrated with engravings taken from marbles, manuscripts and charters, &c., 1st ed., 4°, ½ turk., neat, $10.
428 BIBLIOTHECA Chethamensis, Cat. of Chetham Library at Manchester, 3 vols. 8°, full calf, neat, $3.
429 BOSSANGE, Catalogue et Prix Courants, 3 vols. 8°, ½ turk., neat, valuable list with prices of books and other articles of European commerce, $5.
430 BRUNET'S Manuel du Libraire, ed. 1810, 3 vols. 8°, calf, $2.50
431 ———, Manuel du Libraire, ed. 1821, 3 vols. 8°, ½ turk., $3.
432 CASIRI, Bibliotheca Arabico-Hispana Escurialensis, 2 vols. folio, calf, neat, $6.
433 CATALOGUE Library Brown University, 8°, cloth, $1.50.
434 ——— Friends' Library, 12°, sheep.
435 CHRISTOPHER, Dict. des Auteurs Classiques Grecs et Latins, 2 vols. 8°, sheep, $2.
436 CHURTON, Literary Annual Register, and catalogue raisonné of new publications for 1845, London, 8°, cloth, 50 cents.
437 CLASSAZIONE dei Libri a Stampa dell' I. E. R. Palatina in corrispondenza di nn nuovo ordinamento dello scibile umano di Francesco Palermo, Firenze, 1854, pp. 388, sup. royal 8°, uncut, sewed, $2.
438 CRITICAL and Historical Account of all the Libraries in Foreign Countries, ancient and modern. 18°, sewed, 50 cents.
439 DE BURE, Cat. de la Valliere, 3 vols. 8°, port. and plates, partly priced, ½ turk., $3.
440 DE BURY, Philobiblon, a treatise on the love of books, 12°, cloth, $2.25.
441 ——— do. Excellent traité sur l'amour des livres, par Richard de Bury, notes by Cocheris, 12°, Paris, 1856, cloth, $2.50.
442 DE ROSSI, De Hebraicæ Typographicæ, 12°, sewed, 50 cents.
446 HOTTINGER, Biblio. Orientalis, 4°, vel., $1.
443 FOX, Book of Martyrs, 4°, sheep, new copy, port. and plates, $3.
444 GOSSETT, Sale Catalogue of Library, priced, ½ turk, $1.
445 HORNE, Introduction to the Study of Bibliography, 2 vols. 8°, plates, bds., $3.50.

:ucke aus dem XV Jahr-
h in der Bibliothek des
Beuerberg befinden, 12°,
½ vel., $2.
Initia Typographia, 4°,

1, Catalogue of Library,
·;, $1.
, 8°, ½ turk.; 50 cents.
f Books published from
852, royal 8°, containing
size, price, publisher's
russia, neat, $2.
ibrary Catalogues, 1831-

le Library Cat., 1850, and
. 8°, ½ mor., $2.
Libraries, 8°, sewed, un-

1glish Historical Library,

1697, ½ calf, $1.25.
iri nella Lingua Italiana,

t of Editions of the Holy
thereof, printed in Ame-
, with Introduction and
, sup. royal 8°, ½ turk.,

graphique, Historique et
ares, 2 vols. 8°, calf, $2.
ia, a brief practical guide
, 24°, cloth, 25 cents.
American Libraries, 8°,

ning ofver de fornamsta
rska Handskrifterna nti
Stockholm, 8°, half turk.,

Grammar, 8°, plates, half

ritish and Foreign Theo-
, sewed, 50 cents.

APHY.

aphical Sketches of the
pal Alumni of the Log
r., 50 cents.
3ketch Book, 8°, cloth,
scarce, $2.50.
anorama, 8°, half sheep,
$1.50.
er and Services of James
at, 25 cents.
fe of, 12°, cloth, portrait,

of, 12°, cloth, 50 cents.
', Life of and Narrative
on, 12°, cloth, neat, $1.
and Writings of Isaac
, cloth, portraits, Edin-

rials of Dead in Boston,

Jecimens of Newspaper
onal memoirs, anecdotes
2°, ports., cloth (2 vols. in

en. Wm. Hull, and Hist.
y Clark, 8°, cloth, $1.50.
utobiographical Sketches,
i), $3.
n, and her conspiracy
or of Pennsylvania, 12°,

lord, Life of, 8°, cl., $1.25.

479 CLARY, Discourse on Timothy Farrar, 8°, pamphlet, 25 cents.
480 COLDEN, Life of Robert Fulton, 8°, port., bds., $1.50.
481 COLERIDGE, Biog. Sketches of S. T. Coleridge, thick 12°, cloth, $1.50.
482 CONE, Spencer H., Life of, 12°, cl., port., $1.
483 COOKE, George Frederick, Dunlap's Life of, 2 vols. thick 18°, half cloth, $2.
484 CROSBY'S Annual Obituary Notices of Eminent Persons, who died in 1857–58, 2 vols. 8°, cloth (all pub.), portraits, $4.
485 CUSTIS, Private Memoirs of Washington, notes by Lossing, 8°, portraits, sheep, $3.
486 CUTTER, Life Gen. Lafayette, 12°, plates, cloth, $1.
487 ——, Life Gen. Putnam, 12°, plates, cl., $1.
488 DARLINGTON, Memorials of John Bartram and Humphrey Marshall, with notices of their Botanical Contemporaries, 8°, plates, cl., $2.
489 DEANE, Silas, Papers relating to his case in France, 8°, half mor., $2.
489*DEXTER, Samuel, Life of, 12°, 30 cents.
490 DODDRIDGE, Remarkable Life of Col. James Gardner, slain at Prestonpans, 1745, 12°, sheep, 50 cents.
491 DOUGLAS, Autobiography of Thomas, of Florida, 12°, port., sewed, $1.
492 DRAKE, Daniel Dr., Life of and Notices of Early Settlement of Cincinnati and its Pioneer Citizens, small 8°, cloth, portrait, $1.
493 DRAKE, History and Biography of the Indians of North America, 8°, ports. and plates, cloth, $2.50.
494 ——, Memoir of Sir Walter Raleigh, thin 4°, port., stitched, large paper copy, $3.
495 DUER, Life of Wm. Lord Stirling, 8°, port. and maps, cloth, $1.
496 DUSENBERY, Monument to Gen. Jackson, 25 Eulogies, &c., Proclamation, Farewell Address, Sketch of Life, &c., 12°, port., cloth, $1.
497 EATON, Life Andrew Jackson, and History of War in the South, 8°, port., sheep, $1.
497*—— Life Gen. William, 8°, sheep, portrait, $1.50.
498 FELLOWS, Veil Removed, or Reflections on Humphrey's Essay on the Life of Israel Putnam; Peabody's Life of same, and Swett's Sketch of Bunker Hill, 12°, cloth, 50 cents.
499 FLANDERS, Life and Times of the Chief Justices, 8°, cloth, $2.50.
500 FRANKLIN, Benjamin, Life of, Albany, 1797, 12°, sheep, last leaf wanting, 50 cents.
501 GARDINER, Dictionary of the Army, thick 12°, cloth, $3.
502 GILLIES, Memoirs of a Literary Veteran, 3 vols., 12°, cloth, $1.50.
503 GOULD, Biographical Dictionary of Eminent Artists, 2 vols., 12°, cloth, $2.
503*GRANT'S American Lady, 12°, cloth, 63c.
504 GRAHAM, Life Gen. Morgan, 12°, cloth, $1.
505 GUNN, Memoirs of Rev. John H. Livingston, 8°, bds., $1.25.
506 GURLEY, Life of Ashmun, Colonial Agent in Liberia, 8°, port., cloth, $1.25.
507 HOLCROFT, Life of Baron Trenck, 8°, half morocco, 50 cents.
508 HOLSTEIN, Memoirs of Simon Bolivar, 8°, sheep, $1.25.
509 IRVING, Life of Columbus, 3 vols., 12°, port., half calf, neat, $4.
510 IRVINGIANA, Memorial of Washington Irving, 4°, cloth, 50 cents.
511 JOHNSTON, Charles, Narrative of Captivity among the Indians, 1790, 12°, half cloth, uncut, $1.25.
512 LANMAN, Dictionary of Congress, biographical sketches of its members from the foundation of the government, 8°, cloth, $3.

513 LEAKE, Life and Times of John Lamb, 8°, port. and plates, sheep, $2.
514 LESTER'S Artists of America, 8°, cloth, numerous fine steel portraits, $2.
515 LEGGETT, William, Life and Writings of, 2 vols., 12°, cloth, $1.50.
516 LIFE of P. T. Barnum, 12°, portrait, cloth, 50c.
517 LIFE of Stephen A. Douglas, 12°, port., cl., $1.
518 LOSSING, Our Countrymen, brief memoirs of Eminent Americans, 12°, ports., cl., $1.25.
519 LUNDY, Benjamin, Life, Travels and Opinions of, 12°, sewed, 50 cents.
520 MACKENZIE, Life and Opinions of Benjamin F. Butler and Jesse Hoyt, &c., 8°, stitched, 50c.
521 MALLORY'S Life and Speeches of Henry Clay, 2 vols., 8°, cloth, portrait, monument and view of Ashland, $2 (pub. at $4.50.)
522 MANSFIELD'S Life and Services of Gen. Winfield Scott, thick 12°, port., cloth, 50 cents.
523 MARSHALL, Life Washington, 5 vols., 8°, and Atlas, cloth, stained, $6.
524 MAURY, The Statesmen of America in 1846, 12°, bds., 37 cents.
525 MEMOIR of Nicholas Hill, Member of the Bar of New York, 8°, port., cloth, 75 cents.
526 MEMOIR of Rev. Edward Payson, 18°, port., sheep, 25 cents.
527 MEN of the Time, thick 16° (London, published at $3.50), $2.
528 MOORE, Lives Governors of New Plymouth and Massachusetts Bay, 8°, port., cloth, $1.
529 ———, Memoirs of American Governors, 8°, portraits, cloth, $2.
530 MURPHY, Biographical Sketches New York Legislature, 1858, 12°, paper, 38 cents.
531 NARRATIVE of Jewett, only survivor of crew of ship Boston, captivity of three years at Nootka Sound, with manners of the Natives, 12°, sheep, 50 cents.
532 NEW General Biographical Dictionary, most eminent persons in every nation, 1798, 15 vols., 8°, sheep, $15.
533 NOTICE, Wm. Thaddeus Harris, small 4°, pamphlet, 25 cents.
534 RAYMOND, Biographical Sketches of Distinguished Men of Columbia Co., 8°, stitched, $1.
535 REED, Joseph, Life and Correspondence of, Washington's Military Secretary, &c., 2 vols., 8°, cloth, portrait, $4.
536 ROGERS'S American Biographical Dictionary, 8°, best ed., sheep, $2.50.
537 ROSE, New General Biographical Dictionary, 12 vols., 8°, cloth, $25.
538 RUSH, Washington in Domestic Life, 8°, cl., $1.
539 SABINE'S Am. Loyalists, 8°, cloth, $2.75.
540 SARGENT, Life and Services Henry Clay, 8°, port., cloth, 38 cents.
541 SARRANS, Memoir Gen. Lafayette and French Revolution of 1830, 12°, cloth, $1.
542 SCHOOLCRAFT'S Life of Lewis Cass, 8°, stitched, 25 cents.
543 SPARKS'S Life of Washington, 8°, cl., port., $3.
544 STONE, Life of Brant, 2 vols., 8°, portraits and plates, cloth, $4.
545 SULLIVAN, James, Life of, 2 vols., 8°, cloth, port., $1.
546 SHAW, Life Fourier, 12°, port., paper (published at $1), 25 cents.
547 SHEA, The Fallen Brave, biographical memorial of the American officers who have given their lives for the preservation of the American Union, 4°, 8 portraits, cloth, $3.
548 SIMMS, Life Francis Marion, 12°, plates, cl., $1.
549 SIMPSON, Life and Travels of Thomas Simpson, Arctic Discoverer, 8°, port., cloth (published at $2), $1.
550 SKETCH of Life and Public Services Amos Pilsbury, 8°, port., cloth, $1.

551 SMITH, Recollections of Nettleton, 18°, cloth, 25 cents.
552 SMUCKER, Life Alexander Hamilton, 12°, port., cloth, $1.
553 SPRAGUE, Character of Wilberforce, Address to Literary Societies, Wesleyan University, 8°, pamphlet, 25 cents.
554 STEELE, Life and Time of William Brewster, Chief of the Pilgrims, 8°, plates, cloth, $1.50.
555 THATCHER, Indian Biographies, 12°, cl., $1.
556 THIERS, Mississippi Bubble, a Memoir of John Law, 12°, cloth, $1.
557 THOMAS, Abel, Memoir of, Quaker minister, 12°, half sheep, 62 cents.
558 THOMPSON, Memoir of David Hale, 12°, port., cloth, $1.
558*UNCAS and Miantonimoh, 18°, cloth, 38c.
559 VAN SCHAACK, Henry Cruger, the Colleague of Burke in the British Parliament, 8°, pamphlet, 38 cents.
559*VESPUCIUS, Americus, and his Voyages, 12°, cloth, 50 cents.
560 WARNER, Autobiography of Charles Caldwell, M. D., 8°, port., cloth, $1.50.
561 WEBSTER, Daniel, Discourse on Adams and Jefferson, 1826, 8°, stitched, 25 cents.
562 WESTCOTT'S Life of John Fitch, 12°, cl., $1.
563 WILLIAMS, Life of Te-ho-ra-gwa-ne-gen, alias Thomas Williams, a Chief of the Caughnawaga Tribe of Indians in Canada (with notice of Eleazer Williams his son, the reputed Bourbon), royal 8°, cloth, neat, $1.50.
564 WILMER, Life and Travels of Ferdinand de Soto, Discoverer of the Mississippi, portraits and plates, 8°, cloth, $2.50.
565 WILSON, Eccentric Mirror, male and female characters, ancient and modern, who have been particularly distinguished by extraordinary longevity, conformation, bulk, stature, propensities, &c., 4 vols., 12°, plates, binding cracked, curious work, $8.
566 WIRT, Life Patrick Henry, 12°, port., cl., $1.
567 WOODWARD, Life Gen. Lyon, 12°, port., cloth, $1.50.
568 YOUNG'S Life Cass, cloth, 8°, 75 cents.
569 YOUNG, Life and Character John Thorndike Kirkland, 8°, stitched, 50 cents.

CHRONOLOGY.

570 ALEXANDER, Chronology of the Ancient World. London, 1838, 8°, pp. 64, cloth, 60c.
571 ASPIN, Complete System of Chronology, an universal history abridged. London, 1812, 8°, calf, $1.50.
572 BLAIR'S Chronological Tables, revised and enlarged by Rosse, thick 12°, cloth, $2.
573 BRITISH Chronologist, comprehending every material occurrence, ecclesiastical, civil or military, relative to England and Wales, since the invasion by the Romans. London, 1775, 8°, 3 vols., calf, $3.
574 CHRONOLOGICAL Record of the Remarkable Public Events during the reigns of George III and IV. London, 1826, 8°, cloth, $1.25.
575 DARBY, Mnemonika, a Register of Events, 12°, sheep, 75 cents.
576 EDWARDS, Year Book, thick 12°, cloth, $1.
577 HARDIE, Am. Remembrancer, 12°, sheep, 75c.
577*HIST. Chronological and Geographical American Atlas, North and South America and West Indies, folio, sheep, $6.
579 HISTORICAL Register ; a Chron. Diary of the most remarkable events of Europe. London, 1714–38, 8°, 25 vols. calf, a few vols. slightly cracked, uniform set, $15.

A valuable early record of events during an important period, beginning nearly fifty years before the Annual Register.

578 JACKSON, Chronological Antiquities of the most ancient kingdoms, from the creation of the world for the space of 5000 years, 4°, 3 vols. in 2, half calf, $5.

580 MUNSELL, Chronology of Paper and Paper Making. Albany, 1857, 8°, pp. 110, cloth, extra, $1.50.

581 —— Every Day Book of History and Chronology. New York, 1858, 8°, clo., $2.50

582 PUBLIC Events and Remarkable Occurrences, 1772 to 1822, thick 16°, chart, cloth, $1.

583 PUTNAM, World's Progress; a dictionary of dates, with tabular views of general history, N. Y., 1850, thick 12°, cloth, $1.25.

584 SHALLUS, Chronological Tables for Every Day in the Year, 2 vols. 12°, sheep, $2.

585 TALLENT'S Chronological Tables. London, 1758, folio, with indexes, half sheep, $2.

586 TRUSLER, The Historian's Vade Mecum, 2 vols. 12°, calf, $2.

587 TEGG, Dict. of Chronology, thick 12°, cl., $2.

588 WARDEN, L'Art de Verifier les Dates, Chronologie Historique de l'Amerique, 10 vols. 8°, sheep, $10.

EARLY PRINTED BOOKS, ETC.

589 BAY Psalm Book, literal reprint of; being the earliest version of the Psalms, and the first book printed in America 8° (only 50 copies printed for subscribers), cloth, $12.

590 BOOK of Ruth, illustrated by the Lady Augusta Cadogan. London, small 4°, black letter, 8 plates, cloth, $2.

591 CANTICUM Canticorum, reproduced in fac simile from the Scriverius copy in the British Museum, with an hist. and bib. introduction. London, 1860, folio, vellum, $7.50.

592 HOLTROP, Confessionale ou Beichtspiegel nach den zehn Geboten, reproduit en fac simile d'après l'unique exemplaire conservé au Museum Meermanno-Westreenianum, avec une introduction, cloth, $3.40.

Reprint of an ancient Confessional in fac simile, the original has sold as high as $40.

593 HOLY Bible (the Breeches, or Geneva version), containing the Old and New Testament, Apocrypha, and the Psalms in metre by Sternhold & Hopkins, with musical notes, small 4°, quite complete excepting title page, dark calf, numerous wood cuts, $6.

This is a copy of one of the early editions of the Bible first printed at Geneva by Coverdale and others, 1560, and derives the title by which it is known in commerce, of the Breeches Bible, from Genesis iii. 7: "And the eyes of them both were opened, and they knew that they were naked, and they sewed figge tree leaves together, and made themselves breeches." This version has a great historical as well as a sacred interest attached to it, as it was the first edition furnished to the people in a comparatively portable form, and at a moderate price, and therefore had a large circulation during the reigns of Elizabeth and James I. The communion service bound up with it is of King James's time, as appears from the prayers. The first leaf of Genesis is lost, and its place supplied by another from the translation of James of 1611. The metrical Psalms at the end contain the date of 1610, and the annotations are by Beza, probably.

594 PARALDI, Summe Summarium. Lugdunensis, M. cccc.xvii, square 8°, rubricated, parchment cover, a little wormed, $5.

595 POMPONII Melæ de Orbis Situ libri tres, accuratis sine emendati, una cum commentariis Ioachimi Vadiani Heluetii castigatioribus, et multis in locis auctioribus factis, &c., folio. Basil, 1522, neat, $5.

596 POSTILLE Majores totius anni cum multis Historiis, sive figuris magnis et mediocribus Evangeliorum, etc. Lugdunum, 1527, 4°, vellum, $5

597 TRILOGIUM Anime, non solum religiosis, etc. (three discourses on the soul for preachers and confessors). Nuremberg, Koberger, 1498, thick 4°, original calf, clasps, $5.50.

598 TUTOR to Astronomy and Geography, or an easie and speedy way to know the use of both the Globes, coelestial and terrestial, by Joseph Moxon. London, 1686, small 4°, calf, $1.

HORSE.

600 BAUCHER, Method of Horsemanship, 12°, plates, cloth, $1.

601 OLD Jim Avery's own Farrier and Receipt Book, 12°, portrait and plates, $1.

602 SOLES, Original and Interesting Book on the Horse, 12°, stitched, 25 cents.

603 STEPHEN, Adventures of a Gentleman in Search of a Horse, 12°, plates, $1.

FREE MASONRY.

604 CALCOTT'S Masonry, with additions, 18°, sheep, 50 cents.

605 HARRIS, Discourses, 8°, plates, sheep, $1.50.

606 VOCAL Assistant and Register of the Lodges of Masons in South Carolina and Georgia, 12°, sheep, $1.25.

MILITARY AND NAVAL.

607 BEATSON, Naval and Military Memoirs of Great Britain, 6 vols. 8°, bds., $12.

608 BY LAWS, Muster Roll and Archives of Phil. City Cavalry, 12°, half mor., 75 cents.

609 CITIZEN Soldiers at North Point and Fort McHenry, 1814, 12° (muster roll, attack on Baltimore, &c.), half mor., interleaved, $1.50.

610 COOPER'S Naval History, 2 vols. in 1, 8°, half calf, $2.50.

611 KNOX, Historical Journal of the Campaigns in North America, 1757-60, containing the most remarkable occurrences of that period, particularly the two sieges of Quebec, &c., London, 1769, 2 vols. 4°, map and portraits of Amherst and Wolfe, full calf, $15.

612 MILITARY Trials, Abbot vs. Binney, 1822; Porter vs. Abbot, 1822; Hull vs. Shaw, 1822, thick 8°, half mor., $2.

613 MORDECAI'S Report of Military Commission to Europe and Schon's description of the modern system of Small Arms in European Armies, 4°, plates, $1.25.

614 NAVY Register, 1826, 12°, half mor., 25 cents.

615 RULES and Instructions for Naval Service U. S., 1818, 12°, bds., 37 cents.

616 THREE Years' Service in the War of Extermination in Venezuela and Colombia, 1828, 8°, 2 vols. in 1, half calf, $1.50.

616*SMITH, Monthly Military Repository, 8°, vol. 1, imperfect, 50 cents.

617 WHITWORTH, Collection of the Supplies and Ways and Means from the Revolution to the Present Time, Lond., 1764, 12°, sheep, 50c.

NUMISMATICS.

618 DICKESON, American Numismatic Manual of the currency of the Aborigines, and Colonial. State and U. S. Coins, 4°, cloth, portrait and 20 plates, colored, $5.

619 GOUGE, History of Paper Money and Banking in the U. S., and account of provincial and continental paper money, &c., 8°, stitched, 50c.

620 HICKCOX, Historical Account of American Coinage, with plates, 4°, large paper copy, sewed, uncut, $10 (out of print).

621 PHILIPS, Historical Sketch of the Paper Money issued by Pennsylvania, 8°, pamp., 37c.

622 SATTERLEE, Arrangement of Medals and Tokens struck in honor of the Presidents of the United States and Presidential Candidates, 8°, cloth, $1.

NATURAL HISTORY.

623 AGASSIZ, Contributions to the Natural History of the United States of America, 4 vols. folio (all that are published), cl., plates, $40.

624 CORDA, Contribution to the Knowledge of the different kinds of Brand in Cereals and Blight in Grain, thin 4°, 3 fine pl., sewed, $1.

625 HORSFORD, Solidification of the Coral Reefs of Florida, and source of lime in the growth of Corals, 8°, stitched, 25 cents.

626 NATURAL History of the State of New York, 21 vols. 4°, cloth, and mounted map, $100.

627 RAFINESQUE, Monograph of the Fluveatile Bivalve Shells of the Ohio, 12°, colored plate, cloth, $1.25.

PHILOLOGY.

628 ARTHUR'S Derivation of Family Names, 12°, cloth, $1.25.

629 BARTLETT'S Dict. of Americanisms, 8°, cloth, $2.50.

630 CHAMBERS, Hist. English Language and Literature, with American contributions by Robbins, 12°, cloth, 40 cents.

631 GOURAUD, Cosmophonography, system of writing and printing in all the principal languages (Lord's Prayer in 100 languages), 8°, cloth, $1.

632 HALL'S College Words and Customs, 12°, cloth, $1.50.

633 SIMS, Origin and Derivation of Scottish Surnames, 8°, cloth, neat, $2.

POETRY.

634 ANARCHIAD, written in concert by Humphreys, Barlow, Trumbull and Hopkins, 16°, cloth, 50 cents.

634* BARLOW, Vision of Columbus, 12°, 1787, half calf, $1.

635 CASE, Revolutionary Memorials, 12°, cloth, neat, 30 cents.

636 CROAKERS, by Joseph Rodman Drake and Fitz Greene Halleck, first complete edition, with notes, 2 fine portraits, published by the Bradford Club, on tinted paper, only 150 copies printed, royal 8°, cloth, uncut, out of print, $10.

637 CLARK, Harp of Freedom, with musical notes, 12°, port., cloth, $1.

638 DUNCIAD, The (with notes variorum, being the scholia of the learned M. Scriblerius and others, with the adversaria of Denis, Theobald, Curl, the journalists, &c., index to persons celebrated in the poem, &c., and an appendix containing the New Dunciad as it was found in the year 1741), 4°, calf, red edges, vignette, $2.

639 EOLOPOESIS, American Rejected Addresses, 12°, cloth, 50 cents.

640 EVEREST, Poets and Poetry of Connecticut, 8°, cloth, $1.50.

641 ERSKINE, Gospel Sonnets and Spiritual Songs, 12°, 1806, sheep, 50 cents.

642 FARMER, Fairy of the Stream and other Poems, 12°, bds., 25 cents.

643 FAIRFIELD'S Poems, 8°, cloth, $1.50.

644 HOMER Travestie, London, 2 vols., 8°, half calf, neat, curious plates, $5.

645 HUNTINGTON'S Shadowy Land and other Poems, 8°, cloth, $2.

646 LOYAL Verses of Stansbury and Odell, relating to the American Revolution, notes by Winthrop Sargent, small 4°, paper, uncut, $3.

647 MATTHIAS, Pursuits of Literature, a Satirical Poem, London, 1812, 4° (large paper copy), with appendix and index, half calf, fine copy, $5.

648 MOUNTAIN, Songs of the Wilderness, 12°, plates, cloth, 75 cents.

649 MOUNT Vernon and other Poems, by Rice, 12°, cloth, 38 cents.

650 MOORE'S Songs and Ballads of the American Revolution, 12°, cloth, 75 cents.

651 NEW York Book of Poetry, 8°, cloth, 50c.

652 NOTHING to Eat, 12°, cloth, illustrated, 25c.

653 POETS and Poetry of Vermont, by Miss Hemenway, 12°, $1.

654 SMITH, The Uses of Solitude, 8°, sewed, 50c.

MISCELLANEOUS.

655 ADDISON, The Spectator, 12°, cloth, $1.

656 ADVENTURES of Hunters and Travelers, and Narratives of Border Warfare, 12°, numerous engravings, cloth, 50 cents.

657 ÆSCHYLUS, Tragedies of, translated, Buckley's notes, 12°, cloth, 50 cents.

658 AFRICA and the American Flag, 12°, colored plates, cloth, 62 cents.

659 ALBUM Perdu, 12°, calf, neat, 50 cents.

660 ALCOTT, Library of Health, 4 vols., 12°, cloth, $2.

661 ——, Young Housekeeper, 12°, cloth, 25c.

661 ——, Mother's Medical Guide, 12°, port., cloth, 50 cents.

662 ——, The House I Live in, 16°, cloth, 50c.

663 ALLEN'S Analysis of Saratoga Mineral Springs, 18°, stitched, 25 cents.

664 AMERICAN Cookery, &c., 1808, 18°, 12c.

655* AMERICAN'S Guide; Dec. Independence, Articles of Confederation, Const. U. S., and Constitution of all the States, thick 12°, half morocco, new, $1.25.

656* ANDERSON, Annals of the English Bible, edited by Prime, 8°, half turkey, $2.

657* AS It Is (Life in Washington), 12°, cloth, 50c.

658* ATLANTIC Monthly, 10 vols., 8°, in numbers complete, $12.50.

659* BARING, Alexander, Inquiry into Orders in Council and Examination of Conduct of Great Britain towards the Neutral Commerce of America, 1808, 8°, sewed, $1.

660* BARTLETT, Dictionary of Americanisms, a glossary of words and phrases usually regarded as peculiar to the United States, last edition, 8°, cloth, $2.50.

661* BEAUVALLET, Rachel, and the New World, 12°, cloth, $1.

662* BEDORTHA, Practical Medication or Invalid's Guide, with directions for the Treatment of Disease, 12°, cloth, $1.

663* BEECHER, Riots at Alton, 1838, 12°, cloth, scarce, 50 cents.

664* BIGLAND, Letters on French History, 12°, sheep, 50 cents.

665 BLUNT, American Annual Register, 1826–32 (lacks vol. v), 7 vols. 8°, half cloth, $5.

666 BOISTE, Dictionnaire Universal de la langue Francaise, Manuel Encyclopedique de Grammaire, d'orthographé, de vieux Langage, de Néologie, suivi de synonymes, difficultés de la langue, rimes, homonymes, paronymes, versification, tropes, ponctuation, conjugasions, pronunciation; vocabulaires, mythologie, personages remarquables, geographie ancienne et modern, nomenclature complete d'histoire naturelle; ouvrage classique, adopté pour les bibliothèques et les distributions de prix des collèges, et pouvant tenir lieu de tous les dictionnaires, thick 4°, full turk. mor., valuable work, $6.50.

667 BOSTON Gas Light Co., Trial of, 8°, stitched, 25 cents.
668 BRITISH Almanac, and Year Book of General Information, 26 vols. 12°, with index, hf. calf, neat, fine set, $15.
669 BROTHERHEAD, Amer. Notes and Queries, 8°, cloth, $1.
670 BROWN, Charles Brockden, complete Novels, 6 vols. 12°, cloth, new, $4.
671 —— History of the Shakers, 12°, sheep, $1.
672 —— The Green Mountain Traveler's Entertainment, 12°, cloth, new, 50 cents.
673 BUCKINGHAM, Specimens of Newspaper Literature, with Personal Memoirs and Reminiscences, 2 vols. 12°, portraits, cloth, $2.50.
674 —— The Polyanthus, 4 vols. 8°, half sheep (lacks portraits), $2.
675 BYRON, Repository of Wit and Humor, 12°, cloth, 50 cents.
676 CABINET of Curiosities, natural, artificial and historical, 2 vols. 12°, cloth, $2.
677 CAMPBELL'S Atrocious Judges, 12°, cl., 50c.
678 —— Practical Cook Book, 12°, cloth, 37c.
679 CATALOGUS, Collegii Yalensis, 1859, 8°, pp. 160, stitched, 50 cents.
680 CATECHISM for use of Ev. Lutheran Church, 18°, stitched, 6 cents.
681 CENTRAL American Affairs, and the Enlistment Question, 8°, valuable map, cloth, 50c.
682 CHAMBERS, Cyclopedia of English Literature, a history critical and biographical, of British authors, from the earliest to the present times, 2 vols. royal 8°, sheep, fine copy, $3.25.
683 —— Edinburgh Journal, new series, 20 vols. in 10, sup. roy. 8°, half turk., neat, $20 (pub. at £7:10).
684 —— Handbook of American Literature, 12°, cloth, $1.
685 CHINESE as they are, 8°, p. 116, hf. mor., 50c.
686 CLARE, The Trial, 12°, pp. 70, stitched, 25c.
687 CLARKE'S Commentary on the New Testament royal 8°, sheep, $1.50.
688 COBBETT, Treatise on Corn, 12°, plates (first 2 leaves printed on paper made of husks), sewed, $1.
689 COLOGNE Gazette for the years 1760 and 1782, complete, 2 vols. small 4°, half sheep, $2.
690 COLSON, The Mariner's New Kalendar. London, 1752, small 4°, sheep, last leaf gone, 50c.
691 COLTON, Rights of Labor, 8°, pp. 96, stitched, 10 cents.
692 COMPANION to the Newspaper and Journal of Facts in Politics, Statistics and Public Economy, 2 vols. in 1, small folio, half calf, $1.
693 CONVERSATION between Dominie and Patrick, or the Bible vs. Papacy, 12°, cloth, 25c.
694 CONVERSATIONS on the Present Age of the World in connection with Prophecy, 12°, cloth, $1.
695 COXE, Inquiry into Claims of Harvey to the Discovery of the Circulation of the Blood, 8°, half cloth, 50 cents.
696 CRANDALL, Talks with the People of New York, 8°, stitched (not published), 50 cents.
697 CRIMINAL Statistics of the State of New York, 1856, 8°, cloth, 50 cents.
698 CROSS, Selections of Best Articles in Edinburgh Review, with notes, 6 vols. 8°, sewed, uncut, $5.
699 CYPRESS Wreath, to the Memory of Rev. Geo. R. Williamson, his wife and child, 12°, cloth, 50 cents.
700 CUMMING, Hooper, the whole case of, 8°, bds., $1.50.
701 DANA, The Fireman, accounts of all large fires, losses and expenses, &c., 12°, plates, cloth, $1.

702 DAVIS, The Sailors Companion, 18°, cl., 15c.
703 DE La Hodde, History of the Secret Societies of France, 8°, cloth, $1.25.
704 DE PRADT, Europe and America in 1821, with an examination of the Plan laid before the Spanish Cortes for the Recognition of the Independence of South America, 2 vols., 8°, half cloth, $2.
705 DICTIONNAIRE des Inventions, des Origines, et des Découvertes, royal 8°, half mor., neat, $2.50.
706 DICTIONARY of Merchandise, the history, places of growth, culture, use, and marks of excellency of articles of commerce, with their names in all European languages, 8°, sheep, loose, $1.50.
707 DICTIONARY of Shakesperian Quotations, 12°, cloth, $1.
708 DODSLEY'S Annual Register, first 33 vols., 8°, 1758 to 1791, calf, $25.
709 DRAWINGS and Tintings, by A. B. Street, sup. roy. 8°, half morocco, 50 cents.
710 DWIGHT, System of Universal Geography for Schools, 12°, bds., 25 cents.
711 EASTON, Human Longevity, recording the name, age, place of residence, and year of decease of 1712 persons who attained a century and upwards, 8°, bds., $2.50.
712 ELLIS, Letters on English History, vols. 1 and 3, 8°, cloth, damaged, 50 cents.
713 FAMILY Doctor, complete encyclopedia of Domestic Medicine and Household Surgery, illustrated with all the medicinal plants, 2 vols., 12°, London, cloth, (pub. at $4), $2.
714 FIELDS, Scrap Book (Miscellany), 2d ed., 8°, cloth, $1.
715 FOSTER, Introduction to Study of Geology, &c., 18°, cloth, 25 cents.
716 FREEDLY, Trades and Manufactures of United States, and Sketches of leading manufacturing firms, thick 8°, cloth, $1.
717 FULTON, Treatise on Canal Navigation, &c., 17 plates, 4°, bds., $4.
718 GALLERY of Illustration for 1857, portraits of distinguished persons, with biographical notices and views of celebrated buildings, sup royal 8°, sewed, 50 cents.
719 GIBBINGS, Roman Index Expurgatorius, thick 12°, cloth, $1.
720 GIBBONS, Banks of New York, their Dealers, the Clearing House, and the Panic of 1857, 12°, plates, cloth, $1.
721 GOLDSMITH, Vicar of Wakefield, 18°, cloth, portrait, 50 cents.
722 GUARDIAN Genius of the Federal Union, or patriotic admonitions on the signs of the times respecting human slavery, 1839, 12°, sewed, 50 cents.
723 GUTHRIE'S Modern Geography, or a geographical, historical and commercial grammar, and present state of the several nations of the world, &c., 2 vols., 4°, sheep, $5.
724 HAIGH, Sketches of Buenos Ayres and Chili, 8°, map, half calf, $1.50.
725 HALL, Republican Party and its Candidates, with biographical sketches and ports., cl., 50c.
726 HAMMOND, Hunting Adventures in the Northern Wilds, 12°, cloth, $1.
227 ——, Wild Northern Scenes, or Sporting Adventures with the Rifle and Rod, 12°, plates, cloth, $1.
728 HANDBOOK of Mechanic Institutions, and priced catalogue of suitable books, 8°, cl., 50c.
729 HARSHA, Principles of Hydropathy, &c., 12°, stitched, 25 cents.
730 ——, Thoughts on the Love of Christ, 18°, cloth, 25 cents.

731 HASWELL, Mechanics' Tables, 12°, cl., 25c.
732 HAYWARD, Book of all Religions, 12°, plates, cloth, new, $1.
733 HIND, Solar System, a descriptive treatise upon the Sun, Moon and Planets, 18°, cloth, plates, $1.
734 HISTORY of Harvard College, 8°, pamph., 50c.
735 HOBBES, Thomas of Malmesbury, Complete Works, edited by Sir Wm. Molesworth, 16 vols. 8°, port. and plates, cloth, new, $16.
736 HOPKINS, End of Controversy Controverted (Catholic question), 2 vols cloth, $1.
737 ——— The American Citizen, his Rights and Duties according to the Spirit of the Constitution, 12°, cloth, 50 cents.
738 HUNT'S Library of Commerce, 12°, cloth, 50c.
739 HYDE, Chinese Sugar Cane, 12°, stitched, 25c.
740 IRELAND, From Wall Street to Cashmere, thick 8°, cloth (pub. at $4), numerous pl., $2.
741 JACK Downing's Life and Writings, by himself, 16°, plates, half cloth, 50 cents.
742 JOE Miller's Complete Jest Book, 18°, cl., $1.
743 JOHNSON, Report on the Exhibition of Industry of all Nations held in London, 1851, 8°, cloth, $1.
744 JONES, Characters and Criticisms, 2 vols. 12°, cloth, $1.
745 JUST Vindication of Learning, or an humble address to the high court of Parliament in behalf of the Liberty of the Press. London, 1679, small 4°, half mor., 75 cents.
746 LAMBERT, Handbook of Needlework, 8°, illustrated, cloth, $1.
747 LATTA, Discourse on Psalmody, 8°, sew., 25c.
748 LAYARD, Popular account of the Discoveries at Nineveh, 12°, plates, cloth, $1.
749 LEGENDS of Lampidusa, or the Seven Heroines, 8°, half mor., 50 cents.
750 LESTER, C. Edwards, My Consulship, 2 vols. 12°, cloth, $1.
751 LETTERS to Benj. Franklin from his Family and Friends, 1751–1790, roy. 8°, sewed, uncut, 2 portraits, $2.50.
752 LIBERTY (extracts from authors, ancient and modern, on slavery), compiled by Julius R. Ames, 8°, sewed, $2.
753 ——— of the Press, chiefly as respects Personal Slander, 8°, half mor., 50 cents.
754 LIFT for the Lazy, 12°, cloth, $1.
755 LITTLE, American Cruiser's own Book, 12°, cloth, 50 cents.
756 LOVERS of the Curious Inquire Within, thick 12°, cloth, new, 50 cents.
757 LUCIAN'S Dialogues and other Extracts, literally translated, 18°, bds., 15 cents.
758 McCLUNG, Western Adventure, 1755 to 1794, 12°, half cloth, scarce, $1.25.
759 MALTE Brun, System of Universal Geography, or description of all parts of the world on a new plan, with a complete set of maps and a series of beautiful engravings, 3 vols. 4°, half calf, neat, $15.
760 MANHATTAN Souvenir, 12°, stitched, 25c.
761 MANUSCRIPTS in the Library of the King of France, 2 vols. 8°, calf (one article abstracted), 50 cents.
762 MANVIL, Lucinda, or the Mountain Mourner, 12°, cloth, 25 cents.
763 MEDICAL Addresses, pamphlets, 8°, each 25c.
764 ——— Transactions N. Y. State Society, odd vols., various conditions, 50 cents to $1.
765 MILES, Mohammed the Arabian Prophet, a tragedy, 12°, cloth, 37 cents.
766 MITCHELL, Gospel Crown of Life, thick 12°, cloth, $1.
767 MONROE, View of the Conduct of the Executive in the Foreign affairs of the U. S., 1794–6, 8°, half sheep, $1.75.

768 MONTAGUE, Guide to the Study of Heraldry, 4°, cloth, $1.50.
769 MORPHY, Exploits and Triumphs in Europe, with historical accounts of clubs, biographical sketches of famous players, &c., 12°, portrait, cloth, 50 cents.
770 MOXON, Tutor to Astronomy and Geography, or an easie and speedy way to know the use of both the globes, celestial and terrestrial. London, 1686, small 4°, portrait and numerous plates, calf, $1.
771 ——— Mechanick Exercises, or the Doctrine of Handy Works. London, 1694, 4°, 1st vol. of this very scarce work, with copperplates, illustrating Smithing, Joinery, House Carpentry and Turning, $1.
772 MUNCHAUSEN, Surprising Travels and Adventures of, 12°, plates, cloth, Lond. ed., $1.
773 MUNN, American Orator, &c., 12°, cloth, 75 cents.
774 NEW Dictionary of Quotations, 8°, cloth, top edge gilt.
775 NEW YORK Crystal Palace, sup. royal 8°, numerous folding plates and oil color exterior view, cloth, $2.
776 NEW YORK Session Laws, 1854, 1859, 2 vols. thick 8°, sheep, $1.50.
777 NICHOLSON, British Encyclopedia or Dictionary of the Arts and Sciences, 6 vols. 8°, 150 steel plates full calf, neat, $6.
778 NIEUWENTYT, Het Regt Gebruik der Werelt Beschouwingen, ter ongodisten en ongelovigen aangetoont, thick 4°, copper plates, $1.
779 NILES, Principles and Acts of the Revolution with sketches and remarks on men and things, royal 8°, half mor., $3.
780 NOAH, Discourse on the Restoration of the Jews, map of Land of Jerusalem, 8°, stitched, 50 cents.
781 NORTHERN Traveller, &c., 18°, pp. 432, cloth, maps, 38 cents.
782 NORTON, Handbook of Life Insurance, 12°, stitched, 25 cents.
783 OLDPATH, Lin, or Jewels of the Third Plantation, 12°, cloth, $1.
784 O'CALLAGHAN, List of Editions of the Holy Scriptures printed in America, sup. royal 8°, sewed, uncut, $10.
785 PAMPHLETS, 11 vols., 8°, half sheep, $8.50.
786 PATENT Office Reports, odd vols., cloth.
787 PAULDING, Diverting History of John Bull and Brother Jonathan, 12°, cloth, scarce, $1.
788 MRS. Partington's Carpet Bag of Fun, 150 engravings, 12°, cloth, 50 cents.
789 POLES in the United States, with earliest history of the Sclavonians and of Poland, 16°, cloth, 62 cents.
790 POOLE, Index to Periodical Literature, 8°, cloth, $2.50.
791 POSTLETHWAITE'S Commercial Dictionary, 2 vols., thick folio, lacks 4 leaves, binding broken, otherwise in good order, $6.
792 PREBLE, Voice of God, or Account of Unparalled Fires, &c., 12°, stitched, 50 cents.
793 PROCEEDINGS American Association for Advancement of Science, 1854, charts, sewed, $1.
794 ——— of the Commissioners of Indian Affairs, appointed by law for the Extinguishment of Indian Titles in the State of New York, 3 maps, 4°, half turkey, $10.
796 ——— of the Republican Convention at Chicago, 1860, 8°, cloth, 50 cents.
797 PROMPTER, 12°, bds., 50 cents.
798 PRO-Slavery Argument as maintained by the most distinguished writers of the South, 12°, cloth $1.

799 QUAKERS, Ancient Testimony, Doctrine, &c., 12°, stitched, 25 cents.

——, Brown's History of, 12°, sheep, $1.

800 QUINCY, Journals of Maj. Sam. Shaw, first Am. Consul at Canton, 8°, port., cloth, $1.

801 RAFINESQUE, Genius and Spirit of Hebrew Bible, 12°, stitched, 75 cents.

802 RANKIN, American Slavery, 12°, half cloth, 25 cents.

803 REASON Why, a collection of many hundreds of reasons for things imperfectly understood, 12°, cloth, $1.

804 REVISED Statutes of Wisconsin, thick 8°, sheep, $4.

805 RILEY, Narrative of his Captivity, 12°, plate, best edition, cloth, new, $1.

806 ——, Puddleford Papers or Humors of the West, 12°, cloth, new, 50 cents.

807 ROBINSON, Mexico and her Military Chieftains, 12°, portraits, sewed, 25 cents.

808 SALMON'S Gazetteer of the World, 1768, thick 12°, calf, 50 cents.

809 SAMPSON, Beauties of the Bible, 12°, sheep, 63 cents.

810 ——, Youth's Companion, or a historical dictionary, thick, 12°, sheep, 50 cents.

811 SANDERSON, Republican Landmarks, views and opinions of American Statesmen on Foreign Immigration, and statistics of population, pauperism, crime, &c., 8°, cloth, $1.

812 SATURDAY Magazine, 25 vols. in 13, sup. royal 8°, half mor., $10.

813 SCOTT, Lessons in Elocution, 12°, sheep, 80 cents.

814 SEWARD, W. H., Introduction to the Natural History of the State of New York (MS. annotations by the author), 4°, cloth, $2.50 (only 150 printed).

815 SHERMAN, Slavery in the U. S., a word to the North and South, 12°, cloth, 25 cents.

816 SIMPSON'S Cook Book, with bill of fare for every day in the year, thick 8°, sheep, $1.50.

817 SMITH, American Historical and Literary Curiosities, folio, half turk., new, $8.

818 ——, Catechumen's Guide, 12°, cloth, $1.

819 ——, Illustrations of Faith drawn from the word of God, 18°, cloth, 25 cents.

820 SMYTH, Lectures on Modern History with additions by Sparks, 8°, cloth, $1.25.

821 SPIRIT of Humanity and the Animal's Friend; extracted from the Productions of the enlightened and benevolent of various ages and climes, 12°, half mor., 75 cents.

822 SPIRIT of the Public Journals or Beauties of the American Newspapers. Baltimore, 1806, 18°, half cloth, 30 cents.

823 SPRAGUE, T. Dwight, American Literary Magazine, 2 vols. 8°, portraits, half sheep, $2.

824 STAPP, The Prisoners of Peroto, 1842, 12°, stitched, 25 cents.

825 STEPHENS, Comic Natural History of the Human Race, sup. royal 8°, numerous plates, cloth, worn, $1.50.

826 STERNE, Sentimental Journey, and Letters and Sermons, thick 12°, portrait, cloth, $1.

827 STRANGER, a Literary Paper, by John Cook. Albany, 1814, 8°, half sheep, $1.

828 STREET, Council of Revision of the State of New York, its history, a history of the courts with which its members were connected, biographical sketches of its members, and its vetoes, roy. 8°, half turk., $2.50.

829 STRIKER'S Quarterly Register, 5 vols. 8°, 1848–51, 1st vol. sewed, 4 vols. half turk., $5.

830 TAYLOR, Elements of Thought, or concise explanations of the principal terms employed in the several branches of intellectual philosophy, 12°, cloth, 75 cents.

831 THE Test. London, 1756–7, small folio, 210 pages (conducted by Arthur Murphy, an Irish dramatic and miscellaneous writer, and undertaken chiefly in favor of Mr. Fox, afterwards Lord Holland), half calf, neat, $1.

832 THE Con-Test. London, 1756–7, small folio, 128 pages (uniform in size and style with the preceding; set up by Owen Ruffhead in opposition to the Test), half calf, neat, $2.

833 THOMSON, Domestic Management of the Sick Room, 12°, cloth, 50 cents.

834 THOMAS, Illustrated Annual Register of Rural Affairs, cloth, 50 cents.

835 TICKNOR, History of Spanish Literature, 3 vols. 8°, cloth, $5.

836 TIME'S Telescope, a complete guide to the Almanac, containing explanations of Saints' Days and Holidays, illustrations of history and antiquities, notices of obsolete rites and customs, astronomical occurrences, naturalists' diary, meteorogical remarks, &c., 18 vols. 12°, bds., $9.

837 TREASURY of Knowledge, containing Universal Gazetteer, Epitome of Chronology, and History and Classical Dict., 3 vols. 8°, cl., $3.

838 TRIAL of the Officers and Crew of the Privateer Savannah, on the charge of Piracy, 8°, cloth, $2.50.

839 TRIALS of Rev. John Chester and Mark Tucker, the whole case of the Rev. Hooper Cumming, 8°, bds., $1.50.

840 TROTTER, Financial Position and Credit of such of the States as have contracted Public Debts, &c., 8°, map, cloth, $1.50.

841 TUCKER, Manual for the Guitar, 12°, cl., 25c.

842 TWISS, Oregon Question Examined, 8°, maps, London, cloth, $1.25.

843 TWO Speeches before the N. Y. S. Convention, Sept., 1824, with proceedings of Convention (Vindication of De Witt Clinton), 8°, pp. 8, stitched, 25 cents.

844 TYTLER, Treatise on the Plague and Yellow Fever, with accounts of ancient plagues, 8°, sheep, scarce, $2.50.

845 UNION College, Report of Commissioners, and Argument of Dr. Nott, 2 v. 8°, stitched, $1.

846 VERNES, Le Voyageur sentimental, ou ma promenade à Yverdun, 12°, calf, 75 cents.

847 WALKER, Beauty illustrated chiefly by an Analysis and Classification of Beauty in Woman, 12°, cloth, new, $1.

848 WASHINGTON'S Letters to Joseph Reed during the Revolution, 8°, cloth, 75 cents.

849 —— Letters from 1817, sketches of public characters, 12°, bds., 50 cents.

850 WEBSTER, Daniel, Private Correspondence of, 2 vols., 7°, portraits, cloth, $2.50.

851 —— Noah, Papers on Political, Literary and Moral Subjects, 8°, sheep, $1.

852 WESTERN Border Life, or what Fanny Hunter saw and heard in Kansas and Missouri, 12°, cloth, $1.

853 WILLIS, American Monthly Magazine, 1829, 8°, Nos. 1, 2, 3, 4, 12, in sheets, 50 cents.

854 WINTHROP, Robt. C. Addresses and Speeches of, 8°, cloth, new (pub. at $3), $1.50.

855 WISE, Hist. Israelitish Nation, 8°, cloth, $1.

856 WOOD, Personal Recollections of the Stage, 12°, port., cloth, $1.

857 —— Suppressed History of John Adams's Administration, with notes, 12°, port., cl., $1.

858 WOODBURY, Levi, Writings of, 3 v., 8°, $3.

859 WYNNE, Gen. Hist. British Empire in America, 1760, 2 vols., 8°, calf, old, $3.

860 WYSE, America, its Realities and Resources, policy that led to War of 1812, right of search, Texas and Oregon questions, &c., 3 vols., 8°, cloth, $3.

www.ingramcontent.com/pod-product-compliance
Lightning Source LLC
Chambersburg PA
CBHW030131030726
47498CB00007B/2659